The First North Americans Series

PEOPLE OF THE MASKS

"Flowing imagination, storytelling marvels. The Gears have a fine time drawing the various interclan rivalries and clashes of cultures." —*Kirkus Reviews*

PEOPLE OF THE MIST

"A first-rate murder mystery, anthropological information on pre-European Native America, a slight dash of sex (mostly innocent), and plenty of politics. Whew! The amazing thing is that it is all done so well." —*Booklist* (starred review)

PEOPLE OF THE SILENCE

"Riveting historical fiction series on pre-Columbian North America." —*New Mexico Magazine*

PEOPLE OF THE LIGHTNING

"Brilliantly written book...part of the exciting First North Americans series....The series is an excellent and entertaining way to relive the ancient history of North America....Fascinating, exciting, and educational." —*Lake Worth Herald*

PEOPLE OF THE LAKES

"An adventure saga imbued with a wealth of historical detail....Centers around a totemic mask with great evil power." —*Publishers Weekly*

PEOPLE OF THE SEA

"Adventure, survival, romance, and fantasy all painted on a historical canvas....Good historical fiction, the story transports readers into another time and place." —*School Library Journal*

PEOPLE OF THE RIVER

"A story we cannot afford to ignore." —*The Washington Post*

PEOPLE OF THE EARTH

"A great adventure tale, throbbing with life and death....The most convincing reconstruction of prehistory I have yet read." —Morgan Llywelyn

PEOPLE OF THE FIRE

"The action is intense and satisfying and the characters are vividly portrayed." —*VOYA*

PEOPLE OF THE WOLF

"Rewarding reading to anyone interested in exploring the lives of the earliest inhabitants of North America....Fascinating." —*Locus*

www.Gear—Gear.com

Kathleen O'Neal Gear
and W. Michael Gear

People
of the
Lakes

A TOM DOHERTY ASSOCIATES BOOK
NEW YORK

This is a work of fiction. All the characters and events portrayed in this book are fictitious, and any resemblance to real people or events is purely coincidental.

PEOPLE OF THE LAKES

Copyright © 1994 by Kathleen O'Neal Gear and W. Michael Gear

Cover art by Royo
Maps and interior art by Ellisa Mitchell

A Tor Book
Published by Tom Doherty Associates, LLC
175 Fifth Avenue
New York, NY 10010

www.tor.com

Tor® is a registered trademark of Tom Doherty Associates, LLC.

ISBN 0-812-50747-9
EAN 978-0-812-50747-8
Library of Congress Catalog Card Number: 94-7145

First edition: August 1994
First international mass market edition: April 1995
First mass market edition: September 1995

Printed in the United States of America

0 9 8

In memory of
George H. Davis
August 21, 1921 to October 21, 1992.
He loved elk, horses, high country,
and, above all,
family and friends.
George, we hope they have a crackling-warm fire,
a jar of jalapeños, a plate of backstrap,
and a strong cup of coffee
ready when you get there.
We miss you.
. . . And this one's for you and Shirley.

North

People of the Lakes

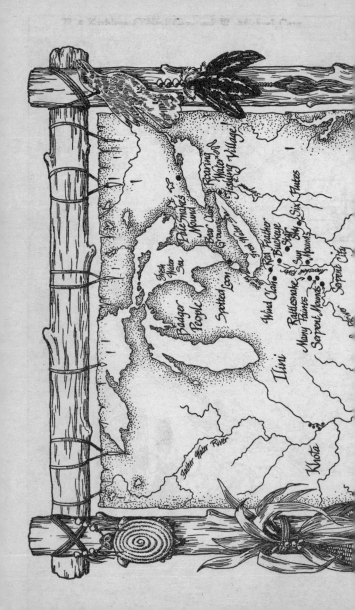

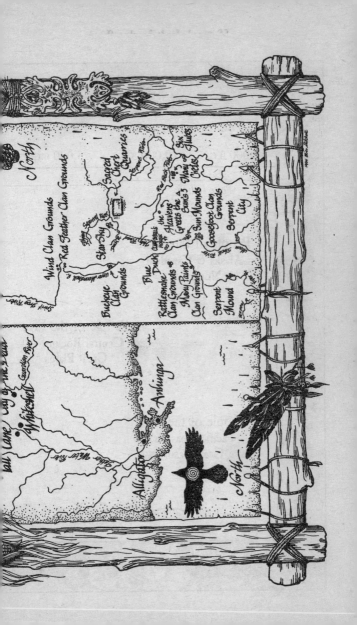

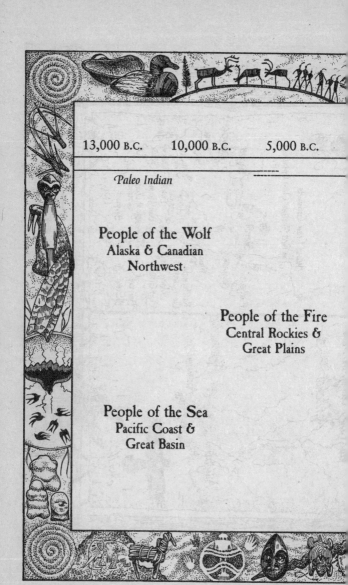

| 13,000 B.C. | 10,000 B.C. | 5,000 B.C. |

Paleo Indian

People of the Wolf
Alaska & Canadian
Northwest

People of the Fire
Central Rockies &
Great Plains

People of the Sea
Pacific Coast &
Great Basin

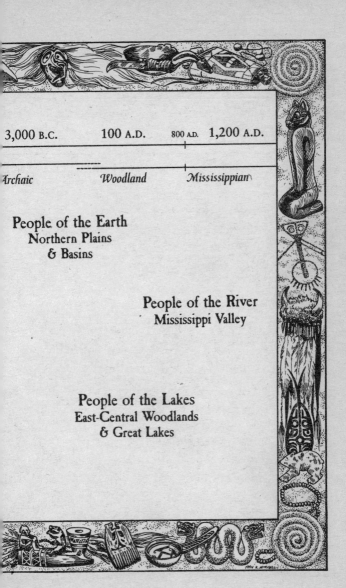

| 3,000 B.C. | 100 A.D. | 800 A.D. | 1,200 A.D. |

| Archaic | Woodland | Mississippian |

People of the Earth
Northern Plains
& Basins

People of the River
Mississippi Valley

People of the Lakes
East-Central Woodlands
& Great Lakes

Acknowledgments

People of the Lakes would not have been possible without the help of a number of people. In the beginning, Michael Seidman—then executive editor at Tor Books—believed we should produce a series of novels about our nation's magnificent pre-contact heritage. He thought the books should educate as well as entertain.

Robert C. Mainfort, Jr., regional archaeologist with the Tennessee Division of Archaeology, provided excavation reports, interpretation, and answered questions about Middle Woodland occupations at Pinson Mounds and in western Tennessee. Mark Norton, Theda Young, and Anita Drury, staff members at the Pinson Mounds State Park in western Tennessee, were also very helpful.

Charles Niquette, of Cultural Resource Analysts, Inc., provided his expertise and archaeological reports relating to Middle Woodland period settlement patterns. Thanks, Chuck. We'll send you a dead armadillo one of these days.

Dennis LaBatt, Nancy Clendenen, and David Griffing—the knowledgeable staff at the Poverty Point Archaeological site outside of Floyd, Louisiana—demonstrated the wonders of the huge Poverty Point site. From the Ohio Historical Society, James Kingery, of the Flint Ridge State Park, proved most helpful, as did Brad Lepper, of Newark Earthworks State Memorial. Brad's work on Ohio Hopewell road systems is remarkable.

We are also indebted to our colleagues within the archaeological profession, specifically to the following: N'omi Greber, R. Berle Clay, Dan Morse, Christopher Hays, Frank Cowan, Richard Yerkes, James Brown, and others who presented papers at the 58th Annual Meetings of the Society for American Archaeology.

Special appreciation is extended to Adrian Gardner, Shirley

Whittington, and Gord Laco, of Saint Marie Among the Hurons. Dawn Barry and Mr. Bancroft, of Serpent Mounds Provincial Park, provided us with a special day of discussion about the Middle Woodland in Ontario. Linda O'Conner and Lisa Roach, of Petroglyphs Provincial Park, opened early and stayed late to facilitate our research. Mima Kapoches, of the Royal Ontario Museum, took time from her busy schedule to discuss Hopewellian interaction spheres.

We would also like to extend sincere thanks to U.S. Forest Service archaeologists Ann Wilson and Gene Driggers, and to U.S. Department of Defense archaeologist Dr. Steven Chomko, for their part in helping to make this book possible. In addition, Dr. Cal Cummings, senior archaeologist for the National Park Service, located elusive field reports, films, and books. Dr. Linda Scott Cummings, of Paleo Research Laboratories, answered endless questions about pollen, fibers, and plant remains recovered from archaeological sites relevant to the story.

Words cannot express what we owe to Lloyd and Julie Schott.

Sierra Adare, our unflagging manager, kept us organized despite ourselves.

We offer our most heartfelt thanks to Harriet McDougal, our brilliant editor, who still edits like they did in the golden days of publishing; and to Linda Quinton, Ralph Arnote, Tom Doherty, Roy Gainsburg, and the superb field force, which has always believed in this project. Our Canadian distributors, Harold and Sylvia Fenn, Rob Howard, and the fine people at H.B. Fenn, have supported us from the beginning. Three cheers to all of you.

Foreword

Around the time of Christ, Middle Woodland peoples lived throughout eastern North America. Remnants of their magnificent cultures are scattered from Ontario to Florida, and spread as far west as Texas and Wisconsin. We know the sites of these cultures by many names: Adena-Hopewell, Havana, Copena, Marksville, Point Peninsula, Crab Orchard, and others. Archaeologists summarize them with a delightfully obtuse technical term: the "Hopewellian Interaction Sphere."

These people remain a marvel—and an enigma. Sophisticated traders, artisans, and monument builders, they nevertheless appear to have had no chiefs, built no cities, and conquered no vast territories. Rather, they traded everywhere, traversing the rivers; and through their trade, they spread the traits of zone-incised pottery, geometric earthworks, exotic burial tombs, and stone and metal trade goods.

Their gigantic ceremonial earthworks and lavish tombs are found throughout the eastern half of the continent, but fewer than a dozen of their domestic sites—the locations where they built their houses and lived their daily lives—have been located or excavated.

Hopewellian cultures domesticated many plants we now consider noxious weeds: goosefoot (*Chenopodium berlandieri*), marsh elder (*Iva annua*), knotweed (*Polygonum erectum*), maygrass (*Phalaris caroliniana*), and, in some places, little barley (*Hordeum pusillum*). Of their domesticates, only sunflower (*Helianthus annus*) and squash (*Cucurbita pepo*) remain as modern crops.

Isolated traces of corn appear around two thousand years ago, but the crop didn't really catch on until about 400 A.D., at the end of the Middle Woodland period; moreover, some researchers believe that corn might have contributed to the demise of the Hopewellian world by producing such food surpluses that the traditional social structure—founded upon small, independent farmsteads and transcontinental trade—collapsed and reformed into what archaeologists call Late Woodland peoples (400 to 800 A.D.). The Late Woodland period is characterized by a sharp decline in mound building and in the absence of exotic trade goods, but villages began to appear. Many of them were fortified by earthen or log enclosures, undoubtedly indicating social stress, perhaps even warfare. The luxury of a food surplus may have made these Woodland peoples targets for raiders from less fortunate cultures.

PEOPLE OF THE LAKES is something of a Hopewellian travelogue that moves from the American Gulf Coast to Rice Lake in Ontario, Canada. We want the reader to experience both the similarities and the differences in Middle Woodland cultures two thousand years ago. In the story, we call the classic Ohio Adena peoples the High Head, and the Ohio Hopewell we designate as the Flat Pipe. Adena is the older culture, dating back to nearly 700 B.C. Hopewell seems to have merged syncretically with Adena to produce a golden age beginning around 1 A.D.

Another center of activity is found in the Illinois and upper Mississippi river valleys. We call this Hopewellian group Havana, and their social organization appears to be the closest to a hereditary chieftainship of any of the Middle Woodland societies. The elite burials at the core of the mounds are almost exclusively male; we assume, therefore, that these were patrilineal clans. In places such as Tennessee, Mississippi, and Louisiana, females were accorded higher status, and were generally buried with more and richer burial goods. This probably indicates a matrilineage in what are known as the Marksville and Miller cultures.

One of our major goals in writing this series of novels is to portray different personalities in the Native American world. Readers of our previous books have met Dreamers, *berdaches,* Healers, and shamans. The Contrary, one of many forms of the sacred clown, is uniquely Native American, and uses the humorous and the profane to communicate deeply serious and sacred lessons. The revelations of Contraries are often as stunning as they are profound. As you come to know Green Spider, we hope you will gain a glimmering of the Contrary's incredible power as a teacher, mystic, and reconciliator of the very duality he represents.

Finally, writing a novel about the Hopewell is a sobering experience for professional archaeologists. The data accumulated in the past century come almost totally from excavations at spectacular burial mounds and geometric earthworks, not from the mundane sites that portray the everyday lives of the people. This is not primarily the fault of the researchers, but rather a fact of life in the struggle to find funding for archaeological work. It is simply easier to gain financial backing for the excavation of a grand architectural marvel than for the humble house of a farmer. Unfortunately, this leaves a critical gap in the information, which means that attempts to portray a dynamic series of interacting cultures may take us so far out on a limb that we end up clinging desperately to leaf tips.

Nevertheless, in the following pages, we've attempted to give you a reasonable reconstruction of Hopewellian lifeways. If we have piqued your interest in the Middle Woodland peoples, we encourage you to consult the bibliography in the back of this book, to visit your nearest archaeological park or monument, and to learn more about this rare and precious era of our North American heritage.

Introduction

State Park Supervisor William L. Jaffman clutched his hands behind his back and inhaled a deep breath of the fresh, storm-scented wind as he walked the nature path that led around the northeast end of the park, opposite the earthwork called "The Circle."

Three people sauntered in a knot just ahead of him: an administrator, an engineer, a political appointee. They laughed and talked, quite oblivious to the magnificence of the Circle, where, two thousand years before, ancient astronomers had charted the cycles of stars that most modern Americans barely knew existed. When Bill had explained the Circle to them earlier, they had stared blankly at him, slightly irritated by his exuberance.

This was a simple matter for them. The state needed thirty-five acres of land. A mere thirty-five—one third of his park—for a new highway project. Their strained smiles had informed him at the outset that nothing he said would change their minds—obviously the future had to take precedence over the past. So all day his heart had been pounding a staccato against his ribs, and now, as they neared the central mound beside the park office, he thought it just might break through and ruin his new khaki uniform shirt.

He calmed himself by studying the maple trees. Every leaf glistened with raindrops from the gentle afternoon shower that had fallen an hour before. Like tears, they dripped down upon him when the wind gusted, splatting on his high forehead and pointed nose, pearling over his brown curly hair.

Was it his imagination, or did he hear soft, pitiful cries coming from inside the Circle? He cocked his head, listening more closely. The whimpers slid around the trunks of trees and crouched amongst the branches. Murmuring to him. Pleading with him. He shouldn't be surprised. Of course the ghosts knew. They had heard today's conversations.

Bill had to jam his hands into his pants pockets and clamp his jaws to keep from shouting. All he really wanted to do was to tell these damnable bureaucrats to go straight to hell, to leave him and his park alone.

But they'd just fire him, and then there would be no one left to fight for the rights of the faithful souls who still lived and worked here.

Ahead, four shiny new state vehicles, Chevy Blazers—one complete with an aerodynamic police-light bar—stood in a short row. Behind them, and across the parking lot, hulked the galvanized-metal maintenance shed. As usual, the garage door hung open, revealing the nose of the tractor where Billy Hanson was no doubt struggling with the bent PTO again. One of the summer temps—a college kid up from the university—had backed it into a concrete guard post.

Jaffman had been a college kid once, and his father had never forgiven him for settling on a degree in archaeology. But that had been a different era, before the coveted MBA rose to such gaudy prominence, an era when kids went off to school to make a difference, to follow their hearts and learn about wonderful new things—not just to learn to make money.

"You're wasting your life," his father, a CPA, had told him. "What's with this? Archaeology? Son, you've got to think about making a living, doing something for your future."

"But, Dad, how can you know where you're going unless you can see the path you walked to get where you are now? I want to know where we came from! What makes us human!"

Even at such a young age, he'd known in his heart that if human beings destroyed the past or continued to deny its relevance to the present, the species was doomed. Civilization was a fragile flower, with a shallow root system. Without vigilant protection and care, the roots would wither and die.

"Hey, Bill? Wake up!" Ed Smith, the state Department of Transportation engineer, called, breaking Bill from his thoughts.

"What is it, Ed?"

Smith had been sent up from the capital, dutifully armed with maps, surveys, and a stack of different-colored notebooks. Smith always wore an off-white shirt—one with a plastic pen guard in its pocket. He kept his gray hair short, and thick, black-framed glasses dominated his thin face.

Anne Seibowitz, state director of Parks and Recreation, and Bill's boss, stood to Smith's right, arms crossed. She wore a lavender twill skirt that hung to mid-calf, and a maroon-and-gray sweater. Her nose always attracted Bill's attention; it looked like someone had pinched the sharp end of it closed with pliers. She wore her black, silver-streaked hair in a short, wavy cut completely in fitting with her status and age. Now she rocked on her Italian boots, unaware of the grass, of the trees, and, no doubt, of the pleading of the ghosts. Her real business, outside of cadging funding from the legislature, was that of scrutinizing visitation numbers, use-fee collection, and the cleanliness of public rest rooms.

Across from Anne stood the suit, Roy Roman, the governor's aide. Around forty, he had blond hair and wore a pale blue shirt, dark blue tie, and had elected a brown tweed sport coat with leather patches on the elbows: the ultimate for an expedition into the paved-trail hinterlands of a state park.

Roman propped his hands on his hips and said, "All right, let's get this started. The governor is very interested in finding a solution to this little problem. We've been getting a lot of heat from people about this highway improvement project. Unfortunately, it has been so blown out of proportion that we've started to get calls from Native American organizations. Maybe because this Soap group got involved."

"Soap Group?" Ed Smith blinked, the effect amplified by his thick lenses. "What does soap have to do with anything? We're building a highway, for God's sake."

"SOPA," Bill explained. "The Society of Professional Archaeologists. Look, you can't expect to bulldoze an Adena-Hopewell site of this importance without stirring up a hornet's nest. This park exists solely to protect the earthworks."

"We *are* protecting the earthworks," Ed said forcefully. "The highway right-of-way is exactly twenty-eight feet and seven inches from the edge of the earthwork. Look, we've been out there. There's nothing but grass in the area we plan to bulldoze. We're *not* going to hurt the earthworks!"

Bill folded his arms across his chest, trying to lessen the ache that swelled with each new gust of wind. "Please," he said.

"I've explained this over and over. Just because you can't see anything, it doesn't mean it's not there. We're talking about archaeology, not—"

"That's ridiculous," Seibowitz responded. "Either there's something there or there isn't! I *personally* walked over that area with Ed, and I didn't see anything but grass either. There's not even a tiny *bump* out there. It's as flat as a pancake."

"There are houses out there," Bill insisted in a precise voice. "We had a field school up two years ago, remember?" She should, she'd tried to do everything she could to stop it. The only reasons Bill had managed to get his state excavation permit were that it didn't cost anything and that the prestige of the university lent status to the Parks Department. "They opened an exploratory trench across that part of the park—right where you want to run your road, Ed. Several domestic artifacts and features were uncovered from that trench. You know, potsherds, stone tools. They even hit a fire pit." When he drew annoyed looks from everyone around him, he added, "You can't *see* the houses. But they're there. Underground!"

"Show me a *house*!" Smith retorted. "What are we talking about? Foundations? Basements? It had better be good, to stop a twenty-million-dollar highway improvement project!"

Bill ground his teeth for a moment. "Listen, Ed. Middle Woodland domestic activities are the least understood aspect of one of the most important cultural periods in the prehistory of the world!"

"Wait a minute." Roman raised his hand. "Middle what?"

Bill exhaled tiredly. How many times did he have to repeat himself? "Middle Woodland. That's what archaeologists call the cultural period into which we fit all the Adena-Hopewell sites like this one. The period lasts from about two hundred B.C. to about four hundred A.D. Middle Woodland is extremely important, but it's largely an enigma."

"What do you mean, an enigma?" Seibowitz asked, frown lines etching her forehead. "To hear the archaeologists talk, everything is an enigma."

Damn you, woman! All the archaeological parks in this state are under your supervision—and you don't even know why they're important! Bill forced himself to remain calm, professional. "All right, think of it like this. These people developed trade relationships that exchanged silver, copper, and furs from Ontario for sharks' teeth, conch shell, and barracuda jaws from the Florida keys. They imported obsidian from as far away as Yellowstone Park in Wyoming. Mica was traded from North Carolina, greenstone from Alabama. Finished goods like platform pipes, and raw materials like Flint Ridge chert, were traded out of Ohio and then up and down all the major rivers. Had white settlers not built the city of Newark, Ohio on top of the earthworks, it would be one of the premier archaeological sites in the world today. The Hopewell people there covered four and a half square *miles* with earth alignments. They built the first road in North America, from Newark, Ohio, to Chillicothe.''

"Yeah, but so what?'' Smith asked. ''We've got a bunch of weird piles of dirt, huge circles, octagons, squares . . . what were they used for?''

"They seem to have been places for worship and scientific study, as well as social centers. We're just beginning to understand them. Most of the complex earthworks were built to chart celestial events—the movements of the sun, moon, and stars. Archaeoastronomy is still in its infancy. I think we're in for a series of shocks as we begin to find out just how sophisticated these people really were.''

"So, it was like an empire? Similar to what they did in Rome?'' Seibowitz asked, her nose looking even more pinched.

"No. It wasn't an empire. And that's one of the big problems.'' Jaffman pressed his toe into the grass as he thought. Birds sang in the trees, but the whimpers still continued, seeming to follow the entourage around the park, rising and falling with the wind. ''The culture appears to have been focused around trade rather than on military conquest. At Pinson Mounds in Tennessee, people piled up over a hundred thousand cubic meters of earth. At the Hopewell site, in Ohio, they mounded almost fifty-four thousand cubic meters of earth. The amount of earth at Newark would have been anyone's guess, probably well over a hundred thousand cubic meters. The point is that it took generations—and considerable planning—to undertake such extraordinary engineering projects. You can't stand on the Eagle Mound inside the Great Circle at Newark, or look across the Octagon there, without being awestruck.''

"Right,'' Smith said. ''Awestruck. Big deal. Some chief told his Indians, 'You boys go dig here, and pile there,' and liking their scalps on their heads, they did.''

Bill tightened his arms, hugging himself. He wondered if Hopewell engineers, two thousand years ago, had that same single-minded lack of imagination. "No chiefs, Ed. Like I said, just farmers who came together on special occasions to build some of the most remarkable earthen monuments in the world.''

Roy Roman shook a strand of blond hair away from his face. "I don't get it. If these folks were so great and they were spread all over the eastern half of North America, why haven't I heard about them?'' He pointed to the low mound of earth near the park office. "That mound doesn't look all that high and mighty.''

Bill answered, "You haven't heard about them because our educational system almost completely ignores the contributions of the native peoples. And . . .'' He exhaled heavily. "In the past four hundred years, we've systematically destroyed just about every major mound site in North America. For centuries, we couldn't even allow ourselves to believe that native peoples built these monuments. It had to be lost Welshmen, Vikings, the lost tribes of Israel, Phoenicians, anyone but our own American Indians. We—''

"You're not gonna turn politically correct on me, are you, Bill?'' Disgust twisted the set of Smith's lips.

"I'm providing you with historical fact, not political opinion.''

"So why is it that we've only got dirt? Circles like this one?'' Roman pointed across the park. "Didn't they do anything else?''

"Of course they did. But their buildings were made of wood, thatch, and bark, and you know how long wood lasts in this climate. Certainly not for two thousand years. The soils all across the eastern half of the continent are wet and highly acidic. If I buried Ed out here and dug him up two thousand years from now, all we'd find would be the lenses from his glasses, the fillings from his teeth, those brass eyelets in his shoes, the snap on his pants, and his zipper. The rest would be gone.''

"Then what's the point?'' Anne Seibowitz asked as she smoothed her lavender skirt. "If nothing's left, why—''

"Because there *is* something left. We recover the copper, silver, stonework, charred remains of magnificent textiles. Tool stone from all over the continent. Pollen grains, charred seeds, charcoal, bits of burned bone, broken pottery, phytoliths, and burials. We've got better tools now. We can even lift blood proteins—thousands of years old—from stone tools. We can isolate the DNA to see if the people were hunting mammoths or other human beings. We can trace each piece of copper we recover right back to the original vein it came from—the same with the chert.''

"Chert?'' Roman asked.

"Most people call it flint." Bill clenched his fists at his sides. "The point is that we need more excavations before we can truly grasp who these people were. We especially need information on their everyday activities. Can you imagine archaeologists trying to reconstruct our North American culture two thousand years from now? If they've only dug up our churches and synagogues, or the World Trade Towers, what do you think they'll say about us?''

Smith tipped his head back, staring at the dark clouds that drifted across the afternoon sky. "Sounds like you want to dig up the whole eastern half of the continent. You park administrators are always—''

"No. That's *not* what I said. I said that ninety-nine percent of it is already gone. You've flown over the entire Midwest, Ed. What do you see when you look out the plane window? One plowed field after another! Then city after city. We have a few tiny, undisturbed places left to look at. *That's all we have.* This is one of those places.''

"Listen, Bill, that's not my problem, okay? My problem is that I've got to run a highway across a corner of this park. The survey is complete; we've condemned and bought up the private ground on either side. We can't save every potsherd in America!''

"No,'' Bill sighed. "We can't. But this site, *this site,* is very important. We—''

"Come on, Bill! You're talking about a big circle and a mound inside a little postage stamp of green grass.''

The wind had died down and, with it, the mourning sounds of the ghosts, but he could still feel them there, watching, listening, praying. "Yes, and they were probably the focal point for a clan, or for a group of clans that occupied over six hundred square miles of this river valley and its tributaries. We have *one hundred acres* left, and you want to blade up thirty-five of them?''

Ed Smith adjusted his black-rimmed glasses and took a step closer, his jaw set. ''Why don't we face some facts, pal? We've got thirteen point six million dollars of Federal highway money going into this new beltway. The beltway is going in because all those nice yuppies have bought houses in the suburbs, right? They don't like waiting in traffic, burning up expensive gasoline in their expensive cars. Now, Mr. Roman here, from the governor's office, was called in because *if* we can get this beltway in fast, a big computer manufacturer is going to build a sixty-million-dollar plant out on Orchard Road.'' He raised a finger. ''Are you following me, Bill? Your entire park budget is fifty grand a year. Getting the picture here? It's priorities we're talking about.''

Bill shoved his hands into his pockets again, straining at his feeling of utter impotence. ''It's always money, isn't it?''

''Welcome to the real world, friend.''

Bill smiled humorlessly, took a deep breath and looked out across the park, meeting dozens of invisible eyes. ''We're supposed to be able to excavate cultural resources as part of Federal highway money.''

''Yeah, well, that hasn't been budgeted,'' Smith stated simply, and began a diligent study of his fingernails. ''Any final decision on such expenditures will come out of the governor's office, but I'll tell you this. DOT has already compromised. We guarantee we can miss the circle out there. You've got to meet us in the middle, Bill. Give a little.''

''Give a little? . . . All right, I will.'' Bill turned to Anne Seibowitz. ''I need twenty thousand dollars to test that thirty-five acres before it's bladed. In six months, with a crew of ten—mostly students and volunteers—we can recover maybe ten percent. That's at least enough for a statistical sample of the domestic activities represented there.''

Her prim mouth pursed into a white line. ''Where do you suppose Parks and Rec could find that kind of money?''

''You spent two hundred and twenty thousand paving the parking lot up at Mallard Lake. You mean you can't find—''

"Be serious!" She looked him up and down. "Recreational visitors must have a place to park so they can go in and spend money at the tourist centers. Parking lots are essential to our operations, Mr. Jaffman. Now if you were asking me for funding for a parking lot, and your visitation numbers could support it, *which they can't,* I'd consider—"

"My God," Bill Jaffman softly replied. He dropped his face into his hands and briskly rubbed his forehead. "You'll give me money for a parking lot, but not a cent to excavate—"

"Tell me something." Roy Roman cracked his knuckles. "Why would this house site be so important?"

Bill swallowed—it was like choking down a knotted sock—and turned to him. "Once again, it's because Middle Woodland houses are so very rare. We're talking about a society that lasted over six hundred years, traded across the continent—and didn't build large urban complexes."

Roman glanced at Seibowitz, but spoke to Bill. "Well, I'll let the governor know what we're dealing with here. I'm sure he'll make the right decision." He paused. "If you just *had* something here. You know, something that people could see besides piles of dirt. Maybe then—"

"I've been trying to get funding for an interpretive center for that very thing for the last three years," Bill replied passionately, and saw Anne's eyes narrow as she readied herself for combat. "With just two or three thousand dollars, I could use my summer volunteers to put in a goosefoot-and-maygrass field, build a charnel hut—maybe construct interpretive exhibits like the superb ones they have at the Cahokia site in Illinois, or at Poverty Point in Louisiana. At Saint Marie Among the Hurons in Ontario, they have a complete Huron longhouse and a living-history program. We could *do* that here! Make it all come alive!"

Anne Seibowitz turned away, looking out past the trees to where the peaked roofs of apartment buildings could be seen. "Bill, you know that visitation has been down here. If your numbers were up, if the public seemed at all interested in your little park, the budget might be—"

"How can I attract visitors without an interpretive center to tell people what they're looking at and why it's important? I need funding, Anne!"

She turned, lifting a thin eyebrow. "Bill, I'll be honest. I can't see how this freeway expansion is going to hurt. Look on the positive side. It might just give you more exposure. People will see the greenery from the highway, and, well . . . who knows? They might just want to stop. When your visitation goes up, perhaps we can find the funding to put in some interpretive exhibits."

Of course thirty-five acres of precious archaeology would be gone by then.

Roy Roman's eyes widened suddenly, as if the light of escape had just been turned on for him. "Yes! It'll *help* visitation!"

Bill felt the final straw settling on his back like a ton of lead. "There are laws to protect state antiquities, you know. If the governor sides with you, Mr. Roman, you won't just have SOPA on your back. The regional tribes will throw a fit. This is a sacred site for them, and once they hear—"

"That's not a threat, is it, Bill?" Anne raised that eyebrow a little farther, and he understood only too well her own threat: *It's easy to get rid of troublemakers like you, buddy boy.* "I know you were trained as an archaeologist, but our state parks are more than just single-use sites. We've got to be responsive to everyone's needs. Joggers, hikers, bird-watchers—"

"*Freeway* builders!" he half-shouted. "Forget it, Anne. I was hired by your predecessor just before she resigned. It was her misguided idea that it made good sense to put an archaeologist in an archaeological state park designed to protect some of the last Adena-Hopewell mounds in this part of the state."

"Bill, you're pushing your—"

"No, I'm just telling it like it is, Anne. I've beaten my head against the wall and the system for years. I still have interpretive signs out here that were written in the *fifties* by little old ladies from the local historical society. They claim these earthworks were forts, for God's sake!"

"At least you've got signs," Roman said. "Some of our parks don't even have that luxury."

Bill raised his arms as if imploring sense. "All right. If we can't interpret this site for the public, we can at least protect it, can't we? *Give me some money to test that area before you blade it!* Or has the governor decided that this state's prehistory isn't important? Is that it? Is that what we're really talking about?''

Anne Seibowitz gave him a cold stare. Roy Roman had backed away and was scrutinizing the maintenance shed as if it had become inordinately fascinating.

Seibowitz—her expression like marble—said, ''I'm sorry to lose you, Bill. I'll have personnel announce the position vacancy in the next mailing.''

He should have been angry, should have raged, tramped up and down and cursed. Instead, only an empty sense of futility opened within him. A wind gust whipped around the park, and the cries rose, shrill and desperate.

Bill stood alone on the nature trail, watching the dignitaries as they got into their vehicles and left. Rain had started again, falling in misty drops, beading on his hot face.

He turned around and walked back toward the Circle to stand at the entry that led inside. He could imagine the shamans, resplendent in colorful costumes, watching him through hollow eyes, knowing in the manner of spirits that another part of their world had been condemned.

''Forgive me,'' Bill whispered. ''I'm sorry.''

The soft roar of traffic in the distance, the barking of dogs, and the occasional slamming of a door, carried across the chain-link fence to this quiet corner of the park. Here, in another six months, there would be a different roar, that of bulldozers, earth-movers, and graders.

He dragged his feet through the grass, noting that it needed to be cut again, and to his surprise, spotted something protruding from amidst the green blades.

Kneeling down, he removed his folding knife from his pocket and chiseled the soil away, exposing polished stone. With careful fingers, he freed the object. It felt cool and heavy in his hand.

The piece had been crafted from banded slate; it was dark and lustrous, probably from the quarries in southern Ohio. Hopewell people had made pendants, gorgets, pipes, all sorts of beautiful stonework. What he now inspected represented some of the finest artistry he'd ever seen.

It was a canoe, with an unusual fox head carved on the

pointed bow. Four people sat inside. The second in line faced backward. Now, what did *that* signify? The specimen was roughly fifteen centimeters long and five centimeters tall.

In the trees behind him, a crow cawed angrily.

Bill looked up and saw the bird perched on the edge of a beech tree that overhung the circular earthwork. "Don't worry," he said wearily. "After all, that moron DOT engineer insisted they would miss the circle by exactly twenty-eight feet and seven whole inches."

The crow flapped its wings in the slanting sunlight, and the sheen from the feathers seemed to glow radiantly.

He gazed down at the canoe again. He couldn't help but think of the carvings he'd seen at Petroglyph Provincial Park, in Ontario. Along with Gitchie Manitou and Nanabush, there were many, many canoe figures. *But none like this. None with a fox-head prow.*

He had studied Hopewell culture ever since graduate school and knew its artwork. Stylistically, this was new. Around him, the grass waved and bobbed, hiding the wealth of information just down under that root mat.

"Damn you, Anne Seibowitz."

The crow made a low, mournful sound, cocking its head, blinking.

Bill sat back on the wet grass, not caring if he stained his uniform. Tomorrow he'd come out with the transit, shoot in the location of the effigy carving, and mail the little canoe down to the university for curation. Then anyone else finding a similar artifact could cross-reference it from the computer curation files—and maybe one of these days, someone would bitch like mad because the key to one more puzzle had been stripped away for a slab of asphalt.

Maybe. . . . A pathetic laugh shook his chest. Who? And by then, Anne Seibowitz would have been promoted to a more influential job. The governor would be in Congress. No one would have to be responsible.

Bracing a hand on the grass, he rose and started back toward the office and the row of shiny trucks, any one of which would have paid for the test excavation he'd pleaded for.

The crow followed him, flying from branch to branch,

squawking. As he walked, he looked down at the four travelers in their canoe. Traders? Is that what they were?

Hopewell traders had crisscrossed the continent, following the rivers, carrying goods all over. It must have been both terrifying and wonderful.

But that was an age of heroes. . . .

He stopped by the admission booth, the ''Gestapo Box'' as he called it, and opened the mailbox to pull out the daily supply of advertisements and junk mail. The *SAA Bulletin,* the newsletter of the Society for American Archaeology, huddled among the dross. Bill chucked the rest into the garbage can and headed for the office, flipping through the newsletter as he walked. In the classified section, jobs were listed.

He paused to read one: ''Navajo Nation archaeological preservation project is currently seeking applications for full-time employment . . .''

A car horn blared in the distance. The crow had gone silent, but now flew down to land on the stack of orange-and-white traffic barricades propped against the rear wall of the office.

''Window Rock, Arizona,'' Bill mused. He glanced at the crow, which peered back at him intently. ''Do you think I could do it? Just throw everything into the truck and go? Uproot my whole life?''

The thought frightened him. Way out there, alone, surrounded by a strange people in an alien land. *So, what's keeping you here?* His relationship with Marge had broken up weeks ago.

He looked down, thinking about the Hopewell traders who had carried entire canoe-loads of obsidian down the river systems. Imagine that, from Yellowstone to the heart of the eastern woodlands. They did it. Two thousand years ago!

He inspected the stone canoe and the faces of the people sitting inside. What would it have been like? Who were they? Heroes? They'd inspired this carving, whoever they were.

The crow hopped to a wheelbarrow handle no more than an arm's distance away. It clucked to get his attention and studied him with one round black eye, then the other, as if measuring his soul.

The stone canoe felt warmer in his fingers.

To the crow, Bill said, ''I've spent my entire life studying the Hopewell people, always living in my head with the ancestors, trying to hear their ghosts, to learn from them." He smiled faintly. "Maybe it's time I go and share my efforts with some living people who care about something besides money. Do you think the Navajo will want to know about the Hopewell? Their roots are Athapaskan, from the Northwest, not Eastern Algonquian. Tell me, crow. Will they care . . . and can I do it?"

The crow launched itself and dove right in front of Bill's face, forcing him to backpedal. Then it flew one big circle around the administration office before heading due west.

Bill gazed back out across the site. The ghosts had gone quiet, somber. His eyes narrowed with thought. "Thank you," he said, "for guiding me."

He tightened his grip on the stone canoe and thought about the adventure that lay ahead. In his heart, he sensed that these heroes from the past envied him.

A very, very old story was told in the dead of winter, late at night, when Owl hooted across the frozen forests. Like all stories, it carried a lesson and a truth for the people. Some say the story came from the High Heads; others, that it was born of the wind and nurtured of the soul. . . .

Once, long ago, in the time of the ancestors, people had refused to care for the Dead, and the earth was filled with ghosts who committed every kind of mischief. Finally, in desperation, the ghosts had appealed to First Man, explaining their plight.

First Man heard their plaintive cries and sent his twin brother, Many Colored Crow, to help them. In those days, Crow possessed feathers so bright they made the painted bunting look dull and lusterless.

Many Colored Crow walked across the land, telling the people about the Dead and their troubles. He explained that if the people would honor and care for their ancestors, the Spirits would reciprocate. They would help the living by bringing messages from the Spirit World. The ghosts would cease harming people and quit playing tricks on them. Everything would be better.

The people heard the words of Many Colored Crow and began to care for the Dead. But so many ghosts walked the land that Many Colored Crow had to do something more. He had been passing through the forest when he found a high hill. Around the base of the hill, he gathered piles of dry brush. Then he climbed to the top and built a fire in a clay pot. He prayed for four days, Singing to the four sacred directions, and the ghosts heard. They came from all over the world to see what Many Colored Crow was doing. On the day of the winter solstice, all the ghosts had finally arrived.

At last, one of the ghosts—a warrior who had died in battle and whose body had been cut up—asked Many Colored Crow, "What are you doing up here on top of this mountain, Singing and Dancing? We have all come to see."

Many Colored Crow raised his hands to the morning sun, saying, "I have brought you here to Sing you to the Land of the Dead. But you cannot go as you are now. You are full of anger, trouble, and evil. You must be cleansed of this before I Sing you to the Land of the Dead."

And saying that, Many Colored Crow picked up the pot with the fire burning inside it and whirled it around his head, scattering the burning embers into the dry brush. The brush instantly caught fire, and the whole mountain was engulfed in flames. The ghosts cried out and tried to escape, but the fire completely surrounded them. In the end, all that remained were ashes. These, Many Colored Crow collected and carried with him to the Land of the Dead, where the souls were finally freed. All the wickedness had been burned away.

In the process, however, Many Colored Crow's brilliant feather colors had vanished, all of them burned a deep black—which is why, to this day, Crow has black feathers.

Prologue

I was young then, foolish and wild. I traveled into the forbidden territory of the High Heads. There I climbed their sacred mountain. Searching . . . I knew not for what. The voice in the Dream told me to go . . . to search for something. I found a rock overhang on the northern side of the mountain where the sandstone had been undercut. A dead man sat there . . . long, long-time dead, and dried out.''

Grandfather's words filled Mica Bird's memory, mingling with his fear.

The young warrior walked in a world of dappled green, where the forest floor cushioned each step. Damp leaves, yellow, brown, and matted, crushed under his moccasined feet. Around him rose the sturdy boles of trees, thick and dark, creating an interwoven maze on the steep slope he climbed. The musky scent of the forest intensified. Vines of wild grape hung like impossible strands of rope, some of them as thick as a man's leg.

Mica Bird stopped, panting, sweat glistening on his brown skin. Overhead, the leafy canopy of the forest interlaced in an emerald miracle; but in this place, where he paused to catch his breath, Mica Bird stood like a wraith in the brooding shadows.

Here, so far into the hills, the oak, hickory, maple, and walnut giants prevailed. He placed a hand on the smooth, silvery bark of a beech, sensing the eternal Power of the ancient tree.

The humid air pressed around him, breathlessly hot, even for this time of deep summer. Though he gasped, the air seemed to offer no relief for his laboring lungs. An earth oven might have been this searing, this miserable.

High overhead, birds chirped and called. The trill of a redstart carried magically. In the distance, the sacred crow cawed and clucked.

Late at night, they had been in the clan house. Mica Bird remembered Grandfather's rasping words: *"I thought it was curious that his people hadn't buried this dead man. That they had just left him sitting there. I stepped under the overhang, looking at the moss that hung down. Not a blade of grass grew in that place of darkness. It was cold—even in the summer heat. My heart beat with fear. Perhaps he had called me, sent his ghost to bother my Dreams."*

At the sudden scurry of sound, Mica Bird wheeled, frantically fumbling to nock a dart in the hook of his atlatl, then saw the gray squirrel that seemed to defy earth as it leaped up a dead sapling, jumped to a branch, and shot across open air to reach another tree.

Mica Bird wiped the beading sweat from his forehead with a trembling hand. This wasn't his country, this land of the High Heads. Here, he was unwelcome—an intruder in this ominous forest.

This place had a strange feel, unlike the rich bottomlands he knew so well. From childhood, he had learned the winding trails that led along the sluggish waters of the Moonshell River. In those familiar haunts, the ghosts of the ancestors watched over their clansmen. At any one of the farmsteads in the Moonshell valley, he could trace a relationship—sometimes back four tens of generations—and claim kinship.

In this forest, people did not live. On steep slopes such as these, fields couldn't be cleared; the land wouldn't produce rich harvests of goosefoot, sunflower, marsh elder, or squash. This place the High Heads kept to themselves, calling it sacred ground.

People traveled the forests, of course, but generally to hunt, or to collect walnuts, acorns, plums, or medicinal plants. In times of war, the clans fled to hilltop fortifications. This mountain, however, remained inviolate; even the High Heads avoided it.

But Grandfather had come here, and so many years later, he'd told Mica Bird: *"A fabric bag lay beside the dead man, and I could tell that it was something important, something precious. The corpse seemed to look at me, pleading. I felt that pleading, even though the eyes were gone—all shrunk away into pits in the skull. Its jaw had dropped open, as if crying out in death.*

"One dried-out hand, like a claw, you know? It lay on that bag. I thought the bag must hold something very valuable."

In the clan-house firelight, Grandfather had looked away, seeing back into the past—into that rock shelter.

Barely twenty winters in age, Mica Bird had grown wiry and tall. As the son of an important man in the clan, his forehead had been tattooed with a black stripe, which accented the firm lines of his jaw and his broad, straight nose. Normally, a serious intent filled his dark brown eyes, but here, in this haunting place, fear glinted instead.

He traveled light, wearing only moccasins and a breechcloth. A mica pendant hung from a leather thong around his neck. His small pack, made from thick strands of double-twisted cord, hung over one shoulder. In his right hand he carried the atlatl, a supple stick a little longer than his forearm. The grip had been carved from the main beam of a white-tailed deer antler. A small black stone carved into the shape of a crow had been lashed to the center of the shaft to act as a counterweight. Finally, a bone hook capped the end.

In his other hand he carried four war darts, each longer than he was tall. A crudely flaked point of black chert tipped each thin shaft, crafted from the arrowwood plant. Turkey feathers fletched the shaft and kept it stable in flight. The butt had been hollowed to fit into the hook at the end of the atlatl.

The atlatl itself acted as an extension of the arm. With it, Mica Bird could catapult one of the darts with enough force to drive it the complete length of a bear's body—as he had proven in the past.

A bear would be easy to deal with compared to the strangeness of this unfamiliar forest. He sensed a presence far more ominous lurking in this shadow-dappled wilderness.

Skin prickled on his neck the way it would if unseen eyes were watching. Ghosts? Is that why the High Heads feared this place so much? Feverish winds brushed his bare chest, and he spun around, searching. The presence seemed to pulse with the wet heat, studying, gauging.

A man had to know how to see in the forest. An odd angle, a shade of color, or a break in the uneven latticework of saplings and tree trunks, might be the only clue available to the hunter. Now he scrutinized the patterns of trunk and limb, of leaf and vine. In the crazy warp and weft of forest, he could find nothing out of place.

Mica Bird swallowed hard. The thick bitterness of thirst coated his tongue.

He eased around a beech tree. Sweat trickled down his chest, refusing to dry in the damp heat.

He proceeded carefully, inspecting the steep slope above him. The old man had to have come here. The stories echoed in Mica Bird's memory. He could hear his grandfather's age-scratchy voice over the crackle of that long-dead fire: "*So I stepped closer, farther under the overhanging rock . . . and I could hear Singing. I swear it. I could hear the voice of an old woman Singing. Like this:*

> "*And among the People?*
> *Come the Brothers!*
> *Born of Sun. One is slayed.*
> *Here, by the long trail, his corpse is laid.*
> *Blood is spread, from the head.*
> *Black one goes . . . aye, he's dead.*
> *He who loves is lost and gone.*
> *Render of the fair heart's Song.*
> *Woman, weep, for naught you know.*
> *Lose forever—or live in snow!*"

Mica Bird shook himself free of a sudden shiver. Yes, those were the words—as clear to him now as they had been that night.

"*I was afraid,*" the old man had said. "*I began to shake, and I couldn't stop. It was as if Power possessed me. I couldn't help myself from reaching for the bag, taking it from the dead man's grasp.*

"*I stepped back then, and tried to breathe, but a coldness had entered my lungs and spread through my soul. I backed away, legs trembling like a newborn fawn's.*

"*When I was outside, beyond the covering of rock, I opened the bag and looked inside. There, as perfect as if it had just been made, lay the Mask.*"

Mica Bird smiled greedily at the very thought of the Mask—and of what it would mean to him. The Mask of Many Colored

Crow had been a thing of awesome beauty. He had seen it only four times in all his life. The last time had been that night. Grandfather had pulled the worn sack over to his side and opened it with reverent fingers to expose the Raven Mask before lifting it free.

In the firelight, it had gleamed. The wooden beak had been carved by a master and stained black. Glistening feathers covered the sides of the oval head, each feather lying flat, as if preened despite the confines of the sack. Funny, could this huge Mask really have appeared so small a bundle when bound by the sack?

Grandfather's arms had begun to tremble, and the old man groaned as if in a struggle. The Mask turned, and the hollow eyes, like two openings into another world, stared at Mica Bird.

The sensation created by those empty orbs had jolted him. A thrill, tingling with the intensity and pleasure of orgasm, had bolted along his nerves, while a sense of empty loss had leached into his soul, hollowing it out.

Since then, that Spirit face had lurked behind his every thought. In his Dreams, the Mask stared at him—and the eyes glowed with Power.

"He who looks through the Mask," Grandfather had stated solemnly, *"sees through the eyes of Many Colored Crow. That long-ago day, I raised the Mask and looked through it. I never saw the world the same way again. It made me—made this clan—all that it is today."*

Mica Bird scaled the steep slope, his legs aching. He paused in the consuming shadow of a shagbark hickory.

Something had happened to Grandfather, had driven him to take the Mask away. For he had worn it for the last time at the Feast of the Dead—the ceremony that marked the summer solstice, when the clan gathered to attend to the ghosts of the ancestors, to bury their dead, and to care for the mighty earthworks of the clan grounds.

Afterward, the old man hadn't been the same. He'd stared with vacant eyes, more bent and crippled than ever. His last words, too, lingered in Mica Bird's ears: *"It has eaten my soul. I should never have taken it. Back . . . it must go back. This is not a thing for men."*

And the next day, the old man had disappeared.

Mica Bird steeled himself and attacked the slope again, fighting upward in the still air. How high was this mountain?

As he climbed through the wavering green shadows, sweat beaded and slipped down his muscular legs.

Why hadn't the High Heads ever mentioned the Mask? Only now did the question fasten itself in his thoughts. Surely they must have heard that Grandfather had it; but no one had come looking for it, demanding it back.

Why not?

The Rattlesnake Clan had gone to war with the Many Paints when their sacred Deer Headdress was stolen. For three years, the two clans had warred upon each other, until a peace was brokered by the Goosefoot Clan and the Headdress had been returned.

Why hadn't the High Heads—with all of their clans and influence—ever mentioned the Mask's disappearance?

Stop thinking about it! Mica Bird sucked in a steadying breath. *You'll drive yourself crazy.*

Perhaps he was crazy already. It had surprised him when he'd realized that he *had* to have the Mask! With it, he would be the next leader of the Shining Bird Clan, and would raise his clan above all the others in the Moonshell valley—even above the clans to the north.

Tumbled boulders, angular fragments of weathered sandstone, poked up through the leaf mat. Mica Bird struggled to catch his breath. The top had to be close now.

Why did it have to be so hot and humid? The very air seemed to sap his strength.

Step by trembling step, he continued his climb.

Through the mass of trees, he could make out the irregular line of stone that marked the mountain's cap. Close, yes. It had to be here somewhere.

He searched for any sign the old man might have made in passing. Grandfather didn't walk so well these days, his body crooked and bowed by age. How had the old man made this steep climb?

Panting and gasping, Mica Bird picked his way over roots and vines until he reached the sullen scarp. The sandstone had blackened with age where it thrust out of the mountain's side.

Sundered and cracked, it nevertheless provided a serious obstacle to any further progress.

Squinting against the burning sweat that streamed down his face, Mica Bird studied the rise. A hill like this would have been fortified in his own territory. War didn't plague the clans often, but when it did, people liked a place to retreat to. The isolated farmsteads might be efficient for farming, but not for defense.

Placing his feet carefully, he worked his way along the broken rock, stepping around holes where trees had fallen, their massive trunks rotting away on the ground.

On one flat surface, a pile of fresh bear manure still drew flies. Mica Bird's grip tightened on his atlatl. Bears didn't usually attack a man, but they could be dangerous if surprised.

The cawing of the crow sounded louder.

So where was this shelter? How far did the sandstone ledge extend?

Or had the old man been blowing wind? Was that it? Had it all been a story? Was that why the High Heads had never mentioned the Mask? Grandfather was clever enough to make up such a story. He could have kept his authority by lies as easily as by the truth.

Feeling suddenly weary, Mica Bird settled on one of the boulders. Mushrooms grew in the molded leaves at his feet. Had the old man hoaxed the clan? Was his Power nothing but illusion? Had his terrifying personal aura been a trick to keep the people under his control?

Stories passed from lip to lip about how Grandfather had looked at a rival through the Mask . . . and killed him dead. Could that have been feint? Perhaps a little water hemlock slipped into a drink?

Mica Bird licked his dry lips, remembering the burning intensity in the old man's eyes. No, it couldn't have been a trick. He could not—would not—believe that.

Standing, he forced himself onward, searching for the dry overhang. He disciplined himself to pay attention, battling to remain vigilant despite his weariness and thirst.

The Mask of Many Colored Crow had to be here. The old man had always done what he said he would do, whether it was the destruction of a rival or the offering of a sacrifice. He must have brought the Mask here, returned it to the shriveled hands of a dead man.

Despite his keen eye, Mica Bird almost missed the place. Cedar trees had grown in a green web over the mouth of the overhang, hiding it. Only the curious odor of musty air caused him to backtrack.

Mica Bird pushed through the supple branches and stared.

The weathered sandstone caprock, splotched with moss and water stains, jutted out from the hilltop to create a small cavern. The roof of the hollow had been stained black by fires, and the rear wall looked rough and irregular. Bare ground lay before him, dark and dry from dung and old fires.

When Mica Bird stepped into the recess, a sudden chill ate into him. Blinking in the gloom, he could make out two shapes leaning against the rear wall. He forced his weak legs to move and stepped into the darkness. The air seemed to swell and billow around him.

"You've come." The old man's voice sounded weary, defeated.

"Grandfather?"

As Mica Bird's vision adjusted, he located his grandfather's withered form where it hunched against the rock in the back. How bent and crooked he appeared. Was this the same man Mica Bird remembered? Where had the broad shoulders gone? What had happened to that arrogant Power that had radiated from Grandfather like heat from a glowing rock? This man, this dried pod of a human, couldn't be the same, could he?

Mica Bird turned his attention to the hunched form propped next to his grandfather. A shriveled corpse. The dead man from the story. The body was just as Grandfather had described it: hollow pits where the eyes had been, mouth open, the expression pleading. One rigid hand hung over empty air, as if patting something. For a long moment, Mica Bird stared, haunted by the desolation reflected in the corpse's posture. As if . . . yes, as if its soul had been looted away and only emptiness remained.

Mica Bird summoned his courage. "I . . . I came for the Mask."

Grandfather's stick-thin arms closed protectively around the familiar fabric bag that lay on his lap. When the old man tilted his head to look up, his face appeared wilted, as if eaten away from the inside. Through the shining white hair and the sunken flesh, the outline of the skull could be seen.

Grandfather whispered, "Leave here. Now, boy. There is nothing here for you. Only sorrow . . . pain."

"I must have the Mask. You can't take that from me."

The old man hunched in silence, staring at the dust before his feet. Finally, he asked, "And what would you have from it? Power? The ability to rule the clan? No, Mica Bird. Leave it here. This thing . . . this cursed thing destroys."

Mica Bird couldn't keep his gaze from straying to the hideous corpse. Brown strips of flesh cleaved to the brittle bones. Dry tufts of dusty hair still clung to the hardened scalp. Once-pliable lips had dried to leather and shrunk to a leering rictus, exposing broken teeth. The tattered remains of brightly dyed clothing—dust-coated and faded—fit the dwindled corpse like sacking. Mice and wood rats had frayed the fine weave. Here and there, beads had fallen from the magnificent breastplate. What had once been the trappings of wealth and status now reeked of mold and decay.

Mica Bird hesitated. Where was its ghost? Hovering in the air? Was that the cold presence Mica Bird sensed?

Finally, he forced himself to meet his grandfather's haunted eyes. "Why did you come here?"

"To die, boy. To die as I have lived. Alone, eaten away with hatred and selfishness. This Mask, its Power is that of death and misery. Don't follow in my footsteps. You'll destroy yourself."

"Then why didn't you bring it back before? Why did you keep it if it's so horrible?"

The old man chuckled evilly. "Because it wouldn't let me. You must understand, boy, that when you look through the Mask, Many Colored Crow lets you *see*. Is that what you want? To see through a Spirit's eyes? To see nothing but the weakness in others? To see how you can hurt people? Use them for your benefit? You will lose all of the beauty in the world. You will never see a sunrise and admire its colors—you'll see only the possibilities that particular day might bring you. Is that what you want?"

Mica Bird straightened. "I would have that Power."

Grandfather made a huffing sound. "You don't know what you ask. Go home. Live your life. Be a farmer, and be happy.

Don't ruin yourself. Don't become another victim of the Mask.''

''Victim? I'll be the most Powerful man among the clans. With the Mask, Star Shell will marry me. I will become the leader of my people. I shall construct the greatest monuments ever built. My name will be spoken from the lips of generations still unborn.''

Grandfather's head slumped forward. ''Yes, it will give you Star Shell. But hear my words. You will never see her through loving eyes. When your children are born, you will see only what they can do for you, or what threat they might be to your status or your goals. You will never see your friends as they are, but for what they can gain you. You will lose that part of you which is human.''

''I don't believe you.''

''I don't suppose you would. But then, I have seen you through eyes different than anyone else's. From the time you were little, I've seen this coming.''

''Then why did you ever show me the Mask?''

''Because it forced me to.'' He coughed and wiped his dirty sleeve over his mouth. ''That night in the clan house. I couldn't stop myself. It wasn't I who showed you the Mask. Raven Hunter . . . he did. He possessed me, as he's possessed me from the moment I first looked through his horrible Mask.''

''Raven Hunter?''

''Many Colored Crow, Bird Man, call him what you will. The Dark Twin, boy. The bloody brother of First Man. For everything there is an opposite. Without both sides, there could be no balance. No harmony. The Mysterious One made the world that way.''

''So, if you are possessed by Many Colored Crow, why does he let you tell me this now?''

''Because I'm dying. For the first time since I looked through the Mask, he's let go, freed my soul. I can see now, see what I've done. Terrible things. Only now, as I die, do I see the mistakes.'' Grandfather sighed wearily. ''But you don't care, do you? Nothing I say will make any difference. That's why the Mask allows me to speak so freely. It knows you've already made your decision. You don't hear my words.''

Mica Bird glanced at the dried corpse again, struggling to

keep from shivering. "You just want to keep the Mask, that's all. A prize you can't give up."

Grandfather grunted and looked up, pity in his eyes. "The Mask has already taken your measure, boy . . . like an engineer laying out an earthwork. It knows what it will gain from you."

"Grandfather," he said, suddenly uncertain, "why didn't the High Heads ever ask for the Mask back?"

The old man could barely shrug. "Why would they? They know that it carries its own curse. Having the Mask was punishment enough for what I did. If a man hides a rattlesnake in a pot and a thief steals it, do you warn him? Or do you let justice follow its own course?"

Squaring his shoulders, Mica Bird forced confidence into his voice. "I am taking the Mask with me."

"So you can build your monuments? Be a great leader?"

"That is the way it will be."

A bitter smile curled the old man's lips. "Is it? Hear me, boy. If you take the Mask, it will destroy you. Any monument you build will be as fleeting as a swallow's song on the wind. Where you walk in your false pride, one day the trees will grow tall and thick. Those whom you would love will flee in terror. What the Mask gives, it takes back threefold."

Mica Bird wet dry lips. Did the corpse have to stare so? It seemed to mock him, exposing the few brown teeth left in the curled wreckage of mouth.

Mica Bird forced his attention to Grandfather. "You . . . you tell me this to keep me from taking the Mask, to keep me from becoming greater than you. That's it, isn't it?"

"Believe what you like. But leave. Now! And never come back. Promise me!"

The passion in the old man's voice almost persuaded him— but not quite. "Die in peace, Grandfather. Die knowing that I will lead our people to a greatness that you can only imagine."

"No! Get out of here! Run, boy. Run . . ."

"You can't stop me." Mica Bird stepped closer.

Lackluster eyes stared up at him. The old man's chest rose and fell, the bones visible through the thin fabric of his beautifully woven shirt. "You . . . you must believe me. You're not as strong as I was. Many Colored Crow knows this. Leave the Mask, Mica Bird. Leave it here with my ghost, or it will devour you before you know what's happened. You're weak . . . too weak. I saw that from the moment you were born.''

Mica Bird cocked his head. "If I'm so weak, why would the Mask choose me the way you say it has?''

"It only needs you for a little while, boy. It only needs you to take it back to the people . . . yes,'' Grandfather said, and his eyes widened as if with realization. "That's it. A strong man will come along, someone ambitious. Then the Mask will break you. Throw you away the same as a man discards a dull flake when it has fulfilled its need.''

Mica Bird reached down, closing his fingers around the heavy fabric of the bag. "Farewell, Grandfather. I will Sing your praises at the Feast of the Dead. And bring your body back with me for proper burial.''

"No!'' the frail voice shrieked. "Leave me here! Don't make me watch!''

"Watch?''

"My ghost will torment you, hound you to . . . to . . .'' When Mica Bird tore the sacred sack away, Grandfather's body stiffened. A croaking sounded from that ancient throat. Then the body went limp, like so many sticks broken loose inside.

"Yes,'' Mica Bird whispered to himself. "I'll take you back, Grandfather. Lay you out in the charnel house . . . have your body oiled and smoked. I'll build a tomb for you. A magnificent tomb. You'll be there. With each Feast of the Dead, you'll watch my greatness grow. I'll lay offerings on your tomb. You'll be proud of me.''

In death, the old man's face had taken on an expression of horror.

Mica Bird stared into those dead eyes, memorizing the expression. Then he straightened and studied the finely woven fabric that covered the Mask. The sack had been beautiful once. He would have another made, even more beautiful.

With anxious fingers, he opened the bag, reverently raising the magnificent Mask to his face so that he could stare out at the world through those eyeholes. The Mask's cool surface seemed to conform to his face. He could sense the Power welling, growing around him as he gazed through the green wall of cedar trees.

He blinked. What was happening? Colors . . . all the colors

were draining from the world, bleeding away like life from a body with a mortal wound. The golden rays of sunlight that streamed through the branches paled to a dusty white, bleaching, sucking at the greens and blues until nothing remained but the mottled shades of thunderheads, and yet . . .

Yes, feel it! Power, flowing through me. Changing, making me great!

Through the eyeholes of the Mask, he glanced back at his grandfather's corpse, seeing a blackened, shriveled thing. *Crow Caller*, the name rose unbidden. *Just like Crow Caller's soul when Wolf Dreamer Danced it away.*

Mica Bird lowered the Mask, awed by the words within him. His grandfather lay next to the desiccated corpse, but different now. Not the grandfather he'd always admired and feared, but a husk—like a maggot casing.

It would be difficult to haul the body back, but the impression it would create on his people would make it all worthwhile. He had to think like a leader now. Everything must be calculated for the greatest effect.

A faint whisper of his grandfather's voice seemed to echo in the hollow of the rocks. *No!* it repeated over and over. *No, don't do this thing! Don't make me watch your destruction!*

Taking a deep breath, Mica Bird replaced the Mask in its sack.

When he turned to the task of bearing his grandfather's body, he thought he heard an old woman's voice Singing:

Taken by sea, their father came,
Born of Sun, of Sun the same.
One must live and one must die.
See the souls rise to the sky.

One

The naked young man lay facedown on the split-cane matting of the temple floor. His name was Green Spider, but now he looked more like a plucked bird than a spider. His arms stuck out like wings, his legs were close together. He might have been dead, so limp did he lie.

Only on close inspection could the faint rise and fall of his bony back be detected. Smooth, coppery skin sparkled with beads of sweat. Arching from the middle of each shoulder blade across to the collarbone, three deep cuts marred his flesh. The blood—an offering to the Spirit World—had trickled down the strips of muscle and bone that composed his sapling-thin body. A bone skewer, split from a deer's cannon bone and ground sharp on both ends, pinned the tight bun of thick black hair in place at the base of his skull. He looked young, no more than twenty-five winters in age.

Despite the awkward angle of his head, part of his face could be seen. Broad cheekbones accented a high brow, and the nose appeared narrow and hooked, like a raptor's beak. Thin shells—each delicately carved into the shape of a spider and dyed bright green—dangled from the lobes of his ears.

For four long days—deprived of food, sleep, and water—he'd lain thus: sweating, praying, falling into the hole in his soul, seeking, seeking . . .

. . . and the Vision had begun to form, that of flight . . . sailing . . . twisting on the predawn currents of cloud and wind.

Far below, the earth waited, gray and somber, locked in the grip of winter. Patches of ice-crusted snow molded around the boles of trees and contoured the mottled yellow-brown leaf mat of the oak-hickory forest.

His strangely acute sight located the winding course of the

Father Water and followed the familiar sinuous shape to the mouth of the Deer River, then turned eastward, up toward the divide. Nestled in clearings, small thatched huts clustered, awaiting the winter solstice sunrise.

There, along the north bank of the Deer River, blocky earthen mounds had been constructed on the high terraces above the swampy bottoms. Some—centrally placed—rose higher than the trees and had an unbroken view of the distant horizon. Each capped with yellow sand, they glistened in the predawn light. Other earthen mounds had been placed along the solstice and equinox lines that radiated out from the towering central mound. These were rectangular, and capped with white sand in preparation for the Dances and offerings. Yet other mounds, smaller and rounded, bore the bones and ashes of the Dead. These mounds had been placed along the lines of the constellations.

"Do you know this place?" a voice asked from the hazy gray distance.

"The City of the Dead."

The humped shapes of charnel houses clustered in the flats between the mounds. Young trees had been harvested for their construction, the butts placed in postholes and bent to stress the wood into firm bows before saplings were woven into the framework and lashed together. The whole had been covered by tightly laced shocks of grass.

On this special day, the Spirits of the Dead waited, already anxious and hungry for the feast in their honor.

"I am giving you a special gift," the voice told him. *"I will let you see through my eyes . . . the eyes of Many Colored Crow."*

And the sense of flight changed, altered, gaining Power and the memory of times long past and places far away. Green Spider circled, drawing the clouds around him like a thick cocoon. In one scaled foot he clutched the Power of lightning, ready to strike. With his keen Spirit Vision, he studied the scene below.

"Many Colored Crow?"

"I have heard you crying for a Vision."

"But I . . . it's so . . ."

"Look down! Observe. This is one of the two holiest days of the year."

Despite the sullen cold of winter, people had braved the chill to journey from isolated farmsteads or from the loose aggregates of oblong houses where they gardened, hunted, and gathered food during the year. From as far away as a six-day walk, they had converged on the mound center of the City of the Dead. They came wrapped in blankets, their feet bound to shield them from the crusted snow. Their backs were bowed, burdened by pots full of food, offerings, or the ashes of those who had died during the preceding year. Some had come along the rivers, paddling canoes through the icy waters of still swamps and meandering streams.

People congregated here four times a year, on the solstices and equinoxes. Some came to bury their Dead, others to honor their ancestors, to bring them food or gifts—to remind the Dead that the living remembered and cherished them. To beg for help in the coming year.

Still others came for the feasting and dancing, for on this winter solstice, the shamans would welcome the new year and invite Father Sun to begin his trip northward. Observances would be kept, and sacred artifacts would be cleaned, their Spirits ritually fed and cared for before being stowed in receptacles within the temple buildings.

The ceremonial societies would Dance and perform the rituals that would ensure a good year for all. The young who sought initiation would be tested. Those who passed the ordeals would be accepted into the secrets of their societies. The structures and enclosures within which these events occurred would be inspected and plans laid for their upkeep. The sacred grounds of the City of the Dead would be policed, and invading saplings chopped out.

During the four days of the ceremonies, clans conducted most of their business. The female clan leaders would decide which crops would be planted in spring. Fields needed to be rotated and farmsteads moved. Hours would be spent in serious council regarding soils, seed crops, and where the forests should be cleared. Internal matters would be dealt with: disputes settled, marriages negotiated, and in some cases, divorces granted.

"Will this Vision give me the Power to call the storms? To control nature and people?"

"No, Green Spider. You seek order, and you will find only Truth. Look at them. See the people? You will never see them the same way again."

As Green Spider gazed down from above, most of those people slept. He turned his attention to the long, thatched temple that stood just south of the highest mound in the central group. There, five men remained awake despite the hour.

Four old men, the Clan Elders, sat inside the temple. They hunched like shriveled toads as they watched a naked young man prone on the floor.

"Me . . . that's me!" Green Spider's senseless body still lay facedown on the mat-covered floor. How pitiful his flesh looked, inert, little more than warm clay.

"Yes, you . . . as you were. Who are those old men who watch you so? Is their faith in you justified?"

"They are the Clan Elders, the old men who see to the rituals. They are the Spiritual guardians of my people."

Green Spider studied the familiar Clan Elders. Summer suns and winter winds had deepened and enriched those walnut complexions with a patina of age. Copper ear spools hung from stretched earlobes, and the wrinkles camouflaged faded tattoos. Mouths puckered around toothless jaws, but their eyes remained bright, sharply focused on Green Spider's inert body.

They wore long winter coats, fringed shawls, and fur-lined moccasins that rose to mid-calf. The cloth, woven from processed nettle and milkweed, had been spun into the finest of fibers before master weavers had strung thread over loom. Great artistry had gone into the weaving, and intricate patterns decorated the carefully dyed cloth. The color represented each Elder's clan affiliation.

The Red Bloods were the clan of the east; to them, the color red was sacred. They dyed it into the stunning fabrics they specialized in producing, and painted it on their bodies for the ceremonials. Blood represented the Power of life that was shared by all living things. With it, the clans renewed the fields in spring and painted themselves after a successful hunt to thank the Spirits of the animals upon which they depended. Old Man Blood carried a conch shell, the symbol of his office.

The Sun Clan held the bench along the south wall and wore the color yellow—symbolizing Father Sun and the life he brought to all living things. This clan maintained the sacred fires in the temples and lit them in the surrounding clan houses for the seasonal rituals. The Sun Clan carried burning brands when new fields were to be cleared or old ones retired, for fire cleansed. Old Man Sun carried fire sticks.

The western bench represented the Sky Clan, who donned blue for their sacred rituals. Blue was the color of water as well as the sky, for the two were interrelated. The sky provided rain for the fields and replenished the rivers for the fish, turtles, and waterfowl. Blue was the color of renewal. Old Man Sky carried a small jar of water.

The northern bench belonged to the Winter Clan, and their color was black, that of war, the hunt, and the winter storms. For what good were blood, sun, sky, and water without courage, strength, and death? Life could not exist without death, nor could the day without the night. All things—be they yearly cycles or lifetimes—must eventually end. And from endings came new beginnings. Old Man North had rattles—crafted from sections of human skulls—tied to his knees so that each step he took rattled the passing of time and the inevitability of death.

Had it not always been so?

"I will be strong enough." Green Spider's soul chilled. Strong enough for what?

"Before I grant you what you seek, I must test you," the voice of Many Colored Crow told him. *"Can you fulfill the needs of Power?"*

All of Green Spider's life, he'd prepared himself to be a Dreamer. He could always sense Power just beyond the fringes of his soul. He craved it, wished to savor it. With Power, he could heal injury, bring rain, cure illness, and encourage crops to grow.

"I will do anything you ask that I may fulfill the needs of Power."

"You seek Truth, Green Spider. If you are strong enough, I will let you experience the essence of Power. Look . . . look at this temple you love so. See it, learn it, remember it."

Flames leaped and flickered in the rock-filled fire pit in the center of the room. The orange gleam washed the magnificently painted walls with their colorful images of First Man, Wolf, Falcon, Spider, Raccoon, Turtle, and Bear. Handprints created a line across the top of the wall, while spirals shone redly between the effigy drawings.

Large pottery jars with conical bases and cord-marked sides

rested beneath the low benches upon which the old men sat. The jars lay canted on their sides, each capped with fabric and tied shut with hemp cordage. Within them lay ashes: the cremated remains of the ancestors. Their Spirits had been called by prayers, the rhythmic clacking of rattles, and the Singing of the Clan Elders. Now they hovered about, watching the young man, hearing his desperate prayers.

Faces of Spirit Animals and people had been carved into four heavy cedar posts that supported the thatched roof overhead. Firelight danced across the faces, and they seemed to change expression—ranging from intense sorrow to a mocking leer as they, too, studied the naked supplicant.

"The temple is the heart of the people," Green Spider said. "The sacred objects are kept here. It is the most holy place of all the clans."

"*And very sacred to you, Green Spider. It has become the center of your life. The clans have nurtured you, cared for you, given you everything you needed to become a Dreamer. Will you become more, Green Spider? Look at those old men. Feel your love for them. Yes, that's right. Savor the warmth rising in your soul.*"

Green Spider looked down, loving each of the old men, remembering the lessons they had taught him. They remained faithful, trusting him. Green Spider loved them with all of his heart as they watched over his senseless body, stoic in their vigil.

"*Love is Powerful, Green Spider. Are you strong enough to deny it?*"

"Deny it? Why?"

"*Love can distract us from Truth—from the reality of Power. Love is a Trickster.*"

The fire had burned down, and Old Man Sun slowly stood, reached for another piece of firewood, and softly chanted as he added it to the fire pit. Then he traced the pattern of a web in the air. According to the beliefs of the people, the Sun Clan had been founded by Spider, who had brought fire to human beings just after the Creation.

The piece of cedarwood crackled and sparked, catching fire. The ghosts shifted as they floated around Green Spider's senseless body and whispered among themselves.

A Song rose from beyond the walls of the temple. The solstice was dawning. The Red Blood Clan stepped out of their houses and into the chilly winter morning, Singing their welcome to the light. People lifted their hands to the east, staring up with expectant faces as they chanted the ritual greeting.

The old men in the temple stirred uneasily. The ceremonies were beginning, and each of the Elders had responsibilities. How long would this vigil last? Four long days had passed since young Green Spider had prostrated himself in the Dream Quest.

Old Man Blood sighed, the action little more than a wheezing exhalation. He fingered the large conch shell and thought for a moment. "We must stay. We promised."

Acceptance brought the barest bobs of heads. They would stay.

"These are honorable friends," Many Colored Crow declared. *"All the better to test your determination. Are you preparing yourself, Green Spider?"*

"Preparing myself?" What did Many Colored Crow mean? Hadn't he already done that?

"Oh, Green Spider, you've barely taken the first step. I have allowed you to fly, to slip into my Spirit wings. If you are strong enough, I will allow you to act in my place. You have made a request of Power. I will grant what you seek . . . if you will grant me what I wish. The way is long, hard, dangerous, and painful. What will you sacrifice to Power?"

"Anything. Just as my people are now sacrificing."

If the Clan Elders would forgo their responsibilities on so important a day, didn't that serve as a lesson for Green Spider? The clans knew the rituals; others—the men who would eventually succeed these ancient Elders—would make the offerings and lead the ceremonies.

"I will do as you wish, Many Colored Crow. Tell me what you desire. You can have anything that is mine to give."

"Not yet," the voice of Many Colored Crow called to him from the distance. *"This is just the beginning. You have a long way to journey yet."*

Green Spider's soul turned its attention to the stirring of the people who shivered and tugged brightly dyed blankets around themselves. Their breath frosted in the icy air.

From the ceremonial huts around the clan mounds, Dancers emerged into the crystal cold of the purple morning. Dressed in their finery, they looked, one by one, toward the tall mound where the Elders should have been. Finding no familiar forms outlined against the heavens, they turned their attention toward the square building at the mound's base. The temple hunched in the gray light; its low palisade and tight cane walls obscured any hint of the Elders' doings. Whispered questions passed back and forth as people clutched their blankets and climbed the mounds to initiate the ceremonies that would bring the birth of a new year.

Faces rose to the galena-gray sky, a wary squint in their eyes as they blew into cupped hands and stamped cold feet. The clouds twisted in the labor pains of a storm being born. Would snowflakes fall—or would freezing rain sheathe the bare, black tree limbs that transformed the rolling horizon into a fuzzy gray blanket?

"Your people seem worried," Many Colored Crow noted.

"They are wondering what has become of the Clan Elders. They know of my search for a Vision."

Green Spider could sense the growing anxiety. Would the rituals be carried out correctly without the guidance of the old men? Would the coming of spring be affected? What did this mean to the lives of ordinary men and women?

Green Spider's Spirit flipped and soared in a spiral over the earthen mounds. Didn't they understand? It would mean that he would be granted his wish; he would be able to intercede, to help them, to control the weather and the storms, illness, and injury. He tried to see it all, the entirety of the clan holdings that would be his responsibility.

Beyond the limits of the City of the Dead, occasional clusters of houses and irregular plots of fields lay under a mantle of frost. They made a patchwork before giving way to the winter-bare forest. Three more moons would have to pass while Father Sun worked ever higher to drive the blackness of winter into its northern lair once again. Then the rich soil could be tilled, the squash planted, and the maygrass and marsh elder gathered during the spring harvest. Knotweed, and goosefoot seeds, would be carefully inspected before being stabbed into the rich, red-brown earth with sharpened digging sticks.

Along the southern border of the City of the Dead, the Deer River meandered through swampy bottoms where drying racks and duck blinds stood. Fish weirs poked up like pickets, and shell beds lay beneath the ice-clotted brown waters. Crusted patches of snow mantled the leaf mat, reeds, and cane that lined the banks of the murky river. Canoes, side by side like pointed pegs, had been pulled up onto the landings where the bluffs sloped gently to the waters. Drying ricks of spindly poles awaited the next harvest, when they would be taken from the meandering channel and back swamps.

Across those sullen waters lay the Sun Clan holdings, random dots of houses and conical storage huts intermixed with the helter-skelter patchwork of fields. There, too, people stepped through door hangings to greet this special morning. Many offered their prayers to the sun and glanced northward toward the high, central mound that dominated the opposite shore.

Green Spider could detect the unease that passed among them, as if each individual felt the weight of Power in the winter air.

"Don't worry," he promised them. "I'm Dreaming for you. I will care for . . . make your lives easier."

"If you're strong enough," Many Colored Crow reminded. *"And were I you, Dreamer, I'd not make a promise I didn't know I could keep. My brother tells me I'm a fool to bet on a man—but he is making his own bets. He has no more sense than I."*

"I will keep my promises."

"And help Power keep its own?"

"Yes! Yes!" The joy of flight surged through him, rapture pulsing with each beat of his shining sable wings.

Within the snug shelters, people scooped the daily meal of hickory nuts, dried berries, or milled goosefoot seeds from the large ceramic jars stowed under the sleeping benches. Some lifted squash from storage cysts cut into the earthen floors as others heated piles of cooking clays for the earth ovens.

Here and there, a canoe passed across the runways in the swamp. Word of the missing Clan Elders was traveling. Exclamations of wonder passed as widened black eyes turned in the direction of the temple.

"It's all right," Green Spider cried, his voice lost in the clouds. "I'm being granted my Vision! Things will be better! I can make them better!"

"Yes, perhaps you can. It would only be fair to tell you,

Green Spider, that if you are truly strong enough to do as I ask, you will never be the same again."

"I want Power!" he cried again. "Anything! Just let me see the Truth!"

"To know the Truth, you, and all that you are, must die. Can you destroy yourself to find what you seek?"

Despite the growing buzz of worried chatter, those who had traveled to the City of the Dead from outlying clan territories huddled about their fires, either telling—or listening to—the winter stories. Stories of Many Colored Crow calling the ghosts, tricking them onto the mountain of fire.

The Dead knew so much more than ordinary folk. People glanced reverently at the beautiful pots that contained the ashes of family members who had died during the preceding year. On this day, they would mix the remains with those of the ancestors in the clan commons of the City of the Dead. None of their loved ones would ever be lonely again.

Ashes came from as far away as the gulf coast. Kin who had died in those distant lands had been cremated, the remains carried up the waterways and over the divides in the packs of Traders. Now the remains were home, in the land of their birth, to rejoin their families.

The charnel houses waited somberly, their roofs hoar-frosted. Within these structures, many corpses had been cared for during the preceding moons. Now the souls would be freed to mingle with the other ghosts.

Excitement swept the people, all of them dressed in their finest fabrics. Gleaming shell, polished copper, or finely ground stone gorgets hung from their necks. Strands of bone, stone, and shell beads rattled gaily on proud chests. Feathers of shocking brightness had been woven into silky black hair, and faces had been painted with painstaking care.

As the Dancers on the mounds gyrated and Sang their prayers to the Spirits, relatives removed corpses from the pole benches in the charnel houses and carried them to the crematories—shallow clay pits filled with ricks of dried hardwood. There the desiccated bodies would be laid out and fire brought from the Sun Clan's temple on the south of the mound complex. The flames would crackle up, returning the flesh into the nothingness from whence it came.

Reverent relatives would pray and Sing to the souls of their departed. The ghosts knew they were remembered and had no reason to linger in the land of the living. Then food, drink, and gifts would be offered on the mound tops, or attached to the poles that canted out at an angle around the bases.

Offerings would also be made to Crow, the carrion bird, the tricky hunter. Because Crow knew the Dead and did them favors, he could bring messages to people here in the world of the living. Therefore, Crow was revered, and his image was often carved on pipes, pounded into pieces of copper, and cut from sheets of mica.

"Yes," Green Spider said, feeling haunted and uneasy. "I will die if it will grant me Power. I will do anything I must to learn the secrets of Power."

"Are you sure? After all, you're only Dreaming, your soul drifting free from your body. You've lain there on the matting for four days and nights without food, without water. You've forced yourself to stay awake, to empty your soul of thoughts. Perhaps you're raving."

"Are you telling me that this is all illusion? I can *see* everywhere . . . the way Crow can see when he circles in the sky!"

"Everything is illusion. But you will have to die before you understand." A pause. *"You will miss the feast."*

Only after the Dead had been cared for could the mourners relax and turn their thoughts to the living and their concerns. Warm houses and anxious families awaited their return—and, of course, the news of the ceremonials. After all, winter was the time of talk around cheery fires, and of socializing. Lapidary work on celts, adzes, atlatl weights, and pipes continued as the people waited for the Planting Moon. Weavers created their works of art. Hunters stalked the uplands, seeking to snare the white-tailed deer, or to ambush turkey or grouse, entangling them with bolas—five thongs tied together at the top and weighted with stones on the ends.

People journeyed to the City of the Dead for other reasons, too. Many came to ask their ancestors for advice, or to plead for help from the Spirit World. Others asked for courage and victory in war, or for the ability to heal the sick and the injured. The love-smitten young often came seeking success in marriage or seduction. Sometimes a person might ask the aid of the ancestors when something was lost, hoping that while they slept, the location would be revealed to them in a dream. Visions of the future might be granted—or warnings of coming trouble.

"Is that all you ask? I will Trade a feast for Power."

"Indeed? A feast for Power? You'd make a poor Trader, Green Spider. And if you will do as I ask, you'll make a Trade such as you never bargained for. A clever Trader would beware."

Green Spider couldn't help but glance down at the Traders' camp that sat just up from the canoe landing. Humans were the same everywhere. Traders and artisans displayed their wares whenever opportunity presented. At solstice, rare goods were exchanged: fine textiles woven from carefully prepared fibers, brightly colored dyes, sharks' teeth and conch shell from the southern seas, effigy pipes from the great earthworks of the Serpent chiefs, copper and silver from the country north of the Fresh Water Seas, delicacies such as maple syrup from the far northeast—even obsidian from a mythical land far to the west where the grizzly bears lived.

"Any Trader worth his calling would do what I'm willing to do."

Many Colored Crow answered with silence.

Solstice ceremonials accomplished many things for the living, as well as for the Dead. Young men met young women, and they smiled at each other. Old women watched the young with appraising eyes, ever alert for new alliances with different kin groups. Negotiations over territory, squabbles, and other frictions were settled. Competitions were held and gambled over. And, of course, after the Dead had been feted, the living feasted and laughed, and celebrated.

Green Spider hovered in the chilly air, watching the sun rise over the platform mound to the southeast. Members of the Blood Clan danced their greeting, peering back occasionally, searching in vain for the withered Elder who normally Sang the blessing and called benedictions down upon them.

"Poor Green Spider," the voice twirled out of the dawn. *"My brother refused to answer your call. You shall not be forsaken. After all, I, too, was once as human as you, and just as anxious to experience Power. I know how your soul seeks."*

Green Spider had heard the old admonition that no one *wanted* to be a Dreamer. The desperate crying in his soul belied it. "I want Power to call the storms and to help my people. I have this craving . . . to find the reason of things. To know everything in its place."

"To know? Oh, Green Spider, I promise, I shall show you everything. Look down there, just above the canoe landing. Do you see that house?"

"A great warrior lives there. A horrible and brooding man."

"Concentrate, Green Spider. I will allow you one of the gifts of Power. You will be able to see into his soul."

At the edge of the bluff, overlooking the precipice leading down to the marshy floodplain, a low mound had been raised to guard one of the canoe landings. Before it stood a single oblong house. Protruding from the four center posts, wooden effigies of Crow, Rattlesnake, Snapping Turtle, and Vulture glared out to the four cardinal directions. On the south side of the big house, two tall posts thrust upward. The wood had been intricately carved to mimic the zigzags of lightning. Faces of the ancestors stared outward, as did the Spirit Animals of War: Eagle, Rattlesnake, Snapping Turtle, and Bobcat. To the top of each pole, a human skull—dyed soot black—had been fixed, the jawbones attached with sinew. The empty orbits stared out over the entrance to the City of the Dead, mindful of the Power and fame of the house's owner.

He was called the Black Skull. His past had been filled with terrible deeds—both inflicted and suffered. Some thought him possessed by malicious Spirits. Others suspected that a more malignant evil lingered in Black Skull's soul. Most believed him to be the greatest warrior who had ever lived. All considered him the most dangerous man alive. No one called him a friend.

Green Spider shook his head as he watched. "He's haunted, terribly. He doesn't like me much. He doesn't like anyone."

"He is a man in pain, searching, as you are. As I am."

"What could Many Colored Crow be searching for?"

"A hero, a Dreamer willing to travel north and recover a sacred Mask. Are you that hero? I will show you Power and Truth, allow you to experience what few other humans have ever experienced, if you will commit yourself to my cause."

Green Spider stared uncertainly at the brooding warrior, the first seeds of doubt cast in his soul. Did he only Dream? Or did he truly fly like the Spirit of Many Colored Crow?

"Concentrate on the warrior, Green Spider. Look into his soul."

As the morning Songs of the Red Bloods filtered through the City of the Dead like predawn mist, Black Skull—armed with his deadly war club—ducked through the low doorway and stepped out to stand between the carved poles. Muscles rolled under the sun-bronzed skin of his massive shoulders. He perched on the balls of his bare feet, poised on powerful legs that corded as he shifted his balanced weight.

Scars crisscrossed his flesh, some of them puckered, others ragged. His face, too, had taken its share of abuse. A Copena war club had crushed the left cheekbone, leaving his face lopsided. The jaw had been broken and had mended askew, which added to the off-balanced effect.

Hefting his war club, Black Skull bounded to the top of the platform mound behind his house.

Despite the wreckage of his face, keen black eyes cataloged the familiar scene, checking, as he did every morning, that everything occupied its place, that nothing had been disturbed in the night. The doorways remained closed on the storage huts, the misty haze of smoke rose lazily over the charnel houses below the death mounds. Here and there, fires crackled up from the crematoriums, accompanied by the chants of mourning relatives.

He nodded, shifting his gaze to the east, where the sunrise remained hidden behind thick clouds. His wealth of blue-black hair had been knotted into a single tight bun at the nape of his neck.

His scarred right hand gripped the heavy war club, made from the stout wood of an old hickory. The weapon had been carefully crafted, thinned, and polished. The warhead consisted of a stream cobble the size of a goose's egg, ground to a sharp point on one end, then grooved. Green sinew had been used to bind it to the rectangular wooden shaft. When the sinew dried, it had shrunk tight around wood and stone. Inset immediately below the cobble were two copper blades—each sharpened into a murderous spike.

As he stared out at the City of the Dead, Black Skull began swinging his club, loosening the muscles in his shoulders. He switched the club from hand to hand, twirling it ever faster as he listened to the weapon's whirring song. Weaving and feinting, he began to leap from foot to foot, shifting and spinning as he twisted and swung his club. With the grace of a dancer, he pirouetted around the terrace on his mound top, aware of the harmonic perfection of his body as he moved.

"I would have to travel with that killer? It is said that he murdered his own mother."

"He did. Her ghost continues to torment him. Like you, he seeks to surround himself with order, with predictability. Unlike you, he is unwilling to look beyond his rage."

With one final leap, Black Skull vaulted into the air, dropping into a crouch as he landed; the wicked club flashed down to stop within a finger's width of the sandy surface of the mound top.

Panting, Black Skull straightened, raising the war club to the blessing light of the new day. From under his feet, he could feel the approval of the ancestors, hear their faint voices as the ghosts of the Winter Clan murmured. Throughout the night, the ancestors had slipped through the walls of his house and lurked about Black Skull's bed, irritating his Dreams, blowing eerily across his face, and whispering into his ear.

Black Skull filled his lungs with the chilly air and watched his breath condense into a frosty cloud. The odor of cook fires carried to him, and he could sense the eyes of the people checking on him, knowing he practiced with his club every morning.

A dog barked, and the crying of a child carried to Black Skull's position atop the Spider mound. In the gray morning, the central temple where the Elders waited seemed particularly ominous.

So they continued their vigil—despite the significance of the day. Black Skull shook his head. No good would come of this.

Green Spider heard Many Colored Crow whisper, *"Go ahead, Black Skull. Worry. It costs nothing more than little pieces of the soul. The time has almost come for me to give my Vision to Green Spider. And, afterward, lonely warrior, your life will never be the same."*

The sun ascended higher in the cloud-strewn sky as the sacred Songs resonated across the hills and the ghosts were freed to their eternal future. Through it all, the young man, Green Spider, continued to lie facedown on the split-cane mat . . . lost in the Spiral.

"Green Spider, hear me. If you are willing to die and give up all that you love, I will grant you knowledge known to no

living man. You may climb the tree of the world, walk the Land of the Dead, and finally I will open your eyes to the Mysterious One. You will have your Truth, Dreamer.''

"And I will go and find your Mask."

"Prepare yourself. The moment has almost arrived."

When the sun reached the highest point in the sky, Green Spider blinked, his aching, tortured body lying on the split-cane mat. He knew what was happening beyond the walls of the temple. As the Feast of the Dead was laid out, people began reaching into steaming cook pots.

Time to die. He could feel Many Colored Crow tighten a taloned foot on the lightning, take aim, and cast. The flickering bolt crackled through the clouds, blasting asunder the temple where Green Spider's body lay.

People whirled, stunned. In the echoes of the thunderbolt, silence fell over the City of the Dead. Tongues of fire crackled in the wreckage of the temple as dry wood ignited. Within seconds, flames leaped and roared, and piteous cries rang out.

Two

My first sensation is of unimaginable blinding light, hot, searing. My eyes are closed, of that I am fairly sure, yet the light penetrates my body like tens of tens of slivers, piercing clean through my soul.

My thoughts are disjointed at first, firming like crystals of ice on a puddle. What . . . what is happening to me?

"You were crying for a Vision," a disembodied voice answers from a great distance.

"Where am I?"

"In the place between life and death."

I am afraid. I twist and turn, seeking to hide from the terrible brilliance. "I can't see! It's burning my eyes out!"

"Of course. Brilliance always blinds. Light gives birth to

Darkness. And Darkness gives birth to Light. All the time, back and forth, back and forth. Never ending. Remember that, Green Spider, you can only see Truth if you look at it backward.''

I am shaking now. I don't understand. All I know is that I feel my flesh burning, burning. . . .

Moon Woman's face shimmered silver-white through the thin film of clouds that rode down out of the northwest. A faint few of the Star People shimmered around her, bright enough to penetrate the nacreous veil. Pale white light bathed the land, illuminating the riverbank and the canoes that lay canted on the beach like fat black lances.

A lone man, tall and muscular, stood with braced feet and stared out over the mighty river. A winter shirt woven of heavy fabric dyed yellow and red hung down past mid-thigh. Leather leggings kept his legs warm above tall moccasins. A foxhide coat draped open over his shoulders—too warm for even this cold time of the year, when the moon deepened after the winter solstice. His breath puffed out in ragged white billows.

His people—the White Shell Clan—called him Otter. Up and down the river, however, he was known by another name: the Water Fox. And what more complimentary name could a Trader have?

The river ran smoothly before him; waves pushed out onto the black surface by the wind that blew across his left shoulder like a sash, and onward, southeastward, across the giant river and onto the breaks that rose in flat-backed, mottled humps on the far bank. In the faded moonlight, the trees created a hazy dove-colored fur on those distant eastern uplands.

Otter's attention, however, centered on his obsession: the river. His life had been altered by the roiling Spirit of the Father Water. On this night, of all nights, he knew the extent of its Power over his soul.

With reverent fingertips, he bent down to touch the gentle lap of water on sand. The surface stretched black and forbidding, and only as his vision traveled out toward the channel did flecks of moon glow dance silver across the waves. He could feel the strength of the current as it flowed southward toward the sea.

Feel it? Feel the call of the river? Powerful, beckoning, like a woman's soft touch, like. . . . It all came back to women, didn't it? For him, it came back to one woman: Red Moccasins.

Otter took a deep breath and filled his lungs with the familiar heady musk of water, the tang of sandy mud, and the pungency of the backswamp. The backswamps were critical to the river people. Otter knew the swamps' quiet ways—ghosts of the old river channel—the water still and spotted with ice that clutched at the brown reeds, cane, and cattails. The smooth mottling of the ice mocked the bulbous bases of the tupelo and moored to the lined columns of cypress trunks.

Somewhere, to his right and behind him, a night predator disturbed the ducks, who quacked warily. Out of the darkness, Owl hooted as he drifted on silent wings. A fish thrashed the water in pursuit—or escape.

The bitter threat of storm traveled on the night wind. Otter could sense frigid air rolling down from the north, and he shivered at the increasing cold.

A cold to mock the chill in my soul. He stuck his hand farther into the icy water, his fingers burrowing down into the cold, dark mud.

Faint laughter carried on the night breeze. He stood, knotting his fist so the sticky mud squeezed out between his fingers in wedge-shaped curls. Turning, looking westward into the wind, he could see the Tall Cane clan houses—the source of the laughter.

Otter had just come from that place, had walked down to the landing where his long, sleek canoe waited with its promise of freedom.

The Tall Cane Clan celebrated for the fourth night with Singing and Dancing, feasting and storytelling, and the exchange of gifts. This marriage was a lucky union between the White Shell Clan and the Tall Cane Clan. All of the lineages were linked now, as if this final marriage created one people out of two.

The clans, their territories facing each other across the river, had been enemies in the distant past. In the beginning, the White Shell Clan had built its clan house and burial mound on the eastern bluffs overlooking the river. The Tall Cane clan house and earthen mound had been built later, when the clan moved downriver. They had chosen to settle on a small rise on the western bank. White Shell warriors had gone to drive the interlopers out of their territory. The Tall Cane Clan had been just as determined to hold their new home. Somewhere, back in the time of the Grandmothers, that feud had ended with a marriage, and so it had been since.

Otter had taken the first opportunity to escape the festivities. He desperately needed time alone to nurse the aching wound in his heart. He had loved her so deeply, so passionately. Here he could look back at the ruins of that love.

How many times had he made his way to this settlement? Those trips had been wondrous with the knowledge that she was waiting, anticipation in her eyes.

All gone now.

Sparkling fires honeyed the thatched roofs and pale walls of the clan house. The light danced and flashed at the incitement of the breeze. Here and there, despite the distance, he could make out the forms of people moving between the fires, casting shadows in his direction.

Her marriage strengthened the bonds between the people, tying the clans closer together. Villages in the central valley didn't realize the frightening changes taking place in the world beyond. Otter had seen them. The number of canoes passing the clan territories had grown by tens of tens over the last year. Young men like himself sought the chance to feed the growing demand for goods above and below the central valley.

We have entered an age of alliances—and, thereby, an age of great danger.

He turned again to the rippling black water. Even now, in the dead of winter, the river whispered, calling to him, drawing at his soul the way it ate at the sandbars and muddy banks.

"Otter?" The soft voice caught him by surprise. He wheeled to find his twin brother standing ghostly in the veiled moonlight. Four Kills looked dashingly handsome in his wedding garb of brightly dyed yellow, black, and red fabrics. A copper hairpiece had been tied into the thick bun at the base of his skull. Alternating layers of bone and shell beads lay thickly across his chest. The half-wash of moonlight gave his fine-featured face a pale delicacy—the eyes shadowed by the prominent brow ridge.

Otter found his voice. "Sorry, brother. You startled me.

The wind, I guess . . . it covered your approach.'' He self-consciously rubbed the tips of his wet fingers on his fox coat and glanced back longingly at the river.

He shouldn't have been surprised. Four Kills would have known he'd come here. They had always shared a bit of soul. So alike, so different, but then, the Father Water had determined that long ago. Perhaps that faraway night on the river had led directly to this meeting. A man couldn't know the workings of Power—they just went on around him, throwing him this way and that, like a stick in the river's roiling brown current.

Four Kills walked down the muddy slope, stopping beside Otter, staring out over the river with him, but seeing the dark bluff where the White Shell clan house and earthworks stood on the other side. That difference marked them. For Otter, the river centered the soul; for Four Kills, it was the clan, and his obligations to Grandmother, that lay at the center.

"I've been feeling your hurt," Four Kills said gently.

Otter reached out to drop an arm around his brother's shoulders. "What would you do? Break the marriage? Defy the clans? Ruin your life, and happiness . . . and hers as well?"

Four Kills paused for a moment, his dark eyes searching Otter's in the moon glow. "If you wanted me to."

Otter tightened his grip on his brother's shoulders, his heart warming. "Yes, you would, wouldn't you? You know, for a man as smart as you are, you can be a real fool sometimes."

"I wouldn't hurt you for anything. Grandmother came to me saying that Red Moccasins had asked for me." He gestured the futility of it. "I haven't slept. I've been torn between happiness and anticipation . . . and tortured by a horrible dread about what you'd say . . . what you'd think. I didn't know what to do, Otter. Do you understand?"

"I understand very well, brother. Twins have Power that way." Otter felt the tug on his soul—the river calling, reminding him of strange places and different peoples.

He pried his thoughts away from the lure and added, "But you should also know that she loves you. I've seen it in her eyes . . . the curious guilt and pain when she looks at me, the stubborn longing when she looks at you."

"But, Otter, she—"

"Wait! Hear me out. Listen to me, brother. Go to her and

love her. Sire her children. You're the man she needs, already listened to in the councils. A solid man who understands the changes in our world. The people here need you. She needs you.''

Four Kills nodded sadly to himself. ''Yes, I know: duty, responsibility, honor. But, Otter, what about us . . . you and me? I can't stand the thought of losing—''

Otter pushed his brother back to face him. ''You won't. Not ever. But your place is here, at her side. She's intelligent, brother. She's going to be a very shrewd leader. You're the right man for her.''

''But you and I . . . Things will change between us.''

''Yes, they will. We will manage.''

''I had hoped you would say that.'' Four Kills paused, his head down. ''I'm glad you came back when you did. It would have seemed like a betrayal if you'd come home after the marriage.''

''I'd never feel betrayed. It's our way, brother. Grandmother makes the alliances, negotiates the marriages. And besides, you really didn't want to refuse, did you?''

Four Kills continued to stare at the damp ground. ''No. You know as well as I that I've always loved her. I've always watched from your shadow. You were the great Trader, Otter, exotic and romantic with your stories of faraway places and wonderful things. Me? I was just a . . . a . . .''

''A strong, capable man who would be there when she needed him,'' Otter finished. The river's current entwined itself in his soul like a lover's caress. The night pressed down upon him. Again the owl hooted into the darkness—the hollow notes like a dead man's flute. ''That's why she initiated the negotiations, brother. Grandmother told me the day I arrived that Red Moccasins had asked for you—first choice.'' He nodded into the darkness. ''She's smart. You'll always be there, while I . . . well, she could just as soon count on the wind.''

Four Kills chuckled softly. ''Couldn't you have stayed home for once? Built a house? Cleared a field? It's not so bad. I do it all the time.''

''I'd die, brother. My soul would wither like a plucked squash blossom in the sun.'' Otter used a thumbnail to scrape the drying mud from his hand. ''I was changed that night I fell into the river. We both know it. Whatever I would have been was washed away. I belong to the Father Water.''

"It's calling you, isn't it?" Four Kills asked. "I can't sense the river's call, but I can feel your need to answer it. You'll be going away again, won't you?"

"Yes, brother. Very soon."

"And it's partly because of me and Red Moccasins. I can feel that, too. The pain it will cause you to be near us."

"That will eventually heal, Four Kills. I've loved her with all of my heart—as have you. I need time to make my peace with the way things will be."

His brother bent down, scooping up mud and packing it into a ball before he threw it out into the river. A satisfying splash sounded. ''Sometimes it's not easy to share souls with a person.''

Otter kicked at the mud with a moccasined toe. "No, I guess it isn't. That's another good reason for me to go. It's not as bad when I'm gone. We don't haunt each other's dreams as much, don't sense each other's feelings.''

"I'll miss you . . . again."

"And I, you."

Four Kills touched Otter on the shoulder. "You know that you always have my love . . . and Red Moccasins' as well."

"I know." Otter pulled loose, stepping to the side of his broad canoe. "Actually, I came down here to get something." He glanced up. "Judging by the laughter, it's about time for the exchange of gifts."

Four Kills crossed his arms against the chill of the night wind. "Yes. In fact, I'd better be getting back."

Otter bent over the gunwale of his canoe, fished around, and found what he was looking for: a heavy, flat slab wrapped in thick folds of sturdy brown fabric. "Here it is. Come on. You're supposed to be at your wife's side."

Four Kills squinted in the darkness. "What is that?"

"Your wedding gift from me. I think you'll like it."

"Something useful?"

"Hardly, but you'll have the wealthiest household in Tall Cane territory." And Otter would incur Grandmother's wrath by giving away such a fabulous prize to his brother's wife's clan. The copper plate he now fingered stretched as long as a man's arm, and half as wide. The heavy metal had been pounded to the thickness of a turtle's shell and polished to a bright luster.

Otter would avoid looking into Red Moccasins' eyes as he uncovered the plate and handed it to her. He would only allow himself to smile at her mother—and then politely step back.

Otter tucked the heavy plate under one arm and gripped his brother's shoulder. "Come on, let's get you back before Grandmother comes raging down on us like a winter storm."

And I'll enjoy watching the Tall Cane Clan's eyes go round at the sight of this much copper in one piece!

Perhaps it was an arrogant act—but it brought satisfaction. Giving a copper plate like this would bolster him enough to bear her presence and to smile as if this were the happiest night of his life.

He glanced sideways at his brother, who watched him warily.

Four Kills would understand—and forgive him this little bit of pride.

That same night, many months' journey to the northeast, sunset had cast golden hues across the hilly, winter-gripped land of the Flat Pipe people and their allies, the High Heads. It was said that of all the peoples on earth, none were so influential as the Flat Pipe, and no ceremonial centers so grand as theirs. Of all the mighty works in the Flat Pipe world, few would argue that StarSky city wasn't the most spectacular of all.

StarSky nestled among the rolling, forested hills in a west-east-trending valley, bounded on the north by the ice-choked Flying Squirrel River and on the south by the smaller Duck River. Their channels joined on the eastern edge of the site, where the canoe landing was situated. A patchwork of fuzzy gray trees and irregular fields covered the slopes to the north and south of the rivers—the beginning of the farmsteads. Sunflower and goosefoot stalks protruded in enough places to give the snowy fields a tawny look.

StarSky had gone quiet in the cold and growing darkness. Footprints crisscrossed pathways through the deep snow and onto the earthen monuments contained within the embankment of the great solar observatory with its huge Octagon. To the southeast, the Great Circle, with its eagle-shaped central mound and high gateway, lay empty this night, none of the Star Society astronomers braving the chill to use the huge lunar observatory.

Clustered throughout the long, linear earthworks, mounds, circles and squares, were the clan houses, society houses, and charnel huts. Threads of smoke rose from the smoke holes, piercing bark-and-thatch roofs before spiraling into the night sky.

One charnel house stood out. It was oblong, peak-roofed with bark, and black smoke curled out of the smoke holes. Such smoke poured out only when a cremation was underway. Blanket-wrapped people had gathered in knots around the doorway. The brightly colored blankets contrasted with the glaring world of white. Headdresses of copper, mica, and glistening beads offset rich black hair, carefully washed and, for the somber occasion, pulled into severe buns and pinned with conch shell-whorl pins. As the people stood silently in the new darkness, their frosty breaths intermingled, as did their grief.

One young woman stepped out of the smoky interior and into the cold. She pulled her blanket tight about her shoulders, as if seeking protection from something besides the cold. Many thought her the most beautiful woman in the world. Full lips balanced the proportions of the firm, straight nose and strong brow. Those eyes—large and dark—should have sparkled with laughter, but now they betrayed the deep sorrow of a bruised soul. Hands like hers were meant for holding, the fingers long and slender. Even as they clutched the blanket, they did so tenderly. Long black hair, shimmering in the fading light, was pulled back now, pinned tightly in mourning instead of billowing in raven waves down her back. One need only glance at her to know that the chill in her soul was colder than the frozen air she now breathed.

Star Shell noted the sympathetic expressions cast her way by grieving relatives. She stopped, staring up at the fading sunset and hugging her blanket even more tightly around her. Her gaze shifted across the broad valley to the northwest, to the heights where the Flying Squirrel earthworks stood to mark the constellation for which the mound had been built.

She knew this valley well. Had the charnel house not blocked the view, she could have seen the trail that led up to the famous chert quarries—placed there by First Man when the world was new. The surface on that high ridge was riddled with huge holes, for countless generations of men had dug the sacred chert from the rocky ground. Part of StarSky city's political strength came from controlling those chert deposits. Traders arrived from all over the world to obtain the large nodules to Trade up and down the river systems.

According to the story, just after the Creation, First Man had battled a mighty monster. With lightning, he killed the beast, and its blood ran into the ground, becoming the multicolored chert. Because of the sacred nature of the stone, it was used only in special ceremonies. A person who petitioned the Spirit World might use the sacred chert to cut off a bit of flesh for an offering, or perhaps to pierce himself and offer the blood. Such offerings were made for the safe return of a relative or very close friend, for success in Trading, or sometimes in hopes of curing a loved one.

Warriors flaked the stone into potent dart points. The secret societies made tools from it with which to carve pipes, atlatls, or mica effigies. In the Potters' Society, blades struck from sacred chert were used to incise the design zones of the ceramic jars and pots.

Star Shell heard the approach of her father; his moccasins crunched in the packed snow as he came to stand beside her.

Polished copper ear spools hung from his earlobes, and his tattooed face looked puckered from the cold. He had snugged a yellow-and-black blanket about his shoulders. For the first time, Star Shell noticed that those once broad shoulders had slumped. When had he aged so?

But then, she too had aged. Not so much in the body, for she was still a young woman—just two tens and four years old. Despite the three children she'd borne Mica Bird, she retained her legendary beauty and her physical endurance. Only her soul had withered.

"It's almost over," her father, Hollow Drill, told her. "When this last fire burns down, we'll collect the ashes. Then I'll build a tomb. When I'm dead, you can bury me there beside her."

"I'll miss her."

He bowed his head. "After all these many winters, it's hard

to think of being away from her—even for the short time I have left.''

"Don't speak like that, Father. I can't bear to think of both of you gone.'' She shivered lightly. "I'll be back for Mother's burial. It will be hard for you. Especially at equinox and solstice. I won't leave you alone.''

"It's a long way." He paused. "And what will your husband say if you miss the rituals at Sun Mounds? You have other responsibilities, Star Shell."

"He'll understand." How easily the lie came to her lips.

"Will he?"

She shrugged, defenseless against his penetrating gaze.

Hollow Drill sighed. "I'm sorry, my daughter. I could have stopped it. Kept you here. Married you to someone else."

"No, Father. He wears the Mask. Nothing can be denied to someone who wears the Mask. It was the same with his grandfather before him."

She shook her head, hating the thoughts that clung to her like fungus on a rotting tree. She feared Mica Bird. Feared him so much it paralyzed her soul.

In the past four years, he had used the Mask time and again. He donned it in heated clan meetings—and his opponents died within days. Tension had divided many of the lineages. Some people had packed up and left, moving to distant places where they had kin. Others stared at him adoringly, in awe of his Power, and did his bidding without question or hesitation.

Since Star Shell's youngest daughter had died, matters had grown worse. Not just the beatings, but other things. He insisted on wearing the Mask before coupling with her. He said it gave Power to his seed. And then, as he covered her, the Mask would be propped beside the bedding—to watch.

If she protested, he beat her into submission before spreading her legs and driving himself painfully inside. His ejaculation made her physically sick.

Do I have to think of this now? She rubbed her cold face to clear her head.

Hollow Drill said nothing. She caught a glimpse of the lines tightening around his broad mouth. She knew that expression— the one that marked deep and serious thought.

"I'll be all right, Father. It's you I'm—"

"Star Shell, I want you to do something for me. I want you to talk to someone. A man arrived here several days ago. His name is Tall Man—an Elder of the High Heads. Some call him 'the Magician.' "

She just stared at Hollow Drill. Who hadn't heard of the Magician? Stories circulated everywhere about the High Heads' most famous and Powerful dwarf. If an infant in the womb was exposed to Power, a dwarf would result. Some said that the Magician was the most Powerful of all. Rumors claimed that he could change himself into an owl or a lizard. Others claimed— often whispering behind shielding hands—that the Magician used the darker Powers of witchcraft to his own benefit. Mysterious deaths were attributed to his Power, as were miraculous cures. Women, so the story went, could not resist his advances. More than one angry husband had died mysteriously after seeking redress for such indiscretions.

Hollow Drill placed a hand on Star Shell's back. "He says he came here to see you."

Star Shell glanced sideways. "What would I want to talk to the Magician for? What does he want with me? I haven't done anything."

"Daughter, the High Heads know all about the Mask. They are an older people than we are. They know about these things. The Mask . . . it was theirs once. Tall Man knows the legends, knows the history of the Mask. Please . . . see him."

At the tone in her father's voice, she nodded. Hadn't she always done his bidding? The chill increased. "If I talk to the Magician, Mica Bird will know. The Mask will tell him. I'll suffer for it."

"The Mask won't know." Hollow Drill sounded so sure of himself. "There are other Powers in the Spirit World besides the Mask." Hollow Drill hesitated. "The Magician, Tall Man, he arrived on the day your mother died. He's been waiting ever since."

Star Shell shifted uneasily, aware of the distance her other relatives had been keeping. Aware of the oily smell of smoke hanging on the still air—smoke from the cremation fire that burned the last of her mother's bones into ash.

Dread filled her, as if she had just stepped upon a dark forest trail. One fraught with peril. "All right, Father. I'll see him. But it won't do any good."

"You don't know that. See Tall Man tonight. Then tomorrow we'll collect your mother's ashes and you can leave. Your brothers will accompany you down the Holy Road, back to Sun Mounds and the Moonshell valley."

She followed in his footsteps as he picked his way along the slick path. Where so many moccasined feet had trod, the snow had been beaten into irregular humps of ice.

Once this land had belonged to the High Heads. They had built the first Sacred Circle here, and buried their dead in the conical mounds. From this rich floodplain at the confluence of the Flying Squirrel River and the Duck River, they had charted the path of the stars and sent Traders out across the world.

According to the legends, three clans had come down from the hills and united to drive the High Heads from the valley. They seized control of the chert quarries. Great Star, the legendary clan leader, had forged a peace. After that, the High Heads married with the Flat Pipe and they lived together, sharing sacred sites, and slowly the people began to grow close. Words from both languages had flowed around each other, and many of the legends had mixed, along with the bloodlines.

Tall Man—the Magician—wanted to see her? *I haven't done anything wrong!*

Star Shell winced. Didn't she have enough to fear? Life with her husband had grown into a nightmare from which she never awoke. At night, in the darkness, she could feel his Power welling around her. He tossed and turned like a man possessed, tortured by dreams she could only guess at. Awake, he walked with his head cocked as if listening to something. At the slightest provocation, he flew into a violent rage.

After hearing of her mother's death, he'd beaten her, a crazed look in his eyes—as though in guilt. The bruises on her body had healed, but those on her soul remained. Had he killed her mother? Why? How could he have done such a thing?

What had become of the young man she'd loved? Only the memory of his handsome face remained. Now, when she looked at him, she saw a stranger. He'd grown thin, his muscles sinking into bone. When he looked into her eyes, she could see the strain in his glassy stare.

Only her first daughter, Silver Water, coming up on her fifth year, had lived. The next two babies had died at birth; it was as if their souls had emerged, seen the horror that lived in that house, and fled.

If only I could escape as well.

For this journey, Star Shell had left Silver Water with her mother-in-law. The girl would be safe there, out of her father's way for the time being. Poor Silver Water . . . the sweet days of carefree childhood had vanished like leaves from a winter-bare tree. Where giggling delight should have filled those large brown eyes, dread haunted that once-innocent face.

Twilight had dwindled by the time they reached the High Head clan house. Although the High Heads no longer lived in the Flying Squirrel valley, they kept a clan house here. The old mound stood to one side of the clearing, a low, conical dome of earth. Beside it, pairs of posts, set out at angles, formed a Sacred Circle. Offerings hung from each of the posts: colored bits of cloth, strips of hide, bundles of herbs, and other precious objects.

Hollow Drill muttered a greeting to the Spirits that dwelt here, and touched his forehead in respect. Star Shell followed his example, feeling the ancient Power of the place. She barely noticed the fluffy snow that crunched underfoot.

The High Heads built perfectly round houses, lashing bark to a pole framework. A heavy fabric covering draped each doorway.

"Greetings!" Hollow Drill sang out. "Hollow Drill and his daughter, Star Shell, have come to see the venerable Tall Man, respected Elder of the High Head peoples."

A young man appeared at the doorway. "Greetings, Hollow Drill and Star Shell. I am to tell you that Tall Man offers you his welcome, and that he shares the terrible grief at the death of your gracious and kind wife and mother. Please, enter. Be welcome here."

Star Shell hesitated as the young man held the hanging aside. Icicles had formed like silver lances on the thatch walls of the clan house. The cold had intensified, or was that only her imagination?

Resigned, she ducked in after her father. The young man allowed the hanging to fall. After the biting cold, the warmth made her nose and cheeks tingle. The air smelled of mint and rose petals mixed with a pungent and soothing incense she couldn't quite place. What Star Shell had mistaken for a distant drum now betrayed itself as her pounding heart.

She stood in a large, high-ceilinged room. A modest fire crackled in the central hearth and cast a rosy glow over the walls. Matting woven of blue-stem grass lined the walls; behind it, she knew, moss had been packed for added warmth.

Decorated pottery lined the walls, and wooden backrests had been placed around the fire pit. Bedding, mostly deerhides and blankets, marked the sleeping area in the rear. A bear skull adorned the southern wall, and medicine bundles of unknown use hung from the soot-encrusted rafters.

Tall Man, the feared High Head shaman, sat on the opposite side of the fire. He rose on stubby legs and spread his arms in greeting. The top of the Magician's head reached no higher than Star Shell's navel. His short legs bowed, as if they'd grown around a river cobble, and his face reminded her of a turtle's, the nose rounded, with the nostrils forward-facing. After his teeth had fallen out, the jaw had receded, which augmented the turtle-like wrinkles on his throat. His skull had been flattened by his having been bound into a cradleboard as an infant to mold the high, broad look for which his people had been named. His gray hair formed a bun at the back of his head, and stone ear spools hung from his earlobes.

Only when she gazed into his faded eyes did she feel the man's Power, so shrouded in mysterious secrecy. And something else—something dark, hidden, and terrifying.

Tall Man wore a magnificent blanket made of interwoven strips of fox fur, rabbit, and feathers. Copper bracelets jingled on his stick-thin arms. His small hands had curled with age, the long nails grown like talons.

"I share your grief." The simple statement proved more eloquent than any long speech.

Hollow Drill nodded. "Thank you, Wise One. It has been a trying moon since her soul passed from her body. The final fires have been lit."

The Magician laced his fingers over his stomach. "We would offer a gift. Please, place this token of our respect with her ashes so that her ghost will know of our deep affection. The memory of the time she nursed Broken Dish has not faded.'' He glanced to one side as a gust of wind shivered the wall. He went slightly pale, then whispered, ''No . . . indeed it has not.''

Star Shell remembered. Broken Dish was one of the High Head clan Elders, a noted Trader who had developed a swelling of the face. Her mother had gone to care for him—and there, she had actually met the Magician. No one else had gone to help. Others feared that whatever horrible thing grew inside Broken Dish's head might also grow in theirs.

The youth, unbidden, stepped forward with an engraved stone tablet. The High Heads valued such tablets, using them to mix ritual body paints for sacred events.

''Her Spirit is honored,'' Hollow Drill said reverently as he accepted the tablet.

Star Shell gazed at the piece of worked slate. The artist's skill showed in the intricate flow of the engraving. She could make out images of a woman, a man, and a wolf, all linked together. On the back, strange symbols had been inscribed. Stains had permeated the slate, some having the rich blackness of old blood, others the crusted silver-white of dried semen.

The piece drew her irresistibly, as if it sucked at the soul.

The Magician explained, ''It is the story of my clan, the Wolf People. It tells of the first days after the Creation of the world. Old Woman is there, along with First Man and his Spirit Helper.'' He smiled. ''You probably know, Star Shell, that your mother's lineage came from the High Heads, long ago. Her ancestors married into Great Star's Clan. You, therefore, are a distant relative of mine.''

''I remember,'' Star Shell replied, fighting to pull her gaze away. She almost sighed when her father placed the tablet into his belt pouch. Didn't he sense the stone's draw?

''Please, seat yourselves. Drink will be provided.''

Tall Man settled against his backrest and folded his short legs beneath him. Star Shell and her father seated themselves across the fire from the Elder, as was proper.

The young man arrived again, bearing a large conch shell full of steaming yaupon. Each in turn drank from the lustrous pink shell. As the bitter black drink settled in her stomach, a warm flush spread through Star Shell's cold body for the first time since she'd heard of her mother's death. Yaupon did that, renewed the body and sharpened the wits.

"May all of your ancestors be praised," Tall Man began. "And may your descendants cherish your Spirits. May First Man shed his blessing upon you. May your fields be fertile, and hunger far from your door."

"And yours," Hollow Drill returned.

The Magician drank again from the shell cup and passed it around. The ritual of greetings continued until the shell was emptied. At that point, Tall Man took a tubular stone pipe from his belt pouch. It had been carved into the shape of a dwarf, long of body, with a decorated sash at the waist. The hair had been parted in the middle and worked into two buns. Hollow ear spools filled the ears.

Tall Man filled the pipe, his movements deliberate. Without spilling a single flake of tobacco, he tamped it with a blunt piece of bone. The youth arrived at just the right moment and offered a smoldering stick with which to light it.

The pipe went around, each person inhaling deeply and blowing smoke out at the ceiling in four puffs.

"May First Man hear our words. May the ghosts of my ancestors speak not of what passes here." Tall Man knocked the dottle from the pipe and reloaded it.

Once again the pipe moved around the circle, until a blue haze filled the room.

"Now then," the Magician began, turning his soft gaze on Star Shell, "you are worried. The Power of the Mask has begun to eat at your soul."

Star Shell glanced uneasily at the youth, who stood to one side, apparently oblivious.

"You may talk, young Star Shell." Tall Man raised a thin eyebrow. "This place is safe."

Star Shell sought to still her pounding heart. "How do you know about the Mask? About me?"

"Power is like smoke." The Magician sucked on his pipe and exhaled a puff. Waving one hand, he set the smoke to swirling. "Stir a part of the smoke, and the other tendrils are affected. The Mask has been stirring Power for many generations of men. Now it is stirring again."

"Why did you come to see me? You did come here for that, didn't you?"

Tall Man's expression sharpened, and as quickly resumed that veiled tranquillity. "It was not an easy journey for me at this time of year, but yes, I came because I knew you would. Remember, girl, we are of the *same* blood. I Dreamed one night last summer. I saw you huddling in fear as your husband donned the Mask and looked down at you. The baby girl you carried in your womb was stillborn three days later. Mica Bird wants a son—one with a piece of Raven Hunter's soul."

"Who? Raven Hunter?"

"The Dark Twin, First Man's brother. You know him as Many Colored Crow. It is he who caused the Mask to be made in the first place. Through it, his Spirit can act in this world. It does so by capturing the soul that looks through the Mask. That is why your husband wears the Mask just before he couples with you."

"He has changed." Star Shell chewed at her lip. "He is not the man I knew. He has become a stranger. Brooding. Dark."

"Mica Bird isn't strong enough to cope with the Mask." Tall Man clasped his hands. "His grandfather was stronger. Nevertheless, it destroyed him, too, in the end. Now, in addition to the Mask's influence, the grandfather's ghost is tormenting Mica Bird. Your husband should never have brought the body back and buried it in the clan grounds."

"Is that what he hears? Is that why his Dreams are tortured?"

"The old man knew that the Mask should not fall to his heirs, but the Mask understood what he planned. Before the old man could take the Mask back to the place where he found it, the Mask spoke to your husband, thereby ensuring it would be recovered."

"But what can I do?"

"For the moment, nothing. As long as Mica Bird wears the Mask, he is too Powerful. His time, however, is limited."

Star Shell stiffened. "I don't understand."

The Magician's expression of sympathy deepened. The compassion of the ages might have been staring at her through those gentle eyes. "Neither does your husband. He is caught in a struggle he can't comprehend. It is tearing him apart."

"Yes, I—I know. But isn't there a way to stop it? To save

Mica Bird?'' She glanced at the honeyed color of the matting and the bundles hanging along the walls. The High Head designs on the large pots seemed to waver in the light.

Tall Man sighed wearily. ''Power discards people it no longer needs. When Power acts, young Star Shell, you must be ready.''

''Ready? For what?''

Tall Man's eyes seemed to expand in the shrunken face. ''Whether you like it or not, Power needs you to restore the balance.''

She shook her head slowly, a heaviness, like a cold rock, in her stomach. *I just want my husband cured of this. Please, can't I have my husband back the way he was?* ''No . . . no . . . not me. I'm not the one you want.''

''There is only one solution, young Star Shell. The Mask must be taken away, placed where men can never retrieve it. First Man has told me of such a place.''

''I'll burn it!''

The wise old eyes measured her. ''You have just cremated your mother—to free her Spirit. Burning will only free the Mask's Spirit. No, First Man has given me a Vision, shown me a place. We must take the Mask there. You and I. Far to the north—at the Roaring Water. There the Mask will be safe, and balance restored.''

''Balance?'' Her voice had gone faint.

''The Mask is not evil, though its Power comes from Darkness. Young Star Shell, you must understand. At the time the Mask was created, it was necessary. It kept the world in balance. The Mask changed the High Heads, brought them into a new age. But then, you will learn these things in due time.''

Star Shell sat in misery, unable to think.

''The problem is, young Star Shell, that Many Colored Crow knows we will seek to remove his Mask. As I told you, when Power is stirred, all the tendrils are affected. Many Colored Crow has chosen his champions, though they know not what they are called for. We are in a race, Star Shell—you to remove the Mask, they to keep it. I must ask you, are you strong enough to see this through?''

Star Shell's lips parted, but she couldn't speak.

''*I* will help you,'' Hollow Drill added.

''No, old friend. First Man has taken a calculated gamble.

Were he to increase the stakes, we could tear the world apart in much the same way Mica Bird is being driven to madness. I have seen the way it must be. This must be done in secrecy. The Mask has touched Star Shell, shown her the terror it holds for those unable to withstand its Power. You, my friend, and your clan, can have no part in this. Power has spoken. It has chosen Star Shell.''

As she watched, the fire sputtered, sending smoke twisting as it rose toward the dark roof.

Three

My gut tightens as I fall through dark nothingness. I spin, weightless, out of control. I am going to die . . .

"Hold on," *a voice commands.*

"A man can't hold on to nothing!"

"Try, just . . . try."

I throw my arms wide, feeling the rush of air as I plunge downward. Then I draw my arms together, embracing . . . the wind. And I slowly tumble sideways, and catch myself by curling my toes.

"But how can this happen? There is nothing here in this terrible darkness to hold to."

"Things work differently here, Green Spider. You have crossed from the world of the living, brought here by Power."

"Where am I?"

"In the City of the Dead."

"Then . . . I am dead?"

"For a while, Dreamer."

"I don't want to be dead . . ."

"You won't be. Not for long."

I tense the muscles in my arms, and I feel feathers bite into the air. Nerving myself, I stroke powerfully, and shoot forward. What wonder . . . have I always shared the soul of a bird?

"This being dead isn't so horrible. I thought it would be, well, a great deal different."

"You are not finished with life. I have chosen you for a special task. And for that task, I will give you a special gift."

"And what gift is that?"

"Green Spider, all of your life you have sought quiet, discipline, and order, and the search has led you in the wrong direction. You must turn around and look through those things to find their beating hearts. I am going to give you the chance. Your eyes are closed now, but when you open them, the patterned illusions of the many worlds of Creation will slip away, and the chaotic wasteland of reality will remain. Open your eyes, Green Spider. Do it now. See!"

Fear clenches my stomach. I open my eyes, and the blinding darkness dies.

I . . . I don't . . . my mouth falls open and I scream. The louder I scream, the more terrible the silence becomes, until I can no longer hear anything at all. And I feel . . . I feel myself disappearing.

It is as if my breath is my soul, and it is escaping into the scream . . . becoming the scream.

Old Yellow Reed sat hunched behind the carved fox head in the bow of the big canoe as it rose and fell on choppy waves. The leaden morning sky reflected off the river with a sullen brilliance. From the time she had been a little girl, sixty winters past, she'd loved sitting in the front of a boat. The way it lanced the water had delighted her, and despite the passing of years—and numerous travels in canoes—it still did.

The storm had unleashed its fury with the morning, sending down veils of frigid rain. The heavy canoe dipped and bucked as it bore Yellow Reed and her daughters across the river toward the White Shell clan house. Craning her neck, the old woman could look back and see Otter's pointed paddle flashing as it propelled them toward the east bank.

She lifted a small, tightly woven reed mat to shield her right side; there the mat caught the brunt of the icy rain that fell from the sky in slushy silver drops. Her hold on it was tenuous. With any luck, a gust of wind wouldn't roar down and rip it right out of her aching fingers.

She wore a heavy shawl about her shoulders, and a thick winter dress beneath that. Nevertheless, cold had seeped into Yellow Reed's bones, and for a woman her age, that meant utter misery.

She sucked her lips over toothless gums and battled the need to shiver violently, wincing at the cold trickle of water that ran from her mat, down her hand and forearm, and dripped persistently from her elbow onto her lap.

"Mother?" Blue Jar asked. She leaned forward under her own mat.

"I'm fine. Just cold and wet, but that will pass as soon as we make shore and I can hobble up to the house. Spider Above knows, I hope that worthless husband of yours has the fires going."

Blue Jar squinted against the storm. "After all these years, Many Turtles is wary of you. I imagine he'll have the house as hot as midsummer."

Yellow Reed chuckled. Blue Jar had just passed four tens and two winters. Her broad face and nose gave her a moonfaced look, and she'd always had heavy eyelids that hinted of sleepiness. Blue Jar, however, was anything but sleepy, lazy, or slow in the head. She had taken over many aspects of the administration of the White Shell Clan.

Water slapped at the hull as the canoe sliced a path through the river, and Yellow Reed smiled at the white splashes of spray that disappeared in the choppy, greenish-brown patterns of wind-pushed wave.

"You did well by your husband." Yellow Reed leaned to the side to hold her reed mat higher against a changing slant of rain. In doing so, she had a better view of Otter paddling in the stern. He seemed oblivious to the weather. Otter wasn't such a bad name for the boy—it fit him.

"I hope Four Kills will be as happy with Red Moccasins as Many Turtles has been with me." Blue Jar hunched under her mat. Rain was dripping off the corner of the plaited grass and into the river, where the rings disappeared in the maze of patterns cast by rain, wind, and wake. The breeze caught their mats, as if struggling to push the canoe sideways.

In misery, Yellow Reed peered back at Otter. With his usual acumen, he corrected immediately, grinning and paddling. The light of challenge lit his eyes.

"Yes," Yellow Reed answered, "he'll do fine. Red Moccasins is no one's fool. Neither is her mother, or grandmother. After all, the girl was smart enough to ask for Four Kills, not for his dashing brother."

Yellow Reed squinted, more in thought than against the rain. *And what was that silly stunt last night, Otter?*

She sucked at her lips the way she did when she was preoccupied. That copper plate had sparked gasps of amazement from the watching people. Red Moccasins had stood speechless, as if rooted.

Four Kills, for his part, had simply nodded, that worshiping smile beaming love at his twin brother—as if he were handed a clan's ransom on a regular basis.

Otter continued to paddle with the deliberate stroke of a master. The water had beaded on his foxhide coat and trickled down the broad planes of his face. He had a strong jaw, firm cheekbones, and the powerful nose of his family. At the moment, a faint smile hung on his generous mouth, and his hair was pulled back in a tight braid. Despite the layers of his clothing, Yellow Reed could sense the powerful muscles that rolled in those shoulders as he pushed the heavy canoe toward the nearing shore.

Yellow Reed said, "Red Moccasins has that younger brother . . . what's his name?"

"Black Water."

"Yes, Black Water. Perhaps we might want to give him a good look."

Blue Jar cocked her head. "Thinking about marrying him to Clay Bowl?" She paused for a moment, raising an eyebrow. "Or are you just hoping to get our copper plate back?"

Yellow Reed gave her a sidelong look. That plate would rankle for a time yet. She flinched under a gust of driven rain. Would summer never come? A brittle chuckle came up her throat. Age must have addled her. No one with sense longed for summer. All summer brought was hard work in the fields, heat, mosquitoes, chiggers, ticks, flies and ants, and centipedes.

She turned her mind back to the problem at hand. Black Water and Clay Bowl? Or should she be thinking in other directions? "Do they like each other?"

Blue Jar shrugged. "She let him into her blankets last night. I think it was her first time. They spent every spare moment staring at each other afterward, so it must have been good between them."

"Huh! What do young boys know about being good in the robes?"

"I think they're planning on practicing." Blue Jar shrugged. "Many Turtles and I did—a lot."

"A lot of good it did you! Twins! And you kept producing boys."

"What about Black Water and Clay Bowl?"

"What would it hurt? Tall Cane Clan has access to that ridge area to the north. Remember when it flooded so badly last year? That ridge was above the water. It might be a good place to plant squash. Not only that, but that backswamp out behind them is almost filled up with silt. In another four, maybe five years, that will be farmable. With the right marriage, we could benefit."

"Unless they keep digging pottery clay out of that backswamp at the rate they are doing now." Blue Jar studied her mother with bland eyes.

"Let them dig. They strain the clay through fabric to keep it fine . . . and they make good pots from it. A person can't have too many pots. Not the way my granddaughters keep dropping them. Either way, we're ahead."

Blue Jar remained pensive for a moment before she asked, "Do you think it's wise to link Clay Bowl to the Tall Canes? We might be better served with a marriage to the City of the Dead. Perhaps among the Black Clan."

Yellow Reed worked her toothless jaw back and forth, her eyes slitting. "It's an idea. What prompted you to think of it?"

Blue Jar leaned forward, gesturing to the rear of the canoe. "The story of that copper plate will travel. Not only that, I've listened to Otter. He's right about the changes on the river. More people are passing each year. The river can carry more than peaceful Traders. It can also carry warriors. The future . . . it's an uncertainty. An alliance with the Black Clan might be worth a great deal. Raiders would think twice . . . and if the worst came true, we'd have a place to go.''

Yellow Reed squinted at the muddy landing they approached. When she looked back at Blue Jar, she asked, ''Worried about the rumors of war among the Serpent Clans up north?''

Blue Jar gave her a shrug. ''Maybe. We need to talk to Otter. Perhaps he heard something on the river. Not all of the Traders stop here to tell the news. With the marriage and all the excitement, well, there hasn't been time to really hear what he has to say.''

Yellow Reed nodded. ''As soon as we're home and I'm warm, let's talk to him.'' She grinned. ''Assuming, of course, that my worthless son-in-law has the fire roaring.''

''I don't think my husband would let his mother-in-law suffer the chills if he could help it. He knows who his friends are.''

Yellow Reed jerked a stiff nod of approval. ''You did well by him, girl.''

The canoe pitched them all forward as it snubbed into the beach. Otter was already over the side, sloshing forward to help Yellow Reed to her feet. Without even straining, he lifted her free, setting her on her feet on the muddy bank.

''I need to see you,'' she said simply. ''Wait until we get settled, then come.''

The thinly veiled delight that had possessed him on the river evaporated as he looked down at her; his face turned as gray and gloomy as the day. ''Yes, Grandmother.''

She stared at the muddy path that led up the slope to the clan house. The thought of climbing all that brought bile to her gut, but Blue Jar offered a steadying arm. In the meantime, she would concentrate on Otter. He'd be wanting to leave soon, to travel north despite the season. Well, perhaps that would be for the best. Young men went crazy when the women they loved married others. Better to send him off than to have him around causing trouble between Red Moccasins and Four Kills.

Several weeks' journey to the south, four slim war canoes traveled upriver. Powerful arms plied the paddles that bore the craft relentlessly northward, away from the crystal-blue gulf waters and the warm breezes. No one could mistake these men—four tens of them. These were Khota warriors, feared throughout the north. Tattooed, scarred, they wore their hair in tight buns, scowling out at the river with hard eyes. In the lead canoe sat a lone woman wrapped in a blanket.

The bow wake rippled out in silvered chevrons across the brown water as the slim Khota war canoe raced forward. From her seat in the bow, Pearl watched the smooth water with a detached indifference. Today, at least, she could be happy that the wind had stopped.

To think any further, to attempt to understand the sudden change that had ripped her from her familiar world, was to realize the enormity of what had happened to her. Better to simply sit and watch with vacant eyes as the winter-brown vegetation passed.

Yes, and pretend you are living a curious sort of dream. That life will return to the way it was.

And the moon might rise in the west.

She was only fooling herself.

Pearl had learned to close her ears to the sound of the Khota warriors as they sang and rhythmically drove their pointed paddles into the river—a melody of swirling, sucking waters, punctuated by tinkling drips. The paddles rose and fell, endlessly lifted for yet another bite. Each stroke propelled her forward, upriver, toward a future she could scarcely imagine.

Pearl sat straight-backed, staring at the wooded banks they passed. Cypress and tupelo waited patiently for summer, while the vines twined through their branches like bleached ropes. The world had dulled to winter shades in response to the cold storms that rolled down from the north.

Perhaps it would work out satisfactorily. Women had traveled the length and breadth of the continent before—and even been happy with their marriages and families. The unsettling dread had to be homesickness. That was all.

Her veins pulsed with the blood of the Anhinga Clan: the Snakebird people. With her marriage to the Khota leader,

Wolf of the Dead, she would ensure her clan's wealth and prosperity.

She lifted her head. Anhinga, yes, that's what she was. Proud, strong, cunning. A hunter. That knowledge had been instilled into her very bones. In the distant past, Anhinga—the hunter bird that swam with its body submerged—had mated with a beautiful human woman, and from her womb had sprung the people who would become the Anhinga Clan.

Her people had always shared behavioral traits with their totemic ancestor. They hunted with serrated spears—like the bird's beak. As the bird spread its wings to the sun, so did the Anhinga spread their arms to its renewing warmth. The Anhinga Clan controlled the mouth of the Great River, known to northern peoples as "The Father Water."

I am Anhinga. I must show these Khota what it means to have the snakebird's blood run in my veins. She felt better at the thought. Stories did that, strengthened people.

The seventh daughter in a matrilineal clan, she should have had the right to choose a mate. Her fate, however, had been sealed when the Khota landed at her village. They called themselves Traders, who, despite their warlike appearance, had come down from the north. But most important of all, they had arrived bearing loads of copper plate, sheets of mica, and greenstone celts.

The young Khota men had been looking for conch shell, marginella for beads, sharks' teeth, and stingray spines—all of them worth a great deal in the north. As they had become familiar with the Anhinga, their haughty manners began to creep past the initial unease of being in a strange land and among strange people.

Bartering for the Trade goods had taken days, especially with the language difficulties—and Grandfather's penchant for long, drawn-out dickering. Despite the sound the strangers made—a sort of swallowing of their words—they'd picked up some of the river pidgin, the universal talk of the Traders, and could make themselves understood.

Pearl had caught the eye of one of the young men, the apparent leader. He'd finally pointed at her and pushed forward all of their remaining copper: some plate, a few ear spools, a hairpiece, and some bracelets. To that they added several ground-stone adzes and made the sign indicating that a Trade was desired.

Pearl could understand male interest. She had a heart-shaped face framed by long black hair that gleamed with bluish tints in the sunlight. Having passed eighteen summers, she'd filled out into a full-figured, lithe woman. She'd seen admiration gleaming in men's eyes as they appraised her high breasts, muscular waist, and smooth thighs. Were it not for her peculiar aversion to clan obligations, she would have been married long ago and surrounded by a squabbling brood of youngsters.

Somehow, the role of dutiful wife had never carried any appeal; she preferred to spend her days standing in the prow of a dugout canoe—atlatl and dart in hand—as the boat prowled the swamps in search of alligator. Her thrill came from tying a bloody bait to a length of braided-hemp line and dropping it into the deep water to draw Snapping Turtle from his muddy lair. No one could stay underwater for as long as Pearl in search of freshwater clams, or of conchs out beyond the surf. Her cousins grudgingly admitted that she could outswim Old Man Catfish himself.

Four moons ago, she'd returned from her most audacious achievement: accompanying some of her cousins on a Trading venture to the Island peoples across the sea. Not many Anhinga men, let alone women, could make such a claim.

She'd heard the joke that no sane man would marry Pearl. After all, who wanted to marry a woman who was better at being a man than a man was? Nor had the Anhinga Clan cared much what she did. She helped keep the pots filled with crawfish, crab, and other delicacies from the swamplands and beaches. Besides, her older sisters had married successfully, and their daughters were now bringing new males and kinship alliances to the clan.

Until the day the stranger had pointed at her, Pearl had been considered eccentric, and was ignored.

The sight of all that copper had unhinged something in Grandfather's soul. His eyes had gleamed in anticipation. By dint of extraordinary effort, he'd finally managed to impart that Pearl could be had—but only in marriage. By this means, Grandfather would establish a kinship relationship with the people in the far north. Thereafter, he could send his canoes full of oyster shell, smoked fish, conch shell, sharks' teeth, palmetto-frond matting, swamp-tree moss, alligator skins, yaupon, colorful feathers, and other goods, to exchange for copper, chert, galena, steatite, obsidian, Knife River flint, quartz crystals, greenstone, effigy pipes, and other exotics. And all that without having to depend on unaligned Traders plying the river.

Days of haggling ensued, much to Pearl's initial amusement. They wanted to marry her to a young man—an important warrior's son—in the far north. Surely this was just Grandfather's way of extending a lucrative Trading session. Only after the agreement had been struck, finalized by the ritual exchange of blood and gifts, did Pearl realize that the Anhinga Clan not only meant to stick with the deal, but hoped to reap substantial benefit from it.

She'd gone to Grandmother, furious at being sold to a bunch of northern barbarians—only to find the old woman gleefully imagining the wealth that would accrue as a result of the union.

"Go, child. You'll bring us fortune."

"Go?" Pearl had demanded, flinging her arms out. "*He* should come *here*!"

The old woman had shaken her head. "Up north, they trace descent through the man. A woman who marries goes to the man's village. To us, it was worth all that copper to send you there. Think, girl. With that copper, we can Trade all along the coast. For each piece of copper plate, the coastal people will fill a canoe with conch shell. Those loads of shell will be following you upriver as soon as we can get them."

"But, *Grandmother*!"

The old woman had studied her from under half-lowered lids. "But what? Pearl, who will you marry here? You've been of age for four years! Men smile at the mention of your name. They respect you, like you. But *marry* you? That's a different thing. What man wants to come here, sire a child in you, and have you leave him in the clan house to raise the infant by himself while you chase around wrestling alligators and teasing water moccasins?"

"But to send me off into the north—"

"You have a duty to the clan—and I wouldn't want to waste you on some backward swamp hunter. Who, after all, is about the only imaginable prospect for you." She'd shaken her head.

"No, girl. This is better. We all serve the clan. That is the lot of women. Responsibility. The Mysterious One made men to be irresponsible, to play through life without a care. But a woman must carry out her duties to her people. Bearers and maintainers. When the Mysterious One made the world, that is how he fashioned us." A withered hand had risen, shooing Pearl away. "Now, I have spoken."

As Pearl stood to leave, Grandmother absentmindedly fingered the new copper bracelet on her thin brown wrist. And a beautifully carved effigy pipe lay beside the fire among Grandmother's things—the ones that would be laid into her burial mound when she and Grandfather died.

Pearl's anger had flared, and it continued to smolder like a buried ember.

As she stared at the flat brown river ahead, she wondered: *Would I have been so different? Wouldn't I want to take exotic items with me when I journey to the Land of the Ancestors?*

Within two tens of days, as soon as Trade goods, wedding gifts, and provisions had been collected, she had mustered all the dignity she possessed and settled herself in the Khota canoe.

She'd considered running away; no one would have been able to catch her. But to have done so would have shamed her family and stained the reputation of her clan for the foreseeable future.

With hollow eyes, she watched the muddy bank sliding past and stared at the huge oak trees that rose in spreading majesty beyond the waving grasses. Tumbled clouds, shot through with sunlight, patched the hazy sky.

Pearl rubbed her face where the spray had dampened her smooth skin. This was going to be no good. Uncomfortably, she shifted on the coarse fabric bag upon which she sat and wished it were filled with anything but seed corn.

Otter stood in the rain watching his grandmother, Yellow Reed, hobble up the path toward the clan house. The old woman clung to Blue Jar's arm, placing each step carefully on the slick mud. The cold wind gusted, driving waves onto the shore to slap against *Wave Dancer* as the big canoe lay canted on the bank.

With the help of five of his cousins, Otter managed to haul the heavy Trading canoe up on the mud bank, and together they turned it over, leaving it to rest on logs embedded in the bank.

Rain continued to fall in bitterly cold sheets from the galena-smeared sky. Water had puddled on the silty sand, flecked here and there by charcoal from the bonfires they lit for night fishing. Angular fragments of pottery from the inevitable broken pot stuck out at odd angles, or had been mashed flat into the mud.

The drying racks—spindly constructions of slim poles—perched like skeletal storks just above the spring flood line. In fall, those racks had bowed under a burden of fish, turtles, ducks, and geese. Now they looked ghostly and forlorn, mocking those warm autumn days when people had laughed, fed the fires, and Sang while brightly colored leaves tumbled down from the bluffs above. Beneath the racks, long fire pits had been dug, where hickory and other hard woods were used to smoke the catch. Now the pits gaped like empty mouths that drooled black stains across the ground as the runoff carried ash down the slope.

The last of the White Shell canoes had landed just downstream from Otter and his party. His cousins called and waved from where they pulled their canoe up onto the beach—then hurried up the path to the clan ground with its earthen mound, temples, and storehouses.

"Let's go get warm!" Jay Bird cried, hugging muscular arms to his wet coat. He squinted against the pelting rain, his wide mouth pressed into a thin-lipped grimace that made his broad face look oddly flat. Droplets of water had beaded in his thick black hair, now pulled tightly into two braids.

"Go on!" Otter pointed to the trail that led up past the drying racks. Shielding his eyes against the slushy rain, he could see that Grandmother's party had already reached the top.

Otter hesitated, running fingers down *Wave Dancer*'s curved hull. Too much moss. No wonder she'd felt sluggish on the way up from the Alligator villages.

The swamps to the south tended to grow moss on anything—even on the turtles and alligators. The only place worse was the Southern Ocean itself. There the Traders fought a constant battle with barnacles, and with saltwater worms that ate holes in their vessels' wooden hulls.

With the touch of a lover, Otter caressed the thinning bow. His soul had gone into building the big Trading canoe. For an entire summer, he and Uncle had searched the forests for the right bald cypress. Bald cypress was a durable wood that resisted rot and splitting; a well-made canoe crafted from the heartwood would last through a man's lifetime, provided that he cared for it.

When they had found the right tree—a towering monster—Otter had said the appropriate prayers and begun the arduous task of felling the swamp giant. To kill the tree, he'd ringed it, using a hafted adze to chip away the gray bark and expose the wood. Next, because the tree stood in a backwater swamp, he'd built a platform of mud and brush around the base of the tree to support his fires. Then he'd burned the ringed area, making sure the flames ate deeply into the green wood.

He'd returned in late fall to find the huge tree dead and partially desiccated. For days, he'd alternately burned and chopped at the base of the trunk, working around it like a beaver. When the tree finally cracked with a thunderous roar and teetered in the breeze, he'd whooped and jumped. The giant seemed to hang for a moment, as if in disbelief that it could reach in any direction but the eternal sky. Slowly it had gathered speed, crashing down and smashing its lesser rivals before smacking the water so hard that it sent white breakers rolling.

Then came the task of limbing the giant. Afterward, with help from his kin, he'd paddled the thick trunk out of the swamp, into the river channel, and onto White Shell territory. Through fall, winter, and spring, he worked, using fire, ground-stone adzes, and hafted chert bifaces to hollow out the interior of the canoe and shape the hull.

Under his hands, she'd slimmed—a sort of oversized gar—sleek, fast, and agile. Despite the extra effort, he shaped the high prow to withstand rough water and worked it into the shape of a fox's head so she could spot trouble and be clever enough to avoid it. To smooth the hull, he used blocks of coarse-grained sandstone. He kept the hull lines straight with cords for guidelines, and listened as Uncle advised him on the proper shape so the heavy canoe would plane the water just right when ten strong men were paddling against the current.

Above the waterline, he'd carved the clan totems: faces of the ancestors and images of Spirit Animals like Many Colored Crow, Spider, Water Serpent, and Snapping Turtle. These he painted, using the brightest colors. With each stage of progress, he ritually poured river water over the wood to ensure that the Power of the Father Water soaked into the grain along with his own sweat, and yes, more than a little blood, too. His soul had joined with that of the wood. He'd felt the canoe's spirit taking form, growing under his hands.

He'd sensed the essence of her spirit and named her *Wave Dancer*, from the way she took to the water, riding high and skipping across the chop.

Finished, she lay pale and sleek, with a beam wide enough that two big men could sit side by side, and long enough that four men could lie head to toe. Fully loaded, she could carry as much as fifteen strong men could manage in the stoutest of packs.

As the rain trickled down his face, he stroked the polished wood. Perhaps if he'd loved *Wave Dancer* less, Red Moccasins might have loved him more. He should have suffered a pang of guilt at that secret knowledge, and it did sadden him. But if only she could have experienced the splendor of the river, perhaps she would have learned to love *Wave Dancer* and the Father Water as he did.

With a critical eye, he glanced down the keel, a strip of oak fastened to the centerline of the hull by means of wooden pegs that had swollen to fit tightly. That trick he'd learned from the saltwater Traders, who carried tobacco, colored feathers, and other goods up from the south. With such a keel, a canoe worked better against the wind and held a truer course. On the other hand, the keel made crabbing against a current considerably more difficult, and sometimes, in fast water, treacherous.

"Tomorrow we'll see about this moss, *Wave Dancer*. We'll be gone soon, girl." He stared along the curving bank. "Northward, taking the shells and feathers upriver. Maybe we'll search out more copper this time . . . or silver. Pan pipes are in demand in the south. They don't weigh much, and we can get many times their weight in conch shell, tobacco, and sharks' teeth."

He gave the pointed bow one last pat, then wound his way through the other beached canoes before following the muddy path upward.

The White Shell had placed their clan house on the high terrace overlooking the Father Water. According to the stories, Old White Shell had been the leader when the people traveled here from the east. It was here that Many Colored Crow appeared in the Elder's Dreams. White Shell had been both a valiant warrior and a pious member of the Star Society. As a result, he gave orders to his daughters that they bury him in a tomb—as Many Colored Crow decreed—and cover it with earth. Since that time, two layers of soil had been added to the burial mound, with Yellow Reed's grandmother and mother buried there along with their brothers. That mound looked somber in the slanting rain, the sloped sides tawny with flattened grass.

Beyond the clan grounds, irregular fields had been cleared from the vine-thick tangle of oak, hickory, and beech. The fields waited, frozen and still; the stubble of last year's knotweed and goosefoot stalks canted this way and that, yellowed and broken. Nearly a third of the fields were grown over with weeds and grass, shot through with slim shoots of newly sprouted trees. These fallow lands would be burned after the next dry spell, and their soil hoed before being replanted in sunflower, amaranth, bottle gourd, and squash.

The White Shell, like most of the farming peoples Otter knew, lived in isolated houses, dispersed over the clan territory. Each household tended its own fields and—after obtaining approval from the Elders—collected the forest bounty within the clan's territory. Large storage pits were excavated into the soil and lined with grass. Bark coverings kept them dry, and often half-shelters were used to protect them from the elements.

Down along the floodplains of the tributaries for a two-day canoe trip up and down the river, similar fields had been cleared for maygrass, tobacco, and little barley. In selected marshes, cane and cattail stands were groomed. Cane provided dart shafts, flooring, and drill stems. Cattail roots were eaten along with the pods, and the leaves were used for matting. Hickory, acorns, walnuts, wild grape, hackberry, sugarberry, wild plums, raspberries, and more, reflected the bounty of forest and river.

Only important structures had been built here, near the

mound: the clan house, a large, oblong building with a bowed roof of thatch; a charnel hut—empty for the moment—built of logs, then roofed with bark-and-cane matting, which was also hung inside for walls; and several storehouses, including the one that now sheltered Otter's Trade goods. Around the periphery lay the lineage houses, where cousins, or cousins' cousins, stayed during the ceremonies, crafting offerings and conducting family business.

As Otter watched, smudges of smoke rose from the peaked roofs of these houses, indicating that fires burned within. Few would be venturing back to their farmsteads on this stormy day.

To build the lineage houses, families had sunk digging sticks into the fertile soil to carve out holes before setting poles as thick as a man's arm. Green branches, stripped of leaves, had been woven between the poles to stiffen the walls, then shocks of grass had been carefully tied in place. Some roofs had been made from sections of bark stripped from ringed trees, while others used grass thatch collected from the flats around the creeks.

Otter slogged his way through the mud toward an opening in the low wall—an earthen embankment as high as his chest—that surrounded the clan grounds. Prior to construction, a peg had been driven into the ground immediately in front of the clan house. A strong cord, nearly a dart's cast in length, had been tied off from the peg. With it, a perfect circle had been scribed around the entire complex. Breaks in the wall marked the locations where the sun could be seen rising and setting on the sacred days.

He paused, looked back across the swollen river. From this height, the Tall Cane clan grounds were barely visible, only a dark swath situated in a wreath of blue smoke curtained by rain.

Four Kills would be learning his new life now, familiarizing himself with one-time friends who had become relatives. From the moment of his marriage, his relationship with his mother-in-law had changed forever. Gone was the old joking and sparring that had amused them by the hour. Now, Four Kills would studiously avoid her. He would refuse to meet her eyes, and never speak directly to her. Even her possessions would be shunned. Any communication between them would be accomplished through intermediaries.

Such was the way of the people. By avoiding one's mother-in-law, domestic tranquillity could be maintained. And if a man really became fond of his wife's mother, he could work like a winter-wary squirrel and buy the right to talk directly to her. It would be like Four Kills to do exactly that.

Otter muttered the ritual greeting to the ancestors who prowled the grounds, then let out a wavering whistle as he started forward. Catcher—his shaggy black, white, and tan dog—appeared, charging from the storeroom.

Otter caught the animal in mid-jump and suffered through the exuberant greeting of wiggles, licks, and whines.

"Did you guard the storehouse? Make sure the pack rats didn't get in and piss on the tobacco? No thieves stole our conch shell?"

Catcher yipped and squirmed, pawing at him with muddy feet. The dog's thick coat was silky black over most of his body, the bib and collar white, with tan trim on the legs, muzzle, and eyebrows. A good Trader's dog knew his duty to the packs and goods that meant livelihood and prosperity. He would guard his packs to the death, making sure that no pests, four-footed, two-footed, or winged, bothered the goods.

Catcher was one of the finest dogs Otter had ever known. For six years now, he and Otter had traveled the length and breadth of the rivers, even going down among the sandy lagoons in the Land of the Manatees to Trade with the people who lived there.

Otter scratched the floppy ears, until Catcher's wiggling nose sought out the strip of fried turtle meat Otter had hidden in his belt pouch.

"What's this? Ah! Yes, a bit of feast from the wedding, isn't it?" He reached in and plucked the tidbit from the pouch.

Catcher trembled with anticipation, his tail lashing the rain. Delighted brown eyes studied the bit of meat, and the ears pricked.

"You sit. That's it. Now . . . wait." Otter placed the brown strip of meat on the top of Catcher's pointed nose. The dog's tail wagged enthusiastically, swiping an arc through the mud. Catcher's eyes started to cross as he tried to focus on the treat tormenting his quivering nose.

"Okay!" Otter clapped his hands.

Catcher made a quick movement of his head, and the jaws

snapped loudly in the blur. The turtle meat vanished. Catcher exploded into happy jumps and circled Otter with pattering feet.

"Good work!" Otter praised as he wrestled with the dog. "You'd better be just as quick with a thief's fingers!"

"Hey!" Jay Bird called from the doorway to the clan house. "Grandmother wants you to get in here. Everyone's waiting on you!"

"I'll be right there! Let me check my packs."

With Catcher dancing beside him, Otter hurried to the storehouse along the western curve of the embankment. The round building sat on raised posts. The walls had been made from split cane laced together with cordage. Shocks of grass thatch effectively shed the rain. The structure protected his goods from sun and storm, and the raised floor discouraged mildew and fungus. His packs remained in the carefully arranged pile he'd left them in. All appeared secure.

Catcher watched with serious brown eyes, his tail slapping back and forth in slow arcs that slung mud this way and that. Otter smiled, knowing that expression: anticipation of the moment when Otter would begin carrying his packs back down to the river—a sign that they'd be off again.

"Catcher? You guard the packs, now. All right?"

Catcher made a grumbling sound and scampered up the pole ladder to settle himself on the packs in the doorway. He snorted a sigh, heedless of the water and mud that dripped on the brightly painted fabric of the packs. Otter raised an eyebrow, gave it up as a lost cause, and turned his steps toward the big clan house.

The clan house served as a meeting place as well as sleeping quarters for visitors to the clan grounds. As leader of the clan, Yellow Reed did little in the way of manual labor. Her needs were supplied by her descendants.

The structure was square but had rounded corners. The interior measured twenty paces long and fifteen across and had been divided into three rooms by cattail matting. A fabric hanging kept the storm from blowing in through the south-facing doorway.

Otter paused, wishing he could simply slip away and nurse his heart. If only he could take some time to think about Red Moccasins and Four Kills. To think about himself. That practical side of his nature could wrap itself around the swelling sense of loss and slowly squeeze it back into nothingness. He could reorder his life the way a shaman ordered the bones before a ceremony. He could put his soul back in harmony.

Resigned, Otter ducked through the low doorway.

Four

From where I soar, I can look down on a green land that gives way to incredibly blue water. A crescent of white beach, the shoreline undercut by waves, lances off toward the horizon on the west. Clouds, a piled magnificence of fluff, fill the sky, dazzled by the high, blazing orb of the sun.

"There," the voice tells me. "Just out from shore. Do you see, Green Spider?"

I tuck my raven's wings and drop like a hunting falcon until I can make out the canoe, a beautiful craft with a fox-head prow rising above the water. Three men and a woman paddle the boat.

"Those are my people!" I cry in delight.

"Yes. And if you look to the east, across the land . . ."

I have to twist in the air to see, arching gracefully away from the huge lake, crossing endless forest. At this height, the leaf canopy billows like small green clouds.

"I see," I answer. "The woman and her daughter. Yes, and there's the sack on her back! So. It is as you said, Many Colored Crow. Yes, at last I understand. I know the way now and can—"

Hard hands grab me from nothingness. Fingers work along my muscles, squeezing, prodding, massaging. I smell flower-scented hickory oil.

In terror, I flip over in the air and wheel around, choking out, "Who are you?"

But the hands are so Powerful. They seize me, rip me from

my journey through the vast blue sky and hurl me downward like a blazing meteor.

And from somewhere, somewhere far below, I hear the faint voices of people I know . . .

". . . time to lay him in his tomb. Poor boy. How could Power have let him die so young?"

I smell fire, hear the Songs my people Sing for the Dead. . . .

The Holy Road had been built straight south from StarSky to the valley of the Moonshell. According to the legends, it had begun as a High Head Trading trail that climbed up over the divide from the Flying Squirrel valley and wound through the wooded hillocks before following one of the creeks to the Moonshell River.

Over the years, the High Heads had refined the route as Trade in exotic goods increased. Despite the distance, the trip could still be made on foot in less time than it would take to paddle a canoe down the Flying Squirrel to the Serpent River, thence downstream to the mouth of the Moonshell and back up.

Generations ago, as the Flat Pipe peoples migrated from their traditional grounds in the hills, they had absorbed the High Head obsession with stars and earthworks. Perhaps, as a young people, their vigor had led them to improve on things the High Heads taught them. Or perhaps the giant monuments resulted from the Sacred Societies, whose membership crossed clan lines. Within the secret walls of the societies, the Elders studied the path of the stars, the ways of the plants and animals, and the arts to which each society laid claim.

A young person's vision, as well as his or her predisposition, would incline him or her to apply to one of the societies. After years of observing the rituals and studying at the feet of the Elders, the youth would memorize the ways of the masters.

The Weavers' Society taught the arts of the loom, textiles, and dyes. The Potters' Society ingrained the ways of finding clay, mixing the right temper, incising designs, painting, and firing. Stoneworkers learned to drill, carve, and polish. Healers had their own very small society, where the Powers of plants, colors, and rituals were instilled and propagated. The influential Warriors' Society trained for the defense of various clan territories and imparted the techniques of warfare.

But the greatest of all was the Star Society, which watched and charted the heavens, and next to it, the engineers, who recreated their observations on earth. The engineers coordinated the building of the great earthworks, each a reflection of the sacred patterns in the heavens. At StarSky, all of the major earthworks served specific functions in the grand master plan. The Great Circle, along with its central bird mound, charted the rising moon at its highest point on the northeastern horizon. The linear embankments charted the rising and setting of the solstice and equinox sun. The observatory, in the western end of the great Octagon, faced the point on the horizon where the summer-solstice sun rose.

From the High Heads, the people had incorporated the Circle, often intermixing it with the square design of their own heritage. The Circle, so the legend said, represented the sky, and the Square the earth and its four corners.

Employing sticks and strings, the alignments were laid out by engineers. Measurements were kept exact by using knots in the string to mark certain distances. Courses of stone would be placed to check the calculations, and if in error, could be adjusted before the societies directed the actual construction of the earthworks during the midsummer ceremonies. At that time, people from the surrounding clans would come, their harvest of maygrass and marsh elder finished. For the two weeks around the solstice, men, women, and children would excavate with digging sticks, loading fresh earth into baskets and piling it on the stone courses. Depending on the purpose of the earthwork, the society leaders insisted on certain kinds of soil, such as clay of the right color. Everything was planned to the last detail.

Year by year, the work proceeded, the knowledge passed from generation to generation within the society. Meanwhile, other societies managed the grounds, pruning back the ever eager forest saplings that rooted in the newly disturbed soil.

The Holy Road had been laid out thus, by line of sight, from tautly stretched string to tautly stretched string. From the eastern entrance to the Octagon, the route ran south, curving around hillsides and leading to the major clan grounds at Sun Mounds.

Star Shell puffed a cold breath, beating her arms against her sides to warm herself. Though similar roads connected the Flat Pipe Clans with each of the major population centers, none were as grand as the Holy Road.

Behind her, the diminutive Tall Man followed in his odd, rolling gait. He carried two packs. The first, and the smaller of the two, was slung crossways to hang under his right arm. It was crafted of finely tanned leather and had been decorated with a wolf motif. From the way it bulged, it seemed to contain lots of odds and ends.

The second pack mounded on the dwarf's back like a shapeless bundle—a soft thing that he used as a pillow when they stopped. This was made of fabric, beautifully dyed and woven with geometrical patterns.

To Star Shell's surprise, the wizened Magician made good time, considering his age and the shortness of his bowed legs. But from the expression on his worn face, the journey was exacting a heavy toll.

They had few cares for shelter, for a different clan occupied each little valley they entered. Travelers, especially Traders, were always welcome, given a hot meal and a place to stay in a warm clan house.

"It's not far," Tall Man puffed as he looked up at the darkening sky. "We're in the Hackberry clan country. The clan house is at the bottom of the valley."

Star Shell glanced up at the brooding sky. Flakes of snow fell, drifting idly to the white ground.

"Why did you come?" she asked.

"You will need me."

"But you won't tell me why?"

"Young Star Shell, there are times when a person shouldn't ask too many questions. I worry about these Flat Pipe people. They must measure and study everything. I've heard the ghosts whispering among themselves. They wonder and marvel at the things men are doing."

"Maybe that's the beauty of being dead. You can watch without worrying."

He made a snuffling sound. "And what makes you think

ghosts are free from worry? Mica Bird's grandfather is harassing Mica Bird for just that reason. He knows the Power of the Mask. It wasn't until the Power abandoned him that he really understood its strength."

"You sound as if you pity him."

The Magician's little feet crunched in the snow. "I knew him. A bright and ambitious young man. He changed—and never realized it until he took the Mask back to the mountain."

"I still have trouble understanding this. Why didn't the High Heads—why didn't *you* go and reclaim the Mask?"

Tall Man walked in silence for a moment. "Sacred objects don't belong to a person. They belong to themselves. People only care for them. Power fills them. True, one of my ancestors made the Mask in the first place. Think of it not as an article of adornment, but rather as a house. Many Colored Crow's Spirit moved into it, that's all. Once that happened, it wasn't just wood and feathers anymore."

She shook her head. "It makes no sense! You tell me that Many Colored Crow is really this Raven Hunter. Many Colored Crow did good things! He came into this world and told people how to care for their ancestors. He rid us of the ghosts that were haunting people. Now you tell me he's wicked."

"Not wicked, young Star Shell. The world balances between opposites. Can you have life without death? Happiness without sorrow? Would you have appetite without starvation? Would you have mice without hawks? Deer without lions? No! It's all a balance. If night never fell, the fireflies would never shine. Were it not for winter, the fields would never replenish themselves. The stars would never gleam unless darkness cloaked the heavens."

She trudged on, saying nothing.

The Magician raised his short arms. "The world is locked together like fingers from both hands, always pulling and struggling. When the High Heads grew complacent and slothful, someone made the Mask. Humans, and the Spirits, too, need that element of competition. Unless you periodically burn an old forest, a new one never grows. Fire and shadow. Always shifting, changing."

She shook her head in frustration.

Tall Man lowered his arms. "The point of all this is that

Raven Hunter's Mask is becoming too Powerful. I don't know why. Perhaps it sucks some of a person's Power into itself when it's worn—like a tick under the skin. Whatever it's done, it sows discord. Discord makes people uncomfortable. Once they are uncomfortable, they work to change the situation.''

"I don't see what's wrong with a little harmony."

"Nothing. Nothing at all. But if all we did was sit around in harmony, what would get done? Think about the clans. They constantly bicker and compete. No matter how fertile a field is, it will grow goosefoot for only so long. Then it ceases to produce healthy plants. Balance is the key. You must have enough harmony to provide security, and enough trouble to keep things moving.''

Star Shell glanced up at the hillsides and the winter-bare trees above the pristine snow. Here and there, fields had been cleared, and she could see a lonely farmstead on one of the terraces. The place looked abandoned. The people had no doubt packed up what was left of their harvest and journeyed to a relative's holdings, where they could socialize the long winter nights away.

That's what winter was for: telling stories, working on weavings, and gossiping with friends. She'd hoped for that once. Now, instead, she struggled along in the cold, her visions of happiness dashed. She hadn't even found time to mourn for her mother. How could things have turned so wretched? What had she done to deserve this?

She gave the Magician a sidelong glance. "You talk a lot, but you haven't told me very much. About the future, I mean.''

"The future?" He clucked to himself. "Do you think knowing the future would make you feel better? What would you say if I told you that tomorrow you would fall through the ice on a river crossing? What if I told you that your body would never be found and that your ghost would spend forever down there in the mud, lost and alone? Would that make you feel better?''

"I'd turn right around and head back to StarSky City and my father's house.''

"That's what I thought. You don't really want to know the future. No one does.''

"But you seem to know, and it doesn't slow you down. When we reach Sun Mounds and face Mica Bird and the Mask, it won't be pleasant for you.''

"No," he admitted heavily. "I won't enjoy any of it. But you must understand, I don't know how things will turn out in the end. I only know what appears probable. Nevertheless, I have accepted certain responsibilities in this matter."

"But why, Tall Man? This is very dangerous. What business is it of yours?"

"Suffering is the business of every human being, Star Shell. If one has the courage, one can save other people from a great deal of pain. That makes it worth the risk, doesn't it?"

"I . . . I don't know." She blinked thoughtfully. "Can't you just give me a hint? What are we walking into? He isn't going to kill us, is he?"

Tall Man sighed. "Very well, I'll let you know this. I promise that you won't die at his hands. But when we arrive at Sun Mounds, you will begin the most horrible days of your life."

She could see the clan house now, a brown lump in the snowy flats on the terrace beside the small creek. Two more days and they would arrive at Sun Mounds. What did that mean for her? For her daughter? Would she ever again see a smile on Silver Water's face? Or was she condemning her daughter to a life of misery?

"I just hope you're wrong, Tall Man."

"So do I." But he didn't sound encouraging.

Otter stepped into warm dampness as he entered the White Shell clan house. The humid air smelled of spiced food, wood smoke, and wet clothing; the sweet pungency of tobacco permeated the whole. A blazing fire crackled in the central hearth, and people had already settled on the benches that lined the walls, or found spots on the crowded floor. Two of Blue Jar's daughters, Clay Bowl and Teal Wing, tended the earth oven, wrapping patties of goosefoot-and-knotweed flour in leaves before dropping them onto the glowing cooking clays.

More cooking clays heated in the roaring flames of the central hearth and would be placed over the top of the patties. Water would be sprinkled onto the clay cubes to explode into steam. Layers of hot clays, patties, and more clays would be alternated until the oven was filled. The contents would then steam and roast for several hours, and the warm hearth would do double duty to heat the house.

Otter took a quick inventory as he shrugged out of his soggy foxhide coat. Not much had changed since last fall. One of the cattail mats that divided the three rooms of the clan house was new. Clusters of gourds still hung from the roof. Most of them were full of seeds that Grandmother used in curing or cooking, or both. Others held leaves, flowers, pollen, and mineral powders for dying textiles in different colors. Net bags of nuts, dried raspberries, sugarberries, and plums hung near the doorway. Strings of dried onions had been tied together with cordage and dangled like shrunken white beads. Soot had coated most of the thatch, roof poles, and cord bindings. The constant smoking of the ceiling kept rot and fungus to a minimum and reduced the number of spiders and insects that lived in the roofing.

The cane walls had been painted in bright, geometric designs—the same as those the women wove into their fine fabrics. The lightning patterns, chevrons, and triangles identified the work of the White Shell Clan, just as other clans used designs peculiar to themselves.

The clan leaders had settled themselves on the floor in the back of the room. Blue Jar, Otter's mother, rested on a reed mat beside the fabric cushion where Grandmother would sit. Round Seed and Red Dye, Otter's aunts, sat in their places to the right of Grandmother's cushion.

Many Turtles, Otter's tall, muscular father, sat behind Blue Jar. The wind and sun had already begun to weather his face into walnut-brown leather. Those clear eyes had fastened themselves on Otter, probing, knowing.

Heavy Rock, Otter's uncle, sat in his place behind Round Seed. A chubby man with a bland face, he had amusement lurking in his heavy-lidded eyes. He knew every hole where the fish settled and could track a wary puma across bare stone. Beside him sat cousin Jay Bird, Round Seed's son.

Along with Aunt Red Dye and her husband, Banded Bird, these were the immediate family, the real power within the clan. More cousins, including Six Shell, Little Wart, and Three Herons, with their families, had jammed themselves in around the walls.

"At last!" Grandmother cried as she stepped through the low fabric-hung doorway in the divider. "Satisfied with the rain, Grandson? You spent enough time standing out in it to sprout."

Otter gave her a crooked grin that he hoped would hide his feelings. "I had to attend to my packs."

She nodded, fully aware of his sham. On age-pained legs, she moved to the center of the room, stepping around respectful relatives. Taking Blue Jar's hand, she eased herself down onto the pillow stuffed with cattail down. Her bones crackled in competition with the fire.

Grandmother looked around as her bony fingers smoothed the tightly woven fabric of her red-and-yellow dress into planes over her lap. As her bright eyes sought out each individual, she inclined her head slightly, her toothless mouth puckering in the wealth of wrinkles. The way her hands worked on the fabric of the dress reminded Otter of a crow's taloned feet, dark with the knowledge and essence of the Dead.

Grandmother waited patiently as Clay Bowl and Teal Wing dropped the last of the leaf-wrapped fish into the earth oven. Steam rolled up from the pit, carrying the aroma of roasting patties.

When the girls had finished, Grandmother sniffed loudly and rubbed her fleshy nose; the action pulled her wrinkles this way and that.

"Well . . ." she began. "May the ancestors and Spirits wish us health and peace. May our crops grow tall and green, and our nets return full when they are cast into the rich waters. May the deer breed and produce fat twins who answer our pleas for meat. May the ducks, geese, and turkeys return to our waters, forests, and fields. May the Great Sun bless our growing plants and ripen our squash. May the blessings of this life and the next fall upon us. First Man, guide us, and ancestors, hear our voices and protect us from evil."

Then the old woman raised her voice in Song, the usual Blessing of the Clan that Many Colored Crow had taught back in the beginning times.

That duty taken care of, Grandmother reached into her belt pouch and brought forth a beautifully crafted stone pipe that Otter had traded for far up the Serpent River. The piece was carved from reddish-brown slate. The flat stem bore the laboriously sculpted image of a falcon's head. She tamped a small twist of tobacco into the bowl and nodded as Teal Wing brought her a glowing ember. Puffing, she blew smoke at the ceiling, at the ground, and then to the cardinal directions.

She made a gesture, and the pipe was taken to Otter, who puffed and inhaled the sweet tobacco that he'd brought up from the south. Carefully, he exhaled in the sacred directions, then handed the pipe back to Grandmother.

"Very well," the old woman said. "We've had a good marriage ceremony. The feasts were wonderful, the celebration superb. Yaupon was drunk by all, and our hearts, souls, and Songs were pure. May the union be as blessed by luck as it was by the gifts showered upon the happy couple." Her obsidian gaze drilled into Otter. "No matter what they might have cost the giver."

To avoid the awkward pause that might have followed, Grandmother quickly stated: "Now, however, we finally have time to hear Otter. He has just recently returned from the Alligator clan villages near the mouth of the river. He brings us shell, sacred yaupon to boil and drink, dried fish, bright feathers, and many other things. Tell us what you have heard on the river, Grandson, and what you suggest that we do with these wonderful gifts you've brought."

Otter stepped to a spot across the fire from his grandmother, glanced around at his relatives, and lowered himself to a sitting position where everyone could see him. The firelight danced on his brightly dyed clothing, the heat causing the soaked fabric to steam. He laced his fingers together before him, his elbows on his knees.

He would start at the beginning, as was good manners. "I followed the river downstream for four tens of days. When I reached the Alligator clan villages, I made shore and asked for Swamp Bear, the chief there. He greeted me as he always has, with warm friendship, much food, and a dry place to sleep.

"For the next couple of weeks, I Traded the copper plate, fine fabrics, galena, pottery, and other goods the White Shell Clan allowed me to carry downriver. In return, I got many wonderful shells, tobacco, raw yaupon, sharks' teeth, and many other goods desired by the people upriver. With the clan's permission, I will take those things north to trade to the people up in the Copper Lands.''

Grandmother glanced around, then shrugged. "The clan will consider this request." She cocked her head. "What did you hear in the south, Otter? What are your words for us? What have you learned? What advice do you have about the coming year?"

Otter took a moment to collect his thoughts. He had expected immediate permission to continue Trading. The request was a formality, since the Trade goods technically belonged to the clan.

"Grandmother, nothing is going to be as it has been. The river Trade is changing. You yourself have seen the increase in the number of canoes passing each year. The demand for Trade is growing. We need to give this change careful thought, and to consider our role in it."

The old woman nodded. "We have suspected as much. Go on."

"Let me tell you about something I heard. Swamp Bear told me that the people living at the mouth of the river, the ones who call themselves the Anhinga, met some Traders, young men from the Khota villages. It seems that these young men decided to take four canoes to the mouth of the Father Water to see if they could Trade with the peoples there. They brought the usual things, of course, but while they were there, they noticed a young girl known as the Pearl. She is a granddaughter of the clan leader . . . the Anhinga are matrilineal. The Khota asked to marry her into the Khota Clan."

Blue Jar leaned forward. "Haven't you told us in the past that the Khota are patrilineal?"

"They are. The rumor is that this girl will go there, to the Khota, to marry Wolf of the Dead, the young war leader." Otter added bitterly, "I hope she enjoys his company."

"She can have him," Grandmother said sourly. "Do the Anhinga know what they've committed their daughter to?"

"I doubt it."

The Anhinga might not know about the Khota, but the White Shell did. Several years back, rumors had circulated that the Khota had been responsible for the death of Otter's uncle. No one would speak Uncle's name now. He had died in violence, and the corpse had not been recovered to be properly cleansed, purified, and placed among the ancestors in the City of the Dead. Instead, the angry ghost still roamed abroad somewhere, committing mischief and mayhem. Mentioning Uncle's name might draw it to White Shell territory. Should that happen, disease, bad luck, crop failures, and death would follow.

News of the atrocity had been particularly difficult for Otter; Uncle had been more to him than just his mother's older brother. Among the White Shell, as with most matrilineal people, Uncle had been responsible for Otter and Four Kill's education. Uncle had raised the boys, taught them, rewarded good behavior and punished them for bad. Many Turtles might have sired Blue Jar's children, but he had no responsibility for raising them other than offering advice every now and then. Many Turtles had enough on his hands with his own sister's children.

Recognizing Otter's obsession with the river, Uncle first took him upriver as a little boy. A famed Trader, Uncle had taught Otter the ways of the river and the peoples who lived on its shores. At the old man's knee, Otter had absorbed the skills of a Trader the way dry moss sucks up water.

Otter himself had paid a stiff price more than once when passing the Khota lands. The Khota were relatively new to the Ilini River, having moved down from the north within the last ten tens of winters. Originally fierce and warlike, they'd driven their predecessors from the country, taken the women, and adopted many of the ways of those they conquered.

Of all peoples, the Khota consistently proved the most troublesome; once they'd stolen an entire canoe-load of greenstone, galena, and steatite that Otter had laboriously paddled upriver. Traders generally tried to slip past the Khota villages at night. Those who tried to pass the villages in daytime were accosted, threatened, sometimes beaten—and always lightened of their loads. Traders categorized the Khota along with mosquitoes, ticks, water moccasins, bad storms, rough water, and other hazards of doing business. After all, the Khota created many fine artifacts, including effigy pipes, gorgets, and other goods that would bring fair profits up- or downriver—provided one could survive the Trading process.

Many Turtles muttered: ''Perhaps this Pearl will enjoy our Trade goods when she arrives there. At least someone will get some good out of them besides the sneaky Khota.''

Grandmother watched Otter through thoughtful eyes. "What do you think it means for us . . . this marriage?''

Otter took a deep breath. ''Trade is going to change over the coming years. The Khota hope to bypass most of the river Traders. They are planning on Trading directly for coastal goods.''

''Is it because so many Traders try to avoid them?'' Round Seed asked.

''I think so,'' Otter replied. ''Even Traders new to the area do their best to sneak their goods through Khota territory. When the Khota openly killed the Serpent City Trader a couple of years ago, they lost a lot of Trade. Tension ran high on the river that year, and the Ilini villages above them threatened war if they ever did it again.''

''They threatened you, didn't they?'' Grandmother retorted. ''Perhaps it would be worth paying Black Skull and some of his warriors to travel with you.''

Otter chuckled. ''It might at that, but what good will that do? Trade is not a matter of war. Making it so would offend Power, maybe turn it against us forever. If the Khota just weren't crazy . . . well, everyone would be happier.''

''We do have an option,'' Many Turtles said quietly. ''We could wait, watch for their canoes, steal from them the way they've stolen from us. Tall Cane Clan would stand with us. So would most of the villages along the Father Water.''

Mutters of assent rose from around the room.

Grandmother stilled them with a raised hand. She studiously avoided glancing toward her son-in-law. ''Someone might think that a good idea. But what would that gain us in the long term?'' She paused. ''As Otter said, they're crazy. Robbing their canoes might bring a whole flotilla downriver—one full of warriors. We'll all join the ancestors one day; let's not rush to do so.''

''It is worth considering,'' Heavy Rock said from his position behind Round Seed. ''A little respect can go a long way toward keeping Trade stable on the river.''

Grandmother steepled her hands. ''Perhaps my daughter's husband should give this some thought: Canoes travel faster than word of mouth. The Khota could land a war party here before anyone was the wiser. They could do a great deal of damage to us. War—no matter what the reasons for it—wouldn't be in our interest.'' She lowered her voice, her eyes gone misty, perhaps in memory of her murdered son. ''Even with the Khota.''

Otter rubbed his hands together. ''I agree. That the Khota have mounted a Trading expedition demonstrates that the number of Traders bypassing their villages has begun to worry them. With normal people, I would expect them to apologize and learn from their past mistakes. With the Khota . . . well, they're just lunatics.''

Grandmother nodded in sage agreement. ''Very well, Otter. You said that Trade on the river is going to change. What do you advise that we do about it?''

''Nothing, Grandmother. Like a flood in spring, you can't stop it.'' He steepled his fingers. ''However, knowing that the flood is coming, you can prepare for it, and use it to better your fields. More and more Traders are going to pass here. Perhaps the White Shell Clan should consider ways to capture part of that Trade?''

''Build a net across the river?'' Round Seed asked.

''I don't think you need to go that far.'' Otter made a simple gesture. ''Part of your work is already done. Traders have always been welcome here. Uncle began that tradition. Make them even more welcome. Perhaps a shelter should be built down at the canoe landing?''

Heavy Rock stirred where he sat behind Round Seed. ''Won't things disappear? I mean, these are strangers, people we don't know. They could be . . . well, you know, untrustworthy.''

''Some will be,'' Otter agreed. ''But I want you to consider this, Uncle. Traders depend on good will. Those who steal, or cause trouble, soon find themselves unwelcome—like the Khota. An unwelcome Trader does little Trading. And the rumors about him soon circulate. After all, a good Trader, like me, doesn't want a bad Trader to prosper. I'll tell everyone that What's-His-Name isn't reliable, and that people should be wary about Trading with him. What's-His-Name will find few villages open to him after a couple of seasons.''

Grandmother patted her knees. ''Not all problems can be avoided, and more good than bad would come from having Traders here. Traders bring luck; you've always heard that, haven't you? Perhaps we should let it be known that a warm stew is always cooking at the landing.''

"That's a lot of effort." Blue Jar looked pensive as she scratched behind her ear. "You have to keep it hot so it doesn't spoil. Sometimes it can be weeks between visits by Traders. That's a lot of wood to collect, and someone must tend the fire all the time." She glanced slyly at Grandmother. "And my husband already has enough to do."

Many Turtles laughed, sneaking a glance at Grandmother from the corner of his eye.

"But you could lay a stack of firewood in the shelter," Red Dye suggested. "And hang bags of precooked patties from the walls. Maybe smoke them so the mold doesn't grow on them."

"I think that just a hut would be enough," Otter said. "Traders would be more than willing to walk up the hill in search of something to eat. Not only that, they'd want to talk, to hear the news, and to sit around a cheerful fire with other people. Make them feel good, and welcome, and they'll be more likely to give you gifts."

Blue Jar looked at her sister. "It might be worth it to make some heavy bags . . . the sturdy kind Traders like to carry. And we might keep some extra pottery jars handy. You know, things that wear out or get broken. Things Traders need."

Grandmother cocked her head thoughtfully. "This will be good for us. As we get more visitors, we'll learn. See what they need . . . and do our best to fill that need."

"I agree, Grandmother." Otter looked around, meeting his relatives' eyes. "If this is done correctly, you could lure most of the Traders to stop here. We are located at the right place on the river. The Deena villages are a day's travel to the north. Yellow Cliffs is a day to the south. Because of the bluff, the White Shell clan grounds are close to the river—not a long walk from where a Trader would have to leave his goods. This is a good place to stop."

"We shall consider it," Grandmother stated, making a sign with her hand that the subject was closed for the moment.

"What is the news here?" Otter resettled himself so the fire would dry his left side.

"Something happened over at the City of the Dead," Grandmother told him soberly. All eyes immediately turned on the old woman. "We're not sure what. A young man from the Broken Mussel Clan—his name was Four Yellow Feathers—passed through the day before the marriage. It appears that the Dreamer, Green Spider, is dead. Killed during the solstice.''

"What?" Many Turtles gasped, propriety forgotten as he stared wide-eyed at Grandmother.

Otter stiffened, his heart skipping a beat.

"Why didn't you say something?" Blue Jar demanded.

Grandmother sat stolidly, her expression neutral as she continued. "This Four Yellow Feathers arrived just before we were to cross the river for the marriage. He saw me here—alone. I, of course, took him for some well-wisher sent by old Willow Thong. Thought he came bearing greetings, or a gift. Instead, he sat there where you are, Otter, lowered his eyes and said that Green Spider was dead." She smacked her leathery palms together. "We had a marriage to attend to, so I said nothing."

"I still don't understand why you didn't tell me." Blue Jar's eyes flashed.

"Why say anything?" Grandmother responded reasonably. "If he's dead, do you think worrying about it would bring him back? If it's a rumor . . . why stir everyone up with it? Apparently, Four Yellow Feathers didn't feel it important enough to paddle across and inform the Tall Cane Clan. Time will tell if it's true or not."

"Mother, in the future—"

Grandmother raised her hand, commanding as always. "Red Moccasins and Four Kills had a wonderful ceremony. Had I started spouting rumors, everyone would have spent the time muttering dire predictions and doing their best to turn the occasion into the end of the world."

Otter slowly shook his head as Grandmother's probing stare bored into him. Green Spider dead? What did it mean?

Many Turtles' lips quivered for a moment. "How . . . how did he die? Does anyone know?"

Only the popping of the fire broke the silence.

Grandmother sighed, and for a moment she stared vacantly, seeing something in her head. She seemed to come to herself again, properly addressing the answer to Blue Jar instead of to Many Turtles. "According to the rumor, it happened on the winter solstice . . . just at the noontime beginning of the Feast of the Dead. As the food was being laid out, a bolt of lightning struck the temple. Green Spider and the Clan Elders were there.

Apparently Green Spider was seeking some sort of Power. The Clan Elders were watching over him. They missed the ceremonies, as a matter of fact.

"The whole temple was burned to the ground. The four old men were scorched as they dragged Green Spider from the flames. Green Spider sat up, eyes wide, but saw no one, heard no one. He is reported to have shouted, 'You are so beautiful! Yes . . . yes . . . I'm coming. Fly . . . fly to the Spiral . . . ' And then he fell over dead."

"What does that mean?" Round Seed wondered. She had placed a hand over her mouth, her frightened eyes fixed on a point over the door.

Grandmother cleared her throat in the familiar growl she used to bring people back to their senses. "How do I know? I told you, this is just what Four Yellow Feathers said."

A stirring of unease sucked at Otter's soul like dark water around a snag.

Five

The evening fire crackled and spit, sending dancing sparks upward into the darkening sky. Pearl sat silently on the weathered gray trunk of a cottonwood. The river had borne the fallen giant down the winding channel, scrubbing the bark away with the same brutal efficiency that had snapped off the tree's branches and limbs. The wiles of current and fate had grounded the giant here, on the crest of a long sand spit that curled out into the murky brown river from the downstream end of a wooded island.

Pearl pulled her blanket tight about her as she gazed across the fire toward the distant eastern bank. In the fading twilight, the river had gone black, roiling and twining in the darkness. Freedom lay there, beyond that surging rush.

She could see the high prows of the canoes in the flickering orange light of the fire; the boats were pulled up on the beach like four weird teeth rising from the damp mud. Water slapped at their sterns, the sound mixing with the bell-like splash of waves on the shore. Beyond the clotted blackness of the eastern uplands, a red wolf sent an eerie call through the trees, only to be mocked by the plaintive *hoo hoo hoooo* of a great horned owl.

Pearl leaned closer to the popping fire to gather more of its warmth. The smell of hickory and sweet gum mixed as the breeze changed and blew warm smoke around her. She leaned back and tilted her head to one side to avoid the worst of the fumes. The blackness of the night weighed on her.

"You all right?" Grizzly Tooth asked in thickly accented Trader talk as he approached and settled on his haunches. He braced his muscular arms loosely on his knees, his fingers dangling.

Pearl nodded, glancing at him from the corner of her eye. Grizzly Tooth couldn't have been more than twenty summers, yet he claimed to have killed ten enemies in battle and to have traveled to a barren land in the far west where he killed a great silver bear.

He looked the part of a warrior, his keen eyes gleaming alertly in a broad-boned face, his nose flat. No trace of humor betrayed itself in his firm mouth. He wore a deerhide shirt that reached to mid-thigh. The leather had been decorated with teeth, most of them human incisors, but there were fangs from bobcat, badger, and fox as well. Large copper ear spools had stretched his earlobes and glinted in the light. He had pulled his long black hair into a bun above his forehead and pinned it with a stiletto crafted from a deer's ulna. The grizzly-bear teeth—from which he drew his name—alternated with long brown claws on his necklace.

From what she'd learned, Grizzly Tooth and her promised husband, Wolf of the Dead, had undergone some sort of ceremony that made them brothers where nature had failed.

She glanced around, hating the dull ache in her soul. The rest of Grizzly Tooth's companions, young, strong, and muscular, either squatted or stood before the other fires, roasting fish, ducks, and a heron they had killed during the day. They laughed, sharing jokes in their guttural language. Periodically, they glanced at her, their black eyes speculative in the firelight.

The Khota were an attractive people, lithe, tall, with broad faces and thin, hooked noses. They covered themselves with ornaments of copper, mica, and shell. For dress, they tended toward tailored hides or coarsely woven textiles that seemed more like matting than the finely woven fabrics Pearl was used to. During cold weather, they draped blankets or fur cloaks over their shoulders. Many used long thongs to lace hide or cloth to their bare legs, twining the laces in a net weave.

Each of the young men carried an atlatl strung to his belt. Thus armed, the Khota were a most formidable party as they moved upriver. Pearl wondered about that. Why did they need forty able-bodied warriors, bristling with darts, to travel the river? Other Traders made the trip by themselves, or at most, in parties of less than ten, depending on the size of the canoes they had to muscle upstream.

Who did the Khota fear? And why? She'd never paid much attention to stories about far-distant peoples. The uneasy thought had settled within her that it might be a serious deficiency in her education.

That morning they had passed the confluence of the Western River. She'd been that far north before. But from there on, she had been seeing country new to her. The journey had taken on a different feeling: one of inevitability.

What would it be like? How would she live with these people? What would this strange northland be like?

The canoes would beach on some strange northern river, and the oddly dressed Khota would crowd around her, nudging, peering, grunting to each other as their stares invaded her. She'd have to walk among them like a curious trophy. Despite the numbing fear, she *must* act with all the pride and bearing of the Anhinga.

How can I do that if they start poking, prodding? The very thought brought a chill to her. Would they resent this woman of the south coming among them? Surely a man as great as this Wolf of the Dead would have women who wanted him, perhaps even loved him. How would they deal with her arrival? Teasing? Testing her courage? Outright hatred?

Pearl knotted her fists. She knew none of their customs. What if she offended their beliefs? Would they understand—or would they shun her for an intruder?

Glancing at the warriors around her, she could remember no moment of sympathy. Of all of them, only Grizzly Tooth regarded her as anything more than a prize. She could read nothing but desire in the eyes of the others—and then only when Grizzly Tooth's attention was elsewhere.

As the fire crackled, she studied the war leader from the corner of her eye. She was the only woman among four tens of men. Could he keep his young men under control? Or would Wolf of the Dead even care if his warriors decided to sate themselves within her?

If you don't think about it, Pearl, maybe it won't happen.

Despite the predatory stare Grizzly Tooth gave her, she forced herself to remember quiet mornings in the backswamps as the mist curled off still water and around the swollen boles of tupelos. She could see the dewdrops, gleaming like crystals on the hanging moss. The lilt of birdsong carried as Alligator floated, only his eyes and nostrils breaking the placid surface of the silky water.

As she stared into the fire, memories of other fires in happier times were kindled. Faces formed, so finely etched in her memory. Brown eyes sparkled, and echoes of laughter broke bright from the lips of friends and family, only to vanish in the emptiness of her soul.

I'm never going to see my people again. I'm headed into the unknown . . . and I'm going to die horribly among the barbarians.

Black Skull dug his decorated paddle into the sluggish water, driving the dugout canoe through the thin sheet of ice that crackled and shattered under the force of their passage. As the boat passed, fragments of ice tinkled and whispered against the hull. The V'ed bow wake washed over the crust, clearing the ice to expose wobbling white bubbles trapped beneath.

The Deer River was bleak at this time of year. The thin dusting of snow that had fallen the night before now vanished in the brightening daylight. Mottled yellow-brown mats of fall leaves carpeted the ground under naked trees half-strangled by ropy masses of dormant vines. In the shadowed hillside fringes of woodland, light-starved saplings cast a chaotic pattern on the forest floor.

Overhead, clots of fluffy white cloud scudded off to the northeast, driven by the relentless south wind. On the north-facing slopes, crusted snow lay blue-white in the shadows. Spears of ice clung to the shadowed limestone outcrops that peered through leaf mold and patchy, reddish-yellow sands.

They've all lost their minds! Black Skull groused at himself. *We're on a fool's errand!*

He craned his neck, studying the next bend. From his position in the war canoe's stern, he had to peer around three men. Two of them were Clan Elders, each dressed in their clan colors. And finally, up in the bow, *he* sat, bolt upright, head erect—facing, of all things, *backwards!*

In spite of his irritation, a sudden need to shiver settled in Black Skull's flesh—and it wasn't incited by the bracing morning air.

Black Skull thrived on discipline and order; he had little time for foolishness. Foolishness in a warrior was a weakness, and no one could accuse Black Skull of weakness. As a child, he'd lived in weakness, and in fear. But Granduncle had shown him the way: the warrior's path. Through discipline and duty, Black Skull had destroyed his tormentor and overcome his weakness. As a warrior, he organized each day, conducted himself with honor and propriety as befitted one of his rank, observed the rituals and taboos of his War Spirits, and obsessed himself with training.

And then lightning struck the temple and Black Skull's ordered life began to dissolve.

I'm cursed with a lunatic . . . on a lunatic's mission. To emphasize his wrath, he used his pointed war paddle to send the canoe flying forward.

From the moment Green Spider had returned from the Dead, he'd been someone, some*thing,* different. The sober-eyed, quiet young man Black Skull had known—and moderately detested—had been replaced by this curiously possessed caricature of that other Green Spider. What had happened to him while he'd been dead? What—or who—had he become?

Black Skull's muscles locked for the briefest of instants as he remembered the horrified face of his mother, her glazed eyes glaring wide at him from the edge of death. Wet, hot blood had leaked down her face in web-like tracery.

He tossed his head the way he would to fling water from his face and hair. . . . *Or blood . . . blood like hers . . . tracing across the numbing skin. Snails left tracks like that blood . . . tracks, the pathways of death . . . and murder.*

He drove the memory away violently, like scattering a covey of quail. The fool had brought all this on—he and his insane babbling.

Black Skull gazed around uneasily, peering into the silent maze of dark tree trunks, hearing the crystal sounds of water and ice. Power seemed to hover in the air around them like an invisible haze—as it had from that fateful moment on the solstice when lightning speared from the sullen sky to destroy the temple.

His mother's memory rarely intruded into Black Skull's dreams, let alone his waking hours. And now she'd returned to haunt him. The raving maniac in the bow had something to do with that. Supposedly, he'd been in the Land of the Dead. Talked to her perhaps?

I ought to crack the idiot's head open.

Black Skull unleashed all the strength in his muscular body, driving the paddle deep into the still water as he battered the canoe through another patch of ice. Imagine, dragging the Clan Elders, the most important people in the world, out into danger like this. It was all insanity!

Behind him, the second canoe, powered by the great warrior, Three Eagles, followed. It carried the other two Clan Elders. They sat like wooden stumps, wrapped in thick blankets woven of feather and cord.

I warned them not to do this thing. They didn't listen to me. Dedication to duty had its failings. If anything happened to the Clan Elders, it would be Black Skull's fault. Yet this demented idiot with the sense of a raving jay had placed them all at risk.

Black Skull cast a suspicious glance at Green Spider. The fool's vacant brown eyes rolled around in their sockets as if they were unhooked. He looked unkempt, his triangular face pale. *That* couldn't be Power.

Black Skull remembered everything that had happened, and he used the memory to cover any trace of his mother—used it the way the clan used a new layer of earth to cover the bones of the Dead in a burial mound.

Just before the lightning struck, Black Skull had been walking toward the temple. He'd felt the hair on his head begin to prickle, and his nerves had crackled like rubbed fox fur.

The bolt had flashed brightly across the cloud-wrapped winter sky, cracking the bones of the world with its thunder. Frying white light had split eerily, touching the flat-topped mound with one fork and splintering the roof of the temple with the other. For one incredulous moment, Black Skull had stood as firmly rooted as one of the old oaks. Then he'd run as he'd never run before.

As he'd charged up, Black Skull had found the Clan Elders dragging Green Spider from the roaring nightmare. The look in their eyes would haunt him forever: sheer glassy-eyed terror.

With his callused hands, Black Skull had beaten the flames from the disoriented old men, shaking them one by one to return them to this world, demanding to know if they were all right.

Somewhere in the horror of the moment, one of the Elders had bent down over Green Spider wailing, *"He's dead!"*

An ominous silence had settled over the City of the Dead, to be broken only by the popping and snapping of the flames.

The rest of that day had passed like a dream. Scattered images still swirled in Black Skull's memory: worried people running in all directions; frantic pleas from cowering individuals with tear-streaked faces; others, mute, who stared up toward the heavens; a little girl lost in the panic, crying past the knotted fist she'd stuffed into her mouth as she ran through the forest of legs, searching for her mother; the wretched expression on Green Spider's dead face as they carried him to the Blood Clan charnel house.

People began to slip away, many leaving their belongings on the ground as if tainted by the horrible event. More followed, until by nightfall, the City of the Dead had been all but abandoned.

The Clan Elders remained, silent, their gazes fixed on Visions that lay outside this world. In spite of the remonstrations of friends, Healers, and concerned relatives, they'd barely responded, choosing to stay in the charnel hut with Green Spider's corpse.

For three days, the grisly vigil continued as Green Spider's relatives trickled back to wash his body, paint it, and begin the ceremonies that would start him on the path to join his ancestors.

What did one do with a man killed by Power? Normal people could lie around in the charnel house until the flesh fell off the body; then the bones could be painted before burial or cremation.

Given the bizarre nature of Green Spider's death, his relatives—with the concurrence of the Clan Elders—had prepared a tomb. They'd dug out a grave and lined it with red clay. Logs were procured from the forest to lay across the tomb. This would be capped with a shallow covering of earth. It would do until a decision could be made on the final disposition of Green Spider's corpse.

On the fourth day, as the morning sun broke the tree-covered horizon into a crystal-cold sky, they'd carried Green Spider to his tomb and laid him on the frozen red clay. When the logs were being placed across the top, Green Spider had suddenly sat bolt upright. Cries of amazement brought Black Skull on a dead run. He'd arrived as Green Spider took a deep breath and opened his eyes.

It took several heartbeats before Green Spider focused and looked around at the shocked faces of the people. Then he smiled lazily and climbed out of the grave.

I should have killed him then, Black Skull thought. *I'd have saved us all a lot of trouble.*

Old woman Many Flowers had gone ashen, her eyes sliding back in her head before she tottered and fell over like a slab of bark. From that moment on, Green Spider had acted strangely. He did things nonsensically—like a maniac.

After he'd eaten, he'd claim he was hungry. When he was hungry, he'd say he was full. If a person told him to sit down, he'd stand up. Ask him to come, and he'd walk away. Tell him to go away, and he'd walk right up.

When asked about it, he simply stated, "I'm fine. The rest of you are going crazy."

Only the Clan Elders seemed to understand. They nodded knowingly and whispered among themselves.

Then Green Spider had lifted a pointed finger and announced: "The time has come to stay here!" He'd looked around, his animated eyes going from face to face, marking each of the Clan Elders and finally pinning Black Skull with a look that nearly curled the warrior's hair.

Green Spider cleared his throat. "Stay away from me, you cowardly Clan Elders. Black Skull, don't you dare come with me. Three Eagles, I don't want you either."

Black Skull glanced over at his friend and sometimes rival. Three Eagles' eyes had gone round. Black Skull slowly took a step backward, his heart pounding like a ceremonial drum. He took another before Old Man Sun clamped a withered hand on his arm and muttered: "Stay where you are! He wants you for something."

"But he just said—"

"Shut up!"

Black Skull froze, glaring hate at the imbecile everyone seemed to take so seriously.

Green Spider pirouetted around in a little dance. "The last place I would want to go is to the White Shell Clan. There's nothing there for me! But then, you didn't hear that from my lips."

To Black Skull's continued confusion, Old Man Sky nodded. "We will get the canoes ready."

Black Skull shot a look at the old man. Had his senses gone the way of Green Spider's? The Dreamer had said he didn't want to go anywhere—and then denied it!

The Elders made immediate preparations. Canoes were provisioned in great haste.

"What are we doing?" Black Skull demanded with unaccustomed assertiveness when he caught Old Man North to one side. "He said he didn't want to go anywhere, let alone to White Shell territory."

Old Man North looked at Black Skull through pitying eyes. "That's just where he wants to go."

"That's insane! He's sick, addled, like a warrior hit in the head. He's not seeing things clearly."

The look of pity intensified in the old man's eyes. "He's

anything but crazy, warrior. He sees more clearly than all the rest of us.''

''But he's—''

''Hush, warrior.'' The Clan Elder placed wrinkled fingers to Black Skull's lips. ''I don't know what Green Spider is doing, but you, of all people, know your duty to the clan. You must do it now.'' Old Man North had hesitated, peering at Black Skull with unsettling intent. ''To live at this time, to see this thing happen, is a marvelous gift. I have known you since you were a little boy. I can't tell you how to see, Black Skull. I'm not sure that you can. Will you bind yourself to your duty? Will you do as your clan asks of you?''

''I know my duty. Upon my soul, I will do anything you order. But this is dangerous! You can't place yourselves at risk! If anything—''

''Black Skull, you and Three Eagles will take me and the rest of the Clan Elders to the White Shell clan house. And you will do anything Green Spider asks of you. Obey, Black Skull, and perhaps you shall learn to see in the miraculous way he does.''

At that, the old man had walked away, his white breath hanging in the air behind him.

And here they were, paddling down the half-frozen channel of the Deer River, headed for the Father Water, and then downstream toward the White Shell clan house. They were taking a terrible chance, exposing the Clan Elders this way. A sudden winter storm could freeze them; a canoe could capsize and one of the Elders could drown. Raiders might capture them. The dangers were too numerous to count.

Black Skull winced. Why would Power hover around an idiot? And what had happened to Green Spider's soul while he'd been dead? Had the ghosts perpetrated some evil? Twisted him to some malignant purpose?

If being dead made you into a fool, Black Skull wasn't sure he wanted any part of it.

Even a brave man like Black Skull had to fear when the Dead rose from their tombs to walk this world again. But Green Spider had come back changed, so different.

And I am bound to him?

At least he would be until they arrived at the White Shell clan house. Then he'd be quit of this madness Green Spider had called down on the Clan Elders. And if Green Spider continued to place the Elders at risk, well, a warrior knew ways to do his duty.

Black Skull looked down at the deadly war club that lay within easy reach of his strong right hand. Beneath the pointed stone war head, the copper spikes glowed eerily in the subdued light.

The morning turned out a great deal more pleasant than Otter expected. Troubled dreams had marred his sleep. He'd dreamed that Red Moccasins had been his—a loving wife who accompanied him as he traveled the river. She had been at his side, dickering for a wealth of copper. He could still see her in the dream, a subtle intimacy in her eyes as she gave him that secret smile of conspiracy. In dreams, the woman you love is always perfect.

He stood beside his overturned canoe, mindful of the sun beating down. Beyond the brown shoreline, the Father Water glinted a wondrous blue. The smell of the river seemed richer this morning, beckoning him to distant places. Otter inhaled; the aroma of mud, musky vegetation, and water seeped through his lungs and into his blood.

He refused to focus his gaze across the river to where the gray haze of swamp cottonwood and the slight blue fog of smoke mixed over the Tall Cane clan grounds.

Red Moccasins would be sitting happily beside Four Kills. Otter's imagination produced the laughter breaking from their lips, the sparkle of love reflected in their eyes. He could see their hands clasping warmly, memories circling around the passion they'd come to share as their bodies locked together under the sleeping robes and—

"Otter?" Grandmother's voice destroyed the tormenting thoughts.

He blinked. Grandmother was tottering down from the drying racks, one hand gripping her gnarled, wooden walking stick. In the sunlight, her white hair gleamed with the purity of newly fallen snow. She wore a yellow-and-red dress decorated with black diamond shapes and lightning zigzags. The clear morning light accented the antiquity of her shriveled face.

She stepped around *Wave Dancer*'s polished prow and thrust her head forward like a hunting heron as she ran thin fingers over the gleaming hull.

"Waxing it?" she asked, squinting at the wood.

"Yes, Grandmother. Too much moss had grown on her. I used chert flakes to scrape the moss off. After that, I used sandstone blocks to scrub her down."

"Why wax? Some magic from the bees?"

Otter rubbed his fingers together, feeling the film that caked them, slick and heavy on his skin. "No, Grandmother. Wax helps to preserve the wood. Feel how smooth she is? Some of the saltwater Traders say the boat will move better through the water. I can't swear it, but it seems to feel that way. *Wave Dancer* likes it. I can sense her approval."

Grandmother walked past him and stopped at the shoreline. She made a grunting sound as she stabbed her walking stick into the lapping waves. They curled over the skid logs set into the landing and ignored her provocation.

Then she balanced on her walking stick: an old heron peering over the sun-silvered waters. The breeze flapped the hem of her dress in slow rhythms. She looked timeless.

Otter shifted from foot to foot, waiting. With a long exhalation, he released the tension and turned back to the boat. A white chunk of beeswax rested on the curve of hull next to the keel. Powered by a vigor he hadn't felt earlier, he rubbed the wax furiously across the wood, friction leaving pale smears on the hull.

"She wasn't for you, you know," Grandmother called, still staring out at the river. "Your destiny was changed, Grandson. The river claimed you. The Water Spirit took you . . . and then sent you back to us."

Otter continued to wax the hull with powerful strokes. He couldn't even remember the event that had changed his life. According to the stories, it had been only a few moons after his birth.

"That night," Grandmother continued as she stared across the river and back into time, "the storm blew up from the south. We were coming down from Deer River, from the City of the

Dead after the summer solstice. How terrible it was. We were out on the river in the dark. Thunderbird flashed sticks of lightning across the sky and shook the whole world with his roaring. The waves rose high on the river, higher than a man stands on dry land."

"That's when I fell overboard," Otter muttered.

"Yes." Grandmother sighed, turning. She approached him with careful steps, her head slightly cocked as she studied him with bird-bright eyes. "We didn't know you'd fallen into the water. When Blue Jar realized what had happened, she screamed in terror, half crazy. Practically had to tie her up to keep her from jumping overboard herself."

Otter braced himself on *Wave Dancer* and stared stupidly at his hand where his strong brown fingers had gouged holes in the wax.

Grandmother sucked lined brown lips over pink gums as she nodded. "The rest of that trip, Blue Jar huddled in the canoe, clutching your brother to her chest. Yes, I remember so well. She had a vacant stare on her face. You would have thought she'd lost both of her boys instead of just one."

"Is that why she always preferred Four Kills?"

Grandmother stood silently, head down, darting the damp mud with her walking stick, perhaps ritually killing something in the past. "I think you've always frightened her. Everyone went out looking for your body, of course. No one expected to find an infant alive. No sooner had she come to accept the fact that you were dead than Uncle discovered you, your cradleboard caught in the driftwood just above the clan grounds." She let her gaze slip to the river. "Now, Grandson, do you wonder that she was afraid?"

"No, I guess not. Who knew what sort of changeling I might have become."

"You never could keep away from the river after that. Your brother would stay in the clan grounds, doing what boys do. But you . . . if you vanished, your mother would panic, and Uncle would find you down here, fooling around in the water. Scold you, she might, but Blue Jar could never break you of your fascination with the river."

"It's in my soul."

The walking stick stabbed out its emphasis. "Of course it is.

Only a fool would think otherwise." A light glinted in those black eyes. "And Red Moccasins is no fool."

"Four Kills is better for her. A brave warrior, smart . . . wise for his age. During that raid three years ago, he killed four of the enemy and earned his name. People already listen to him in councils."

"I'm glad to hear those words from you. I'd half feared you'd grown jealous of your brother. Twins . . . they make a person nervous. And you know the stories."

"About First Man and his twin brother? If you'll recall, Many Colored Crow was that brother."

"He was indeed." She appraised him from the corner of her eye. "The brother of the Dead, of the Darkness. How does it work out between you and Four Kills? Opposites crossed? If so, which of you is Light . . . and which Dark?"

Otter chuckled. "He is Light, Grandmother. And yes, I am the Dark one. Lost in the storm, bathed by lightning and thunder. Cast to the dark waves, I still float. But jealous?" He shook his head wistfully. "Not of my brother. I feel him—" he pressed his hand to his breast "—here, inside. He loves her with all of his heart, Grandmother. And she loves him."

Her eyebrow lifted skeptically.

"You must understand, Grandmother. He is me, what I might have been. No woman could turn me against Four Kills. A woman would have to turn me against myself first."

"That's been known to happen," she said and raised a hand to shade her brow as she studied the rolling river. "Look at you. You can't wait to push your canoe back into the river, load her up, and paddle like a frantic rodent for the north. You'd think you had more in common with those strangers than you do with your own relatives."

"You know better than that." Otter relinquished the wax and bent to pick up the thick folded square of nettle-and-milkweed fabric. Doubling it, he began the arduous job of buffing this last section. With powerful strokes, he worked the wax into the wood, seeing the pale streaks become clear, the rich grain of the wood leaping out at him.

"But you can't stay, can you?" she insisted. "The thought of him and her . . . just over there—" she pointed with her walking stick "—eats at you."

"He is her husband. I have no part in it."

"And that copper plate you gave them?" She snorted loudly. "Quite the gift. The *clan* forgives you such generosity with *its* wealth."

Here it came. Mentally girded for war, Otter bent his head to the side to meet those glinting eyes. "Not *all* of what I accumulate belongs to the clan!"

"Indeed?" she asked mildly. "*You* belong to the clan—and, therefore, so does anything you own. Just as a woman's children, and her children's children, belong to the clan." A pause, then her voice dropped to emphasize the point. "And I told you the clan forgave you."

Otter remained silent, continuing to wax his boat.

"Besides," Grandmother granted, "the story of that gift will travel up and down the river. Such stories serve a purpose."

"Are you always so crafty? Always seeking some advantage?"

"Absolutely. I'm a Trader . . . just like you. Ah, you see, Otter, we're not so different, you and I. Each of us seeks an advantage. You in your barter for goods, I in the accumulation of obligations, good will, and alliances for my clan and territory."

"It's all Trade?"

"What else would it be? Just because you're young, Otter, you're no wide-eyed innocent. You've seen more of people and places than most old men who've died and been burned to ashes. You know a great deal more than you ever let on." She made a twirling gesture with her bony hand. "So why don't you and I make a bargain—a Trade, if you will?"

"And what would that be, Grandmother?"

"If you give me honesty, I'll give you freedom."

"I already have it, or are you threatening to take *Wave Dancer* away from me, along with all my copper plate?"

"Yes, you have your precious freedom, or whatever it is that you think freedom is." She pointed the walking stick northward. "You could go up there. I'm sure there are clans along the Serpent River that would leap at the chance to adopt you into their ranks. Hmm? Give you your choice of wives, of fine houses and honors." She paused. "They'd be fools not to."

"Yes, Grandmother, I suppose there are people who would take me."

"Good." She bowed her head, frowning at the holes she'd poked into the mud with the walking stick. "I don't think the others understand what you've been trying to tell them. Our world is about to change. That thought worries me."

"Don't judge them too harshly." Otter fingered a nick in the wood. "Not even the Traders really understand. They look at the rise in demand and think it's just good luck—or their own special Power."

Grandmother finally said, "I'm an old woman. I need you, Otter. More than that, the clan needs you. Your mother will need you even more. You heard that silly talk about raiding Khota canoes that might come downriver?"

"Mother wouldn't allow it. She's smarter than that."

"Ah, she might know that instinctively, but does she have the experience to argue against it? That's the question. She's a bright woman, I know. She makes most of the decisions these days; but leadership is more than wisdom. You need to understand what's happening beyond your territory. Events upriver are going to affect your people. Like it or not, she's going to need your eyes, ears . . . and experience."

Otter buffed the wood with circular swipes of the cloth. "Are you really that worried that I might run away?"

He flinched when her hand settled on his arm. "Yes, Grandson. What's to stop you? The woman you have loved since you were a child just married your brother. You're not one of us, Otter. Not in the sense that the other men are. You could not care less about clearing new fields. Hanging snares for deer in the forest runs and collecting nuts aren't in your soul. Sitting beside a warm fire, watching your children play on the floor while you carve a new steatite pipe and gossip about your sister-in-law's relatives—none of that suits you." She made a wistful sound. "The big ceremonial centers along the Serpent River, the Moon River, and the Ilini, they're exciting . . . more so than this little squalid clan ground on the riverbank."

"And your Trade?"

"I give you the goods, your canoe, anything you want. Go where you will, Trade what you want . . . but come back with what you learn."

"I'll be back," he promised, and at that moment, he heard the shout from above and looked up.

Many Turtles hollered again, pointing out across the river.

"What is it?" Grandmother hopped from one foot to the other, trying to see across the sun-bright water.

Otter shaded his eyes, making out the silhouettes paralleling the far bank. "The Khota, I think. Four canoes, each with ten . . . no, the lead canoe has eleven in it. Yes, the Khota, bearing the Anhinga woman, Pearl, northward to her betrothed." He made a clicking with his tongue. "Lucky girl."

Grandmother had spotted them, her expression grim as the long, deadly canoes passed. "So she's on her way to Wolf of the Dead? His father is Blood Wolf. His grandfather was Killer Wolf, as I recall . . . and wasn't the great-grandfather Man Eating Wolf, or something like that?"

"Something like that."

"They do seem to enjoy colorful names, don't they?"

Otter clenched his fist, squeezing the rag. "I guess they do. But then, if you're nothing more than two-legged vermin, maybe that's how you entertain yourself."

"Wolf of the Dead," Grandmother mused, eyes half-closed. "He's the one who claims he turns himself into a wolf, isn't he?"

"That's him. But I don't think he can. If he did, the wolves would come from miles around to hunt him down. No self-respecting wolf would allow him into their midst."

"It is said," Grandmother added softly, "that Blood Wolf killed your Uncle."

"More than that is said. Uncle wouldn't let them rob him. He had the nerve to stand up to them. They killed him, all right. Filthy animals. All of them."

"I remember hearing when I was a young girl about how the Khota moved into the Ilini valley. About the way they killed . . . and the fate of the women they enslaved. I hope this Pearl knows what she's in for."

"One of the times I was Trading with the Anhinga, I saw her. She's a beautiful girl, but half-wild herself. Swims, dives. Uses an atlatl better than most men. Her clan decided that she would never be of any use to them. They let her run wild. Said that no man would want her."

The canoes were moving fast, flying upriver to the cadence

of paddles that flashed as they caught the sun. Otter watched them, the simmering hatred burning within.

"You should see the expression on your face," the old woman said. "You look like something's made you sick to your stomach."

"I always feel that way when I have to think about the Khota." He stood, feet braced, watching the war canoes as they passed safely out of sight. "Poor girl. No matter if she is wild, she deserves better than she's going to get at their hands."

Otter remembered Wolf of the Dead. At times, a bestial gleam lit the Khota warrior's eyes, as if he really was filled with violent Power. Sometimes he lost all sense, screaming, slashing the air with his war club. Perhaps he couldn't turn himself into a wolf, but something possessed him on those occasions. Something brutal and wicked.

If Pearl were smart, she'd drown herself in the river before she ever saw that gleam grow in her future husband's eyes.

Six

I clamp my hands over my ears to keep the terrible Silence out. Still, it grows louder, louder, until I can't stand it. I sit up in my blankets, gasping in pain . . . and suddenly the pain is gone. So . . . it wanted to wake me. Why?

I look up at the night sky, so bright. Thousands of the Star People gaze down at me through twinkling eyes.

Faint voices echo inside my head. Ghosts. Only ghosts shout so loudly.

They grow clearer. Along with the crackling of the fire, shouts rise in horror.

That fool young man must have the Mask on again. Otherwise, I wouldn't be able to hear the voices of the ghosts from this distance.

I shake my head, lie down once more and pull up my blankets.

There is nothing worse than an angry bunch of dead people tormenting the living, and demanding that everyone within earshot listen.

I close my eyes and try to sleep.

The storm that had been threatening for days finally broke on Star Shell and Tall Man. They had left the Salamander clan house, where they had spent the night, but had made scant progress before the sullen gray skies opened and fluffy snow fell.

Rather than brave the storm, they cut off from the Holy Road to Blue Duck territory. Shuffling through knee-deep snow, they entered the earthen embankment marking the clan grounds. Star Shell chanted the ritual blessing to the ghosts that inhabited the place. Was it just the storm, or did she sense the brooding disapproval of the Spirits? Wreaths of snow twisted down from the dismal sky, shrouding the grounds. They could barely see the charnel house as they trudged past, and the burial mound had become a shapeless mass.

Fatigue sapped the strength from Star Shell's legs as she led the way to the clan house and stopped before the door flap. Snow capped the high, rounded roof.

"Greetings!" Star Shell called out, numb and shivering. Snow had matted her blanket and melted on her exposed face to trickle down and drip from her chin.

A head poked out past the deerhide hanging over the doorway. "Who's there?"

"Star Shell, from the Shining Bird Clan of the Sun Mounds, and Tall Man, Elder of the High Heads. We ask your permission to enter."

The head ducked back inside, much to Star Shell's surprise.

"It's snowing!" To Tall Man, she added, "Perhaps they're conducting clan business."

The dwarf stood in silence, the mounded snow on his blanket making him look more like a stump than a person.

A thickly built man ducked through the flap, tucking a blanket around himself. He walked forward through the dimpled snow, head cocked. "Star Shell? What brings you here?"

At the cold tone, Star Shell gaped. "It's snowing too hard to travel any farther!" She blinked through the fast-falling flakes. "Robin? What's the matter?"

He studied her cautiously as his blanket began to whiten. He had a thin-lipped mouth under wide cheekbones. His broad nose looked mashed onto his face, and those hard eyes were slitted, hostile.

"Mica Bird sent you?"

"No. I've been away . . . at StarSky. My mother died. I had to attend to the rituals. Are you conducting clan business? Did we come at a bad time?"

He watched her in stony silence.

Tall Man spoke up suddenly. "Indeed, I think we did come at a bad time." He stepped forward. "Robin, of the Blue Duck Clan, I am Tall Man, an Elder of the High Head peoples. What has happened? Why do you act as if we come bringing trouble instead of as weary and cold travelers seeking a warm fire and shelter from the storm?"

"Forgive me, Elder. I didn't recognize you. Blue Duck welcomes you to our territories and we offer our warmest welcome."

"I thank Robin for his kind words, and the Blue Duck for their welcome."

Robin fastened on Star Shell. "But you, woman, are a different story. Perhaps the Elder is unaware of who he travels with."

"What's happened?" Star Shell asked.

"How long have you been away?"

"More than a moon." She stiffened. "It's Mica Bird, isn't it? He's done something. He . . . or the Mask."

Robin hesitated, licked his lips nervously and stamped a foot in the snow. "You're his wife. Of his clan. You're no friend of ours. Leave this place." He glanced at Tall Man. "Honored Elder, please enter and share our fire. We have heard of the great Magician." He paused, his gaze straying back to Star Shell. "Although you travel in strange company."

"Wait." Tall Man lifted a shivering hand. "Tell us what has happened. Star Shell is not your enemy. Grant me this, Robin.

Let us at least warm ourselves, and tell us what has happened. Hear Star Shell out, and then if you still believe her harmful, we will leave.''

Robin squinted for a moment, then jerked a nod. ''Out of respect for you, Elder, we will listen. Otherwise, she could freeze to death in the snow for all the Blue Duck care.''

''May your ancestors be blessed,'' Tall Man replied.

Star Shell's dread grew as the old man followed Robin into the clan house. She shook snow off of her blanket before she ducked through the hanging, miserably wet and chilled.

The clan house had been built along lines similar to those in the rest of the Moonshell valley. The structure consisted of two oblong rooms connected by a covered walkway. The first of these rooms—the one she now stood in—served for entertaining visitors and for clan business discussions. She could cross it in ten paces lengthwise and seven crossways. The rear section, equally large, was reserved for rituals and the storage of sacred objects.

The room contained two fires that crackled and smoked; the smell of goosefoot cakes and venison added a rich aroma to the smoke-heavy air. Trophies hung from the ribbed interior wall, including war clubs, textiles, and dusty bags. Star Shell's gaze passed over what looked like pottery at first, and only on second glance did she notice that painted skulls had been hung with the other trophies. Skulls, relics of the War Society—why would they bring them here?

She turned her attention to the people. To her surprise, no less than four tens of people, including the clan leaders, were present. They lined the wall benches and sat on blankets on the floor, their backs oddly stiff. Had their arrival halted a heated debate in mid-utterance? The old women studied her with open sourness, the young men with the fierce anger of stinging insult in their eyes.

Robin had removed the wet blanket and stood illuminated by the fire. His crossed arms emphasized their slabs of muscle. The thick fabric shirt didn't disguise his deep chest and broad shoulders. Copper ear spools gleamed, and he wore his hair in a tight bun at the back of his head. Thick wraps of fabric covered his legs above high moccasins. His only other ornamentation was a breastplate made of split human jawbones that created chevrons on either side of a gray slate gorget.

Star Shell could see no sympathy in those reptilian eyes. He'd been different once, years ago, when he made the journey to StarSky specifically to court her. At the time, she wouldn't consider his suit. He'd been little more than a farmer's son, and she, the beautiful Star Shell.

How arrogant I was then. He is right to hate me. But the man who watched her with such seething anger was driven by more than a once-spurned courtship.

Tall Man tottered forward on his short legs, the exertion of the journey plain on his weary face. "Winter is not the time for an old man like me to be floundering about in hip-deep snow." He smiled at the fire as people cleared a path for him. In obvious relief, the dwarf extended his hands toward the blaze and sighed.

For her part, Star Shell stood stupidly, desperately unsure of what to do next.

"Come," Robin beckoned. "We don't have to like having you here, but if so respected an Elder as Tall Man speaks for you, we will hear you out."

Torn between a desire to run and a yearning for the fire, Star Shell inched forward.

For long moments, no one spoke. The Magician, looking like a happy child, grinned into the fire. Star Shell couldn't help but be aware of the snow melting and dripping off of her. What she must look like! A miserable camp dog, soaked to the skin.

Tall Man turned around to warm his backside, oddly oblivious to the pulsing animosity that radiated from the Blue Duck people. They stared woodenly—as hard as the sooty posts that supported the clan house. The only sound came from the snapping of the fires.

Star Shell managed to find her voice as she cataloged the implacable faces. "Where is Catfish? And Woodpecker? And Broken Pipe? I don't see Old Tree, or Warm Soil."

"Catfish is dead," Robin said curtly. "Ask your husband why."

"Ah," Tall Man said evenly. "And the others whom Star

Shell notes are missing . . . they have no doubt gone to talk to the other clans. Am I correct?''

Smoldering glares provided the answer. Star Shell closed her eyes; a new sense of desolation invaded the pit of her stomach. Woodpecker, Broken Pipe, and Warm Soil were members of the Warrior Society. They would be the ones sent to formulate alliances with the other clans. The Blue Duck must have been discussing warfare when she and Tall Man arrived, unbidden and unwelcome, out of the storm.

''Don't do this,'' she whispered. ''No.''

At a gesture from Robin, two of the young men moved to block the doorway. They stood with arms crossed, anger on their faces.

''Going to war would do more harm than good,'' Tall Man said, apparently unaware of the growing danger. ''You will need to organize yourselves, call in the warriors from the outlying farmsteads in the foothills up and down your territory. The other clans, those who would join you, must do the same. You can't strike for another moon yet, and by that time, Mica Bird will have rallied the Shining Bird Clan. Not only that, but you must consider that some clans won't join you and that others will side with Mica Bird.''

''Honorable Elder, Mica Bird isn't going to find out,'' Robin asserted, his eyes gone to slits as he studied Star Shell.

Her heart had risen, pounding. Involuntarily, her hand rose to her throat, as if she could ward away fear's suffocation. Blessed Spirits, would she be the first to pay for Catfish's death?

''He already knows.'' The Magician cocked his head, his eyes thoughtful as he looked up at Robin. ''That, or he will as soon as he dons the Mask. It will tell him.''

''That's how he killed Catfish!'' Robin roared. ''And we're going to make sure it will never happen again! Don't you understand, Elder? Mica Bird has gone too far! And this isn't the only clan he has enraged! People up and down the valley are thirsting for his blood! We want to stop this madness! Blood can only be repaid with blood!''

Star Shell's voice caught in her throat. ''What happened?''

Loathing soured Robin's face as he stared at her. ''Your husband beat Catfish's son. Used a digging stick to gouge one of his eyes out. Then he tried to castrate the boy. He would have done it, too, if Old Slate hadn't heard the boy's shrieks and stopped it. And why? Because the boy was caught coupling with Mica Bird's sister.

"Catfish, quite naturally, flew into a rage and stormed down to Sun Mounds to exact a fair retribution. Mica Bird offered to meet him in the clan house—alone. Except it would seem that when Catfish entered, your husband was wearing the Mask.

"Hear this, *woman*. Two of your clansmen dumped the body out in the snow, where Woodpecker found it, half chewed by wolves."

"You don't want to go to war," Tall Man insisted.

"Pardon me, respected Elder, but why not?" Robin demanded. "Do the High Heads expect us to live like this? To be treated like camp dogs? Kicked around and murdered at Mica Bird's pleasure?"

"Indeed not." Tall Man rotated to dry his front again. Steam was rising off his backside. The effect made the little Elder appear as magical as his name. "However, members of the venerable Blue Duck Clan, consider what you will start. This is not some border skirmish between one clan and another over pilfered storage pits, or slighted pride. You seek a blood vengeance that will rip the valley apart. And then what? This cannot be brought to a conclusion before midsummer at the earliest. What will you do? Retreat to the hilltops? Live behind the clan fortifications? Do you have enough provisions to see you through? How long can you live in the snow up there? When will you plant your fields? As this drags out, the Traders will avoid you."

"Then what do you counsel, respected Elder?" Robin asked, raising an uncompromising eyebrow.

"I will deal with Mica Bird."

Incredulous stares centered on Tall Man.

"You?" Robin smiled at the absurdity. "Honorable Magician, we know your reputation, but in all seriousness . . ."

The Magician's expression changed for the first time as he fastened a gleaming stare on Robin. Perhaps it was a trick of the firelight, but he seemed to grow, his eyes expanding into great, luminous orbs. "Do you always judge a man by his size, young Robin?"

The burly man stepped back a pace, his flat features losing some of their color. "No, Elder." Then he took a deep breath. "But let us say that you do punish Mica Bird. That still doesn't solve our problem. Someone else from the Shining Bird Clan will pick up the Mask and look through it. It will all begin again. We've dealt with Mica Bird, and before that, his grandfather. Now it's our turn."

Tall Man fingered his shriveled chin as he pondered the warrior's words. "I see. And I suppose the other clans would like the Mask, too?"

"I cannot speak for the other clans." Robin's answer was plain enough. All of the clans along the Moonshell had seen the Power granted by the Mask. Everyone would be entertaining the same thoughts as Robin.

Tall Man smiled easily. "Yes, young Robin, I think we're in agreement. The Shining Bird Clan has had the Mask long enough for one people. Let us see what we can do about that."

"And her?" Robin pointed a finger at Star Shell.

"Oh, she's on our side. Believe me."

Robin spun on the ball of his foot, his fist clenched at Star Shell. "What about your clan obligations? What about your responsibility to your husband? How do you answer that, woman?"

Star Shell forced herself to stiffen. "I was born of the StarSky Clan, man of the Blue Duck. As you well know, I was StarSky before I married Mica Bird. Catfish's son wasn't the first person Mica Bird beat and degraded. My husband practiced on me. I have my own reasons to hate him."

Robin's stare pierced her, measuring. From deep inside, she forced herself to remember the empty eyes of the Mask—watching as Mica Bird ripped away the blanket and beat her naked body until she gasped in surrender.

She could feel his hard hands as he rolled her over, driving a knee between her legs. Then the pain as he drove himself mercilessly inside, grunting as he took her.

Her anger rose in response. Yes, the time had come for her to do something about Mica Bird—and that accursed Mask.

Robin nodded, a reluctant acceptance in his eyes. "Very well, Star Shell of the StarSky Clan. We take your word . . . for the moment. But remember, the time for retribution has come. If you betray us, if you won't help us get the Mask, we'll remember. And if that happens, you'll wish I'd ordered your death here, tonight. I promise you that."

Black Skull couldn't shake the sense of impending disaster—and it was all Green Spider's fault.

Sunlight flickered in dazzling silver beams from the wind-choppy water as Black Skull continued to throw his weight into the paddle. His canoe shot forward with the speed of a thrown dart, while in the canoe following him, Three Eagles struggled at the end of his endurance to match the pace.

Black Skull refused to let up, especially now. At sight of those four strange war canoes—paddles flashing in stroke after measured stroke—a lance of icy dread had shot through his soul. He was responsible for the four most important men in the world, and he had only himself and Three Eagles to protect them. He shot a glance over his shoulder, checking. Those strange canoes should be far upriver by now. Still, he couldn't rest until the Clan Elders were safe.

Foolishness! This whole silly journey is the work of insanity! Only a complete idiot would place his faith in the Power of the Spirit World to protect him. A wise man backed up his beliefs with five tens of seasoned warriors and their atlatls and darts.

Green Spider . . . it all came back to Green Spider. The gibbering idiot was the cause of all this craziness. Possessed, that was it. Something evil had taken over the silly young man's soul. Some malignant ghost had sneaked into the City of the Dead, undetected by the Ancestor Spirits, and fastened on the boy.

Everything he does is contrary to any kind of sense. Contrary to the simplest rules of behavior that even a child knows. Contrary to the way the world is supposed to work. Contrary to—

Black Skull's hair prickled across his scalp. He'd heard of Contraries—but they were beings of legend, half amusing, a curiosity of Power when it interacted with the world of men.

Was that what Old Man North had wanted him to discover for himself?

Black Skull shook his head, refusing to believe. More likely, the lightning had fried all the sense out of Green Spider's soul when it hit.

Black Skull understood the world and the things in it to be orderly. Everything in its place. A man planned his objective, then pursued it through discipline and hard work. Life was like war. You could be dealt unexpected blows, but the prepared warrior applied a counterstrategy and sought to regain the initiative. The more desperate the situation, the more dogged the response, until tenacity brought victory.

The approach was simple. Now, as he glared at Green Spider through slitted eyes, he thought of another simple solution to his problem. This madness would end if he could get his fingers around the fool's skinny throat when the Clan Elders weren't watching.

Or will I incur the wrath of Power? And that presented a problem. Was Green Spider truly a Contrary? Had he been touched by Power? Or just made into an idiot?

As a child, Black Skull had believed in the Power of the Spirit World. He'd prayed to it to come and save him from Mother, from her sneering dislike and the way she looked at him with such loathing. She'd told him how disgusting he was.

He'd been a lonely boy, unable to fit into the rough-and-tumble society of other children. As a result of his shy ways, he'd always ended up as the butt of the cruel, practical jokes children play. That, coupled with general snubbing by his peers, drove him farther into himself, and ever closer to his only friend and benefactor: Granduncle.

Granduncle, not Power, had shown Black Skull how to save himself. Granduncle had taught him relentless discipline, practice, and unflinching obedience. No one sneered at Black Skull these days. In the end, he had triumphed—even over Mother.

What would Granduncle say if he could see Black Skull now, responsible for a fool's venture—the four Clan Elders at perilous risk from the simplest of calamities?

He could still see the old man, as thin and brittle as last summer's goosefoot stalks. Granduncle sat with his bad leg out straight, his rheumy black eyes staring into the past, seeing other days, other times. The firelight flickered across the grass-shock walls of his house and sent the wavering shadows of roof poles across the soot-thick thatch above. Net bags were tied up there in the rafters, each with a trophy—a dead warrior's skull—staring hollowly out through the confining cordage. The old man's atlatl hung from a thong on the wall behind him. Long, deadly darts, tipped by crudely chipped stone points, leaned against the cane room divider, their polished wooden shafts gleaming blood-red in the firelight.

Granduncle understood Black Skull's humiliation at the hands of the children that day. And that other humiliation inflicted by his mother as she beat and spit upon him, and then shamed him with her probing fingers. The old man had waited, squinting as they sat in silence.

Black Skull had been staring raptly at the scar on Granduncle's wounded knee when the old man spoke: "Boy, everything in the world, the rocks, the trees, the creatures, and men—all are different. No two things are exactly alike. Not even two seeds from the same pod are the same. Power sorts them."

The old man nodded as he affirmed some internal thought. "Human beings are the same as the seeds. All different. And just as no two plants grow up to be identical, neither do human beings. Some, like Dreamers, have old souls, souls that are trained through time and allowed to see things ordinary people can't. Some souls are women, others are men. Some are meant to be Traders, and others to be warriors." A twinkle grew in his eye. "And some, of course, are meant to be just stupid."

"Which am I, Granduncle?" Black Skull had reached down to pull on the old man's big toe with anxious fingers. The answer was particularly important to him. Earlier that day, the other children had called him stupid after they tricked him into falling into the mud. To make matters worse, he was wearing his best ceremonial clothing. At sight of him, his mother had called him stupid, too. Then the odd light had come to her eyes. Her broad mouth had hardened, her voice sharpening as she berated him. Louder, always louder, until everyone could hear. As her rage built, she pushed him, then hit him. When he began to whimper, she kicked him. That day she'd driven him, cowering, out the door. He'd tripped, falling into the mud again. There, as he was wallowing and pleading, she'd kicked him one last time.

"Stupid boy! Stupid! Live in mud, for all I care!"

He'd lain there—calling on Power to come and save him—motionless, trembling at the expectation of another blow. With eyes closed and mud cold on his hot skin, he'd heard her stalk away, still ranting.

Stupid. The thought of being stupid for the rest of his life horrified him. If he weren't stupid, maybe Mother wouldn't beat him.

Granduncle considered, his lips pressed into a serious line. "I've watched you, boy. I've seen your soul. You're meant to be a warrior. It's in the way you walk, in the set of your head and how you see things. You watch the world the way a warrior does. That's your gift, boy. What you do with it is up to you. Your mother has tried to beat it out of you. Power gave you the soul of a warrior, but it's up to you to become one . . . no matter what your mother does."

"A warrior?" Not stupid! His mother, his friends, they were all wrong—and Granduncle was right! "How?"

"You must train your muscle and bone. Pain can be controlled, fatigue denied. Skill and balance must be honed, just like a ground-stone ax, lest it grow dull and awkward." The old man's eyes had gleamed in the firelight. "Duty, boy. Discipline, order, *respect!*" He knotted a fist and shook it. "Those things rule a warrior's life!"

That night had changed Black Skull's life.

As he paddled, he could still see the old man's face just as it had been that night long ago. The firelight had turned his weathered skin golden, accenting both the shadowed wrinkles and the tight crow's-feet around the eyes. The leathery hands had knuckles like walnut burls as Granduncle rested them on his swollen knee—the one the Copena war dart had maimed.

The dart had driven in between the knee bones, just back of the kneecap, and lodged there, leaving the leg forever pinned in that position.

The words had eaten into Black Skull's soul like termites into a log. "Practice, boy. Be what you are . . . and let other people be what they must be. To do otherwise is to act against Power. Follow your way as a warrior, boy. But remember, you must follow it better than any other man. Dedicate yourself. Learn." Fire had burned in the old man's eyes.

Fire, yes. Fire as bright as the day Granduncle had called Black Skull to that last final test. *"She's possessed, boy. The lineage Elders have spoken. Kill her. Are you a warrior . . . or a boy?"* The words echoed hollowly over the years of memory.

War had become his Dance; when he fought, his soul floated free of the darkness of the flesh and surrounded him like smoke. To be a warrior, however, was more than simply cracking heads and ripping out throats. The true warrior used his ability to think, to win without risking body and limb. The best warrior could defeat his enemies without shedding blood.

That ethic of the true warrior goaded Black Skull now, pricking his soul with poisoned barbs for allowing himself to be lured out of the City of the Dead with the most important men in the world—and only two warriors to guard them.

Those four canoes full of strange warriors had knotted his guts with fear. How easy it would have been for them to turn, to capture the soul of the Four Clans, and the lunatic Green Spider—without more than a minor scuffle.

I couldn't have stopped them!

The thought twisted Black Skull's soul around the way a young girl spins cordage from nettle and milkweed.

The warrior redoubled his efforts at the paddle, making the canoe literally skip across the waves. When it became apparent that Three Eagles couldn't equal his effort, Black Skull swallowed a curse and slowed, using his paddle to steer with as the second boat closed the distance.

How much farther could it be to the White Shell clan house?

Black Skull studied the tree-lined banks with a practiced eye, keeping their craft at least a dart's throw from the screen of brush and trees. Recesses in the bank could conceal war canoes with ranks of fresh paddlers; therefore, he steered closer to the center of the river when passing such dangers. At other times, he followed the fastest current downstream.

I should have brought four more boats, each loaded with armed men. The Elders, however, had told him otherwise—and part of a warrior's duty depended on obedience to his Elders.

It was all Green Spider's fault. Before his return from death, he'd been nothing more than an inoffensive—if skinny—young man with unfocused eyes. He was known to forget where he was and frequently he lost what he was saying halfway through a sentence. He also had a habit of seeing things that eluded even the keen eyes of a warrior like Black Skull.

Granduncle had defined it nicely that night long ago: *People are different.* But Green Spider's gaze now chilled Black Skull to the bone, and he had to wonder. If Green Spider would involve him today in something as silly as traveling under-strength through uncertain territory, what would he do in the future?

"Dreamers," Black Skull whispered to himself. "Trouble."

At that exact moment, Green Spider grabbed the gunwales of the canoe and craned his skinny body to stare back into Black Skull's worried eyes. The Contrary's pupils seemed to expand, enlarging his eyes.

"Salvation, warrior," Green Spider announced in his absent voice. "The Mask . . . that's all that counts."

"What? What Mask?"

But by that time, Green Spider's eyes had lost their focus, and he bent over the side of the canoe to stare at the water passing so rapidly past the hull.

"There!" Old Man Blood cried, pointing at the eastern bluffs.

Relief washed through Black Skull. A plume of blue smoke rose from the forest, marking White Shell territory. Clearing a new field, no doubt. Tawny-walled houses, some thatched, others bark-roofed, dotted the high bluff. At the river, a canoe landing could be seen, with the usual drying racks, beached canoes, and fire pits.

A cry carried faintly to them as someone spied their approach. Squinting against the sun, Black Skull could make out people—like colored dots—running to the lip of the bluff.

Raising his hand, Black Skull signaled to the following canoe and used his paddle to heel his craft shoreward. With a final burst of energy, he powered the boat toward the landing.

Here, at least, he could commandeer several canoe-loads of warriors—protection for the return journey. And if the White Shell Clan couldn't provide enough bodies and atlatls, he'd levy some from the Tall Cane Clan, across the river. The Elders and the Dreamer would travel in safety this time—and the Elders could rot before he'd let them talk him out of it.

The dugout canoe jolted—almost tumbling Green Spider backward over the bow—as it hit the shore and plowed mud for a full third of its length up the beach. The Contrary jumped out and looked around owlishly, while the Elders grunted. Old Man North had slid off his seat, and he cast an angry look Black Skull's way.

Before the old man could open his mouth, however, Black Skull had leaped lightly into the water, picked up his atlatl and darts, and secured his war club to his belt.

He waded ashore warily, searching the beached canoes and the surrounding brush, ensuring the safety of the landing.

"Warriors!" Old Man Blood was muttering as he glared at Black Skull. "He's in *your* clan, do something with him!"

"What do you expect," Old Man North cried. "He's doing what warriors do! Keeping us safe!"

"Safe? I think he broke my back when he drove the canoe ashore! What was he trying to do? Paddle us up the bluff and into the clan grounds? What do we have to worry about, anyway? Green Spider would have seen any danger in his Dream!"

Green Spider's voice rattled Black Skull to his bones. "We'll all be murdered here. Five tens of warriors are charging down to kill us even now!" He screamed and scrambled back into the canoe, where he covered his head with his arms.

Black Skull's heart jumped like a bullfrog in glowing coals. He crouched, a dart nocked. Warily, he pivoted on the balls of his feet. "Get back in the canoe! Warn the others! I'll cover your escape!"

"He's a Contrary," Old Man Blood reminded sourly. "We're perfectly safe."

"But he . . ." Black Skull straightened. The danger charging down upon them consisted of two little girls: one about eight, the other perhaps ten. They skipped down the steep slope, shouting and laughing.

"Who's here?" the older girl called as she perched on a limestone rock above them.

Black Skull drew himself up, filling his lungs. "The four Clan Elders of the City of the Dead, their warrior, the Black Skull, and . . . and Green Spider."

The girl cocked her head, giggling. "Sure you are. And I'm Many Colored Crow! Who should I tell Grandmother is *really* here to see her?"

The eight-year-old had slid to a stop several paces in front of Black Skull. She frowned as she inspected him. Turning, she shouted: "He's ugly enough to be the Black Skull!"

The older girl laughed again, her eyes sparkling with mischief.

Black Skull exhaled wearily, aware of the amusement in Old Man Blood's eyes. Old Man North, his bony hands clasped behind his back, stared out at the river to keep Black Skull from seeing his stifled laughter. Green Spider had climbed out of the canoe again, and now he thoughtfully studied a big Trading vessel that rested upside down on skids. The wood shone, lustrous and polished. Brightly colored carvings lined the hull above the waterline.

Black Skull lifted his war club, shaking it. "Tell your grandmother that the Black Skull is here to *eat little girls*!" He thrust the club toward the path to the clan grounds. "Now, go announce our arrival!"

The eight-year-old backed up, her eyes suddenly large. She spun on her heel and shot up the trail, even passing her sister on the way.

"How do these people raise their children? Don't they teach them anything? What do they expect? That I'm not who I say I am?"

Green Spider's absent gaze shifted from the canoe to Black Skull. "We are never who we say we are."

Black Skull felt his face begin to twitch, and he struggled for control. Ever since the Copena war club had crushed his cheekbone, he'd had trouble with the muscles.

"It's a long way up." Old Man North studied the path that led to the clan grounds. "I suppose we should start. Black Skull, go find this Otter. He's supposed to be a Trader here."

Black Skull stamped his foot to settle his crawling nerves, then charged up the rutted way, his dart still nocked in his atlatl. The second canoe had beached. Three Eagles had wilted in the stern, exhausted, his paddle across the gunwales.

Black Skull bounded clear of the top of the bluff to find the two girls chattering excitedly to a group of women who stood before the opening to the clan grounds. They stopped short, staring at him with wide eyes. He dropped to a defensive crouch and gave the curving earthworks a careful inspection for any hint of danger.

All that worry and frustration on the river had fed the desire to kill something—and all that awaited him here was a covey of wide-eyed women!

Taking a deep breath, he threw his head back, withdrawing the dart from his atlatl. The women stood frozen. And he realized what a sight he must have been as he vaulted over the crest, ready to cast.

"I am called the Black Skull! I announce the arrival of the Four Clan Elders of the City of the Dead. And with them comes Green Spider. He seeks a man of the White Shell Clan, known as Otter!"

"You *are* Black Skull! I saw you once." A middle-aged woman stepped forward, peering up at him. "But we heard that Green Spider died . . . on the solstice."

"Green Spider returned from the Dead. I have escorted him here!"

A shrunken old woman, growling and muttering to herself, pushed through the clot of women. "It's *him*!" She wet her lips nervously. "What . . . what do you want here?"

"The Trader, Otter. The Four Clan Elders and Green Spider would speak with him."

The old woman placed a hand on the arm of the first woman who had spoken—as if for support. "Blue Jar? What's happening?" She looked back at Black Skull, then saw Green Spider as he topped the rise. He was walking backward, pulling Old

Man North up the slope by his withered hands. "I am . . . I am Yellow Reed, White Shell Clan Elder—grandmother to Otter. What . . . what do you want from us?"

"I have told you, Grandmother," Black Skull growled, hating this whole silly charade. They looked as if ghosts had just stepped into their world. Were these outlying clans so simple after all? Didn't they know anything?

"W-Welcome," the old woman stuttered, openly staring as the fool stumbled around backwards. "This way. Come. Tea will be made. Food brought. And . . . and Otter will be fetched. Immediately." But she stood rooted in place as the rest of the Elders arrived, out of breath, to stand behind Black Skull.

Green Spider circled the group, running backwards now, like a demented antelope, until he came to old Yellow Reed. His gaze wobbled as he blithely announced: "May all your children drop dead, and may you suffer horribly forever, Yellow Reed. I hate having to meet your son. He and I will become great enemies."

The old woman gaped, a strangled sound issuing from her throat. "Wh—what?"

A moan rose from the other women. Seeing them about to break and run, Black Skull leaped forward. "No! You don't understand! It's all right!"

"It's all wrong!" Green Spider shrieked in his high-pitched voice. "Everything is wrong. Nothing is right. Wrong, wrong, wrong—"

"It's all *right*!" Black Skull bellowed, grabbing Blue Jar, who seemed the most likely to keep her head. "He's Dreamed, you see. Become a Contrary! Do you *understand*?"

"That is the truth," Old Man Blood said as he smiled and cuddled his pink conch shell to his chest. "We've come here to find young Otter. I think we need him very badly."

"I don't need him at all," Green Spider said, making faces at the horror-struck little girls. "I hope he stays away all day."

Black Skull rubbed his flushed face with a nervous hand.

"A Contrary?" old Yellow Reed asked, as if from far away.

"A Contrary." Black Skull assured her. "He does everything in reverse. Something about his Vision while he was dead.''

"Oh. Well, come to the clan house and we'll . . . we'll talk," the old woman whispered, seeming to gather her wits. "This just doesn't . . . doesn't . . ."

" . . . happen to us every day," Blue Jar finished.

My thoughts exactly. Black Skull shot a scathing look at the oblivious Green Spider. *And as soon as I'm free of this maniac, I swear it . . . I'm going to* kill *something!*

Seven

Otter knew a great deal about stone axes. For example, greenstone from the mountains south of the bend of the Guardian River was highly prized by all peoples. When ground to shape and polished, the stone took on a gemlike luster. Basalt, too, made good ax heads and adzes. To begin with, it could be formed by flaking and, if in a hurry, could be used in such condition. Better, however, to grind it into the final shape, since the edge angle could be controlled for a sharp, yet durable cutting tool.

The one thing Otter really knew was that he'd much rather Trade ax heads than use them. For the moment, he had a use-polished handle clamped in his knotted hands. The thing was raising blisters on his palms. The paddles had left their share of calluses, of course, but the adze he now used had rubbed the skin raw. Besides which, his back felt like it had been hammered by mad Khota tribesmen swinging mauls.

Nevertheless, he persevered, crouched over, close to his work as the adze *thwock-thwocked* to the steady rhythm of his aching attack on the base of the basswood tree.

Sweat beaded to trickle down from his armpits and across his ribs, where the shirt soaked it up. An odor of smoke lingered pungent and heavy in the cool air.

"Need a break?" Four Kills asked as he walked up, a clamshell hoe in one hand. Charcoal-stained clumps of dirt clung to the white shell, and soot had smudged the fabric leggings tied with nettle-fiber cord around Four Kills' calves.

"Are you absolutely positive you don't want to burn this one down like all the rest?" Otter made a pained face as he straightened and tossed the adze from hand to hand. Blood began to rush through cramped places, bringing new life.

Four Kills had that pleasant smile on his face, the reassuring one that made the recipient feel that everything would be fine in the end. Charcoal had smeared down the side of his nose. "This tree—" Four Kills patted the bark tenderly "—will give us many wonderful things. We'll peel off the brown outer bark and strip the white inner layer. Once we boil that down, I will have enough fiber to twist and braid one of my ropes. Maybe even better than the last one I made. You know how much people will Trade for one of my ropes. No one on the river makes a stronger rope."

"No, no one makes a stronger rope." Otter rapped the bark with the adze. "And the rest of the tree will be dried, and the soft white wood will be used to make bowls, loom shuttles, fish traps, net floats, statues, masks. Anything that needs to be lightweight or takes lots of carving."

Four Kills continued to smile blandly. "The basswood is one of our most treasured trees. I make my strongest ropes from them." He shook his head. "But they seem to be getting rare. And you want to burn it down?"

"You're on the edge of their range here." Otter looked out over the smoking rubble of the new field. Last winter, the women had chosen this section of the forest, with its rich, loamy soil, to prepare for fields.

That decision made, the men had begun work. Using adzes, they'd ringed the giant trees, cutting away the bark and building fires at the bases to kill the forest giants. The basswood had been left, however, its value well worth the effort to chop it down rather than burn it through, in order to save the precious bark.

With the trees dead, weeds had grown under the skeletal branches, and new saplings had started up. Now the burning had begun again—as soon as the ground had dried after the rains.

The weeds and winter-dry grasses had been set afire, charring the ancient leaf mat and clearing the land for tilling.

Even as Otter looked around the new field, a gang of children were carrying wood to the fires that ringed the bases of ancient elms, oaks, and hickories. Day after day, the fires would burn and the blue pall of smoke would rise to drift over the canopy of endless forest. As the flames died down, the charcoal would be chipped away to expose virgin wood. Then the fires would be lit again to eat their way into the heart of the tree. One by one, the trees would topple. The branches, vines, and finally the trunks, would be rendered to ash to fertilize the soil. By mid-summer, only squash, goosefoot, and sunflowers would be growing here.

"When are you leaving?" Four Kills asked in the stretching silence. "I can feel your soul chafing, brother."

Otter ran his fingers down the hickory handle to the place where the original branch had Y'ed. There, offset at an angle, the stone adze had been hafted, glued in place by gumweed sap, and bound by deer tendon that had shrunk-dried in the sun. "Within the week."

"Or maybe as soon as you cut this tree down?" Four Kills joked, a wry smile on his lips.

My smile, Otter realized. The one he wore when he was on the river, feeling the Power of the Water Spirits that coiled and surged in the main channel. The same smile he used when Trading: slightly chiding, mocking without malice, as if he shared a grand irony with the entire world. That smile always broke down the resistance, overcame distrust, and made his opponent feel at ease.

Can I smile that way anymore? Maybe just not here.

"You're wrong," Otter answered, jabbing the adze, handle-first, at the tree. "I might leave *before* I cut it down. Leave it for you. Something to remember me by."

Four Kills slapped him on the shoulder. "May the Dead bless you, brother—and may all your relatives be as ugly as you are."

Otter squinted, curling his mouth into an expression of distaste. "Don't you wish." He sucked at his lips, a bitter taste of thirst in his mouth. "Are you sure you don't want to go with me? Maybe paddle up and steal Pearl from the Khota?''

Four Kills slowly shook his head. ''I have enough to worry about here, let alone losing my head like they say Uncle did. Besides, you remember how I did that one time when I went with you.'' The grin returned. ''It's the one thing different between us, brother.''

''I could use you. It's a tough trip—just one man paddling that big canoe clear up to the Copper Lands.''

They paused, listening to the children squealing as they charged back and forth, making a game of the search for firewood.

Four Kills shielded his eyes with his hand as he glanced up at the forest canopy. ''She wants you to come to the house before you leave. She says that if you will, she'll make a grand feast. Fill you full the way a man ought to be before he has to paddle a big canoe clear up north.''

A flying squirrel, disturbed by the smoke swirling up around its tree, glided silently to the forest. With the grace of its kind, it cupped its body to brake on the air, dropped onto the bark of a living tree, and vanished into the forest.

Four Kills wondered, ''How do they do that?''

''Magical.'' Otter chewed at his lip. ''I might come. I don't know, I . . .''

A warm hand settled on his shoulder. ''It's all right, brother. I was just told to ask you. She feels, well, sad. She's worried that you'll avoid us forever.''

''I'll be around.''

''I told her that. You're me, and I'm you. I know how it will be. She just doesn't understand that it will take time.'' Four Kills shrugged. ''I'll tell her that you've got clan business. Something about . . . I don't know, how about the Trading? Whether you should go to the Copper Lands or up the Serpent River to the clans up there.''

''I've heard that trouble is brewing among the Serpent Clans,'' Otter grunted.

''Trouble?'' Four Kills raised an eyebrow. ''Really?''

''Rumor. You know how it is. A Trader stopped last night for a meal and to dicker for some hickory oil for his lamps. He said that he heard it from a Trader who came down Serpent

River. Mica Bird, one of the leaders of Sun Mounds, was causing trouble. The other clans are either jealous or anxious over the growth of Sun Mounds' Power. Mica Bird is a strange character. I've met him. Moody, obsessed with authority. According to the story, he uses some sort of dangerous Spirit Power to gain his ends. Something about a Mask that turns him into some kind of sorcerer.''

''Very well, I'll tell Red Moccasins that's come up. It isn't serious, is it? I don't sense that you're terribly worried about it.''

''Worry? About two chiefs squabbling over clan prestige? That's clear up on the Moonshell River. To even get there, you have to travel way up the Serpent River. Why should I worry? I'm going the other way—up to the lakes at the source of the Father Water.''

Four Kills shifted uneasily, arms crossed. ''I know where the Copper Lands are. That route will take you past the Ilini River. The Khota will be trying to get you . . . just like they did Uncle.'' He paused, bit his lip. ''That's always worried me. We didn't carry Uncle's ashes to the City of the Dead. His ghost is up there somewhere, wandering around, causing trouble.''

''I'm not going near the Khota, either. They're a half-day's journey up the Ilini River. I'm heading straight up the Father Water—and right to the Copper Lands. Maybe I'll get some of those pan pipes. And some silver. The Trade for them in the south is very good now.''

''So, even if it comes to war among the Serpent Clans, it won't make any difference?''

Otter shook his head as he ran a toughened finger down the smooth wood of the adze shaft. ''I've heard them squabble before. If Mica Bird doesn't make an overture to his rivals, some raiding parties will be sent out. A couple of fights will be fought. Honor will be upheld, and one of the other clans that's getting irritated by it all will broker a peace through one of the societies.''

Four Kills gave Otter a shy grin and propped his hands on his hips. ''You amaze me. You talk of strange clans and far-off wars—and you're so confident about it all. You know these men who seem like something out of a story, and can guess what they will do so far away.''

''Ah, Four Kills, my warrior brother, people are people, whether they are arguing about who took whose hickory nuts in the storage house or debating the boundaries of great clans far up the Serpent River. Personalities, be they chieftains or fishermen, are the same. Only the degree of importance differs.''

Four Kills continued to stare up at the tops of the skeletal trees to where the flying squirrel had fled. ''This time . . . I wish you wouldn't go.''

Otter's voice dropped. ''You know I have to. You know why.''

Four Kills sighed, his gaze locked on the sky. ''Maybe it's the talk of war.''

In that instant, Otter could feel it, the unease that he'd assumed was tied to Red Moccasins and the invitation to eat with them. ''What is it, brother?''

Four Kills shivered, then shrugged it off. ''I had a Dream last night. Water, falling in endless cascades that turned from crystal-clear to a white as bright as snow. Thunder . . . everywhere, roaring and booming, drowning all the sound in the land as the earth shook beneath it. The water fell and fell, like a river running over a cliff and hammering the rock. Spray rose from the roar, catching the sunlight to splinter into ten tens of rainbows as the mist was carried out of the gorge.''

''Sounds like quite a place.'' Otter thunked his adze against the tree trunk, bruising the outer bark of the basswood. ''Did you see ghosts, too?''

Four Kills pursed his lips and narrowed his eyes, looking back into the Dream. ''I didn't see a ghost, brother. Just the body. It came rolling out of the thundering rush of water that pounded the whirlpool under the falls. There, amid the foam, the body whirled and twirled, played with by the Water Spirits as if they were making it Dance in a playful way all their own. Like a stick in a flood.''

''Go on.''

Four Kills scuffed the ground with his soot-packed moccasins. ''The body came spinning in the water, the arms out wide, the head bobbing like a net float with black hair spreading around it like stream moss. So delicate.

"I was standing there on a black rock, with the foamy waves lapping at my feet. Cold, Otter. I was shivering in the drenching spray as the body came whirling about in the sucking whirlpools. A ray of sunlight pierced the sky then, shimmering through the dancing spray and silvering the droplets and striking gold from them as it lit your face. You were dead, brother, and your soul was still Dancing in the water."

Otter had been entranced by Four Kills' voice. Now he shook himself of the horrible image. Clearing his thoughts, he chuckled to lighten Four Kills' melancholy.

"You've always feared the river, brother." Otter reached out, mimicking his brother's grip on his shoulder. "I know of no such waterfall in the Copper Lands."

"Don't go." Four Kills met his sober stare. "It's the Power of Twins, brother. I can feel it. Maybe you've covered it with sorrow over Red Moccasins, but I don't want you going. Not now, not until we can divine the meaning of this. Perhaps it was Uncle's ghost that whispered in my Dreams last night. A message, from the Dead."

Otter was framing his reply when the sharp cry scattered his thoughts.

"Uncle Otter!" The childish voice belonged to Tiny Turtle, Red Dye's youngest daughter, a chubby girl of about eight summers. She came trotting doggedly across the smoking field, ash churning up about her moccasined feet. "Uncle Otter! You gotta come quick!"

Otter and Four Kills bent down, each reaching out instinctively. Tiny Turtle panted to a confused stop, searching their identical faces. "Uncle Otter?"

Four Kills chuckled and dropped his arms.

"That's me," Otter confided. "You must have run all the way from the clan grounds to be this winded."

"I did!" She nodded as she ran into his arms. He could feel the heat of her exertions through the thin fabric dress she wore. The skirt had been decorated with circles of clamshell drilled through the center and bound by hemp thread. "You've got to come immediately. Grandmother sent me to find you. It's mergentcy."

"Emergency? What's happened?" He glanced up, noting Four Kills' paling expression. The revelation of the Dream was bad enough. Now this?

"Two canoes—war canoes—arrived from the City of the Dead. Some old men . . . important men. Clan Elders. They brought Green Spider to see you."

Otter squinted suspiciously. "I thought Green Spider was dead."

"He was!" Tiny Turtle asserted, wide-eyed with the gravity of the whole situation. "But he's come alive again! And he wants to see you! He brought the Black Skull with him! The Four Old Men came, too! Just to see you, Uncle Otter! You gotta hurry!"

"The Black Skull?" Four Kills mumbled disbelievingly. "To see Otter?"

Otter gave Tiny Turtle his best grin. "You're sure you've got this right? Maybe the names you heard were—"

"No!" Tiny Turtle squirmed, breaking free to wave her arms up and down like frantic wings. "Grandmother told me the names. And, Uncle Otter, I've never seen her like this. She looked scared. You know, with her eyes gone funny and her mouth hanging loose. She barely looked at me. I mean, she didn't even recognize me when she ordered me to find you! And I'm her *favorite*! She's told me so!"

"I believe you. We'd better hurry then. Can you run all the way back with me?"

"I can!" Tiny Turtle asserted, jerking her chin in a nod.

Otter straightened, dropping the adze. "Let's go. Come on, brother. If it's Green Spider and Black Skull, something's really wrong."

"It started with that Dream," Four Kills growled. "Ghosts . . . blowing across my face all night. And you . . . floating dead in the water."

"The only time I Dance is on land," Otter quipped in return as he led the run across the smoldering field.

When Star Shell had finally stepped out of the Blue Duck clan house that morning, it was into a pristine world. The virgin mantle of snow had blanketed the clan grounds with a delicate purity. The sky seemed bluer, the air crisp and invigorating. Sunlight had sparkled off snow crystals, while the charnel hut, clan house, society houses, and storehouses were capped by fluffy whiteness. The ridge-shaped lump of the burial mound had looked soft in the morning light. The only tracks to mar the freshness had been those of the Star shaman who had climbed the platform mound to Sing his welcome to the new day.

Once Star Shell would have gasped and marveled at the sight. But, for her, the morning had been a lie, an illusion of peace and beauty following a night of horrid Dreams of death, blood, and war.

Now, as she trudged down the Holy Road ahead of Tall Man, she could recall that beauty and try to place it into her soul. Maybe she could draw on that to assure herself that all was not misery and fear. Perhaps, as she walked the familiar way into the Sun Mounds, she could find courage to look forward to another morning like that. One now obscured by the uncertainties of the future.

She glanced back to where the Magician followed in her tracks, his white breath fogging in the afternoon sunlight. His small size confused her, the intuitive urge always nagging at her to act protectively. She had to remind herself that this was a capable Elder, not a child. Tonight it would be deadly cold when the sun went down. If things went wrong at Sun Mounds, it might be the cold chill of death she would feel instead of that of the night.

Tall Man swung along in his rolling walk, his stumpy legs shuffling snow. The two packs bobbed with each step he took. His wizened expression reflected nothing more than an amused contentment. Did he feel nothing? Was his soul unaffected by the tremors and terrors that ate at hers?

"How can you remain so calm?"

He glanced up at her, his eyes as bright as a chipmunk's, then stared out over the wide valley. Most of the trees had been cut down here, leaving only a patchwork of forest intermingled with the stubbly fields of farmsteads. Rounded houses stood at the sides of the fields, some with people near at hand dragging in firewood or attending to various tasks. His thoughtful gaze looked beyond, to the dark gray mat of trees that marked the uplands to either side.

"I suppose it's because I understand too much," he finally answered. "It's a good day, young Star Shell. The sun has been bright enough to hurt the eyes as it shines off of the new snow. Clean, don't you think? Even the works of humans are muffled by the freshness of the snow."

This was Goosefoot Clan territory, theoretically friends of the Shining Bird Clan. But as they had passed people, no one had raised a hand to wave or to call out a greeting. A dark shadow might have fallen over the souls here, despite the brightness of the day.

They followed the Holy Road down to the broad expanse of the Moonshell, then turned as the river meandered next to the road. The channel was obscured by snow, the location of the ice marked only by the rushes and river grasses that humped the shoreline.

She could remember the way the river looked in summer, broad, lazy, the current slowed by silt. Out there in the brown waters, young men would be diving from canoes, swimming down to finger the mud for shellfish, and perchance, for the added bonus of a pearl.

On those hazy days of summer, the banks would be green with growth, the clouds floating serenely. She'd marveled at the Moonshell the first time she'd seen it. Now it only reminded her of the present, of the ordeal to come.

The upright post that marked the transition into Shining Bird territory stood like a sentinel with a lopsided cap of snow. On reluctant legs, she plodded onward, hating the thought of what it meant.

"We're here. In another hand's time, we'll be at the mounds." And she could see them, the earthworks glistening with fresh snow. Even at this distance, the faint smear of smoke could be seen rising from the clan grounds. Too much smoke for an ordinary winter's day. A lot of people had congregated at Sun Mounds for something, and she could pretty well guess the reason.

"It can't come to war," Tall Man stated simply. "The results would be disastrous."

"Why do you care so much? Do the High Heads really mind if the Flat Pipe destroy themselves?"

One corner of his mouth turned up wryly. "And who, exactly, are the High Heads? Where do the distinctions lie between our peoples? Think about it, Star Shell. Our peoples have run together like the waters of two different rivers running down the same channel. Can you separate the waters? Over east of here, across the hills and down south of the Serpent River, a lot of High Head clans still exist—but we've got Flat Pipe clans in some drainages just as you have a couple of High Head clans here. We marry people back and forth, some following the rituals of High Heads, others of Flat Pipes. In another five or ten generations, will we still be able to tell the difference? Even our languages have grown together."

She mulled that for a moment. "So if it comes to fighting, High Heads will be drawn into it."

"You're part High Head—and you've been drawn into it." He grunted his disgust. "No, it's more than that. Think about the way we live. All the clans have their territories, but we still depend upon each other. Sure, sometimes a squabble breaks out—like the time that deer headdress got stolen. The affected clans retreated to their hilltop forts, and raiding parties crossed back and forth, but it was all brought to a stop because it caused too many problems for the rest of the clans."

He puffed a weary sigh. "This is different. Or it could be. What would happen to us if everyone went to war? The Trade would be cut off, that's what. We need each other. If a harvest fails among the Blue Duck, the Rattlesnake send their excess to make up the difference. When that happens, the Blue Duck Clan sends some of their blankets in return for the favor, or perhaps they volunteer labor on some of the earthworks.

"And consider another of the ramifications we face. True, we're very good at the way we farm the land. We use the rich bottomlands for fields, but to do this, we must have little farms scattered out all over. If serious warfare broke out, what would happen? Easy pickings for war parties, don't you think? What would the consequences be if we spent a summer raiding each other's isolated farms? Do you think any fields would be planted?''

"No, they'd be left to the weeds.''

"Ah, indeed, young Star Shell. That's right. And next winter, people would starve. Bad things happen when a man sees his family starving to death in front of his eyes. He picks up his atlatl and darts and strikes out to take the food he needs from others. Generally, that means he goes down the trail to the next farm to get it.''

"The societies wouldn't allow that to happen. The engineers would stop it. So would the Star Society, and the Pipemakers. If they didn't, they'd have members killing each other.''

"When it comes to keeping your children alive, Star Shell, that might not be a consideration.'' He snorted to himself. "No, young friend, we'd tear ourselves apart. Like an old blanket gone suddenly rotten, we'd pull the weave into strands that could never be put back together again.''

That image stuck in her mind. If anger got too far out of hand, how would the summer ceremonies be conducted? If no one cared about anything but killing, who would organize the labor details to work on the clan grounds? If the Traders avoided the country, who would bring in pipestone? Mica? Copper? Who would carry out sacred chert from the quarries around StarSky? Who would coordinate the rituals to care for the ancestors?

And if people stopped caring for the ghosts, would the ghosts extract their revenge? Would they ruin the relationship with the Spirit World? *And I thought a ghost didn't need to worry!*

Worse, would the Spirit World react angrily if the proper ceremonies weren't carried out?

"But Many Colored Crow started this whole mess!'' she growled to herself.

"I caught only a bit of that, but I think you're starting to understand.'' His voice sounded too cheerful. "Like fingers woven together, always pulling. First Man for harmony and the Dream of the One. Raven Hunter for struggle and conflict. The balance must be achieved . . . in the Spirit World as well as in the world of men.''

He paused. "That, young Star Shell, is why I'm so calm. You, too, must learn to balance. Pain lies ahead, but we'll face it when we get there. For the moment, enjoy the beauty. Sniff the air. Listen for the cries of the hawk on the wind. Suffer when you must; enjoy when you can.''

She gave him a weary grin. "You know, I'm starting to like you.''

"Indeed, alas, poor Star Shell, more's the pity, reality being what it is. Were you anyone else, I should revel in that admission."

"I don't understand."

His eyes had taken on a snake-like, hypnotic depth. "I don't suppose you would. Forget it, girl. Concentrate on finding your balance."

She did. But try as she might, she couldn't coax anything but dread from her soul.

As they closed the distance to Sun Mounds, Star Shell imagined the scene as she confronted Mica Bird. What would she say? *"All right, this is it. I'm leaving you. And taking the Mask with me."*

Indeed?

The crazed gleam would light his eyes. He'd beat her half to death and rape her in front of that hideous Mask.

So what could she do? Walk in, pick up a war club, and crack his skull open?

Over her shoulder, she said, "This is going to be a great deal more difficult than I thought."

"I'm glad you've begun to realize that. Robin isn't the only person in the Moonshell valley who is thinking about the Mask and the Power it would give him. They're all going to want it. Our task isn't an easy one."

"I was thinking about how to face Mica Bird. What's he going to do?"

"What he must."

She searched herself, grappling with the image of fighting him. "I don't think I can kill him, Tall Man. I just . . . well, it's not in me. He's my husband. The father of my daughter. I mean, I . . . What am I going to do?"

"Were I you, I'd be thinking of where I would go."

"Do you know something I don't?"

"Yes. And don't ask me more. I won't tell you what I've

seen. Where *will* you go? What will you do? You must get the Mask away from here. Men like Robin and the other clan warriors want that Mask, girl. You will have no friends." His voice lowered. "Everyone will be searching for you."

She could make out the familiar lines of Sun Mounds now, see the individual roofs where they poked up over the earthen enclosure. Children should have been playing in the snow, sliding down the earthworks on deerhides. People should be out and about, but here, too, the outlying houses were silent, only tendrils of smoke rising from the bark roofs.

"Something's not right."

The Magician remained silent.

And her daughter? Would Silver Water still be safe at Mica Bird's mother's farmstead? Yes, she would. Old Gray Deer wouldn't let anything happen to her granddaughter.

What do I do? What am I walking into?

She turned off the Holy Road, following a beaten track that led to the eastern equinox opening in the earthen perimeter. At least people had walked this today. It wasn't as if the clan grounds had been abandoned.

The sick feeling in her stomach grew worse as she covered that final distance. The sun had begun to slant into the southwestern sky, ready to dip behind the far bluffs that marked the uplands on the other side of Many Colors Creek.

At the entrance, Star Shell muttered the ritual greetings to the ancestral ghosts . . . and felt the chill within her soul, as if the ghosts were trying to warn her about something terrible.

It's going to hurt me.

No, don't think that. After all, Tall Man still accompanied her. Despite his small size and great age, he'd shown himself more than a match for the troubles they'd already encountered.

Her heart in her throat, she entered the clan grounds, noting the familiar structures, the charnel hut, the burial mound with its—

Star Shell caught her breath. A gaping hole had been dug into the side of the humped earthen mound that marked Mica Bird's grandfather's tomb. The hole gaped blackly in the sloped side, like a mortal wound in an otherworldly beast. Clods of dirt had been scattered about wildly; they spattered the dimple-trodden snow like day-old blood, coagulated and black.

Who would have dared to . . . She closed her eyes, a dizzy horror eating at her.

No. Not even he would have the nerve for that!

She swallowed hard, sensing the wrath of the ghosts. A frantic horror spurred her to run forward, past the defiled mound, around the charnel house.

"No! Wait!" Tall Man cried from behind her. "Wait!"

She ignored him, dashing with all her might for the clan house. People stood in a mass before the humped structure, silent, gazing uneasily at the door flap. They seemed paralyzed, unaware of the cold.

Terror flowed bright with her blood as Star Shell ran panting to the knot of people.

"What's happened?" she demanded. "What's going on? Have you all lost your minds?"

"Mama!" Silver Water cried out, breaking free from her grandmother's arms and flinging herself at Star Shell.

For the briefest of instants, Star Shell bent down, hugging her daughter to her. Endless tears had streaked Silver Water's face; a wretched fear lay in those wide, dark eyes.

"I'm home, baby. It's going to be all right." Taking her daughter's hand in hers, she stood to face Gray Deer, her mother-in-law. "What's gone wrong here?"

The old woman had a distant stare, one of panicked horror. "He wasn't strong enough. He . . . he's mad. Possessed!"

Star Shell fought the trembling fear that threatened to betray her. "Where?" But she knew. A few eyes had turned in her direction before they fixed again on the clan house doorway. "Silver Water, stay with your grandmother."

"No!" Gray Deer insisted, clawing at Star Shell's blanket. "Don't go in there! He's wearing the Mask. Crazy! Mad, I tell you. He's been running around screaming, digging into graves. He'll kill you! Just like the others!"

Star Shell thrust her daughter into Gray Deer's arms and turned for the door flap just as Tall Man came puffing and wheezing through the stunned crowd.

Worry glittered in the High Head Elder's eyes as he glanced around uneasily. He was muttering something under his breath in a language she couldn't understand. It sounded a great deal like a warding spell.

Star Shell could sense the evil, heavy brooding—a malignancy twisting around them like polluted smoke. Taking a deep breath, she strode purposely for the door flap on the silent clan house. She must face him. In there. Now.

Tall Man scuttled up to her, reaching out. "Wait!"

"If you've got Power, now's the time to use it."

"The danger isn't with Mica Bird! *It's the Mask!* Be careful. Leave it to me!" He twisted then, sliding out of his backpack and fumbling with the straps.

She barely heard him, finding a fire-hardened hickory digging stick thrust into the snow before the doorway. No doubt the one Mica Bird had used to desecrate his grandfather's grave with. She had to tug to free it from the frozen ground, but the weight reassured her.

Thus armed, she took a deep breath and ducked through the door flap. Like most of the big clan houses, this one had been built in two sections, joined by a narrow passage in the middle. The outer—the one she was now in—was reserved for visitors, general clan meetings, and secular activities.

The interior of the clan house was dark, eerie. The feeling of malicious Power hovering in the cold air strengthened. In the sudden silence, Star Shell could hear the frantic beating of her heart. Unseen things moved, stirring the air.

"Mica Bird? Where are you?"

Silence.

The door hanging shifted, and in her fear, Star Shell whirled, bringing up the digging stick. She stopped a split instant before she brained Tall Man. He looked about warily. A rolled bundle of wolfhide filled his stunted arms.

"Careful," the Magician warned. It took a moment before she realized that he didn't refer to the fact that she'd almost killed him.

"Mica Bird?" she called again, stepping into the center of the dark room. A creaking sound came from down the dark passage that led into the rear.

She blinked, trying to clear her vision. Why did it have to be so dark? Did something move back there in the shadows? "Mica Bird? It's Star Shell. I'm back. Where are you?"

The faint creak sounded again.

Her eyes were adapting to the low light. She took another step, noticing the faint glow of embers in the main fire hearth. Familiar benches lined the far wall. Ceramic pots lay scattered about, most of them broken. Spilled goosefoot seeds grated underfoot.

What if he was wearing the Mask? What if he used it on her? She had no defense.

She kicked something that rolled hollowly, unevenly, to one side. Glancing down, she gasped and backed a step. The broken skull lay on its side like a cracked egg, its empty eye sockets staring vacantly. Peering closely, she could see broken bones strewn all over the floor—splintered as if they'd been smacked by a hammerstone.

His grandfather! A sob caught in her throat; the urge to vomit tickled her stomach.

In horror, she whispered, "Oh, Mica Bird, what have you done?" She crept forward, glancing into the passage that led to the rear section.

Shattered pottery crunched under her wet moccasins as she entered the narrow passage. The place smelled of seasoned wood, smoke, and leather.

Blessed Spirits, will this never end? She tightened her grip on the digging stick, painfully aware of the Magician's footsteps scuffing the floor behind her.

The darkness pressed down, suffocating despite the cold air that stirred. A somber presence seemed to linger in the murk, drifting over her, threatening, measuring.

Grandfather's ghost. It had to be.

She ceased to battle the trembling in her legs and stepped into the rear section. The creaking was louder now, the sound like straining wood. Yes, something moved in the rear of the room. Something in the air, floating, drifting.

Her mouth had gone dry; the digging stick shook as she lifted it, ready to strike. In a bare whisper, she asked, "Mica Bird?"

She could see it now, dangling, spinning slowly in time to the creaking of the wood.

No! It couldn't be!

The Magician stepped around her warily, angling off to one

side. He made a clucking sound, like a scolding grouse, and picked something up from the floor; then, as if burned, he let out a cry and hastily dropped it, muttering to himself as he wrestled with the wolfhide. She knew the shape of the Mask.

Star Shell stood rooted, barely aware of Tall Man's movements. Her eyes had fixed on the body of her husband where it spun in the air.

He hung naked, his head oddly cocked to one side. In the dim light, she could see the tongue, swollen and protruding, the glassy eyes bulged out in terror. And yes, there it was: a thick twist of rope that suspended him from the heavy rafter. The harsh fiber had cut deeply into the puffy flesh of Mica Bird's neck.

"I've got it," the Magician groaned. "It's covered, girl. Don't—whatever you do—don't take the Mask out of this sack."

She barely heard. Mica Bird's body slowed to a stop—that glassy stare drilling into her—then began rotating slowly in the other direction.

The rafter creaked again.

Eight

For the life of him, Otter couldn't understand. Why had the Clan Elders come for him? What could he give them that they couldn't find in the City of the Dead? Nagging worry ate at his gut as he hurried from the forest path and across the clearing into the outskirts of the White Shell clan grounds.

When Otter strode through the summer solstice opening and into view of the clan house, he found a knot of excited people gathered. Otter shot Four Kills a wary look and pushed his way forward.

Grandmother appeared to have everything in order. From the way she looked, she seemed to have overcome her shock; her eyes had taken on that obsidian-sharp edge of cunning.

The four Clan Elders sat on a long bench in the sunlight outside Grandmother's house. Everyone who had been within the clan grounds and all the people from the nearest farmsteads were clustered about. Anxious to see and hear everything, they were nevertheless cowed wide-eyed by the august presence of the visitors.

Otter and Four Kills found people backing away, leaving an opening for them, while Tiny Turtle walked shyly beside them, eager to maintain her importance despite wobbling legs and the finger she suddenly needed to chew on.

Otter knew the Black Skull on sight. No one else looked like that. The crisscrossing scars only seemed to accent the crushed cheek and offset jaw. The warrior's eyes, however, burned with an intensity Otter had rarely seen. The man seemed to smolder, and that fearsome face twitched like a nest of mice under thin fabric. One powerful fist clutched the atlatl handle, while the other had clamped to the war club. Sunlight flashed on the polished copper spikes set so wickedly into the wood.

Stories circulated about this man. It was said that he'd killed his own mother, struck her down on orders from his family. In one fight with the Copena, he had killed six of their warriors, chased down the remaining five who fled and dispatched them one by one as they collapsed from exhaustion along the trial.

When Otter met the warrior's eyes, he gazed on Death.

He had to force his attention to the others. Grandmother stood to one side, that thoughtful look on her face as she tried to absorb the meaning of this encounter, and, no doubt, to determine how the White Shell Clan could prosper from it.

Otter bowed politely to the seated Elders in the order of the directions: Blood, Sun, Sky, and Winter. One by one, white heads bobbed in reply. No more hallowed men could be found throughout the world. What were they doing here?

Finally, Otter faced a skinny, thin-nosed man, little older than himself. A Dreamer—especially one just returned from the Dead—should appear Powerful. Something about him should instill that sense of reverence and awe. By looking at him, a man should understand that here was a human being who had looked upon the face of the Great Mystery.

Instead, Green Spider grinned sheepishly, his expression somehow slack, his gaze sliding this way and that, as if he had problems with focusing his attention on any one thing. A turkey-feather cape hung over his bony shoulders, and every rib on the man's body stuck out like skin stretched over a coil of rope. A thick twist of brown fabric wrapped his waist. Two legs, like warped spindles of cedar, ended in big, sandal-clad feet.

On his first trip south with Uncle, Otter had been introduced to the noted Anhinga shaman, Fell Through the Sky. At the time, the old Dreamer had been alive for over eight tens of years. No more than withered flesh on bone, that frail Elder could have been blown away by a child's fan. Nevertheless, he'd radiated Power. One could feel it like heat from a fire pit.

In contrast, Green Spider had squatted down and now used his finger to trace circles in the dirt around a broken potsherd that had been pressed into the tan earth by a careless heel.

Blue Jar stood just behind Grandmother's shoulder, a hand to her mouth, anxiety bright in her eyes.

Four Kills bowed to the Clan Elders, tense, missing nothing as he instinctively positioned himself between Black Skull and Grandmother.

Otter placed his hand to his breast. "I am Otter, son of Blue Jar and grandson of Yellow Reed of the White Shell Clan. I understand the Clan Elders of the City of the Dead wished to speak with me." He shouldn't be this nervous. How many times had he landed at a strange clan ground, walked up the bank to the opening in the earthworks and faced suspicious eyes and nocked darts? He'd always maintained some sense of serenity, even while distrustful dogs barked, growled, and snapped at his heels.

Steeling himself, Otter forced that disarming smile to his lips and tried to quiet the frantic pounding of his heart.

Old Man Blood inclined his head as he fingered his pink conch shell. "We are pleased to meet you, Otter. May your life be long and may you enjoy good health. May your sisters have many children and may they all grow to old age."

"Thank you, Elder. The White Shell Clan is honored with

your presence. All that we have is at your disposal. Feel free to remain with us for as long as you like. We hope we may be of service.''

"Well said," Old Man Sky told him, looking around. "I'm afraid our arrival shocked many here."

Otter shifted uneasily, glancing at Grandmother. She immediately seized the opportunity to speak: "The effect was somewhat like having First Man walk into your camp, Respected Elder. You caught us by surprise." She jabbed Blue Jar, amusement in her eyes. "As soon as some of us find our tongues, we'll be a great deal more hospitable!"

Chuckles came from the Elders; the tension began to recede . . . for everyone, that is, except the Black Skull, who continued to seethe. Four Kills—ever attentive to such things—remained wary.

"We are all potsherds," Green Spider mumbled, frowning at the sherd he'd encircled. When he looked up, scanning the faces around him, most had turned uneasy again. "Did you realize that? You can see your lives copied in the potsherds. From mud and water we're made. Once born, we're molded by a great many fingers, dried in our childhood, fired in the passions of our youth. As adults, we're vessels, doing our work, carrying our goods, storing things for the Spirit World. Then, one day, we're dropped to smash on the ground. What's left? Fragments. Some return to the earth. Other pieces, like those of the soul, are ground up for grog and used in new pots."

Black Skull growled, "I'll never see a crushed pot the same way again."

And Otter realized where the warrior's smoldering hostility centered.

Green Spider stared up absently, then pushed himself to his feet. With uncertain steps, he approached Otter; but those vacant eyes seemed to stare right through him to something on the other side of the world.

Green Spider reached out and placed cold hands on the Trader's shoulders. Smudges of mud rubbed off on the fabric. "Are you ready, Otter? It's a long way to the Roaring Water."

"Roaring Water?" Otter glanced uneasily at the Clan Elders.

"First three . . . then four," Green Spider went on. "And . . .

and finally, six less one. Who will the one be? Do you know? Can you guess?" He paused, frowning as his attention wandered. "Yes. That's what we must do. Time means everything . . . especially if you're at the wrong place. It means nothing when you arrive where you need to be at the right moment. And for what? Will the world cease if a young girl dies? Will Power cease to pulse if a sacred Mask is drowned?"

"Drowned?" Otter tore his gaze away to glance anxiously at Four Kills. Images of his corpse Dancing in the current lingered.

"It doesn't have to happen that way," Green Spider insisted. "Four Kills Dreamed only one of many outcomes."

Frost settled on Otter's soul. "How . . . how do you know about my brother's Dream?"

Green Spider's eyes seemed to expand, sharpening with a terrible intensity. "The Power of water pumps with your blood. The Water Spirits took you and gave you your life. They can take you back just as easily—as Four Kills Dreamed. A hero must be tested."

"Tested? A hero? *Me?*"

Green Spider reached up, pressing his fingers against Otter's face, feeling about as if to learn the shape of the bones beneath the flesh. Otter endured.

"Do you know the single greatest truth, Otter?"

"I don't— Well, it depends, doesn't it? Which great truth are we talking about?"

Green Spider grabbed the soft part of Otter's nose, bending it back and forth. "The single greatest truth is that you must lose yourself to find yourself. It sounds so very simple, but it's so very hard to do. Not just for Dreamers, but for everyone. You can't be a hero, Otter, unless you're willing to give up what you want the most."

"How about you, Green Spider? Have you lost yourself?"

He nodded, a dreamy indolence in his eyes. "Yes, Trader. I wanted order. I was desperate for it. I needed to understand the way Power worked, and the why of everything in the world. Many Colored Crow showed me. Did you know that nothing is ordered, Otter?"

"I have often feared that might be the case."

Green Spider tugged at one of Otter's braids, then leaned close, placing a conspiratorial hand over his mouth. Otter hunched over to listen intently—and jerked back in alarm when Green Spider shouted at the top of his lungs: *"All of the worlds of Creation were made as a jumble!"*

Otter clapped a hand to his assaulted ear. "Are you *crazy*? You didn't need to shout!"

"Of course I did," Green Spider said simply as he turned around and paced away in steps that stretched his skinny legs to the limit. There, in the center of the crowd, he whirled like a stork in a pond and cocked his head. Cupping both hands to his mouth and filling his lungs until his ribs looked as if they would pop, he whispered in a voice Otter could barely hear, "You wouldn't have heard me otherwise."

Black Skull sighed audibly, his battle-scarred hands clenching the war club so tight that his fingers whitened.

"What is all this?" Four Kills asked, stepping close to Black Skull.

My question exactly, Otter thought. He glanced nervously at the Clan Elders. They sat—each like a lump of wood—with faint smiles on their faces. Looking closely, Otter could see places where their hair was singed. The temple had supposedly been hit by lightning. Perhaps it had addled Green Spider's soul? Too much Spirit Power? Could it singe a man's Spirit the way it did hair? Burn away the ability to think clearly?

Black Skull had leaned closer to Four Kills. "The fool says he's a Contrary. Does everything backwards—and he's *proud* of it!"

"Not proud!" Green Spider corrected, prancing over to face the warrior. He looked very puny beside Black Skull. "I'm free, Killer of Men. Free because *I* know what the snare looks like! To be free, you must live and breathe inside the rope. That's the only way to keep from stepping in it and getting caught!"

Black Skull's jaw clenched. "You want a rope? I'll give you rope, just the size of your neck. I—"

"A Contrary!" Otter cried, and clapped his hands.

Grandmother stepped forward, a glint in her eyes as she stared at Green Spider. "Why didn't I see it? It's been so long . . ."

Four Kills turned, as if sensing Otter's understanding. "Do you know what this means?"

Otter studied Green Spider with new interest. "I've met Contraries. Most people guard them like the last sack of squash seeds in a famine. They're good luck. Powerful."

"Bad luck! *Bad luck!*" Green Spider insisted, and he began spinning around with his arms outstretched. "No Power! I'm so weak I couldn't even poke a hole in water!"

By this time, Green Spider was whirling around so wildly that people were diving out of the way of his whipping arms. Finally, he staggered and stopped, weaving on his feet as his head continued to jerk spastically to the side. He stumbled forward dizzily, reeling and careening until he smacked into the wall of Grandmother's house, exclaiming, "Thank the blessed Spirits! I can still walk straight!"

Grandmother asked suddenly, "Why did you come here? What do you want with Otter?"

She'd addressed her question to the Clan Elders, but Green Spider spoke as he fingered the walls, then began chipping at the tightly bundled grass with a thumbnail. "I don't want Otter. I hope I never see him again." Then he wheeled, clapping his right hand over his eyes, pointing with his left at Otter and crying, "I see you!"

From where they watched along the peripheries, the rest of the clanspeople stood wide-eyed and dumbfounded. Many had pulled blankets over their heads, and mothers had grabbed up their children. Even Red Dye had snagged Tiny Turtle away.

Old Man Blood cleared his throat. "Yellow Reed, we have come to ask your permission to have your grandson, Otter, carry Green Spider to a place he has seen in his Vision. We—the four of us—believe it to be so important that we came ourselves to ask you to grant this favor."

"We would be most honored," Old Man Sun added. "We understand that you might have other obligations that Otter needs to fulfill, but we can only stress that you would be granting us—and the clans—a great boon."

"We will be happy to compensate you for the use of your grandson," Old Man Sky continued. "Perhaps you have some needs that the clans could attend to? A house to be built? A field to be cleared? A son you would like to marry to someone? We will be happy to discuss anything you would like.''

"And I would add,'' Old Man North stated, "that a great deal of status will accrue to the White Shell Clan for undertaking such a journey. People will be talking about your grandson throughout the territories. One never knows the ramifications of fame. I'm sure that Otter's reputation as a Trader would be greatly enhanced. This could be very beneficial for you and your clan.''

"But why Otter?'' Blue Jar demanded, finding her tongue and stepping forward. "Why did you choose my son?''

"We didn't,'' Old Man Blood replied, hooking a thumb toward Green Spider. "He did.''

"Not me!'' cried Green Spider as he shook his head furiously. "I don't even like Otter.''

Grandmother jabbed her walking stick at the ground, her head bowed. "I imagine the White Shell Clan won't object.'' She cocked her head. "But the final decision will be Otter's.''

People whispered back and forth, wondering why Grandmother didn't simply order him to go. The old woman's black eyes fixed on him, gleaming. He could read her thoughts. *I gave you my word.*

"He won't go! He won't go!'' Green Spider began chanting in a singsong voice. "He doesn't like me, either.''

"Where am I supposed to take him?'' Otter turned to Green Spider. "Do you know the way?''

"Downstream to the Fresh Water Sea, then eastward to the Roaring Water.''

Otter licked his lips and placed his hands on Green Spider's bony shoulders. "I know a little about Contrary Power. But you must understand that I'm like a child . . . without your wisdom. Can you talk to me as an adult to a child? Can you tell me the way?''

Green Spider's expression pinched, as though thought took great effort. "I've only flown over it—it's not the same as being there. My feathers got awfully cold, though. I can tell you that. And I'll know places when I see them. We must follow the Father Water north.''

"Oh, that's a big help!'' Black Skull grumbled. "He's *flown* over it! Good luck, Trader, you're going to need it.''

Green Spider whooped and flapped his arms like a crane

soaring up from a pond. "But you don't need to call on luck, do you, warrior? You won't need luck to survive, will you?"

Black Skull crossed his thick arms, tossed his head back. "My path isn't yours, Green Spider."

The Contrary clucked like a crow. "No two paths are alike, warrior. Not even in the same boat. I can tell right now, you will enjoy this trip. It won't challenge a man like you . . . not at all."

Black Skull's abused face darkened. "What are you talking about? The only place I'm going is back to the City of the Dead!"

What were the Contrary's words? First three, then four, then six, less one? Otter spun on his heel, looking at the Clan Elders. "I take it that I'm supposed to pack for three?"

"As Green Spider wishes," Old Man North replied mildly. "The great warrior, Black Skull, comes from my clan. He will do as the Contrary wishes."

"Wait! *No, I won't!*" Black Skull rushed forward. "Please. Not this! Go upriver with that . . . that . . ." The muscles in his ruined face jumped and knotted beyond control. "He's crazy!"

Old Man North stood, taking a pained step to face the defiant warrior. "If Green Spider wants you to go, I am asking you to go. I can't force you, Black Skull. That isn't our way. If you decide not to go, I understand. It is a fearsome journey, and filled with many dangers. Someone must maintain the honor of the Black Clan. I will offer myself in your place."

Black Skull's mighty muscles flexed and bunched like twisted oak. Tendons, like vines, popped, and his fingers knotted into fists. He bowed his head, and his crooked jaw worked back and forth.

Old Man North raised a thin hand, touching Black Skull gently. The warrior flinched. "Black Skull, do you remember when Green Spider returned from the Dead? He got up off the bench in the charnel hut and led me and the rest of the Elders up to the top of the high mound. There we sat down among the ashes of the Dead and he told us of his Vision. He told us about Otter, and taking the canoe north. You are in the Vision. You are there.''

"Doing what?'' Black Skull's deep voice had dropped to a faint rasp.

"Confronting the challenges you must face. This is a matter of Power, Black Skull. You have been chosen—perhaps because you are the greatest warrior ever to live.''

Black Skull nodded, then glanced at the watching people. Stiffening, he drew his war club and shook it. "I'm *not* afraid! But I ask you, would you want to be stuck in the same canoe with *him*? For days on end?''

Green Spider made a croaking sound and hopped to a spot in front of the fuming Black Skull. "The Contrary has a puzzle for you.''

"I *don't* want to hear it.''

"When we find the Roaring Water, you'll be the ugliest man in the world. Now . . . is the Contrary saying that forward . . . or backward? You must decide.''

Black Skull's muscles bunched like serpents under his scarred hide. Then he jerked a curt nod at the Clan Elders and pushed through the crowd.

"Should be a fascinating trip,'' Otter muttered from the side of his mouth.

Four Kills placed a restraining hand on Otter's shoulder. "Brother, I don't care what's at stake. That Dream last night . . . Listen, don't do this. You didn't feel the terror that I did. I mean, I . . . I don't want you to die. I need you too much.''

Otter patted his brother's hand. He could sense Four Kills' fear—like a dark wind within the soul. "I think it's meant to be, brother. You have a new life to live now. Our paths split that night on the river. And, brother, search your feelings. There, in your soul, that part of you that is me. I was leaving for the north anyway. I want to do this. I *need* to do this.''

Otter bit back a cry at the expression of loss in his brother's eyes. "You're already mourning me.''

"Who will bury your body?'' Four Kills bowed his head. "And care for your soul so it doesn't become a homeless ghost?''

Water patted and slapped off the bow as the sleek canoe continued to shoot forward into the twilight. The land had changed, growing colder and familiar plants were becoming rare along the banks of the Father Water.

For Pearl, the endless monotony of the river had become a sort of torture. She'd picked a handful of winter-dry dogtail grass. To keep herself from madness, she worked the leaves into a series of complicated knots, creating an Anhinga prayer mat. She'd never made one before, although she'd been taught the difficult knots as a child. Prayer mats were made only in the direst of situations, and then laid on the burial mounds of the ancestors in a desperate quest for aid.

Pearl had no mound now, no ancestral ghosts around to hear her pleas.

When would this misery end? Her body ached from constantly sitting on her sack of maize seeds, and to make matters worse, she had started her Bleeding Time. When she squirmed from the discomfort, the men behind her made hissing sounds.

She'd come to hate them. They never left her alone. When she went into the forest to strip the soft inner bark of trees to use as an absorbent, they followed and jeered.

Somewhere, the roles had changed between them. From escorts, they'd grown into captors, and she'd found herself a virtual prisoner instead of an exalted and precious bride.

"Woman, you spend all day riding in the canoe. After that, we wait on you all night. From now on, you will cook for us," Grizzly Tooth had ordered. Then, last night, he'd forced her to carry all the bedrolls up to camp.

"To teach you to serve men," he'd added.

And what can I do about it? The thought had been nagging at her for days. She'd become nothing more than their slave. Somehow, there had to be a way to escape, or to fight back. But how?

They made sure that someone always stayed close to her—even on the occasions when she retreated to the bushes to relieve herself. Granted, Pearl had never been shy. People who travel on small boats can't afford that luxury. Nevertheless, she'd never been the subject of intense observation when she attended to the by-processes of digestion.

Where once the Khota warriors had stared at her with something of a reverence, she could now detect open desire among the majority of them—and outright lust in the eyes of a certain few.

The warrior called Eats Dogs would fix his gaze on her full chest and rub his jaw as his eyes went glassy. Round Scar, on the other hand, was the worst violator of her privacy, always stalking her, grinning at the swing of her hips, seeking to touch her muscular thighs when he helped her into the boat.

Today had been particularly trying. One Arm had slowed whenever he passed her, lifting his nose, sniffing like a male dog around a receptive bitch.

Grizzly Tooth noticed the shift in behavior and sensed the increasing tension. Despite his role as nominal leader and best friend to her future husband, he'd taken to giving her guarded glances, his thoughts veiled.

And perhaps he'd been right to do so. More than once he'd caught her staring back downriver, the longing for home welling in her eyes while the empty ache of loneliness grew in her gut.

As the canoe lanced the waves and turned toward a long sandbar that jutted from the shore, she pondered her options. There were only two: run away, or surrender meekly to whatever fate her clan had sold her into. Glancing at the warriors in the canoes beside her, that latter option seemed less and less desirable.

She'd grown sick of everything Khota. The chore of learning Khota language exhausted her very soul. The endless repetition of words tangled her tongue and frustrated her. However, coupled with Trade pidgin, she'd come to be fairly proficient as long as she didn't need to say anything rapidly. To her, the language still seemed to be that of a people who sneezed a lot.

The boat slid up on the sandy mud with a *shish*ing sound, and Pearl sighed, pushing painfully to her feet. The miserable, prickling sensation of numb legs returning to life had to be endured before she could trust herself to step out.

"Weak, woman?" Round Scar asked as he stepped out and placed his oar in the canoe. The wood thunked hollowly. "Maybe you need me to help you carry all the blankets up to camp?"

"May the leeches suck your blood," she rattled off in her own tongue. Then in the Trade pidgin, she added, "I'm fine. You?"

Round Scar chuckled and hefted the weight of his atlatl as he and several others pulled darts and fanned out to investigate the approaches to the camping spot.

The worst of the prickling over, Pearl trusted her legs to take her up onto the spit of sand. Others had camped here in the past. Several charcoal stains indicated where hearths had been dug out. Bits of broken pottery hinted that someone had dropped a food jar—or else the vessel had been broken in a canoe and the remains tossed out here.

Behind the sand spit lay a brackish backwater from which cypress had begun to grow, and tall cane lined the crumbled bank where the forest started. Sparse grass shaded into brush, and finally into dense forest. Even as she considered the site, several of the warriors trotted past her toward the trees, perhaps to hunt meat for the camp.

Pearl walked down to the head of the backwater, screening herself with brush. She squatted and pulled her skirt up, thankful to relieve her full bladder and change her absorbent. At the last stop, she'd tucked a thick loop of bark into the top of her moccasin, and now she removed it.

One Arm walked up behind her, grinning, sniffing. "Aren't you done yet, woman?"

"Just a moment longer." She took her time replacing her old absorbent with new. There *had* to be a way to pay these arrogant—

The plant stood right before her. Brown, dead, but the oval leaves couldn't be mistaken. They had grown straight out of the now-desiccated stalk: no stems. The seeds were long gone, but the many-forked umbels remained.

They wanted her to do all the cooking, did they? She picked up a twig and dug at the dirt as though burying her old absorbent, which was her habit. One Arm would expect it.

The plant might be dormant, but the roots would still be there, waiting, full of the Power that flowering spurge was noted for.

Pearl gripped her precious root, stuffed it into the top of her moccasin, and stood up.

One Arm had a crafty gleam in his eyes. He lifted his breech-clout, pointing at his enlarging penis. "You want this? Maybe tonight? When everybody else is asleep?"

She shook her head, placing her feet carefully as she backed away.

"I'm good!" he insisted. "*Real* good! Make you happy."

"I'm for Dead Wolf," she insisted. "Remember him? Your war leader?"

He laughed at that, wagging his engorged penis. "I'll come to you tonight. Make you happy, yes?"

"No!"

She slipped to the side as he grabbed for her. With a twist of her body, she avoided his fingers and sprinted for the camp. Behind her, he laughed.

Seeking to recover some sense of dignity, she strode forward purposefully, her head held high, back arched.

Grizzly Tooth had used a splintered piece of driftwood to dig out one of the fire pits. He looked up, noting her expression and the flashing anger in her eyes.

"Trouble?" he asked.

"One Arm wants me. Offered to crawl into my robes."

Grizzly Tooth nodded. "You're the only woman. What do you expect? Now stop causing trouble and go pack our blankets up to camp."

"Does Dead Wolf want his warriors sticking themselves in his woman?"

Grizzly Tooth sighed. "It's Wolf of the Dead . . . not Dead Wolf. And the answer is no. You stay within my sight. Besides, the way you talk Khota, you might mean no and say yes. It sounds like you're talking with too much food in your mouth."

"Khota don't talk like real people."

They watched her like hawks as she lugged their gear up to the camp. As she worked, she studied the bedrolls in her hands, and a sly smile curled her lips.

She carried one of the cook pots to Grizzly Tooth's fire and set it on the sand, watching as he placed kindling in the hollowed-out fire pit. He opened a small pottery jar he'd taken from the canoe and poured gray ash on the ground before bending down to blow on it. A puff of fine powder blew away, but several embers glowed redly to life. These, Grizzly Tooth plucked up with twigs and settled at the base of the tinder. Lowering his face, he gently blew, and the embers ignited the twigs and frayed grasses.

The stew was built on a stock of goosefoot seeds, fish netted that day, five ducks, and what was left of last night's deer. Pearl ate as she worked, filling herself before she surreptitiously added the final ingredient: the spurge root.

As the fire crackled and the stew steamed, Grizzly Tooth watched her. "You're thinking about running off. Trying to escape—to make your way back downriver."

She met his thoughtful glance, then turned her attention to her prayer mat. As her cold fingers worked another of the knots and pulled it tight, she said, "Why would I do that? If I did, I would dishonor my people."

Doing so *would* dishonor her family and people. It bothered her that she cared so little about the consequences of her proposed action. She should care. Her people had made a promise. And if she slipped away from these captors, the shame would be theirs forever.

And what if they are shamed? So what? I didn't want to be married in the first place.

"I would not run away," Grizzly Tooth said casually as he fed sticks to the fire. "We have forty warriors here. Many of these men are excellent trackers, excellent swimmers."

He nodded at the crackling fire, satisfied with the way it climbed the water-smoothed sticks. Then he moved back, settling himself casually beside her. "There is something you should know about the Khota. We have many failings, as do all peoples. Sometimes we fight amongst ourselves. Other times we travel long distances to raid and steal from other peoples. We have even robbed Traders, and sometimes killed them."

"I've heard the rumors."

Grizzly Tooth shrugged, his eyes still on the fire. "Maybe these things are good for us . . . or maybe not. But you must understand that we are vigorous, strong. A kind of fire burns in our hearts that does not burn in the hearts of other people.''

Warriors were starting to trickle into the camp as night fell. Some carried wood. Others brought poles for shelters. They drove the pole ends into the sand and unrolled cattail matting from the canoes to provide a covering in case it should rain. As they prepared their own fire pits, they came, nodded to Grizzly Tooth, and lit brands with which to light their fires.

''I would tell you a story to make my point,'' Grizzly Tooth continued. ''In the time of my great-great-great-grandfather, a marriage was made between one of our leaders, Strong Wind, and the people who lived at the mouth of the Ilini River.

''The woman was brought to our camp in the north, in the Land of Many Lakes, where we were hunters. The ceremonies were held and the vows exchanged between our people and hers. Then, that night, when he took her, she went inexplicably crazy. She drove a deer-bone dagger into his side and broke a good, oak war club over his head. Then she slipped away into the night. She stole a canoe and traveled down the Father Water, heading for her people, who lived at the mouth of the Ilini River.

''Miraculously, Strong Wind lived. His relatives held a big feast, and for four days and nights, they Danced, calling upon the ghosts of the ancestors to heal Strong Wind, and upon the other clans of the Khota to join them in avenging the insult to Strong Wind.''

''Maybe he deserved what he got?''

''Maybe he did, but the Spirit World heard the call for help. With news of Strong Wind's recovery, all the clans of the Khota sent warriors.'' Grizzly Tooth gave her a cool stare. ''Ten tens of canoes were assembled. Together, they paddled rapidly downstream to repay the Ilini woman and her relatives. Everyone, young, old, they were all killed. Today, in that place where the Ilini woman once lived, lie the clan territories to which you are being carried.''

She stared down at her fingers, slim and brown where they gripped the tan grasses of the prayer mat, which contrasted to the buff-colored fabric of her nettle-and-milkweed-fiber skirt. The chilly air lanced through the thin dress as the breeze on the river changed.

In her entire life, she'd never been as cold as during the two moons she'd been on the river. Now she huddled closer to the fire, and Grizzly Tooth, with a nod of his head, signaled one of the warriors who lurked around the peripheries to find her a blanket.

"Why do you think I would escape?"

"I've seen the look in your eyes. We have come a long way from your lands. If I were you, I might want to run away also."

"I would not dishonor my people."

Grizzly Tooth tossed a stick into the fire. "I got the feeling they didn't think much of you as it was. They said you made men uncomfortable. That it was better for you to go north. Establish a Trading relationship with the Khota. That no one would marry you at home. That you would be better—"

"Do not discuss my clan with me."

An owl hooted out in the forest.

"Let me tell you something." Grizzly Tooth rolled onto his side, staring at her in the firelight. "You're not marrying just a man."

"What is he then? *Berdache?*"

Grizzly Tooth's voice dropped, and the owl hooted again. "I told you what the clan would do if you ran away. But Wolf of the Dead, he isn't like other men. He'll hunt you, find you, and when he does, he'll deal with you in *his* way."

Grizzly Tooth glanced away, uneasy, a hoarseness in his voice. "He's not just a man. He's . . . well, like his father before him."

Pearl noticed that the warriors had started to gather close, their eyes shining in the flickering light.

"Are you trying to frighten me? Alone in the swamps, I used to hunt alligators. I've traveled far out into the sea, traveled by the stars. You can't scare me."

Grizzly Tooth pinched his lip in his teeth, then knotted a fist. "Your husband isn't all-human. Do you understand? When the Power is on him, he turns into a wolf."

"A wolf?" Pearl shifted uneasily, seeing the sober belief in the eyes of the warriors. An unbidden shiver slipped down her spine, prickling her skin.

"Wolf of the Dead," Grizzly Tooth whispered. "That's why you can't run away from him. He'll find you. The Dead will tell him where you're running to—and he'll follow. Sniff you out in his wolf form. You can't hide from a creature like that.''

He really believes what he's saying! Her soul went cold. The watching warriors nodded in slow assent. She barely kept herself from twisting the prayer mat she clutched so desperately.

Grizzly Tooth gave her a sympathetic look, then lowered his eyes. After several seconds of silence, he got to his feet, making a gesture to the warriors. ''Some of you have started to desire this woman. See that you do not. She is for Wolf of the Dead.'' Then he studied Pearl, his fingers to his chin. ''I want at least three of you watching her all the time. Spell yourselves through the night. She'll try to run away now that she knows the truth.''

Pearl didn't sleep well that night—but then, neither did the Khota. All night long they moaned and groaned and ran back and forth from camp to the river, grumbling about their twisting guts. Several of them tripped over her in their haste to get to a place where they could relieve themselves. Even then the moans continued, laced with curses.

Pearl smiled to herself. How fortunate she had been to find the flowering spurge. . . .

Nine

Despite the fact that a forest surrounded the White Shell clan grounds, firewood was always a scarce commodity, especially since people had been living on the site for generations. As a result, all the branches, deadfall, and forest litter had been collected for a day's walk in any direction. The forest behind the clan grounds flourished—but living wood burns poorly. Sometimes, people would ring a tree, wait for it to die and dry out, then hope to topple it before a major celebration. However, that took advance planning.

The arrival of the Clan Elders, Black Skull, and Green Spider might have proved something of an embarrassment for old Yellow Reed and her clan. Perhaps the Contrary willed it, or perhaps it was just the right time, but one of the smaller hickory trees had fallen. From the splintered branches, the children pulled enough wood to feed the fires. And the White Shell clan grounds needed many fires on this night.

Word had spread, and now canoe after canoe landed as Tall Cane people arrived. They came to see the noted Elders, the famous Black Skull, and to hear about Green Spider's Vision that had led him to become a Contrary.

Night had fallen with a crystalline clarity that made the chill intense. The stars seemed to press down in a way Otter had seen only in the far north.

He watched people crowd around the crackling bonfire before the large clan house. Flames illuminated the faces of the Elders as they stood waiting, hands clasped before them. Their wizened features puckered as they concentrated on what they would say.

People, wrapped in blankets and heavy coats, whispered excitedly. Flickers of firelight caught momentary glimpses of their animated expressions. Black eyes sparkled, and wonderment could be seen in the set of mouth or eyebrow. The plaza murmured with pensive anticipation. Meanwhile, boisterous children slipped through the mass of adults like minnows through a net. They crowded close to the fire long enough to warm first one side, then the other, before turning to wiggle away into the night again amidst giggles and laughter.

Otter stood in the rear—off to one side, where he could slip away if he wanted to. As he waited, he took note of the visitors and was aware of Hard Clay and her family. And there stood Slim Turtle with her relatives. And behind her—

Otter's heart skipped. Red Moccasins couldn't be mistaken for any other—, tall and elegant, the firelight gleaming on her perfect face. She'd parted her hair differently, on the right side, in the style of a married woman. As Otter watched, she bent her head, whispering something to Four Kills, who stood at her side, holding her hand.

Otter knew that slight frown. Lines formed between her eyebrows, and the serious set of the mouth caused dimples at the corners of her lips.

Go away, Otter. You're only hurting yourself. He even started to leave, half-turning when he noticed the Elders.

Old Man Blood moved at last, standing and composing himself. He nodded at one of the children, who brought him a finely beaded, red pipe-bag. People hushed as he ceremonially loaded the pipe with tobacco and lit it with a burning stick from the fire. One by one, the Clan Elders passed the pipe between them.

Together, they raised their faces to the night sky and Sang, their old voices wavering and twining together in the Blessing Song. The lilting notes carried on the still night. As if in response, the stars seemed to pulse with the rhythm of the words.

A silence fell over the expectant crowd. Then Old Man Blood began the story about how Green Spider had fasted, purified himself in the sweat lodge, chanted, and Danced. How he'd entered the temple four days before the solstice and cried for a Vision, finally passing into a trance. And then, on the day of the solstice, lightning had struck.

"We pulled him from the burning building," Old Man Sun took over the narrative. "We, ourselves, were burned. You can see where patches of our hair are singed." He pulled back a sleeve, exposing healing skin. "Our flesh still renews itself."

"We thought that Green Spider was dead," Old Man Sky explained. "He showed no sign of life, so we had his body carried to the charnel hut and laid there among the other corpses. He was washed, his flesh rubbed with hickory oil. For four days, he lay like that—dead in the charnel hut. On that last day, we went for him, to carry him to a log tomb we had cut into the ground just to the north of the Temple Mound."

Old Man North nodded his assent. "We dug the pit into the ground and lined it with clay. Into that pit we placed cane matting, and then several layers of fine cloth to cushion the body and show our respect. With great care, we laid Green Spider into the tomb, placing a drinking shell beside his head and copper plate upon his chest. Logs had been brought from the forest to lay over the tomb. Other young men had been sent upriver in canoes to find sandstone slabs to lay across the top, as is our custom.''

''And then . . .'' Old Man Blood hesitated ''. . . then we ordered the young men to place the logs. They had lifted the first and were struggling to set it across the tomb—''

''—when he woke up!'' cried Old Man Sun. ''Sat up! Right there in the tomb! He blinked, groaned, and rubbed his eyes.''

''People stood as if they had been turned to wood,'' Old Man Sky insisted. ''Green Spider climbed to his feet, wobbling, weak and sick. He called out to us, and we rushed forward, asking him what had happened.''

Otter shifted and flexed his knees to ease the cramp in his legs. As he crossed his arms, he happened to glance across the fire. His stare locked with that of Red Moccasins; he could read the misery in those large dark eyes, which seemed to suck at his soul with worry and pain.

Otter forced himself to look away as Old Man North raised his hands to the crowd, his ancient face possessed of wonder. ''He told us he had been to speak to the Dead, that he had been given a Vision. Listen, my people. Hear Green Spider. He has seen a young girl floating in a river. Behind the child, a woman flounders in the water, coughing, spitting, her arms splashing as she tries to reach the child. In the struggle, she loses a sacred bundle that is strapped to her back.''

''The water begins to move faster,'' Old Man Blood cried. ''It rushes around rocks, sucking and whirling. The pretty little girl is torn beyond the mother's reach as she spins away in the foaming rapids.''

''A roaring can be heard! It grows louder and louder.'' Old Man Sun shook an age-spotted fist. ''Power fills the air, and the helpless child is tossed on the angry waves, crashing this way and that as water pounds the rocks into fury. At the last minute, it seems that the innocent girl might be spared, for a mat of debris lies just ahead, just at the edge of the tumbling water.''

''But this is not to be.'' Old Man Sky tilted his face toward the star-speckled heavens. ''A twist of the current carries the child away from the piled logs and sticks. She cries out, spitting water as she grabs onto the floating bundle. She tears at it, and a beautiful Mask floats free. Meanwhile, the woman manages to grasp onto a rock, clinging desperately as she watches in horror. Her child and the bundle are carried on by the rapid current, carried over the edge. Together, they vanish, falling among the rainbows of spray that rise up from the roaring depths.''

''At that point, Green Spider looked out over the land.'' Old Man North seemed to slump. ''There he saw all the world, and the peoples upon it. Tears were in their eyes, and the souls of the Dead were sad. The plants in the fields wilted, and the deer hid themselves in the thickets. Clouds covered the sky, but no rain fell. The land became as winter.''

People swayed on their feet, somber as they cast furtive glances at each other. The silence seemed to hold them as firmly as a basswood rope.

''Then the Spirit of Many Colored Crow approached Green Spider,'' Old Man Blood related. ''He told him—as I am telling you—that if Green Spider would become a Contrary, Many Colored Crow would show him a way to save the woman, the little girl, and the Sacred Mask . . . but that to do so would take a great deal of courage and dedication.''

''So Green Spider followed the Spirit of Many Colored Crow,'' Old Man Sun declared, raising his hands again. ''And Many Colored Crow began to teach Green Spider the way of the Contrary.''

''And that was when First Man appeared out of a haze as golden as when the sunlight pierces the morning mist,'' Old Man Sky cried. ''First Man, assuming the shape of a wolf, then of a Thunderbird, and then of a rattlesnake, demanded to know what Many Colored Crow was doing! Many Colored Crow explained that Green Spider would become a Contrary, and would save the new Dreamer!''

''And then,'' Old Man North bellowed as he shook his fists, ''First Man and Many Colored Crow argued. They fought back and forth as they had when the world was new. The Earth Mother was awakened by their noise and came up from her cave in the underworld and scolded them, and told them they were acting like children!

''First Man smiled at his brother, and golden light shot out to gleam on the rainbow feathers of Many Colored Crow. And

First Man said: 'Very well, I will let Green Spider try to save the child. If he will become a Contrary, he will become a good man. Power does not always work as we would wish it, brother.' ''

Old Man Blood cradled his conch shell to his breast. "Many Colored Crow looked at his brother, First Man, and said, 'Your Spiral is shifting. Your Dream is no longer only yours. All we can do is wait—and try to prepare the people.' And at that, First Man nodded, and vanished.

"So Green Spider was taught the pathway of the Contrary. Then he was introduced to his ancestors, who gave him a feast in the City of the Dead. They all gave him advice on being a good Contrary. Finally, when they thought they had prepared him, they sent him back to us."

"And that's when he woke up in the tomb," Old Man Sky told them. "That is the Vision, the experience he had when he was dead."

"And that is why we have come here," Old Man North added. "The advice that Green Spider got from the Land of the Dead was to take Black Skull and Otter with him on his journey northward toward the Roaring Water. The ancestors said that if they all did their best, they could save this Spirit Mask and this child, this Dreamer."

So, I was chosen.

Otter glanced up, meeting Red Moccasins' eyes again, noting how her lips had parted. She shook her head, then tried to smile bravely. She whispered something to Four Kills and started to work through the crowd.

Otter eased away into the darkness. Of course she'd want to talk to him. But what could she say now that would make things any different? The words were exhausted between them.

He ducked around Grandmother's house, circling the side of the crowd where the old woman had just been. Then he cut behind Red Dye's house. Head down, he traced his way through the dark clan grounds and paused at the hump of the burial mound. So much was happening. A knot of frustration choked at the base of his throat. He could feel the ghosts of his ancestors, and they seemed to whisper to him. Straining, he failed to catch their words, and nodded out of respect before ambling forward aimlessly. Out of habit, he checked the storage hut.

Catcher greeted him happily. His tail lashed the air—fit to cut ghosts in two. The hot, happy tongue licked Otter's hand, and Catcher jumped and bounded.

"Soon, my friend," Otter promised, dropping down to wrestle with the shaggy dog. "Everything all right? No thieves in the night have come to take our goods?"

Catcher made a muffled sound as he stretched his front end and yawned. The stretch moved back to stiffly extended hind legs and a curved tail.

Otter smiled wanly, grabbing hold of the dog, hugging him close. For a long moment, he savored the warmth, burying his face in the animal's fur. The dry scent of the dog soothed the ache in his soul. Red Moccasins' face floated there, haunting him, twisting the hurt that lived like a blade inside him.

Catcher, predictably, had been delighted with the attention at first; but—as any dog worth his name would do—he began to wiggle, desperate to escape the hug. After all, it wouldn't do for a guard dog of Catcher's renown to be seen clutched in an embrace like a silly puppy!

Otter sighed, the moment of solace forever past. "You're a good guard, Catcher. You stay here and watch things. There's going to be a feast tonight. I'll bring you some bits of meat, and maybe a couple of cakes."

As Catcher climbed nimbly back into the storage hut, his tail whapped at Otter's legs. The dog curled around a couple of times and flopped onto the top pack with a thud.

Otter cocked his head, listening. The chatter of excited voices filled the night as people talked about Green Spider's Vision. Someone laughed. Otter melted back into the shadows as two people—a boy barely past his manhood and a young girl from Tall Cane, Wet Bone's daughter—slipped past into the darkness. A shared blanket lay over their shoulders. In their groping preoccupation, they hadn't noticed Otter's shadowy presence.

He waited for a moment, hearing their steps crunch on the dry leaves behind the storage hut. A gasp was followed by a soft voice and the rasping of clothing.

Otter ghosted into the night, following the curving wall that marked the perimeter of the clan grounds. Once, not so long ago, he too had slipped away into the night with a woman. That had been more than four moons past. He'd just returned from the north, his canoe brimming with goods.

The moon had gleamed whitely, halfway through its cycle but bathing the land with soft light as they had walked out in the warm fall evening. He'd draped her blanket about them, a symbolic gesture.

"I can't put off marriage any longer," she'd told him. "I'm getting too old as it is."

"So . . . marry me. Grandmother would understand. I think she expects it." He'd lifted her hand, touching the tips of her fingers to his lips. "Most people speak of it as a foregone conclusion. They think you just need to choose: me, or Four Kills."

"What if I chose him?"

"He's a good man. The best I know. And if you didn't marry me, I wouldn't want you married to anyone else." But she'd always preferred Otter. Perhaps it had been unfair to his brother, but Otter had always been the exciting one, the Trader who ventured off to strange places and returned with exotic items that brought joy to Red Moccasins' eyes.

They'd walked out onto a narrow spit of sand that jutted into the river. "We always come here," Red Moccasins had sighed.

"Isn't it a beautiful spot? You can hear the water. Feel the freedom."

"Freedom?" she'd wondered thoughtfully as he stepped behind her and hugged her close.

"You can feel the Power of the river here, ebbing, flowing. Close your eyes, Red Moccasins. It lives, throbbing almost like the blood in your veins."

His hands had moved up to massage her full breasts. She'd relaxed then, leaning back against him, breathing deeply as she savored his touch. "Would you stay with me? Now, I mean? Wait until next summer to travel south to the Alligator Clans?"

He'd deftly settled the blanket onto the sand before nibbling at her ear, aware of her response.

"Next summer?" he'd muttered as she turned in his arms and unfastened the laces of his shirt. She'd helped him pull the garment over his head. He'd shuddered as she reached down to run tickling fingers under his testicles. His scrotum tightened at her light touch.

With a lithe shrug, she slipped out of her dress and stood tall and proud before him in the half light of the moon. The river breeze teased the wealth of her thick black hair tangled in a shining mass around her shoulders.

She stepped close and pressed herself against him—as if she could squeeze the whole of him inside of her, keep him safely there forever. Then she settled onto the coarsely woven blanket and pulled him to her. He could remember her gasping delight as he entered her and their hips locked. They'd waited for a moment, savoring the sublime unity before they began the ancient dance.

They'd coupled with a passion that night, rested, found each other's bodies again and fulfilled the honeyed sensations once more.

He'd awakened in her arms, suffused with a deep satisfaction. Her warmth seemed to pervade him, as if their hearts beat as one. Reaching up, he'd lifted a long black strand of hair away from her beautiful face and watched her as dawn purpled the horizon.

She moved to him, and to his amazement, the stirring of his loins brought them both to renewed passion.

In the limp afterglow, she'd wound her arms around him, then tricked him so that she could lick the end of his nose. He laughed, his reflection in her eyes.

"Will you stay with me?" she asked again.

"I won't be gone that long, beloved. If you must marry, tell them yes. Tell them I'll marry you upon the return from the south. The time to go is now. I have this new copper—big plates—and some of the fabrics can't wait. Neither can the packs of dried meat."

She'd seemed to fade then. "I understand, Otter. It's the river. But do you understand? I can't tell you I'll be yours when you come back. I'm a woman . . . with responsibilities of my own."

"I understand, but I promise—"

"It's morning. I've got to get back."

They'd dressed, and he'd helped her comb out her glossy black hair.

Just before they separated, she'd hugged him close and whispered, "Be careful, Otter. May your River Spirit cherish you as much as I do."

And then she'd gone.

He'd been so drowned in the memory, he'd only half-known where he was or what he was doing. During the reverie, he'd walked down the steep, zigzagging path that led to the canoe landing.

He paused for a moment and took stock. A fire had been burning in one of the fire pits—a landing light for anyone crossing the river from Tall Cane territory. Untended, it had dwindled to red coals from which periodic flickers of flame valiantly shot up.

Otter found the woodpile the children had left and added a couple of splintered limbs to the coals. As the flames danced up, he thrust his thumbs into his belt. His breath puffed frosty against the night sky.

The familiar musk of the river soothed him, and he sniffed to draw it deeply into his lungs. A man might do the same with the scent of the woman he loved—breathe it in and hold it in his lungs to enjoy it for as long as he could.

As he walked toward the water, his fingers traced the smooth curve of hull on *Wave Dancer*. At the water's edge, he crouched to wet the tips of his fingers. Closing his eyes, he could feel the Power, endless, roiling, moving. The river pulsed and lived within its banks.

Otter exhaled wearily; at last he understood Red Moccasins' words on that day they'd parted. He straightened, crossing his arms as he leaned against *Wave Dancer*'s stern. A chill wind blew down from the north. Up there, at the head of the river, the land would be shrouded in ice and snow. Fierce blizzards would be roaring down Moonshell River, driven by all the anger of the north.

How much time do we have to get to the Roaring Water? How will we know where to find it?

Presumably, Green Spider had that knowledge locked away inside his Contrary head. But even if he tried to explain, could Otter translate it? Would it all be backward jabber?

"Can you spare a woman a moment?"

Otter stiffened; his heart skipped at the sound of her voice.

Despite the flutters in his breast, he forced himself to relax. Turning, he found her silhouetted against the light of the landing fire.

"I didn't hear you. You startled me."

She gave him that curious nod of acceptance, a half-cocked bob of the head. "Otter, I had to come. I had to talk to you. To see if there were any way I could . . . I don't know, stop you from feeling the way you do." She slapped frustrated hands against her thighs and turned away. "Now that I'm down here, I feel pretty silly. There's nothing I can say, is there?"

"No."

She stared at him, fists knotted, and in an agonized voice, said, "I did what I *had* to do, Otter. No matter how much I loved you, I couldn't spend the rest of my life alone. I couldn't stand to have only a sliver of your life while the river and Trade had the rest. Don't you see?"

He glared at her. "So you chose the next-best thing. My brother."

"I took *your* advice—the way I always have. You yourself told me that if I didn't marry you, you'd prefer that I marry him." She bowed her head. "Look at me, ready to rip you into pieces. I've been hating your return, knowing how hard it was going to be. And now I'm just mad at you, Otter." She paused, her gaze fixed out over the inky waters of the river. "I guess it's because I'm still so terribly in love with you."

"And what about Four Kills?"

She rubbed the back of her neck, kicking at the muddy beach. "I love him just as much . . . but differently. I guess I knew that twins had magic, but I didn't know how much I could get bound up in it." She kicked harder at the ground. "The two of you . . . he's like the earth, stable, secure, warm, and tender. You, Otter, you're water—just like your Spirit out there. Tempestuous, exciting, rain and storm, flood and renewal, all in one."

She sniffed, and he realized she was battling tears. Her shivers came half from the chill, half from her shaking emotions.

He reached for her, to pull her into his arms. "You did the right thing, beloved." The scent of her refreshed his memory, made him hearken back to the other times when they'd slipped away into the darkness to share their bodies.

"I know," she whispered. "You would have destroyed me, Otter. In the end, you would have driven me mad with loneliness. I would have gone to Four Kills anyway. I'd have gone to him because he looked like you, acted like you." She smiled wistfully. "It wouldn't have been as if I hadn't shared his blanket, either."

"I knew that you had shared his blanket."

"He told you?"

"Never. It was enough to know that he loved you with all his heart."

She seemed to wilt against him. "The worst time was always just after you left. I went to him as often as he or I could get away. I could pretend he was you. And in the end, I knew you would never be there for me . . . and he would always be."

Otter ran his hands through her hair. "And if I asked you now? Would you share my blanket?"

She tensed, then trembled. "Don't ask that. Please."

He pushed her away, aware of his rising desire. "I guess I can't, beloved. I can feel his acceptance even if we did. He loves us both. Go back to him. We've said what we need to."

She hugged him so desperately that she drove the breath from him. Hot tears tickled on his neck. "This time, Otter, be even more careful than usual. I don't understand why Power has come for you, but it's dangerous. Stay alive, Otter. For me . . . for Four Kills. If you died, he'd . . . Just be careful!"

She grabbed his head to kiss him passionately, as if demanding his very soul. Then she whirled and ran for the trail.

Otter stood still for a moment, his soul gone numb, before he started along the shore, stepping around the canoes, brooding.

He stopped short at the sight of the crouched figure that sat perched on one of the overturned hulls.

Barely distinguishable from the darkness, the man rose on cat feet. In a deep voice, the Black Skull said, "Forgive me, Trader. The opportunity didn't present itself to say anything. And afterward . . . well, I had hoped you would walk the other way."

Otter struggled to find a response, but he could only manage to nod.

"If you will excuse me, I must go and guard that addled lunatic." At that, the warrior rose and disappeared into the darkness on ghost-quiet feet.

Ten

I sit cross-legged, my eyes fixed on the wavering dance of flames.

I can hear the Mask clearly now, or rather, the world around the Mask. It is as though the eyeholes funnel sound to me.

Earlier, one ghost had been shrieking in anger; now two rage at each other. The frightening part is that they are ghosts, and will rage at each other through eternity.

From somewhere in that distant land, a cackling laughter begins. Faint tremors of Power vibrate in the air around me, surging, seeking . . .

Firelight cast eerie shadows over the assembled leaders of the Shining Bird Clan. Star Shell watched them through vacant eyes, barely aware of the fear that sank sharp talons into her belly. In her mind's eye, the grisly image of Mica Bird's swinging body dominated everything else. She shivered at the memory of his bugged-out eyes, the purple tongue protruding through swollen lips.

People had gathered in the Potters' Society house—for no one would enter the clan house again. Mica Bird's tormented ghost still seethed there, locked behind a barricaded doorway. Frantic measures had been taken. Posts had been scavenged and set in holes hurriedly excavated into the frozen soil. This time, the posts faced inward to keep Mica Bird's angry spirit at bay. Branches of cedar, plucked from living trees, dangled on thongs tied to the tips of the poles. Hung so, they created a Spiritual barrier to the ghost.

Now the stricken clan would decide what measures to take.

The Potters' house consisted of a bent-pole frame roughly fifteen paces across. Sections of bark had been tied over the framework to shelter the contents and the women who worked here. Baskets of clay and ceramic jars of water lined the back wall. Large bowls held sand and grog for temper. Old bits of fabric and thick cord had been wound around paddles, to impress decorations into the wet clay of newly made pots. A stack of sharpened awls lay in a basket and were used for punctating and incising the clan's unique designs. Other jars held special clays that allowed the maker to add a brightly colored slip.

Men and women packed the room. Tall Man sat to Star Shell's right, preoccupied with his own thoughts. Frown lines had deepened his wizened face. To her left, Silver Water clutched Star Shell's arm, her eyes wide with a terror she was just beginning to understand. Her young face mirrored the tragedy and fear that hid in her small body. Silver Water's grip tightened, as if she could draw strength from her mother's flesh.

Gray Deer, Mica Bird's mother, sat on the other side of Silver Water. She had draped a mourning blanket over her head to cover her expression of misery and horror.

"We are all here," Old Slate, of the Branch Water lineage and the keeper of the Potters' house, declared uneasily. "Let us attend to the rituals."

Star Shell joined the invocation, uttering the prayers to First Man without thinking the words. When they called for the Blessing of Many Colored Crow, her voice caught in her throat. Glancing to the side, she noticed that Tall Man called for the blessing as reverently as the rest. Then they Sang to the ancestors, calling on the ghosts to help them, to whisper advice in people's Dreams that they might make proper decisions regarding this sudden calamity.

Old Slate lit her silt-stone pipe and sucked. She blew smoke to the sacred directions, then called upon the gathered people.

"Hear me, my clanspeople. A terrible thing has happened. My cousin's son, for reasons known only to Power and the ancestors, was possessed by something evil. We've seen it coming—and did nothing. Perhaps now we will pay for that disregard. Then again, perhaps we can think of a way to deal with this and get on about our lives. Do I hear any thoughts?"

Bad Tooth stood and looked around the assembly. Her four tens of years showed in the lines that time had eaten into her face. She fumbled at the edge of the blanket she'd wrapped around her stooped shoulders, worry in her eyes. "For the moment, my cousin's ghost is contained. So is that of his grandfather. We have locked them up together. But this is only a temporary measure. We must act to ensure that these ghosts remain safely contained."

Mutters of assent came in response.

Skinny Porcupine sighed as he stood. He wore a black blanket over one shoulder and sucked at his toothless mouth. "The clan house must be burned. Many Colored Crow taught people that lesson when he gathered the angry ghosts on the Sacred Mountain and burned it. We must do the same."

Reaches Far, also of the Branch Water lineage, stood then, his hands clasped before him. "I agree that we must burn the clan house. But before we do, we must hold a Dance and a feast. We must ask the ancestors to help us keep my cousins' ghosts contained. With their help, we can set better guard posts, and then build a mound on top of the ashes."

Reaches Far lifted his head and looked around. "After that, we must cleanse the clan grounds—and all of the people who work to build the mound must spend four days in the sweat lodge. When this is done, they must fast for ten days and nights. After they fast, they must sweat again and be rubbed clean with fresh cedar."

Whispers of assent signified agreement.

Gray Deer remained slumped as she said, "That will purify the clan grounds. But we have another problem—the Mask. What shall be done with it?"

"Burn it!" Old Slate cried.

People turned to stare at her in horror.

Old Slate spread her hands. "The change came over my

cousin after he retrieved the Mask from wherever his grandfather had taken it. Why do I not hear agreement that it should be burned?''

Fat Lips, an overweight man of the High Pole lineage, tugged at the blanket he wore as he looked around with sullen eyes. ''The Mask belongs to Many Colored Crow. It is not ours. It is a thing of Power. We have no right to destroy it. If we do, Many Colored Crow might be offended.''

Around the room, a few heads nodded.

''How do we know it belongs to Many Colored Crow?'' Reaches Far asked. ''Perhaps the evil within it made someone say that. To protect it. Maybe it lies as well as kills.''

Grunts sounded.

Fat Lips said, ''We know that it causes trouble. In the past moon, people have disappeared from the Holy Road. Or, when you do see them, they hurry past. How often have people stopped in to ask the news? They are avoiding us.''

Star Shell hesitated, then forced herself to speak. ''Many of the clans are thinking of calling up their warriors. Some with whom I've spoken want the Mask for themselves.''

A startled silence greeted her words. The ring of somber faces glanced back and forth. The smell of too many people mixed with the earth-musty scents of clay.

''Who?'' Old Slate asked.

''The Blue Duck, for one,'' Star Shell said softly. ''There will be others. Many see the Mask as a way to gain authority and status through Power. They would like to be known as wearers of the Mask. It offers a great deal to the ambitious.''

Gray Deer sighed. ''Yes, the Mask served my husband's father well. Think back, people. Remember what our clan was like before the coming of the Mask? We lived from hand to mouth. Our clan grounds were small, and the Goosefoot Clan, the Many Paints, the Rattlesnake Clan, and the Blue Ducks never took us seriously. The Mask helped to build this clan. Our harvests improved. Others watched and took note. They would see their influence grow, too.''

Tall Man rose to his feet, a diminutive caricature in the fire's glow. ''An Elder of the High Heads requests permission to speak.''

Old Slate glanced around, then nodded. ''We have heard of

the Magician. He is known as a wise man. Let the Elder speak.''

Tall Man clasped his small hands before him. ''As you know, the High Heads are an old people. A long time ago—so the legends say—one of my people received a Vision. It is said that Many Colored Crow called to him, took him to fly among the golden clouds of the Spirit World. In the Vision, Many Colored Crow gave this person directions about how to build the Mask.

''For many generations, the Mask helped people . . . and sometimes it hindered them. Some, those who were strong enough, used the Mask to accomplish great things. Others, those too weak to deal with the Power, became evil and were destroyed. Finally, one man, seeing the pain he had caused, took the Mask and hid it on a mountain. From that time onward, no one went near that mountain.

''At the same time this was happening, a new people, the Flat Pipe, came into our valleys. At first we fought. Then a peace was made, and we lived side by side, often sharing territories. Together, we have prospered. Trade increased, and the ancestors were happy.

''Finally, the one of whom we have spoken here, retrieved the Mask. It had been lost for a long time. Many had forgotten the Mask and its Power. The situation was discussed among those who remembered, but a decision was reached to do nothing. It was thought that perhaps the Flat Pipes could use the Mask in a way we never did.

''I think now that it was a mistake. As long as the Mask is worn by men, it will cause discord and trouble. It has grown, become too Powerful. I believe it is not a thing for human beings anymore.''

''Burn it,'' Old Slate muttered.

People nodded, a resolve growing.

''I would counsel my friends, the Shining Bird Clan, not to burn the Mask.'' Tall Man looked about impassively.

Open stares were turned his way.

''What then?'' Old Slate demanded. ''Star Shell tells us that the clans are thinking about going to war. I believe Star Shell when she says that some would claim the Mask for their own. Is that what we want? I ask the Elder of the High Heads, why shouldn't we burn the Mask and be done with it?''

Tall Man looked up and spread his short arms. "I don't think that would be wise. Just like burning the corpse frees the soul of the dead, so would burning the Mask free its Power. Do you want that kind of Power drifting around you like smoke? The ghosts of the ancestors would be helpless to prevent any retribution by Many Colored Crow. If you—"

"Then what do we do?" Fat Lips interrupted rudely. "We have this thing here, among us. And worse, we now have a couple of angry ghosts within the clan grounds. We've had a tomb defiled. You did this to us! You High Heads, you made the Mask in the first place!"

"Enough!" Old Slate snapped. She took a deep breath. "Forgive my cousin, Elder of the High Heads. We are all scared, shocked by what has happened to us."

The Magician smiled beneficently, ignoring Fat Lips' sour expression. "I understand. But allow me to finish. The Mask must be removed from the Moonshell valley. After that, things here will settle down. Angry passions will cool and people will be glad to blame the recent troubles on the Mask instead of on the Shining Bird Clan."

"Who would take the Mask away?" Old Slate asked.

Star Shell raised her head, a dull feeling in her breast. "I will take the responsibility. My husband brought it here. His wife will take it away."

Mutters of assent, along with a nodding of heads, followed.

Old Slate pursed her thin lips. "And where will you take it? To StarSky? To your father? StarSky is strong enough without your father wearing the Mask. He doesn't need its Power to add to StarSky's authority. Or would you hide the Mask someplace? If it was found once, it can be found again."

Tall Man raised a hand. "If the good Shining Bird Clan would hear my words again, I will tell you that I know of a place where the Mask can be placed."

"Where?" demanded Fat Lips. "In a High Head clan house? Is that your plan? Do you want the High Heads to grow in Power?"

Suspicious eyes turned toward Tall Man.

"I have no such desire. The Mask—"

"You want it back!" Fat Lips crossed his arms defiantly. "That's it, isn't it, Magician? Maybe it happened like this.

Maybe the Mask *was* hidden. And now that it has been found; you see an opportunity to possess it yourself.''

Fat Lips nodded as he glanced around. ''I've heard of you, Magician. Curious, isn't it, that a man known for poisons, seductions, and trickery would come to us at just this time. The Mask would give you a great deal of Power. With it, you could become the leader of the High Heads. That's what you're after, isn't it?''

Tall Man remained nonplused. ''Hardly. I—''

''I say no!'' Fat Lips shook his head. ''I say we keep it here, or destroy it. If we can't use it, no one else should.''

Tall Man bowed slightly. ''Were I ignorant of my people's past, I myself might think in those terms, gracious Fat Lips. However, let me tell you something about the High Heads that you may not know. When your people moved down out of the forests and into the river valleys, the High Heads were already here. The question might be asked, how did you manage to drive us out of our lands? Not because of your prowess as warriors, for we won most of the wars we fought against you.''

''But not all,'' Fat Lips growled.

''No, not all.'' Tall Man steepled his hands. ''But we could have. After all, we outnumbered you. It might be said that your access to Spirit Power was greater than ours; but if that were the case, why have you adopted so many of our rituals? Learned our Healing Songs, and studied our knowledge of the sun, moon, and stars?''

Fat Lips stamped an angry foot. ''He's stalling, seeking to distract us.''

''Let him finish!'' Old Slate clapped her hands to accent her point.

Tall Man studied Fat Lips with pensive eyes. ''The point is this: At the time your people moved into these lands, the High Heads were warring and squabbling with each other over the Mask. Had we not been raiding each other, stealing back and forth, and accusing each other of every kind of misdeed, we might have paid more attention to the Flat Pipe farms that were cropping up in our territories.''

Tall Man held up a hand. ''Hear me out. I do not wish to have those days back. I would not see the clan territories become

High Head territories again. We are greater together than we were apart. My relatives are half High Head, half Flat Pipe. Should I seek to harm my own relatives? These days we are so mixed that it is difficult to tell what is separate.

"I would see us all avoid the conflict and hatred that developed the last time the Mask was loose among people. Think about it. The lust for the Power of the Mask would tear our societies apart. Would you see the Holy Road closed because of warfare? Would you see the Traders stop coming, stop bringing big shells from the south? Stop bringing obsidian from the far west? Yaupon? Bear teeth? Caribou hide from the north?"

"That is worth considering," Old Slate muttered as if to herself. "We must use sacred flint from the StarSky quarries when we cut ourselves for the solstice rituals. The pipe-makers must have stone from the north bank of the Serpent River. Everything we make depends on something coming from another place."

"Indeed, wise Old Slate, that is the case," Tall Man replied. "And with whom would you war? Fighting with the Blue Duck Clan means that you would be fighting against relatives, wouldn't it? How many of you have daughters or granddaughters who have married into Blue Duck? How many of your sons are married to women from the Goosefoot Clan?"

Old Slate nodded sadly. "My oldest daughter is married to a Blue Duck man."

Fat Lips shook his head stubbornly. "We only have your word that things would go that far."

"And you have mine," Star Shell added, finally forcing herself to stand up. "This whole discussion is becoming silly. If you need proof that the Mask creates division and misery—" she thrust out her arm, pointing "—look around you! Then go look at my husband's body swinging from that rope in the clan house."

She stared at the silent people. "Last night, at the Blue Duck clan house, Robin would have *killed* me! Do you understand? He would have killed me only because I was my husband's wife! Messages of war are being carried from clan house to clan house, stirring up anger and resentment against the Shining Bird Clan. People are angry—angry enough to kill!"

She stepped out so that the fire illuminated her face and glanced up at the bark roof, choosing her words with care. "Fear is blowing across the clan territories like the winter wind. Why? Because of the Mask. With it, my husband killed good men. He did it by looking at them. Not by driving a dart through someone, but with just *a look*."

Star Shell closed her eyes for a moment, steadying herself. "We may be too late as it is. Tall Man has had Visions ... Visions granted by First Man. Many Colored Crow knows we will try to defeat the Mask. He is already acting to ensure that it remains with us."

"But why?" Old Slate asked. "That is the one thing I can't understand. Many Colored Crow is our *friend*! Why would he have such a thing built?"

"May I answer?" Tall Man asked.

Old Slate gave a sweep of her arm, urging him to do so.

Tall Man cleared his throat. "In the beginning, the Creator made two brothers. One, First Man; the second, Many Colored Crow. They fought for their visions of what the world should be. First Man won. That doesn't keep Many Colored Crow from trying to see his vision finally triumph."

At the expressions generated by his words, Tall Man responded, "Many Colored Crow isn't evil. I'm not trying to say that. He was born to balance First Man. If you think of the world as a fire, you would readily understand that unless the fire were stirred every once in a while, the embers would burn out."

"People are not fires," Fat Lips said condescendingly.

"Aren't they?" Tall Man countered. "My people, the High Heads, had just about burned out. We were losing our heat. It was at that time that Many Colored Crow's Mask was made. Within a lifetime, we were smoldering again. When the Flat Pipe peoples added new fuel to an old flame, we began to burn brightly. A people, like a fire, must be stirred up. You see, when a fire is stirred, the shadow is mixed with the light."

"That doesn't make the Mask sound so bad," Old Slate observed.

"It does if you consider that given too much wood, the fire will grow out of control and burn your house down," Tall Man riposted. "Remember the Hero Twins. First Man and Many Colored Crow are constantly struggling, balancing each other. The Mask of Many Colored Crow has done what it was supposed to do for our people. Now the time has come to remove it."

"That *will* anger Many Colored Crow," Old Slate reminded.

"Yes, but it will please First Man," the High Head dwarf insisted. "And if you will wait to make a final decision, I can offer you a way out of this dilemma."

"How?" Fat Lips demanded. "We will anger one side of the Spirit World or the other, no matter what we do."

"That might be true," Tall Man said with a sad smile. "However, before the ghosts of my ancestors, I give you my word that I will provide you with a way out by tomorrow night."

Old Slate licked her lips and glanced around. Everyone was nervous, unsure, afraid. "What do we do in the meantime?"

The Magician clasped his hands. "For now, go to your beds. The angry ghosts of your cousin and his grandfather are contained for the night. Still, I would place a sprig of cedar at the doorways of your sleeping quarters, and do not go outside—just in case." A wry smile bent his lips. "And, believe me, I have a great deal of experience with angry ghosts.

"Tomorrow, first thing. Set fire to the clan house. Surround it with every person you can find. Have everyone wave cedar branches at the flames from first light until dark. Try to keep the guardian posts from burning. Then, after dark tomorrow night, you will see how the problem of the Mask can be solved without angering either side of the Spirit World."

"By tomorrow night?" Old Slate repeated dubiously. "Why not now?"

Tall Man's oddly shaped head bowed over his chest. "Because the first and most important worry is those ghosts over in the clan house. The Mask must come second." He glanced up, taking the measure of each face. "I know of what I speak, especially when it comes to vengeful ghosts. I can only offer my advice. Will you take it?"

Murmurs of assent, enough to win the vote, made the rounds of anxious clanspeople.

"Just until tomorrow night?" Old Slate asked.

"I promise," the Magician said solemnly.

Old Slate sighed wearily. "All right, Elder of the High Heads. We will follow your advice." To the people, Old Slate said,

"Let's go and try to sleep. Do as the Elder says; place cedar in the doorways, and perhaps over the beds, too. And please, stay inside tonight."

From the frightened looks that Star Shell saw, there would be no disobedience. People stood and walked hurriedly toward the doorway.

Old Slate stopped before Tall Man. "Thank you, Elder, for your kind advice." Her eyes glinted. "However, I must say that I, too, find it curious that you would arrive at just this time."

"Power sent me, wise Old Slate. To tell the truth, I would rather have stayed next to a warm fire in my own clan house."

Old Slate managed a faint smile, and left. Only Fat Lips hesitated, a look of distrust in his eyes. Then he too ducked out into the night.

Tall Man reached up to pat Star Shell on the arm. "Come, you and I must take a walk. We have things to discuss."

Star Shell gave him a worried look, then glanced at Silver Water.

"Bring your daughter. She's coming with us."

"What? Why? What if . . . if *his* ghost has managed to—"

"Shh!" The Magician glanced back and forth furtively as he led Star Shell and Silver Water out into the frigid night. The sky was frosted with stars. The clan grounds could be seen clearly in the snow.

Tall Man pointed to the ominous, dark clan house. "His ghost is safely contained. But we must hurry. I must get the Mask and we must be gone from this place!"

"Gone?" Star Shell tensed.

Silver Water looked up, her face panicked. "Mama? What?"

"Gone," the Magician insisted. "And by tomorrow night, we'll be far north of here."

"But you said—"

"I said I'd give them a way out. Keep Many Colored Crow's wrath from falling on the Shining Bird Clan. They'll understand by tomorrow night. By the night after that, so will Robin, the Blue Duck, and any other clan with desires to obtain the Mask." He smiled ironically. "I'm a Magician . . . and I'm about to make the Mask disappear. However, the fact remains that we must be far from here when they make that discovery.''

"But I don't understand!"

Tall Man paused in the night, looking at her with sober eyes. "Then you had better start to. I have made my bargain with Power. I mean to do everything within my ability to save you and Silver Water. A great many people will do anything to get the Mask. They will kill you, your daughter, or me for it. They will stop at nothing, Star Shell.''

Silver Water walks beside her mother on the icy path. The earth-works cast long, cold shadows that eat at her skin and make her shiver. Tall Man is taking them away, far away.

Silver Water swallows hard. A big black bubble is swelling up in her throat, choking her. She feels sick. What will Little Fern do without her? Fern's father hurts his daughter . . . worse, even, than Silver Water's father used to hurt her. Fern and Silver Water have always held each other when things got really bad. They've sneaked out of their blankets and run to the other's lineage house, where they whispered through the night. Who will hold Fern now? Will she be all alone?

Silver Water blinks back her tears and looks around. Starlit eyes study her. Tens of tens of them. They stare from holes in the ground, holes in the rocks—holes in the world.

Tall Man sees them, too. Silver Water can tell. He stares right at them.

Silver Water clutches her mother's hand so hard that her own fingers ache. Her heart is pounding. She struggles to put each of her moccasins on the least shiny spots, to avoid the ice in the path, and listens to the sounds of night.

The worst sound comes from the darkness; it breathes, in and out, huge shuddering gasps like the lungs of a dying Spirit creature. They must be walking inside the creature, through the middle of its chest. Silver Water's eyes widen. If she looks hard, she can see the blacker-than-black outline of the creature's body; it lies all around her. In the manner of a mother grouse protecting its young, its vast wings snug down over Sun Mounds.

Warm. Clear as a quartz crystal, but there. The stars gleam fuzzily through dim feathers.

Softly, her mother says, "I can feel them, Tall Man."

"Who?"

"The ghosts who roam these grounds. They're saying goodbye. It's almost as though I can see them watching us."

"Oh, yes, they are. Most of them are hiding tonight, tucked away in any hollow they can find. They're more frightened than we are."

"No one could be more frightened than I am."

Silver Water can taste her mother's words on the back of her tongue—cold and bitter—as if she's eaten poison seeds that have been buried from the beginning of time.

Up ahead, two society houses sit side by side, and she wonders what will happen when they reach the enormous black beak that hangs down between the houses, the tip touching the ground. The path leads directly to it. Smoke rises from the houses' smoke holes, and the beak wavers—almost as though it floats on that thin, blue-gray layer.

Silver Water glances at her mother, then at Tall Man. Neither of them seems to see it.

Slithery waves of heat radiate from its faint shadows. She can feel them tingling on her arms and face. The worst thing would be if the beak opens and tears them to pieces. She flinches, wishing she could take back the thought and stuff it into the corners of her soul, where she couldn't see it. But then it would just peek out at her—like the tens of tens of starlit eyes.

As they get closer, the black beak parts, and Silver Water tips her chin up to look down the Spirit creature's throat.

All she sees is smoke, spiraling away into nothingness, but she can feel the creature's warm breath. It smells like hickory and maple.

"I have friends here, Tall Man," her mother says. "Will I ever come back?"

"I cannot answer that. Not yet. Not until we see which way Power wants to take us."

Silver Water thinks about that. About Power.

She turns to look over her shoulder at the forbidden clan house. She is being dragged along by her mother, and she cranes her neck. Her feet slip and slide on the ice, but her mother doesn't seem to notice. A pale green glow oozes from the pores of the roof, and she thinks she sees her father's hands reaching out of the green, clawing at the freedom beyond the imprisoning thatch. . . . Power took her father. It took him and blew him around just like a dandelion seed in a cyclone.

Silver Water bites her lip and turns to concentrate on the pack that rides Tall Man's hunched back. The Mask is whispering in the dwarf's ear, threatening, laughing, sobbing . . .

She doesn't know if the dwarf hears, but she does. The waves of despair and anger are enough to make Silver Water lag as far behind as she can. The sadness is the worst. It stalks about with the stealth of Wolf on a blood trail, hunting, hunting desperately for someone, anyone, who will listen.

She wants to listen. But she is too afraid.

Lifting a hand, she tucks a finger into her mouth and quietly sucks on it while she watches the toes of her moccasins appear and disappear.

Somewhere deep down in her soul, she hears her father crying. Crying and crying, as if he can't get enough air.

Eleven

Four Kills could feel the excitement. People stood about the fires in knots, their frosty breaths spinning in the cold air as they discussed the day's events and speculated on what they meant for the future. Overhead, stars shimmered and danced on a soot-black sky. Firelight wavered in golden patterns on thatched house walls to accent the shaggy, scalloped effect of the grass bundles lashed to the frames.

He sensed a gravity beneath the facade of excitement. Awed looks kept being cast in the direction of the Clan Elders. The four old men sat illuminated by the fire that had been built in front of Grandmother's house. Grandmother and Blue Jar sat to either side of the Elders, nodding occasionally as something was said. From Grandmother's relaxed posture, she was clearly oblivious to the unease.

Four Kills shook himself. *Trouble is waiting somewhere in the shadows. Someone will get hurt before this is over.* Images of the Dream kept replaying in his memory. Otter's dead body continued to swirl in the foam-topped green water. His brother's face, so familiar, mocked him with its agony.

Don't do this, Otter. Don't go.

Four Kills placed a hand to his stomach, as if the action would still the churning. Perhaps if he hadn't married Red Moccasins? Would that have made a difference? Guilt wedged into his soul with the sure chill of a polished ax head. He'd felt Otter's loss; it was pervasive, as deep and wounding as it would have been for him.

We share too much, brother. In finding my happiness, I have cursed you.

Had Red Moccasins found Otter? What would come of that meeting? Could she make a peace? Or would she surrender to him for one last time?

The problem with loving two people that you knew so intimately was that you couldn't condemn either of them.

Maybe we're like the Hero Twins. We both want the same woman. Unlike the Hero Twins, however, Four Kills and Otter would never go to war with each other.

To keep his mind from images of Red Moccasins and Otter—and of what they might be doing together out in the night—Four Kills studied Grandmother's house through slitted eyes. The Contrary sat within, locked away, doing whatever it was that Contraries did when alone.

What was it like? How did a man who did everything backward feel? Or even think? Did he have to concentrate all the time, always on guard against making a slip and acting like a real person? Or did the touch of Power simply alter him, turn him into something not quite human? In the plaza earlier, Black Skull had reacted as though the latter were the case. The warrior's expression had been the same as if he'd been ordered to travel with a water moccasin for a companion.

Even as he thought about it, Black Skull emerged out of the night and entered the clan house. He had to stoop to get his huge shoulders through the doorway. Four Kills could believe he was the most dangerous man alive. *I wouldn't want to face him.*

Red Moccasins appeared at Four Kills' elbow, a hollow longing in her eyes. She slipped an arm around his waist, clutching to him the way she would to a log in floodwaters.

"It's all right," Four Kills said gently. "He isn't ready to talk to you. Not yet. The wound is too fresh."

In the shadowed firelight, she closed her eyes, her head bowed as the silken black hair spilled forward. Even in her pain, her beauty stunned him. For a moment, Four Kills had to remind himself that she had chosen him, not Otter. This magnificent woman was his wife . . . his alone.

And at the thought, regret grew again.

She shook her head. "He's . . . Oh, Four Kills, I knew it would happen."

"He loves you."

She took a deep breath and nodded.

"And you still love him," Four Kills added, shifting his gaze to the fire, where people crowded around with their bowls. The feasting had begun, celebrating the arrival of the Clan Elders and Green Spider. Despite the misgivings that gnawed at his soul, he would force himself to be happy. And at what price? Otter, the Black Skull, and Green Spider would leave in the morning, bearing themselves off into the unknown. And if they never returned . . .

"He's hurt, Four Kills. I didn't know how much until now. He asked me if I— I would have gone with him. No, that's not right. I wanted to. I *wanted* to have him . . . one last time."

Four Kills steeled himself, forcing calm into his voice. "I know. It's all right. He's my brother. Take my blanket, and the two of you can—"

"No." She looked up at him, her dark eyes gleaming. "He pushed me away. He said that you would understand if we did. And that's why he couldn't . . . maybe because he loves you so much."

And now I love him even more.

Four Kills hugged her tightly to him, closing his eyes as he savored the feeling of her body pressed against his. "He'll survive this. We all will. He needs time. So do we."

Despite himself, Four Kills looked back at Grandmother's house. There, inside, Green Spider waited with Black Skull as his guard. For what? When would the Contrary come out to feast? After all, this was his doing.

Grandmother had evacuated the house—the ultimate honor to visiting guests. She'd moved herself into Blue Jar's house, giving her dwelling and possessions over to the use of the Clan Elders, their warriors, and the Contrary.

For long moments, Four Kills studied the house in the firelight. Everything had gone wrong, like the earth shifting beneath his feet. Did the answer lie there, with Green Spider? Had the Contrary seen something in his Vision? Of all the Traders, why had he come after Otter?

"What is it?" Red Moccasins watched him soberly.

"Nothing. I . . ." He hugged her one last time. "Are you all right? Can you spare me for a while?"

She gave him that probing look. "Leave Otter alone. He doesn't need any more complications."

"I'm not going after Otter. Get yourself a bowl. The food's hot and the night's cold. Better enjoy the stew while it lasts. I'll be back." He kissed her on the head and bent down to retrieve one of the wooden bowls.

"Where are you going?"

"To take Green Spider a bowl of stew. You know, just being hospitable."

"You mean you don't think he's ever coming out? To get his own food?"

"I don't know, but this way, he will understand that we care."

"Four Kills, don't you dare do anything that—"

"Shhh! Trust me." *Because I'm going to find out what Green Spider knows if it gets my neck broken!*

He dipped a helping from one of the boiling pots and threaded his way through the clusters of people until he reached the doorway of the clan house. Grandmother sat cocooned in layers of blanket as she talked to the four Clan Elders. Four Kills could feel her anxious gaze.

"May I help?" Old Man Sun had risen to his feet, the effort accompanied by the muffled crackling of bones and joints.

"I brought food for Green Spider. A plate of stew. Since his arrival, I haven't seen him eat anything. It wouldn't do for him to think that the White Shell Clan was miserly."

Old Man Sun smiled graciously. "Your thoughtfulness is most welcome, son of Blue Jar. I am sure that Green Spider will appreciate your gesture of hospitality and friendship. I will take the bowl in to him with your warm wishes for his comfort."

"Thank you for your kindness, Elder; but I wouldn't want you to have to interrupt your conversation with—"

"Four Kills," Grandmother called in her warning voice. "The Clan Elder knows what's best. Perhaps the Contrary doesn't wish to be disturbed by stripling boys."

Old Man Sun's smiling expression sharpened. "Ah, I understand, young Four Kills. You wish to extend your courtesy in person. But, please, allow me to accompany you. It would be, well, better if I helped you to present your compliments to Green Spider."

Grandmother's voice had taken on an edge. "Four Kills, take that bowl right back where you—"

Old Man Sun's raised hand cut her off. "Green Spider will be most pleased to see him, I'm sure."

As the wizened Elder ducked through the hanging, Four Kills caught Grandmother's scathing glare. Before she could say more, Old Man Blood tactfully distracted her—at least for the moment—with a question about the designs woven into her blanket.

Four Kills ducked inside, and almost ducked right back out. His heart rose to thump in his throat.

Green Spider knelt in the dim red glow of the fire's burned-out coals, naked. His clothes lay on the floor beside him, and in front of him he had a bowl of white paint. He had smeared his body with black charcoal and painted long white lines down his arms and legs, paying particular attention to the disconnected bones in his fingers and toes. At this moment, he was patiently drawing lines across his narrow chest, atop the bars of ribs. He looked just like a skeleton risen from a moldering tomb. A skeleton without a head, since he hadn't started painting his face yet.

"What . . . what's he doing?" Four Kills asked Black Skull,

who stood stoically by the door, a depressed expression on his ugly face.

The warrior's mouth puckered. "The fool says he's painting himself inside-out."

"What for?"

"How do I know? He's demented."

"Didn't you ask him?"

"Certainly I asked. He said that flesh was a snare and that he had to get rid of it before he stepped into it and it caught him. He said that living inside his bones was like living inside 'the rope.' Does that make sense to you? Of course not. It doesn't make sense to anyone with a human brain."

Four Kills swallowed convulsively.

"Come," Old Man Sun said with a smile.

The Clan Elder settled himself carefully on one of the benches to the Contrary's right. He leaned forward, his thin old arms bracing himself like struts. He studied the Contrary for a moment, his ancient eyes—set deep in the mass of wrinkles—gleaming with excitement.

Four Kills knelt to one side, the bowl balanced in his fingers. He could feel the heat of the stew. He waited awkwardly, wondering if Green Spider wouldn't at least look at him, acknowledge his presence.

The Contrary stared thoughtfully at the white paint on his fingertip, and then down at his crotch. "Now that's interesting." He glanced up quizzically. "What happens to the bone? I mean, where does it go?"

"What bone?" Black Skull asked.

"The one in my penis. What do you think? Should I paint it, too?"

"Spare me," the warrior whispered as he rolled his eyes at the roof.

"Oh, I couldn't," Green Spider said seriously as he ran a line of white down his male part. "I can't even spare myself."

"Green Spider?" Old Man Sun finally said. "The worthless being before you is Four Kills, son of Blue Jar of the White Shell Clan. As a measure of his disrespect, he brings you this foul-tasting mess in the hopes that you will starve to death."

Four Kills swiveled his head to gape and stare at the Elder.

Horror shot across his panicked nerves. "No! Wait! What are you *saying*? That's not why—"

Old Man Sun waved him down with a fragile hand. "It really is rude of Four Kills to insult you with such unconcern, don't you think, Green Spider?"

To Four Kills' wretched astonishment, Green Spider agreed: "Four Kills is a most vile man. He can take that disgusting stuff and throw it into the river. Let him poison the fish instead of me. May all of his ancestors spit on his manhood, and all of his sister's children be born blind and without arms and legs."

Old Man Sun turned amused eyes on the stunned Four Kills. "Green Spider is delighted. Please hand him the bowl of stew. Go ahead. What's this? You snake-bit, boy? Or just froze from the neck down?"

Fighting the tremble that betrayed his hands, Four Kills handed the bowl over to the living skeleton, fully expecting Green Spider to dash it against the walls. Instead, the Contrary finished painting his last rib line, cleaned his fingers on the dirt floor, and sniffed the steam with a heavenly expression. He took the bowl and lifted the rim to his lips, drinking deeply, his throat working. When he'd drained the liquid, he plucked out pieces of fish meat, hickory nuts, and sunflowers with his fingers before popping them into his mouth.

Green Spider summoned a satisfied belch from deep in his gut and sighed contentedly. "I wouldn't feed vomit like that to my enemy's dog."

A crushing weight flattened Four Kills' soul. What now? Just get up and leave? Or was it better to simply bolt through the door and go drown himself in the river?

Before he could summon the courage to act, Green Spider had turned those weirdly unfocused eyes on him, saying, "You're a thief and a coward, Four Kills. I don't have time to waste on your silly problems."

Any response lay stillborn in Four Kills' chest.

"What did you wish to ask Green Spider?" Old Man Sun asked in a kindly voice. "You must remember, he's a Contrary. The more important the occasion, the more backward he behaves."

"Not backward, young Sun . . . forward . . . always forward," Green Spider insisted.

"Speak to him, Four Kills," Old Man Sun prompted. "Talk the way you normally would. The Contrary will answer in his own way—just the opposite of what he means."

Four Kills—who had slain four enemies in battle—now found that his courage had fled. He stared into the Contrary's dizzy gaze and suffered the sensation of his soul come adrift in muddy brown floodwaters.

"Why did you want to see Green Spider?" Old Man Sun asked with that warm, fatherly tone.

"My Dream," Four Kills managed. "I saw . . . Otter . . . drowned. Is that right, Green Spider? Will he die?"

"No one ever dies, do they?" Green Spider smiled wistfully. "I died. As you can see, it's made a mess of me."

Four Kills didn't experience any surge of relief.

Green Spider's eyes focused for a moment. "Do you fear death, warrior?"

"I fear for Otter's soul."

"His fate will be dictated by Power—and his actions. Not yours."

Four Kills wet his lips. "Of all the Traders, why did you choose him?"

"I chose nothing. Power chose everything. I am the master of nothing . . . and everything." The eyes lost focus again. "Backward is forward. Many Colored Crow, blacker than black, spirals in the golden light. He who runs happily toward danger is he who is the most frightened. Terror brings peace; and happiness is always filled with sorrow."

Four Kills anxiously fingered his feather-wrapped blanket— a wedding gift made of fine down spun around cordage. Now he would have readily given it up to be free of the sense of futility that possessed him.

"You are blinded by your sight," Green Spider continued. "Deafened by your ears. Calloused by your heart." His expression went blank. "By leaving, Otter will find himself at home."

"But will he survive this journey? I've Dreamed of his body swirling in the water."

"To gain everything, you must lose everything. Is Otter different than the rest of us? Than First Man and Many Colored Crow?"

"I don't understand."

Green Spider seemed to stiffen, his glassy vision locked on some invisible scene. He cried, *"Born of ice . . . the mother's womb!"*

Four Kills shot a desperate look at Old Man Sun. "What's he saying?"

Old Man Sun's face glowed rapturously.

"Born of Sun, of Sun the same."

Four Kills squirmed, his fingers locked tight in his thick blanket as he glanced back and forth between the three men.

"One must live, and one must die."

Sweat had begun to bead on Four Kills' face, and a cold, clammy feeling traced along his abdomen. "Please, I just want to know what you see . . . what's going to happen to Otter. He's going to die, isn't he? Isn't that what you're trying to tell me?"

Green Spider said nothing and sat motionless as his eyes swam out of focus.

"Ask what you will of me. I—I'll do anything you wish!" Four Kills insisted.

Green Spider remained silent. He dipped his finger into the bowl of white paint again and turned his attention to painting rib bones on his shirt, which lay spread on the floor at his side. Black Skull sneered at the sight.

"That is all," Old Man Sun stated softly as he rose to his feet. "He will say no more."

"But it wasn't an answer!"

Old Man Sun gestured for Four Kills to rise. "He told you everything."

"He spoke in riddles!" Four Kills protested as he got to his feet.

"I warned you," Black Skull reminded. "He's an idiot."

"It only seems that way to you." Old Man Sun wobbled toward the door. "He sees this world, this part of Creation, as illusion. You are lucky that he told you as much as he did."

Twelve

The Black Skull hadn't slept well after the feast. At the first graying of dawn, he'd slipped out of the White Shell house. On the seclusion of the beach, he'd practiced with his war club, swinging it while he darted back and forth. After having worked up a fine sweat, he'd stripped and charged into the river.

He swam out into the current, challenged by the gurgling suck of the water. The deep cold leached into his flesh as he flexed and dove into the darkness. With water bubbling in his ears, he fought his way down.

I should feel fear. But he didn't. Instead, the river's Spirit surged against him with its probing force, massaging his hot muscles with cold fingers. His ears began to ache.

Black Skull jackknifed and shot up. He broke the surface, puffing for breath as gooseflesh rose on his scarred hide. He flipped water from his face and paddled against the current. Sticks and bits of flotsam pattered off his skin. Overhead, the sky had gone rosy with dawn.

Floating a dart's cast from the shore, he spotted the Trader, a gigantic pack on his back as he picked his way down the path in the soft light.

Black Skull flipped and dove. Strong strokes drove him down until he touched bottom. Despite the pain in his ears, he could hear the pulse of the river, the sound of it like hollow echoes. He groped in darkness, the mud soft under his prying fingers. Were there no shellfish here? The chill from the cold water had begun to sap his strength. Shivers racked him. Unable to find more than weeds, he shot to the surface and sucked in a new breath.

The Trader had almost reached the drying racks, so Black Skull summoned all of his strength and raced toward the shore in a flurry of powerful strokes. By the time the Trader reached his canoe, Black Skull's feet dragged bottom. He emerged from the water—unable to stop his violent shivering, panting from the effort of the swim.

Under the Trader's watchful gaze, Black Skull began wiping water from his numb body. The air burned the cold in deeper.

"The currents out there are dangerous," the Trader told him evenly. "I'd have an older brother today if he hadn't dived to the bottom looking for freshwater mussels and pearls."

"I didn't find him down there." Black Skull shook himself and walked to his blanket, cape, and war shirt. With the blanket, he dried himself, then pulled his shirt on. He belted his waist and hung his atlatl there. Against the bitter chill, he swirled his turkey-feather cape over his shoulders.

The Trader had deposited his pack and was watching him, his head cocked.

Black Skull picked up his war club and walked over to the Trader. He paused, letting his gaze scan the seething waters. He took Otter's measure, aware that the handsome young man didn't spend as much time staring as most, wondering at Black Skull's scars, or giving him that gushy look of adoration and embarrassed enthusiasm at being in his presence.

"So, Trader, we'll go upriver together, you, me, and the fool."

"So it would seem, warrior. You didn't look very happy about it yesterday."

Black Skull made the growling sound he used to warn people, then tilted his broken face to give it the most frightening angle. "My duty should be here, with my people. Not sailing off into strange lands to battle with wild peoples. I have lived, fought, and killed to keep *this* land safe. This land here, where our ancestors dwell. Not some far-off place."

Otter didn't react to his fierce visage. Instead, a faint smile traced his lips, a twinkle lit his eye. "They're not wild up there, Black Skull. We'll travel up to the Serpent River, then up to the Moonshell, which will take us to the Holy Road. From there, we'll travel to StarSky City. After that, I don't know the way. But we'll go a lot farther north. They aren't wild, warrior. Like the Alligator Clans to the south, the Serpent peoples think of us as being half animal. Savage."

Black Skull fingered the use-polished hilt on his war club. "I can't believe such a thing. Their Traders come to us. They marvel, Otter. I've seen the wonder in their eyes when they visit the City of the Dead. They say they'd never expected to find such a place.''

''You are quite correct, Black Skull.'' Otter propped a foot on one of the smaller canoes, leaning forward and lacing his fingers. ''And when you see some of their incredible clan grounds, and meet their Elders, you will react in the same way. Who knows? If we time it correctly, you might be able to stand atop the Temple of the Sun and watch the stars on the solstice.''

''What of their warriors?''

Otter shrugged. ''They have some very good ones. The Khota once squabbled with the Six Flutes, one of the Serpent Clans. When the Khota came paddling up to raid, the Six Flutes' warriors sent the Khota right back downriver—with about half as many paddlers, I might add.''

''Then these warriors have Power?''

''It's not so much that they have Power. It's that . . . well, there're a lot of them. Most of the men are warriors as well as farmers. They work as a practiced team in a fight. The people come together for the ceremonials, like we do. Part of that time is dedicated to war training. The rest is for games, feasts, prayers and offerings, but they *do* practice war. The War Societies ensure that.''

''Perhaps we should do it that way.''

''We could never make it work. They have powerful societies that cross clan boundaries. Think of it like a piece of cloth. The clans might be thought of as the warp and the societies the weft. Together, they hold the Serpent Clans together. If the leader of a society orders something, the people within that society do what they are told. Here, if a clan leader asks something, the people talk about it for a while, then half of them do it and the other half don't.''

''Who makes the Serpent Clans take orders?'' Black Skull asked.

''Men like you. Men initiated into the society and who make sure that its rules are followed.'' The Trader paused thoughtfully. ''In the case of the Warrior Society in the Moonshell valley, it's a man by the name of Robin. I can't remember which clan he belongs to, but he's been initiated, tested, and proven. Through courage and dedication, he's been given the leadership of that society. Except in unusual circumstances, any warrior will follow his orders—no matter what clan he belongs to.''

Black Skull nodded, looking out over the river. "A lot could be said for such a way of doing things."

"I thought you called them wild."

"They probably are." Black Skull studied the Trader from the corner of his eye. "You might be telling me this to trick me. You, and the fool."

"And why would I do that?"

"Traders are born to trickery."

"And you, warrior?"

"I was born to discipline and order."

Otter paused for a moment. "You don't like Green Spider, do you?"

"I can't believe Power would work this way. I don't approve of it. I didn't approve of coming here. We passed four war canoes on the river. If they'd wanted to hurt the Elders, I couldn't have stopped them. Now I'm expected to leave here—and who will guard the Elders on their way back to the City of the Dead?"

"Four Kills and the White Shell Clan."

"Four Kills may have fought bravely once, but he doesn't have my skill. Nothing must happen to the Clan Elders. It would reflect on me."

Otter frowned slightly. "Warrior, I don't know what to tell you. It seems that Green Spider—and his Vision—have changed our lives. As of yesterday, your duty lies with the Contrary."

"And yours, Trader?"

"I'm a Trader. That's what I do. This is just another form of Trade. Along with my other goods, I carry you and Green Spider."

"You make it sound easy."

Otter's facile smile grew. "A journey is never as easy as you would hope, warrior, and it is often more difficult than you ever believed it would be."

Black Skull growled to himself. "Now you sound like the fool." He paused. "What about this Vision? Do you believe it? I saw the lightning strike, found the Clan Elders as they pulled Green Spider from the burning temple. I could feel the Power . . . but was it there to enlighten Green Spider, or just to kill him? The latter would seem more likely. Unfortunately, he survived despite the Mysterious One's efforts."

Otter made a helpless gesture. "I've met Contraries before, Black Skull. I've met the Anhinga, Fell Through the Sky, and one in the Ilini territories—but I was allowed to see each of them only once. They are considered very holy. It is said that Contraries see things more clearly than other Holy Ones untouched by their truth. I know only enough to have recognized what Green Spider became."

"Oh, just wait until you sit in the same canoe with him." Black Skull shook his head. "He has become very simple. Like a child. He had no right to risk the Clan Elders."

Otter gave him a curious inspection. "Do you question the ways of Power, warrior?"

Black Skull snorted his derision. "Not in the slightest, Trader. I know what I am. Power made me that. Green Spider is different. He was becoming a great Dreamer. A Healer who could make people well. This last time, when he went to Dream the solstice, it was to seek Power to Dream the rains and see the future." Black Skull ground his poorly occluded teeth. "And look what happened to him. He came back a fool!"

"Power works in mysterious ways."

The way the Trader said it, it galled. He appeared to think that it was all right to load up, travel across the known world with a lunatic—and hope to live through it!

I'm not stuck with two *maniacs, am I?*

Black Skull pointed at the Trader with his war club. "I want you to help me keep him under control, Trader. I want this to be as orderly as we can make it. I want to get up there, find that place, and see if any Mask is floating there. If so, we'll grab it and get back here. I don't want trouble. Do you understand?"

Otter tensed but didn't break his easy stance—the insolent foot still propped on the canoe hull. "Let's get something straight, Black Skull. When we're on the river, I give the orders. When we're dealing with other people, I give the orders. When it comes to fighting, you can give them. Otherwise, when you're in my boat and among people I know how to deal with, you do as I say.''

Cool anger stirred in Black Skull's breast. Through clenched teeth, he hissed, ''Do you *know* who I am?''

''Everyone in this part of the world has heard of the Black Skull. You could kill me before I could blink. That doesn't change the fact that in my boat, you do as I say. Among people whose customs you don't know, you'll act as I tell you to. If you can't agree to that, right here, right now, we'll go see the Clan Elders and let them decide.''

Black Skull controlled the urge to slap the man alongside the head with the flat of his war club. Insolence, sheer audacious *insolence*! Black Skull's soul thrilled. The heady tranquillity of combat pumped in his blood as his mind cleared.

Otter remained calmly propped on the canoe, his fingers still laced together.

For that instant, Black Skull balanced on the edge of murder, fully aware that before the Trader could raise so much as an arm, his skull would be splintered, his body dead before it hit the ground. Nevertheless, Otter waited patiently, evincing only the slightest tightening of the eyes, a faint pressing of the lips. In the floating clarity, Black Skull could see the artery in the Trader's neck pulsing.

Discipline! Black Skull took a cautious step back and willed himself into relaxation. Drawing a deep breath, he stilled his anxious soul, quieting the deadly natures within. A warrior must maintain his control, prove his discipline. This was not the time.

''You are a very brave man, Trader.'' With a flick of the wrist, Black Skull flipped his war club up to rest on his shoulder. ''We will still see the Clan Elders about who gives orders on your boat. If they tell me I must, I will do as you say.''

Otter nodded carefully and straightened. The trembling of his legs betrayed just how terrified he had been. He walked off awkwardly, the way a man did when he couldn't trust his knees not to buckle.

I may end up having to kill him, but at least he's a man worthy of respect.

Black Skull followed Otter up the steep trail, intuition telling him the Clan Elders were going to side with the Trader.

To his chagrin, they did.

Otter glanced around as he made the last trip from the storage house. Catcher dashed back and forth in zigzags, his tail wagging furiously and uncontrollable squealing sounds uttering from his throat.

High clouds had moved up from the south to obscure the sun. The wind had risen, blowing the chill off the choppy water with enough strength to lance it through blankets and coats. Gusts moaned in the naked gray branches of the trees and whimpered along the thatch siding of the buildings. Here and there, the wind played curiously with the last of fall's leaves where they had piled in nooks and sheltered recesses.

The familiar clan grounds now elicited a sense of sorrow, as they had on previous departures. Trails had been beaten into the flattened brown grass. The clan house, with its weather-beaten thatch, looked gray and dingy in the morning light.

Around the rectangular mound, prayer offerings had been tied to the guardian posts that stuck out at an angle from the ground. The offerings danced in the cold wind, carrying their messages to the Spirit World. Pleas for him and his party. He'd seen Blue Jar placing one as he'd entered the grounds after his confrontation with Black Skull.

He hefted the coarsely woven fabric bag that held his few personal possessions: an atlatl, his flute, a bola, a platform effigy pipe, a small ceramic jar of earth taken from the burial mound, and his fire sticks. He had already packed an ax, an adze, several coils of rope, a neatly folded net, and the two dozen long darts for his atlatl. Another clay jar neatly stowed in *Wave Dancer* contained cord and fishhooks crafted from bone. The rest of the cargo consisted of the clan's Trade goods: tobacco, conch and marginella shell, bolts of fabric, several pieces of copper plate, palmetto matting, sharks' teeth, yaupon, and the other items he'd

Traded for in the south. From White Shell he had included fine fabrics for Trade, and sealed jars of goosefoot, marsh elder, sunflower seeds, and squash for supplies.

He lowered his bag as he stepped between the offering poles and knelt at the foot of the humped burial mound. Only the greatest leaders were placed in the mounds. The tomb was cut into the ground, lined with logs, and the mound of soil placed above. This way, the leader rested at the symbolic heart of the earth, there to continue to work for the people, to plead their case to the Earth Mother, and to converse with the Guardian Spirits.

Lifting his arms, he wet his lips and Sang, "Ancestors? It is I, Otter, son of Blue Jar. I ask you, please help keep my people safe. Protect them from illness and trouble. Allow no evil to enter the clan grounds. Keep my family and friends healthy, prosperous, and happy." He bowed his head. "I'm going far away. While I'm gone, I will honor your memory. I hope you will ask the Spirit World to watch over me."

From the pouch at his belt, he took a thin blade of sacred chert from the distant StarSky quarries. Pulling back his left sleeve, he exposed the bronze skin of his wrist. There, beside a parallel series of barely visible scars, he made a quick incision. Replacing the sacred chert, he squeezed his forearm until several drops of rich, red blood beaded and dripped onto the dark soil.

Was it the wind, or did he hear the ghosts rustling as they scented the blood he'd offered?

He turned then, and picked up his pack before striding purposefully toward the western break in the earthworks. The vague murmurings of the dead still haunted him—a sensing rather than the barely audible whispers he strained to hear.

He approached the gap in the earthen perimeter wall and cast one last look at the enclosure. Here he'd grown from boyhood into a man. Ever since that first farewell with Uncle, he had sensed that one day he would leave—and never come back.

Had that day come?

Catcher bounded and jumped about, knowing instinctively that the dreary days of guarding the storehouse had ended. The time had come to venture forth again—onto the river, with its smells and the lazy days of sleep, curled on the packs.

A Trader's dog didn't always live a life of drudgery.

For Otter, the sense of excitement had been building, overcoming the low point he'd suffered last night in Red Moccasins' arms. The river called, and with it, the most prestigious expedition he'd ever undertaken.

"Come on, Catcher. Let's go."

The dog snorted happily as it bounded forward. Otter placed his moccasined feet on the worn trail.

The sky didn't look promising; high layers of cloud had an ugly look, that of a storm pushing up from the ocean. The diffused light gave the river a look like tarnished and smudged silver.

Hardly an auspicious day. By tomorrow they'd be lucky if they weren't soaked to the bone and miserable.

Perhaps Green Spider had been granted his control over the weather. It would be a small bit of blessing. Wouldn't Power want its Contrary to travel in ease?

Otter shook his head. According to the stories, Power never made anything easy on people. Maybe the Spirits took some perverted joy in inflicting every conceivable misery on those it chose to do its bidding.

Like including Black Skull as part of the package.

Otter stilled a shiver, the image of the warrior's violent gaze frozen in his mind. Even now, fingers of time after the morning confrontation, he couldn't imagine how he'd met that deadly, single-minded stare. He'd looked into those black eyes, and the effect had been horrifying.

Yet, I faced him down. I'm either braver than I thought I was, or five times more the fool!

The shiver broke free and sent spasms through his muscles. Blame it on the biting wind. That was it.

I'm stuck between Black Skull, a man whose sole purpose is wielding death, and Green Spider, a Contrary who can't even give a straight answer.

Power had a rotten sense of humor.

The canoe landing swarmed with people, both White Shell and Tall Cane. He could see the Clan Elders waiting patiently in the crowd. Spotting Green Spider proved even easier. People had granted him a wide berth, clearly not caring to get too close to a man of such Power. One never knew what might rub off.

The Contrary seemed oblivious. He stood smiling benignly at the trees. The white bones painted on his black clothing looked startlingly real, down to the tiniest of toe joints on his moccasins.

Otter located the warrior. Black Skull stood to one side, his muscular arms crossed. Even from this distance, Otter could see the arrogance reflected in that erect stance. How was he going to manage such a long journey with the overbearing man?

Four Kills noted Otter's approach and broke away, followed by Blue Jar. Four Kills, too, had dressed in his best; his buckskins were tanned to a honeyed glow. He wore his hair in a knot over his forehead, pale marginella beads gleamed against his black locks. A thick blanket, interwoven with strips of soft beaver and goose down, was folded over his left arm, and a thick coil of rope filled his right.

At the foot of the slope, Otter met his brother and lifted his bag. "This is the last of it."

Four Kills forced a smile, worry bright in his eyes. "I wish you weren't going."

"Your tongue will grow tired of saying that, brother."

"But it's true." Four Kills raised his arm, extending the blanket. "I want you to take this. It will be cold up there. You're going way up into the north. It's not much, but Red Moccasins and I . . . well, you'll need this."

Otter ran his fingers over the blanket, feeling the smooth warmth of it. The workmanship was superb, the weave as thick as a man's finger. "Thank you. I can tell from looking at it that I won't spend any cold nights." *Nor will you, brother, with Red Moccasins at your side.*

"And here, this is the rope I was telling you about. I've never made a better one, or one as strong." Four Kills smiled. "Perhaps I anticipated that you would need it. It's my best work, Otter. Maybe it will save your life. Take it. Along with my love, it's the most important thing I can give you."

"I'll take good care of it, I promise." Otter studied the fine workmanship. The rope was twined out of right- and left-hand twists, all tightly wrapped. Had he been able to find the purchase, he could have hung the world with a rope this fine.

Four Kills' smile faded. "Be careful. And no, my tongue won't grow tired of telling you that." He glanced away. "I talked to Green Spider last night, or tried to. I'm not sure of what he was really trying to tell me. He . . . he was in the process of painting himself inside-out.''

Otter smiled. "He does look inside-out, doesn't he? Curious things, Contraries. What did he say?''

"Not very much, just that it will be dangerous for you.''

"The river always is.''

Blue Jar had stopped several paces behind. Now she stepped forward, extending a small leather sack, the top drawn tightly closed with a cord. "This is for you. A Trader, a friend of my brother's, saw it in a Khota village. He Traded two pipes and a sheet of mica for this. Later, when he came this way, I Traded him a hot meal and a comfortable night's sleep in return.''

Her fingers closed on Otter's as he started to open the bag. "Not now. Later. When you're on the river and have time to think. Promise me.''

"Very well, Mother.'' Otter weighted the bag in his hand. Heavy. But what would it be? And from the Khota?

His mother's eyes bored into his. "You've always been different, Otter. And perhaps because of that, I've tended to favor Four Kills.''

"Mother, I've never—''

"No. Hear me out. We both know the way of it. I just wanted you to understand that I'm so very proud of you. I only wish . . . well, that I could have had you all to myself instead of sharing you with the river.''

"You have me, Mother.'' He took her into his arms, hugging her. Her responding hug was powerful.

"I'll be careful.''

"See that you do.'' And at that, she stepped back, the shine of tears in her eyes.

Otter patted her shoulder and took a deep breath. Catcher had already threaded the maze of human legs and leaped onto the stowed packs. He stared back from *Wave Dancer,* his tail swishing as if to say, "Well, what are we waiting for?''

Walking beside his mother and brother, Otter said his farewells as family and friends crowded around. Finally, he faced Old Man North.

The wizened Elder stared up at him with eyes that gleamed

like obsidian. "May Power go with you, Otter, son of Blue Jar. You, of all of your party, have the most courage."

"Me?"

Old Man North made a gesture of assent with his gnarled hands. "Green Spider lives wrapped in his Vision, disconnected with the realities he must face in this world. The Black Skull, despite his bluster and haughty posture, is frightened of the unknown. Be kind to him, Otter. He'll need your help."

Otter glanced at the burly warrior, who still stood at the edge of the crowd. Not a trace of unease could be detected in his graven-stone expression, but the black eyes burned with a frightening intensity. One that boded violence rather than fear.

"Trust me," the Elder stated. "He can't allow anyone to see his vulnerability. Reassure him, if you can."

I'd rather try to reassure a water moccasin than Black Skull!
"I will do my best, Elder."

The old man patted him with a wrinkled hand and gave way to the others. Only as Otter turned to go did he suddenly find himself face-to-face with Red Moccasins. For that startling instant, they stared into each other's eyes. He sought to capture every detail of her smooth skin, her delicate nose, the graceful line of eyebrow. Her full lips parted slightly, showing the white gleam of even teeth. She radiated the allure that had always captivated him.

After long moments, she murmured, "Good-bye, Otter," then spun and ran away through the crowd.

A dizzy rush of memories swept him. Times they had sat together by the fire, laughing, talking. Moments of shared joy when he'd brought her special presents from faraway places. The way she smiled shyly at him at some moments, then cast sultry glances at others. Other times: walking hand in hand; canoeing out onto the river; the times they'd set fishing lines, or nets. The fall hunts when they prowled the backwaters, bolas in hand to bring down the wily ducks.

Different visions, woven from imagination and desire—those of a warm house, children, her welcoming arms. The life he might have had with her.

Gone now. Gone.

"Trader?" Black Skull's gruff voice intruded. "If you stand there much longer, your feet will sprout roots. The sooner we're off on this mad venture, the sooner we'll return.''

Otter ignored the warrior and sloshed through the cold water to stow his possessions in *Wave Dancer*. Green Spider had already seated himself in the hollow between the packs amidships and was talking animatedly to Catcher. The Contrary and the dog seemed instant best friends. Catcher had even allowed Green Spider to scratch his ears, a favor he granted only to a select few.

Otter balanced himself on one of the packs and wrung out his moccasins and leggings before seating himself in the stern. Black Skull was in the process of settling himself in the bow, carefully arranging his war darts within easy reach and so that the fletching didn't get mashed.

"Let's go!" Otter cried and raised his hand to Four Kills.

Jay Bird, Four Kills, and some others pushed the big canoe off the beach with a grating of muddy sand.

Otter backwatered, then turned the prow into the current. He drove his paddle into the sullen water, forcing the canoe forward. Black Skull, with consummate skill, caught his rhythm, and *Wave Dancer* sliced through the chop.

Black Skull was staring back at the bank. "If they don't get the Clan Elders home safe, I'll kill every one of them.''

"They'll all die!" Green Spider crowed as he rearranged himself backwards on the packs amidships. "Each of the Elders, dead . . . dead . . . dead . . . dead. Four deads.''

"Shut up!" Black Skull growled, which prompted Green Spider to chatter on like a happy finch. "Four deads, four deads, four deads, four deads!''

"Which way?" Black Skull called back over the babbling of the Contrary's voice.

"Across the river. The current isn't as strong there.''

Together they threw their weight into the task, angling across toward the far shore. Otter glanced behind him, seeing a whole flotilla of canoes launching in pursuit as the clans followed. Such an opportunity was not to be missed. Many of the boats would travel with them until dark before veering off to catch the current and race home.

Otter bent himself to the effort of driving the big canoe on its way. Catcher, perched on the packs, lifted his nose to the wind, sniffing eagerly. His thick black, white, and tan fur rippled and fluffed as he stood proudly.

"This will be a long, hard walk," Green Spider proclaimed to no one in general. "My legs are already tired!" Then he picked up his paddle, making a mess of trying to row the wrong way. In the process, he splashed water all over the warrior.

"Fool! I'm going to step back there and *break that paddle over your head*!"

"Green Spider?" Otter said nervously. "I think that Black Skull and I can do the paddling." The Contrary paddled all the harder, and Black Skull started to stand up, saying, "That's it, fool. Paddle a little harder and I'm going to shove that oar down your throat!"

Green Spider promptly laid his paddle down and sighed.

Black Skull growled an unintelligible curse under his breath. *Everything backwards.* "Should be an interesting trip," Otter muttered to himself. But when he looked back, Red Moccasins stood on the shore, her eyes shaded by a slim brown hand.

Leave it. Leave it all behind you.

Thirteen

I lie wrapped in my blankets, warm, drowsy. On the other side of the dead fire, I sense movement. Swaying . . . rocking . . . I hear feet crunching snow. From far off, across the land, the Mask cries out to me.

Its Power has been restricted, the effect like strangulation.

So . . . they've fled into the brilliant darkness.

It has begun.

Star Shell led the way as they walked through the silent winter night. Myriads of stars dusted the velvet black of the moonless sky, their gleam providing enough illumination to allow them to proceed northward along the Holy Road without tripping or losing their way. Bitter cold ate through Star Shell's blanket and moccasins. With each step, the frozen crust crunched and groaned, until the very snow seemed to share her wretched burden.

The snow had taken on a bluish glow that washed the cleared fields beyond the low embankments that marked the Holy Road. Dark patches of trees blotted the flat bottoms of the Moonshell valley. The distant hills lay like pale, sleeping monsters, furred with trees. They cast mounded silhouettes against the sooty distance of the night sky. Despite the fresh chill of the clear air stinging her nose, the odor of death remained in her nostrils.

Star Shell glanced down at her daughter. Silver Water clutched her hand tightly, and her little legs pumped to keep pace.

"Are you all right, baby?"

"Cold, Mama. And I'm scared."

From behind them, Tall Man said sympathetically, "I'm sorry, Silver Water. It will be cold tonight—and probably for a long time afterward. But you had to come with us."

The Magician plodded along on his short, bowed legs. The pack with the Mask perched like an awkward hump on his back, while the smaller bag, adorned by the wolf's head, swung under his left arm. Star Shell wondered—didn't he ever feel the exhaustion that sapped her to the bone?

"Why?" she demanded. "What does a little girl have to do with this?"

"Her father killed himself," Tall Man said gravely. "Do you think the Shining Bird Clan would ever forget? Do you want her growing up with the likes of Fat Lips constantly reminding her?" He added sadly, "How ironic. Power works across generations. Some saved . . . some condemned."

What was that haunted look in his depthless eyes? Star Shell bit back the urge to shiver and studied the little man. "Is everything ruined?"

"No, young Star Shell." She could make out his grin in the

cold darkness. "Not as long as you and Silver Water are alive and well, and we have the Mask. As long as that is the case, everything is saved."

Ill at ease, she turned her attention northward to study the trace of the Holy Road. Here the clans had built parallel earthworks to either side of the beaten track to mark the route. Over the years, the entire road would be contained within the straight banks of dirt. Someday a person would be able to walk the whole way from Sun Mounds to StarSky, bounded by the earthworks—like the walls of the tunnel through which First Man had led the people into this world.

"Where are we going, Mama?" Silver Water asked.

"Away, baby. Far away, where we will be safe. We'll go to StarSky and you'll meet my father. You'll be warm then." But could she believe that? The prickling presence of the Mask lay just behind her. How did the Magician muster the strength to carry it, to be that close to it?

She caught the faint outline of an owl as it glided silently across a fallow field to her right. The domed farmstead sat quiet, abandoned, buried under mounds of white. It would be another two, maybe three, moons before the owners returned and began the ritual of planting, caring, and watering.

Star Shell slipped on a slick spot, caught her balance, and paid more attention to the uneven track. Her feet had begun to ache from the cold. "Do you seriously believe for a moment that Robin won't guess we went north? He knows I'm StarSky. He'll immediately think I ran to my birth clan."

"I'm counting on that." Tall Man seemed unconcerned.

"That's where we're headed, isn't it?"

"What made you think that?"

"We're on the Holy Road. We have to take the Mask north to the Roaring Water. Wouldn't we go to StarSky, recruit aid, and travel on to Buckeye clan grounds and then onward?"

"In the middle of the winter? Think, Star Shell. News of your husband will travel faster than sunlight at dawn. It won't take Robin long to figure out that we're running. You don't believe that a woman, a little girl, and a short Elder could outrun warriors, do you?"

"Then why are we on the Holy Road?"

"But only for the moment, young Star Shell. We must hurry

for the time being, true, but I have a destination in mind. We'll be well into Blue Duck territory by morning. After that, we can rest for a couple of days and recover our strength at a farmstead I know of.''

''A High Head holding?'' Star Shell flinched as the owl hooted in the night. ''Robin will look there, too.''

''But will he know which farmstead to investigate?'' The Magician strode along in his rolling walk, seemingly as fresh as when they'd started from StarSky so many days ago.

Everything had happened so quickly. Finding her husband, the meeting in the Potters' Society house, fleeing into the night. Now, realizing the extent of their plight, things began to look ever more hopeless.

Why don't we just let Robin have the Mask? Then I'll take Silver Water and run away. Get as far from the Blue Duck Clan and the Moonshell valley as we can.

Star Shell concentrated on placing one foot ahead of the other as white breath twined from her nose and mouth. Frost had formed around the blanket that covered her head. The chill had eaten into her feet, and snow crusted her moccasins. She'd never be warm again.

''I'm hungry, Mama,'' Silver Water said in the tone that proclaimed want and worry.

''We'll eat soon.'' But what? They'd left without thinking to take rations. Everything had been so hurried, so desperate.

Despite the silence of the night, she could hear the creaking sound. Would she ever close her eyes and not see that gruesome corpse twisting slowly in the air? No, that sight would always slip into her dreams, stalking the peace she craved.

Knowing that his soul still cleaved to Sun Mounds, she could not look back lest the tenuous link between them might be strengthened. Lest somehow his diseased ghost might find the courage to brave the warding posts and pursue her across this frozen land.

Tomorrow, with sunrise, it would be better. She would know then that they had fired the clan house and that the flames had licked up around that hanging horror.

Her imagination played with her, conjuring the flames from the floor matting. They leaped along the walls and blackened the wooden posts before roaring through the cattail matting and bursting violently through the roof thatch to shoot into the sky.

In tongues of yellow, they curled around her husband's feet and caught new life. Spirals of heat worked up his legs. She could see his face now, shining in the dancing light. The flames jumped and cavorted, casting their crystalline reflections in his bugged-out eyes. Then his hair burst into a headdress of writhing fire, sparks spinning away to vanish like teardrops from memory.

Star Shell stumbled, her feet unsteady.

"Mama?" Silver Water cried.

Trembling, Star Shell dropped to her knees, heedless of her daughter's clinging hand. She bowed her head and broke into uncontrolled sobbing.

"Mama? What's wrong?" Silver Water shrilled before she too surrendered to frightened tears.

Star Shell pulled her daughter to her. Together, they cried, each lost in her own sorrow. *It's all right! By tomorrow, his flesh will be reduced to ashes. The rope will be nothing but charred fibers that fray and break to spill those wretched bones onto the fiery floor.* The cold biting into her knees brought Star Shell back to the night, back to the road.

She wiped the tears from her eyes and stared at her daughter. Silver Water looked as fragile as the starlight that shone on her small face. Her big eyes were as dark as her long black hair that spilled out from under the disheveled blanket.

"Are you all right, baby?"

"I'm cold, Mama. I want to go home. I want to get warm. Please? Can we go home now?"

"I'm sorry, Silver Water. We can't. Not for a long time." *If ever.*

A gentle hand settled on Star Shell's shoulder. Tall Man patted her softly. "Sometimes wrongs get passed down from one generation to the next. I wish this hadn't had to happen to you."

Star Shell said bitterly, "Yes, I know. But it doesn't look like we have any choice, does it?"

His gaze grew remote, as if seeing into another time and place. "No. The only choice is atonement. Someone must pay for the mistakes of the past."

"Mama? Why do we have to go away?" Silver Water looked hesitantly from Star Shell to Tall Man.

Star Shell struggled to her feet and paused only long enough to wipe the tears from her shivering daughter's face. "Come on, sweetheart, let's go. We'll be warmer when we're walking."

"Mama, I don't want to—"

"Hush, baby. We must be brave now. And strong."

Relying on willpower, Star Shell tugged her daughter along. One step ahead of the other. If she concentrated on that, she might be able to suppress both memories and imagination.

Otter fed sticks into a cheerful fire that crackled and spit sparks. A second fire, built earlier, had burned down to glowing red coals that shimmered with the breeze off the river.

They had camped on a damp beach, half mud and half sand. Behind them, the forest rose in a tangle of interlocked branches and sullen trunks wrapped in tendons of bare vines. Thick clouds had darkened overhead, a promise of the blackest of winter nights. Nevertheless, the river corded and flowed, its pulse mixing with Otter's own.

He scented the musky air, drinking the river's Power into his soul to buoy his damp spirits. The heady excitement engendered by a new voyage should have been bursting within, but a subtle foreboding ate at his soul.

Misty rain had fallen through most of the morning, soaking them, and now Green Spider sat humped over the red sheen of the coals, his vulture-like attention on a ceramic cook pot that Otter had placed on its four stumpy legs in the coals. Steam rose from the bubbling broth within, sending a mouthwatering aroma into the chilly air.

Waves slapped against the sandy shore, while wind whispered through the bare branches of the trees behind their camp.

Otter glanced down to where *Wave Dancer* rested on the shore to the south, the fox-headed prow barely visible in the fading light. Catcher was prowling the beach, sniffing here and there.

"This food is too cold to eat," Green Spider observed. He

wrinkled his nose. "Manure smells better than that stuff!"

"Going to be that good, huh?" Otter asked, raising an eyebrow.

"I wouldn't trust you to cook a rock."

"Good, I'll cook you one tomorrow, assuming, that is, that we can find a rock."

"We'll find them everywhere!" Green Spider grinned down at the thick stew.

"Is that a fact?" Otter gestured with a piece of firewood. "You know why people down here in the valley use cooking clays, don't you? It's because they don't have any rocks bigger than sand. And besides, cooking clays can be molded to shape so they heat differently."

"I never knew that." Green Spider's forehead lined. "This isn't ready to eat yet."

"All right, take your bowl and dip some out." Then Otter cocked his head. "Better be sure to leave some for Black Skull. He's already looking for an excuse to pull off your arms and legs."

Green Spider twisted around and grabbed his worn wooden bowl. He dipped hot stew from the pot, settled back on his haunches, and blew noisily to cool the boiling liquid.

Black Skull seemed to materialize out of the darkness, the only sound of his passage the grinding of sand underfoot. Like a menacing bear, he crouched opposite the fire and stared his disgust across the flames at Green Spider.

"Find anything?" Otter asked.

The warrior shook his misshapen head. "Only old tracks. Whoever camped here before us spent just one night. It must have been the war party I saw when I was coming downstream with the Elders."

"The Khota," Otter grunted.

"They had a woman with them."

Otter told him the story about Pearl and her betrothal to Wolf of the Dead.

"This Wolf of the Dead," Black Skull said. "Is he a Powerful warrior?"

Otter paused, staring at the ground before him. "In his country, he is as well known as you are around the City of the Dead. He's quite the killer—but beyond that, you and he are as different as night and day. He doesn't have your warm and winning personality.''

Black Skull studied him with glittering eyes, while Green Spider slurped noisily at his stew. ''You leave me puzzled sometimes, Trader, but I'll ignore that for now. You don't seem to like these Khota. You have dealt with them, I take it?''

Otter took his bowl and dipped out some of the stew. ''They killed my Uncle. They've stolen from me. Given my way, I'd never have to deal with them again.''

Black Skull stared out at the night as he fingered his crooked chin. Then he shook his head. ''To think that the Clan Elders passed so close to such a danger.'' He gave Green Spider an acid glare.

Otter blew on his stew to cool it. ''Sometimes, warrior, it is safer to travel inconspicuously.''

''I've never been inconspicuous in my life,'' Black Skull growled.

Otter sipped his stew. That morning he'd been lucky enough to bring down a mallard with his bola. Now the rich, dark meat, coupled with goosefoot flour as a thickening agent, made a wonderful meal.

''Khota,'' Green Spider muttered. ''What lovely people. So friendly and hospitable. The finest pearls are fished out of the deepest waters. I'm looking forward to meeting them. Warm embraces . . . all the way around. And such lazy hunters!''

Otter took a swallow and said, ''We're going up the Serpent River. We're not going close to the Khota.''

''Not if we can help it,'' Green Spider amended—or did he?

''See anything besides tracks?'' Otter asked Black Skull in an effort to maintain the conversation.

''Nothing. Only a patch of bloody grass. It smelled like old deer blood. From the tracks, the Khota killed it. There are deer bones scattered around the other fire pits they left. Oh, and there's this.'' Black Skull produced a twist of grass that had been woven into a square, the knots intricate.

Otter took the piece and studied it curiously. ''I've seen this before. It's a prayer offering. The Anhinga make them. Most of the ones I've seen are larger. They're generally placed on the burial mounds to ask for aid from the ancestors.''

''Anhinga? So maybe this Pearl made it?''

Otter fingered the woven grass. ''I'd say that she's caught on to the trouble she's in. The poor girl must be scared to death.'' He sipped his soup and considered the prayer mat. ''Generally, the Anhinga don't make these unless the situation is dire. You know, someone is very sick, about to die. Or maybe someone is badly hurt.''

Black Skull reached for his bowl. As he dipped it full, he shot an angry glance at Green Spider, who was tracing patterns in the sand, apparently oblivious. Black Skull drank, grunted satisfaction, and nodded. ''I'm surprised. This is excellent, Trader. You'd make some warrior a good wife.''

A cold gust pelted them with sand and whipped the fire around. Otter shielded his bowl and drank the last of his stew. On impulse, he folded the prayer mat and tucked it into his shirt.

''Tell me more about these Khota,'' Black Skull asked. ''Do they normally travel downriver this far?''

''No. Usually they like to wait for the Traders to come to them. Why take a chance on the river when you can do your dirty work on your own ground?'' He paused, his voice dropping. ''And some people have long memories.''

Black Skull pursed his lips. ''I thought so. I've only heard them mentioned. I've never known one of their Traders to come to the City of the Dead.''

''You wouldn't want them to. They only bring trouble.''

''Trouble?'' Black Skull grinned. With his broken jaw, it wasn't pretty. ''They'd only bring me trouble once, Trader.''

''Is everything so simple for you?''

Black Skull's piercing gaze gleamed in the firelight. ''In battle, there are but two outcomes—and the only one I know is victory. That's all there is, Trader. You win, or you lose.''

Green Spider piped up, ''And you've always lost!''

Black Skull spit into the fire. ''I've always won!''

''Win, win, win, always win,'' Green Spider chirped.

''What I'd give to shut you up!''

To change the subject, Otter asked, ''Green Spider, I want you to concentrate. Can you do that for me? Can you play a game? Remember how it was to be backwards. Can you talk to me like that?''

Green Spider's attention focused. "Yes," he mumbled, "I remember."

"Why have the three of us been chosen to save this Mask? Why not someone who lives close to the Roaring Water? Why are we traveling so far to attempt this?"

Black Skull's attention had sharpened the way a fox's does when a grouse flutters with a broken wing.

Green Spider looked pained. His mouth puckered as if searching for words. "We aren't expected."

"Expected by whom?" Black Skull had stiffened.

"The gamblers."

"What gamblers?" Black Skull leaned forward, his head slightly cocked.

Green Spider stared into his bowl as if he could see things in the last of the liquid. "Gamblers, dwarfs, children."

"You see!" Black Skull threw up his arms. "You try to make sense out of him and what do you get? Irritation, that's what! I ought to smack him in the head a couple of times. See if *that* straightens out his tongue!"

"Yes, warrior," Green Spider whispered. "Follow your nature. Be what you've been—not what you could be. Smack them all. Lift your club and split the world." A pause. "She's told him, you know. She's made a point of it . . . as if he didn't already know."

"He? Who is he? Who's told him? She made what point? What are you babbling about?"

Power swelled in Green Spider's eyes, burning blackly as he locked his gaze with the warrior's. They stared at each other, sharing an intensity Otter could only wonder about.

Green Spider said, "Your mother. She's told the Burning Wolf."

"Bah!" Black Skull growled. "He's a raving fool." The warrior drank down his bowl of stew and got to his feet. The muscles in his face were twitching as he glared at the Contrary, but the usual arrogance had faded. Instead, something else, a glint of fear perhaps, flickered in those black eyes. In silence, Black Skull turned on his heel and walked down to *Wave Dancer*. There he gathered his blankets.

Otter studied Green Spider suspiciously. "Why do you torment him so?"

The Contrary's gaze seemed to focus at the base of the fire. "Which stone cuts with the sharpest edge, Trader?"

Otter thought for a moment. "Obsidian."

"Yes, sharp—and deadly. The Black Skull is obsidian. Like it, he cuts through life. So clean and painlessly." Green Spider's focus seemed to fade.

"Go on."

"What happens when you bend an obsidian blade, Trader?"

"It snaps."

Green Spider shivered, and sighed. "The Black Skull needs to turn himself inside-out before he cuts off his own head and suffocates."

"I see."

Without a word more, Green Spider stood, hummed to himself while he did a little Dance, then pirouetted back to the fire and flopped down atop his bedding. He rolled himself up in his blankets and began to snore, loudly.

Otter glanced nervously at the dark lump where Black Skull had bedded down by the canoe. Catcher sniffed at the warrior's bed, then trotted toward the fire. He stretched, shook himself, and circled several times before dropping on the sand at Green Spider's feet. With pricked ears, he watched Otter for a moment, then yawned.

Otter fed another piece of wood into the fire. The flames flickered merrily. What had that exchange been about? Black Skull had, so the story went, killed his mother. Beyond that, not much had ever been said—and the White Shell didn't have many ties with the Black Clan.

Otter glanced at the warrior's blanketed form again. A man didn't just kill his mother and go on about life. His family would exact retribution for such a grisly crime ... unless, of course, the family had sanctioned it. And if it had, that would account for the lack of gossip floating about the country.

Otter rubbed his tired face. Why, of all people, had Power called on him to take this unlikely pair north? Couldn't Power have found just as gullible a Trader at the City of the Dead? The place would have been crawling with them during the solstice.

And gamblers? He studied Green Spider from the corner of

his eye. The Contrary had tried to tell them, but as usual, the import had been hidden in twisted meanings.

Does the world really hang in the balance as the Clan Elders insist? Or is Black Skull right? Are we all on a fool's errand? And if that's the case, what will it cost us?

Otter shifted, suddenly aware of the little leather bag his mother had given him. He fished it out and studied it. Blue Jar said that a Trader had brought it down from the Khota. That Trader had paid handsomely for this—yet Blue Jar said she had obtained it for a mere night's rest and a hot meal.

Otter pulled the mouth of the sack open and turned it upside down. A piece of copper, bound in cord, fell out. Even before he unwound it, he recognized the familiar ornament. The polished piece had been drilled through the middle and hung on the braided cord. In the firelight, the copper likeness of a falcon stared up at him. A freshwater pearl had been set for an eye; it seemed to burn in the yellow light.

In all the years Otter had known him, Uncle had never taken the copper falcon from around his neck.

Otter bowed his head, his fist knotting on the cool metal.

When he finally took a deep breath and looked up, he caught the gleam of firelight in Green Spider's eyes. The Contrary said nothing, but watched him with an unwavering intensity.

Fourteen

Pearl waited in the dark shelter, feigning sleep. Tonight, on this narrow island in the middle of the river, she would make her escape. The Khota felt secure. That feeling—along with the yellow valerian she'd laced into the stew—might prove to be her only edge.

Yellow valerian had been used by Anhinga Healers for generations as a sedative. The problem with hunting herbs in the middle of the winter, and under guard at that, was that a person couldn't always find what she was looking for. The plants were dead, and the only clue might be a few twisted brown stalks and some curled tan leaves. In this case, Pearl had been able to infuse only one small root into the evening meal.

She waited for the right moment. Patience, she counseled herself. Her blankets were so warm. As tendrils of weariness threaded past her guard, she too drifted off . . . to dream. . . .

Sunlight shimmered on turquoise waters, sparking bits of silver off the waves. Pearl balanced in her slim canoe, her spear poised as the boat rose and fell. To her right, breakers rolled onto a white beach that gave way to salt grasses and dunes. Farther inland, she could see the dark green belt of pines and cypress that marked the backwaters.

As the warm sea breeze caressed her skin, she searched the clear water for her prey. Above the flat horizon, massed white thunderheads promised hot afternoon showers as they were driven ashore by the gulf winds. The musky odor of the warm water filled her nostrils, and white salt stains marked her smooth brown skin. She shook her head to flip the tangled black mass of her hair away from her eyes.

There! The dark shape moved in the crystal depths. With a smooth motion, Pearl launched the spear with its serrated bone point. The lanyard rope streamed out behind, drawing coils of braided cord from the bottom of the canoe.

She'd judged accurately, seeing the spear slip through the water and into the big red fish. Water thrashed, and the heavy spear bucked hard before it slapped underwater.

Pearl jumped down, grabbing the rope in callused hands. Careful, too hard a pull would jerk the barbed point free and the huge fish would escape.

With skilled hands, she played the fish in, aware that if she took too long, the sharks would be drawn and all she'd get would be the satisfaction of a good cast.

As the panicked fish battled for its life, she could hear its frantic drumming. Now she could reach the wooden spear, and through it, control the movement of the red fish. Keeping pressure to the side, she caused the fish to crab against the boat. There, straining, she could reach over the side. As the canoe rocked, she slipped a hand inside the gills, feeling the spines.

The red fish thrashed desperately at the invasion of her fingers. With a deft jerk, Pearl pulled the flopping monster into the boat.

She grinned at her catch, noting the familiar black spot at the root of its tail. The fish slapped the carved wood with its body, blood leaking down the golden-red scales to smear on the wet wood.

Pearl used a deer-bone awl to work the barbed point free of the tender meat. For a moment, she glanced down at her prize, watching the jaws work as it gasped for breath.

The dream shredded itself, and some sense of urgency goaded Pearl awake. She lay for a moment, remembering the freedom, the sea, the still waters of the swamp—how glorious life had been. Then she blinked her eyes open at the cold plop of rain on her face. Occasional drops fell through the matted roof of the hasty shelter the Khota had built.

She stared into the darkness. How much of the night remained? She propped herself on one arm and looked out beyond the shelter. So dark. Rain beat on the hard-packed sand and hissed and spat in fires burned down to smoldering coals.

Chill air crept into Pearl's blankets as she sat up. To her right lay One Arm's slumped body. His chest rose and fell with each sleeping breath. At the mouth of the shelter, Eats Dogs had curled into a ball. Rhythmic breathing told her that he too slept soundly.

Pearl drew her feet up. With the care instilled by a lifetime of hunting, she eased from the blankets. Fear charged both nerve and muscle as she placed her feet carefully.

Holding her breath, her heart battering at her ribs, she stepped over Eats Dogs and out into the cold rain. In a low crouch, she hurried warily across the camp. Bitter wind gusted out of the north; its bite sliced into her as she made her way to the beach.

She reached the first of the canoes and took stock. Nothing

moved. Any sound she'd made had been covered by the rain. As another gust of wind worried at her, she bent and put all of her weight into pushing the canoe. The heavy dugout wouldn't budge.

Gritting her teeth, she tried rocking it, but made no headway.

Pearl bit off a curse and moved to the next of the canoes. Her plan had been to shove all of the craft into the water, to let the current carry them away, while she stole the last one.

The third canoe hadn't been pulled as high onto the beach. She grunted, throwing every bit of her strength into lifting and shoving. Her feet dug into the wet sand as she inched the canoe back into the slapping waves.

Well, one canoe would be better than none. With it, she could reach the creek mouth she'd spotted that afternoon. She would paddle up the creek as far as she could go, hide out for as long as she needed to let pursuit vanish downriver, and then go in search of shelter.

She could wait it out. Let them forget about her. Enough fish, ducks, and shellfish could be found to keep her belly full in the meantime. She might not make it back to the Anhinga lands until late summer, but she'd get there.

She could hear water slapping the stern of the canoe. Another good hard shove and—

"If you'd wait until morning, we'd help you," Grizzly Tooth called from the darkness.

Pearl froze for an instant, fear running bright through her veins.

"Wake up, my warriors!" Grizzly Tooth shouted. "Our woman is trying to escape!"

Pearl fumbled in the canoe, searching for a dart, a weapon, anything. Her fingers clutched onto a thong as she turned to run. A bola!

Her feet beating into the sand, she sprinted down the beach. She sorted out the bola, finding the knot that bound the separate cords together. The stone weights rattled and knocked at each pounding pace.

"She's heading down the island!" Grizzly Tooth bellowed. "Cut her off!"

The angry shouts of men filled the night. Pearl ran as she'd never run before. How far did the sand go before it turned to mud?

Behind, she could hear the muffled steps of a pursuer. She forced herself to greater effort. Now, or never! She had to break free! This would be her only chance.

She could hear his panting breath. Too close.

She slowed, whirling the bola, casting it low at the legs of her pursuer; she heard him go down, grunting at the fall, and she turned and pelted onward, sprinting blindly through the rain-lashed night.

Sometime in the past, another storm had fallen the old cottonwood. The current of the river had carried it to this slow backwater and beached it. Silt had settled as the water slowed around the snag, and now only one rotted branch rose above the sand.

At the last instant, Pearl saw the pale wood. She tried to cut her pace, to set herself for a jump, but she managed poorly. Her trailing foot hung on the branch, spilling her full on her face on the beach.

Impact knocked the breath from her. Stunned, she gasped, digging her fingers into the sand. Agony burned through her, but still she forced herself to crawl toward the water.

Feet pounded in the night, men called.

Pearl couldn't stop herself from coughing.

"Over here!" a voice cried.

She dragged herself forward, her lungs starved. Flickers of light, like dancing fireflies, sparkled in her vision. She slapped a hand into the chilly water, then lurched forward. A wave slapped her full in the face. Icy water shocked her hot flesh.

A hand grabbed her foot, drawing her backward.

"Got her!" an excited voice cried.

Pearl went limp, gasping, finally recovering enough breath to cry.

The hard hands pulled her back onto the sand, and a heavy body fell on her, pinning her in place. She barely caught some of the words. " . . . tried to . . . you could escape?"

Dark shapes appeared around her.

Grizzly Tooth bent down, his necklace rattling. "Good thing that tree was there, huh, woman? As it is, you almost broke my neck back there. You'll pay." He straightened, and she saw that he was limping. "Tie her up. Take her back. From now on, she stays tied."

Pearl let her head fall to the damp sand. Rain beat steadily on her face. Then she was jerked up and thrown over a muscular shoulder.

Wave Dancer cut through the placid water like a dart through air, the wake streaming out in a V as Otter guided her up the winding stream. Overhead, the branches intermingled and laced together in a thicket. Squirrels darted across, shaking the limbs and vines. Birds chirped around them.

Black Skull had grown tense and irritable. He glanced uneasily to each side, starting at the forest sounds.

And well he might be edgy, Otter decided. Six days of traveling with the warrior and the Contrary had him more than a little jumpy himself.

Black Skull's nervous reaction seemed to stem from something besides just his disdain of the Contrary. As they had proceeded north, Black Skull's mood had grown more sullen. At night, Otter had observed the warrior lying awake, staring around uneasily, or up and prowling the perimeter of the camp on silent feet.

Something about Black Skull's manner reminded Otter of a child who'd lost his way in the forest. But what did the warrior have to fear?

They rounded yet another bend in the creek. Here the roots of an elm had curled down the crumbling brown bank for a hold in the murky water. Brown grasses hung in tufts, and saplings crowded the shore, striving for the sky.

Otter used his paddle as a rudder to round a series of wooden floats that marked the location of a trotline. "We're getting close."

Black Skull turned his head, his eyes narrowed. "I don't see the purpose in this."

Green Spider sat in the middle of the canoe, backwards as usual, legs crossed. He dragged his fingers in the muddy water, muttering, "Purpose, purpose, always a purpose."

Catcher balanced on a pack, nose searching the wind. His tail cut slow arcs in the air.

"We're stopping at Green Turtle village to Trade with old Long Squirrel for shirts. They produce a luxurious kind of fabric here. I'm not sure how they do it . . . the clan is very close-mouthed about it. They do something with milkweed and cottonwood fluff. Then they dye it purple. They'll Trade a shirt for a couple of sharks' teeth."

"A shirt for sharks' teeth?" Black Skull frowned. "But why do we need a purple shirt?"

"We need one of these purple shirts to Trade to Meadowlark, clan leader at Brown Water. Meadowlark likes purple shirts. He has come to believe that wearing anything purple gives him special Power. Of course the problem with purple is that it fades over time. So Meadowlark is always looking for purple clothing. For the shirt, Meadowlark will give us a couple of his badger bowls."

"His what?" Black Skull shot a look of annoyance Otter's way.

"Badger bowls. Meadowlark's potters make a bowl that has a badger's head on one side and a tail on the other. They're the handles, you see. Only the Brown Water potters make them."

"So, what do we do with the badger bowls? What do we need them for?"

"We need the badger bowls to Trade with Elk's Foot. He's the head Elder of the Cottonwood Clan. He's got a passion for these badger bowls. He leaves them as offerings to one of his ancestors. He fills them with seeds and places them on the top of the clan burial mound, a gesture of respect for his great-grandfather's ghost. In return, we'll get a couple of pots of his honey beer."

"And that we drink?"

"No, we take the honey beer and Trade it to Great Ring at Hilltop. The Hilltop holdings are located just south of the mouth of the Serpent River. For the honey beer, Great Ring will Trade a tanned buffalo robe that came out of the plains this last fall."

"And we'll Trade the buffalo robe to someone?" Black Skull was shaking his head.

"You're catching on."

"You never get to keep any of the worthwhile goods. You just Trade them away to someone else. Sounds dreary to me, Trader." Black Skull grumbled to himself and gave the paddle all of his effort.

Green Spider had ceased to drag his hands in the water and now stared with fascination as droplets fell from his fingertips to form rings that spread over the canoe's wake. He squinted at the rings, bending over the side of the canoe to watch them melt into the wake and vanish.

After a time, Black Skull shipped his paddle and turned halfway around. "So why don't we just Trade the sharks' teeth for the buffalo robe and be done with it?"

Otter counterbalanced for the way Green Spider leaned over the side, trying to watch the water. "Because every Trader who goes upriver tries to Trade sharks' teeth to Great Ring. Look, Hilltop is situated right under the confluence, which means that everything that passes up and down the river goes by his clan's ground. Now I happen to know he likes that honey beer, but he and Elk's Foot have hated each other for years. Great Ring doesn't get much honey beer as a result."

"Then let's give him more sharks' teeth and save the time," Black Skull insisted.

Otter sighed, "You're just not good at this, Black Skull."

"But I don't—"

"Never mind!"

Star Shell blinked herself awake. The Dream had been horrifying. She'd been surrounded by burning corpses, all of them reaching for her with fingers of fire. A mountain, consumed in flames, had risen into a reddish, smoke-choked sky. Not a mountain like those she knew, but a huge slab of rock that jutted upward in steep majesty. The high, timbered slopes had been ablaze, and there men screamed as they burned to death.

A fat man, dressed in skins, had run toward her, waving his arms in the flames while sparks fell around him, setting trees ablaze.

She massaged her tired eyes with gentle fingers, as if she

could rub away the vivid images: flames, men burning, burning as her husband's body should have burned by now. She'd had Power Dreams before—haunting visions of people and places far away—but the terror of this one didn't fade from her soul.

Easy, Star Shell. You're exhausted, that's all. As soon as the horror of your husband's death fades, it will be all right.

Star Shell looked up at the roof of the small hut. Sections of bark had been overlapped and tied to the bowed rafter poles with rough cordage. The place looked old, in need of repair.

"Awake?" a reedy voice asked.

Star Shell turned her head. An old woman crouched over a small, smoldering fire. She wore a faded, worn blanket that had unraveled at the edges. Where once-bright colors had made it a thing of beauty, now smudges of dirt and ash sullied it.

Silver threads had won the battle with gray in the old woman's hair, which she wore pulled back in a severe bun. Ancient brown eyes looked out from a mass of wrinkles, and her undershot jaw proved that all of the teeth had fallen out.

An old dog, its muzzle gone white with age, lifted its head to glance longingly at the old woman. The tail slapped the ground twice before the dog yawned. Then it dropped its head back onto the filthy brown fabric it slept on and huffed a heavy sigh.

The hag shook her head at the animal, then glanced at Star Shell with rheumy eyes. "It's almost morning. You've slept a long time."

Star Shell sat up and looked around the small hut. Silver Water's body was little more than a small mound in the blankets. Tall Man's face was visible only from the nose up. The rest of him lay covered in another grease-crusted blanket.

Here and there, faint traces of snow had worked between cracks in the bark siding. Old spiderwebs rippled along the walls as the air currents played with them. A mouse zipped around one of the half-rotted posts and out through a hole.

"Quite a surprise," the old woman said simply. "I don't get many visitors in the dead of winter. And the Magician, well, he's about the last person I would have suspected."

"He came directly here. Called you a friend."

The old woman nodded and added another crooked branch to

the glowing coals. The little fire bathed her face in red, augmenting the shadowed lines of her wrinkles. Her head bobbed loosely on a turkey-wattled neck.

"Oh, yes . . . but from a long time ago. He saved my sister's life. Drove the evil out of her body. It would have killed her, but for him. Mostly dead, she was . . . when the Magician came."

Star Shell pulled the blanket back, moving with care so as not to awaken the others. She stepped carefully over her daughter's bundled form and squatted across from the old woman before she extended cold hands to the fire.

"You're a member of the Blue Duck Clan. Is that why you let us stay here? Because he saved your sister?"

The old woman shrugged like a hunching of bones. "Blue Duck? Now, yes, perhaps. But not then. I was of the Six Flutes Clan then. I didn't come here until I married my fourth husband." The old woman's head continued to wobble. "Husbands don't last. I've worn out four of them."

"No," Star Shell whispered absently. "Husbands don't last."

"Four," the old woman muttered, staring into the red coals. "But imagine my surprise to see the Magician. Funny thing, that. To look up and see you people walking out of the forest as I was out saying prayers to the morning. And dragging a little girl around in wintertime. What's the Magician coming to?"

"We shouldn't stay here. We'll be trouble for you. We're not very popular with the Blue Duck Clan these days."

"The Magician said something about that. Stay as long as you like."

Star Shell frowned. "What about food? We're only a moon past the winter solstice. We can't eat all of your food."

The old woman chuckled. "The great benefit of all those grandchildren and great-grandchildren is that they bring you food. I've more than enough. What I don't eat by spring harvest goes to the mice." Her gaze drifted off. "I always hated mice. Fought them all of my life. Now they keep me company."

Star Shell blushed. "I hope you forgive me. I've forgotten your name."

"Eh? Oh. Which one?"

"How many names do you have?"

"A bunch. Mostly I was known as Clamshell." She stared at the fire. "Wasn't the name I was given at my coming of age, of course." Her head seemed to wobble worse as she gazed into the fire. "Well, what do they expect."

Star Shell said, "Excuse me?"

"The men. They started calling me Clamshell." She worked her toothless gums and grinned. "Because I could tighten up on them, you see. Used all of my muscles down there. Like working damp clay with powerful fingers. And they liked it. Other women didn't give them that."

Clamshell seemed to drift off. "So many fights. Five men . . . killed . . . They fought over me. Can I help it? I was beautiful then. Even more beautiful than you. Supple and strong."

The old woman smiled and blinked. "What sort of life could a woman have, married to a Trader like that? Always gone. Only saw him once every two years. The rest of the time he was off on the rivers. Gone way west, you know. Way west, where the world rises to meet the sky. He carried obsidian. They buried him down in the Six Flutes' mound. Covered him with his own cache of obsidian. Enough to fill a canoe."

Clamshell scratched her head with her left hand. Her forearm was bent and knotted. She noticed Star Shell's gaze and explained: "Second husband did that. Caught me locked together with a Trader from down south someplace." She smacked her lips. "I always had a weakness for Traders."

Star Shell huddled closer to the fire. How much of this was true? How much the wild imagination of a lonely old woman? "You must have had quite a life."

Clamshell's head wobbled even more. "I've got few regrets . . . outside of getting old. These young men, they don't look twice at me anymore. Although the women, they seem to get along better with me now. Used to have a terrible time with women, especially if I was sneaking off with their men at night."

Another mouse scurried along the wall. The rodent stopped, hunched, nose quivering, before it shot into the shadows.

"Never deny your nature, girl. That's the one truth I learned in life." Clamshell scratched at her head again and reached for one of the small sticks from a dwindling pile. "Follow your soul and your talents. I was the most beautiful and desired woman in the world in my time. Men came from everywhere . . . some just to look.''

Clamshell's head steadied for a moment. ''Can you imagine that, girl? Men crossed the world just to look, just to be able to go back and say that they'd seen me.''

''It must have been wonderful.'' Humor the old woman. After all, she'd provided them with a warm—if dirty—bed, and a safe day's sleep. That had to be worth listening to a few flights of imagination.

Clamshell glanced at her. ''You look pretty miserable, girl. Well, pay it no mind, for things will get better. And having the Magician for a friend, you can't do much better than that.''

''People are looking for us.''

''They won't find you here.''

''What if they follow our tracks?''

Clamshell scratched her head again. ''Pesky lice. It took long enough to get to liking mice. Lice, though, there's no way to make terms with them.''

Star Shell stiffened, suddenly feeling crawly all over.

Clamshell seemed not to have noticed. ''Don't you worry about tracks, child. The snow started again just after you got here. Any tracks are long buried. You don't leave here, ain't nobody going to know.''

An itch began to burn in Star Shell's hair. ''What about your family? Don't they come out to see you?''

''Not while it's snowing.'' Clamshell chuckled to herself. ''I suppose they'd just as soon wait till spring. Each year they do that. I guess they're hoping to find me all chewed down to bones. Won't have to come up and plant my fields that way. Won't have to bring me part of their harvest every fall.''

Star Shell glanced around the little hut. The few pots were plain, undecorated. An old digging stick stood along one wall, its tip blunted. Several fabric sacks hung from the cross braces, most with holes in them.

''What do you do out here all winter?''

''Talk to the old dog over there, him and the mice, mostly.'' Clamshell scratched again. ''That old dog, he's the last man in my life. And would you look at him? Just sleeps all the time. Can hardly walk without hobbling, let alone break into a run. But he listens.''

She smacked her lips. "And the mice listen real close—not like most people, who've got their souls clotted up with worries all the time. Mice listen to me like the men used to listen. Sometimes the mice fight—and I know they're fighting over me. Just like the men used to do."

Star Shell shifted uneasily, annoyed by the pride in the old woman's voice. It didn't seem the sort of thing to gloat over.

Clamshell snorted to herself. "No, mostly I sit and watch the fire. You can see things in fire. You got to learn to train your eyes, but you can see things. Mostly, you see the past. I've trained myself. Watched the fire for years to gain the sight. See? You look in there now, and you can see Stone Wall. Yes, he's just the way he was before I married him. Young, strong. Look at the expression on his face. Just like the time I put the water snake in his blankets."

Star Shell leaned over—and saw only coals. Try as she might, she couldn't make out any kind of picture. Then it dawned on her. "You . . . you said his name? And he's dead? Don't you worry—"

"About calling his ghost?" She waved it off. "I've been trying for years. I don't think there's anything to that. I've called out the names of all my dead lovers. They never come. No, they never do." She seemed to drift off. "Let them haunt me. I wish they would. We could look into the fire and talk at night. Remember the old times."

Star Shell glanced around nervously.

Clamshell said something under her breath, then tottered slowly to her feet. She winced painfully, straightening. "A person gets a little knotty out here."

"Knotty?"

"Like an old tree. You know, filled with knots and bends. Not like the old days. No . . . not at all. The men could have told you."

Star Shell scratched at a new itch behind her ear. "How long have you had lice?"

"Hmm? Oh, lice. I don't know. I used to make a point of husking black-walnut rinds. You know, mashing them and boiling everything in the juices. Got so I couldn't hold the pestle and mash them anymore. Too much trouble. Turns all your fabric brown. Besides, lice aren't very big. Just little bits of things, you know. They can't eat much.''

Star Shell scratched at her side. "I'll keep that in mind.''

Clamshell glanced at her from the corner of her eye. "What's in that pack the Magician's carrying?''

Star Shell hesitated. "Some kind of sacred thing. I don't know. Why?''

The old woman shook her head, muttering to herself. She half turned, her ancient eyes on the pack. "Thought I heard it calling to me. You know, trying to form pictures in the fire.''

"Don't you ever sleep?''

"Not much. Funny thing, isn't it? You'd think that the older you got, the more you'd need to sleep. Me, it seems as if I never do anymore. That, or I sleep while I'm awake. Can't tell the difference between dreaming at night and dreaming during the day.'' She cocked her head. "Of course, when I'm young, and the men are with me, I must be dreaming.''

Clamshell made faces as she stretched her bent body. Then she slowly settled before the fire again.

"I want to thank you for hiding us here. I hope we won't be any trouble.''

"No trouble. Not when it's the Magician.''

"How long have you known him?''

Clamshell's head stabilized for a moment. "Since I was . . . oh, let's see. He saved my sister's life. Did I tell you about that?''

"Yes.''

"For a long time, child. A long time. Dwarfs have Power, you know. And him, well, he has more Power than anyone I know.'' She blinked at the fire. "Thought his child would be short . . . like him. But he came out normal.''

"You had his child?'' Star Shall gaped, then glanced at the mounded blankets where Tall Man slept.

"A long time ago,'' the old woman whispered. "A long, long time ago.''

Fifteen

Morning had dawned clear and crisp as they paddled into the main current of the Father Water and bent their course to the north. Black Skull had to concede that the Trading session at the Green Turtle clan grounds hadn't been so bad after all. In fact, he felt fine for the first time since leaving the City of the Dead.

And to think I was nervous.

The canoe wobbled, and Black Skull glanced behind him. Green Spider was playing a silly game with the Trader's dog, Catcher. He'd skitter his fingers across the top of the heavy fabric pack like they were some sort of curious bug; then, as the dog slapped a paw at the crawling thing, the lunatic would grab the dog's nose and make a whooping noise. For the dog, this was all splendid joy, happy whimpers, and tail-wagging.

For those engaged in the serious business of propelling the canoe, it meant no little pitching, bobbing, and rocking as mutt and lunatic cavorted amidships.

Yes, it was the fool's fault. How could a man—a warrior—maintain any semblance of discipline in the face of a gibbering idiot like Green Spider?

The river rolled and coiled placidly this morning, the smooth surface reflecting the light like smudged silver. Overhead a V of geese honked and flapped toward the knotted woods and the quiet backswamp that no doubt lay there. A cool breeze—not even enough to mar the water—blew from the south.

Black Skull's muscles warmed to the paddle, and he relished making the big canoe fly over the calm water. The Trader was a good partner in a canoe. He had strength and superb stamina; but then, what should Black Skull expect? Otter had been paddling all of his life. He seemed to live for it.

"Left!" the Trader called. "Work for that backwater. See,

where the surface is glassy and smooth. We'll make good time there.''

Black Skull put his back to the task as *Wave Dancer* arrowed for the stiller water. They worked in closer to shore, taking the inside of the river's curve. Marshy grasses and canebrakes bearded the shallows they skirted, while farther back, cottonwoods had found a tenuous hold in the muddy bank.

Black Skull bit off a curse as Green Spider and the cur tipped the boat dangerously to the left.

A lone duck quacked as it skimmed low over the water, veering wide around the canoe. The air carried the musky scent of the big river, thick and cloying in the nostrils.

Black Skull grinned. Despite the annoyance of Green Spider's game, it had turned out to be a fine morning after an even finer night in Green Turtle village. *Yes, I could come to like this.*

In fact, why should a man return to the City of the Dead when he could be treated so magnificently by these little isolated clans?

They'd put in at a small canoe landing below Green Turtle clan holdings, unseen and unheralded. Otter had rummaged through one of his packs while Green Spider waded ashore and began poking his finger into the mud.

Black Skull had taken up his weapons, nervous at the silence. Unease had stalked him all the way up the little tributary to the Green Turtle landing. Nerves, that was all. The result of too many days in the presence of the fool. What warrior wouldn't expect the worst after listening to the lunatic's ravings for days on end?

"You won't need those," Otter had told him.

Black Skull remembered his bristling response: "I go nowhere without my weapons."

"Leave them." Otter's voice had been cool, those black eyes commanding.

Black Skull had grunted, ignoring the Trader as he stalked up the slope, but Otter had stepped in front of him, blocking the way.

"I said, leave the weapons. We agreed. The Clan Elders agreed. This is my responsibility."

Black Skull had smoldered, his rage building.

"Danger abounds!" Green Spider had shrieked as he

laughed, clapped his hands, and pirouetted up to them. "Listen to the warrior, Trader! He's right, always right! Take your darts and club! Let's all go fight, fight, fight!"

That bit of silliness had changed Black Skull's mind. He'd offer himself naked to the Copena before he'd allow the fool to mock him. Black Skull had given the Contrary a seething glare, wishing he could knock the smirk off the pest's thin face.

And to Black Skull's surprise, Otter had conceded, "At least leave your atlatl and darts. No one will bother them. Catcher will be on guard." The Trader had smiled faintly. "After all, it wouldn't do for the Black Skull to show up at Green Turtle village empty-handed."

"Very well, Trader. I will leave the atlatl and darts."

Nevertheless, his nerves had hummed as they walked up the slope and out into the open.

Green Turtle village consisted of a scattering of huts dotting a long hillock. A child saw them first, calling out and charging toward them.

"The Water Fox!" came the cry.

At the happy sound, Black Skull's sense of dread lessened. At least they spoke a language that a human being could understand. He wouldn't have to muddle his way through in Trader pidgin.

By the time they'd reached the outskirts of the settlement, an old man, supported by two equally old women, had hobbled to the head of the growing crowd.

"Long Squirrel and his two wives," Otter had whispered from the side of his mouth.

"*Two* wives!" Black Skull stared. He'd seen such things before. Traders from the north often had more than one wife, but that had struck him as a curious peculiarity. Here he saw people who actually lived that way. "These people are patrilineal." Black Skull had never heard of a matrilineal people with more than one wife.

"That's right." Then Otter raised his voice. "Long Squirrel! You look fit, as spry as ever!"

"Ah, ha!" the old man cried. "Water Fox! You have come again. For a new shirt, perhaps?"

"May all of your grandchildren be healthy and happy. The blessings of Many Colored Crow on you and all of your clan!"

While they chattered on, Black Skull found himself standing to the rear, casting about nervously for some hint of what to expect. Somehow, in his preoccupation, he missed his introduction. A calm had fallen, and all eyes were upon him.

"*The* Black Skull?" Long Squirrel had whispered in awe, his mouth agape. "Here? In *our* clan holdings?"

"And Green Spider, the great Dreamer," Otter proclaimed with a flourish. "We have business in the north, my old friend. Green Spider has had a Vision, become a Contrary."

More gasps.

But of course Green Spider immediately ruined any solemnity and order the situation might have had. He flapped his arms and proclaimed at the top of his lungs, "Down is up, and up is down, and all the leaves blow 'round and 'round." Then his vision seemed to clear, and he asked, "Are we going to stand here all day?"

To which he promptly sat down.

Long Squirrel seemed at a complete loss for words. One of his more sensible wives gathered her wits and waved them toward the houses. "Come, we will feed you. Make a place for you to stay. Everyone! Bring food for our guests! Children, gather firewood. Hurry!"

Green Spider had jumped to his feet and started off back toward the canoes. Otter noticed and called, "Green Spider, go away and never come back!"

The Contrary promptly changed direction and led the shocked procession into the village.

Black Skull chuckled to himself as he remembered. Long Squirrel had provided not only an endless hot meal, but he'd cleaned out a house just for Black Skull's use. So many gifts had been showered on them that it would have taken two extra canoes to carry them all. Artfully, the Trader had given it all back, most of the wealth going to recent widows and to a poor family whose house had burned down a couple of nights earlier. No wonder the Green Turtle people liked the Water Fox.

That night at the fire, the clanspeople had listened wide-eyed as Black Skull recounted stories of battles fought and won. They'd been a wonderful audience, gasping at his ferocious expressions, their souls drinking in every word. At Long Squirrel's insistence, he'd twirled his war club and brought cries of amazement and awe from the assembled people.

Black Skull had seen worship reflected in those eyes. They had understood the sort of warrior he was. Then, after he'd retired to his bedding, two young women had ghosted in out of the darkness and slipped under his blanket. Closing his eyes, he could remember their warmth, the softness of their skin against his. Tireless, they had taken turns, each stroking his manhood to reawakened vigor when he thought himself drained. He could hear their soft cries, feel their flesh tighten in ecstasy at his pulsing release.

They'd left in the faint graying of dawn, whispering excitedly to themselves about the strong children they would bear from his seed.

It was a wonder he could even wield a paddle this morning.

The canoe wobbled again as Green Spider began wrestling with Catcher.

"Be still!" Black Skull thundered. "You'll tip us over!"

Green Spider immediately stood up, waving his hands and dancing around. The canoe rocked and bobbed dangerously.

"Dance!" Otter shouted in the stern. "Go wild, Green Spider, like a young ferret in spring!"

The Contrary promptly seated himself and crossed his arms, as motionless as a stump. Catcher cocked his head, then pawed at Green Spider and whined.

"One of these days," Black Skull grumbled to himself in promise.

"What was that?" Otter called.

Seeking to recover his rhythm with the paddle, Black Skull thought for a moment. "Trader, have you ever considered? We could just brain the fool. That, or strangle him. I'll even cut his throat, if you'd like. We could weight the body down and sink it in a backswamp. After that, we'll hole up in some nice place like Green Turtle and go back to the Elders next spring with some story we've made up. No one will ever know the difference."

When he glanced back, Green Spider was miming having his throat cut, choking, and stabbing himself, but Otter was grinning.

"I don't think we'd better kill him yet."

"Oh? Much more of his foolishness and I'm going to break this paddle over his idiot head."

"Don't," Otter chimed back. "I beg you. Let's keep him alive. Long Squirrel was so engrossed by the two of you that he never thought to haggle over the purple shirts. I got four of them—and he never asked for *anything* in return!"

You don't know how lucky it is that you have these," Star Shell declared. She lifted the long wooden pestle—crafted from the trunk of a small tree—and thumped it down on the dried paw-paw seeds in the old mortar. Like most, the mortar had been hollowed out of a stump. She worked in a constant rhythm, *ta-tunk, ta-tunk.*

Tall Man sat in a half-shelter, little more than a south-facing arbor that cut the wind and shaded a person in the summer, while sunning him in the winter. The farmstead sat in a cove where a small tributary trickled out of a narrow valley before joining Blue Duck Creek, which ran westward through the hills toward Moonshell River.

Clamshell's holding consisted of her small hut, a couple of fields, the arbor, and several storage pits excavated into the ground before the arbor. Trees screened the small farm from the main trail that ran on the other side of Blue Duck Creek. Beyond the worn pestle and mortar, the old woman's only large pot was now steaming over a small fire.

The morning sun had burned through the last remnants of the storm, which now fled eastward as billowy clouds. The land gleamed in the white clarity of a fresh snow. Their tracks, once so damning, appeared only as dimples in the white.

"I always go prepared," Tall Man said easily. "I keep a lot of the necessities in that little pack. You never know when you'll need something critical."

Star Shell continued to mash the dried brown seeds. "I hope this is enough. I'm being eaten alive."

"It will be. I know that tree. The seeds are particularly virulent."

Star Shell inspected the crushed hulls and nodded, reaching

down to rub the powder off the bottom of the pestle.

"Stop!" Tall Man cried. "Don't touch it!" He stood up on his too-short legs and waddled over to hand her a long blade of sacred chert. "Use this. Scrape off the excess carefully. It probably wouldn't hurt you, but let's not take chances. I know that particular tree. I followed rumors for two years to find it."

"Rumors?" Star Shell asked as she took the chert blade and shaved the powder from the pestle.

"I heard of people dying. Everyone knows that pawpaw fruits are excellent fare but that the seeds are poisonous. It turns out that a little girl had eaten one of the seeds because she didn't know any better. For days she lingered with her soul half out of her body. Perhaps in that state it met an evil ghost, I don't know. But something malicious worked on the girl's soul. Over the years, other people were poisoned. It turned out that it was the girl—not so little by this time—who was causing all the problems. She'd taken to slipping ground seeds into the food of people she didn't like. I finally got her to show me the tree."

"Nice child," Star Shell commented as she used the flake to scrape up the powder from the hollow in the mortar and pile it into a mussel shell Tall Man had provided. The notion returned to her that the Magician had spent a great deal of his life in the company of nefarious characters.

"Poor old Clamshell." He inspected the powder. "It hadn't occurred to me that she'd slipped so much. She knows better than to let lice take over her house. She used to be so fastidious."

Star Shell paused awkwardly. "She says you fathered one of her children."

Tall Man turned away and poured the contents of the mussel shell into the pot of steaming water. "There, let it steep for a while. Then we can soak the blankets and our clothing in it. As for us, a good scrubbing in the creek will take care of any other little pests. We'll rub ourselves with some walnut rinds that I'm carrying. That should cure most of the trouble."

Star Shell pointed at the worn mortar. "What about the residue? Someone will use this mortar again."

"Burn it out. It needs to be reshaped anyway."

Star Shell placed the pestle to one side and studied the dwarf. "You don't strike me as a fatherly type."

He finally sighed at the sight of Star Shell's arched eyebrow. "Yes, she had my child. Or claims she did. With Clamshell, it was hard to say whose child was whose."

"She claims to have been quite a lover."

Tall Man smiled and fingered his chin. "Yes, she was. Made a study of it. Had quite a reputation."

Star Shell stared up at the rounded shoulders of the wooded hills. An eagle soared across the open patch of sky, then vanished behind the trees. "Is that why you didn't stay with her?"

Tall Man stared into the steaming water. "No. It wasn't that at all. I . . . well, I couldn't. That's all. Sometimes people get themselves into . . . I guess you could call them situations. I was young, you see. And she was the Evening Star."

Star Shell started at the name. "But I thought that was just a story!"

Tall Man glanced back at the house. "No, young Star Shell. She was the most beautiful woman in the world. Men came from all the corners of the earth just to look at her. To my knowledge, at least four men died in fights over her."

"She says five."

"Five, then. It doesn't matter."

Star Shell placed her hands on her hips. "So why didn't you stay with her? Last night she spoke very affectionately of you."

"She was married, not that that ever stopped her. No, I . . ." He glanced up uneasily, seeing Star Shell's confusion. "I did something. It was a long time ago."

"The way she talked, I guess you could say she had some regrets. Maybe her husband wouldn't have mattered."

"In her eyes, a husband never mattered."

"Then is that why you didn't stay with her? Because she wouldn't be loyal?"

Tall Man squinted up at the sun. "Star Shell, you must understand. She was like a fragrant flower. She drew men to her like bees to the bloom. To love and couple was simply her nature. Some women are by nature fine potters. Some women have the talent for weaving, dying, clan politics, or healing. In the case of the Evening Star, hers was coupling. That was where Power gave her her greatest art. Generally, a man and a woman learn each other over time. She knew intuitively how to make the greatest pleasure out of coupling."

"So I'm right. You didn't want everyone sharing her bed?"

He seemed to hedge. "No, I wouldn't have wanted that."

She studied him, a frown chiseling her brow. "Why do I get the feeling that you're not telling me everything?"

"You've been too close to Power for too long. You're starting to read souls." He sighed in defeat. "I suppose you might say that she and the Mask share a great deal in common. Wherever the Evening Star went, controversy, trouble, and ferment followed. Nevertheless, I would have accepted that."

Star Shell cocked her head. "You keep avoiding the reason, Tall Man. Should I ask Clamshell?"

"She doesn't know." He dropped his gaze to the trampled snow. "And I'd prefer to keep it that way. One of these days her ghost will probably find out."

"Her ghost?"

"Ghosts learn a great deal more than the living do, my girl. They see through the lies perpetrated by the living."

"I won't tell her. But I think I need to know. This is important, isn't it?"

"Why do you think that?"

"I don't know. A hunch."

Tall Man patiently packed the snow down with one of his small feet. "I poisoned her husband. He was a Trader. Brought obsidian from the far west. I was young. In love—and carried away with Power and all the things it had taught me. I thought that if he was . . ."

"Out of the way?" Star Shell crossed her arms.

"Yes. Out of the way. The Six Flutes Clan shared a valley with my clan. I'd loved her for years. Oh, she was so much older than I, but you've got to understand. She was the most beautiful woman in the world. And she had, well, an attraction that overwhelmed a man's sense. It was her form of Power, and through it, she married one of the most prestigious men among the Flat Pipe people. Obsidian is a rare and important stone. The Trader she married was renowned. If he'd stayed at home more, perhaps things would have turned out differently."

"All right, you killed him. That's pretty drastic. If you could go that far, why didn't you marry her?"

Tall Man continued to tramp the snow flat, each step a deliberate act. "I'd never killed a man before. The poison I chose, water hemlock, has a deadly root. I made him a tea of it, used mint leaves to cover the taste. I watched him die. How could I go to her after that?"

"And her sister?"

"A simple treatment of gumweed eased her stomach complaint." He glanced up. "Listen to me, Star Shell. Deep down in her soul, she loved that Trader. No matter that she shared her blankets with others, she *loved* him. She never loved another in that same way. I ask you, never let her know what I did."

To hide her unease, Star Shell stared at the mortar, where the virulent powder had left its stain. "I'll fetch some kindling. Burn this out. Then we'll scrape it down to wood again. Meanwhile, you go and fetch Clamshell's blankets. I'm tired of lice."

The Magician nodded, turning slow steps toward the bark-covered house. As he did, the old woman and her dog stepped out into the sunlight. Clamshell shaded her eyes with a gnarled hand. Silver Water slipped out through the door, chattering animatedly to the old woman and patting the rickety old dog.

How many other secrets do you hide within that diminutive soul of yours, Magician? One thing's for sure. I won't ever underestimate you.

Wave Dancer bucked and rolled as Otter steered the big canoe across the open water. Gusts of wind interspersed with sheets of rain slapped at them. Even Green Spider seemed cowed by the weather. Moisture had ruined the bones he'd painted on his shirt. Now the pigments dripped from the fabric in a gray sludge. He hunched under a blanket, reaching out periodically to pat Catcher. The dog had curled into a wet lump and lay shivering on the packs.

The only sounds were the sigh of wind, the hiss of rain on wood and water, the chop smacking the hull, and the bell-like sound of the paddles stroking and lifting.

Traveling upriver took a keen eye and an intuitive sense, developed from long familiarity with wind and water. Otter used all of his skills to read the river, judging where the path of least resistance lay. Generally, they traveled close to shore, away from the boiling center of the current. But on the Father Water, that meant crossing and recrossing the channel as it wound around in wide loops. Sometimes side channels offered the best route, but these changed over time, some silted in or the passage blocked by a fallen tree.

Nevertheless, they made good time, thanks in part to Black Skull's endless strength. The warrior had a natural sense of balance, and used all of his body. He might have been matching himself against the river—another battle to be fought, another challenge to be won. From early morning to late evening, his pointed paddle dug deeply into the roiling water, always pushing them onward.

Thick forest ran right up to the banks along this stretch of river, the dripping trees dark and brooding. People didn't live close to the water here, for the floodplain was too broad. Instead, they built inland, where higher ground ensured that their settlements wouldn't wash away in the spring flooding. A Trader had to know which tributaries to take to reach each of the clan territories.

Two canoes had passed them that morning, headed downstream, carried in the center of the current.

"Tree coming!" Black Skull shouted and rose to his knees, crabbing sideways with his paddle.

The mass of branches rolled down on them like a dangerous water monster as the forest giant tumbled in the current. Otter threw himself into the paddle, and *Wave Dancer* angled to the right of the danger. They passed well clear of the mess. Ugly spears of broken branches lifted from the brown waters, dripping as they arched over and dove again.

"As we go north," Otter warned, "there will be more of them. There always are as spring washes the roots out from under them. After a while, the branches get broken off or worn away, and if the tree was green, it won't float high in the water. Sometimes all the warning you get is the wave pattern off the trunk."

"Great place, this river of yours!"

"Just around this bend there's an island. Night is coming. Let's stop early and build a fire, dry out."

"As you say, Trader."

True to Otter's memory, the island offered shelter. He and Black Skull leaped ashore, grabbed the fox head, and pulled *Wave Dancer* up on the wet sand. Catcher bailed off the packs, dove into the shallows, then trotted onto the shore and shook copiously.

"Just like a dog," Black Skull observed as he twisted the tail of his heavy leather shirt to wring the water out. "People are half-drowned and a dog has to come shake right beside them."

Otter turned his attention to the campsite. The river was eroding away the sides of the small island despite the stubborn resistance of the trees. Farther up from the sandy spit they'd landed on, roots clung desperately to what dirt remained. In another ten years, nothing but a low sandbar would be left.

Otter wiped water from his face. "Black Skull, go see if you can find some dry wood. I'll put some tinder together and shake the embers out of the fire pot."

The warrior reached for his atlatl and darts, checking the delicate feathers.

"Don't you ever go anywhere without your weapons?" Otter asked.

Black Skull gave him a disapproving scowl and stalked off for the narrow band of woods.

"He must never be what he is," Green Spider observed. "Therefore he is always what he is not."

Otter bent over the packs and fished out the thick-walled clay pot that held their embers. The sides were pleasingly hot. "He's become stranger and stranger. I thought he'd pick a fight the other night in Meadowlark's clan house. Why does he have to be so difficult?"

Green Spider's disconnected gaze seemed to sharpen. "The meat of the snapping turtle is very delicate."

Otter hesitated, shivering now that he'd stopped paddling. "What does that have to do with Black Skull?"

"Why, not one thing." Green Spider, his arms outstretched, pirouetted around on the sand while gray water trickled body paint from the blanket corners.

Otter shook his head and walked up to the tree line. From the looks of the place, they'd stopped at yet another Khota camp. The shelters still stood, and with a little effort, they could be patched up. Several fire pits marred the silty sand. Otter used his hands to dig one out and pinched the charcoal between his fingers. Not more than two days old.

He picked his way into the remnant of forest and kicked around, finding dry grass beneath a section of bark. Cupping the tinder, he returned to the fire pit and huddled over it to protect his prize from the rain. From the pot he coaxed a couple of embers and blew on them until they glowed. Then he poked them into the tinder with a wet stick.

Flames crackled, and he added damp twigs. The fire smoked but stayed alight. When he looked up, Green Spider was watching, his expression quizzical.

"Guard this, will you? And don't drip on the fire. I want it kept as wet as the river."

Green Spider grinned and knelt down to protect the vulnerable flames from the worst of the rain.

Otter returned to his foraging and found enough wood that was only damp instead of soggy to keep his fire going. Entrusting that to Green Spider, he searched out his adze in the canoe and attacked some of the larger logs, hacking off the wet wood to expose the dry. These he added to the blaze, and by the time Black Skull reappeared, he had a toasty fire crackling.

"Find anything?" Otter asked. Black Skull shouldered past him and went to rummage in the canoe before walking off down the shoreline.

Otter chewed his lip for a moment, battling an urge to confront the ugly warrior.

"Better do it now," Green Spider whispered at his side. "Now, now, now. Before it's too late."

Otter frowned. Did that mean, "Do it now and Black Skull will likely break your neck"? He shook his head, thinking about it. A few days before, they'd been facing Meadowlark and his clan. The talk had been in Trade pidgin. Trouble began only after the introductions.

"He doesn't seem to know who I am," Black Skull had muttered, looking half baffled by the quick interchange. The languages were completely different. And then Black Skull had said: *"I'll teach the gobbling grouse just who the Black Skull is!"*

Only Green Spider's sudden decision to leap up and start running around in circles, gobbling, and flapping imaginary wings, had kept a melee from evolving out of Black Skull's surly behavior. That, and a curt reminder from Otter about whose territory they stood in, and who had been given authority by the Clan Elders.

Otter rose from the fire and stepped into the trees. At times, late at night, he was convinced that this entire journey was headed for disaster. Black Skull was going to explode at the least opportune moment. Green Spider wasn't going to know which way to go. *Power, you'd better have a good Trade in mind to even this out.*

But Power rarely Traded in respect to value. Offer a piece of copper and Power would give you a rock in return.

Otter was pulling another log out when Black Skull appeared from the trees. He traveled silently, his moccasined feet moving ghostlike on the leaf mat. The big warrior looked grim. "You'd better come look."

Otter dropped the log and followed Black Skull down to the beach. A ways above *Wave Dancer*'s landing, long marks could be seen in the sand, along with dimpled tracks.

Black Skull bent down, pointing. "Canoes, four of them. They beached here. The tracks have mostly been washed out by the rain, but you can still read them. These dimpled ones here, that's where they pushed the canoes out. But look at these, up here by the bow. See how deep they are? And smaller. Like a boy, or a woman, tried to push the boat out."

Black Skull moved to the second. "Same thing here."

Otter pursed his lips as cold water trickled down his face. "What makes you think that wasn't where they pushed the canoe off?"

"Whoever was trying to push the boat off didn't succeed. You don't see any other small tracks following the boat down as it slid into the water. Come."

Black Skull pointed at the brown sand. "See here? The tracks turn. From the way they twist and dig in, the woman was running. See how the stride lengthens? Look close at this track here.

See how the heel pushed deeply into the sand and the toes gouged?''

"But I don't—"

"You're not a tracker. How do you run, Trader? The heel hits first, and you push off with your toes. That's why the track breaks like this. And down here, a man, a big man, is running behind her, see? His stride is greater than hers."

They followed the tracks down past where *Wave Dancer* lay canted on the sand.

"Look at this!" Black Skull squatted to finger a smooth depression. "Someone fell here. Look, see this? That's where he pushed up. Before the rain, you'd have seen a palm print. And what's this?"

Black Skull plucked a strand of leather from the sand. Tugging gently, he pulled it loose, including the polished stone tied to the end.

"A bola weight?" Otter reached down to examine it. Bola stones were ground into long teardrop shapes, the tips pointed.

Black Skull chuckled. "This Pearl, she's canny. She brought down this man who was chasing her."

Otter bent low, squinting at the sand. "So did she get away?"

Black Skull stood, slapping the sand from his hands. "Let's see."

They worked out the tracks to the point where a broken branch as thick as a man's arm protruded from the sand.

"She would have been able to jump that," Otter exclaimed. "I know Pearl. She's half wildcat."

"Would she have seen it in the dark, Trader? And yes, here, on the other side, look. She fell. From these tracks here, another man came in and pounced on her. See the drag marks? Like he pulled her back from the water."

Otter sighed and straightened. "Too bad. I wish she'd gotten away."

Black Skull stared out at the river. "She almost did. Not that it would have done her much good."

"She'd be free. According to the stories her people tell about her, she can outswim a catfish."

Black Skull shrugged. "I've been swimming in your river, Trader. And that was considerably south of here. How long would she have lasted in that cold? Not long enough to make the shore. Not at night.''

Otter reached down to touch the cold water. Black Skull was right. Not even Pearl could have lasted long in that.

Black Skull wiped rain from his face. ''Better for her that they caught her. She may be a captive, but at least she's alive.''

As the warrior turned back toward the fire, Otter stared at the depressions in the damp sand. Unconsciously, he patted the prayer mat he'd placed in his shirt. It now rested over his heart.

''Maybe. But knowing the Khota, perhaps she'd rather be dead.''

Sixteen

I can feel the luminous darkness stirring, awakening, like the black depths of a mighty thunderstorm about to be unleashed.

I lean back in the canoe, my head close to Catcher's. The dog's breath warms my upturned face. And I marvel at that. That I experience it at all. This elusive world grows more slippery for me every day. The Mask and its suffering have become my reality. The depths of its sorrow are stunning. The emotion twines within me with barbed tendrils, squeezing, stinging, and comes out of me like a volcano, erupting in hearty laughter.

And I know . . . I know . . . I must force myself to sit in the midst of that laughter, because if I do, it will teach me everything.

The smoldering pile of ashes did little to soothe Robin's anger. Guard posts canted inward like ungainly teeth blunted by the green sprigs of sacred cedar. Some of the posts had been scorched in the fire, but they still stood, hemming the ghosts within.

"You came for my cousin," Old Slate said. The blanket draped around her weary shoulders had been beautiful once. Between smudges of ash and dirt, a hawk pattern could be seen. She pointed with a thin arm. "There he is. Go on. Walk in there and get him."

Robin turned uneasily and glanced back at the warriors who had followed him to Sun Mounds. They shifted, staring around uncertainly and clutching their weapons. Some wore cloaks of twined rabbit fur; others used finely woven blankets for covering. Thick winter moccasins rose high on their legs, protection against the deep snow. The Shining Bird people stood separate, clustered in little groups. They huddled under soot-stained blankets, children peeking around from behind them.

They'd come expecting brutal war, but no one from the Shining Bird Clan had met Robin at the opening to the earthworks. No challenges had been hurled over the snow-clad fields. Instead, they simply stared at him with haggard eyes, their faces smudged with soot as his warriors trotted into the clan grounds. Most of the Shining Bird stood stoop-shouldered, and not a weapon could be seen anywhere.

Ash darkened the trampled snow of Sun Mounds. Occasional flakes still fell from the brooding sky. Robin could feel the tension in the air as the ghosts that lived in the place watched and whispered among themselves.

He studied the ashes, a pensive set to his lips. His enemy was dead. Over the years he'd come to hate Mica Bird. His rival had had everything—the benefits of status birth, the Mask, clan leadership, Star Shell, and the list went on. Was this where it ended, in smoldering ashes?

He fingered the war club at his waist, running his fingertips along the smooth wood. A thick blanket woven from split feather, cord, and strips of rabbit fur hung from his shoulders. The human-jawbone breastplate covered his chest. He could feel the cold eating into his earlobes through the copper ear spools that marked him as an influential man. No, there had to be more.

He had been the sixth son of a farmer, his father nothing more than a man from an inconsequential lineage, eking out a living on poor, rocky soils. They'd lived in a hilly valley along the upper margins of Blue Duck territory. In those places he'd learned to run, hide, hunt, and track. Even as a boy, he'd derided his brothers for their limited dreams of simple wives and back-forest fields.

At the time of his passage to manhood, when he took the name Robin—the darting hunter bird of the forest floor—he'd made up his mind to take a different path. The decision hadn't been a hard one to make, not after watching his brothers follow in their father's footsteps. Robin, of whom people expected so little, would have so much more. No matter what the cost.

He had dedicated himself to that task, consumed by the need to advance himself through politics and war. Power had favored him, for status had come rapidly, helped by the ruthless efficiency with which he attacked both problems and foes. He had already risen to leadership of his War Society, but now he wanted to go farther. It would not be enough to be the first man of his lineage to be buried in his own earthen mound; he would have all people know his name.

The living shall kneel before me! All the generations of men shall know my name. When I am dead, the ghosts of the ancestors shall receive me with humble, bowed heads.

Now, staring out at the ruin of the Shining Bird clan house, he told himself that the unease clawing at the edges of his soul was caused by the howlings of the two ghosts . . . nothing more.

His warriors looked as if they'd rather be anywhere but here, witnessing Shining Bird clan's terror. What could he expect? He'd led them here for a fight, and now the old woman offered him only burned ashes and the ghost of his enemy.

Old Slate took a deep breath, raising her clenched hands. Tendons stood out on her thin old arms. "He hung himself. First he ripped a hole into his grandfather's grave and pulled out the bones, and then he went into the clan house and . . . did what he did."

"My clansman, my cousin, is dead. His son is maimed, blinded in one eye. I have come to avenge them, and I will see to it that I make my cousin's ghost rest easier." Robin straightened. "Where is Star Shell?"

Old Slate shook her head. "I don't know."

"What about the High Head dwarf, the Magician?"

Old Slate appeared beyond deception. "I don't know that either."

"It's the Mask!" Fat Lips cried, stepping close. His hair hung in loose strands; panic glittered in his eyes. "That's what did this to us."

Robin bent down to glare into Old Slate's face. "Where is the Mask? Did you burn it, too?"

Old Slate rubbed a dirty hand over her wrinkled face, smearing the soot. "No. The Magician brought it out. At least I think he did. We were all so shocked. I mean, that my cousin would . . . would . . ."

"Your cousin did us all a favor," Robin concluded. "But this isn't finished. Not for me or for my warriors. *I want that Mask!*"

Old Slate just shrugged.

Fat Lips pushed his way closer. "That Magician, he stole it! Stole it, I tell you. We'd be a lot better off if we'd burned it like we said!"

Robin placed a hand on Fat Lip's shoulders. "Where is Star Shell? Where did she take the Mask?"

Fat Lips slowly shook his head, giving Robin a blank stare. "Gone. Somewhere. Gone. That's all. She took her daughter and left. The Magician said he'd solve our problems after we burned the clan house. We did that yesterday. We were supposed to meet again, afterward, you see. And he'd tell us how to solve the problem of the Mask."

"What were his exact words, do you remember?"

Fat Lips frowned, his mouth working. Then he nodded. "I think he said, 'If you wait to make a final decision, I can offer you a way out of this dilemma by tomorrow night.' Yes, that's what it was, wasn't it?"

Old Slate jerked a weary nod. "That's what he said."

Fat Lips rubbed the back of his neck. "That would have been last night. That's when he said he'd offer us a way out."

"Fools!" Robin hissed. "He was planning all along to take the Mask! Why didn't you realize it? And no one saw them after that?"

"No." Fat Lips glanced around. "I've asked. They disappeared."

"So, that was the way out," Old Slate mused. "The Magician

knew you'd be coming here, that you'd want the Mask.'' Her shrewd eyes sharpened. "Robin, take my advice. Go home. Shining Bird Clan will help you appease your angry ghost. We'll come and make offerings at his burial. The Mask has created enough trouble. Let it go.''

"I *want* that Mask!''

Old Slate seemed to have recovered some of her spirit. "Why? So you can go the way of my cousin? Look out there at the ashes, Robin. Is that how you hope to end? Your ghost hemmed in by guardian stakes? Feared by all? No. Mark my words, boy. Follow that Mask and your soul will spend eternity forgotten in the cold darkness.''

He stiffened. "Perhaps I would rather serve Many Colored Crow than take your advice.''

The old woman shook her head. "You want to serve yourself. I expect the Mask knows that, too.''

Robin spun on his heel and walked back to where Woodpecker stood. Meeting the warrior's eyes, he ordered, "Divide into small parties. Scout out all the roads. They can't have gone far. Star Shell, her daughter, and the Magician shouldn't be too hard to track.''

Woodpecker's thin body belied his strength and endurance. He wore a feather cape over his thick winter shirt. Fabric leggings kept his legs warm. He glanced uncomfortably at the sky. "In the beginning, it was just Star Shell and Mica Bird. But the Magician's involved now. I don't need to remind you of how Powerful a dwarf is.''

"I know, and yes, my friend, I understand the danger. But I will be very, very careful.'' Robin lowered his voice. "I've swallowed a pearl wrapped in mint leaves.''

"That's protection against sorcery!''

"Precisely.'' Robin gripped Woodpecker's shoulder. "Now, assemble the search parties. Our quarry can't be far ahead of us.''

Woodpecker didn't look convinced. "It's going to snow again. The tracks will be hard to find.''

"They went north—to StarSky. I can feel it.''

"Why not south? Down toward Serpent City? Once they reach the river, they can go in any direction. Or west, to the Many Paints. For that matter, the Magician might have taken the Mask east, where most of the High Head Clans live. Or to their clans south of the Serpent River.''

''Star Shell has been the spoiled daughter of privilege all of her life. She will run to her father.'' Robin was already staring northward, up the wide valley of the Moonshell. *That's the way she will have gone.* ''But just in case, send scouting parties in every direction. I will take no chances with this.''

Woodpecker exhaled a frosty breath, then trotted back to the warriors and issued orders.

When he caught them, he'd have to act quickly, take no chances. If possible, he'd kill the dwarf from ambush, give him no opportunity to cast a spell or don the Mask. If ambush was impossible, he'd just walk up, smiling and warm, and dash the Magician's brains out before the little dwarf could suspect anything.

Robin chuckled at the vision. *And then I will have everything. Influence and status, the Mask . . . and Star Shell!*

He noted Old Slate's pensive gaze. She was looking at him in the way she'd stare at a dying man. He waved her away with disgust and followed Woodpecker. By nightfall, he'd be far to the north.

The Anhinga were experts at catching alligators, and Pearl had caught more than her share. Her people ate the meat, tanned the skins, and rendered the fat to mix with insecticidal plants. This ointment they smeared on their bodies for protection during mosquito season.

The Anhinga often trapped the alligators alive—at least the smaller ones—and carried them back to camp. In doing so, they used a thong to tie the mouth shut so the animal couldn't bite, and they bound the legs tightly to the body with cord.

Pearl now knew what the alligator felt like, for the Khota had bound her in much the same way. Like an alligator, she could wiggle, but that was about all. Any respect the Khota might have had for her vanished. Instead of a bride, she had become a war trophy, except that Grizzly Tooth insisted none of the men touch her.

Grandmother, did you know I would be treated like this? Would you have sold me had you known they were going to carry me bound like a piece of meat?

Desolate, Pearl stared out at the banks of the river. She knew the price of her life, she had watched it pass from Khota to Anhinga hands. She could see her grandmother's brown fingers tracing the cool surfaces of copper. Each piece of metal would be earned by Pearl's suffering in a far-off land. Those stroking fingers that glided over the polished metal might have been flaying away bits of her own soul.

I hate you . . . I spit upon everything Anhinga! She would never look downriver again without experiencing that feeling of betrayal.

Patches of snow—the first she'd ever seen—whitened the ground in the shadow of the trees. The eastern bank of the river rose into tall bluffs, their rounded and worn tops blurred by a fuzz of winter-bare tree branches. To the west, the forest grew to the banks of the river. In places she could see back along quiet waterways thick with ice, and beyond them to gray sandstone cliffs that loomed like half-hidden sentries.

A year ago at this time, she'd been on a deepwater Trading canoe, far out in the gulf. The season of horrible storms had passed, and she'd joined some of her cousins, saltwater Traders. They'd traveled to the islands to obtain tobacco, shells, and sweet cane. If only she were so free now.

Closing her eyes, she could remember the smell of the breeze as the big canoe rose on the crests and slid into the troughs. How marvelous the water had been, a blue so rich that it hurt the eyes. Dolphins had leaped and plunged, keeping company with their vessel until the head Trader, Bleeding Starfish, had harpooned a young one.

What a fight that had been, the dolphin making wailing sounds and pulling their canoe so fast that water boiled white around the bow.

When they finally landed the puffing prize, it had taken several thrusts of a dart to kill it, the blood clouding the water around them. Without fire, they'd eaten the rich red meat raw.

And then my luck began to turn.

No more dolphins had appeared. The weather had grown worse and the swells had mounted. By the time they'd weathered the storms and made shore, they were so far off course that it took them weeks of paddling down the coast to reach Anhinga territory.

Bleeding Starfish had known the way. And on that journey, he'd taught her to read the stars and the patterns of the waves. Beyond the excitement of making the crossing and seeing new lands and people, that knowledge might have been the only good to come from that trip. For within weeks of their homecoming, the Khota had arrived.

Now, when she looked up at the sky, she could tell how far north they were. She watched the heavens, studying the changes in the guiding stars, noting how the familiar constellations had shifted southward. No matter what, if she escaped, she could find her way home, pick a path across land or sea. Every day the cold grew more intense—and so did her desperation.

She studied the Khota, always in hope that she could detect some weakness that would allow her to escape.

And if she did, she promised she would never eat the dolphin's meat again.

A moan, followed by an uneasy laugh, caused her to turn. The warrior known as Rotten Mouth—because all of his teeth had fallen out—had hung his bare bottom over the edge of the canoe. He had spent most of the morning sweating and vomiting over the side. Now he was experiencing the second phase.

Pearl glanced across to one of the other canoes. Big Toe and White Squirrel were looking a little peaked, too. They had shared Rotten Mouth's dinner the night before.

Pearl sighed. *No, I will never eat dolphin again—and if Rotten Mouth and his friends knew, they'd never eat dogbane again, either.*

In Clamshell's hut, the firelight flickered. The old woman who had once been known as the Evening Star studied the beautifully wrought fabric pack that lay beside the Magician's blankets. For the moment, her unsteady head had ceased its uncontrollable wobble. She listened, straining to catch something at the edge of her hearing.

She half rose, then placed bony fingers to her lips as she glanced suspiciously at the sleeping forms of her guests.

The old dog raised its head, eyes glowing as they reflected the firelight. It watched as she stood on curiously steady feet and made her way over the sleeping visitors to the fabric pack.

Her fingers traced the patterns of the brightly dyed geometric figures. With a firm resolve, she picked up the pack and carefully retraced her way to the fire.

She didn't hear the old dog whine and turn away. Ears back, it curled into a ball, as if against the brunt of a coming storm. With that cowed expression of canine distrust, the dog glanced at the old woman and growled.

Heedless, Clamshell's age-curled fingers undid the cords that bound the pack together. Eagerly, she slipped the fabric off and unfolded the supple wolfhide to see what lay within. . . .

A troubled Star Shell lay on her side in the thick nest of blankets. Her sleep-haunted cries came only as stifled whimpers, muffled by her clamped jaws and the bedding.

In her Dream, she stood on a rocky plain, windswept and desolate. Overhead, a tortured sky roiled and billowed with twisting black clouds. Wind buffeted her naked body, pelting it with stinging grains of sand and tearing at her hair. She staggered on uneven rocks that bit painfully into her bare feet and hunched against the blasting sand, trying in vain to shield her tender flesh.

As wind wailed and moaned over the cracked and broken ground, it sang in voices known to no human. The howling air smelled of drought and dust. Wicked lightning flashed in the blackness.

Grit blew into her eyes, and she raised an arm to shield her face. The weird lightning continued to sear the sky above her, splitting into blinding strands of jagged light that burst in all directions.

Star Shell fought to cry out, terrified by the forces that surrounded her; but even as she drew breath, the gale tore it from her lungs. She stumbled ahead uncertainly, shrinking against the driving wind. Somewhere she had to find shelter.

Where? In every direction, the sere landscape stretched featurelessly. And then something caught her eye.

Before her, a white speck could be seen hovering over the rocky ground. Against the blackened sky, it seemed to glow—as if an unseen shaft of light fell upon it.

Star Shell drove herself toward it, half-sobbing as the angular rocks cut and bruised her feet. The wind whipped itself to a fury, blasting her with its full wrath. Barely sheltered by her raised arm, she continued step by staggering step until she could discover the nature of the white object.

What she saw amazed her. A beautiful ceramic bowl floated on the air. She had never seen such a perfectly crafted object—as if the Earth Mother herself might have willed the finest of her white clay to form the delicate shape. No clumsy human fingers could have coiled such a perfect, thin-walled vessel. Only freshly fallen snow matched the purity of color. Had some Spirit Being crafted this?

The wind died into an eerie silence as Star Shell walked to the bowl and stood on tiptoe to peer inside.

She cried out in delight and pulled back her long black hair to see better. The designs on the inside had been painted with great intricacy and detail, the shapes irregular, the colors brighter than any human-made paints. Within that thin ceramic shell lay the entire world.

Water bounded three sides of the land, east, south, and along the far west. On the northern side of the bowl, she could see white snowfields fading into green basins. Mountains, rounded and worn, ran down from the ice-packed plains. Silver rivers threaded out of verdant valleys and followed their twisting courses to the sea.

The scene seemed to expand, to broaden, until she could make out the tiny details of forests, creeks, and plains.

Looking closer, she was overtaken with wonder. She could see herds of animals, smell the richness of vegetation. The faint sighing of the wind, of the leaves and the water, lingered at the edge of her senses.

The beasts she saw surprised her. While some were animals she knew, others defied description. Monster creatures walked the land, along with deer, foxes, beaver, and raccoons. Some had long trunks that made Star Shell think their tails had grown from their faces. Others looked like oddly shaped bears, furry, with three hooked claws for toes, which they used for pulling succulent branches down to prehensile lips. Oversized wolves, weirdly misshapen bears, long-toothed lions, and fleet-footed grazers—all these delighted her.

As she watched, Star Shell realized that the ice was melting in the north. To her amazement, the vantage shifted, until she seemed to have fallen into the bowl, and whimsical air currents carried her above a grassy plain.

In the distance, the ice still rose, white and gleaming. A Song lilted on the wind—a human Song. Star Shell watched as a lone wolf, magnificent in its rippling coat, ran powerfully toward the south. Behind it, following in its tracks, came people: human hunters streaming out of the ice.

They began filling the land, crossing the plains, following natural pathways through the mountains. At the swollen rivers, they hesitated only long enough to lash rafts together and pole across the braided channels to the far banks.

As they went, they killed the giant beasts and lived off of the succulent flesh. More and more humans walked the land, all of them hunting their way across the world. As they spread, the animals became fewer and fewer. She watched a worried man on a far western beach struggle to draw a maze in the sand, only to have his efforts washed away by the pounding surf.

Hot winds blew, and the last of the great beasts vanished. Deserts spread around fading lakes, and people watched in alarm. Soaring, she looked down on a blazing mountain, oddly familiar to her. In the foothills beneath the flame-swept mountain, people Danced.

Others came down from the north, bringing new ways and warring with the peoples they found. In the glow of a fire, a beautiful woman and a crippled man raised a bundle to the flames, and thunder cracked in the distance.

As if borne on the wings of Eagle, she was carried to the east. There at the edge of the endless blue ocean, wide rivers poured into a large bay. A man and a woman crouched on a mound of shells and talked thoughtfully while serene water flowed past. They studied a small fetish that lay between them.

Again she was carried aloft, across the bones of old mountains and into a land she was familiar with. She stared down on StarSky, seeing the immense geometry of the Octagon, the Great Circle, and the earth-lined ways.

The wind rushed her northward to an immense freshwater sea, then along its undercut shores to a river. The clear water seemed to seethe and was hemmed by tree-lined banks. She hovered over an island where the river split and could hear a faint roaring like endless thunder. As the channels rejoined, she saw twirling white mist rising to the west.

For long moments she studied the scene, feeling her heart race. The Mask stared back at her from the mists, slowly sinking into the roar of the mighty falls. It dropped from sight like a rock from a child's hand. Down, down into the engulfing torrent.

Star Shell screamed, twisting and pulling back.

She staggered on the jumbled rock, and the bowl fell, dashing itself to tiny white shards on the jagged black stones.

With a start, she came awake, sitting bolt upright while cold sweat ran down her sides.

"What is it?" the Magician demanded, sitting up in his blankets.

Blinking owlishly at the wall of Clamshell's cramped hut, Star Shell gulped the chilly air. "Dream. Horrible and wonderful. I saw a bowl. And the world was inside it."

She placed a knotted fist against her heart. "And the bowl fell . . . and shattered."

She exhaled wearily and closed her eyes. The vision from the Dream filled her, as perfectly as before. Fragments of the bowl gleamed whitely on the cracked rock.

"Power is loose," the Magician said softly. "Go back to sleep."

Star Shell could hear the old dog's low whining. She turned, and her next breath died in her throat.

Old Clamshell's face had a tortured expression. That glassy look—one of a soul looted clean—might have been Mica Bird's. Clamshell slumped next to the fire, the Mask clasped in her stone-dead hands.

The Magician cried out and threw off his warm blankets.

The Raven image gleamed in the firelight. Shimmering coals

reflected like mottled blood on the polished jet beak. The black feather ruff shone with ghostly brilliance, scarlet, green, blue, and violet. Those eyes, nothing more than black holes, stared fixedly across the room.

Star Shell turned her head, following the gaze to see—

Silver Water sat like stone, her blankets partly fallen away from her small body. Her young face had gone slack amidst the tangle of her long black hair. She seemed drained of color, and her large eyes were wide as she stared into the Mask's unswerving gaze.

"No!" Star Shell screamed as she dove for her daughter.

In the silence, the old dog howled.

Robin came awake with a start. He lay on his back, huddled in his blankets beside the fire in the Hackberry clan house. He stared up at the dark ceiling, where the sooty rafters were barely illuminated by the glowing coals. He'd heard a cry, not detected by his ears but within his soul, and now he could feel sweat beading on his cold skin.

What kind of cry did the soul hear? Then the words whispered on the winter wind.

"Listen, warrior, I have little time. For the moment, I am free of the Magician's entrapment."

"Who are you?" Robin whispered softly.

"That which you desire. Do not fear the Magician, warrior. I have touched his soul. Dwarf though he may be, his Power is dwindling, dying, rotting from within."

"Where are you?"

"I am staring at the child. She is so beautiful, but too young despite her affinity for Power. Look at her. She hears the Song, has already learned it. You, however, are strong, Robin of the Blue Duck. You can save me from the Magician. Come for me. Quickly, the Magician awakes! The bowl is broken. Come for me . . . come . . ."

Robin sat up, glancing around. His heart beat like a pot drum in a ceremony; his whole body was pulsing. Woodpecker and the rest of his warriors were wrapped in their blankets, sleeping uneasily, as if plagued by bad dreams.

Robin tapped Woodpecker, and the warrior's eyes snapped open. "What is it?"

"Did you hear the voice?"

Woodpecker sat up, his fingers searching out his war club. "By the ancestors, Power is loose on the night. What voice? Do you fear treachery on the part of Hackberry Clan?"

Robin gestured restraint, frowning. "Not Hackberry. The Mask. It called to me, but I Dreamed it awake. Do you understand? It woke me before it spoke."

Woodpecker lifted a questioning eyebrow.

Robin clenched a fist. "The Mask called to me, gave me this message: 'Do not fear the Magician, warrior. I have touched his soul. Dwarf though he may be, his Power is dwindling, dying, rotting from within.' Do you know what that means?"

Woodpecker slowly shook his head.

Robin smiled grimly. "The Magician is weak, my friend. His Power is rotting from within. But Robin's Power is growing. Soon I'll have the Mask. *It wants me!*"

Woodpecker swallowed hard, his brow furrowing. "I believe it did call to you, War Leader. Just before you woke me, I was Dreaming of water. It was roiling and foaming, deep and green, almost alive. I looked up, and high above, I saw you sailing through the air in a large canoe. It was as if you were a bird."

"The Mask of Many Colored Crow." Robin rubbed his chin. "Yes, a bird. Go to sleep, my friend. Worry not about the Magician. Robin, war leader of the Blue Duck, shall deal with him in time. The Mask has told that it will be so."

The sun lay just under the horizon as Black Skull crept through the tall stands of maygrass. Snow lay in thin wisps, crunching underfoot as he took step after careful step. This day would be cloudless, cheerful after the latest of the rains. Nevertheless, like every other day in his recent past, Black Skull would hate this one, too.

Only in dreams did he have peace. There his soul could once again walk the City of the Dead. In the shadows of the tall burial mounds, amidst the presence of familiar ghosts, Black Skull reigned supreme. People greeted him with respect and watched in approval as he practiced with his club or cast his war darts farther than any other man alive.

The Trader prevented him even this small justice. Fingers of time ago, Otter had rousted Black Skull from his dreams with, "Come on, get up. There are ducks in the marsh back of camp."

Why did it take so much effort to keep from grabbing the Trader by the neck and squeezing until those smug brown eyes popped out of their sockets?

"Discipline." Grandfather's words haunted him from beyond the grave. Throughout his life, Black Skull had lived by that single rule—and now he'd come to hate it.

He'd risen to a chilly predawn morning, frost thick on everything. The Trader had already moved on, down to the many-times-cursed canoe, where he fished around for his bola.

Discipline! It had brought a shivering Black Skull here, to this grassy bank. Frost now coated his clothing, and the chill threatened to coax shivers from his scarred hide. Despite it all, Black Skull gripped his bola in his knotted right fist and caught the Trader's hand signal to move to the left.

With the grace of a hunting cat, the warrior eased through the tall grass, hearing the subdued quacking of ducks as they paddled around.

Glancing above the brown mat of grass, Black Skull caught the Trader's curt nod. Then he leaped forward, crashing through the grass.

The pond beyond exploded with a fluttering of wings and the panicked quacking of ducks. The Trader had timed his cast perfectly, whirling the bola around his head and sending it out in a graceful arc. Like talons from an outstretched raptor's foot, the weighted stones spread, their thongs making a whirring sound as the bola cut through the clean air.

A perfect throw! The bola tangled with a rising mallard and fouled the frantic wings, causing the bird to somersault in the air. Feathers floated free, spiraling down in the flapping bird's wake.

The duck landed in the grass with a thump.

Amidst the quacking cries of the departing survivors, the Trader raced around the thin layer of ice that had formed a cresent on the margins of the pond. His shadow reflected in the rippling black water.

Black Skull watched from across the pond as the Trader thrashed through the grass, finally leaping on the squawking duck. Straightening, the Trader clasped his flapping victim by the head and spun it, breaking the neck. The bird quivered and stilled.

Black Skull looked down at the bola in his hand. Those polished black stones had been given to him by a Trader from up north. Each stone had been painstakingly ground into a teardrop shape and polished to a deep luster; then a hole had been drilled through the narrow top for the thong. From a quarry up on Serpent River, the Trader had said.

The last thing Black Skull wanted to see was that quarry. And now fate was taking him there—or at least nearby.

"Couldn't get a clear throw?" the Trader asked as he approached, mashing down the tawny grass.

"No," Black Skull said shortly.

Why hadn't he thrown? For a moment, the question nagged at him. *Because I just didn't care,* the answer came back.

The silly grin on the Trader's face mocked him, as if Otter could see inside him, gauge the meanderings within Black Skull's being.

In an attempt to avoid that grin, Black Skull turned away and walked vigorously back toward the camp, where the silly fool, Green Spider, no doubt still slept.

The Trader had to trot to catch up. From the corner of his eye, Black Skull could see the pursed mouth, the unease that had replaced the Trader's excitement.

"Could we talk?"

Black Skull spun on one foot, planting the other. "About what?"

Not expecting such a quick stop, Otter overran him by several paces. The Trader backtracked, suddenly unsure. He glanced around at the pink morning, inspecting the white-gray branches of the trees. The buds hadn't even formed this far north. And they had how much farther to go?

"Are you all right?" The question sounded awkward.

"I'm fine, Trader. You?"

Unease could be read in every line of Otter's body. In the set of the shoulders, the shifting of moccasins. Then came that disarming grin that Black Skull had become so familiar with.

"Don't use that Water Fox smile with me, Trader." Black Skull had seen it work its magic. The times were becoming too numerous to recount. He'd seen it with Meadowlark—the stupid fool—and with fat Elk's Foot at the Cottonwood clan holdings.

There the talk had all been of "the Water Fox," and worse, of the fool, Green Spider. And he, the greatest of all warriors who ever lived, had stood in the shadows.

At least Meadowlark had heard of him. That simpleton, Elk's Foot, hadn't even batted an eye. Just smiled, and through pidgin, bid Black Skull welcome in his clucking tongue.

The rage had started then. Hadn't they known? Where was the warm welcome with which Long Squirrel had greeted him? Oh, Meadowlark would have learned, all right. Black Skull had bided his time, waiting until late at night when he could stand it no longer, then he'd risen on light feet to reach for Meadowlark. Meadowlark would have eaten one of his precious badger bowls—that is, if *the fool* hadn't bounded into the middle of the room and tried pouring water on the fire to make it burn brighter.

"You've been silent," Otter managed at last, "ever since we stopped at the Brown Water Clan." He paused, glancing at Black Skull. "I thought it might have been because I reminded you of what Old Man North said back at White Shell."

"Does this have a purpose?"

"Tonight, if we don't have problems, we should arrive at the Hilltop clan grounds. Great Ring is a very important man. Critical for us, since he knows all the gossip. He can tell us a good deal about what's happening up the Serpent River."

"And what is it that you want of me?" *Not to cave in some silly fool's head when he asks me if I'm a warrior?*

Otter placed callused hands on his hips, the duck dangling limply. "I thought we might come to some sort of understanding. Maybe I could do something, change something. Make it easier for you. I know—"

"You could start by stopping this silly chatter. You make as much sense as those ducks back there.'' Black Skull made three steps before Otter was at his side.

"What does it take?'' the Trader demanded hotly. "Another bolt of lightning? We've got a long way to go. It won't be pleasant if you insist on acting like a big dumb rock!''

Black Skull reacted instinctively. He let the bola drop as his hands flashed out to clamp around Otter's neck. For a delightful moment, he replayed the image of the Trader killing the duck, enjoying it in his soul. At the last instant, some vestige of restraint stopped him from tightening his grip beyond reprieve.

Under the inexorable pressure, the Trader's mouth opened, the tongue pushed up. His eyes glazed with a spreading panic as they bulged outward.

"A long way to go?'' Black Skull asked evenly. "Then perhaps we should go kick that idiot Green Spider out of his warm blankets and head upriver. What do you say to that, eh, Water Fox?'' With that, he shoved the Trader away, leaving him staggering and pale, feeling of his throat with a worried hand.

Black Skull retrieved his bola and bulled forward, fueled by a sense of well-meted justice.

Of course, he shouldn't blame the Trader. He was every bit as mired in the mud of this insane trip as he. The blame belonged to the fool—and his silly Vision of Many Colored Crow, and Masks, and saving the world.

At that moment, as if they'd heard him, several of the black birds soared over the treetops, cawing and rasping to each other. The rising sun caught their feathers in a sheen of ebony as they darted artfully through the air. The hoarse sound of beating wings carried on the still morning.

He executed the throw with polished perfection, the arm flexed, shoulders rolling, as he whirled the bola. He extended in a perfect cast, sending the weapon up at an angle, the weighted tips whistling. The birds moved rapidly. One of the toughest targets he'd ever tried.

The lead crow reacted a second too late, seeking to cup the air with its wings while the others slipped and dove. The hesitation was the bird's undoing. The bola embraced the startled crow in a stranglehold.

Black Skull shielded his eyes with his hand, but the first rays of morning sunlight blinded him as he followed the falling bird down. Blinking in the afterimage, his vision filled with a ghostly face; his mother's features were etched by brightness. Did he hear her coarse laughter?

As the bird plummeted to the ground, it let out a curious screech, then disappeared behind the tree line. Black Skull heard its body thud. The vision—tracery of sunlight, or imagination—vanished from his eyes.

No matter. He'd killed his mother with the same disciplined efficiency that he'd killed the crow.

When he broke through the thin belt of oaks, he found Green Spider bolt upright in his blanket. The Contrary had a comical expression on his thin face as he gaped at the shiny, black-feathered mass that had fallen at his feet. The bird had a broken neck, and it seemed to be staring directly into the fool's eyes.

Otter rushed into camp a moment later, one hand held to his bruised neck.

"Not a bad cast. Don't you agree?" Black Skull said evenly as he untangled the broken bird from the bola thongs. Some of the futility seemed to have bled off. Not much, but enough to get him through this day.

"Oh, a good cast indeed," the fool whispered. He turned to stare at Black Skull with eerie, haunted eyes; then he laughed hysterically, tears running down his cheeks.

Seventeen

Star Shell held Silver Water in a crushing embrace, desperate to protect her daughter. Tall Man, like some oversized doll figure, scuttled around the perimeter of the little hut. His undersized feet kept wadding up the crumpled blankets. When he was close enough, he reached out, his stubby fingers plucking up the wolfhide.

He advanced with the cape held before him, the way he would if he were about to net a trapped rabbit.

Star Shell could sense the menace, heavy in the air like greasy smoke. Sweat, despite the cold, had beaded on the Magician's face, the sheen accenting his turtle-like features.

Tall Man charged forward, enfolding the Mask in the wolf-hide. The Mask appeared to resist. The old woman's talon-like fingers remained knotted in the edges. With a cry, he wrestled it out of her frozen grip. He sat down hard then—the action sudden, as if his feet had slipped out from under him.

Tall Man heaved a weary sigh and stared across Clamshell's body. "Is your daughter all right?"

"Baby?" Star Shell peered down. "Are you all right? Baby, talk to me."

"Mama?" Silver Water looked up, those large eyes eerie, depthless.

"Did the Mask hurt you?" That choking desperation continued to tighten in her throat.

"It talked to me." Silver Water lowered her gaze, her attention thoughtful as she considered Clamshell's dead body.

The old dog moaned now, as if it had been kicked by a careless stranger.

Star Shell stopped her jaw from trembling. "What . . . what happened? What did it say?"

"Stories, Mama. It told me stories. And it Sang Songs."

Tall Man hung his head, saying in wooden tones, "Clamshell. She took the Mask out of its covering."

Star Shell swallowed, some sense of control coming back to her. "She asked about it the other night. I told her it was a sacred thing. Maybe it's my fault. I didn't give her a very good answer."

"She always was a curious one." Tall Man used one hand to rub his face. "Leaving well enough alone wasn't among her ways of dealing with the world."

"It called her," Silver Water whispered absently. "It called, Mama. Not loud, but you could hear it."

Tall Man leaned forward, his expression sharpening. "It called? And you heard it?"

With the wariness of a hunted animal, Star Shell asked, "What does that mean?"

Tall Man didn't respond for several moments. "Probably nothing."

"Nothing? Clamshell's dead! My husband's dead! My daughter hears that thing . . . and you say *nothing*!"

He glared at her, the tone in his voice commanding. "Don't panic! It's contained. Within the wolfhide. We caught it in time. All we have to do is get the Mask to the Roaring Water, throw it over the edge, and Power will take care of itself."

The prickling worry refused to abate. "Why is Clamshell dead?"

Tall Man's sympathetic gaze returned to the old woman. "Evening Star, my poor old love." His welling sadness betrayed itself. "You had to look into those eyeholes, didn't you?"

"And . . . and what happened? What did the Mask do to her?"

He glanced at Star Shell, then back at the corpse. "She was the most beautiful woman to have ever lived. You should have seen her in her youth. Radiant, alluring. And now, in old age, she looked into the Mask—not through it. Instead of seeing the world as Many Colored Crow would see it, she saw herself reflected there." He paused. "The fulfillment of every nightmare she ever had about aging."

Tall Man slipped the wolfhide-bound Mask back into the fabric bag. Then he reached over and closed Clamshell's eyelids over the death stare. "She saw what she had become, Star Shell. Not what she dreamed herself to be, but what she really was. In all her life, she never saw herself as she was. What a shock to see herself now, in this condition. Old, ugly . . . well, that's not so bad for most of us. But she lived behind a sort of Mask all of her life. Tonight she finally saw through it."

Star Shell closed her eyes, tightening her hold on Silver Water until her daughter squirmed and complained, "Mama, you're hurting me!"

"Oh, I'm sorry. I'm sorry, baby." She patted Silver Water's hair gently. "And what did my daughter see?"

Tall Man smiled reassuringly. "She's a child, Star Shell. Children generally see themselves as they are, or at least as they want to be. That's the blessing of youth."

Star Shell frowned, glanced at the dead woman, and slowly

shook her head. "No, Tall Man. *What happened to my daughter?* You tell me."

For a moment, their stares locked, a battle of wills escalating. Then, abruptly, his eyes went limpid and sympathetic. "I don't know, Star Shell." He looked at Silver Water. "Did the Mask ask you to do anything? To hurt anybody?"

Silver Water shook her head as she nestled against Star Shell's side.

"Silver Water?" Star Shell asked.

"It just told stories, Mama. About people a long time ago when the world was new. That's all. I promise."

"I believe you, baby." But did she? Could she? She raised a skeptical eyebrow. "Tall Man, I don't understand. A lot of people looked at the Mask when my husband wore it. He ... they died only when he willed it. *I* looked at the accursed thing when he wore it. Even when it lay by the bed and watched ..." She shook her head, seeking to gather scattered thoughts. "*It never killed anyone on its own!* Not like it did Clamshell."

"No, I suppose it didn't. Try to understand. The Mask is not a thing. Power lives within it. Power, this Power, is acting alone. It is seeking to accomplish its own ends, whatever they might be."

"You mean it's alive?"

"Of course it's alive. Though in a way you do not yet understand. It has no feet or hands. It can't move or create on its own. It needs a human to serve those purposes. Without a wearer, the Mask is lost, struggling to reach out to anyone who can act as a bridge between it and the world, so that its Power may soar free again." Tall Man threw wood on the fire, and the flames shed light on the grubby insides of Clamshell's house.

Star Shell forced herself to think. "The wolfhide. Why does it smother the Mask's Power?"

"Wolf—the Spirit Helper of First Man—has a special kind of Power. This hide did not come from an ordinary wolf, but from a Spirit Animal. A black wolf with gleaming amber eyes. I had to seek him out. I hunted him for four moons. And finally, when I had proven myself worthy, he came to me, allowed me to kill him for his pelt."

"You've known that this . . . this journey . . . was coming for a long time, haven't you?"

Tall Man nodded uncomfortably. "We all make our gambles, Star Shell. Power has to position itself. As among men, plans must come to fruition. The right people must be chosen."

Chosen. The words chilled her. *Why did it have to choose me and my little daughter?*

"Come," Tall Man said gently. "Help me prepare Evening Star's body. She needs someone to care for her ghost. To wash her and make her ready."

Star Shell managed to nod an unsure assent. She looked down at Silver Water. The events of the last couple of days would have taken a toll on any adult, but something had changed in Silver Water's expression. She didn't look as young anymore.

Silver Water crouches behind a clump of bushes and peers out at the world through the winter-bare tangle of stems. She is so frightened that she can't catch her breath. It comes in quick, shallow gasps, like the breathing of a rabbit in a snare. *Who are all these people?* They began arriving at dawn, and now there are dozens of them. All men. She hasn't seen them, *not really,* but she senses them here. When the wind creaks the tree limbs, she hears voices, and every so often she glimpses a face in the wavering, windblown shadows. Have they come for Clamshell's funeral?

Ten body-lengths away, her mother and Tall Man are laboring over Clamshell's body. They have laid the naked old woman on a beautiful red-and-blue blanket and are gently rubbing hickory oil into the withered flesh of her arms while they speak softly to each other. Tears streak the dwarf's cheeks, but his voice is strong, as if only his eyes are sad. He doesn't see the men, though they have crowded around him—disguised as flitters of shadow. Silver Water tilts her head to listen better, but catches only a few words:

" . . . loved her so much," Tall Man says.

Her mother nods. "Well, she won't have to dream of her old lovers anymore. Soon she'll . . ."

"Yes," Tall Man answers. "She must be looking forward to that."

Clamshell's gray hair has been combed and twisted into a bun on top of her head. A copper pin secures the bun. It glints in the cold white sunshine filtering through the leafless filigree of branches. Triangles of light decorate the forest floor. They shudder and shimmer, as if the wind is playing, shattering them into tens of tens of pieces, then delightedly fitting them back together again.

Silver Water glances around, wondering if that's who all the men are. Clamshell's old lovers?

A gust of wind sweeps the forest, and a low, pulsing groan meanders through the trees. It must be the men talking to each other. At the root of that groan is hurt and longing. When Silver Water tries to imitate the sound, it tastes like green pawpaw fruit in her mouth, sour now, but with a promise of sweetness to come. This comforts Silver Water, though she isn't sure why. Maybe the men are telling Clamshell how sorry they are that she's dead, and describing the wonders of the afterlife, hoping to make her feel better.

She wishes they would go over and tell the same thing to the old dog who lies faithfully by Clamshell's side. Though he is perfectly still and quiet, his white muzzle propped on his paws, he's been whining inside his head, whining and whimpering, and begging Clamshell not to leave him here alone. Not once all day has he taken his huge, forlorn eyes from Clamshell's face.

When Silver Water concentrates, she can feel the dog's ache in her heart. It is like looking up from the bottom of a cold, cold lake, knowing your lungs are full of water and that you'll never be able to swim to the sunshine.

Silver Water gets hot and cold and sweaty. Somewhere in a secret place in her soul, her father's hands reach out through a green, watery glow, and she hears sounds of angry breathing, moccasins on a hide-covered floor. His fingers are hot—boiling grease poured on her body—and she is drowning . . .

Silver Water's legs go weak. She sits back hard, and the secret place flies away, plummeting down, down, like a falcon, until it is nothing but a tiny black dot on her bright soul. Her mouth has dried out. She clutches a handful of snow and chews it to melting. It is cold. Not hot. She is sitting in a forest, listening to men's voices. But not his voice.

Silver Water slips her hands between the stems and parts them to peer out. Clamshell is different. Silver Water senses that she is absorbed by the feel of hands on her body, massaging, stroking. Wavering shatters of light dance across her breasts. They must be warm. She seems to like that.

Silver Water's mother straightens up, and looking around pensively, says, "Tall Man, where did you put the Mask? Is it still inside Clamshell's house?"

"Yes. I left it by the fire. I didn't want my old love to have to see it. Not after last night."

"Good. I don't want to have to see it, either."

Silver Water takes a deep breath and lets it out slowly. Tall Man said that when children look into the eyeholes of the Mask, they see themselves as they are, or as they want to be. This doesn't make any sense.

She didn't see herself at all. Snake eyes had filled the sockets. Shiny, like golden suns racing toward her.

Four days later, after the prayers had been uttered and firewood dragged in, they scooped coals from the fire pit and poured them on the tinder at the foot of the pyre they'd built for Evening Star. The old woman lay supine atop the rick of wood they'd piled in the middle of her floor.

As the flames leaped up, Star Shell followed Tall Man outside into the dusk and swung the pack she'd made onto her shoulder. This time, they would have food and a few necessities for their travels.

As the flames crackled along the bark walls, Tall Man picked up Evening Star's sturdy hardwood digging stick. The old dog was staring mournfully at the burning house. In a lightning movement, the dwarf swung the heavy stick down in an arc. He caught the dog just behind the ears, the blow hard enough to snap the neck.

For a brief few seconds, the dog kicked, its muscles jerking in spasms. The tongue lolled from its open jaws.

"Why did you do that?" Star Shell demanded as she dropped to her knees and began stroking its gray side, watching as the aged eyes went dim.

"Kindness, Star Shell," Tall Man said sympathetically. "This old hound would have died from loneliness. I think he loved Clamshell more than all the other men in her life put together did." He grabbed the tail and grunted, pulling the animal against the corner of the house, where it would be certain to be engulfed by the fire. "This way, he can go with her to meet the ancestors. He would have wanted to." Then Tall Man shouldered his pack and started across the snowy field.

As Star Shell struggled to her feet, she noticed that Silver Water was looking into the dead dog's eyes, smiling. Couldn't her daughter remember petting the old beast? How could she smile?

"Come on," Star Shell ordered, sounding harsher than she meant to. As they plodded in Tall Man's short tracks, she looked back. The flames shot red and angry into the evening sky. Darkness would be falling soon enough to hide the telltale pall of black smoke.

She hadn't really listened to the Song Silver Water was Singing. Now she turned.

Silver Water sang:

"Feathers colored, the dead are laid.
Logs across and dirt is made.
Lazy sloth, in baskets carried—
Sun man, and woman high are married."

"What is that song, baby?"

Silver Water looked up with her depthless eyes. "Nothing, Mama, just a Song I learned."

"Learned where?"

Silver Water pointed. "We'd better hurry. Tall Man is way ahead."

She dashed after the dwarf.

Star Shell bit back the urge to grab her daughter and shake the truth out of her. *This isn't the time. She's had enough trouble for now.*

The snow had turned rotten in the warm days following Clamshell's death. It made slushy sounds under Star Shell's moccasins.

Behind her, the fire crackled and snapped in a roaring inferno. Did it spin some final Visions for Evening Star? And if so, would she see them differently because she had dared to look into the Mask?

The chert flake had turned slippery with blood and fat. Pearl wiped it on the hem of her skirt to clean the edge, then returned to the chore of butchering the white-tailed deer that Six Fingers and Tailless Cougar had brought in.

Glacial wind blew down from the northwest, and occasional flakes of snow twirled through the trees and over the ashen waters of the river. To dispel the gloom of the evening, the Khota had built large fires that crackled and spat sparks into the wind.

Pearl had slit the white belly open. Now she reached into the steaming gut cavity, the musky aroma of deer bathing her. With knowing hands, she severed the tissue that restrained the squirming intestines, which she lifted out. Similarly, she cut the diaphragm, and hot red blood spilled in from the wounded lungs.

Heart, liver, and kidneys she placed on the damp leaves to one side. The punctured lungs and trachea she threw out. It was while she was emptying the intestines that she noticed the tapeworm. She cut off a section of intestine, knotting one end and slipping a section of the worm into the other end, which she tied off. This she carefully tucked into a fold of her shirt.

"Hurry up!" One Arm called. "Paddling your lazy body upriver has made us all hungry!"

Of course he was hungry; the marsh marigold she'd seasoned his catfish with had proved such a powerful purgative that he'd been empty for two miserable days.

After she'd cut off the deer's quarters and placed them to roast on the various warriors' fires, she took a moment to scrape the blood from her fingernails and study the camp. Soon Grizzly Tooth would order her to be bound up like a stuffed turkey. For the time being, she could enjoy moving around.

At that moment, Big Toe cried out, bent double, and threw up all over his bedding. Pearl managed to keep a sober face. Must have been the bit of dogbane root she'd fed him for breakfast.

Grizzly Tooth rose from his fire, shaking his head. He started in the sick warrior's direction before glancing suspiciously at Pearl. He hesitated, giving her a careful scrutiny from narrowed eyes. "I am sometimes led to wonder. My warriors seem to spend most of the time being sick. They were not nearly so sick on the way downriver."

Too bad I couldn't find the water-hemlock root or I would have cured your worry a long time ago—and mine, too. "Maybe your warriors shouldn't venture so far from home." Pearl flicked dried blood from the cuticle of her thumb. "Are all Khota such weaklings?"

"I might be led to believe that it was a mistake to let you cook."

"What are you suggesting?"

"No one started getting sick until *you* started cooking!"

Pearl smacked her hands on her thighs, an act that drew the attention of the entire camp. "You think that I, a captive woman, watched every minute and tied up like a camp dog, am poisoning your thin-blooded warriors? When am I doing this? How?"

Grizzly Tooth muttered to himself, turning to watch Big Toe puke again. "I don't know. But perhaps I shall not let you cook anymore."

"You seem to reverse your orders often, War Leader, but that's fine with me. If you'll remember, I didn't want to cook for your weaklings in the first place. Make One Arm cook. He would be better at 'women's work' than I am. Or maybe Big Toe. Now there's a strong warrior, just look at him! Or perhaps even you, Grizzly Tooth. Why don't you cook for your underlings?"

The warriors listened with clamped jaws, their gazes carefully averted to such fascinating sights as the sand between their feet. A complete silence had fallen on the camp.

Grizzly Tooth's fists knotted. His face had gone dark. "You cook, woman! And if I find you messing with our food, I'll twist your arm off of your body. Wolf of the Dead will forgive a little discipline to his bride.''

At that, Grizzly Tooth stalked off to his fire.

Pearl smiled secretly to herself and walked over to where Round Scar was scratching madly at his side. A wicked red rash could be seen beneath the gaps of his clothing.

''Looks bad,'' Pearl told him.

''That true? You poisoning our food?''

Pearl snorted. ''Half the time, you're the warrior who is watching me. Have you seen me pick anything I didn't eat myself?'' Of course, in Round Scar's case, Pearl had slipped crushed water-pepper plant into his bedding as she carried it up from the canoe. She'd found the dried stems at the water's edge and grabbed up what she could.

Big Toe exploded again, his stomach pumping vigorously but without much visible effect this time. Pearl watched with mild interest. ''I sure feel sorry for him. Must be the river water up here.''

''He's pretty sick.''

''I'd help him,'' Pearl sighed, ''but I'd probably be accused of trying to poison him.''

Round Scar scratched at his rash again, brows furrowed. ''How would you help him?''

''Deer intestine. You don't see deer throw up, do you? They just chew cud and it goes right back down. A bit of deer intestine calms the stomach. My grandmother told me that.''

''Deer intestine, huh?'' Round Scar scratched at his head. Too bad that skin irritants lost their strength during the winter. Had it been summer, she could have driven half of them to slit their own throats.

''I just butchered that deer.'' She handed Round Scar the short section of intestine. ''If Big Toe had a friend, well, he might take this over to him.''

Round Scar studied the gray-white slip of flesh, then glanced at Big Toe, who was on all fours, wiping his mouth. He gave Pearl one last uneasy glance.

''Oh, come on,'' she chided. ''What could I have done to it since I cut up that deer? Boiled it in yew leaves for a couple of days? Mixed it with fresh buckeye seeds? Maybe I cursed it with some terrible Anhinga magic?''

Round Scar ripped the section of intestine from her hand, and instead of taking it to his friend, plopped it into his own mouth. His throat convulsed as he swallowed it down.

"There. Now *I* won't have to worry about throwing up from this river water."

Pearl nodded approvingly, then walked off to check the deer meat cooking on the fires. Who was she to chastise Round Scar? Besides, Big Toe might have thrown up again and wasted a perfectly good tapeworm.

Eighteen

Such aching loneliness!

I feel as if I've eaten crushed obsidian and it is churning away inside me, slicing my soul to nothingness.

Oh, Many Colored Crow, hear me! How much longer must I bear this anguish?

Everything in the world is weeping, weeping . . .

Yet I stare out through dry eyes.

Has any human ever been forced to endure such unbearable isolation?

. . . Is this how you felt when you were a living man? Fighting with your brother over your visions of what the world would be?

Despite the warm, clear day, the journey upriver grew ever gloomier as Otter mulled over his cloudy doubts. What had started as premonition had been driven home with startling swiftness that morning. He fingered his throat, still sore from Black Skull's mauling.

Normally quick of reflex, Otter hadn't even seen the warrior's blurred motion. One moment he was raging at Black Skull, and an eyeblink later, his throat felt like an ax head clamped in a green-stem handle.

From *Wave Dancer*'s stern, he watched the warrior's corded muscles bunching and flowing under that heavy cape. Black Skull never missed a stroke, but if anything, his manner was more relaxed.

Immediately in front of Otter, Green Spider sat like a stump. The Contrary's hands, normally in and out of the water, Catcher's mouth, and anything else they fancied, were neatly folded in his lap. Green Spider didn't even glance at the passing flotsam, the birds, or the landmarks that generally absorbed him.

Well, Black Skull, we've found that you can intimidate as well as kill.

The eastern side of the river had risen into stern headlands topped by a mat of trees. Otter knew that horizon well. One by one, he ticked off the landmarks, realizing that they would reach Hilltop clan grounds well before nightfall.

And then what? Did he dare stop and garner the information he so desperately needed from Great Ring? Or would it be better to simply push on, gambling ignorance against Black Skull's insane anger.

The snapping turtle's meat is tender. An eel was as slippery as a Contrary's lessons.

As they rounded a bend, Otter could see a familiar bluff on the eastern bank. The Hilltop had cleared a field there, which accounted for the flattened look.

Green Spider picked that moment to raise his head. Drawn and pale, his thin visage had an even more sobering effect. With uncharacteristic directness, the Contrary said, "You must stop."

Glancing nervously past Green Spider's shoulder, Otter said, "We don't really need a buffalo robe."

The Contrary's eyes lost focus. "You're too brave for your own good. With courage like yours, we're all in safe hands. Pass on, good Trader. The currents are at your command."

And at that, he turned away.

Otter took a deep breath, wincing at the effect on his tormented throat.

What more could I do? I tried talking to him. And what did it get me? Half strangled, that's what.

Just how was he going to deal with Black Skull? Wait until he wasn't looking and drive a dart through his back? Use the point of a paddle and kill the warrior in his sleep?

Otter barely noticed when Green Spider gazed at him again. "Power has made its choice. The gaming pieces are placed. The gambler never wins if he withdraws the pieces after his only throw."

"What's all this business about gamblers?"

"At sunrise, a crow could have gambled on seeing sunset. In your youth, you would have gambled on marrying the woman you loved. On the morning of the solstice, the Black Skull would have gambled that nothing on this earth would have frightened him. We always know more than we think we do."

"And we never know as much," Otter retorted. "Only a fool talks to a Contrary without becoming more confused than when he started."

"See, you've begun to learn the order of things."

"But I just said I got more confused."

"At the rate you're learning, life will no longer hold many mysteries for you."

In disgust, Otter bent his back to the paddle. "Green Spider, you're a worrisome bother, did you know that?"

"Paddle hard. You can be long past the Hilltop Clan by dark. Few will know."

Otter growled, then cut it short as Black Skull laughed and called back, "You truly *are* learning, Trader. Only a fool would talk to an idiot like Green Spider."

The tickle of fear still ate at Otter's gut as they rounded the final loop in the river below the Hilltop clan grounds. He could see them now, the peaked roofs rising just above the bluff.

With a muttered curse, Otter ordered, "Take it in. We'll land just below their drying racks." And Power help him if Black Skull acted like his normal self.

By the time they beached, the usual flock of children had gathered on the bluffs, along with a few adults. Winter was like that. More people congregated in the clan grounds, but fewer Traders passed. In the summertime, Otter had beached *Wave Dancer* beside as many as ten Traders' canoes and no one had noticed his arrival until he was announcing himself at the clan house.

After stowing his gear, securing the pottery bowls of honey beer, and advising Catcher to guard well, they started up the trail past the drying racks and half-shelters. As usual, he led the way, Green Spider and the brooding Black Skull following. The warrior, he noted, carried his heavy war club, the copper spikes freshly polished.

As they neared the top, Black Skull muttered, "Introduce me first, Trader. Let's see what they do."

Do? Otter paused reflectively. *You thrice-cursed fool, you wouldn't dare pick a fight.* Meeting the warrior's black eyes, however, he saw that it was a distinct possibility. Otter continued on his way. How did he handle this? What approach could he use to defuse his companion's terrible wrath?

Naught but ill would come of the killing of that crow.

Black Skull demanded, "Tell me about these people, Trader. Who are they? What are they like?"

Could this be a way to lessen the chance of trouble? Otter said, "Hilltop's one of the most important places on the river. I've spent a great deal of time here and tried to learn the customs." In the process, he'd picked up a smattering of their language. "I'm an adopted member of a local family. My brother's name is Owl Eye."

"And what is this Owl Eye like?"

"A man about my age. Just like any other man, I suppose. I like him."

Through Owl Eye, Otter could warn Great Ring, and Black Skull would never be the wiser—but that would cast a cloud over what should otherwise prove a congenial meeting.

How would Great Ring respond to any kind of challenge? The thought laid frost on Otter's thoughts. Hilltop had a proud warrior tradition, and any offense . . . Yes, that just might be the way out of this: Let Great Ring's warriors kill Black Skull.

Clanspeople waited at the circular embankment as Otter's party crested the top of the bluff. At the opening that faced the river, Otter stopped and offered his compliments to the ancestral ghosts. Green Spider jabbered incomprehensibly, seeming to see things Otter couldn't.

"The ghosts wish us well in Many Colored Crow's quest," Green Spider announced.

Before Otter could reply, a voice cried out happily from the crowd. "Water Fox!" Owl Eye spoke in pidgin. "It's good to see you—but a bit early, isn't it? The snow's still deep in the north."

Otter easily picked out his adopted brother: slim, muscular, with a bearhide cape draped over his shoulders. Owl Eye's strong cheekbones dominated his triangular face and cast shadows on his tattooed cheeks. His straight black hair was pulled back into a tight bun in the fashion of Hilltop warriors.

Otter raised his hand. "Brother! Greetings! Snow in the north, you say? You know me, I'm slow. By the time I make it upriver, the leaves will be turning colors."

Chuckles broke out. Otter indicated his companions, the gesture awkward because of the two jars of honey beer he carried. "I've got help this year. Maybe I can be there by harvest instead of first snowfall. Now, how's that new baby of yours, my nephew?"

"Nephew?" Black Skull grunted.

Otter told him, "Hilltop practices cross-cousin marriage. A man is expected to marry his mother's brother's daughter—who, of course, is in a different clan since Hilltop is a patrilineal society."

"That's crazy!" Black Skull shook his head, glancing uneasily at the surrounding people.

"Why? They have their reasons, Black Skull. Just like your Winter Clan is matrilineal. Hilltop does it this way to ensure that lineages maintain control of fertile fields through generations. And just so you know ahead of time, not only is a man expected to marry his cross-cousin, but he's also expected to practice sororate, which means that when a man is married to a woman, he is expected to marry her sisters also."

"Sisters? Blessed Spirits, you mean a man marries a whole family?"

"That's the idea. The people here claim that it keeps divorces from disrupting alliances between the clans—a serious problem for a people who depend on group harmony and cooperation. They've got a lot of enemies upcountry."

"So, this Owl Eye—" Black Skull eyed the young man who

had stopped while they talked "—is married to all of his wives' sisters?"

"Not yet. But he will be. Since Owl Eye is young, he's been able to afford only one wife, but the last time I was here, he was working on bride price for his wife's sister."

"I don't believe it!" Black Skull muttered, a slight look of bewilderment in his eyes. "Who'd have thought people could be so different?"

"Well, they are." *And I hope you remember that, Killer of Men. It might save your stupid life one of these days.*

Owl Eye stepped forward, slapping Otter on the back with just enough vigor to keep from spilling the honey beer. "You ask about your nephew? That baby is no baby. He's wobbling around on two feet! Come, I'll announce you." He paused, a serious look in his clear brown eyes. "Otter? Are you all right?"

Did his worry show? Otter forced that disarming smile to his lips. "Healthy enough to wrestle that baby of yours."

Hilltop clan grounds were laid out in a circle, the domed charnel huts scattered to the north and south of the central burial mound. The clan house lay just behind the square ceremonial mound, in line with the eastern equinox break in the surrounding earthen wall. Despite the wealth enjoyed by Hilltop, the structures were small, partly because the tribes upcountry from them found hunting, collecting, and periodic raiding more profitable than trying to farm the rocky hills. The teachings of Many Colored Crow had never penetrated much beyond the river here. Hilltop's warrior traditions flourished because of that constant friction.

At the thought of Many Colored Crow, dread grew in Otter's soul. Black Skull just had to kill a crow that morning, didn't he? Glancing back, Otter noted that the warrior had an angry expression on his deformed face. The muscles even twitched occasionally.

They crossed the clan grounds, Otter's party surrounded by chattering people. Owl Eye kept peering curiously at Black Skull, and then at the Contrary. Two more unlikely companions couldn't have been found. Finally, Owl Eye noted: "The big warrior, he brings a club with him. Tell me, brother, from the look in his eye, he might be tempted to use it. You don't bring trouble, do you?''

Otter gave a quick laugh, then lowered his voice, saying in the Hilltop tongue, ''He is a great warrior among the clans at the City of the Dead. Up here, he's but another warrior.'' In that instant, Otter thought he'd found a way out. ''Sometimes it is difficult to discover you are not as great as you thought. He could be made to cause trouble, but only if pushed.''

''I see.'' Owl Eye grinned as if continuing their small talk. ''Thank you for your honest words.''

''A Trader's craft depends on honest words.''

''And dishonest ones even more, eh, Water Fox?''

Otter let out a cry of dismay. ''I am stung!''

At the clan house, Owl Eye raised his voice. ''Clanspeople, my good brother, the Trader Water Fox has arrived! Dear brother, greetings! You and your friends are welcome among us. Enter our clan house. The Elders await you—and whatever it is that you carry in those jars you guard so protectively.''

Laughter broke out as eyes danced merrily. The ceramic jars held no secrets.

Otter ducked, entering first. His eyes took a moment to adjust after the bright sunshine outside. People had already crowded inside. The Hilltop clan house differed little from others, with the exception that atlatls, darts, and bits of clothing hung from the smoke-stained walls. Here and there, a jawless skull had been tied up by cords—a trophy of the wars with the nomadic peoples in the hills.

The main room measured twenty paces in length and perhaps fifteen in width. Benches lined the walls, and matting had been laid across the floor where people now sat. A wealth of ceramic jars and pots, bearing characteristics from peoples all up and down the river, had been stowed under the benches and were visible between legging-clad calves.

Great Ring sat in the place of honor across from the central fire. The Hilltop Clan was patrilineal, so, unlike the White Shell Clan, the men sat in front, the women just behind them, where they could whisper counsel.

Otter stopped before the fire, lowering his pots of honey beer. ''Great Ring, may your lineage prosper, and all of your children's children grow tall and strong. May the ghosts of your ancestors forever smile upon you and grant you wisdom. May Many Colored Crow shed his grace upon your people and lands." *And may he forgive Black Skull for killing that poor crow!*

"Water Fox." Great Ring stood, a wiry old man, his face scarred and one eye missing. Despite his age, his hair remained glossy and black, bound in the bun of a warrior. He held himself erect despite an old wound to his leg that had left the knee stiff and slightly bent. A bearhide cape hung from his shoulders. Through the open front, his weathered brown chest looked like carved walnut.

Great Ring raised a sprig of sacred cedar in his hand, waving it in gentle strokes in Otter's direction. He chanted a blessing on Otter, his clan, offspring, and ancestors. Finally, the ritual greeting finished, the clan leader asked, "Who are these companions you have brought among us?"

Otter gestured at Black Skull, stating in the Hilltop tongue, "This is the Black Skull, the greatest warrior among the clans of the City of the Dead. His trip has been hard. As a favor, I would ask you to treat him with the greatest honor. His triumphs, venerable Great Ring, are many and valiant. He is known far and wide to the south and east. Perhaps you have heard of him?"

There, would it work? For the moment, Black Skull was staring at Great Ring's stiff leg, an unusual softness in those black eyes.

Great Ring studied Otter for a moment, then nodded at Black Skull. "I have heard of you, Black Skull. Sometimes I did not believe the stories. You must be a very great warrior! You're about as ugly as I am."

Otter translated, his wary eyes on Black Skull. A neutral smile curled the warrior's lips at the mention of being ugly. "I am honored to be here in your land. May the Spirits and Power guard you and your people. Perhaps later we can share stories."

Great Ring nodded, slapping a callused hand to his knee. "We will do that, Black Skull!"

Otter grabbed the Contrary—who was completely absorbed by a string frayed from his shirt—and pulled him forward gently. "And this is Green Spider. A Dreamer from the City of the

Dead. Great Ring, honored members of the Hilltop Clan, I must warn you, this Dreamer has Contrary Power.''

People began whispering back and forth, their interest sharpening. Otter caught the stiffening in Black Skull's muscles. What was it with him? Couldn't he bend just a little?

In pidgin, Great Ring asked the Contrary, "We have heard of your kind of Power. Please, all of you come and be seated. Share our fire."

Green Spider pivoted on one heel, starting steadfastly for the door.

At which point Otter cried, "That's it! Go away, Green Spider. These people don't want you by their fire. They hope you go far away and never shed your grace on them."

Green Spider vented a loud sigh, clapped his hands and leaped back to the fire, where he flopped down cross-legged and cocked his head. He made a face and began picking at the packed floor with a sliver of wood he'd found. Several people gasped as the Contrary levered out a clod of dirt and plopped it into his mouth, chewing thoughtfully for a second. Then he gave a satisfied smile.

Black Skull watched the Contrary, and his facial muscles twitched in disgust. He growled, "Stop it, fool! That's enough."

Green Spider continued, heedless of the warrior's threat.

Great Ring watched nervously, then gestured to a young warrior, who immediately produced the leader's pipe. The piece had been carved of fine gray slate into the form of a kneeling warrior who held the bowl in his hands.

Hilltop people stared unabashed at both warrior and Contrary while the clan leader Sang a prayer and tamped his tobacco into place. The young attendant thrust the end of a twig into the fire and lit Great Ring's pipe.

As more prayers were humbly offered, the pipe made the rounds, periodically pausing long enough to have the dottle knocked out before refilling. After the stone pipe had passed among the principals, Great Ring settled awkwardly, his stiff leg out. Bracing callused hands on his knees, he asked, "What brings you to favor us with your presence here at Hilltop, Water Fox? From the nature of your companions, you are not on any ordinary journey. Tell us your tale."

Otter collected himself, glancing around at the shining eyes of those who watched. "I will let the great Black Skull tell the story." In his own tongue, Otter told the warrior, "The Hilltop Clans would hear the story of our journey. If you would be great, tell it that way."

Otter's heart skipped at the gamble. If Black Skull insisted that the Contrary was a fool, disaster would befall them. Of that, he had no doubt.

For an instant, their gazes locked. Then Black Skull nodded and stood. He propped the pointed tip of his war club between his feet, his gnarled hands gripping the handle. "I am a warrior," he stated bluntly. "One who fights men . . . not a teller of stories. However, this is the way it happened . . ."

Otter translated, using Hilltop words, and where they failed, filling in with Trader pidgin. Black Skull faithfully reported the story of Green Spider's Vision Quest on the solstice, then told of the lightning strike and Green Spider's return from the Dead. When he told of Green Spider's Vision, the only sound in the clan house came from the crackling of the fire. Never had Otter seen such an entranced audience. The mention of the Mask, of the drowning women, and dread settling over the world, caused many of the Hilltop people to place hands to their mouths.

Black Skull faithfully reported the facts of their journey, recounting the fearful sight of the Khota canoes, and then of the arrival at the White Shell Clan and the journey upriver.

"I do not claim to understand Power, outside of how it affects a warrior's life." Black Skull paused thoughtfully. "Yet I am here, in your clan grounds. I would rather be home."

"Far from home! Far, far, far from home!" Green Spider chanted. "The warrior always gets what he wishes." His eyes suddenly focused in his emaciated face. "And Black Skull wishes more than any other."

To thwart any hot reply from Black Skull, Otter quickly stated, "That is our story. Power has chosen us to make this journey to the far north to save the Mask of Many Colored Crow. By doing so, perhaps we can save the world from Green Spider's frightful Vision."

Great Ring nodded, then spoke into the silence. "You are most brave, Water Fox." He looked up at Black Skull, his single eye glinting. "And you, warrior, are most worthy." He glanced uneasily at Green Spider, and for the first time, Otter noted that during the recounting, a space had mysteriously opened around the Contrary. Green Spider was chipping at another piece of the pale soil with his splinter.

Great Ring studied the stone pipe in his hands, then looked up. "You are welcome among us, Contrary. We are honored by your presence."

"My presence brings only pain." Green Spider's expression had grown slack as he stared into the fire and absently rolled the dirt clod between his fingers. "So much pain. The dwarf was wrong, you see. The old woman saw more than age. She saw her own solitary life for the first time, stripped of all the imaginary companions she had enjoyed. So sad to have the blanket lifted from one's eyes."

"What's he saying?" Black Skull muttered, distaste creeping into the set of his mouth.

"I don't know," Otter admitted. Then he explained to Great Ring, "He's a Contrary. When Power is on him, like now, most of what he says is backward . . . though it's hard to know what is backward and what forward. When we first met, he told me he never wanted to see me again. It's confusing sometimes."

Great Ring nodded, his one eye wistful. "One never knows the ways of Power." Then he seemed to shake himself. "How will you travel to this place, this Roaring Water?"

"Up the Serpent River. From there, up the Moonshell and—"

"I wouldn't," Owl Eye broke in. People began to whisper.

Otter lifted an eyebrow. "It's the shortest route."

"Did you pass a Trader on the river?" Great Ring asked. "Headed downstream?"

"At least two. Both were running with the current, moving fast. Neither stopped to exchange news."

Great Ring tapped his knobby chin with a finger. "Yes, the news would be traveling rapidly. What Black Skull tells us about the Mask is most interesting. The Mask of Many Colored Crow."

Otter's scalp prickled. "You know something?"

Great Ring's face turned sly, his empty eye socket so much like a skull's. "Indeed I do . . . but it might be Traded for those two jars of honey beer. After all, they'd be better off in my belly than in Fat Elk's.''

"One jar of beer. For the other, you will need to find three tanned buffalo hides. It will be cold upriver."

Great Ring cocked his head. "The information is worth both jars—but I admire your skill, Water Fox. Of all Traders, you are the most audacious. For your daring, you could have been a warrior."

Black Skull snorted, picking the content from the Trader pidgin.

"The Mask, the Mask," Green Spider whispered as if to himself. "Souls Dance in its reflection."

The jitters had wiggled into Otter's gut like roundworms. Still, he couldn't help but say, "Two buffalo robes."

Great Ring had fastened that piercing eye on him, reading him as worry battled with the need for barter. The clan leader listened as one of his wives leaned forward to murmur in his ear. He nodded, grinning at Otter. "Done, Trader. My gracious wife has reminded me that by your very presence, we are gaining a great deal. We shall tell the story of your visit for years to come, no matter what your fate. However, I would advise you not to travel the land of the Serpent Clans."

Otter's back had straightened. "It's the most direct route."

Great Ring had gestured, and now his young warrior stepped around the fire to retrieve the honey beer. "Not when the Serpent Clans are going to war, Water Fox."

"War?" Otter paused to measure Great Ring's words. "Are you sure? The Serpent Clans might have their differences, but I would never have believed that the societies would let it go to war. The results will be disastrous."

Otter could imagine that same smile on Great Ring's lips as he looked down at the dead body of a slain enemy. "Usually, I would agree. However, you should know that many of the clans are allying against the Shining Bird Clan. There is a certain young man, a leader of the Shining Bird known as Mica Bird."

"And he . . . he has a Sacred Mask." Frost settled in Otter's blood.

"Yes, indeed." Great Ring winced as he moved his maimed leg into another position. "The Trader who passed reported that fear and distrust are growing among the Serpent Clans. This Mica Bird has started killing people. Not in the usual way, mind you, but simply by looking through the Mask.''

Otter glanced uneasily at Green Spider. The Contrary stared absently into the fire, a silly grin on his lips as he chewed on yet another dirt clod. Then he pointed into the flames. "You don't see that just every day, do you?"

"I don't understand this," Black Skull growled, ignoring the Contrary's prattle. "Is this the same Mask we're after?"

"I see them!" Green Spider threw his arms wide and bent down to peer intently at the fire. "Warriors, passing single file through the snow. Ashes dance in the wind. See the wind curling around the charred posts? It blows black, filled with soot from the burned clan house. He still hangs, the ghost twisting from the cord. Accursed by memories of life. Every weakness grows on his soul—like mushrooms on a rotting log."

Then, as though he'd never said anything, Green Spider leaned back, yawning, his eyes as vacant as an old hut.

"What else do you see?" Otter demanded, grabbing the Contrary's thin shoulders and shaking him.

"Not you, that's for certain," Green Spider mumbled. "My stomach is so full, it will burst wide open and blow brown slime all over the room."

Otter groaned his frustration. "We'll feed you when we get a chance . . . and *stop* eating dirt!"

His expression slack, Green Spider methodically pried out another clod and swallowed it. "I'm a cannibal. Eating the Earth Mother. Chewing the flesh from her bones. Cannibal . . . cannibal . . . cannibal!"

Otter tried to shake off his discomfort, noting that even Great Ring had been shocked into a loss of words. "How old was that information, Owl Eye?"

"Three moons, little more." Owl Eye was the first to recover his tongue, but though he spoke to Otter, his gaze might have been glued with pine pitch to the Contrary.

"If Mica Bird was creating consternation when I saw him last, three winters ago, he must be even more of a terror now," Otter said.

Owl Eye nodded soberly. "We've heard stories. They say the Mask has possessed his soul. This is not the first time we've heard of him killing someone by looking through it.''

"But what if it's true?"

Black Skull had cocked his head. "Then talk of sorcery will be running through the land like rabbits. That sort of thing breeds fear and unrest. For the first time, I begin to see why I was chosen, Trader." A wicked smile curled his lips. "Your friend, Great Ring, is right. There will be war. And none of these societies will be able to stop it."

Otter started to respond, but whirled when Green Spider crumpled limply to his side and his eyes rolled back in his head so that just the whites showed.

"I'm going to burst," Green Spider whispered miserably. "War or no war." He reached out with bony fingers and industriously scratched at the floor for another dirt clod.

Otter sighed and turned. "Great Ring, would you mind if we helped ourselves to your stew? If we don't put real food into him soon, I'm afraid you'll end up living in a hole."

Nineteen

Pearl crouched before the small fire, her attention fixed on Round Scar as he poked at the flames with a bent twig. The Khota had passed the confluence of the Serpent River with the Father Water that morning. Not far beyond it, Grizzly Tooth had located a murky tributary running off to the west and turned the boats into it.

The Khota had traveled up a winding stream so narrow that they'd pulled the canoes along by grabbing the brush and branches that overhung the waterway.

"Hidden place," Grizzly Tooth had told her when they beached the canoes on a section of collapsed bank. As they'd manhandled her from the canoe, she'd caught a glimpse up the twisting channel and saw that no further travel was possible.

Bleached limbs choked the entire route several paces beyond the landing.

Snow had squealed underfoot as they dragged her along a whitetail trail through the tangled forest. The distance hadn't been far. Here in this little clearing hemmed by trees, they'd paused long enough to build a fire, check her bonds, and leave Round Scar as a guard.

So she sat, hunched as close to the warmth of the fire as she could get. To avoid the look he gave her, she turned her attention to anything that might distract her. Interlaced branches made patterns against the gray sky. The threat of snow lay heavily in the air. With a little imagination, she could see faces in the patterns on tree bark. But her efforts wore out quickly.

"What are they doing?" she finally asked. Anything except suffer under that constant lustful stare the warrior gave her. It was one thing to be desired, another to read a man's expression as he mentally raped her over and over again.

"Raid," he grunted, rubbing a hand along the line of his blunt jaw. "Supplies are low. Ice covers the shallows, and we haven't netted many fish." He gestured around. "This thick brush, you got to have a stand, ambush the deer trails. We don't have time for that. Birds haven't come this far north yet. Too cold."

"And just who are you raiding out here?"

Round Scar grinned and scratched at his roached hair. "Trader told Grizzly Tooth about a little clan that lives near here. Not far."

As if in reply, faint screams broke out, carried by the breeze that blew from the west.

"I guess our warriors found it!" Round Scar chuckled and stood. He kicked at the frozen snow for a moment, exposing the tan grasses beneath. Another burst of faint screams carried on the chilly air.

Seeing Pearl's expression, he laughed. "Relax, woman. My friends, they'll be busy for a while. Got to kill the wounded. Find the food caches. Maybe leave some babies in these women they catch. How does it feel to know that every warrior who captures a woman will close his eyes and imagine it's you that he's taking?"

Pearl sneered her disgust. "How much farther to the Khota villages?"

Round Scar shrugged. "Not far. We'll be there by the time the moon is full. How about that? You ready to be married? Wolf of the Dead, he'll use you up, you know? Then maybe I'll buy what's left from him. You'd like that?"

"I'd rather be married to a skunk. At least the smell wouldn't be so bad."

Round Scar studied her, his face expressionless. "You're brave, did you know that? You've kept your courage. I thought you'd break by now. You're worthy of Wolf of the Dead. A prize by any man's standard."

She gave him a grim smile. "I'm Pearl of the Anhinga. If Dead Wolf has any sense, he'll let me go the second he sees me." She cocked her head. Was this an opportunity? "A prize? What about you, Round Scar? You wouldn't make a bad man for a woman like me. You've got strong shoulders. You're no coward, either."

Round Scar glanced sideways at the trail leading toward the village. Screams could still be heard. He resettled himself, suspicion in his black eyes. "What are you talking about?"

"You and me. Just the two of us."

Round Scar grinned. "Right now? Before they get back?"

"No, stupid! I'm talking about you and I running away! About us getting into one of the canoes and slipping downriver." She gave him her seductive smile. "And then, Round Scar, we'll have plenty of time to see just how much man you are."

He hesitated, that familiar lustful gleam in his eyes.

"You and me," she goaded. "If you've the courage to win a prize like me." *And as soon as you turn your back, I'm going to split your head with an oak paddle!*

Round Scar made a face as he rubbed his chin. She could see desire fighting with good sense. At last he shook his head. "No, it's not worth my life."

"Oh, come, your life? They'd *never* catch us!"

Round Scar snorted and spit into the tiny fire. "You don't understand. Wolf of the Dead would find you. Then he'd find me. He'd slit my belly open and let my guts fall out. He'd leave me to die like that. It takes a long time. You don't know him. He'd turn himself into a wolf . . . *smell* us out. You can't run, not from Wolf of the Dead."

"I *know* we can," Pearl maintained. But she could see that she'd lost. If the opportunity had presented itself earlier, she might have had a chance. Round Scar had been one of the worst of the warriors, driven by lust. Now, however, so close to his unholy leader, his desire—and evidently his courage—had gone to water.

Pearl studied him from under lowered lids, aware that he avoided her gaze.

"It's not too late," she insisted, refusing to give up.

Round Scar gave her a flat look of warning. "Maybe downriver I might have been tempted. You would make a perfect wife for a warrior. But not here, not this close to Wolf of the Dead. And because I desire you so much, I will give you a word of advice, woman. Do not run from him. Instead, if you would live comfortably—if not happily—dedicate your life to pleasing him."

"And if I don't?"

"He will find a terrible way to kill you. Maybe by skinning your pretty hide off of you a hand's measure at a time. Maybe he'll burn you to death, a little piece a day until you're half-cooked, half-raw. He might cut open places on your body and put maggots inside. He does strange things with maggots."

A notion—and an uncomfortably awkward one at that—crawled around inside Black Skull like a curious sort of mouse. He sat to one side of the fire they shared in Owl Eye's small house.

Since the beginning of this lunatic journey up the river, he'd become no stranger to notions—all of them bad—or to misgivings, either. Misgivings plagued him every moment of the day. His Dreams had turned particularly bothersome. Here, far up the river, no friendly ghosts whispered in his ears at night. The Spirits of his ancestors lived far away, safe within the City of the Dead. From the moment he'd left the City of the Dead, their protection had been denied him.

How had he ever ended up here, with such strange people? People who were supposed to marry their cousins, no less. And not marry just one, but all of them. A man heard of such things, of course. Traders brought stories, or even had curious behaviors themselves, but to see such a thing!

What more don't you know? He pushed the question from consideration. A warrior need know only discipline, strength, courage, and duty.

To Black Skull's right, Owl Eye and Otter talked as they bent over some scratches they'd made in the ash-ridden dirt. To his left, the Contrary sat immobile. Nevertheless, Green Spider watched Otter with a sort of detached curiosity, as if all of his attention were on the Trader. In the rear sat a young woman, Owl Eye's wife. Comely and delicate, she was nursing an infant. She appeared subdued by her august visitors. As she cradled the baby, her wide brown eyes kept shifting from person to person. Like a worried doe, Black Skull thought.

He studied the patterns created by the framework of saplings and branches laced together to form the hut. Thin, overlapping sections of bark were lashed to the outside, and on the whole, the place was snug. Bundles of dried food hung from the ceiling, much of it stored in netting.

It continued to plague Black Skull that somehow he'd made a mistake, but he wasn't quite sure of what the notion meant. Not just the mistake of coming on this idiot adventure in the first place, but that *he'd erred.*

It all went back to that morning when he'd killed the silly crow and put the Trader in his place. In effect, he'd achieved leadership, gathered the Power to himself as all war leaders should. Knowing that he'd established his authority, he should have been relieved.

Then why am I not?

Despite his unacknowledged domination of the Trader and the lunatic, that silly notion wouldn't leave him alone. Many Colored Crow had little to do with war or battle. Those Spirit Beings were Snapping Turtle, Hawk, Bobcat, and Water Moccasin. They gave Power to a warrior. Why should a crow be different than a duck when it came to hunting? Crow might have meaning to the lunatic, and who knew, maybe to the Trader, too; but not to a warrior.

Black Skull took a deep breath, drove the matter from his ordered thoughts, and bent forward.

"What are you discussing?"

Otter and Owl Eye glanced up. They'd been drawing in the ashes at the fire's edge. The Trader explained: "We've been discussing the route north."

"You've told me enough times. Up Serpent River to the Moonshell, then—"

"No," Otter said, refusing to meet his eyes. "Not now."

Black Skull gave the Trader and his alleged brother a hard look. "Why not? You yourself said it's the most direct route."

Otter vented an exasperated sigh. He'd pulled his long hair back and plaited it into a braid that hung down his back, leaving his flat face unobscured. His skin had taken on a pale pink flush. Fear? "Didn't you hear the talk about war?"

"Of course. That's why I'm included in this mad venture. If there's a war to be fought, you need a warrior. Obviously, I was chosen for that purpose. To fight our way through the war among the Serpent Clans."

"Is everything so simple for you? Just beat your way through life with a club?"

You sure straightened out after I grabbed you by the throat, Trader. "I obtain my ends—and generally with a great deal of satisfaction."

Green Spider mumbled to himself, "Like dull obsidian, so dull it has to hack its way through the world."

Otter paused thoughtfully, as if truly considering the Contrary's nonsensical statement; he again hunched over the doodlings in the ashes.

"What's he babbling about?" Black Skull asked.

"Nothing. At least, I doubt you'd find it interesting."

Every day the fool looks more and more like a lost child—and the Trader panders to him!

Otter distracted the warrior by pointing to the drawing and chattering to Owl Eye in that turkey talk the Hilltop people spoke. Black Skull leaned forward. The lines and scratches made little sense to him.

"What is that?"

Otter pointed to a hole pressed into the gray ash. "That's Hilltop. This line is the Father Water. And here, a day's travel north, is the confluence with the Serpent River." A series of dots followed the line of the river. "Those are the different clan grounds along the Serpent River . . . until here. This dot represents Serpent City, the clan at the mouth of the Moon-shell. From there we pass more clans until we reach Sun Mounds. That's this dot. The next line is the Holy Road north to StarSky."

"And that other line you've drawn?" Black Skull pointed, hunching forward on his knees.

"The Father Water. It takes us north through the narrows to the confluence of the Ilini River. These dots mark the clan grounds we would pass."

Black Skull cocked his head. "The Khota are up the Ilini."

"That's right. They are at this dot." Otter pointed. The line continued up to a big round circle. "These dots up to the Fresh Water Sea are the Ilini clans we'll pass."

"Wait a minute. You said we weren't going that way." Black Skull could feel the muscles in his face start to spasm—and wished mightily that he could control them.

Otter lowered his voice, his fists balling. He swallowed hard, as if nerving himself for a final assault. "You can kill me any time. We know that, don't we? It's my canoe. _I_ choose the way we go."

Green Spider chirped, "Kill him, warrior. Kill him!"

Owl Eye might not have known the language, but he caught the undertones. Now he rocked back, his gleaming eyes on Black Skull.

That unsettling notion he'd been feeling broke free to scamper about Black Skull's soul. For a second, he fought the urge to push the confrontation; then he became aware of the interest in the fool's eyes. More than just a matter of wills was at play here. From Otter's posture, it was apparent that even the smallest of pushes would break something inside him.

Do I want to break him? Black Skull hesitated, then reduced the tension by asking, "What does going that way get us? It's longer. You said so yourself."

Green Spider poked at the dirt with a skinny finger. The fool wasn't going to start eating it again, was he? That idiocy had totally amazed the Hilltop people.

"It's safer." Otter glanced at the fool. "Green Spider saw the Fresh Water Sea in his Vision. I didn't understand why at first. I do now. In Green Spider's Vision, we're on the Fresh

Water Sea. Not fighting with the Serpent Clans—who, in any case, we can't beat.''

''Try me.''

''I don't doubt your courage, Black Skull, or your ability. On the other hand, if four canoe-loads of Khota made you nervous, you should remember that the Six Flutes sent them running.'' Otter raised a hand to forestall Black Skull's response. ''Tell me, is it better to win with a fight . . . or to win without one?''

And to think I allowed him to save face just now. ''Without. Any good warrior knows that.''

Otter nodded. ''That's what makes you a good war leader.''

Black Skull studied the words, but found nothing placating in them. Despite his building frustration at seeing the plans changed, he couldn't smack the Trader around for outflanking him on his own ground.

''How much longer to go around?''

''Three weeks?'' Otter turned to Owl Eye, asking the question in Hilltop tongue.

Owl Eye chattered back.

Otter translated. ''Maybe three weeks. It depends on the weather. If we time it right, we can reach the Fresh Water Sea in the fifth moon. That's the calm moon.''

''This Ilini River flows out of the Fresh Water Sea?''

''No, but a swamp called Mud Lake lies at the headwaters. The western side flows into the Ilini, the eastern into the Fresh Water Sea.''

Black Skull contemplatively rubbed his broken chin. ''And how big is this Fresh Water Sea?''

Otter shrugged, asking the question of Owl Eye. He translated: ''The Traders who cross it say it is very wide. Some say it is one sea, others that it is more, all hooked together. I can only tell you what I've heard.''

And what could one believe from a Trader? ''Well, it can't be much wider than the Father Water. There can't be any more water in the world than what's flowing down the Father Water.''

Otter started to say something, a curious look in his eyes. Then he just shrugged. ''Probably.''

''What about these Khota?'' Black Skull pointed at the dot

on the line representing the Ilini River. "You've had trouble with them before."

Otter gave him a blank look. "Perhaps, warrior, that's why Power sent you."

Four long war canoes with flashing paddles. Black Skull could recall the worry with which he'd watched them pass. "Yes, perhaps that is why Power sent me."

A thrill swelled within him. The Trader might fear the Khota, but Black Skull would not. A brush with a few Khota might be just what Power had in mind.

From across the fire, Green Spider chanted in a singsong voice, "Obsidian bends, just a little bit. How much more before rock gives way to tender meat? Watch yourself, Snapping Turtle, the water's deep!"

"We'll take your longer route," Black Skull said.

That night, Black Skull Dreamed: Like a bit of wood in a roiling flood, *Wave Dancer* bobbed in waves taller than any man. Pitching and diving, the canoe rose on a high crest of water, only to drop into a deep trough so that seething water rose on all sides. The canoe pitched upward again, to cant on a high peak before the drop.

Rigid with terror, Black Skull threw his weight into the paddle, driving the canoe forward from one ridge of water to another. On either side, the tortured waves threatened to rush downward and crush him beneath their weight.

A way out! He must find it! But as the canoe bucked and leaped up another wall of water, an endless violence of waves stretched in every direction.

He cried out then, lost. In the storm clouds above, a weird wind whistled, blowing spray off the choppy peaks around him. Pausing only long enough to wipe his soaked face, Black Skull watched in horror. *Wave Dancer* was thrown high, then slipped down into the next trough like a cast dart. The fox-headed bow dove deep, allowing a frothing-white boil into the canoe.

The wailing of the wind had changed, and in that last horrible moment, he could hear the laughter, so familiar. From the depths of the grave, his mother laughed with her rasping, throaty chuckle.

The paddle was wrenched from Black Skull's hand as the canoe wallowed in the trough. In desperation, he clung to the slippery gunwales. He gaped in horror as the next wall of water crashed down, sending him deep into the cold, leaching blackness.

Hollow Drill stared up at the endless blue of the unseasonably springlike sky. More storms would roll down from the northwest before winter was finished, but for now, he enjoyed the reprieve.

He walked along the southern wall of the huge Octagon, barely seeing the stippled tracks that had melted through the snow to expose bare grass. Here and there, despite the desires of the engineers, children had crisscrossed the earthworks, but their telltale snow-slides were fading under the warm sun.

The Engineers' Society took some things too seriously, but then, when it was one's own works, who didn't?

He nodded as the hobbling Elder of the Wild Plum lineage approached. Crest Grass should have been long dead and burned to ashes, yet the shriveled old man continued to live on in spite of no teeth, pain in his swollen joints, and one blind eye.

"May your ancestors bless you, Hollow Drill," the Elder called, stopping to prop himself on his walking stick. Crest Grass's back curved like a throwing stick, and he could no longer straighten it. Instead, his skinny neck curved backward to allow him to see straight. On this day, the old man wore a blanket woven from feathers and strips of rabbit fur. The flaps dangled down on either side of his hollow stomach like folded wings.

A buzzard looks like you, old man. "Greetings, Crest Grass. May your ancestors smile on your lineage and all of your grandchildren."

"Hah! Let them. I won't be among them for at least another spring yet." He worked his toothless gums, which made his fleshy mouth pucker and pulse under the huge curving eminence of his nose. He wore his silver hair in a bun over his forehead; gossamer strands had escaped and wavered like antennae in the morning light. "Sometimes I wonder if the ancestors even want me to join them. They keep passing me by. Took my great-granddaughter the other day, though. Poor little thing. Everything she ate went right through her. She wasted into a little bundle of bones. Her face shrank up, and in the end, I had more meat on me than she did."

"I share my sorrow with you." Hollow Drill dropped his gaze to the mushy snow the old man stood in. The Elder had wrapped his feet in layers of cloth, but the fabric had absorbed so much melted snow and dirt that his feet resembled a bear's dark brown paws.

"Your wife . . . now that was a loss." Crest Grass wobbled slightly on his propped stick. "The ghosts of the ancestors are richer and we the poorer until Many Colored Crow comes to whisk us to her company."

Would it always be so hard to talk about his wife's death? "I'll be with her soon."

"What's this?" Crest Grass blinked, as if trying to make his bad eye see. "You're young yet. Might be that the Spirits will pass you by as they did me. My only hope is that ghosts don't have bodies that fall apart like those of the living. Funny thing, isn't it? Getting old. You'd think the Mysterious One would have made us different."

"Indeed."

Crest Grass sighed. "I should make my way along. Thought I'd go sit on the mound." He meant the burial mound, of course, the one where his friends and family had been buried, or where their ashes were scattered. "I can visit that way. Listen to their voices. I either think I hear them, or else I do. Don't know which is which anymore."

"Give them my kind wishes." Hollow Drill started on, passing the Elder. Having ghosts close did help drive away loneliness. Ghosts loved to talk.

Once a Trader had told him that some of the savage peoples in the far west *feared* the ghosts of their ancestors. What kind of life would that be? Your loved ones shunned and avoided— and just because they'd passed from this existence into a different one? How much better to know that the ancestors watched over you and your family. What would it be like not to have the Dead hovering near, giving advice, scolding?

"Oh! By the way. What did those warriors want?" Crest Grass, instead of turning, walked his way around his stick to face Hollow Drill.

"Warriors?" A crow cawed from the roof of a charnel house on the other side of the earthen embankment.

"The ones who wanted to see you." Crest Grass blinked a little harder. "Arrived at the Warrior Society house. A whole big party of them. From somewhere south . . . uh, Blue Duck and Rattlesnake. Had some Many Paints with them. Goosefoot, too, I think. Wanted to see you."

"I didn't know anyone had come. I've been out at my cousins' . . . the ones northwest of here by the Flying Squirrel mound. Are you sure they're looking for me?"

"You'd better go." Crest Grass began pivoting back around his planted stick toward the direction to which he'd been headed. "That war leader, Robin, he was as cold as river ice, and most impatient to see you."

South! With news about Star Shell? It had to be.

"Thank you, Elder. Greet your ancestors for me." Hollow Drill cut off at an angle, circling the marshy lake that lay between the Octagon and the Great Circle. In defiance of the engineers, he cut across one of the low embankments and hurried toward the Warrior Society house. Across the trampled flats he could see a number of shelters around the squat building. Just how many warriors had come up from the south?

Two moons had passed since Star Shell left StarSky with the Magician. Stories had drifted up the Holy Road—tales of Star Shell's husband and the terrible things he'd done. And then, a moon ago, came the horrible tale of the suicide. Through those long days, Hollow Drill had waited, vainly hoping that Star Shell would arrive. Instead, he'd heard nothing but rumors that turned ever more wild.

He'd been told that Star Shell and the High Head dwarf, Tall Man, had disappeared—and with them, the terrible Mask. Later, he'd heard that she'd become a witch, wearing the Mask and walking the trails at night, invisible to human eyes. Some said she and the dwarf had become lovers, vanishing into the forests and looting abandoned farmsteads in the dark hours.

All Hollow Drill knew was that his daughter was in serious trouble—but he'd known that before his wife's funeral.

I sent her south with Tall Man. Better that I had just forbidden her to return to Sun Mounds. Except that he couldn't do that. Not when she was a man's wife, had a child to care for, and obligations to the lineage she'd married into.

That pointless waiting had forced him to put off visiting his cousins in the first place. Now, what if she'd come? Found him missing? No, she'd have gone to her brother's holding next. There she would have found safety.

Hollow Drill passed the first of the shelters built by the visiting warriors. At least two men had slept here. Glancing about, he counted more than three tens of the small shelters; and what about the warriors who would have been accommodated within the Warrior Society house? His heart went cold. He shielded his eyes from the glare of sun off snow. A sizable crowd had gathered before the house.

Even as he approached, five and ten warriors came trotting up the Holy Road. They looked travel-worn, their leggings soaked and muddy. They wore war shirts and carried wicker shields; their darts gleamed in the sunlight. These men moved warily, as if expecting trouble. They trotted like wolves on the hunt.

Hollow Drill walked slowly toward the throng that stood before the Warrior Society house.

The building was at least forty paces long and nearly that wide. StarSky could muster a great many warriors when the need arose, and one out of four men among the clans belonged to the Warrior Society.

"Hollow Drill!" someone called. "Here he comes."

A path opened before him as all eyes centered on his approach.

Three Beavers, one of the Chokecherry clan members from StarSky, trotted out to meet him. "Where have you been?"

"At my cousins'. What is all this? What's happening?"

Three Beavers gave him an uneasy appraisal. "Your daughter, is she here?"

"No."

"The warriors from the Moonshell Clans have come searching for her. You've heard the stories about the Mask? This war leader—Robin—wants it." Three Beavers hesitated. "He means to have it. No matter what."

"What do you mean, no matter what?"

"What I said. And make no doubt about it." Three Beavers placed a warning hand on Hollow Drill's arm. "If you're hiding her, don't play games, Elder. They will kill us all, if necessary, to find her."

By this time, others had come to stand around them. Hollow Drill nodded to those he knew, but in a multi-clan center such as StarSky, there were many he didn't know. The Moonshell warriors stood unmoving, watching him from their position before the door. Some had started rattling sticks on the wicker of their shields, a demonstration of anger.

"Strike no sparks," Three Beavers warned. "The tinder is very dry."

Hollow Drill nodded as he threaded his way to the Warrior Society house.

"Go in," a warrior ordered. "Robin is waiting for you."

Hollow Drill felt his throat go dry. What kind of trouble was Star Shell in? He could feel the tension and the hostility between the StarSky warriors and the southerners. Dry tinder indeed.

He ducked through the doorway into a place he'd never been before, for Hollow Drill had never been called to war. His preference and duty had been in public works, and he had served as the leader and spokesman of a clan. The babble of talk died at his entry. He blinked, waiting a moment for his eyes to adjust.

The big room was packed with warriors, and smoke hung low enough to sting his eyes. The room smelled of unwashed humanity, damp fabric, and smoke-cured leather.

As he started to pick his way forward, men shuffled to either side to clear a path. His eyes gradually adjusted. War trophies hung on the walls: painted skulls, masks and fetishes, darts, and clubs—but not so many of the latter as would be normal. Most had found their way into anxious hands.

The awareness knotted his belly—intense enough to bend him double were he not the center of attention. If this dry tinder ignited, a bloodbath would result. So many hostile eyes. The wrath of the clans seemed to be poised, and it would all fall on him.

At the big central fire, the principals rose.

Hollow Drill stopped before them, a hand to his cramping

belly. He nodded to those he knew, but his attention was on the strangers. One, burly and blunt-faced, wore a heavy blanket with the image of a duck woven into the blue fabric. A breastplate of human jaws hung on either side of a ground-slate gorget. He had to be Robin. The man beside Robin was leaner, spare, but no less deadly. Neither had friendly eyes.

Six Bears, leader of the Warrior Society, stood on the other side of the fire. He nodded apprehensively at Hollow Drill. Six Bears wore a cougar hide over his shoulder: the emblem of his office. With a dart, he'd single-handedly hunted and killed the animal—proof of his courage and ability to lead the Warrior Society.

Galena Ferret, Six Bears' second-in-command, stood at his side, his brawny arms crossed. So did Thick Cord, head of the Engineers' Society. Green Pod, of the Star Society. Big Hand, who oversaw the sacred chert quarries. So, too, did the society leaders for the weavers, the potters, the pipe carvers, and others. Many of the Clan Elders—Hollow Drill's peers—sat behind Six Bears, each watching intently.

Six Bears spoke kindly. "Hollow Drill, may your ancestors shed their blessings on you. May all of your children be well and your grandchildren happy."

At mention of his children being well, blunt-faced Robin seemed to sour even further.

"These men—" with an outstretched arm, Six Bears indicated the warriors "—have come in search of something they say your daughter has stolen. A Mask, the Mask of Many Colored Crow. They say they must have it back. This warrior—" Six Bears confirmed Hollow Drill's suspicion "—is called Robin, leader of the Warrior Society of the Moonshell valley. He is of the Blue Duck Clan. Beside him stands Woodpecker, also of his clan."

Hollow Drill hoped his voice wouldn't crack as he faced Robin. "I am Hollow Drill, of the StarSky Clan. Ask what you will of me. In the presence of my ancestors, I will tell you all that I know." *And let us pray that it is enough.*

A flicker of irony twitched at the corner of Robin's hard lips. "Your daughter is Star Shell? The same Star Shell who married into the Sun Mound Clan?"

"She is."

"Then you know what has happened? About the murder of my cousin by Star Shell's husband? About the theft of the Mask?"

Hollow Drill swallowed, and he feared the whole room heard. "Some. I have heard about what happened to my daughter's husband. Also about the disappearance of the Mask. About your cousin or his death, I know nothing."

"Where is your daughter?" Robin seemed perched to spring.

"As the ghosts of my ancestors bear witness, War Leader Robin, I do not know. I have not seen her or heard from her since the night she left StarSky. That was over two moons ago, before the events you speak of. I can tell you nothing more."

Six Bears seemed to sigh with relief.

"*If* we are to believe you," Robin said with a snort.

"He is one of our Elders!" Six Bears protested. "Hollow Drill has told you the truth!"

Robin studied the old leader with deadly eyes. "Men have been known to lie when the safety of one of their children is at stake."

"Not Hollow Drill," Six Bears growled. Mutters of assent came from the society leaders.

Robin seemed unimpressed. "What of the High Head dwarf, the Magician? Have you seen him?"

"He was here." The words seemed to twist from Hollow Drill's throat. "He left on the night my daughter did."

"And what," Robin asked mildly, "did the Magician want with your daughter?"

Hollow Drill hesitated.

"Please," Six Bears said gently. "Tell us, Hollow Drill." The leader of the StarSky Warrior Society gestured behind him to the society leaders, the most influential men and women in the StarSky holdings. "We have discussed this. All of the societies want to see this matter brought to a satisfactory resolution. We find ourselves in a very dangerous situation, one we haven't faced in a long time. Talk of war has been heard. If we cannot bring this to a conclusion, hostilities are certain. No one wants that, old friend."

"I would urge my friend, Hollow Drill, to speak," Thick Cord advised from where he sat. "I have known Hollow Drill's heart to be that of a good man. He has always worked with us in the Engineers' Society. He has organized his clan well, and provided labor on the earthworks. He has always helped us in the past. I would wish that he work with us now to bring this situation to an end before real trouble can be born.''

Hollow Drill experienced a sinking within his soul. He could not defy the societies, even if he truly wished to. ''The High Head Elder, Tall Man, arrived just after the winter solstice—at the time of my wife's death. He sent a young man to see me. The young man requested that I bring Star Shell to see Tall Man, saying that perhaps the Magician could help her. On the night of my wife's cremation, I went with Star Shell to see the Magician. They talked about the Mask, about what it was doing to my daughter's husband.''

Hollow Drill recounted the conversation to the best of his ability. Someone coughed in the back of the room. He could hear people shuffling nervously. ''So, you see, Robin,'' Hollow Drill finished, ''they may have taken the Mask, but I cannot tell you where. I would say only this to you. The Mask was made by the High Heads. They know of its Power. If you, who wish it so badly, were a wise man, you'd let it go to wherever the High Heads think it belongs.''

''To their clan houses? So that they might use it against us?'' Robin cried. ''You may save your advice, Elder!''

Hollow Drill stiffened as if struck. ''If you won't take mine, perhaps you had better seek my daughter's husband's. I imagine he would talk to you, War Leader Robin. As I am given to understand, his ghost is lonely within the guardian stakes at Sun Mounds.''

A ripple ran through the crowd.

Robin stepped close, so close that Hollow Drill could smell venison on his breath. ''If you have lied, old man, we will return to StarSky—and women will wail in empty houses. The bodies that lie in your charnel huts will be missing heads on that day.''

Gasps of hard-jawed outrage escaped the StarSky warriors, and some of those seated rose on muscular legs. War clubs balanced in knotted fists.

One wrong word, Hollow Drill told himself, and we're all dead.

At that moment, Woodpecker raised his hands. ''*Hear me!*

My cousin's words were misspoken. We seek *only* the Mask . . . and vengeance for our cousin's death! Not a war with StarSky! My cousin apologizes for any unintended slight to the noble people of StarSky and her allied clans.''

Robin glanced around at the hard faces of the StarSky people. Cold reality leached into his soul, and his face paled. ''Forgive me.'' He placed a hand to his heart. ''My business lies with Star Shell, not with the clans of StarSky. Perhaps my grief has led me to words spoken in pain over my cousin's unjust death.''

''You are forgiven,'' Six Bears stated, ice in his voice. ''We have heard from Hollow Drill. Star Shell, and this Mask you seek, are not at StarSky.''

''And if they should come here?'' Robin asked hotly.

Six Bears crossed his arms. ''As leader of the Warrior Society at StarSky, I do not believe that will be my business.''

''Would it become your business if my warriors come here looking?''

Six Bears met the younger man's hard glare with one of his own. ''Let me ask you this, War Leader. Where is your real purpose? Do you wish a war with StarSky? If so, I give you my word that one can be arranged. Or do you wish to find Star Shell and the Mask? If the latter, do you wish to spend time and energy watching your warriors die instead of seeking that which you say you desire? The answer is yours to give, War Leader.''

Robin trembled, anger bright in his flushed face.

Woodpecker cried, ''We seek only Star Shell and the Mask!'' In a lower voice, he added, ''We have no quarrel with StarSky, her clans, or warriors.'' At that, Woodpecker laid a hard hand on his cousin's shoulder. ''Come, we have done all we can do here.''

Robin shrugged the hand away and spun on his heel, signaling his men. Not a word was spoken as he and his warriors left the room.

Hollow Drill stared disconsolately at the packed-earth floor. His soul had collapsed like a punctured fish bladder.

Six Bears stepped across the fire and took Hollow Drill's hand. His voice turned sympathetic. ''I don't know what trouble your daughter has become involved with, but I sincerely hope she can find a way out . . . without forcing us to go to war.''

''It's the Mask.'' Hollow Drill shook his head, his heart as stone-cold as on the day his wife died. ''It brings misery, old friend, to anyone who has anything to do with it.''

Twenty

Warm winds and sunny days had brought a long-overdue melt. On northern slopes, hollows formed in the snow around the black boles of trees, and the water-rotten drifts sagged in retreat. The creeks swelled and flexed as ice melted to fill rivulets. The tributaries rose, spilling their banks and flooding fertile fields along the winding courses. On the south-facing meadows, the first tentative blades of grass poked green spindles toward the sun and a new season.

Wave Dancer passed through murky waters with arrow-like grace as she crossed the confluence of the Serpent River and the Father Waters. Otter had seen the river like this before, but only in the wettest of years. The flood has risen above the Father Water's banks. To the east, waves lapped at the slopes that rose to rounded headlands, while in the west, the flood vanished into the tangle of trees and vines. Looking across the expanse, the brownish water took on a silver sheen.

Black Skull just gaped at the sight, shaking his head. Green Spider delighted in the matted flotsam freed by the flood.

Otter followed a route near the western trees, where yellow-brown foam bobbed in soapy patches. Black sticks, bits of bark and other debris dotted the surface. The still air smelled of mud, wet wood, and the musky vapors of the water.

''This is all the water in the world!'' Black Skull cried. ''Where does it all go?''

''Up, up, up into the sky!'' Green Spider shrieked. ''It flies like a bird. North, ever north!''

Black Skull shot a slitted glance back at the Contrary. ''I

know a way of finding out, fool. I could wring your scrawny neck, throw what's left overboard, and see which way your miserable corpse floats!''

Green Spider laced his fingers in his lap and sighed. ''Killer of Men, soon you will stand upon a desert the likes of which you would never have believed. Sand stretches as far as you can see, blowing, spiraling around and around. Will your corpse float? Float, float, in all that blowing sand?''

Black Skull shook his head. ''This is a fool's quest.''

Indeed, Otter agreed, *and I'm the biggest fool of all for leaving White Shell. I should have turned them down. I didn't have to come on this insane journey.*

The image of Red Moccasins' face formed on the heels of that thought, and he knew he'd just lied to himself. A fist tightened around his heart. He would have taken any excuse to escape proximity to her and Four Kills.

Catcher stood up on one of the packs, stretching and yawning before taking a couple of turns and resettling, his nose dangling over the side as he watched the opaque water pass.

''Where are we going to camp tonight, Trader?'' Black Skull indicated the endless water. ''Do you think you can find high ground anywhere?''

Otter continued paddling, watching *Wave Dancer's* wake as it rippled the water-soaked tree trunks to either side. ''We will find no high ground, warrior. Not around the confluence. We could land over on the bluffs, but you'd have to climb to find a flat place to sleep. Most likely we'll spend tonight sleeping in the boat, tied off to a tree. North of here, the sandstone forms protective overhangs. We'll have good camps for the next couple of nights.''

''And what then?''

''The river widens out just below the confluence of the Big Muddy—what some call the Moon River. A half day's journey above that, we'll find the mouth of the Ilini River. From there on, we'll make better time. The Ilini's current isn't as swift, or the channel as wide.''

''And that's where we'll find the Khota,'' Black Skull said easily.

''That's where we'll try to avoid the Khota,'' Otter amended. That night, after they'd tied off and eaten a cold dinner of goosefoot-and-sunflower-seed bread, Otter removed his flute from its sack. Green Spider had leaned against the packs, making his bed in the center of the canoe. Black Skull had arranged his bed so that his head was pillowed by the fox-head bow.

Otter wet his lips and blew, sending the haunting notes across the dark water. He played the loon song, a piece he'd learned in the far north. Next, he played the harvest song, which the High Heads who lived in the hilly lands south of the Serpent River sang in the fall. He played the hanging-moss song of the Alligator Clans, and finally, the spring-buffalo song of the hunter-farmer peoples who lived up the Big Muddy River.

"You are good, Trader." Black Skull spoke from the darkness. "Many of those songs are new to my ear."

"I try to learn something wherever I go." Otter fingered the smooth wood. The flute had been a gift from Uncle. He couldn't help but look northward.

"How long have you been playing?"

"Since I was a boy. I didn't really get much practice until I started Trading on the river." He paused, remembering. "We played every night."

"We?"

"Uncle and I."

"The one the Khota killed?"

"He was more than my teacher and disciplinarian. He was my friend. Probably the best friend I'll ever have." Otter's loneliness grew, gnawing like a disease in his soul. Was life nothing but a series of losses? Uncle? Red Moccasins? Four Kills? Precious people slipped away, but new ones didn't come to fill those gaps.

"A friend?" Black Skull queried.

"A friend," Otter replied, lost in his musings. He reached into his shirt, fingering the copper effigy he now wore around his neck. A fish splashed in the darkness, and an owl hooted over the water. Overhead, the stars shimmered and gleamed. The faint glow on the horizon indicated that the half-moon was about to rise.

"I've never had a friend," Black Skull said quietly.

With your fun-loving personality, it's no wonder. Aloud, Otter said, "There must have been someone."

"Granduncle. He saved me, taught me." The warrior paused. "Do you know what it's like to be different? I was ridiculed. People made fun of me. My mother, she . . ." Black Skull lapsed into silence.

After long moments, Otter said, "I know what it's like to be different. I was claimed by the river. It took me when I was an infant. I should have drowned, but it gave me back. Uncle, he understood."

"Perhaps we are more alike than I thought." Black Skull shifted, rocking the canoe.

Alike? *Me and Black Skull?* The man had no friends. Otter, however, couldn't count all of his. Clear from Smoking Bear in the Copper Lands to Fat Snake in the Coral Islands, Otter had friends. "I'll give you some of mine. How about Long Squirrel? You liked him."

"Is he really your friend, Trader?"

"Of course he is. He—"

"Would you bet your life on him? Die for him?"

Would he? Otter stared out into the darkness. How many people could he say that about? Four Kills, obviously, but . . . who else?

"When you talk in terms of your life, it's not so easy, is it?" Black Skull prodded. "These people you meet in your Trade, they're likable, true, but only to the extent that such relationships facilitate the movement of goods. How many *real* friends do you have, Trader?"

Catcher. He would willingly give his life to save Catcher's. He looked at the black, white, and brown dog where it slept on the packs, and warmth filled him. Yes, and with no regrets.

Black Skull waited for an answer, then chuckled in the darkness. "No, deny it all you wish, but you and I are more alike than you want to believe."

"Did you really kill your mother?"

Now it was Black Skull's turn to be silent. His ruined face twitched in the moonlight. At last he spoke, his voice gravelly. "She was possessed, Trader. An evil woman, driven by demons. She used to do things, terrible things. When I was a child, if I did something wrong, as all children can't help but do . . ." A pause. "She'd beat me, Trader. Burn me. Punish me for things I didn't deserve to be punished for. Not like that."

Otter stroked his flute.

"Once she broke my arm. Threw me across the room in a wild rage. No one stopped her. The man she'd married, the one who sired me, I think—she'd driven him away years earlier. That's not to say that she didn't have lots of men. She liked men. Finally, she started luring boys into her bed. You must understand, she was possessed."

"And your clan?"

"They suspected. Granduncle, he finally cornered me, asked me. I was scared to death. Mother would kill me if I told. Granduncle would kill me if I didn't."

"People must have known," Otter countered, thinking about how everyone knew everything in a clan holding.

"They did. The clan leaders had gone to Granduncle with their decision. Mother was hurting people. Being wicked. The responsibility was my granduncle's, but he was too old. I had to tell him what she did to me. What I'd seen her do to other people."

The silence stretched again.

Otter said, "Then it was your granduncle's responsibility to end—"

"He couldn't kill her." Black Skull sounded hoarse. "He was too old, too crippled from the wars. It fell to me. I was just strong enough. I . . . I crept up from behind. While she was asleep. Scared, so terribly scared that she'd wake up, turn around, see me."

"But you did it?"

"I did it." Black Skull made a snorting sound. "People are funny, Trader. They feared me after that. No matter that my family . . . that *I* was responsible for my mother's behavior. We still trace our descent through the females, not like these Hilltop people. With that one stroke of the war club, I became something terrible. I know that she was wicked, evil, possessed by demons. But, Trader, what if you'd been forced to kill Blue Jar? How would people look at you?"

Otter knew. No matter how necessary the justice, that look of revulsion would have lurked in everyone's eyes. "So you followed the warrior's path?"

"That I did. Granduncle showed me the way. Taught me to order my life. He gave me the discipline to become the best that ever lived. So, you see, I still guard my people. And now, for the most part, I don't see that look in their eyes. But I will never forgive them for what they made me do."

"You can't blame yourself. You did what you had to, for the good of your clan."

Black Skull grunted neutrally. "I've made peace with my soul. She was a monster preying on the innocent. She hurt me. Humiliated me. Shamed me until I hated myself more than I hated her. Something horrible had grown in her soul. You can't let people like that live, or they will infect society with their pus and rot. But . . ." He looked down at his hands, spreading them open as if to the cleansing air. "But no one should make a boy responsible."

"No. You're right. I've never heard of such a thing before."

Black Skull snorted uneasily. "I've never told this to anyone, except Granduncle before he died." A pause. "I wouldn't want to hear any talk of this, Trader."

"I would never betray your words, warrior. It will be our secret."

Green Spider resettled on the packs; he gently added, "And not mine."

The eastern sky had brightened, cloud-speckled, turning pink with morning. A chilly breeze blew from the east. Star Shell shivered and pulled her blanket tighter around her. From the trail they climbed, the horizon spread out like a black-mounded silhouette of hills and distant trees.

Star Shell squeezed Silver Water's cold hand, whispering, "It's almost time, baby."

The climb to this weathered peak had taken most of the night, the going slow and treacherous in the inky blackness. The zig-zagging route up had been choked with roots—slick and frozen, hidden by branches—and every other malice of a forest trail. Not only that, but despite the warm spell, the predawn chill was sharp. Her belly rumbling with hunger, Star Shell struggled to keep her teeth from chattering.

Silver Water seemed to be listening to something beyond her mother's hearing. When that happened, Star Shell couldn't help but stiffen, fearing what it might be. Since the night at the old woman's hut, Silver Water had been different, quiet, perhaps resigned to her flight across the hilly country.

Or is it something else? The Mask? Don't even think it. But Star Shell wondered.

This morning marked the spring equinox: one of the four high holy days of the people. On this day, all across the world, men and women would be offering prayers to the Spirit World, to the Mysterious One, First Man, and Many Colored Crow.

"It's time," Tall Man said.

The young man named Greets the Sun nodded and smiled as he led them across a rocky meadow to a small earthen mound. He was younger than Star Shell, stately and handsome, bearing a subtle dignity. His wide forehead had been achieved by the binding of his head as an infant, as Tall Man's head had been similarly bound.

Tall Man had led the way here, eastward from the Blue Duck Clan. His knowledge of the back trails had surprised Star Shell, as did his familiarity with isolated farmsteads and the people who lived in them.

Instead of dropping down into the Red Buck valley and the settlements there, Tall Man had led them along the hilly divide between the Moonshell and Red Buck drainages until they arrived at Greets the Sun's small house.

This hilltop lay within the bounds of Greets the Sun's lineage territory, a high, rocky valley fed by several small springs and a temperamental creek. Greets the Sun himself lived at the base of the hill they'd climbed the night before.

"He's something of a hermit, but simple in nature," Tall Man had told her as they walked up to the small house. "From the time he was a boy, you could see that Power had touched him. He never played as the other children did. Rather, he preferred to be alone, to spend time in the forest, or listening to the birds."

The house had looked a little dilapidated, but nothing like old Clamshell's place. And the thought had crossed Star Shell's mind that perhaps fugitives couldn't expect to stay in neat, warm clan houses while they were on the run.

"What does he do up here?" Star Shell had asked.

Tall Man shrugged. "A little farming . . . but not enough. He starts a field every year, but generally he forgets to weed it or to care for it in any way. He's never been able to see things through. Mostly, he listens to the Spirits and talks to the Mysterious One. He speaks to the animals, calls the clouds, and watches the stars. He was initiated into the Star Society at a very young age, but lost interest. To get back to your question, he's a hermit. His family brings food to him to augment what he collects. He does some Healing, and sometimes he'll Dream things for people. Tell them where to find lost objects."

She hadn't been prepared for that first moment when her gaze locked with Greets the Sun's. At the door of his shabby house, she'd looked into those soft brown eyes and seen his soul reflected there—warmth and tenderness, along with deep sympathy and concern. Then he had smiled at her, joy creating a radiance on the smooth planes of his face.

"Welcome to my house," he said simply. "The birds have been Singing your arrival."

Even Silver Water had taken to him, smiling shyly when he reached down to pat her head and smooth her tangled black hair.

From that moment, the weather had warmed, the snow had begun to melt, and a subtle peace had taken root in Star Shell's heart.

Now, as she climbed up on the small earthen mound atop the hill, she raised her arms, Singing the traditional greeting to the sun as it rose on the halfway journey to the north. Beside her, Tall Man had knelt and was praying for health, happiness, and rains. Across from her, Greets the Sun held his arms wide, Singing in the tongue of the High Heads, rapture shining from his handsome face.

In that instant, Star Shell's heart skipped. The young hermit's radiance seemed to mirror that of the sun as the first rays touched his face, turning the skin golden and honeyed. Had she ever seen such a beautiful man?

I pray to you, Sun, she pleaded, *let me find a way to be rid of this terrible Mask. Grant me peace. Let me find beauty. Let me rest.* She couldn't allow herself to pray for this beautiful young man who had begun to absorb her.

As one, they lifted slivers of sacred chert, making incisions in the skin of their shoulders. Star Shell barely felt the bite of the sharp stone. Her blood welled in a red bead before trickling down her soft skin, dark in the first light of morning.

She bent down, pulling back Silver Water's shirt to expose the pale skin of her shoulder. "Did you say the prayers you wanted, baby?"

"Yes, Mama. I prayed for what I wanted most." Silver Water's eyes seemed to expand in her small face, and for a moment, Star Shell was locked in their hypnotic gaze.

"Mama," Silver Water broke the spell. "Can I make the cuts? I want to make my offering by myself."

Star Shell swallowed hard, then nodded. "Yes, of course. You won't cut too deep? You won't be afraid?"

"No, Mama. The most sacred offering comes from us, from our own acts." Silver Water took the sharp chert, frowning as the colored stone dimpled her shoulder. Without hesitation, she sliced herself on one shoulder, then on the other.

"That's good, sweetheart," Star Shell praised. Then she turned to look at the sun again, now a huge crimson sphere just above the misty horizon.

Greets the Sun was still Singing, his arms outstretched.

Silver Water pulled on Star Shell's skirt so she'd lean down. "You like Greets the Sun, don't you, Mama?"

Star Shell sneaked a glance at the young man, so absorbed by his prayers. "I don't even know him. We met him only a couple of days ago. Your father . . ." She sighed, whispering, "I don't have time to like anybody."

Silver Water watched her. "Mama, maybe we could stay here. Maybe Power will give you Greets the Sun. He's nice. I like him, Mama."

"Yes, baby, he is nice." *Too bad your father couldn't have been like him.* And as she thought it, she caught herself studying Greets the Sun again. How tall and straight he stood. His shoulders were broad, powerful, and despite his hermetical life, he seemed fresh and clean, his long black hair gleaming in the morning light.

What was it about him? Where did that magnetic attraction come from?

"I think it will be a good spring," Greets the Sun said, and he threw his head back, inhaling the fresh morning air, his smooth chest swelling. He had such a look of satisfaction. "Indeed, a good day to be alive."

"Yes, it is," Tall Man agreed, dabbing at the blood that seeped from the cuts on his shoulders. He shrugged back into his travel-worn coat and picked up the sack that contained the Mask.

Greets the Sun pulled his shirt back on and stepped around Tall Man. He might have been speaking only to Star Shell. "For this day's feast, I have something special: a turkey! Last night, when you weren't looking, I slipped away and cleaned out my fire pit. I wrapped the turkey first in clay and then in fabric and buried it in the hot coals. It should be about ready."

"That sounds wonderful."

As they walked, she was painfully aware of his scent: like the sweet, tangy musk of a fall buck. Tall Man and Silver Water had taken the lead on the treacherous trail that wound down through the trees.

"I'm glad you came here," Greets the Sun told her. "You've brought happiness into my little valley."

"I thought you liked to be alone."

"I do." He seemed puzzled for a moment. "You're not like other people. Power has touched you . . . and something else. I feel terrible grief coming from you."

"My husband is dead. Only two moons ago."

He studied her, those brown eyes probing. "My soul aches with yours. Did you love him a great deal?"

"Once . . . once I did. He had a kind of Power. Or maybe it was just . . ." *The Mask.* A shudder climbed her spine on icy ants' feet. "No, now that I think about it, maybe I didn't love him."

"I'm sorry. It's a terrible thing never to have loved."

She gave him a glance from the corner of her eye as she sidestepped down a steep place. "What about you, Greets the Sun? Have you ever loved?"

"All the time. Every day I love." He gave her a shy smile.

"I think I love you. I think I have loved you from the first moment I looked into your eyes."

"But you know so little about me."

"I know that you're beautiful, that you've been hurt, and that you're weary and sad. I don't think that people feel sad unless they have a beauty of the soul."

"Let me see if I understand. You think people who suffer are beautiful?"

"They are, you know. They understand more of the Mysterious One."

"They understand more . . ." She slipped then, stumbling. On lightning feet, he was close to her, catching her, steadying her in warm, protective arms. His strong brown hands were sure, the fingers gentle where they touched her. His eyes had widened, their lashes long and black, glistening in the morning. She could trace every detail of his perfect face, see the slight widening of his nostrils as he caught her scent.

In that instant, his face so close to hers, she felt an electric excitement run through her like fingers of lightning.

With reluctance, she stepped back, smiled her thanks, and concentrated on her feet, making sure that he wouldn't have another opportunity to stir her soul so.

Why, Star Shell? Why is this happening? He's just a handsome young man. What's wrong with you anyway, that you're as ready for him as a camp dog in heat?

She forced her heartbeat to slow, aware that he, too, had been affected by the brief encounter. With bent head, and putting one step after another, she made her way down the trail.

When she glanced up, she could see that the buds were full, ready to burst into new leaves. Sprigs of grass and the first green tendrils of the flowers had awakened on the forest floor. Even the moss on the downed tree trunks gleamed with the promise of spring, of new life.

Is that what I want? New life? New love? She turned to look back furtively, watching him as he stepped lithely down the trail. He walked with the balanced control of a hunting cougar. No move wasted, a man in harmony with himself and his world.

She couldn't allow herself that surrender. It was too soon.

Twenty-one

Days of warm rain, coupled with the melt, had worked upon the land; the Ilini River overflowed its banks in full flood. Water had backed up into the flats, leaving murky openings among the trees. Pearl watched fearfully as the Khota war canoes approached homecoming.

They had turned off on one of the bends of the Father Water, passed under a headland, and followed the Ilini north, the river running close to the western bluffs. The channel ran wide and slow as a result of the flood.

"This is good," Grizzly Tooth said, pointing to the flooded areas. "The backwaters are refilled with fish. The fields are being renewed with the silt."

"Harvest will be good this year," Round Scar agreed. "Unless, of course, late rains flood out the maygrass and little barley. That's happened too often lately."

Flood it all out! Let them starve! Pearl sat on her sack of seed corn, still bound and as hopeless as she'd ever been.

Perhaps her tormenting of the Khota had done more harm than good. Not that she was the slightest bit sorry for their various sufferings, but Grizzly Tooth—though never able to catch her in the act—had grown ever more vigilant. Only the Khota warriors' ignorance of plants and her own furtiveness had saved her.

The hills didn't seem as intensely forested as they had been farther south; most of the trees appeared to be oak or hickory, and brushy hazel grew around the margins of open meadows. Here and there, mottled scars from fires could be seen. Clearing brush?

Then she noticed the rickety-looking tower on one of the points. A lookout? For whom?

Grizzly Tooth rose to his feet, and balancing against the

rhythm of the paddlers, jabbed his pointed oar at the sky five times.

Shading her eyes against the sunset-lit sky, Pearl could see the silhouette of a sentry clambering down from the perch.

"They know we're coming," Grizzly Tooth said with satisfaction as he regained his seat.

"Look!" Dog Trot pointed. "That's where Wolf of the Dead ambushed the Fat Blankets!"

"And there's where the Two Throws Clan started their new field!" Round Scar cried. Even as he spoke, two slim canoes emerged from the trees, one heaving to, the other racing off upriver.

Grizzly Tooth called, "The word is being taken to the clans! My warriors, we're home! We're heroes! We've done it! Accomplished what no Khota has done before!"

Wild cries and whoops split the air. They put their backs into it, their muscles rippling; the canoes seemed to leap ahead with a new grace as they skimmed the brown water.

Think, Pearl. Look, learn! During the confusion of the homecoming, an opportunity to escape might present itself. People would be milling around, excited, greeting old friends. She turned her attention to the irregular western bluffs. She could see the silhouette of the bun-shaped earthen mounds on the tops of the ridges. From there, the vantage would overlook the tree-choked tributaries. Smoke coiled up from some of those mound complexes, leaving blue traceries against the evening sky.

Darkness was falling. She needed to have at least a rudimentary understanding of the terrain. Where could she run to? The land was more open here, the forest purposely kept at bay.

The lone canoe was within hailing distance now. Cries of greeting carried across the water.

"What news?" Grizzly Tooth called.

"Not much, War Leader! A couple of raids, a few Traders robbed. Your families and clans are well. With the warming, women have been harvesting groundnut to add to the supplies. How was your trip?"

"Wonderful! We have seen things that just . . . well, you wouldn't believe!" Grizzly Tooth cried before he whooped again.

With a flourish that belied almost four moons of hard labor

spent in paddling up the river, the Khota heeled the canoes into a swollen tributary, the channel barely discernible between the waterlogged trees. More canoes came into view, sliding out from among the trees, racing down the channel: people hurrying to welcome the travelers.

Pearl got her first look at the everyday Khota and found them particularly well dressed with gleaming ornaments of mica, galena, copper, and shell. They wore their hair pinned in tight buns at the tops of their heads. For the most part, clothing consisted of long shirts that fell to mid-thigh and were belted at the waist. Long moccasins, the leather dyed a rich russet, rose to above the knee. The preferred color for apparel appeared to be a bright yellow, although reds, blues, and browns could be seen. Their fabric motifs, woven or painted, always portrayed a stylized purple wolf, no doubt dyed from pokeweed berries.

"Who is that woman?" a man called. Pearl noted his white teeth as he grinned.

"We have brought a wife for Wolf of the Dead!" Grizzly Tooth called back. "A marriage to bind us to the Anhinga people. We have made an agreement with them. We have a Trading partner!"

More whoops rose in happiness. They did indeed sound like wolves.

The narrow watercourse ended in a waterlogged landing at a fork of the creek. Here the ground sloped up toward the valley headland to the northwest. The Khota settlement had been placed at the mouth of an eastward-flowing creek that had cut through the uplands. Mounds marked the northern and southern sides of the Khota valley. Laughing and shouting with excitement, people streamed down the paths that led from the village complex on the uplands.

As Pearl expected, the Khota warriors' arrival turned into a rush of confusion. They had reached the clan grounds before full dark. From the moment the canoe grounded, people crowded about, everyone eager to gawk and chatter and grab at *her*. Talk centered on Wolf of the Dead's new wife. Where did she come from? How much had they paid? What sort of savage was she? Could she talk like a human being?

Strong hands lifted her from the canoe. Round Scar, Grizzly Tooth, and Dog Trot formed a guard around her, giving her some slight protection from the surging crowd that threatened to press too close.

Pearl crouched, her teeth gritted, wanting to snarl like the wild animal they thought she was. *I am Anhinga!* The thought fought through her panic, causing her to stand straight, head back, proud. "Grizzly Tooth, cut these thongs from my arms and legs. I will not be treated like a beast."

The Khota had gone silent, staring with wide brown eyes. Hands that reached for her stopped, frozen in space. The odor of smoke-scented, sweaty human bodies bore down on her.

"She talks!" someone whispered.

Then the crush started again, and Pearl was touched, prodded, and explored by their stinking fingers. Her head high, she endured the melee of extended arms, shoving bodies, and insolent stares.

She felt, rather than saw, the bonds being cut between her ankles. At least she could walk—and if the opportunity arose, run.

The mass started to move uphill. The warriors laughed, only halfheartedly struggling to protect her from the mob, mainly enjoying the homecoming excitement.

In the confusion, Pearl glimpsed Khota houses, most of them covered with weather-grayed thatch and connected by dirt paths. Square in construction, the houses stretched roughly four paces across. The roofs were constructed with rafters and a center pole. Drying racks and sunshades stood before storage pits filled with pottery.

A hand reached out to grope her breast, and Pearl brought her elbow down with force enough to elicit a yelp. Laughter greeted the action—an invitation to attempt more intimate baiting of this strange woman.

"Here!" Grizzly Tooth roared. "Back away! Is this any way to treat a stranger among us?"

"Better than the way we treat most strangers!" a pug-nosed young man responded, bringing more laughter. "By the way, how many children did you and your warriors plant in her?"

A bowlegged man shouted, "Yes, tell us! Is Wolf of the Dead getting a field with the crop already sprouted?"

"No one has touched her!" Grizzly Tooth yelled, then grinned. "But that doesn't mean we haven't thought about it!"

Peals of laughter broke from the crowd.

In Anhinga, Pearl hissed, "You are all flies—maggots in putrid meat. May you choke on the excrement of your own filthy habits."

"What did she say?"

"Wasn't nice!"

"Wolf of the Dead will take that foreign insolence out of her!"

But by then, the way had become steeper as they climbed the bluff, taking the water-worn trail up to the tall house that stood there at the edge of the cracked, gray-sandstone rim. Despite the restricted trail and the irregular slope, people scrambled in a mad procession. The nightmare continued as Pearl was jostled, insulted, and abused. *I'll never forgive them for this humiliation. Never. I swear it!*

And then they swarmed out onto the sandstone flats before the house that guarded the rim with such authority. The crowd went suddenly quiet, smiles shooting back and forth, heads craning to see.

Pearl managed to orient herself. To the west, the sun had dropped below the silhouette-blackened tree line to cast an orange glow on the high clouds. Below them, the valley of the Ilini stretched north-south. In the faint haze of evening, the flooded brown river snaked close to the western terraces, which inclined to talus slopes along the broken rim. Eastward, beyond the river, irregular plots of fields faded into a patchwork of timber and brush rising to the far uplands— flat-topped, and no doubt sandstone-capped like the one on which she now stood.

"My leader!" Grizzly Tooth called out in the gathering dusk. "Your war leader and brother, Grizzly Tooth, has returned from the journey on which you sent him! I come to report triumph. No warrior is missing, wounded, or dead. We have returned to you with conch shell, barracuda teeth, yaupon, tobacco, fine fabrics, and the wealth of the southern lands. We have created an alliance with the Anhinga peoples. In token of their respect for the great Wolf of the Dead of the Khota people, they have sent a gift, a wife!"

The mob thundered approbation.

Two young men stepped out of the doorway, each bearing a

burning cane torch that cast a yellow light over the expectant people.

Pearl shivered, and her heart began to pound. The tension among the watching people boded evil. Where was he?

She licked her lips, glancing around uneasily. All eyes remained on the torch-lit doorway. *Come on, let's get this over with!*

The hanging, a sunset-orange cloth, trembled, then parted as a long, lean wolf's head stared out, peering this way and that. The animal looked slightly misshapen, and much too large for—

He stepped out then. Not a wolf, but half-man, half-wolf. The long muzzle had grown out of a man's face. The hide covered the skull; the ears pricked slightly back in the manner of lupine threat. Long white teeth gleamed in the firelight.

"My ffffriend," Wolf of the Dead spoke awkwardly, his pronunciation slurred. "Powerrr comes wiff you."

Grizzly Tooth dropped to his knees, inclining his head. "I, and your warriors, have done that which you asked. We have Trading partners. The river Trade is ours now. No one can interfere. The Traders cannot deprive us of our rightful wealth."

"Gooood, my ffffriend."

Pearl could do nothing but stare at the horrible creature illuminated by the firelight. Its posture was that of a man, the hide that of an animal, clear down to the bushy tail that hung between his very human legs. Then the monster turned gleaming eyes on her, and Pearl's soul wailed.

"This woman," Grizzly Tooth explained, "is a daughter of the Anhinga leader's family. The Anhinga present this girl, Pearl, to you as a wife. By joining with her, you join with the Anhinga."

The wolf leaned its head back, and from its throat broke the most eerie of howls. Pearl watched with glazed eyes, seeing the inside of the wolf's mouth, seeing the tongue move. No human mouth lay behind a cunning mask. This *creature* was real!

"Thennn we suuud join teeese Anhingaaa." The nightmare creature stepped up to Pearl, its glittering eyes, in deep sockets, inspecting her. Two human hands extended from the wolf skin. She flinched as they explored her breasts, then moved up to caress her face.

"Verrry beeeutifulll," the abomination hissed in its distorted voice. Pearl felt the cords binding her wrists being cut.

Run! the panicked voice of her soul cried—the command stumbling against paralyzed muscles. Before she could regain control of herself, hard hands had grabbed her from behind. She tried to thrash, to strike out, but they had her, ripping her shirt off over her shoulders, untying her belt. As she screamed, cloth tore and the wolf laughed, the slurring sound hideous.

Too many hands held her, turning her, shredding away the last of her clothing. She tried to twist, aware of the grunting warriors who fought her down. She managed to land on her knees, hunching up in a protective posture. Fear—worse than anything she'd ever experienced—burst brightly through her trembling body.

Someone had grabbed a handful of her long hair and was pulling her forward, stretching her out. The horror, more than the pain, defeated her.

She could turn her head and see past the warriors who restrained her. People watched with an awed expectation mirrored in their rapt eyes. Expectation of what?

She started when soft wolf fur slid across her naked back. Then she became aware of the warmth of his body, of his hoarse breathing. Wolf of the Dead was crouching over her, bending down.

She screamed as his hips conformed to her buttocks. She could feel his penis hardening between her legs. Gasping and trembling, she fought. Too many hands held her down. His arms curled around her ribs; his fingers cupped her breasts.

"Yesss," that inhuman voice hissed. "Now you becommme Wolfff of theee Dead's wiiffe."

She could only scream—and scream—and scream again.

Wave Dancer drifted forward, and not for the first time, Otter prayed that the fox head on his canoe would see, would guide them past any danger.

The night had begun as clear; sunset had reflected from a few high clouds fading from an indigo sky. Now half of the night sky had been blotted black by high clouds. Moonrise wouldn't come for another couple of hands' movement. As a result, Otter navigated by instinct, by the surge of the current, by the darker mass of trees just off to his right.

"Cry in the breeze, cry in the light, cry with the wind, cry for the fight. Cry with the leaves, cry for the grass, cry without sight. Cry for the innocence, cry for the strength of the woman tonight." Green Spider's singsong voice had a sad note.

"Shut up, fool," Black Skull growled, speaking for the first time since nightfall. "You'll get us all killed."

Green Spider whistled and chirped, closely imitating the night song of a robin.

"If you whistle a little louder, Green Spider, Wolf of the Dead will invite you to his house," Otter whispered. "He really likes Contraries."

Green Spider went absolutely silent, and Black Skull chuckled under his breath.

Water dripped musically from the lifted paddles. Periodically a muted thump sounded as some bit of flotsam hit the hull, or a paddle bumped it.

Otter struggled to see in the darkness. He'd cocked his head in a vain effort to hear better. Water lapping against the trees, the subtle night sounds of fish, and sometimes a rustling of the breeze, were the only disturbances in the smothering silence.

"I don't like this," Black Skull whispered.

"You'd have liked passing their territory by day even less."

"There's something dishonorable in sneaking around like this. A real warrior travels fearlessly."

Otter squinted into the darkness. Uncle's ghost was here, somewhere. The copper falcon lay cool against the skin of Otter's chest. "Are you trying to say you're a little scared out here in the darkness, Black Skull?" Otter felt the canoe shiver as the big warrior stiffened, and added, "Which means you're doing better than I am. I'm terrified."

"I'm just nervous. You can't see well enough to spot one of those twirling trees floating down on you," Black Skull retorted.

"And if we do get in trouble and the Khota catch us, they'll know we were trying to slip past them. They have a very unreasonable response to Traders who sneak past them."

"Uncle knows," Green Spider said softly. A wretched chill ran down Otter's spine as the Contrary continued. "He watches, seeing from the shadows, looking into the souls of men. There in the dark places, the weaknesses are many. She won't succeed, but this is a time for action. The time is near.''

Otter needed three tries before he could ask, ''What are you saying, Green Spider? Uncle's ghost is here? Watching us?''

''You're blinded because the light is too strong,'' Green Spider said. ''Squint a little and you'll be able to see better.''

Black Skull snorted irritably. ''He's raving, Trader. That's all. Let's just pass these vermin. We'll all feel better.''

Otter paddled forward slowly. Yes, he even tried squinting, and the world only got darker—if that was possible.

Uncle? Are you out there? I have your copper falcon. I know the truth. One day, I promise, I'll pay them back.

''A light,'' Black Skull's voice interrupted. ''Up there, to the left, on the hill.''

Otter could barely see the warrior's gesture as he lifted his oar and pointed. The dancing light appeared little more than a flicker.

''I know where we are now. That's their lower lookout tower. If we were attempting to pass in the daytime, by now they'd have a runner on the way to the clan grounds to alert the warriors. We'd be met by war canoes and directed up to the Khota clan house for a thorough robbing.''

''I'd like to do a little robbing of my own,'' Black Skull declared.

''Thief! Thief!'' Green Spider erupted. ''Get ready to run, thief! Steal their hearts and guts. As the Khota chase, so do they lose.''

''Shut up!'' Black Skull twisted around, rocking the canoe. ''I've got half a mind to throw you out, fool. If you want to shout your silly head off—''

''It's all right,'' Otter soothed, trying to quiet both of them. ''The river runs fairly straight through here. Let's just concentrate on making it past their holdings. I want to be in Ilini territory by morning.'' *Please, Many Colored Crow!*

The stars had moved less than half a hand when Black Skull's low warning came. ''Look. Another fire up there to the west.''

Otter saw it through the screen of bud-rich treetops. ''That's the main mound complex,'' he said. ''If you look just south of there, you should see a smaller fire on the southern rim of the

Khota valley. There will be more. They have farmsteads and lineage mounds along the bluffs and terraces for the next twenty or thirty dart casts along here. Now is the time to be quiet and to pray that no one is out fooling around in the night.''

"Except fools like us," Green Spider amended. "People will be glad we were out."

"Idiot!" Black Skull cursed.

At that moment, distant shouts broke out. Even as Otter watched, the flames in the watch fires danced up, following one after another along the bluffs.

The trip-hammer of his heart competed with the icy fear that gripped his guts. "I don't know how, but they must have spotted us!"

Every nerve in Pearl's body tingled. She crouched in the corner of Wolf of the Dead's house, her naked back pressed against the prickly thatch of the walls; sweat trickled down her belly and sides. Strands of her long black hair stuck to her breasts, partially shielding them from his hot gaze.

In the middle of the floor, coals glowed in a clay-lined hearth. The hearth's reddish gleam transformed Wolf of the Dead into an unearthly abomination. He had ceased talking. Now a low growl issued from his muzzle as he stalked stiffly around the room on all fours. His long nose sniffed at his sleeping mat, then nudged the atlatls, darts, axes, and other implements that lay in neat order atop the bench along the northern wall. Copper, conch shell, sheets of mica, large nodules of galena, and vitreous obsidian lined the other benches and filled the zone-incised jars that sat beneath them. Bolts of fine fabric, dyed in every color imaginable, hung from the rafters. Net bags of sacred chert, enough to ceremonially bleed the entire world, swung from pegs in the walls. As he moved from object to object, his gaze never left her.

Terror had twisted its fingers in Pearl's guts. An eerie yellow sheen plated his eyes; the way he acted reminded her of the red wolves that sometimes prowled at the edges of Anhinga fires.

He'd pulled back the door flap to allow the cold night wind

to bathe the place. A way to escape? Through the opening, she could see the Khota people, no more than a dart's cast away, cavorting before the huge bonfire in the center of the mound complex. Laughter and shouts echoed across the bluff. Several warriors had broken into a dance and were leaping and twisting like evil Forest Spirits on a raid for human souls. A single shout and they'd be on her.

Would the celebration continue all night? People had left them alone more than a full hand of time ago, to continue their "mating" rituals, they'd said, but she suspected they'd witnessed Wolf of the Dead's perversities so many times before that they really preferred hearing Grizzly Tooth's stories of the southern clans.

Think, Pearl. Think! You can get out of this! She wet dry lips and said, "Wolf of the Dead." Her voice trembled. She fought to steady it. "What more do you want of me? You've already taken me in front of the entire village. Didn't their cheers and praise satisfy you? We are alone now. If I am to be your wife, you must speak to me like a man!"

And he was a man, wasn't he? Didn't she see the way the wolf hide hung like a blanket instead of a true hide? But the head . . . how could that be?

Wolf of the Dead tilted his head to gaze at her through one glinting eye. He lifted his right hand, extended it and lightly placed it on the floor; then he did the same with the left and moved toward her with the stealth of a starving beast. When he halted beside an elaborately decorated pot, Pearl swallowed convulsively. He'd stopped breathing . . . at least his chest no longer rose and fell. Slowly, his huge gray head lowered while the muscles of his arms and legs tensed, bulging. She'd seen real wolves do the same thing just before they leaped on a rabbit and tore it to pieces.

Pearl extended her arms along the walls, bracing herself for his attack. Her movements seemed to thrill him. A strange sound rumbled in his throat—half human laugh and half wolfish snarl.

He sprang so fast that it stunned her. She dove aside, but his massive arms tightened around her waist as he dragged her to the floor. "No! Please!" She screamed and kicked, clawing at his flesh until the blood ran hotly over her hands.

He let out a ghastly howl, exposing wolfish canines. Pearl

screamed hoarsely as he lunged for her throat. She rolled, trying to get away—and her groping fingers brushed polished wood beneath the bench on the western wall. Twisting, she managed to plant a foot in the middle of his chest. Terror-mad, she braced herself and thrust him backward. As she scrambled away, she pulled the war club from beneath the bench. The wolf's head had canted slightly to the side. He reached up with both hands, resettling his head. Pearl rose on her knees, and she could see his eyes filling the dark holes in the wolf's head. She watched those eyes widen as she set herself, tightened her grip, brought the club down—with no mercy whatsoever.

The cracking blow took him in the left temple. He swayed for a moment before pitching face-first to the floor in a heap. She lifted the club again, surprised to see that she'd split the hard ash. He didn't move.

Pearl rose to her feet and backed away.

Use your head now or you're dead! She threw the broken war club down next to his shoulder and sobbed soundlessly. He lay with one arm sprawled out, the other under his body.

They would kill her now. Of that, Pearl was completely certain. Nor would it be a quick and painless death. She'd heard enough of Grizzly Tooth's hideous stories on the way upriver to know that.

She leaned against the wall and fought to control herself. The tears had stopped, but the spasmodic shudders in her chest continued, as though her heart were bursting its seams with each rhythmic beat.

She'd killed him. Wolf of the Dead obviously hadn't expected her to react so violently. A proper captive, after all, knew her place, knew she had no choice but to obey her new husband's wishes.

But I am Pearl of the Anhinga! In my veins runs the blood of the snakebird.

She reached down, seized the wolfhide and tore it from his body. The long muzzle resisted, then fell free as his head rolled to the side. Pearl frowned in the dim glow of the coals. His face looked as human as any she'd ever seen—but the places where the front teeth should have been were empty. She turned the wolf's head, looking into the mouth, and nodded before casting the thing onto the coals.

The mask had been cleverly constructed. The wolf's head was real. The back of the hard palate of the skull had fit neatly into the gap where Wolf of the Dead's front teeth had been knocked out, mating wolf skull to human head. No wonder he'd talked so strangely and slurred his words.

The acrid odor of burning wolf hair filled the room as the hide smoldered, then burst into flames.

She had to hurry. Rubbing nervous hands on her thighs as if to clean them, she made her decision. She slipped on a beautiful yellow shirt with a red-and-black wolf design woven into the front. The long war moccasins with thick soles were too big, but she tied them on her feet anyway.

She filled a leather bag with fire sticks, sacred chert, obsidian, and copper needles, slipped its lacings over a thick leather belt that she tied to her waist. Wolf of the Dead's atlatl didn't balance quite right for her, but she took it nevertheless. Finally, she noted the sack of Anhinga seed corn that she'd sat on all the way up the Father Water. In no way would the Khota get any profit from her—or from her clan. She tied the atlatl to her belt and hoisted the sack of seeds over her shoulder. If nothing else, she'd throw the corn into the river rather than let the Khota have it.

On impulse, she spun around and kicked the fire, shooting coals all over the inside of the room. Before she even ducked through the door flap, flames had begun licking their way up the thatch walls.

Over by the ceremonial mound, the Khota danced and shouted, their laughter roiling the night air like a current in the river. Shadows wavered as bodies interposed themselves between Wolf of the Dead's doorway and the bonfire. The closest of the spectators had their backs to her for the moment. That wouldn't last. The barbaric Anhinga woman, and what Wolf of the Dead was doing to her inside his house, would be on many people's minds.

Keep your wits, Pearl. She nerved herself to walk arrogantly toward the trail that led down the talus to the flats and the canoe landing. *If you panic now, you're dead.*

The dark shadows in the gap through the caprock gave her the first stirrings of hope. She was barely a third of the way down the trail when the flames burst through the walls of Wolf of the Dead's house and roared up into the sky.

Cries rose on the night, followed by inky silhouettes running along the rim. Pearl hurried, afraid to break into a run, afraid to maintain her slow pace.

"What is it?" a Khota voice called from the darkness ahead of her.

"Fire!" Pearl prayed her accent would suffice. "Hurry!"

The man charged past her, scrambling up the slope.

Pearl's knees almost buckled with relief. She slipped and slid the rest of the way to the bottom. If only she'd had a better chance to study the country with an eye for escape.

A voice shouted from the bluff, "The woman has escaped! Round Scar! Dog Trot! Quickly! She'll try to take a canoe! Run, you fools!"

Pearl's heart sank. She knew that commanding voice: Grizzly Tooth's.

She could hear them coming, pounding down the hill, charging recklessly through the night: warriors intent on cutting her off. Pearl veered from the trail and dashed blindly along the faintly visible dirt tracks that linked farmsteads on the lower terrace.

"Run downhill," she gasped to herself. "Find the river!"

Maybe, just maybe, there would be a canoe there, even a fishing or pearl-diving boat. A log, anything that would support her weight.

She gasped as she ran. A dark image materialized out of the night. Instinctively, she dropped a shoulder, rammed the person flat . . . recovered after several staggering steps and sprinted onward. An angry woman yelped behind her, more indignant than vengeful.

Throw the corn away! It's not worth your life! But she clung doggedly to the thick sack, driving herself forward. She tripped and fell knocking the wind from her lungs on the cold ground. For precious seconds, she gasped life back into her fevered body, then clawed her way to her feet and raced on through the blackness.

"She's running!" came the faint shout from behind her. "Down! Toward the river!"

Branches lashed at her when she reached the belt of trees

along the floodplain. Within ten tens of paces, her feet splashed in water. Now which way?

North. They'd think she'd head south, toward home, no matter how far away. Pearl waded into the shallow water, winding her way upriver through the blackness, feeling with one hand and her feet. Curse these Khota, couldn't they have left a canoe tied off for her?

Splashes sounded behind her, but not close enough to panic her. She was still ahead, and like the swamps back home, this water would leave no trail. By the Power of the great Anhinga, she might just make it!

At that moment, she stepped into nothingness and sank into cold, black water.

She paddled up, coughing, spitting muddy water. Blessed air filled her lungs before the current twisted her around again. She flailed wildly at the bitter water with one hand, the other holding firmly to her sack of corn.

"Filthy Khota leeches," she hissed. "May pus-eating worms infest your testicles!"

She coughed again. The heavy moccasins, so good for the trail, dragged at her feet in the water. How long could she last before the cold robbed her of the ability to swim?

The current coiled around her, wrenching her legs, sucking her under again. Pearl fought her way back to the surface, trying to stroke with her one hand.

Turn loose the corn! But she couldn't. That seed corn was all that was left of her world. Assuming she could escape, she'd need it. If nothing else, she could eat it, but more likely she could Trade it to these northern people. Her cousins had taught her the value of exotics—and corn would be very exotic. Besides, this was the best seed corn the Anhinga had, each kernel carefully selected for size, or for the health of the plant from which it came.

The water sucked her under again. She thrashed her way to the surface, battling the sack. Then again, having a sack of corn didn't do a drowned corpse much good, did it?

Frantic, she brought the sack down from her shoulder and prepared to drop it, knowing she was going to die in the darkness anyway.

But a hand firmly clasped her arm and dragged her up through the layers of water, coughing and wheezing.

Somehow, some way, they'd found her. She went limp, finally defeated. "Go ahead," she rasped. "Khota *filth*! Kill me now."

"Not a chance," a deep voice said from the darkness, and powerful arms hoisted her up into a canoe.

Twenty-two

Grizzly Tooth had been attending to his duty, uttering the prayers for a safe homecoming and offering food, copper, and mica to the ancestral ghosts at the great burial mound, when he caught the faint odor of burning hair on the night breeze. Some premonition had caused him to turn, taking several steps back toward Wolf of the Dead's house. So it was he who first saw the flames burst through the thatch, then ignite like a huge torch.

He broke into a run before he believed what he was witnessing. The clan leader's house on fire? How?

Pearl!

Grizzly Tooth had watched the girl's face as Wolf of the Dead mated with her. The Khota leader had done it in the manner of a dominant wolf, from behind, with his pack watching that it might understand his supremacy.

Grizzly Tooth had come to understand Pearl, even to respect her. The horrible look of shock and fear as they stripped her and held her had given way to humiliation and disgust as Wolf of the Dead mounted her. A wild look had come to her, as if she were taken by a sudden insanity.

I shouldn't have let her out of my sight.

Even as he ran up to the blazing house, he knew that the structure was lost. Others arrived, gaping at the crackling roar.

"Have you seen Wolf of the Dead?" Grizzly Tooth demanded. Then, before anyone could answer, he dove through the doorway and into the blaze.

Smoke and whirling sparks clouded his vision. He put up his arms to ward away the heat, then saw his leader on the floor. Coughing in the acrid air, he bent down, his watering eyes narrowed to slits. By feel, he pulled Wolf of the Dead from the raging inferno and out into the night just as the burning roof collapsed.

Despite seared lungs, he bellowed, ''The woman has escaped! Round Scar! Dog Trot! Quickly! She'll try to take a canoe! Run, you fools!''

Then he bent to help Wolf of the Dead, gently turning him over to place his ear on his blood-brother's chest. There, faintly, the heart still beat. A mottled bruise and hard lump were rising on the left side of the Khota leader's head.

''Is he alive?'' One Arm asked, bending down out of the sea of people who had gathered.

''He lives ... but this woman, she must not. Find her! Quickly! I want her before the night is over!''

Live, my friend. You can't die on me now. If you do, it will be my fault. All my fault. Grizzly Tooth blinked to clear his vision. It took a moment to recognize the stench of his own burned hair. The pain, forgotten in the emergency, now grew excruciating where his skin was blistered and peeling. His eyes ached like hot stones.

He looked up at the burning building, anger raging brightly within. *Pearl, I can understand your horror, but you will pay for this. And when I'm done, you and your Anhinga will wish you'd never been born!*

He knotted a fist, wincing at the burns on his hand. *Before the ghosts of my ancestors, I swear it!*

Perhaps the winter of my soul is over. That thought reassured Star Shell as she walked along the irregular path, aware of fresh deer tracks on the dark soil.

She let her fingers touch the twigs and bushes, all full-budded, ready to burst into leaf. Bright sunlight washed down out of a blue sky to accent the new green of grass and the shoots of flowers rising to the burgeoning season. Around her, the high, bowl-shaped valley curved to embrace her with its warmth. Just up ahead, the slope rose to the observatory, where they had worshiped on the equinox. Scrappy patches of outcropping rock dotted the hillside where the trees didn't obscure them. Birdsong carried on the clear spring air. The land was coming alive, ready to greet the fourth moon of the year.

Star Shell climbed over a moss-mottled limestone outcrop and stopped. Water trickled along a rocky bottom, ending in a stone-lined pool dammed by the fallen trunks of trees. She hurried down, bending over to look at her reflection in the mirrored surface. Testing the water with a finger, she found it cool but acceptable, and she slipped off her dress before she waded in. The water's bite invigorated her skin as she settled in the sunlight on the northern side of the pool.

Splashing and dousing her head, she dredged handfuls of sand from the bottom. She scrubbed herself, twisting like a trout in the clear water. For the first time in moons, she felt clean and fresh.

When she finally rose, her skin tingled from the scrubbing as well as from the chill. She bent over to wring out her dripping hair.

"In the stories, this is when the enemy warriors find you and steal you away."

Star Shell stifled a cry and whirled. Greets the Sun stood on the rocks, his head cocked. The sunlight picked a bluish tinge out of his raven-smooth hair. Zigzag patterns were woven into the warp and weft of the light-blue shirt that hung down to mid-thigh. His muscular legs were braced, his hands on his hips.

"You frightened me."

He gave her that magical smile and spread his hands. "I could leave . . . come back after you've dressed."

She looked down at her naked body, startlingly aware that she was a handsome woman, full-figured. The long days on the trail had taken some of her roundness, but her muscles had been toned. She straightened proudly. "What did you want?"

He suddenly turned a shade pale. "I should apologize. I saw you from above." He waved toward the slope. "I thought

I'd come talk to you. Then, well, I walked over the top, and . . ."

She chuckled, seeing his confusion. Wading out of the water, she continued wringing out her hair. "And you didn't know what to do but stand there and gawk."

He tried to shrug again, but failed and lowered his eyes. "You're a beautiful woman. You stir things within me, Star Shell."

She pulled her dress over her head, studying him from the corner of her eye. "You do things to me, too, Greets the Sun."

His look of confusion grew. "I do?"

She walked over to a tilted slab of limestone and seated herself, leaning back so that the heat of the sun could drive the chill from her body. With careful fingers, she fluffed her hair to dry it. "Yes, you do."

Unsteadily, he walked down and sat on the rock beside her. "Most women aren't interested in me."

"You're a very handsome man. I find that hard to believe."

His smile was a fleeting thing, the soft vulnerability in his eyes bringing a flutter to her soul. *This* man would never hurt her. He didn't seem to have a violent bone in his body. *I could trust him.*

Greets the Sun frowned. "Women lose interest in me. I've never known what to say to them. And most of all, I hated the pressure to marry." He picked up an acorn and pitched it away. "I wasn't ready for that, don't you see? The Power wasn't right. I wasn't made for clan politics. There's more than family and gossip and clearing fields and building things."

"What?"

"The Mysterious One." He tilted his head, the light playing on the strong angles of his cheeks. "I suppose I take things too seriously, always looking for what lies beneath. I've been looking for beauty, Star Shell."

"Looking for beauty." She averted her gaze to the pond, settled out to crystal clarity again. "I've seen so much ugliness in the last years. It's hard to believe that beauty exists anymore. Except perhaps here."

"You're beautiful."

She smiled before daring to reach over to clasp his hand in hers. For a long moment, she savored his warm touch, and with her eyes, she traced the patterns the veins made in that soft skin. "I haven't felt that way. Not until today . . . when I caught you staring at me. For that brief moment, I saw myself reflected in your eyes. I could forget the rest, if only for a moment."

"You could forget forever, Star Shell."

She shook her head wearily. "It would be nice to think that. But no, I can't forget. There are men out there, warriors, hunting me. Hunting the Mask."

"You could stay here." He said it so simply.

"And if they came here? Word of my whereabouts will spread eventually."

His muscles tensed slightly as he shifted to gesture at the hilly country. "I know this place, Star Shell. I've tracked the deer and the badger, stalked the cougar and the fox. I can hide you here, and I can protect you and Silver Water."

"You believe that, don't you?"

He reached up, allowing his fingers to trace the line of her jaw. His touch sent a shiver through her. "I believe that. I think you do, too."

The stirrings within had built to a honeyed warmth. "Why is this happening?"

"What?"

She laughed at herself, and at the hesitation in his eyes. "You're a handsome man. I've never met a man like you, strong, but without rage." She shook her head, watching the lines of his throat where the golden skin curved into the light-blue fabric. "I keep fighting within myself when you're around."

His hand tightened on hers. "Why? I don't scare you, do I? I don't mean to. If it's something I'm doing . . ."

She took a deep breath, feeling her pulse rising. "I don't know. I've never wanted a man so much. But I just can't help thinking that maybe you're a trap."

His gaze drifted over the rugged country, a softness in his full lips. "I give you my word, Star Shell, that I'll never trap you. I'll never hurt you. You're too beautiful to be hurt. And besides, I think you've been hurt enough."

He looked so vulnerable, yet so trusting in her presence. In the days since she'd been living in his house, he'd never once tried to impress her. Not once had he openly made a sexual advance. But every time she was near him, desire clouded her thoughts.

Why are you fighting it?

"Yes, I've been hurt. My husband . . . he hurt me a great deal. Maybe he took the love out of me, Greets the Sun. Maybe, in the end, he ruined me the way he ruined everyone else. He burned his fear so deeply into me, I may never trust a man again."

He shifted, probing her with those beautiful eyes. "Am I like your husband?"

"Don't be silly. Of course not."

"Then maybe you can trust some men and not others. Star Shell, you're safe here. No one, nothing, can harm you. If you would be free, be safe, you've got to take the first step. You will have to decide what you want to do with the rest of your life."

His face was so close to hers that she could see the yearning in his soul. His hand brushed her breast, the gesture innocent. She didn't mean to reach up and run her hand over his chest, but he shivered, his muscles tensing.

She could sense the edge, so close now. The pulse rushing in her veins drove her onward. Her breathing had deepened, and the warmth was spreading through her pelvis. His arms had gone around her, and he'd buried his face in her hair, inhaling her scent.

My decision. The thought seemed to echo from so far away. She'd passed the edge now, had fallen into that torrent of want. Her hands peeled away his shirt. She didn't remember untying his breechcloth, but he groaned when she gripped his stiffened penis.

"You're sure?" he whispered.

"Yes." She let loose of him only long enough to slip off her dress and stretch out on the warm rock.

No man had ever treated her with the gentle care that he did. His caress of her breasts and throat only served to deepen her longing for him. She closed her eyes and arched to meet him as he slid inside. He had barely begun to move when the ecstatic rush shot through her pelvis in pulsing delight.

Why now? a remote part of her wondered. *Why is this happening? I am on the run. I can't stay here.*

Any other thoughts eroded away as her body accommodated to his and began to build for yet another burst of fulfillment.

Otter knew they were in trouble. He'd lost the current. Floating through a flooded forest, bumping off trees in pitch blackness, with Khota shouting angrily and engaged in a search, a man had the right to be a little nervous. Therefore, at the sound of splashing—the sort a person wading might make—Otter hissed for silence.

He heard the Khota flounder off into deep water; then came the muttered curse. At first it didn't register. However, as he raised his fire-hardened paddle to brain the hapless Khota, the accent triggered something in his memory.

The little things in life can often have the greatest of effects. Instead of striking, Otter used his paddle to ease *Wave Dancer* forward, alongside the struggling figure in the water. He leaned over and grabbed at the flounderer, latching onto flesh. For a second, the captive struggled, then went limp, saying, "Go ahead, Khota *filth*! Kill me now."

"Not a chance," Otter said in the Trade tongue. Then he lifted her, cantilevering with his hips to keep from capsizing the canoe. "If you're running from the Khota, you're among friends."

He helped her raise a heavy, wet sack, holding it aloft long enough to let the water drain before flopping it into the canoe. "Black Skull, take us out, away from the fires. We've missed the channel."

"I gathered that, Trader. Who have you caught back there?"

"A woman."

"Just what we need," came the sour reply.

"Who are you?" she asked.

He could sense her shivering. "My name is Otter. And yours?"

"What are we doing?" Black Skull was twisting back and

forth as he tried to see in the darkness. "What's going on?"

"Stealing from the thieves!" Green Spider chortled. "Who is the craftier, Killer of Men? The thief, or the thief's thief?"

"Quiet!" Otter hissed. "Are you running from the Khota?"

Her voice was guarded now. "I was to be Wolf of the Dead's wife."

"Pearl? Of the Anhinga?" In her tongue, he reassured her. "May your ancestors bless you, and may your days be filled with happiness."

"Who *are* you?" she hissed.

Otter took a stroke with the paddle to send them angling away from the shouts on shore. "I am Otter, a Trader of the White Shell Clan. Let's see, it's been three years since I Traded with the Anhinga. Last year, I stayed with the Alligator Clan. We'd heard rumors that you'd been promised to Wolf of the Dead. He's a real treasure, isn't he?"

"Why are you out here?" she demanded.

"Would someone tell me what's going on?" Black Skull rocked the canoe as he turned backwards. "Who is this woman?"

"It appears that we just rescued Pearl," Otter surmised. "Now we'd better put some thought and effort into getting as far from here as we can. The ten-times cursed Khota are going to be swarming like kicked bees. And personally, I don't want to get stung!"

"Bees, bees, always licking up the nectar," Green Spider advised. "Go slowly, Trader. The slower, the better. Khota hospitality is well known. Such kind people! You've got all night to lounge around. The lazy Trader makes the most."

"Right." Otter dug deeply with his paddle, driving *Wave Dancer* into the night. "Black Skull, keep a close eye out—" The canoe bumped and jolted on a tree.

"I think I get the idea," Black Skull muttered, crabbing sideways and batting at the branches.

"If we capsize, I don't need to remind you—"

"I said I *understand*."

"What are you doing here?" Pearl demanded again. Her teeth had begun to chatter.

"Trying to sneak past the Khota holdings before morning. Picking you up might make things a little more difficult. Are they hunting you? Is that what the big fires up on the bluff are about?''

''I burned Wolf of the Dead's house down.''

Otter missed a stroke. ''You set his house on fire?''

''Yes.''

The way she said it, he knew there was more to it. ''Then he was somewhat annoyed?''

''I didn't wait around to find out.''

Her shivers had degenerated into violent shaking. ''Are you all right?'' he asked gently. ''Green Spider, hand Pearl my fox coat. Then wrap her in a blanket.''

''I'm fine,'' she insisted, but she shook more than ever.

''You're out of danger now.'' Otter stared out at the night, listening to the distant shouts. Water lapped on the tree trunks.

Foolish words, those. They wouldn't be out of danger until the Khota lands were far behind them—and if Pearl had enraged Wolf of the Dead, maybe not even then.

Star Shell awoke from happy dreams. She smiled, pulling the warm blankets up to her chin. Faint rays of morning sunlight pierced pinholes in the thatch. Greets the Sun had built a snug, if small, house for himself. Star Shell stretched before she snaked her hand under the blanket in search of Greets the Sun. Her questing fingers found only cold bedding.

Well, it was morning. A man had a right to get up and greet the day. And she knew he always offered prayers to the morning.

She closed her eyes, savoring the memories of the night. She had moved her bedding, placing it beside Greets the Sun's. Tall Man had watched her actions with curiously cold eyes. The little man's expression might have been carved from unyielding oak. Why? What could have upset him so? Surely he couldn't be jealous?

Silver Water had just given her a dreamy smile before crawling into her own bedding.

Out of respect, she and Greets the Sun had waited until the others were soundly asleep before slipping into each other's arms. She blinked, stifling a yawn, her flesh and soul still warm with the memory of his ardent body.

She had never guessed that a man could be so gentle, yet so strong. From the moment of their arrival, he'd shown her nothing but consideration. How odd not to have recognized it, but after all the lonely, miserable years, that quality had been leached out of her life like poisons from acorns.

She hugged herself to compensate for the bursting joy in her heart. *I love him! Wonderful, dizzy love!*

What could possibly have caused that horrified look on Tall Man's face?

The birds were singing in the trees behind the house. Reluctantly, Star Shell forced herself to sit up and slip her dress over her head. She wrapped her blanket about her shoulders, picked up a pot half full of water, and ducked outside.

On her return from ablution and necessity, Tall Man surprised her. She'd have sworn he was still mounded in his blankets when she left, but here he sat, his back propped against the wall of the house, smoking his stone effigy pipe in the sunshine.

"Good morning, Tall Man. Did you sleep well?"

"The nice thing about growing old is that you generally grow hard of hearing." The ironic humor didn't extend to those eerie black eyes. They communicated a dark foreboding, an increasing desperation. "Walk with me, Star Shell."

She paused, setting the now-empty water pot on the ground and drawing her blanket tighter around her. "Let me fetch my moccasins."

They walked out on the trail that led eastward along the valley bottom. Signs of spring met them everywhere, from the delicate green fuzz of opening buds overhead to the unusual birdsong carrying in the mild air as the migrant species returned.

"I thought we were pretty quiet," Star Shell began. "We didn't mean to disturb you."

His voice was coldly precise. "I would like to believe that I have become your friend."

"You have."

"Very well. Keep in mind that I am now talking to you as a friend, Star Shell. You think you love him, don't you?"

She nodded, her head down as she watched her feet. Her moccasins pressed broken leaves into the rich soil. "He's the most wonderful man. He's kind, gentle. When he smiles, his soul radiates. He's the first pure man I've ever met.''

'' . . . A *pure* man? Not anymore, it would seem. My fault. All my fault.''

''What does that mean?''

''Nothing, girl. Let me think.'' Tall Man fingered his chin with one hand; the other clutched his pipe so hard that the tendons stood out on his wrist. ''I hadn't thought of that when I brought you here. What woman would find a boy like that . . .'' He shook his head. ''I was *only* seeking a hiding place where Robin's warriors wouldn't come looking.''

''You don't need to apologize! This could be the most wonderful thing that's ever happened to me.''

''Could it?'' Tall Man glanced uneasily at her from the corner of his eye. ''It could be ruination for all of us. You, him . . . me. Look, forget that for the moment. What about the *Mask*, Star Shell?''

''What about it? We'll wait here for two moons, then start north. Robin can't keep his warriors hunting around the holdings for that long. By the time he hears we're headed north, we'll be long out of the country.''

''Two moons? Do you really believe that we have that much time? Greets the Sun has relatives who worry a great deal about him. They do check on him every so often—and they're a very traditional High Head family. How do you suppose they will react to a man of their lineage and clan bedding his . . . a stranger? The talk will go all over the territories.''

''We'll hide. Greets the Sun has already told me that we're safe here. Even if Robin comes, he can protect us.''

Tall Man fixed his concentration on a moldering deer carcass that lay beside the trail. The ribs had gone mottled gray, and strands of ligament hung down where the crows had pecked. Leaves had blown in to mat the insides of the rib cage and pelvis. ''And you believed him?''

Why are you acting this way? You sound as if I'd done something horrible. ''Yes. He . . . he knows the countryside. Knows places where no one would look.''

Tall Man stopped suddenly, his head cocked as he threw his stubby arms wide. ''Has the Mask blinded you this badly, Star Shell? Can't you see what it's up to?''

"The Mask?" She shook her head in confusion. "What does this have to do with the Mask? I don't understand your words."

Tall Man turned his pipe in his short fingers. "When you see Greets the Sun, you see a kind and handsome hero who will protect you from both the evil that you carry and the vengeful warriors who follow you. You see a vigorous young man who beams when he looks into your eyes.

"I, on the other hand, see a strapping boy who has avoided every responsibility that has ever come his way. When his clan negotiated a marriage, he ran off. When the time to plant rolled around, he vanished into the hills. He was initiated into the Star Society, then lost interest and left after four moons. The only commitment he's *kept* was the one he made to avoid responsibility. But so be it, men must follow the calling of their souls. Greets the Sun's goal is to live up here like a hermit, hunting, gathering nuts and berries, and living on his family's surplus."

"Are you jealous?" Star Shell crossed her arms, aware of the uneasy beat of her heart.

He gave her a veiled glance. "Don't be silly. My time for jealousies—at least of the flesh—is long past. No, Star Shell, I'm curious about you . . . about the good sense that I've come to expect from you. Remember Robin? I want you to think back, to recall the hatred that fired his eyes that night in the Blue Duck clan house. Now, look at me, Star Shell. Do you seriously believe that young Greets the Sun could protect you from *that* man? That vicious, vengeful killer? Could Greets the Sun, who has never faced up to any difficulty in his life, hide you from warriors used to sniffing out their enemies' trails like wolves?"

She struggled for words, suffering the first erosion of joy.

"And let me ask you this . . ." Tall Man's eyes had begun to blaze. "How do you see your life? Let's assume that, for once in his life, Greets the Sun is correct. Let's say he can successfully hide you up here. Is that how you want to live? Do you plan to be a hermit for the rest of your life? What about Silver Water? Is she to be condemned to this life as well? And what if, may the ancestors forgive . . . you have a *child* by him?"

She started. He'd spit the word "child" with unmitigated disgust.

Tall Man raised his hands, the pipe clutched like a baton. "You're not *married*, Star Shell. You can't be! His clan doesn't . . . *won't* recognize you. I know them. These are very traditional people. When they learn who you are, what your husband did, and of your association with the Mask, they will never, *never* consent to a marriage—no matter what status your clan has in StarSky City."

A cold futility had emptied the warmth from her soul. "Why are you doing this? Saying all this?"

Wistful compassion replaced the dark desperation in the shaman's wrinkled face. "Star Shell, I understand what you've been through, and I know how tempting it is to escape into a dream. As a young man, I did that myself, as you well know. I understand the appeal of an offer of safety after so much fear. But it's an *illusion*, Star Shell. A horrible trap that you don't understand. A disaster that will condemn you. There is *no* safety. Not in this place, and not in this young man."

She stared at him, uncomprehending as fear built within her.

Tall Man wet his thin brown lips. "Please, Star Shell, you must believe me. He will destroy you. For your sake—if not for mine—you must never touch him again."

Star Shell turned away. She intended to walk only a few paces and regain control of herself but her steps quickly became a trot, then a desperate run. A silver shimmer of tears tried to blind her. She ran her heart out, crashing through the sapling trees, pounding across the leaves.

With the graying of dawn, Otter heeled *Wave Dancer* into a sluggish and muddy channel. Was this the right way? Had he remembered correctly? The flood made memory tricky at best. He peered around in the shadowy murk of tree trunks and lapping water. This had to be the way. He stroked with his paddle, driving them eastward. Everything was wet; cold dew had dampened the packs and beaded on the canoe's waxed wood.

Pearl had curled up like a child, her knees drawn to her chest as she huddled under Otter's fox-fur coat. The shining wealth of her long black hair spilled over the thick pack that cushioned her head. Her face had a delicate, sweet innocence in sleep, one that Otter's soul couldn't help but respond to.

"What are you doing?" Black Skull demanded as his wary eyes searched the flooded forest. He'd lifted his paddle, its droplets making rings on the smooth surface.

"Daylight is breaking. We'd better find a spot where we can lie low."

"I don't understand, Trader. They'll be hunting up and down the river for this woman. We'd be better off to paddle like scared rats for the north. Outrun them."

"I've thought about that, but if Wolf of the Dead has any sense, which I know he does, he'll have already sent fast war canoes up and down the main channel to post observers on the high spots. Think, warrior—he's looking for a lone woman. With daybreak, they'll know that she didn't steal any canoe and that she must still be close. If they see *Wave Dancer,* they're going to break their backs to catch us. They'll want to find out who we are."

"And that would be so good!" Green Spider chortled. "Such a boring feast they would give in our honor! Yawn, yawn, yawn. I'd sleep right through it." The Contrary stared at Pearl, his thin face pensive. One skinny arm dangled overboard, where his fingers could drag in the cold water. Catcher lay beside him, nose to tail on a roll of palmetto matting.

"Indeed," Otter agreed. "That is, if being dead is like sleeping."

"I'm not sure I like this," Black Skull groused. "Proceed, Trader. Find a place for us to hide."

They wound around; the channel was marked only by the denser band of trees to either side and the narrow ribbon of water that threaded through drowned brush. Pearl twitched now, uttering muffled cries that betrayed terrifying nightmares.

And if you'd been a captive of the Khota, Otter, you'd be possessed by horrors too.

"There." Otter pointed with his paddle. Off to the right, a hummock of brush stuck out of the water. "From the height of that hazelnut, there ought to be dry land behind it. If we are where I think we are, this is an old levee from the river. A localized high spot.''

"There's a lot of brush here. Good cover." Black Skull peered around suspiciously at the few tall oak and hickory trees, all with splendid canopies. "There ought to be more trees."

"It's an Ilini trick that the Khota learned. If you burn the forest out—get rid of the elm, ash, and maple—the nut trees produce better. Hazelnut grows around the grove edges, which it couldn't do in thick forest. The other advantage is that you can compete with the squirrels for the nut crop. If the squirrels can't jump from tree to tree, they have to run up the trunk. So, you see, you get a double harvest: additional nut yields and a place to set squirrel traps for a tasty stew."

"Smart people, these Khota."

"Dumb," Green Spider countered as he splashed the water, apparently fascinated by the droplet patterns. "As dumb as rocks and twice as soft."

Black Skull lifted a threatening fist. "I'd like to beat some sense into you, fool. But I get the feeling that if I knocked your head off, it would just roll around and spill emptiness all over everything."

Green Spider nodded. "Emptiness. Yes. It never hurts to spread Truth around, Killer of Men."

Black Skull glared back at Green Spider. "As soon as I don't need to worry about any Khota war party, I'm going to twist your arm around a couple of times, just for the pleasure of hearing you scream."

"The louder the scream, the greater the silence. Silence so profound it's deafening." Then the Contrary took a deep breath, threw his head back and mimed a wrenching but perfectly silent scream.

Black Skull's broken face twitched in frustration. He turned back to paddling, and Otter could hear the warrior muttering to himself. They worked their way around the edge of the hazel thicket, finally finding a winding channel that seemed to offer them haven. They pulled *Wave Dancer* along by hand, using the overhanging branches.

The noise of their passage brought Pearl awake with a start. Wide-eyed, she sat up, raising an involuntary hand to her heart. She took a deep breath with the realization of where she was and applied herself to helping them pull the boat through the brush.

"Where are we?" she asked, glancing nervously at Otter.

"Hopefully, a hiding place where we can avoid Khota hunters during the daylight."

Otter could see panic glittering in her eyes. Well, you couldn't blame her. He was more than a little frightened himself.

"Ground," Black Skull said as he stepped over the side into the dense brush. He grasped the carved fox-head bow, and muscles bulged as he pulled the heavy canoe forward.

"That's good," Otter decided as the canoe began to list in the mud. One by one, they clambered out and pushed through the brush, coming upon a small, dry clearing before them. Thickets screened them on all sides.

Pearl held back. She gave Otter a particularly detailed inspection. Green Spider she almost dismissed at a glance. Black Skull, however, caused her such a start when he turned around to face her that she involuntarily took a step backward into the water.

"Perhaps I should tell you our names again." Otter gave her his ingratiating smile. "I am Otter, of the White Shell Clan. My skinny companion here is Green Spider, a Contrary from the Blood Clan of the City of the Dead. The warrior is Black Skull, of the Winter Clan of the City of the Dead. We are on our way northward, across the freshwater seas."

By her face, Otter could tell that Black Skull's mangled face and scarred body unnerved her. Her furtive glances at the terrain indicated that she was determining the quickest route of escape.

Despite her haggard appearance, the smudges of mud left by the floodwaters, and the bits of twigs and other detritus in her hair, she would catch any man's eye. The Khota war shirt didn't hide the full curve of her breasts. The belt emphasized her trim waistline, and then rounded hips gave way to long, muscular legs. Even with the terror in those shining eyes, any man would call her a beauty.

"Black Skull—" Otter shook himself free of her spell "—go see if there's anyone around. If I'm right that this is an old levee, it should be a long, skinny island. I'd hate to find out there was a house, or a field, just beyond that line of brush."

The warrior nodded, taking his club, atlatl, and darts from the boat before he padded off into the hazel thicket.

Otter then waded back to *Wave Dancer,* where he removed blankets and a couple of sealed jars. Green Spider took the opportunity to roll around on the dry grass, wrestling with Catcher. The dog growled and jumped, its tail lashing the air with joy. Pearl watched with a brittle sharpness in her eyes.

Otter dumped his load on the ground and motioned her over. She came, but with the same wariness that a starving wolf pup might have used.

"Sit. Please." Otter gestured to a spot as he used a deer-bone awl to pry the wax seal from one of the jars. He'd Traded for the dried-berry pemmican at Hilltop, expecting to need exactly such a hasty meal as this. In the middle of Khota territory, they could afford no fires.

Pearl knelt, and Otter gave her a friendly appraisal. "You can leave any time you wish, woman of the Anhinga. But you are welcome, and should feel safe among us." He offered the jar of dried fruit. "Eat. It's a combination of grapes, strawberries, blueberries, and raspberries sealed in a mixture of shredded deer meat and buffalo fat."

She tried it, made a face as she chewed and swallowed, then dipped a slim hand in for a second helping. "Why should I feel safe with you?"

"Well, I don't know. Maybe because we hate the Khota as much as you do . . . perhaps even more than you do. We followed you upriver. Read the stories of your captivity in the abandoned campsites." He gave her a nod of admiration. "You're a brave woman. Perhaps one day you'll tell me what happened back there. Most women would have given up, accepted their fate."

She wet her lips and swallowed hard, avoiding his eyes as she ate ravenously.

"The Khota killed my Uncle," Otter continued. "And they've robbed me several times in the past. I want you to hear my words. No matter what, we will never give you up to them."

"Yes we will!" Green Spider whispered, bounding on his hands and knees like a dog. Then he giggled and flattened out, crawling forward on his belly. He wiggled up to within an arm's length of a suddenly horrified Pearl and stuck his tongue out in a very reptilian manner.

"He's a Contrary," Otter tried to explain. "Everything he says is backward. Please, I give you my word, you're safe among us."

Green Spider wormed his way closer to Pearl, who in turn edged closer to Otter. Her face had gone pale.

"Green Spider," Otter said, "I think she's plenty brave. Why don't you come a little closer now? I think Pearl wants you to fall all over her."

For once, the Contrary ignored him.

"He lives," Green Spider said, hissing like a snake. "The club broke when you hit him. The thick fur of the wolf mask cushioned the blow. Before he could burn, his old friend pulled him out of the fire. Feel the anger, Woman of the Water! So much anger . . . burning in your soul and his. If it should meet, how terrifying, for it will turn into the final peace, that of the Dead. But for which of you?"

She spun to peer at Otter. "What's he saying? He can't mean . . ." Horror glazed her eyes. "Last night Green Spider was with you, wasn't he?"

"He was." Otter leaned forward to within inches of Green Spider's face and said, "Keep this up, Contrary. She loves it. You're not scaring her at all."

In his hissing-snake voice, Green Spider responded, "Good. I didn't want to scare her. After all, she's safe with us. You said so yourself."

Otter clamped his jaw and straightened to glance around at the hazel. He could sense Uncle's ghost out there, watching, calling, but the message couldn't quite be heard over the trilling of the birds and the droning of the insects.

Pearl closed her eyes and knotted a hand in the fabric over her heart. To Otter, she said, "Did . . . did you hear him say that he lived? That the club broke? That his old friend saved him?"

"That's what he said."

"But he's a Contrary. Did he mean it forward or backward? Is Wolf of the Dead alive or dead?"

Otter could see the pulse racing under the silky skin of her neck. He had his own jitters now. "I'm never sure of what he means."

Her horrified stare riveted on Green Spider, who watched her with motionless eyes, looking just like the reptile he imitated.

Green Spider hissed, "What do you see down there, in the roots of your soul, Woman of the Water? Has he destroyed you? Or will you fight back? How will you accept this fear? Will you be a coward, let it eat at your soul the way cactus acid eats shell? Or will you reach through the fire, here, now, knowing that the flesh will sear in agony, but then it will heal?"

Otter slapped his hands to his knees, attempting to act casually. "If I were to guess, I'd suppose he meant that Wolf of the Dead is still alive. Too bad, too. I'd have given anything—"

"How does he . . . I mean, he wasn't there, was he? He was with you! He can't know that! It's . . ."

"Impossible?" Otter rubbed his face, feeling the night's fatigue. "He's a Contrary, Pearl. Possessed by Power. He knows many things no one else does. Like where we're supposed to go. He's seen it all in a Vision. The Clan Elders believed him. I believe him. And since we're talking about miracles, I'm even coming to think that Black Skull believes him, too."

At that, Green Spider flipped over on his back and crossed his arms on his stomach. "That pemmican stinks. I'll bet it tastes vile. You know, like that slime on rotting fish."

Otter handed the Contrary the jar. "Pearl, believe me, you get used to him." Catcher came over and curled up beside Otter. He patted the dog as he leaned back on a rolled-up blanket. "Well . . . mostly."

Pearl had barely moved; she cast worried eyes on the happy Green Spider, who with unrivaled gusto was shoveling the fatty mix from the jar into his mouth.

Her voice sounded distant when she said, "I've heard of a Trader called the Water Fox . . . from the White Shell Clan."

"That's me."

She stood slowly, as if checking to make sure that her legs would hold her. "You have a reputation for being a good and honest man. I thank you for pulling me from the water last night. But I . . . I'd better be going. I'll just bring you trouble."

"Indeed you will," Green Spider garbled through a mouth crammed with food. "You'll kill us all. Your time is coming, Pearl. It's in the stars. They shine for you."

Otter put out his hand to Pearl. "Wait." He turned his attention on Green Spider. "You've seen her? In the Vision?"

Green Spider chuckled. "I'm blind, Trader. The world is filled with so much light that everything you look at is in total darkness."

"Tell me . . . if Pearl leaves, goes her own way, what will happen? Green Spider, please. Talk to me so I'll understand."

The Contrary licked his fingers one by one, his unfocused gaze fixing on the end of his thumb. "She was brought to us for a reason." He seemed to start; then he stared intently at Pearl. "The dolphin can find its way. Can you? Can you see the darkness between the stars?"

Pearl's frightened eyes widened. "I'm leaving, Water Fox. Again, I thank you and your friends. I won't be any more burden to you. You can keep the sack of corn. I was going to Trade it—and maybe I have. For my life." She nodded at Green Spider. "We're even."

Otter sighed and stood, spreading his arms wide. "You're free to go. But if I know this river, and I think I do, we're on an island. It will be a wet escape. Travel with us at least as far as the Ilini territories. We'll be there in a day or two. You'll be able to find a Trader there who'll manage to sneak you down past the Khota lands and take you home. That, or you can cut overland to the Father Water. It's only a couple of days' walk to the west."

"No. Thank you, I . . . I just . . ." Turning, she sprinted into the brush and disappeared.

Otter whirled to Green Spider. "We need her? You're sure?"

Green Spider's eyes had gone vacant again. He was laboriously picking a dry blade of bluestem grass into little hairs of fiber. "Not at all. She wouldn't even be good company for a dead muskrat."

"Green Spider, couldn't you have been a little kinder? She's hurt! Scared! And all you did was to frighten her even more! I ought to kick the fat out of you!" He threw his hands up. "Oh, never mind."

"Have you ever noticed the way grass is put together? How do you think the Mysterious One ever managed to think up the arrangement for all these little fibers?" Green Spider cocked his head as he prodded the leaf with a stubby fingertip.

"All right, I'll go get her." As Otter started on Pearl's trail, Green Spider locked a strong hand around his ankle, saying, "That which you chase runs the quickest. That which you run from follows the fastest."

Otter closed his eyes in frustration, then opened one a slit. "You know, sometimes I feel a lot of sympathy for Black Skull."

Twenty-three

I sit here on her sack of corn, my hands clasped tightly in my lap, waiting. I am afraid.

She was just here, stealing from the canoe. When the birds saw her, their songs died in their throats. The squirrels stopped their chatter.

Now I am alone again.

Otter is gone. Black Skull is gone. Even Catcher has abandoned me, unable to bear the look in my eyes.

He knows. So do all the other animals.

No matter what this frightened woman's decision, suffering and death will be the result.

I drop my head in my hands and close my eyes. A background of stars blazes to life on the fabric of my soul. Glorious! Too many to count. Stars like frost crystals spreading endlessly across a grassy meadow on a cold spring morning. They gleam and twinkle at me.

But they are mute.

Perhaps it is because I am so very tired that I do not understand how this woman might hear them speak. But I trust that it is so.

And if I am wrong . . .

I exhale wearily. Otter. Poor, poor Otter. He feels responsible for all of us. What will he do when faced with our deaths?

She found him on the top of the ridge where the sandstone jutted out to create a small cliff. Greets the Sun lay on his side, a bronzed hero against the gray-mottled rock. In appreciation of the unseasonable weather and the warm sun, he wore only a breechcloth, though his blanket was folded under him for a pad.

For a moment, Star Shell stood still, enjoying the way the sun gleamed on his supple skin and shining hair. With her eyes, she traced the swell of his muscles as they curved along his tawny sides; she remembered the feel of them under her hands as they tensed at that moment of sexual release.

Tall Man told me never to touch him. How could anything be wrong with touching a man like Greets the Sun? If only Tall Man hadn't been so sure of himself. How can this be bad?

When she started forward, he turned, smiling radiantly at her approach. ''Come, sit with me. I've been listening to the hawks. This is mating season. From here you can watch them wheeling and diving, grabbing at each other with their feet as they tumble in the air.''

She stretched out beside him, and he curled around her, pointing over the rugged tree-covered hills. ''There,'' he said, ''two redtails. The female is the larger. She still hasn't made up her mind about this male. Watch, they'll come closer. In a bit, they'll be hovering right out here in front of us. The air rises first here on a warm day. They like that. It makes it easier for them to float.''

The problem was the Mask. Solve that, and everything would work out. She struggled with what she would say. The sun warmed her body, even touching the conflict in her soul. The right path had to be here somewhere. She leaned her head against his shoulder, aware of his crushed-leaf, fall-buck scent.

''I have come to love you, Star Shell,'' he told her dreamily.

''Me? You love me?''

He laughed, the sound as free as the cry of the hawks. ''Yes, I love you as I never thought to love any woman! You have touched my heart with fire and melted my soul.''

He clasped her to him, his hand tracing the swell of her breasts. And in the moment of her confusion, she surrendered to him again, turning to face him as she wiggled from her clothing. She savored the heat of the sun and their coupling, aware of the glistening sweat and the exertion. Her muscles ached as she locked her legs around him. Her cries mingled with those of the hawks. And afterward, she refused to turn him loose, refused to allow him to roll away.

His face had flushed, and perspiration beaded on the bridge of his nose. He panted for breath, his lungs laboring in time to hers.

"I never knew it could be like this," he whispered.

She tightened her hold, driven by new desperation. "I need you to help me. Will you?"

He smiled, brimming happiness. "I would do anything for you."

"Will you go away with me? Help Tall Man and me with what we must do?"

"I love you. I'll help you. Where do you and Tall Man have to go? I can take you there. I know most of the places around here."

"It's far to the north, Greets the Sun. Very far. We must go to the Roaring Water."

He frowned. "I've never heard of it."

"Many days' walk to the north, there's a big freshwater sea. You know of that?"

He nodded.

"If you follow the shore around to the east, there's a river that drains the freshwater sea. The Roaring Water is there. That's where we must go."

He hesitated. "You mean . . . not around here?"

Her heart ached. "No. Far away."

Greets the Sun pushed back, forcing her to loosen her hold as he rolled away. He stared out over the basin of his valley. "Does this thing you have to do . . . must it be done so far away?"

"I'm afraid so." She took his hand. "It's very important. Will you come with us? It will be a great adventure. And you and I, we'll be together."

He smiled. "Together."

"Yes, and when we throw the Mask into the Roaring Water, we can come back. Go to StarSky and have my father, the great Hollow Drill, send word to your clan." She ran her fingers down the side of his head. "We'll be together forever, Greets the Sun. You and I and Silver Water. We'll come back here . . . and live the rest of our lives listening to the hawks."

"Married, you mean?"

" . . . Yes."

His frown deepened. "This journey? It would take five days? Ten?"

"More. Maybe three moons."

He bit his lip, rising to his feet and wrapping his breechcloth about his waist. His face mirrored sudden uncertainty as he stared out over the greening vista. In the distance, the rumpled hills looked bluish.

Star Shell ran her finger around a pit in the rough limestone and chipped at lichen with a fingernail. "I have to do only this one thing, and then we'll have forever together. We'll rise every morning and climb the hill to greet the day."

He nodded then, smiling down at her. "I will help you."

She sank back laughing in joy and relief. "I knew it! I knew you'd come with me!"

He reached over and stroked her cheek. "I'll see you at the house in a little while. I have to do some things first. Prepare to leave and . . . and make some offerings. It won't take long. I'll see you then." He started toward the forest, his head down.

"I'll be there!" she called. "I love you!"

He turned at the edge of the trees and waved back. "I love you, too!"

She took a deep breath and watched the blue eternity of sky. The breeze cooled her as it dried the last of the perspiration from her body.

Finally, she sat up and collected her clothing. *You were wrong, Tall Man. He loves me. And because he loves me, he will help me do what I must.*

She stood, stretching lithely, her head thrown back to the warm gaze of the sun. The breeze blew her long black hair about her, tickling her skin. The desperation that had followed Tall Man's words had vanished like last winter's crusted snow.

Pearl had found a thicket of hazel with a tiny, leaf-lined hollow in the middle. She'd crawled in, careful to make sure she didn't break or bruise any branches, or leave sign of her passage. There she curled into a ball, dozing and worrying in the soft spring sunlight. Only another hand of time or so remained before the shadows of evening would creep into her sanctuary and steal the warmth. She wanted to enjoy it for as long as she could.

Birdsong carried on the same breeze that bore the musky odor of wet earth, flood, and damp timber. She could see spring in the branches that surrounded her, the ends of twigs supple with sap, the buds ready to burst, and catkins almost to flower. Even the rough gray bark seemed to swell with the promise of warm weather.

Pearl clutched the atlatl she had taken, aware that it had been *his*, but the desire to pitch it as far as she could didn't outweigh the knowledge that her very life might depend on possessing it.

Panicked she might be, but she could take some comfort in the fact that her mind still functioned. Even after fleeing from the Traders, she'd doubled back, slipped up to their canoe and lifted a half-dozen of the Trader's darts from where they rested behind the sleeping Contrary. That sackful of corn was more than enough Trade for the rescue and a handful of darts.

I should have taken more. Things I could Trade, or use, like blankets.

She stared absently at the double-toothed leaves that she lay on. She hadn't planned on falling asleep in the Trader's boat. Her dreams had repeated the horrible scene at the Khota clan grounds as she walked up the bluff to Wolf of the Dead's house ... and the degradation as they stripped her, forced her down and held her while their leader prepared himself.

She began to tremble, remembering. Every bit of her being had been invaded by their staring eyes, her humiliation mirrored in their awed expressions. And then had come that instant of horrified numbness as he mounted her as if she were a filthy camp dog.

Pearl winced at the bruises on her breasts. He'd squeezed and twisted them in an effort to make her gasp in time to the movement of his hips. His piercing howl had announced the moment when he'd pulsed wetly inside her.

"He's alive," she whispered to herself. "And he'll come looking for me . . . he'll gather his warriors and they'll come, too. Just like they did for the Ilini woman." And that woman— so the story went—had died horribly.

How had the Contrary known?

"What do you see down there, in the roots of your soul, Woman of the Water? Has he destroyed you? Or will you fight back?"

How could she fight ten tens of warriors? Alone. With only six darts.

Pearl curled more deeply into the leaves and moldy nut husks. She couldn't shake the image of the Water Fox's sympathetic eyes. He'd known, and he'd tried to soothe her fears.

Why didn't I make certain Wolf of the Dead's skull was bashed in? It would have taken but a moment! Then if I'd heard a heartbeat, I could have driven a dart through his chest.

Her fist crumpled the dry leaves. The only consolation she could imagine was that if he did find her, and if he killed her, her ghost would never leave him alone. She would haunt this river valley forever, terrorizing those who passed this way as he had terrorized her. Pay them back, Trade in a way not even the Water Fox could understand. Terror for terror.

"I was never afraid of anything," she whispered softly to herself. "Nothing could scare Pearl. Not alligators. Not even the great wide sea with its storms and swells."

Her life had changed when she ate the dolphin's tender meat. She could see that rich, red blood leak down the hewn hull of the canoe, hear the young dolphin squeak and chatter in fear and pain. She could hear its tail slapping at the wood while strong men—

Pearl quivered and shook beyond control now, fear pumping hotly through her body with each stroke of her racing heart. Fear . . . fear, a thing alive, devouring her whole.

"How will you accept this fear?" the Contrary asked again out of the sucking silence. *"Will you be a coward, let it eat at your soul the way cactus acid eats shell? Or will you reach through the fire, here, now, knowing that the flesh will sear in agony, but then it will heal?"*

Pearl tried to swallow, but her throat had gone dry. She whispered, "I may be afraid, Contrary, but I'm no coward. No man could turn me against myself that way—not even Wolf of the Dead."

Hushed voices eddied from the trees behind her, and Pearl froze. Men's voices, speaking furtively. She could make out a few words. Khota! Hunters after prey, outlining the way they would hunt.

They were closer now. Her heart sought to burst through her ribs. They would hear her quaking muscles, smell her fear on the breeze.

Stealthy footsteps hissed through the grass as they passed beyond her thicket.

" . . . camp up ahead . . . and a dog, so watch the wind. Move to surround . . ." and the voices faded away.

Relief rushed through her. They weren't hunting *her*! It was the Trader and his companions they sought! Euphoria made her want to jump up, shout and dance, whoop to the very skies and the sinking sun.

Lie still, be quiet, and they will never suspect that you're here.

She closed her eyes, cursing herself for a fool. The sack of corn would give her away. The Khota would find it in the canoe. They'd know. And she'd taken some of the Trader's darts. How would he defend himself?

You are Pearl of the Anhinga! Get up . . . The order chafed at her like sharkskin on raw meat.

She gathered herself, summoning strength from her nerves and muscles. *Prove you're not a coward, woman.*

Wolf of the Dead howled triumphantly in her imagination as she crawled forward.

Tired to the bone, Otter stared up uneasily at the evening. He lay uncomfortably on the dry grass. Overhead, flying Vs of birds winged northward as they followed the waterways. In the distance, he could hear the endless honking of geese. The sky had gone from blue to lavender as the shadows lengthened into dusk. The songs of the birds gathered a throatier intensity as night approached.

Otter blinked and stretched. Unaccustomed to sleeping during daylight hours, he hadn't slept well. The thought of Pearl venturing out on her own plagued him. He hadn't been able to find her—but then, he wasn't much of a tracker. He shifted on the uneven ground, wiggling his shoulders around a hummock that tortured his back.

When he had finally managed to drift off, Uncle's ghost had drifted in, whispering warnings and reminding him of the atrocities committed by the Khota. The result had been fretful naps instead of refreshing sleep.

He pillowed his head on his arm. Black Skull was snoring, the sound reminiscent of a gouge dragging over uneven wood. Catcher kicked, then made a weary canine sigh.

Otter sat up and rolled his blanket. Finches flitted about in the trees, and the first frogs had crawled from the mud to croak their greetings to spring. A robin darted across the clearing, then stopped with its black head cocked to look and listen before racing forward again.

Black Skull lay with his crooked mouth open, his closed eyes flickering with dreams. Green Spider had stretched out on his stomach, half out of his blanket. His cheek rested on Pearl's sack of corn, and one arm was thrust out like a lance. Catcher was lost in doggish dreams, his paws quivering and his nose wiggling.

Otter walked over to the brush to drain his water. He yawned and rubbed the back of his neck. High above, an eagle spiraled on the last golden rays of the day. Two squirrels chattered annoyance at each other in the distance.

When he'd finished, Otter began clearing their camp, carrying things back to the canoe.

Black Skull had awakened, though he made no move to rise from his blankets. "The woman is still gone?"

"I guess she didn't come back." Otter picked up the empty

jar of pemmican and began flicking the ants out of it. "I'd hoped she would realize that we were the best way off the island."

"She must make her own way, Trader. Though I must admit, she was one of the most pleasant women to look at that I've seen in a long time." Black Skull threw back his blankets and sat up. He scowled at Green Spider—for practice, if nothing else—and scratched at his matted hair with one hand. "I'll be glad to be gone from this place. How long until we're away from the Khota?"

"If we get a little moonlight tonight, enough to see the main channel by, we could make the Ilini boundary by morning."

"*Ilini?*" a man's voice asked from the brush.

Black Skull sprang to his feet, catlike. But the surrounding warriors who stepped out of the hazel were prepared, their darts nocked in atlatls, their war clubs held ready.

"Greetings!" a big warrior called out. "So you are looking for the Ilini? I am known as Eats Dogs." He glanced around, noting the canoe back in the brush.

"Down," Otter commanded to Catcher as the dog bounded up, growling. "Catcher, *down!* They'll kill you as soon as look at you."

"What was that?" Eats Dogs asked with a cocked head. "I don't know that tongue."

Otter answered in the Trade pidgin. "Pardon me, noble Eats Dogs. We are Traders bound northward in search of the great Khota." He spread his arms wide. They ought to like that. "I must confess, the river has tricked us. We lost the main channel in the flood and floundered around in the trees, searching for the Khota territories."

The Khota warriors had closed their circle, each man wary. Two tens and one of them. They looked like the vicious predators they were, their long shirts belted at the waist, each decorated by a brightly dyed wolf effigy. Copper, shell, mica, and bone ornaments gleamed in shining black hair drawn into round buns at the tops of their heads.

Eats Dogs grinned as he shook his head. Ropy muscles rippled on his arms. His hair bun was pinned with a long spike made from a human ulna, and squares had been tattooed into his cheeks. A wicked war club bobbed in his hand.

"I see, Trader. Odd, isn't it, that you would sleep by day? A smart traveler would use the sun to orient himself.'' He barked orders to the others, who tensed.

Otter flashed his famous smile. ''Great Eats Dogs, we've been lost! This is the first *dry* piece of ground we've seen in a long time. After three nights of sleeping in a canoe tied to a tree, do you mean to say you wouldn't take the opportunity for a nap on Mother Earth?''

''Clever,'' Eats Dogs admitted. ''But it won't be up to me to say, Trader. Wolf of the Dead will deal with you. I'm sorry to report, he's not been happy this last day.''

Black Skull had stiffened, his command of Trade pidgin evidently much greater than Otter had guessed.

Green Spider picked that moment to sit up in his bedding. He threw his head back, squawking and cawing like a crow, then thrust out his arms and flapped them wildly.

''What is this?'' Eats Dogs asked, a sneer tugging up the corner of his lip.

''This,'' Otter gestured, ''is Green Spider. A Contrary from the City of the Dead.''

Eats Dogs squinted at Green Spider, apparently unimpressed, then took a step closer to Otter. ''I know you. The Water Fox, isn't it?''

''I am honored at your memory.''

''So was your Uncle,'' Eats Dogs said quietly. ''And you are a great deal like him, aren't you?''

Otter could feel Uncle's copper effigy burning against his chest where it lay under his shirt.

''Careful, Trader,'' Black Skull said evenly in their own tongue. ''Discipline.''

Otter hadn't realized that his hands had knotted into fists. He took a deep breath, stifling his welling rage. ''He got lost in floods too?''

''A good joke.'' Eats Dogs laughed loudly. ''You three will come with us. Your canoe will be brought to the Khota clan grounds.''

At that, Green Spider stood up, pointing at the sky. In perfect Trade pidgin, he shouted, ''Look! The sun! It burns with the blackness of the rainbow! The wings of Many Colored Crow are spread, and for many, the white light of darkness is coming!''

"What?" Eats Dogs turned, his attention on the Contrary who Danced around the camp, spinning and diving and soaring for them.

He hopped before Eats Dogs. "Your wife's lover will thank us for this day," Green Spider told the surprised Khota. "He has wished for your death so that she might be free of you. What? Did you think her robes empty when you traveled far to the south? Ah! But then you didn't look closely when you crawled into your still-warm bed last night, did you? In the darkness, you didn't see the swelling of her belly. And then the war call came!"

Eats Dogs had stiffened, glancing about. Several of his warriors looked away, and in that instant, Eats Dogs saw the truth of the Contrary's words. He slapped Green Spider with enough strength to flatten him.

"Get up, dog! Now!"

Green Spider laughed, wiping at the blood that began to leak from his nose. "You shouldn't tickle people like that. You'll make them giggle all the time."

Rage ran like fire through Otter's veins. He stepped forward to help Green Spider to his feet. The Contrary, however, leaped into the air like a desperate mullet. "Truth is pleasure, is it not, Eater of Dogs? Shall I pleasure you more and tell you that your line will die with you today?"

"Mad!" "Possessed!" "Spirit-haunted!" Whispers were escaping the Khota warriors, enough of the words familiar for Otter to garner their meaning. He noted that Black Skull was now three steps farther away, almost unobserved by the Khota, so fascinated were they with Green Spider.

"Kill them!" Eats Dogs screamed suddenly. "I will not hear this!"

The warriors hesitated, suddenly unsure.

"Only a fool harms a Contrary!" Otter cried, opening his arms to the warriors. "Is that what you want? To be hounded by Power for the rest of your days? He is one of Power's own!"

"*If* he's a Contrary!" Eats Dogs bellowed, anger and humiliation on his face. "*I* say he's a Trader's trick! This . . . this *beast* is no Contrary! If he is, then Power strike me down!"

The Khota warriors shifted nervously.

Green Spider broke out in peals of eerie laughter until he had to hold his sides.

Eats Dogs filled his lungs to bellow yet another order, but the hiss, followed by a meaty spat, made him stumble. Anyone who'd heard an atlatl-driven dart hit home knew that sound. The impact drove Eats Dogs forward a couple of steps. He glanced down wide-eyed at the bloody dart point that protruded from under his sternum.

We're going to die. The thought rolled around inside Otter during that first stunned instant. At least two tens and one of warriors had them surrounded—and Black Skull had only managed to crouch down.

A second *hiss-spat* caused another warrior to stagger and sink to his knees, a dart transfixing his side. He grabbed at the bloody point before the most gruesome of screams broke his lips.

The Khota shrieked war cries as Eats Dogs toppled forward, the weight of his body driving the dart partway back out of the bleeding wound. Yet another dart smacked home, and the Khota responded by driving darts aimlessly into the surrounding thickets of hazel.

Black Skull exploded from his crouch. His vicious war club was in his hand. He moved in a blur, twisting, flashing, the cracking sounds of his club on flesh a horror to the ear.

Catcher couldn't contain himself. His fighting growl turned half howl, and he launched himself on a man, driving him down, ripping his face and throat in unleashed fury.

And through it all, Green Spider Danced like a happy child, whirling, whooping, and Singing. He pirouetted, pranced, capered over bodies, and clapped his hands. In the midst of the battle, his face beamed radiantly, streaks of blood from his leaking nose making lightning patterns over his lips and chin.

Otter had frozen, gaping at the twisting, whirling Black Skull. The warrior never lost a step as he mowed through the Khota warriors. Yet another dart arched downward in the fading light, this one pinning a Khota warrior's leg to the ground. The man bellowed and fell, pawing at the hardwood shaft that held him.

Out of the fog of disbelief, Otter turned and ran for *Wave Dancer*. He grabbed the first thing he found—his paddle—and charged into the melee. With all the strength in his muscular shoulders, he jabbed a face, then swung the sharp edge into the warrior's neck. The Khota's head snapped sideways as he fell.

Otter pivoted, using the fire-hardened point like a lance to impale a charging warrior, literally scooping the man up and driving him into the ground. Before the stunned warrior could recover, Otter chopped the paddle edge across his victim's throat.

Otter yanked his paddle up, using it to catch a war club that arched down to brain him. In that instant, he stood face-to-face, breathing the man's foul breath, staring into his frightened eyes. Each strained, a battle of pure brawn, all thought of finesse vanished in the bloody haze of the moment. The Khota broke, leaping back and setting himself for another blow. Otter jabbed at him with the paddle, backing him, and as the man turned to run, Otter charged, slamming his hardwood paddle into the angle of neck and shoulder.

The Khota collapsed, and Otter was on him, beating, slashing, battering. A cry broke Otter's lips as he rose high, driving the point of his paddle into the man's chest the way he would a spear into a sturgeon.

Otter threw himself sideways when Black Skull's club sizzled past his shoulder and the sharpened copper spikes slashed the throat of another attacker who had raced up behind him.

Rolling, Otter got to his knees. The fallen Khota warrior clasped futile hands at the welling fountain of blood bubbling from his throat. Then Otter looked for Black Skull, but the warrior had already turned, searching for other opponents.

Otter gripped his paddle to prop himself up, unnerved by the incredible spray of blood and the glazed terror in the dying Khota's eyes.

"So many!" Green Spider chuckled as he danced by. "Look at them dancing in the light! So much life, so little death! Spirals all the way around."

"Watch my back," Black Skull growled to Otter. "They can still kill us!"

Otter staggered, his starved lungs heaving, and stared at the bodies. One or two twitched, kicked, or reached out their hands as they lay dying. Black Skull prowled the perimeter; he poised on the balls of his feet, ready to leap or dodge, eyes on the brush.

Darts had been driven through five of the dead or dying. The warrior with the pinned leg had never freed himself—his skull had been crushed by Black Skull's war club. Otter had dispatched three. Catcher had jumped one. That left twelve. All lay there with broken skulls, ripped throats, and the gory wreckage of what had once been heads.

"We should have been dead," Otter whispered hoarsely to himself. He'd started to shake. "Two tens and one against three. We should have been dead! You killed . . . killed seventeen men, Black Skull!"

"I killed twelve, Trader." Black Skull's eyes narrowed, peering into the brush. "You can come out, friend," he called in pidgin. "I, for one, would know your name. The Black Skull will Sing your honor!"

"We should have been *dead*!" Otter could only stumble about on unsteady legs.

"Well, we're not," Black Skull told him pointedly. "Come out, friend."

Pearl eased out of the brush with her atlatl in her hand. No emotion showed on her beautiful face.

Black Skull nodded to her, admiration in his eyes. "You saved my life, woman. I did not see that warrior until he stood. By then, it was too late for me to do anything about him. I would have you know my gratitude."

"Call it a Trade," she answered. "You saved me last night. I paid you back today. That's the end of it."

Black Skull jerked his head toward Otter. "Help him kill the ones still breathing. We must hurry."

"Kill the ones . . ." Otter swallowed hard, fingering his deadly oar. *It's just like clubbing a deer in a snare.*

Pearl nodded, but the lines around her mouth drew tight. She looked at the faces as though she knew them. Picking up a miscast dart, she began moving among the dying, kicking them to see if they moved, lancing their chests even if they didn't, making certain. She used her dart expertly.

As if spearing a huge fish, Otter thought.

He found a groaning Khota trying to crawl away, lifted his paddle and selected the right place: just where the curve of the skull met the back of the neck. He swung with all of his strength. Another wounded Khota propped himself up on locked arms, his eyes closed against the blood leaking down the side of his head.

Otter swung. With each stroke, the vertebra crackled and the victim twitched or jerked into death. *They can't feel it,* Otter told himself. *It's all right. Just like stunning fish.*

Aware of the trembling in his muscles, he finished his task and saw Pearl finishing hers. His intestines wanted to knot and void, and a tickle in his stomach warned of a desire to vomit.

A hard hand settled on his shoulder, and he looked into Black Skull's concerned eyes. "Are you hurt? Or is it the jitters?"

"Jitters."

Black Skull gave him a reassuring nod. His voice turned curiously compassionate. "It will go away, Otter. You did well. Not even your brother could have fought better here today."

Otter stood staring at his hand as he opened and closed it, watching the fingers move. *Alive . . . still alive. And so many are dead.*

"The sooner we leave here, the better," Black Skull decided. "Trader, pack the canoe."

Otter did so, his actions automatic. Few items remained to be packed, so it didn't take long. He tried not to look as Black Skull looted the bodies of the dead of whatever he could find— mostly Khota ornaments and weapons. Green Spider had resumed his Singing and hopped around like a child at a ceremonial. Periodically, he stopped gleefully over a dead Khota, dipped his finger in the man's blood and drew beautiful designs on the face or chest of the corpse. Arms crossed, Pearl watched him curiously.

Otter walked on legs that threatened to buckle beneath him, fighting through the stiff hazel, wading out to *Wave Dancer,* shoving the bloody oar down next to a pack. Catcher jumped up on his pack, licking at the gore caked on his muzzle. "We're ready, Black Skull. Let's go."

Pearl and Black Skull helped him push the boat back and kept it steady when Green Spider splashed through the water and leaped in.

They climbed aboard one at a time, taking the places they'd occupied last night.

When they floated out onto the somber floodwaters, Pearl turned to Otter. "I guess I had to come." Her hands knotted, the muscles on her firm forearms taut. "I don't know. I just had to. Maybe the Contrary knows why."

"It's because you can see the darkness between the stars," Green Spider said seriously, his attention on his fingertips where clots of red had glued to his nails and cuticles.

"I wish he wouldn't do that," Pearl said, more to herself than to Otter.

"That makes three of us," he told her frankly.

Black Skull grunted in agreement.

Twenty-four

Do you think he's all right?" Star Shell fed sticks into the fire. She had refused to waste a balmy evening indoors. The spring storms would be coming, bringing fitful gusts of wind and cold, pelting rain. This was not an opportunity to be missed.

Tall Man said nothing. He sat hunched against the outside wall of the house; he'd been using a deer-ulna awl to poke holes around a moccasin sole, preparatory to stitching. Now he laid his work aside. "I'm a little surprised at the change in your attitude, Star Shell. When you ran off this morning, you seemed anything but happy. Now you seem as carefree as a chickadee."

She poked at the fire, looking up at the last purple tints of sunset over the ridge. The fat-budded branches cast irregular patterns against the luminous evening sky. A nightjar chirped in the trees. "I asked him to come with me. He said he would."

Tall Man crossed his stubby legs, a pinched look dominating his turtle-like features. Was it her imagination, or did he look defeated? "He said he'd go with you?"

She pulled her long hair back over her shoulder. "He told me he loves me. You are my friend, Tall Man. I will always listen to, and treasure, your advice. But Greets the Sun and I, we love each other."

Tall Man closed his eyes for a moment, as if in pain, then picked up his moccasin sole again, bending it, testing the suppleness of the leather. "Well, very good. It will be a blessing to have another strong body. He will be a . . . an asset to our party."

Star Shell glanced up, hearing his desperation.

Tall Man kept his face lowered. "The sun has set, girl. The morning will come early. I, for one, am going to find my blankets and get some sleep."

As he stood and reached for the door flap, she said, "You don't believe he'll do it, do you?"

"We shall see." Then he vanished inside.

Star Shell waited before the house, periodically feeding wood to the fire—wood she and Silver Water had gathered that afternoon. The stewpot sat near the flames, the stew too hot to eat but too cool to boil. He'd be happy when he found a hot meal waiting for him.

How long would he be?

The stars had moved a hand's distance across the sky before Greets the Sun emerged from the dark forest. She smiled up at him as he approached, then walked out to hug him. For long moments she stood enfolded in his arms, listening to the rhythms of their combined heartbeats.

"I have hot stew for you."

"Thank you." He turned her loose and went to squat next to the fire. He burned his fingers on the pot, then used a stick to move it away from the flames. "I've been thinking."

"What about?" She settled next to him, taking his hand. The sense of rightness had returned.

"About what we discussed up on the ridge. Do you love me?"

"Yes! What a foolish question."

His serious gaze turned on her. "If you really love me, Star Shell, you'll stay here with me. I see that now. It's a test . . . a test of how much you believe in me, in us. If you say you'll stay here and forget this journey of yours, I will ask my clan . . . no, I will *demand* that they allow us to marry. I will have my clan send a runner to your father to negotiate the marriage."

She sat quietly, trying to frame her response.

"Love works two ways, Star Shell. It can't be just what you want. It must be what I want, too."

"What about the Mask?"

"What about it? We'll take it out and hang it in a tree somewhere. Dig a hole and bury it! No one will know where it is."

"But it has to be thrown into the Roaring Water."

"How do you *know* that?" he asked reasonably. "Did you have the Vision?"

"No. Tall Man did."

Greets the Sun gave her his radiant smile. "Then if he's really so driven by the Mask, let *him* take it north. I'll protect you here. I give you my word. If you love me, you'll stay."

Star Shell stared into the fire, watching the flames leap and dance on the ash wood. You could see things in a fire, or so an old woman had said once.

"The Mask has done terrible things," Star Shell whispered.

"I'm not interested in the Mask, Star Shell. As long as its Spirit goes away and leaves us in peace, what difference will it make? You have an old man's word that it must be taken to this place in the north. That's all."

"Tall Man is a respected Elder, not just an old man."

"I know." He reached out, his strong fingers turning her chin. As he looked into her eyes, he added, "I have no fear of the Magician. If you love me, Star Shell, you must trust me. Can you do that? Love and trust at the same time?"

She bit her lip and nodded, her soul wrenching at the surrender.

Greets the Sun lifted the bowl of stew. "Thank you for your trust, Star Shell."

She knotted her hands in the fabric of her dress. "Please, let me think. Just for tonight. That's all. Let me sort it out. I do trust you, Greets the Sun. I do love you . . . so deeply that it's tearing me apart. But I've shared so much with Tall Man. We've seen things that . . . well, you wouldn't believe."

His happy smile had returned. "Of course. We'll talk more in the morning." He drank the last of his stew and bent down to kiss the top of her head. "I will dream of you, Star Shell. I will dream of you as my wife."

She smiled then, taking his hand and pressing it to her cheek. "Maybe I'll slip into your robes tonight."

"You will find me warm and waiting," he promised before he ducked through the doorway.

She sighed wearily, throwing another cracked branch onto the fire. What did she owe Tall Man? How correct was his Vision? Did the Mask really have to be taken north and thrown into the depths as the Magician said? And if she turned Greets the Sun down, they'd never have another chance for happiness.

Tell him to go with you.

Didn't he have as much right as she did? He had offered protection and marriage. How could she balance that against her demand that he accept the risks and dangers of a journey into the distant north?

I'm asking too much, and he's being reasonable in return.

Tall Man would be crushed. He would disguise his miserable disappointment under good cheer, walking off to whatever fate would be his. And the Mask's.

It is all right, Star Shell. He's had his life, made his own mistakes. You have a right to your life.

High above, a streak of light burned greenish as a star fell across the sky.

Yes, I have my choice: I can stay here and live with this kind man who loves me, or I can follow an old man's Vision into who knows what.

Robin and his warriors would be out there, but Greets the Sun could send them word that the Mask was gone. His clan would see to it.

Star Shell rubbed her shins, hating the decision she'd just made. Tall Man *would* understand. He knew about affairs of the heart. She'd seen the longing in his eyes when he talked about Clamshell and the things he'd done to win a love that he couldn't claim. Put in that perspective, he'd understand why she'd chosen Greets the Sun.

She stood. She'd tell him in the morning.

Taking one last look at the stars, she turned toward the door flap, her loins already warming at the thought of Greets the Sun in his blankets. She'd slide in next to him and whisper her decision. Then, after they'd joined, she'd lock herself around him again, knowing that they would marry and be happy here.

She lifted the door flap, and paused. Had it not been such a still night, Star Shell would never have heard the soft whisper.

"It will be all right," Silver Water's muted voice said. "He won't hurt my mother. I won't let him. I won't, I won't."

Star Shell ducked through the flap. The fire flared, and Star Shell could see Silver Water in the bright flicker of the flames. The child had crawled out of her blankets to huddle before the pack in which lay the Mask of Many Colored Crow.

The memory of a swinging corpse flashed in Star Shell's mind.

"What . . . what are you doing, baby?"

"Nothing, Mama. Just talking to myself." Silver Water sat back and gazed up innocently at her. Tall Man's head had raised from his blankets, those knowing eyes absorbing it all.

Star Shell's soul writhed. Her daughter had never lied to her before.

She squeezed her eyes closed.

Oh, Many Colored Crow, you can't have my daughter! Never!

Silver Water curls beneath her blankets, her cold hands tucked between her knees, watching the Mask pack. It sits across the fire, gleaming red in the glow of the coals. Tall Man is watching it, too. Can he hear the voice? She isn't sure. The dwarf has his head cocked, as though listening hard. Maybe he hears it. He looks a little frightened.

Silver Water wets her dry lips and turns silently to glance over her shoulder. Greets the Sun's robes are still empty. Her mother and Greets the Sun had quarreled. Her mother sleeps fitfully behind her, black hair cascading across her face. Silver Water is glad she's asleep. Her mother wouldn't like it if she knew that Silver Water was still listening to the Mask.

Tall Man smiles at Silver Water. He looks strange in the reddish light, scary. His teeth gleam, orange and pointed.

Only Silver Water's eyes see him. Her soul is far away . . . carried by the voice coming out of the Mask.

It is her voice.

But not her voice now. Her voice years from now.

It has mesmerized Silver Water. How can the Mask hold her grown-up voice inside itself? It holds her voice, and a brilliant flood of moonlight, and a man Dancing in warm, swirling mist. They Dance as one in the Mask. It is odd to know that someday she will have this sultry silver voice.

Tall Man silently rolls to his side and stares directly at her. He mouths the words, *What do you hear?*

So he doesn't know.

She blinks and pretends she didn't understand him.

He props himself up on one elbow and leans toward her whispering, "What is the Mask saying to you?"

His gray braids dangle like short snakes, framing his withered cheeks. When he glances uncomfortably at the Mask, she can see that he really is afraid.

Silver Water whispers back, "She's telling me about you. About the things you've done."

Tall Man's face slackens. "*She?*" A tremor has entered his voice. "Who is *she?*"

It is the way he says it that makes Silver Water tug her blankets up to cover half of her face. The basswood fabric smells like wet dirt. "You know," she answers, and grits her teeth hard.

Tall Man seems to go weak. He lies back and stares unblinking at the ceiling, but his chest is going up and down very fast.

Silver Water studies the Mask pack and thinks: *I am inside it. It swallowed me.*

And from some great distance, a man's voice murmurs, *You don't look like a sorcerer, girl.*

"I'm not a sorcerer," she answers, but no one hears, because the words just walked across her soul. Her teeth are still gritted and groaning against each other.

The dwarf rolls to his opposite side, turning away from Silver Water.

She rubs her nose where the blanket has made it itch. Two owls *hoo-hoo* outside, the calls interrupting each other. It is mating season. They sound eager. Wings whir in the darkness, and Silver Water sits up halfway, listening to these owls who are not afraid. Their calls move closer together, until they seem to be coming from the same place. She holds her breath.

Listening . . . wondering.

Black widow spiders eat their mates. She's seen them do it.

The male is much smaller. Usually, the female bites off his head, then slowly chews up the rest of his body.

Is that what the Mask did to her? Gobbled up her soul in a mating ritual? Is that why her grown-up voice lives there now, in the Mask's belly?

Silver Water quietly slides backward until her bottom touches her mother's legs. Sleepily, her mother reaches out and puts a hand on Silver Water's shoulder. She breathes a sigh of relief.

That's what drove her father mad. Hearing his own voice come out of the Mask's mouth. He couldn't stand it. But what he had heard was a little boy's voice—and it was always angry. Silver Water used to hear it talking to him, whining and demanding. It shouted a lot.

And it made her father cry in huge, breathless sobs.

When he cried, he did bad things. Things that hurt people. Things that hurt Silver Water. And her mother.

That's why she never spoke to that little boy when he called her name. Over and over, he called, "*Silver Water? Silver Water?*" Oh, how he had wanted her to answer.

But Silver Water had hated that boy.

She tips her head back to peer at the Mask pack again. As breaths of wind seep through the walls and blow across the coals, crimson light hesitantly reaches across the floor to stroke the pack. It is a loving gesture.

Silver Water understands why. Tonight, for the first time, she knows that the boy is truly dead.

Grizzly Tooth was no stranger to brutal warfare, but what he saw disturbed even him.

The narrow island was one of the few places close to the east bank of the river where the floods never reached. The land had been ripe for a farmstead for years; however, the people's energies had been directed to the borderlands—settlement on the peripheries being necessary to remind the surrounding folk, especially the Ilini, that these holdings were now, and forever, Khota territory.

Nevertheless, this little island just north of Broken Loom

Creek had been useful for catching Traders in the past. Now it seemed that Eats Dogs had done exactly that—and something had gone terribly wrong.

Wolf of the Dead bent over one of the bodies, waving away the pesky spring flies. "Big Woodpecker," he muttered, staring at the ravaged flesh still clinging to the shattered facial bones.

He placed a hand on the ground, catching his balance as he tottered. Wolf of the Dead hadn't fully recovered from Pearl's attack. Most of his hair had been burned off, and crushed willow plasters had been applied to the worst of his burns. Sometimes he stopped short, wincing from the terrible pain. Or he'd lose his thoughts. Grizzly Tooth had seen enough men hit in the head to know the symptoms.

Overhead in the hickory tree, the crows cawed and the magpies chattered, demanding the departure of the Khota so they could return to their feast.

"I don't understand," Grizzly Tooth said thoughtfully. "No bodies have been carried off. No drag marks. Just one canoe—and you can't tell me that one canoe carried enough warriors to do this!"

Wolf of the Dead rose, swayed on his feet and closed his eyes. Grizzly Tooth steadied him with a painfully blistered hand. "Sit, old friend. Let me study this."

Wolf of the Dead nodded, settling to the ground beside the corpse. He took several deep breaths, the shells and copper effigies on his chest rising and falling with his labored breathing. His ear spools of shining black stone caught the light.

Grizzly Tooth noted the seething anger of his warriors as they walked among the dead, pointing out friends. Most of the bodies had been looted of ornaments—often pieces that had been handed down through generations from father to son. Most peculiarly, many of the dead had been painted with their own blood; designs of fish, birds, spirals, and circles had been dabbed on the exposed flesh.

Why? What did that signify? Grizzly Tooth could think of no enemies who would do that. Were these strangers, then? Some unknown threat?

Grizzly Tooth walked over to Fast Mouse, one of the best trackers. Fast Mouse was slim of build and wore a stained-yellow shirt. He was crouched, his elbows on his knees as he frowned at the rumpled grass.

"How many?" Grizzly Tooth asked.

Fast Mouse answered, "I see three men: one heavy, one medium, one light. I see one dog . . . and one woman."

"Woman?" Grizzly Tooth tensed.

"Woman," Fast Mouse said. "She came down the trail, hurrying, as if running to catch up."

"Pearl," Grizzly Tooth said. "It must be. But where were the others?"

"No others."

"Don't be a fool! There must have been others. Look around you! Two tens and one of our finest warriors are dead! And you say no others?"

Fast Mouse shook his head, his eyes perplexed. "No others, War Leader. The woman, however . . . she threw all of the darts. I found the place where she was hidden in the brush back there. Some of our warriors, they shot darts into the brush, but wildly, not at a target they could see."

Grizzly Tooth turned, spreading his arms. "And you would tell me that three men, one woman, and a dog did *this*?"

Fast Mouse rose, his head bowed. "War Leader, I've walked this place up and down. The sign is in the ground for all to see. The attackers hid here during the day. My guess is that they were sneaking through our territory, traveling by night. Our warriors surprised them in their beds just as evening was falling. You can follow the tracks, see how Eats Dogs laid out the ambush. It was done correctly. Eats Dogs made no mistakes. Then the woman hidden in the brush started killing the men." Fast Mouse shook his hands in confusion. "And after that, it all fell apart! Like an old rotted basket, it came unraveled. But I can tell you this—the big man, he killed most of our warriors. I don't understand how, but he did. Ten and two. I can show you the tracks."

Grizzly Tooth could read the truth in Fast Mouse's eyes— but he couldn't believe it.

"We have to follow them," Grizzly Tooth said.

Wolf of the Dead finally managed to overcome his dizziness and stand. "I agree. Follow them and kill them. No one must learn of this thing. And we killed *none* of them?"

"No, my leader." Grizzly Tooth offered his arm, taking Wolf of the Dead over to the muddy trough where the canoe had been. "But we can find them. Look, there in the mud. This canoe . . . it had a keel."

"A what?"

"A keel. The saltwater Traders use them. It's a thing from the south. And here, see this track, great leader? I *know* that track. I saw it often enough coming up the river from the Anhinga lands. Pearl made that track." And perhaps that explained the curious designs painted on the Dead. It must be a southern ritual. What had she been doing? Cursing their Spirits to oblivion?

Wolf of the Dead squatted down, running his fingers over the marks in the drying mud. When he looked up, an odd glitter lit his eyes. "We will find them, my friend. And when we do, we shall make their deaths so hideous that the stories will be told for generations. No one, *no one* will ever dare to cross the Khota again!"

Twenty-five

Wind gusted ferociously out of the night sky, soughing through the thick mat of branches. Around them, the forest shivered and swayed with the onslaught of the storm. The faint moonlight overhead failed to penetrate the interwoven trees, and soon the storm would overwhelm even that. Did they always have to flee in the dark of night? Did they always have to run when they couldn't see where to put their feet? Star Shell couldn't worry about the brewing tempest.

She had to destroy the Mask before it could destroy her daughter.

"Mama?" Silver Water asked, perhaps sensing her thoughts. The little girl looked like an inky blob moving down the twisting trail.

"Just walk, baby." The fierce wind lashed the swaying branches again, a melody for this late-night exodus. Star Shell forced herself onward, the swift pace more of a punishment than a matter of necessity. Roots tried to snake out and trip her feet. Shadows shrouded holes, uneven ground, and lurking rocks that could twist an ankle or send a person on a painful tumble.

"I would not have guessed that you would come to your senses so soon," Tall Man muttered as he picked his way behind her. She didn't need to look back to see the ugly bulk of the Mask's pack bulging on his back. She could *feel* its presence.

It wants my daughter . . . my darling baby. Why? Why would it want a little girl? How could Silver Water help it with its wicked goals? It all went back to that night when the old woman died. That was when the link had been formed.

I should have turned north then, ignored Robin and his warriors, and traveled straight to the Roaring Water.

Silver Water stumbled, her muffled sob added to Star Shell's determination to get as far as possible from Greets the Sun's isolated little house.

"Mama, I'm tired. I want to—"

"Walk, daughter. You'll have plenty of time to sleep later."

They passed from the trees into a clearing. Star Shell dropped back to walk alongside of Tall Man. "It was a trap, wasn't it? Greets the Sun, I mean. He was so perfect. He offered me everything I didn't have."

"Yes, I think so. And, I must say, one so cunningly wrought that I wasn't absolutely certain—not even when I was so desperate to get you to leave." He walked with his head down, trying to watch his feet in the darkness. "Only when Silver Water's words woke me did I fully understand the lengths to which the Mask would go to distract you from your mission."

"How is it talking to my daughter?" With every step, the coldness grew in her soul.

"I don't know," Tall Man confided. "Bound as it is with the wolfhide, it shouldn't be able to. That night when old . . . you know, my old lover, she took the Mask from the pack. Silver Water was staring at it, Singing that Song afterward. Somehow, through some—"

"She will *never* see it again, do you understand?"

"Yes, yes, of course, but—"

"Never, Tall Man."

"I *understand*, Star Shell. Now, before you kill an old man by running his legs off, what are we doing? Where are we going? Do you have something in mind? Or are you just running like a deer from a cougar's scream, without thought?"

She almost missed a step. "I guess I'm just running."

"And there's something more, isn't there?"

"Mama," Silver Water complained, "I'm tired."

"Remember that night we left Sun Mounds? It's like that again, baby—but not so cold."

Yes, Tall Man, there's more. I need to push myself tonight, to forget the look on Greets the Sun's face when we started packing. Those soft eyes, so wounded, so gently disbelieving.

Star Shell lowered her voice as Tall Man fell in step beside her. "Did Greets the Sun know? Was he involved with the Mask?"

"I really don't think so, Star Shell. I've known the boy since he was born. I doubt that you could find a devious thought anywhere in his soul—and even if he had one, he wouldn't have the slightest idea of what to do with it."

"You don't like him very much, do you?"

"No, it's not that. I like the boy a great deal. We wouldn't have gone there if I didn't *like* him. It's just that he's such a simpleton. That's why the thought of you and him . . . It defies all reason that you'd fall in love with him."

"He's *not* a simpleton."

"Perhaps I read him wrongly, then."

"Perhaps you do."

After a pause, Tall Man asked, "Star Shell, where *are* we going? If you continue down this trail, you'll run into Blue Shroud's farmstead. They have a rather nasty dog . . . or at least they used to. He was getting old, but Blue Shroud is the type to replace one nasty dog with another."

"What do you have against nasty dogs?"

"You've forgotten what it's like to be my size and meet a nasty dog—especially a *big* nasty dog."

"What do you suggest?"

"Ahead of us, where the trail dips down and crosses the creek, a faint path runs downstream on our side. Instead of crossing, let's take the path. It will lead us back up again, but it ends at a rock shelter where hunters camp. From there we can climb to the ridge top, cross the Shroud Clan's fortifications, and take the ridge trail clear down to the Red Buck bottoms.''

''And then, Tall Man? I want to get rid of that horrible Mask. The sooner, the better. I want to go north, Magician. I want this over with!''

As if in answer, lightning flashed whitely across the torn and ragged clouds. The first drops of rain spattered down, and then the fury of the storm broke loose above them.

Dawn had begun to blue the eastern horizon, but Otter and his party continued paddling up the main channel of the Ilini River. Otter felt his way, seeking the weakest current, crisscrossing the channel to make the fastest time. Outside of Black Skull asking an occasional question about the river or their direction, no one had spoken.

Otter continued to fret, torn between guilt and elation over the single most shocking event of his life. The battle on Levee Island played over and over in his head until it had taken on a dreamlike existence. *Did it really happen? Or was it a dream, the kind of fanciful creation of an imaginative soul? Did I really kill those men?*

Haunting eyes, possessed of fear and disbelief, stared at him from his memory. He tightened his hands on the paddle, the feel of it as it crushed bone and flesh memorized in the fiber of his body. He could still hear the sickening impact of wood on flesh. Through the eye of his soul, he watched them die again, and again. Until he died, those warriors would spasm and twitch. Khota loved—just like real people. How many lives, beyond those of the warriors, had been destroyed? Women would weep. Children would cry. Parents would surrender to the aching emptiness of the soul.

Otter applied himself to paddling.

Their ghosts are free, Otter. You'll never pass this section of river again without looking over your shoulder, fearing lest the angry Dead descend upon you.

As it was, he stared uneasily at the dark shadows, at the places where mist hung over the water. Did their ghosts already lurk there? Ready to pounce on a man's soul in enraged retribution?

The temperature had dropped in the night, and the thin sliver of moon wore a faint golden halo, indicating moisture in the air. How soon would the spring storms strike?

Otter leaned forward to set the paddle and used his body weight to propel them forward in the endless rhythm.

"Have you thought about a place to camp?" Black Skull asked quietly. On this voyage, he had learned how far a voice could carry over water.

"That will depend on where we are." In a few moments, Otter had his answer. "That point . . . up on the bluff to the west. See the wooden tower? That's the northern Khota look-out."

"Then what do you suggest, Trader?" Black Skull squinted at the faint outline cast against the purple dawn sky.

"I say we run for it. The flood is dropping, but if we cling to the trees, our outline will be obscured by the branches' shadows. Ilini territory is just ahead, Black Skull."

"Then run we will."

"You need more paddles," Pearl said. "Green Spider, you're no good at this. And you're facing in the wrong direction anyway. Give me your paddle."

The Contrary smiled and clutched his paddle to his chest as if it were a precious infant.

She had spoken the truth, of course. Green Spider rarely dipped his paddle more than halfway, and when he wasn't paddling against them, he was pushing water. Pearl reached over and gently tugged on the paddle until Green Spider relinquished it.

Then she paddled with the strength of a desperation that Otter understood fully. *Wave Dancer* leaped ahead as they bent their backs to the river.

He glanced up nervously at the bluff where the tower stood. *Are the Khota awake up there? Watching? Perhaps relatives of some of the dead warriors who lie so still on Levee Island?*

"And if we pass that lookout?" Pearl asked over her shoulder. "We're safe then?"

Otter chuckled wryly. "All that means is that we're out of Khota territory. But safe? That's another story. The Ilini may or may not protect us, depending on how much they want to risk. That, in turn, will depend on how stirred up the Khota really are. Let me ask you flatly, how mad was Wolf of the Dead?"

She couldn't hide the sudden shiver. "If he's alive—the way the fool says he is—he's going to be plenty mad. Grizzly Tooth will be boiling, too. He didn't care for me even before . . . And besides, we've humiliated them in battle."

"The Khota needed humiliating." Otter measured the distance to the Khota tower. The structure had been built on a sandstone outcrop where the river ran close to the base of the bluff. He didn't remember that it was this close—no more than three dart casts up the hill.

Pearl gripped her paddle harder. "You think I don't know that? I spent the last four moons living with them. But they have their own sense of honor, and we've spit in their faces by killing those warriors. They'll have to make us pay."

"Pay? How?" Black Skull asked, his paddle flashing in the growing glow of morning.

"With our lives," Pearl said shortly. "If they catch us, it won't be pretty."

"Last time they caught us, it wasn't pretty either," Black Skull reminded darkly.

"You were lucky I happened to be hiding in the bushes, or it would have been even 'prettier,' " Pearl retorted.

"Woman, I for one am glad you were there."

Otter smiled. Odd that Pearl had coaxed some humanity from Black Skull, or perhaps it was just winning the battle that had turned him courteous.

Fatigue weighted Otter's arms and shoulders. His lungs began to labor. Pearl must be having a hard time, too, but she showed no signs of slowing down. She kept up with them perfectly, though perspiration darkened her skin and she gasped for breath.

Faint lavender light drained the gray from the world, and Otter could see well now. The water lay calm in the morning shadows under the trees. Bud-fuzzy branches screened the outline of the lookout tower. Ahead, the smooth water had taken on a silver sheen. Odd bits of flotsam broke the glassy surface.

Otter watched Pearl's slender body curve sinuously with each stroke of the paddle. The motion of her shoulders pulled the fabric taut across her muscular buttocks and back and accented her narrow waist. The shining black hair swayed with the movement.

But for Pearl stealing his darts and acting when she did, they'd all be prisoners of the Khota. Otter considered it. No matter how he thought it through, he couldn't imagine Red Moccasins reacting with Pearl's cool efficiency—especially after as harrowing a time as the Anhinga woman must have had at Wolf of the Dead's hands. At the critical instant, Pearl had used her atlatl with a deliberate deadliness.

Would I have done so well? The question plagued Otter. He'd never killed a man before. What would he have done had he been out there in the brush?

With a newfound respect, he watched Pearl paddling. What would a man have to do to prove himself worthy of a woman such as Pearl?

"So why did you throw in with us?" Otter whispered as they drew even with the tower. "You could have lain there, hidden under those hazelnut bushes, and they'd never have found you."

"In spite of what you think, I make mistakes every now and then. Saving your worthless hides might have been one of them," she told him dryly, glancing up toward the tower.

At that moment, a faint cry carried down from the bluffs.

"What's that?" Black Skull demanded.

"How could they see us?" Even as Otter glanced around, he understood. "The wake!"

Wave Dancer's very speed was mirrored and betrayed by the spreading V of wave that she sent rippling across the surface of the water.

"Of all the rotten luck," Black Skull hissed under his breath. "Paddle! Hurry, paddle with all you've got!"

"Water can bear and water can betray, the Khota can see us by the light of day," Green Spider sang out happily. "And I'd say that if we are going to die, we'd better turn around and go the other way.''

''If we make it out of this mess, I swear I'm going to strangle him,'' Black Skull promised.

Green Spider grabbed his throat with both hands, his face reflecting panic and desperation as he gasped for air. His eyeballs rolled back in his head as he stiffened and flopped over backward. Catcher, fascinated by the entire performance, climbed over the packs to lick Green Spider's slack face, his tail making slow arcs of appreciation.

How could the fool mock them during such desperate moments? Didn't he understand their danger?

Otter had no more strength to waste on wondering. He labored on the paddle, feeling the strain on arms, shoulders, and back. Pearl panted in earnest; every time she threw a glance downstream, her imagination spurred her to redoubled efforts. Black Skull paused long enough to shrug out of his coat and change his seat. A damp sheen glistened on his skin as the heavy muscles knotted and rolled under his scarred hide.

''Yes!'' Otter rasped as the river bent to the east. ''Around that bend is Ilini territory!''

Gasping and wheezing, they angled across the channel, gaining a little leeway from the sluggish current. A blood-red sun hung over the irregular horizon now, and light streamed through the tops of the trees as they rounded the bend and passed the Ilini territorial marker. It jutted up from the muddy water, a stout wooden pole with a bear's head carved in the top.

''What's that?'' Black Skull demanded, jerking his head toward yet another high tower on a truncated bluff ahead of them.

''Ilini tower.'' Otter's breath tore as his muscles cramped. ''Like the Khota one we just passed. You'd have a tower, too, if you had Khota for neighbors.''

They maintained the killing pace, forcing *Wave Dancer* to glide along the curving line of trees until Otter used his paddle to send them back across the main current when the river bent northward again. They rounded yet another of the bends in the wide ribbon of water.

''Slow down,'' Otter ordered. ''It's time . . . to get our wind.'' He coughed a couple of times, allowing his pace to dwindle. ''No telling . . . what that lookout could get to . . . chase us.''

Green Spider stood up in the canoe, his skinny arms raised to the morning sun. "A black, black day! Greetings, my dark friend. We thank you for your cool touch and illuminating darkness."

"Is he always like that?" Pearl asked, refusing to look at the Contrary.

"Sometimes he's worse." Black Skull glanced over his shoulder, then rocked the canoe heartily.

Green Spider yipped, clawing at the air, and barely saved himself from pitching headfirst into the water.

For the first time in days, Otter laughed. Black Skull joined in, and Catcher barked happily. The best Pearl could manage was a smile.

The gaiety was short-lived. Green Spider saw them first and pointed ahead. "A sight for weary eyes, my friends."

Otter shot a look over his shoulder and saw the long, slim shape of a Khota war canoe rounding the bend.

"I guess we're paddling again." Pearl's voice had a jagged quality.

"So far, there's only one." Black Skull renewed his powerful strokes, driving *Wave Dancer* ahead. "Let's see how many come after us. We're in Ilini waters now, aren't we?"

"We are," Otter agreed.

"And they watch their Khota neighbors?" Black Skull jerked his head toward the Ilini tower.

"Like turkeys watch a fox."

"Then they probably know that we're in their water?"

"Probably. It depends on how alert that lookout is."

"Well, if only one Khota canoe is following, what will they do? Try to pick a fight on the open water?"

"They're just foul enough to try it," Pearl warned.

Otter took another look over his shoulder. The Khota war canoe came on with lightning swiftness, the sleek shape closing the distance. He could count four flashing paddles.

"How many do you see?" Otter asked.

Pearl stood up, her paddle dripping water. "One canoe, four men on the paddles, that's all, Trader. We're evenly matched. No second canoe in sight."

"Then we may have a chance."

"What do you mean?" Pearl asked. "They're fresh. We've been paddling all night."

Otter thought for a moment.

"I know that look," Black Skull said with a faint smile. "What are you thinking, Otter?"

"They couldn't know about the fight on the levee; we'll have outraced the news this far northward. That means they're just looking for Pearl. The rest of the Khota will be beating the brush for her farther south. What could they know? Only that a Trader has slipped through their net."

"Then why are they following?" Pearl asked, worry bright in her eyes.

"To find out who we are. Put yourself in their place. That northern clan leader is no idiot. He wouldn't have a fool in charge of a border territory. Whoever he is, he'll have received word that Pearl has escaped. All right, so he spots us. He'll send a second canoe racing downstream with the information that we've passed. This canoe—the one that's following—will try to catch us. They'll want to know if Pearl is aboard. That's all."

"So?" Black Skull asked.

"Yes, so?" Pearl demanded. Otter noted that her knuckles were white around the paddle.

"So what if none of these Khota following us have ever seen Pearl?"

"I say we wing a dart at them." Black Skull squinted back downriver, gauging the distance. "They'd never get close enough to get a look."

"And you'll confirm every suspicion. Pearl, quickly, before they get much closer, look into the pack in front of you. You'll find a shirt in there. It's done in the manner of all White Shell weavings. Slip it on and be sure that it completely covers that yellow Khota shirt you're wearing."

"I don't like this," Black Skull muttered, reaching down to make sure his darts were easily at hand.

"Trust me, warrior," Otter said as Pearl dug into the pack and took out one of his heavy shirts. As she slipped it over her head, Otter added, "That gray pot that's sitting behind Green Spider . . . yes, that one. Stuff it under your shirt . . . wife."

"Wife?" she cried, shooting him a startled look.

"Wife!" Otter insisted. "Now. Hurry up! They're getting close."

While Otter kept *Wave Dancer* pointed away from the approaching Khota canoe, Pearl wrestled the big round pot under her shirt, stretching the White Shell fabric tight.

Black Skull began chuckling. "Trader, you're as devious as any fox I know. This might just work."

Pearl blinked, staring down at her protruding belly.

"Let me handle this," Otter reminded. "Pearl, you're Tall Cane Clan, all right? Barely fluent in Trade tongue, and when you do speak it, do so roughly, like it's new to you. Your name is . . . is . . ."

"Fat Frog!" Green Spider cried.

"Right, Fat Frog!" Otter agreed. "We just paddled straight up the river, all right? Stopped at the Khota clan grounds and traded for . . . for . . ."

"Ornaments!" Black Skull said, indicating the sack of loot he'd taken from the dead warriors.

"Right! And Wolf of the Dead himself took ten jars of honey beer in return."

"And a couple of badger bowls," Black Skull added.

"See, you are getting good at this." Otter noticed that the Khota had closed the distance. They'd be hollering soon. "Oh, and Green Spider? When the Khota catch up with us, I want you to howl, scream, and talk so much that no one can get a word in unless they drive it into the conversation with a mallet, understand?"

"No!" the Contrary responded.

"Good."

"You there!" The cry carried across the water. "Hold up!"

Otter brought *Wave Dancer* neatly around, using his paddle to backwater. In pidgin, he shouted back, "We already made our contribution to Khota health and wealth!"

"No weapons out," Black Skull barely whispered.

Otter could see that Pearl had gone tight with fear. She wouldn't break, would she? If so, it could all come apart very fast indeed.

The Khota canoe skipped across the water, the four men as sweat-damp as Otter's party. "Who are you?"

"Four Kills! A Trader of the White Shell people. Who are you?"

"Charcoal Thumb, a warrior of the Khota. You have just come from Khota territory."

"Indeed," Otter replied as the Khota canoe came to rest no more than ten paces off their beam. "And we're now in Ilini territory—as the post back there marks. What does Wolf of the Dead want now?"

The four Khota warriors were staring openly at Pearl, muttering among themselves.

Black Skull bellowed, "He already got our honey beer. Ten pots of it! And our badger bowls. Do you know how valuable badger bowls are? And my purple shirt. I had to Trade Long Squirrel ten tens of sharks' teeth for that purple shirt!"

"All right, all right," Otter hissed from the side of his mouth. "Don't overdo it."

"Who is this woman?" Charcoal Thumb demanded.

"Her name is Fat Frog. A woman of the Tall Cane people. She's my wife."

"We're looking for a woman," Charcoal Thumb stated as he squinted at Pearl.

"I might make you a good deal on this one," Otter told him. "Do you know how many stops a pregnant woman has to make? We'd be most of the way upriver if she didn't have to get out of the boat every half a heartbeat. What an ordeal."

Several of the Khota chuckled. Pearl twisted around, her dark eyes flashing. Whatever that look meant, it boded ill for the future.

Otter added, "This child of hers is coming in another moon. If you think I've got trouble now, just wait until it shits stinky brown goo all over my boat! How about I Trade you straight across? One of your young men, of good wind, strong in the shoulders, for this woman? Oh, and the young man must bring his own paddle and take orders without backtalk."

More Khota laughter broke out.

"Is that right, woman?" Charcoal Thumb asked as the Khota crabbed their canoe closer to *Wave Dancer*.

In pidgin, Pearl responded through gritted teeth. "I did *not* want this trip!" Then, in Anhinga, she told him some other things that Otter couldn't understand, but the tone spoke volumes.

The Khota continued to laugh, all but Charcoal Thumb. The suspicion didn't ebb from his eyes. "What did you Trade for with Wolf of the Dead, White Shell man?"

Black Skull lifted the sack of ornaments. "For all that honey beer, the badger pots, and my purple shirt, we get some trinkets. Do you know what these will be worth?"

Khota expressions remained neutral. Charcoal Thumb said, "You could go back and complain to Wolf of the Dead."

Otter shrugged. "It is of no consequence. We'll be talking to him on the return trip, won't we? It's the price of Trade, isn't it, warrior? We don't have to like it, but we cross Khota territory, drink their water, camp on their land, and fish in their river. Better to Trade for peace than to pay for war."

"And where will you go to Trade?"

"The Ilini. Beyond that, we hope to make it to the Fresh Water Sea. We'll travel north along the shore to the Copper Lands. We have heard of fine warm furs Traded down from the north. Silver fills the ground in the north, too. We would like some of that. Maybe take those things back to Trade around the City of the Dead and among the Copena."

"Copena?" Black Skull growled with a curse. "Not so long as I'm alive, we won't!"

Charcoal Thumb muttered something under his breath in Khota. In pidgin, he said, "Go your way, Trader."

At that, the Khota backpaddled, turning and drifting downriver with the current.

Black Skull sat high in the bow, watching them go as Otter began driving *Wave Dancer* northward. As the Khota passed out of dart range, the warrior began to smile. He knotted a fist, driving it into the palm of his other hand with a loud pop. "You are a worthy man, Otter. You would swindle Many Colored Crow himself out of his feathers."

Pearl wiggled uncomfortably, "delivering" her storage pot. "Fat Frog? *Fat Frog!* I will never forgive you for that. I'd rather be bitten by a water moccasin than be married to you, you leech!"

"What?" Otter cried. "Our first fight! And the baby's not due for another moon at least!"

Pearl grinned then, the first real spirit in her eyes. She leaned forward as she replaced the bowl and shucked off his shirt. "Enjoy your imagination, Trader. The only thing you'll plant inside me is a headache."

Otter glanced back downriver, watching as the Khota paddled around the bend. "They'll be back."

"W—what?" Pearl whirled, her arms braced on the gunwales.

"Charcoal Thumb. Eventually he's going to find out that we tricked him. He'll be just as anxious to hunt us down as Wolf of the Dead is."

Twenty-six

Beneath the jutting stone ledge, Star Shell sat hunched into a ball, knees tight against her chest, her damp blanket about her shoulders. Dawn had arrived gray and dreary. Rain continued to pelt the forest with a soft pattering sound. Water dripped from the spring-ripe branches to spatter on the sodden forest floor. As she exhaled, her breath spun whitely before vanishing in the chill. Thunder growled across the brooding hills and rolled away into a faded challenge.

The hunter's camp had turned out to be little more than a hollow under a cracked sandstone overhang. Beneath it, the ground had eroded to leave an uncomfortable slope on which to perch—and if a person tried to lie down, head safely uphill, his feet would stick out beyond the drip line and get soaked.

Silver Water lay bundled in a hollow they'd scooped from the charcoal-stained soil. Glancing at her daughter, Star Shell's heart ached. Silver Water looked so innocent and sweet in the blankets. Her little girl's face had relaxed, the mouth parted and large eyes closed. Hoary bits of mist clung to her long lashes.

"She's sleeping soundly," Tall Man said.

"She shouldn't be here. It's not fair. My little girl ought to be playing with her friends, making dolls by stuffing rabbit hide with twists of grass. She should be running, jumping, squabbling with friends.'' Star Shell leaned her head back, exhausted. ''What happened to ruin that? Where did it all turn bad?''

''With your husband.'' Tall Man cocked his head as he stared out at the streaks of rain slanting from the galena sky. ''Or perhaps with your husband's grandfather. Or with the last High Head to wear the Mask. It might even go clear back to the man who made it.

''I don't know, Star Shell. If a man drowns in a river, at what point did the water get too deep? Was it in the drop of rain at the top of the mountain? In the freshet on the way to the creek? When the little creek met another and became a bigger creek? You can trace the water all the way to the Salt Water, but the man is still drowned.''

She picked up a stick to scratch at the flecks of charcoal and fire-reddened rock that littered the inside of the shelter. Here and there, bits of bone, burned bluish-black, marked the meals of previous inhabitants. The muscles in her back had cramped. ''I want this over with, Tall Man. We've been running for almost two moons. I'm tired. I'm heartsick.''

''I know, young Star Shell, but it wasn't safe to just start northward. Robin would have tracked us down. You would be dead at best, his captive at worst. Your daughter would have been destroyed along with you. Do you think that StarSky would rally its warriors to rescue a single woman who got in trouble over one of Sun Mounds' religious objects?''

''No.'' She watched cardinals dropping down from the trees in a flutter of red wings to pick among the leaves. It would have been far too dangerous. Not even her beloved father would have dared to suggest such foolishness.

''Then what would you have? You and your daughter dead in a most unsatisfying way, and Robin would be wearing the Mask.''

She did not need to imagine how Robin would have treated her, or Silver Water. Their deaths would not have been pleasant.

She sighed, thinking back to the illusion offered by Greets the Sun. Of all the traps the Mask could have set, that of happiness, safety, and love had been the most devious. The dreamy peace in his honest brown eyes, the warm strength of his body coupling with hers . . .

Would I have been so blinded by his love that I'd have failed to see the Mask working on my daughter?

"Someday," Tall Man promised, "when you look back on this, the lessons will be bittersweet and worthwhile. These days, Star Shell, are the most wonderful of your life."

"If that's supposed to be a joke, I'm not laughing."

"I'm utterly serious." He rubbed his stubby hands together, generating a bit of warmth. "You see, you're vibrantly alive. This adventure will be the most exciting and important event in your life. No matter where you go from here, you will forever look back on these days with awe and enchantment."

"Tall Man, I'm scared, tired, hungry, and hopeless."

"That is true. More than that, however, you're heroic. What a priceless opportunity has been given to you."

"I'll Trade it." *I would have . . . for a dreamy young man and a Hilltop valley.*

"All heroes say that."

She doodled on the ground with her stick, looking at him from the corner of her eye. "What about you? Are you a hero? Is this your priceless opportunity?"

He shook his wizened head sadly. "No, I'm a fool. In the beginning, I thought I would make a deal. Peace in the afterlife. In return, First Man asked me to save the people from the corrupting influence of the Mask. Indeed, I was the one who would set off, rescue the beautiful young Star Shell and pluck the Mask from the very hands of the unworthy."

The rain had picked up to the point that the cardinals retreated to the trees for protection. Bits of cloud wound like wreaths through the rain-darkened forest. "My failings have always been vanity, arrogance, and pride. To be a dwarf . . . that is the most privileged of human states. A dwarf need but walk the clan grounds and all of his desires will be fulfilled. Women will flock to him, hoping for his luck and blessing. Food, of course, is provided without second thought. He need only admire the finest of ornaments, houses, or fields, and they will be bestowed as gifts from the admiring owners. What greater good can come than from the giving of a gift to a magical dwarf?"

"You sound bitter."

"I am." Tall Man spread his arms. "I have watched the illusion pass from my eyes like clouds before a midday sun. I am nothing! *Nothing!* Little more than a parasite. And an arrogant one at that."

"None of this would be happening if it were not for you." Star Shell reached out, taking his hand in hers. "You always know what to do. I'd be lost without you."

His lips quivered, and he refused to look at her. "Yes, you would. And that's why I was sent. It wasn't me, Star Shell. In my vanity, I naturally assumed that *I* was the focus of Power's interest. Fool that I am."

"You're no fool."

"But I am. It's you, Star Shell. You are the focus of Power's interest. I am only a guide and advisor. Power has cast its lot with you. When I am no longer necessary, I shall be discarded like a broken pot."

"I think you're wrong," she said, but the words sounded lame, halfhearted. "You'll see."

But see what? Her answers had fled. All that remained was to take the Mask northward. Throw the thing into the Roaring Water, and then they could see about memories and legends.

The pain inside Wolf of the Dead's skull made him wonder if someone hadn't driven a splintered hardwood stake clear through his brain. The agony had hit him with a stunning suddenness that blurred his vision and made him gasp. He reached up and grabbed his head to make sure it hadn't cracked in two.

He bent over, his vision going gray and narrowing as if he were looking through a long, dusky hole.

"Leader?" Grizzly Tooth asked. The softly spoken word hammered with the impact of a granite-headed maul.

"I'm . . . all right. A moment, that's all. I just need . . . a moment." He forced himself to breathe, to live, to endure the pain. The anguish drained away, and he could blink his eyes, force his trembling muscles to respond to his commands again.

"Leader?" Grizzly Tooth repeated.

Wolf of the Dead managed to look up. He squinted, his eyes

blurry, and saw again the war canoe in which he sat. The slim boat glided aimlessly across the water. All the warriors had stopped, their paddles frozen, to watch him worriedly.

"Pain, that's all." Wolf of the Dead drew more cool air into his fevered lungs; the freshness drove the pain farther away. "It will heal."

Grizzly Tooth squatted before him. "Leader, if I'd had any idea she'd strike, I would have—"

"No, you did your duty, my friend. We just misjudged her animal nature. Who would have guessed her to be so wild, unbreakable."

"Canoe!" one of the warriors behind him announced. "It's coming downriver, fast."

Grizzly Tooth stood up and turned, superbly balanced in the narrow boat as he shaded his eyes to look upriver. "The way they're plying their paddles, they have news. Quickly, let's go meet them."

Wolf of the Dead didn't trust himself to look. The shimmering dizziness could easily return. What had gone wrong? What should have been a four-day celebration had turned into a prolonged search for one skinny girl, and one of his most trusted men had been ambushed and killed by unknown Traders—one of them a woman. The same woman, so Grizzly Tooth said, who had brained him and burned down his house.

Double images wavered when he finally glanced up at the canoe racing toward them. Through the blur, he couldn't quite see who it might be.

"Thumb Clan," Grizzly Tooth said. "That figures."

But the girl was from the south. She should have run in that direction. How could he think when all he wanted to do was to go home, crawl into warm blankets and sleep, and heal, and sleep some more?

"Leader!" a voice called from the other boat. "We have had word from the northern lookouts. A Trader passed the frontier this morning. Four people. Three men and a woman. They tried to sneak past just before dawn, but our lookouts caught them."

"What did they do?"

"Nothing, Leader. Nothing! They did not know what to look for. They let the Trader and his party go."

The information refused to fit into Wolf of the Dead's thoughts.

"It's them," Grizzly Tooth snapped. The popping sound as he smacked his fist into a callused palm nearly shattered Wolf of the Dead's skull as if it were an old cracked pot. "They've eluded us."

The canoe rocked as Grizzly Tooth peered into Wolf of the Dead's unfocused eyes. "Leader, I understand how head wounds affect a man. We must go after them! If they carry the story to the Ilini, tell them that they could insult our leader, burn his house, and kill so many warriors, we will never be safe again. Do you understand?"

"What?" Wolf of the Dead couldn't put the fragments of his thoughts back into place.

"The Ilini, Leader. They outnumber us. We keep them at bay only with our reputation. If they ever unite against us, they could drive our people from this land."

"Yes, yes." It had begun to make sense. The dead warriors . . . their killers had fled northward, to the hated Ilini. Of course. "We must kill them. Just as soon as we find and kill this woman who attacked me."

Grizzly Tooth bent down. "Leader, I think—as I told you— I think she's with the Traders."

"But what if she's not? What if you were wrong about the footprints? This could be some other woman." There, he'd started to think again.

"It won't matter," Grizzly Tooth replied. "We'll say that Pearl is with them. Given the threat to our northern border, we must go and kill these Traders. We'll have to parade their heads back through Ilini territory so that all can see how we repay treachery. And if Pearl's with them, so much the better. If she's not, we'll finish this business, then send an expedition south, to the Anhinga. If Pearl is there, we'll kill her. If not, we'll tell the Anhinga how their daughter disgraced them, and demand more marriages. A showing of northern wealth will overcome any reservations on their part. I know that old woman—Pearl's grandmother—and what drives her."

"Very well. Call the warriors. You're right, of course. To the North. We must find these Traders." *And when we do, they're going to die slowly, over many days, so that all of the Ilini can watch.*

Yes, his thoughts were coming back together. He licked his lips, hardly aware of the gap where his teeth had been knocked out when he was a young man.

That had hurt—but not nearly as much as his cracked head hurt now. Pain must be repaid with pain. Humiliation with humiliation. That was the Khota way.

Once before, a woman had done this.

Her people had wailed for generations.

Twenty-seven

I sense the ripples and changes in the Spirit World. The Mask is moving again, carried along muddy forest trails. I can smell the newborn grass and the earliest wildflowers. Cool breezes rustle through budding leaves.

Power ebbs and flows, Many Colored Crow Dances around First Man, sparring, each of them searching for a new opening, a new way to defeat the other.

Those who bet on human beings must always be prepared, for no matter how a man might start the race, he can't always be counted on to finish it.

I lift my hand. And stare. The blood I washed away long ago still stains the edges of my fingernails.

"So many people," Black Skull remarked as they paddled in the eastern lee of the Ilini River's main current. A faint haze of green shaded the first newly burst buds on the lines of trees that clung to the riverbank. The endless flights of birds darkened the skyways as the flocks flew northward with the spring.

Three canoes currently paddled on courses parallel to *Wave Dancer*'s. Otter's expedition had already been hailed and inspected by the warriors who guarded the border. They had passed more than two tens of canoes pursuing their own business on the water.

"The Ilini are plentiful and prosperous," Otter said with a yawn. He lifted his paddle and raised it high overhead as he stretched out the knotted muscles in his shoulders. They'd been paddling for a full night and day—and had raced the Khota in the bargain. Some relief had come from taking turns. Pearl was a good paddler, and Green Spider, uncharacteristically, had done his share, for once curiously conscious of *this* world.

Otter grinned in anticipation. They'd spend the night sleeping in peace in an Ilini clan house. Otter guided *Wave Dancer* into a small drainage that wound eastward, the course marked by green ash, elm, silver maple, and pin oak.

Mud rings on the tree bark indicated that the water had dropped the depth of a man's arm. Otter saw open patches visible through the trees. The plots still held puddled water or slick mud that had settled after the flooding. "Fields for marsh elder and little barley. After the rains, they'll produce well."

"You're sure there's a village up here?" Pearl asked.

"Oh, the Water Fox knows everything," Black Skull said with a flourish of his hand. Then he gave Otter a crooked grin. Green Spider tipped his head back, belched, and cried, "Nothing! Nothing at all!"

"Greetings, Traders!" a voice called in pidgin, and a canoe slid out of one of the tree-screened backwaters to reveal a man and a woman, each wearing stained, brown clothing. They looked wet and muddy. Their hair was pulled up and tied off at the back of the skull. "You are welcome to Hazel Clan territory. Where are you from?"

"From downriver!" Otter called back. "And fairly won!"

"May the Khota rot!" the Ilini woman returned, but she was smiling as they paddled alongside. *Wave Dancer* dwarfed their little dugout. The man had a broad face, lined by humor and too much sun. His broad shoulders suggested endless exposure to hard work and long familiarity with the paddle. The woman appeared stoutly built, and from the laugh lines and crow's-feet at the corners of her eyes, she shared her husband's enjoyment of life.

"You've had a bit of luck!" Catfish and suckers lay in the canoe bottom, along with piles of damp netting. Long-handled gigs with splay-barbed points lay to one side with atlatl darts, coils of twine, and a broken fish trap.

The man chuckled, wiping a mud-speckled hand under his nose. "We built a weir at a place I know of in the backswamp. When it floods, the fish swim in. When the waters drop, the only way out is blocked by the weir. Those we don't catch in the fish traps, we net."

"We might Trade for a couple of those fish," Otter told him, accenting the words with one of his winning smiles.

The man seemed to notice Black Skull for the first time and stopped short. His wife caught his interest and stared, too. "This man? He has been hurt?"

Black Skull spoke. "I'm a warrior."

The Ilini glanced uneasily at Otter. "Must Traders now carry warriors to pass the vile Khota?"

"No. We're on a journey to the far north." Otter indicated Green Spider, who had leaned over the side of the canoe and was trying to sink a stick with his forefinger. He poked it down into the water, only to look slightly surprised when it bobbed up again. Otter smiled and said, "Green Spider is a Contrary. Many Colored Crow gave him a Vision, and now we follow it northward."

"A Vision! From Many Colored Crow?" The man spoke rapidly to his wife in Ilini. Then he stared unabashed at Green Spider. "I . . . we are blessed. Forgive me. I am called Three Legs, and my wife was originally named Woman Who Walks With Mist In The Morning. As you would no doubt guess, it was shortened. We call her Baker now."

"Baker?" Pearl asked.

"For the breads she makes with goosefoot, hazelnut, and duck potato."

Otter indicated Pearl. "This beautiful woman is Pearl, from the far-off Anhinga Clan. And I am known as the Water Fox, a Trader of the White Shell people."

"Ah! We are honored to meet you," Baker exclaimed, nodding. "You have come from very far away. No wonder you look tired. I would imagine that after passing the Khota, you are ready for a hot meal and a good night's rest. My husband's brother is clan leader here. Our lineage has farmed and hunted this land from the time First Man walked the earth and gave the Ilini the rules of life. Come, be welcome among us. We will lead the way.''

At that, the man backwatered to turn the canoe, and he and his wife paddled up the winding watercourse.

''That's more like it,'' Black Skull growled over his shoulder.

''Maybe.'' Pearl appeared pensive. ''They weren't sure what to make of your story about Green Spider's Vision.''

''How do you know that?'' Black Skull asked.

''I read people well,'' she replied flatly.

The Hazel clan grounds sat on the northern bank of the creek, at the point where a headland came sloping down from the bluffs. The main mound had been built on a high terrace overlooking the landing and was surrounded by the various clan and society houses. Three Legs shouted at the top of his lungs, announcing the arrival of Traders. People turned to stare.

The air was redolent with the smell of wood smoke as *Wave Dancer* beached at the landing. Continued cries from their escorts brought people running from all directions. Dogs barked and children shrieked. Smiles filled the Ilini faces as people clasped their hands and chattered to each other.

''Quite a greeting,'' Pearl remarked as she jumped over the side and helped to pull *Wave Dancer* onto the packed soil of the landing. Drying racks and canoe rests lined the bank.

''The Khota have slowed Trade considerably,'' Otter replied. ''That's why Wolf of the Dead sent his best friend downriver to your people. Traders are bypassing the area. The Ilini are starved for goods—especially for the goods they need for their burials and sacred rites.''

Catcher growled at the camp dogs that came to sniff at his canoe and was rewarded when one of the Ilini adults instructed the older children to kick and cuff the camp dogs out of Catcher's range.

Three Legs shouted the names of Otter and his party, indicating each with a nod of the head. Then he almost pushed Otter up the slope.

After the ritual greetings to the ghosts, Otter and his party were escorted to the clan house. Along the way, Otter noticed that people had dropped what they were doing at the arrival of the newcomers. A section of basswood bark, half-shredded into cordage, lay beside a pile of limestone rocks, pestle and mortar, and a half-filled ceramic jar, where someone had been turning the gray rock into temper for pottery; a hickory stave stood propped on a shelter amidst a wealth of white curled shavings, the stave beginning to taper into a new fishing spear; water boiled in large, thick-walled pots that squatted in a fire. Camp dogs fought over a meaty deer skull from which the tongue, hide, and brains had been removed. How prosperous these people were that they hadn't bothered to render the head meat!

Broken nut shells, squash rinds, and hulls from sunflower seeds had been kicked out of the main paths, some hastily swept into gaping storage pits that had emptied over the winter.

"Come," Three Legs called, elbowing his way forward with Baker at his side. Behind them, the people trooped along in happy retinue.

The large, dark clan house smelled of sooty fires, dusty earth, fabrics, and thatch. No benches lined the walls, but large jars, many of them decorated with punctations and incised designs, had been placed there on their conical bottoms. Baskets and net bags hung from the walls. In the rear, ceremonial masks had been suspended—the visages of laughing old men, curve-nosed women, deer, raccoons, and frogs. All were exquisitely carved, and ornamented with mica, shell, and copper inlay.

People crowded in, filling the place.

Behind the fire, the clan leader stood. He was dressed in a colorful blue-and-white-patterned blanket, a buff-colored shirt, and high moccasins. His face had little resemblance to Three Legs', being rather long and narrow. A tight bun, held in place by a long copper pin, adorned the top of his head.

The Ilini leader spread his arms wide. "Greetings, Traders. I, Silent Owl, bid you welcome to the holdings of the Hazel Clan. May your sons all be strong, and may your children's children continue to bring honor and wealth to Many Colored Crow, to your ancestors, and to your clan."

Otter responded with a greeting of his own. Even as they went through the rituals, young boys hurried in with firewood, building up the blaze in the central hearth.

Otter offered Silent Owl a bit of tobacco to start the pipe for the traditional prayers. After Otter had drawn deeply and exhaled the sweet smoke, he passed the pipe first to Green Spider, then to Black Skull, and finally, to Pearl.

When ghosts and Spirits had been attended to, the clan leader pressed a hand to his chest. "I am Silent Owl, son of Great Owl. I declare you my guests and ask that you be seated."

As usual, Green Spider promptly started for the door. Otter had to tell him to go away before the Contrary came back and flopped himself before the fire. Otter proceeded with the introductions, aware that Black Skull seemed curiously at ease. What had changed in the warrior's attitude toward strangers? Was it the battle at Levee Island? A little blood, and he was fine?

Silent Owl raised his voice. "Someone go and bring these Traders food!"

Pearl had seated herself behind Otter, farther back than she needed to. Why? Maybe she'd just had enough of people and worry and all that went with it. So be it. He could understand her reticence.

Silent Owl exhaled a mouthful of blue smoke. "You have successfully passed the Khota. And with a mostly full canoe." He smiled then. "I think I know who you are . . . the one they call the Water Fox. Your boat has been described to us by other Traders. Your reputation for honesty and Power in Trade has traveled far and wide. You are a friend of the Ilini."

"I am so known among many peoples," Otter said. Then he related their passage through the Khota lands, briefly mentioning the battle at Levee Island.

"We killed two tens and one of their warriors," Black Skull growled in Otter's tongue. "Don't you want to tell them of that?"

Otter hesitated, but by then, Silent Owl's curiosity had been piqued. He turned back. "Noble Clan Leader, I'm afraid that we had more than a little trouble with the Khota. We were forced to kill some of their warriors."

"Some?" Black Skull cried, smacking his fist to his breast.

"How many?" Silent Owl asked.

"Two tens and one!" Black Skull bellowed.

Otter winced. *Why didn't I think? I should have told him to keep quiet. Too late now.*

Gasps sounded from the people listening. Excited whispering followed.

Silent Owl leaned back, his gaze shifting from the proud Black Skull to Otter. "You act apologetic, Water Fox. The Ilini will not weep for a few Khota dead, but tell me, how did you ambush them? How many of your party did you lose?"

"We did not ambush them," Black Skull stated bluntly in pidgin. "They attacked us. And we needed no help in killing their pitiful excuses for men."

Silent Owl's eyes widened. "Oh, for such an ugly man, you tell a very beautiful story."

"Lies, lies, all lies!" Green Spider cried out as he jumped to his feet and flapped his arms. The Contrary looked around the suddenly quiet room. "I ask you, who is alive . . . and who dead? I would say that Eats Dogs and his twenty are experiencing the unbounded exuberance of life, while that Khota leader and his war chief—whose names we can't speak—are but Spirits . . . ghosts. The sort of shadows we can only appeal to in prayers! Gone, gone, here and gone."

"What is he saying?" Silent Owl asked uneasily.

"Stop!" Green Spider motioned everyone in the room to remain where they were, though no one would have even entertained the thought of leaving. "I can't stand this rushing about. *Relax!* We are in no hurry!"

"Idiot!" Black Skull muttered under his breath. Then he added, "The fool distracted the Khota long enough for me to get my club."

"Forget that!" Green Spider pounced like a weasel and pointed a skinny finger into Black Skull's face. "That never happened, Killer of Men. They are alive! More so now than when you, Pearl, and Otter killed them."

Silent Owl leaned toward Otter, his hand indicating the warrior and the Contrary. "What *is* this?"

Otter shifted uneasily. "A message, noble clan leader. The Contrary is warning us of something. But I—"

"Not *you*, great Trader!" Green Spider whirled around, dropping to all fours to stare into Otter's eyes. "Relax, man of the White Shell. Take your time. No one follows you. They wouldn't dare. Not with the Killer of Men in your company. Or with fragile Pearl to dissuade them."

Otter's heart started to pound. "I see."

"You see what?" Black Skull asked, scowling uneasily at Green Spider.

Something akin to panic had grown in Pearl's beautiful dark eyes. She leaned forward to whisper to the warrior, "He's a lunatic!"

Black Skull nodded wearily.

Otter avoided Green Spider's peering eyes, craning his neck to see the Hazel clan leader. "I ask your advice, great Silent Owl of the Ilini. What will the Khota do? We have killed two tens and one of their warriors when they would have taken us, robbed us of our goods, and harmed this woman."

Silent Owl looked uneasily from face to face, studying them. "This is true then? You did kill their warriors?"

Black Skull reached into his shirt and tossed a copper effigy across the fire. Silent Owl caught it with a snap of the fist, holding the piece up for inspection. Firelight gleamed on burnished copper, although stains of red blood mottled the edges. The piece looked like a turtle's head, with two freshwater pearls inlaid for eyes.

Black Skull indicated Pearl. "Her first dart killed him. He was the war leader of the party that tried to capture us."

Silent Owl tossed the ornament back too quickly—the way he would were it hot to the touch. He rubbed his fingers on his blanket for a moment. "I know that piece. It was worn by Eats Dogs."

The mutterings of the crowd had taken an ominous tone. Expressions had hardened, some with skepticism, some with satisfaction.

"That was his name," Otter agreed, his stomach churning. This night might not find him resting so well after all.

Silent Owl's long face looked pinched in the firelight. He glanced furtively at the onlookers, then back at Otter, Black Skull, Pearl, and Green Spider. His hesitation broke when Green Spider began slinking around the fire, his movements particularly catlike. The Contrary sniffed a couple of times in Silent Owl's direction, then rolled back on his haunches.

Silent Owl spoke tensely. "You have asked my advice. To you, this killing might seem like a remarkable stunt—assuming your words are true, which I still doubt. But let us agree that you did this thing. Perhaps it was the Power of this Contrary. Perhaps the skill of this warrior. I am more inclined to believe that you ambushed the Khota, trapped them somehow and—''

''I have told you,'' Black Skull bristled, ''that they surrounded *us*.''

''It's all right.'' Otter raised his hand to stop any further outbursts. ''Please continue, Silent Owl. I await the counsel of your words.''

To Otter's immense displeasure, Green Spider threw back his head and belched in the crudest of fashions. Then he said, ''Think this through, renowned clan leader. We offer you the fulfillment of your greatest wish. The greatest gain always comes with the greatest wish. Chance flies with the speed of a swallow, darting this way and that. Will you allow the bird to fly and pursue the desire of your people?''

The clan leader studied Green Spider with narrowed eyes before he spoke. ''As I was saying, we live beside the Khota. Not so long ago, within our memory, they came down from the north, took that land where they now live. That was Ilini land. We fought them then, and we fight them now—distant cousins though they might be.''

Three Legs and one of the old women had leaned forward, each speaking in Ilini. Something in their manner hinted at trouble.

Silent Owl raised a hand to silence his counselors and addressed himself to Otter. ''If you have killed one of their war parties—no matter what your justification—they will follow you. I advise you to rest this night. Eat your fill and sleep in peace. But if I were you, I would be gone with the first morning light.''

Green Spider jumped around, still on all fours. ''Never! Not the Khota! Cowards all—and afraid to fight. I can see them now, trembling in their lodges. They wouldn't walk across a deer trail, let alone chase us across the world. No, they'd allow the Water Fox to spit in the faces of their ancestors and insult their leaders! They laugh! They cower! See them?''

Otter closed his eyes for a moment, imagining the Khota as they whipped themselves into a seething rage. He could see Wolf of the Dead, that ugly visage twisted in hatred. When he opened his eyes again, Silent Owl's counselors were whispering once more, casting wary glances toward Otter and Black Skull.

The Hazel clan leader waved them off and said: "You're in a lot of trouble, Trader. Your Contrary might act like a fool, but I think I'd study what he says. He knows more than any of us."

A weary inevitability weighted Otter's soul. The Contrary was watching him, but this time, those normally vacant eyes had a deadly intensity.

Pearl lay flat on her back, a blanket pulled up to her chin. She should have been asleep, but unease nagged at her. She stared up at the dark thatch roof and listened to the warrior, Black Skull, snoring in his bedroll. She could hear a dog barking somewhere on the other side of the grass-and-pole wall of the Ilini clan house. The animal sounded distant, perhaps down by the edge of the fields near the foot of the slope.

Sleep no longer provided rest. Instead, the nightmares strangled any peace she might have found. Wolf of the Dead, the Khota, that horrifying night—all came back to be relived. The humiliation sawed constantly at her soul.

She'd hoped that killing those Khota would help, and perhaps it had. She couldn't be sure, but Eats Dogs might have been one of the warriors who'd held her that night. One Arm and Round Scar, yes, she could remember them. And Grizzly Tooth, of course. Some of the debt had been repaid, but she would never heal, not all the way. Even now when she accidentally touched Otter or Black Skull, the contact tripped shivers and a strangling revulsion.

A baby squalled somewhere.

Pearl rose soundlessly to her feet and wrapped her blanket around her. She stepped over the warrior's bedding and hesitated. The Contrary's bedroll lay flat and empty in the faint light.

Stealthily, she ducked through the doorway. Only the tied-back hanging rustled on her clothing.

The night air smelled of water, damp earth, and humans:

smoke, housing, manure, and decomposition. The growing moon angled light over the Ilini clan grounds. At another time, the soft rhythms of the night would have soothed her. Here, they were but an illusion.

Pearl tugged her blanket tight against the cold night air. The Khota would pursue her. She'd known that from those first days on the river. Neither forgiveness nor understanding played any part in Khota culture.

She crossed her arms, hugging herself. The moon hung over the eastern horizon, a shining crescent. For as far as she could see in the half-light, fields dotted the land before giving way to stands of trees. This valley was a lush place, producing all that the Ilini needed. The tall society houses and large burial mound were indicative of industry and activity.

With so many resources, why didn't the Ilini mass their numbers and retake the land the Khota had stolen? Or had the Ilini, too, accepted the myth of Khota invincibility?

She sensed, rather than saw, movement and turned to see the Trader duck out of the doorway she'd just exited. He wore his fox coat against the night's chill.

"Couldn't sleep either," he confessed as he tucked his thumbs into his belt. "I should be in there sleeping as soundly as a corpse in a tomb. Instead, I just kept running things through my mind. Tired and worried, I guess."

"It's not a time for easy sleeping." In the pale light, she studied his face, noting the strong angle of the jaw, the thin nose and straightforward eyes. Such a handsome man, well respected, and talented. His every action toward her had been generous and thoughtful. His wife must consider herself a very lucky woman.

Why did I never find such a man? And, if I had, would I have had the sense to ask for him? No, she wouldn't have. Among the Anhinga, she'd never have seen past the entrapment of family and clan duties. For the first time, she experienced a pang of regret, an unfamiliar loneliness welling inside her. Among the Anhinga, she could come and go, share moments with kin and friends. Among the Khota, she'd been buoyed by the battle of wits, plotting escape and revenge. Tonight, here in the thin moonlight in this strange village, the truth of her situation finally settled on her. She would be alone, friendless, for the rest of her life.

The Anhinga would not take her back. She was a woman adrift, without family, lineage, or clan to give her identity. She belonged nowhere. Without clan to speak for her, what clan would marry her? Word would travel up and down the rivers.

She glanced uncertainly at the handsome man standing beside her, suddenly curious. Would Otter and his friends still be as kind when it occurred to them that she was so totally alone and vulnerable?

Otter broke the silence, asking, "I still don't understand. Why did you fight for us? You could have hidden . . . waited. You didn't need to kill that warrior. No one would have known you were anywhere around."

She chose her words with care. "I don't know. Perhaps I couldn't bear the thought of anyone falling into Khota hands. They would have humiliated you before they killed you . . . and they were in a mood to kill."

"I thought maybe it was more than that."

She studied him for a moment, balancing his serious concern against her vulnerable circumstance. *He pulled me out of the river, and since then, he's been only kind.* "Actually, it was. It had to do with something the Contrary said. About fear, and cowardice, and how I would live. I wanted to hide and let them pass. The Contrary said that I had to make a decision. That I had to live or die—and I chose to live, to face my fears."

Otter's smile indicated that he'd already figured that out. "You could stay here. The Ilini would hide you until a Trader comes by who is headed downriver. He could manage somehow to get you home."

"Am I to understand that you don't want me to go with you?" The question brought her a sudden anxiety. "Haven't I carried my weight?"

Amusement twisted his lips. "Oh, yes, more than I would ever have expected from such a slender woman. I just wanted you to know that you have options. And—" he hesitated and exhaled a heavy breath "—I also want you to know that I can find you a way home. I know almost all the Traders who pass here. I could leave a message, explain—"

"No." She gazed up at the thousands of stars that dusted the heavens. He would figure it out anyway, so she said: ''Tell me, what would I have to go home to? My clan . . . my people, they sold me for copper plate. The Anhinga would consider my return dishonorable. They gave me in alleged marriage to that bloodsucking leech, Wolf of the Dead. Toothless, two-footed trash that he is.''

I should have driven something sharp through his anus and pinned him in the fire. Perhaps then he would know how I felt being penetrated by him.

''Do you want to tell me about it?''

Of all the stupid questions. ''No. Thank you.''

''Pearl, I want you to understand. They'll come after us. And even if we do outrun the Khota, there are other dangers ahead. The Fresh Water Sea, strange people, unknown lands. Myself, I've never been past the passage to the Fresh Water Sea. I can't tell you what we'll find out there. Possibly people even worse than the Khota.''

''Why are you so worried about me?''

''I don't know.'' He shrugged those broad shoulders. ''Given the way you throw a dart, you can take excellent care of yourself. I just don't want you to—''

''Stop it.''

''Stop what?''

''Worrying about me. Otter, no matter what, I'm on my own. I can't . . . I won't return to the Anhinga. Neither they nor I could stand it if I did. I definitely don't want to stay here. These people are scared to death of the things we told them. For a while, back in the clan house, Silent Owl was asking Three Legs and that Bone Jar woman whether or not it wouldn't be better to just tie us up and give us back to the Khota.''

Otter straightened, staring at her. ''You speak their tongue?''

''It's like Khota. A bit different accent, but similar enough. Silent Owl said they were cousins of some sort. I know the Khota tongue. I spent all those moons listening to it as I traveled upriver . . . learning it in spite of myself. I guess it proved good for something.''

''What else did they say?''

She rubbed her arms as she looked up. What had the Contrary meant when he asked if she could see the blackness between the stars? ''Some of them don't believe that we could have killed two tens and one of the Khota—especially not Eats Dogs and his raiders. They're split on that, but the concensus is that if we did kill that many Khota, Wolf of the Dead will stop at nothing—not even a desperate war with the Ilini—to capture us.''

"I thought as much." He frowned, lips pursed. "I'm not a good judge of things when the Khota are involved. They killed my Uncle. They've robbed me in the past. When I think of them, anger builds and I lose what little sense I have.''

"Otter, listen to me. A great many of these Ilini that you like so much wouldn't hesitate to turn you over to the Khota. The only thing that's saved us so far is that they don't know I was Wolf of the Dead's wife, and they're scared witless of skinny little Green Spider.''

"Wife? I thought—''

"Never mind. Getting back to the point, they hate the Khota, true, but we might be more trouble to them than their hate is worth. If they knew how much they could gain by handing us over . . . well, it frightens me.''

"I didn't want Black Skull to bring up the matter of the killed warriors. Rot him, he doesn't have the sense to know when to shut his mouth.''

"But he can sure fight." She grinned at the memory.

"Indeed. Had you not cast your dart when you did, and had he not been the warrior he is renowned as, we'd have been lost.''

She gave him a sober appraisal. Grandmother had once told her that a man's face mirrored his soul. If so, Otter's soul was attractive, strong, gentle, and smart. Barring Grandmother's failings—of which Pearl had become more than aware—she'd found no guile or deceit in his words or actions.

"Be honest with me," Pearl said. "I've heard of you. You're supposed to be one of the most successful Traders on the river. And Black Skull is no ordinary warrior, but the best I've ever seen, maybe the best in the whole world. And Green Spider, he is certainly a Contrary. Tell me what this is really all about.''

Otter took a breath, held it for a moment, then let it out filled with words. "It's about a Mask—a special Mask, one in the land of the Serpent Clans. On the winter solstice, Green Spider was killed by lightning. While he was dead, he flew over the world with Many Colored Crow and saw this journey unfolding. It ends up at a big waterfall some place on the other side of the Fresh Water Sea. We have to get there and save the Mask. I'm sure there's more, but that's all that Green Spider has revealed.''

She raised an eyebrow. ''Why didn't Many Colored Crow find someone closer to home? Surely they have Traders, Contraries, and warriors in the land of the Serpent Clans.''

Otter lifted his hands in supplication. ''I don't know. Black Skull definitely did *not* want to go anywhere except back to the City of the Dead. Green Spider . . . well, you know what he's like. He wanted Black Skull and me to take him north. The warrior couldn't refuse.''

''And you, Trader? Why did you come on this journey?''

He looked away. ''I—I needed to.''

''Running away?''

''Perhaps.''

''Can't control your wife, or is it that your in-laws make you too miserable? I've heard that a lot of men go into Trading for that reason.''

''I have no in-laws.''

Pearl's brows raised. What woman wouldn't jump at the chance to marry this man? Handsome, strong, and at the same time, enchantingly vulnerable—a perfect alliance for any aspiring clan. ''Something wrong with your White Shell people? A bit of scandal, or gossip?''

He chuckled, making a throwaway motion. ''Stop it, Fat Frog. It's nothing like that.''

''*Fat Frog!*'' She folded her arms. ''Tell me and I'll shut up.''

''A Trade then,'' he countered, turning to stare at her. ''I'll tell you why I ran away . . . if you'll tell me what happened with Wolf of the Dead.''

Curse him for understanding and using that tenderness. ''No Trade.''

He relaxed, the easy smile slipping back in place. ''Then we have established the value that each of us places on private matters.''

She sidestepped. ''What do you know about Green Spider?''

''What can anyone know about a Contrary? Half the time

you're laughing at him; the other half, you're scared stiff that he knows something you don't.''

"You seem to think he knows where to go. How to get there.''

"He's seen the way. I must trust that.''

"And he warns you about things before they happen?''

"Sometimes, but never with an outright statement like, 'Take that left channel or you're going to capsize and drown.' He'll tell you just the opposite of what he wants you to do. You saw him do that earlier tonight in the Ilini clan house. All that business about Wolf of the Dead not caring what we did to him. That was all a pointed warning.''

"I was close enough on Levee Island to hear him talk about Eats Dogs' wife having a lover. Eats Dogs seemed to believe it.''

Otter laced his hands behind his back. "It seems impossible, but Green Spider knows a great deal more than he tells—and you can't pry it out of him. If you put too much pressure on him, he goes empty, becomes a silly fool with that dislocated look in his eyes. If you ask me, he knew exactly what he was saying to Eats Dogs, knew exactly the reaction it would evoke, and exactly when your dart would strike home. Pearl, he'd seen that encounter before it happened.''

Pearl, what have you become involved with? She steepled her fingers before her mouth. *How could Green Spider have known about the dolphin?* And he had known that she was about to lose her soul to fear. She asked, "Then why didn't he warn you about the Khota? Give you time to escape? We didn't *have* to kill those warriors. If we hadn't, you wouldn't be in this mess.''

"Well, unless . . .''

"What?''

"Unless those warriors *did* have to die, to force you to come with us. It's as if . . . well, Power is using us, but who knows for how many different purposes?''

Power is using us? She shivered, suddenly aware of the shadows, of the way the moonlight played tricks on the eyes. Did Power stalk her? Why had the Trader's canoe happened to be there just when she desperately needed it? What were the chances that a fugitive would find rescue in the black of night in a flooded river?

Eerie premonition came to her. "Wolf of the Dead is alive because Power didn't want me to kill him. Power saved him—not the wolf mask."

"What?"

She lifted a hand to still him, grasping for the pattern; but it turned illusive, slipping away. "So Power is driving us to this waterfall?"

"Yes, as far as I—" Otter froze, staring out across the moon-lit fields.

Pearl turned to see. There, out in the goosefoot fields, she could see a man and a dog. The man jumped, turned, and ran, then circled and darted back the way he'd come. From the flopping clothing and the loose-limbed gait, she could recognize Green Spider. The big dog copied his antics, obviously enjoying the play.

"If that's Catcher," Otter promised, "I'm going to beat him to death for leaving the canoe and the packs!"

"No." She placed a hand on his arm, hardly aware of what she'd done. "Wait. There's something odd . . ."

Deceived by the distance, she thought at first she was indeed watching the Contrary at play with Catcher. Then the animal sped across the stubble and came to rest beside the man.

"That's no dog, Trader. That's a wolf."

Twenty-eight

I have the freedom to choose. I could have refused. It was, after all, nothing more than a cry in the darkness. But that soft whimper touched my heart—and so I rose and went out to meet the wolf.

Strange, of all the souls in nature, only human beings and Power place any importance on human promises. The other creatures learned of our perfidy long ago.

But I did not refuse . . . and his words have confused me. What had been one clear path now forks.

Yet each trail leads me to the same destination.

He asked little of me. Gave me no time limit for deciding. But when I hesitated, he did ask me to remember that no decision was, in itself, a decision.

I must never let that thought stray far from my soul. . . .

White flashes of lightning zigzagged across the ragged clouds, followed by thunder that shook the ground and rolled off the forested hills. Every freshet ran, every puddle brimmed, patterned by the widening ripples of raindrops. Swollen creeks overflowed their banks and washed over the alluvial bottoms in leaden sheets.

Every inch of Star Shell's body was cold and soaked. Her moccasins squished, each step wringing as much water out of the soggy leather as the next accumulated.

Images of Greets the Sun's dry house clung to her like midsummer cobwebs. Warmth, fire, security—all gone. He would never again smile for her, never reach out with those strong, gentle hands.

Star Shell rehitched her pack on her back and gave the low, dark clouds an inspection filled with misery. In no direction could she see the incipient shine of clearing skies, only the constant threat of more rain.

"I'm shivering," Silver Water declared. "I want to go home. I want my grandma."

"I know, baby. But we've got to keep going. We'll find a place to get warm soon."

"Down there." Tall Man pointed across a flat that now looked more like a shallow lake. "That's the Red Buck bottomlands. Past those fields we'll find a small earthen enclosure with a society house. They'll take us in."

"More of your friends, Magician? So far, each friend we've met has paid dearly for our arrival." She arched an eyebrow, and the water running down her cold face changed course.

"You have a better idea then, young Star Shell? Night is coming."

"Mama, let's go there! I'm freezing," Silver Water insisted. As wet as she was, her hair soaked and stringy, she looked like a very miserable little girl.

It's not her fault. Why does she have to suffer? Star Shell glared angrily at the Mask pack before slogging through the wet grass. Clinging berry bushes impeded the path that led down the slope to the rain-dappled brown waters. Distant thunder echoed in the hills.

She hesitated, looking across the sullen pools. Stalks from last year's harvest stood in mute testament to the water's depth—mid-thigh deep. Silver Water and Tall Man might find themselves wet to the chest. Did it matter? They were all soaked through and through.

Doggedly, Star Shell started forward into the shallows. Her feet sank in slippery mud. Looking between the boles of trees that lined the fields, she saw water in every direction.

"Mama, I don't like this!" Silver Water waded deeper, her eyes casting about uncertainly. Her mouth puckered with discomfort.

"Just follow me, little one. I won't let you drown," her mother said, then added, "It's just like pearl diving, Cricket. This is what pearl divers do."

Silver Water appeared to be slightly mollified.

They waded across the field and entered a maze of trees that reached upward to the charcoal skies. Star Shell slipped, sloshed about, and recovered. A dead squirrel floated past, its head down, its tail stuck straight out behind a fan of dark fur. Star Shell winced and looked away.

"Look, Mama, a squirrel. It's dead."

"Leave it alone, baby. Let it be dead by itself."

Star Shell glanced back to where Tall Man labored through the mucky water, the Mask pack bowing his back.

How does he stand being so close to that thing? And what did he mean when he said that he was incidental to this entire tragedy?

"Head more to the left," Tall Man called. "In this water, among these trees, you can lose your way, go around and around."

"Since you know the way . . ." Star Shell gestured him forward, the action slinging droplets from her waterlogged fringes.

"That way." He pointed. "Go on. It will take me longer than you."

She hadn't liked the idea of following behind the Mask anyway, so she picked a line of sight from tree to tree in the direction he'd indicated.

Branches, bits of foliage and bark, floated past—the leavings of the years since the last such flood. But the muddy land finally reappeared, and Star Shell waded the last steps to a grassy hummock. Through the trees, she could see a clearing, and beyond that, an earthen embankment. Either her imagination tricked her or the faint odor of smoke lingered on the rain-purified air.

Climbing through the rain and gathering darkness, she made her way around the circumference of the sacred enclosure. Instead of the low spots normally used to mark the solstice, lunar movements, and other celestial events, tall posts had been set at the highest part of the berm. Each had been painted a different color and topped with a carved head—either animal or human. One or two, she saw, looked like monsters. Something about them, the weathered look, or the fact that many stood slightly askew, conjured the sense of abandonment and neglect.

"He's getting careless," a caustic Tall Man said. She shot a look over her shoulder to see the dwarf fingering a two-year-old sapling. "All of these should have been chopped out." He pointed to the numerous young trees that climbed the slope toward the Circle.

Concerned only with her own misery, Star Shell shivered and hurried forward. She thought she saw a single opening—it was hard to tell in the misty rain—on the eastern side of the Circle, and hesitated uncertainly.

"Where are we, Mama?" Silver Water asked uneasily.

"At the Heavens," Tall Man told them. Then he raised his voice and spoke in a language Star Shell had never heard. As the singsong words rolled off the Magician's tongue, he lifted his hands, holding them outward toward the dark and rainy skies. He shifted to face inward, toward the opening. The words sounded hard on the throat, guttural and strained, but the language had a sense of poetry to it.

When he had finished, Star Shell asked, "Should I call a blessing for the ghosts?"

"You could if you wished, but there are no ghosts here. No, the blessing has been called—and with greater eloquence than you could ever muster, young Star Shell." He paused. "Though I'm not sure of how much longer such words will be spoken in the world of men."

Tall Man then ambled through the gap, his awkward gait giving him a wobbling motion. Suddenly he threw his arms up in frustration. "Look! This is a disgrace! Weeds are growing out of the barrow pit inside the Circle!"

Star Shell waited until the pack containing the Mask moved ahead before she grabbed her daughter's hand and followed. Now flooded, the barrow pit inside the wall was indeed full of weeds, and upon closer inspection, young trees as well.

The rest of the interior of the Circle brimmed with new grass and ever-widening puddles. Instead of walking toward the center, Tall Man angled across toward the northwest. At the precise center, she could see a series of posts set in a circle around a small mound—as was the wont of the High Heads. The posts were short, leaning outward, and each had a standard, or tassel, flying from its end.

"Look at this!" Tall Man kicked at another young tree, this one little more than a shoot that had found root in the thick grass. "Inside the Circle! What's he doing? Spending so much time after dark with the stars that he misses things like this?"

"It's just a tree," Silver Water remarked.

Tall Man spun on a stiff leg to face her. "Would you allow a tree to grow in the clan grounds at Sun Mounds?"

"I guess not."

The beaten path they followed ended at a bark-sided hut covered with a gabled roof. Smoke—perhaps she'd been right when she thought she smelled it—hung in a bluish wreath about the top of the building and hinted at hickory wood burning within.

"Greetings!" Tall Man stopped before the door flap and swung the Mask pack from his shoulder. "Tall Man, Magician of the High Heads, asks who might be within!"

After several long moments, an old man stuck his head through the door flap. He squinted against the rain and tilted his head back as if to see better. "Tall Man did you say? Is that you?"

"Of course it's me! Would I have announced myself if it wasn't?"

"What are you doing here?" the Elder demanded. "The whole countryside is searching for you. They say that you have the Mask of Many Colored Crow—and that you've been murdering people and doing witchcraft all over the place."

"Who says?"

"Why, people do. Are you?"

"Of course not! I don't need the Mask to do witchcraft. You know that."

"Then why are you here?"

"Because, you old fool, you just said that the whole countryside is searching for me. Who would think—or dare—to look here? I thought this place would be safe."

"I suppose it might be." The old man pulled back slightly as a gust of rain pelted out of the darkness. "Nobody comes here anymore . . . except the trees, of course. Each summer I have to take a hoe and chop the saplings out."

"You missed more than a few. What do you do, wait until they grow up so tall that you can't see the sky?"

"I see *fine*! You haven't been talking to my idiot grandson, have you? Did he send you up here to bother me? He's worse than a wood tick in the folds of a man's scrotum."

"We need a place to stay."

"I thought you had one. Down at the Many Circles'."

"I do. We need a place to stay now, here. Have you lost all of the sense you used to have?"

"I don't know. Have I?"

"So it would seem," Tall Man declared indignantly. "It's getting dark!"

"Stars are rising," the Elder said, his voice softening. "Two-Headed Dog is at the zenith tonight. Right overhead, on the plumb pole."

Another gust of wind drove cold rain down in a vigorous burst. The old man drew his head back again, something like a turtle into its shell, and he cried, "It's raining out there, did you know that?"

"Of course, you silly old—"

"Don't call *me* silly!" the Elder replied, wagging a warning finger in Tall Man's direction. "I'm not the one standing out in the rain!"

"Well, blessed First Man save us, *can we come in out of the rain*?"

"Of course! What sort of friend would I be to leave you out in the storm when there's a perfectly good house here?" And the turtle head ducked back into the house shell for good this time.

Tall Man glanced at Star Shell. "He might be a little worse than I remember. If so, bear with him. We won't be here long . . . and he was a very great man once."

"What is this place?" Star Shell asked, staring around at the rain-splashed grounds.

"It's called 'the Heavens.' It's an observatory, one that hasn't been used much since the Flat Pipe have intermarried with the High Heads. This is still a place of old knowledge. No one knows when it was built . . . back in the First Days, I suppose. It's not very well situated. Some of the hills block the view of the horizon." Tall Man ducked under the flap.

Star Shell stood dripping and uncomfortable, unwilling to enter the society house. The Heavens had a feel of age, of old Power lying in wait. No good would come of this.

"Mama? I'm cold." Silver Water tugged at her hand.

"Are you coming?" Tall Man's head popped out of the doorway the way the Elder's had done earlier.

"Let's go in, Mama," Silver Water mumbled miserably. "I'm cold, and hungry, and tired. It looks warm in there. And dry, Mama. Maybe it's dry."

Star Shell ducked down, pushing her pack ahead of her through the doorway, and stopped wide-eyed as Silver Water scuttled through behind her.

It took a moment for Star Shell to realize what she saw. The entire inside of the house was draped with dark blue fabric on which had been painted white dots, apparently at random. A fire—hickory, indeed—crackled and popped in the center of the room. The Elder had retreated to the far side and now squinted down his fleshy nose as he studied them. He wore an old blanket over his thin shoulders, the fabric blue like the wall hangings and covered with white dots. Worn-out moccasins had been laced optimistically to his feet, and a thick loin cloth twisted about his waist.

Tall Man placed the Mask pack carefully to one side and shrugged out of his dripping coat.

"So that's the famous Star Shell?" the old man asked. "Come here, woman. Bring your daughter. Let me look at you."

Star Shell overcame her reluctance and took Silver Water's hand before she stepped up to the fire. In the glow, she and the old man studied each other. His gray hair had been gathered and spilled down his back. The eyes were faded, slightly gray in the firelight, like a dead fox's. Wrinkled brown skin bunched under the jaw and hung loosely from his cheeks and throat. The fleshy nose was hooked like a hawk's. Once-bright tattoos had faded on his leathery skin, and thick ceramic ear spools filled his earlobes.

"Yes, Elder. I am Star Shell, and this is my daughter, Silver Water. We thank you for your welcome and hospitality."

"You do? I would have left you standing in the rain were it not for the Magician demanding to be let in." No change of expression appeared on his shrunken face.

"Show some manners, Stargazer," Tall Man reproved while he fussed with his wet clothing. "Or have you gazed into the heavens for so long you've forgotten that you, too, are human?"

Star Shell's heart skipped. Stargazer? The High Head holy man? Was that who this ancient bag of bones was?

"That's right," Tall Man said as he saw Star Shell's shock. "I couldn't think of any other place to take you where tongues wouldn't wag and we wouldn't get into trouble. This Mask, it's a trial. People are just too curious. I learned that from my old lover."

"*Which* old lover?" Stargazer demanded. "I'm surprised that you can keep them straight."

The Magician looked acidly at his old friend.

Star Shell grew uncomfortably aware of the water dripping from her drenched clothing to puddle on the dirt floor. As soon as Stargazer noticed what a mess she was making, well, who knew what his reaction would be? He might turn her into a slug on a dry tree or something equally horrible.

Silver Water tucked a dirty finger in her mouth. She seemed

fascinated by the white dots on the dark background of the room's hangings. The rest of the household reflected a caring hand; each jar was neatly in its place. All of the ceramics were beautifully crafted ceremonial ware, with intricate designs and workmanship.

"You must make yourself at home, young Star Shell," Tall Man said kindly. "Stargazer couldn't care less about your comfort. People have never been high on the list of his concerns."

As if to emphasize that, Stargazer asked, "What are you doing here, Magician?"

"Surely I can spend a night with an old friend. Give us a good rest, and perhaps the news, and we'll be on our way in the morning." Tall Man waved at the soot-thick roof where rain pounded. "You're not going to observe the sky tonight."

"I can see the stars just fine from here," Stargazer growled as he seated himself. He extended a thin arm, one finger pointing upward at an angle. "The Fox constellation lies there." The arm moved. "The Hero Twins rise in the east, the seven prominent stars just visible over the horizon. To the west, early in the evening, Spider sinks . . . never to rise again until the fall equinox approaches. And then Spider comes from the east! And the Planting star, it waits just under the eastern horizon. The Hero Twins will rise and make way for the Planting star. All chasing Spider away."

"Odd, isn't it?" Tall Man had stripped down to his loincloth and was spreading his clothing over a couple of big pots to dry. "Spider is the harbinger of winter, yet in the First Days, it was Spider who brought fire to man. You'd think Spider would dance around the sky to be a summer constellation."

"Yes, but Spider is also the Trickster!" Stargazer turned his head to the west, where the constellation lay hidden behind the storm. "We are all tricked by life, old friend. Everything is temporary. Nothing remains. Of all the mysteries I've ever considered, the most perplexing is why the Mysterious One made the world—and men—so fragile."

"Fragile?" Tall Man asked as he walked over to the fire, extending his hands. "Star Shell, get out of that wet clothing. Warm up. You'll need to dry your bedding. Silver Water's, too."

"Fragile," Stargazer insisted, turning his odd gray gaze on

Tall Man. With a finger, he pointed to his head. "Generation upon generation have accumulated the knowledge that I keep here. And when I am gone, Magician, it will go with me. None of the young come here to study. They go to StarSky, or Great Serpent, or to the Flat Pipe places on the Moonshell. They enter the Star societies there and study those new things. Not the old things. Not *our* things."

As Star Shell undressed and spread her wet clothing before the fire, she noticed that Tall Man looked particularly somber. The Magician said, "It's a lot of the same knowledge. The same movement of stars and the same change of seasons. Places like StarSky, they're just bigger. They serve more people."

"But the old ways," Stargazer insisted, "are dying. Even here, old friend. Simple things. My son doesn't even say the blessing in the old language anymore. He says it in common tongue, not ritual words."

"It was said tonight in the ritual language," Tall Man replied.

"I am pleased to hear that. And after I am gone, and you are gone, and a handful of others are gone? Who then will say the blessing? The world is changing, and it frightens me. Power is shifting, playing games. The ways of our fathers are fading, like a yellow fabric in the sun."

"I noticed that the path was not as well worn as it used to be." Tall Man paused, uncertainty on his weary face. "Do you still show the stars to people?"

"On those rare instances when they come. Most come seeking the answers to the silliest of questions. They want to know who they will marry. Will the Trading be good? Should I be buried with a copper gorget or a mica gorget? Will my husband find out about the affair I'm having?" The old man kept his gaze fixed on the ceiling as he pointed upward. "But for the storm, you'd see Flying Bat beginning his ascendance."

Star Shell caught herself looking, trying to decide which constellation Flying Bat might be. "Would that be River Otter, or Black Bear, to the Flat Pipe?"

"You see?" Stargazer's voice filled with lonely disgust as he turned gray-dead eyes on Star Shell. "Who couldn't recognize Flying Bat? No one has the wisdom of the Elders." His voice broke. "It will be gone. What was the Mysterious One up to the time he made this world? Truth should not change with the generations. Truth is Truth.''

Tall Man asked, "Are you all right?"

"Of course, fool! Don't I look all right? I'm just disgusted, that's all. Enraged by the world and the injustices within it. Now I hear you're a witch?"

"I've always been a sorcerer. It's never bothered you before."

"Are you still murdering people?"

Star Shell's hands clenched involuntarily.

"No." Tall Man sighed, rubbing his face. "I gave that up many years ago. The ghosts kept bothering me every time I'd go near where someone that I had killed was buried."

"Will you tell me truly, old friend?" Stargazer asked as he studied Star Shell with those empty eyes. "Do you still look up at the stars and remember their right names? Or are you, too, prey to these new Flat Pipe ways?"

Tall Man pointed at the pack that carried the Mask of Many Colored Crow. "There's your answer, old friend."

"She's a young woman. And Flat Pipe at that! Didn't know where to find Flying Bat! And what are you doing with a pretty young woman? At your age! Still sating your endless lust! You should be home telling your grandchildren the old stories."

Tall Man cocked his head uneasily. On tiptoes, he moved silently across the room. Stargazer's gaze remained on Star Shell, his expression distasteful.

Tall Man made no sound as he waved his hand to one side of Stargazer's head. Only when the waving hand came between the Elder and the fire did he receive a reaction.

Stargazer's head bobbed as if he were searching for something. "What foolishness are you up to? More witching, you silly little man? Get you around a Power object like that Mask and you think you're a clown!"

Tall Man sighed as he placed his small hand on Stargazer's thin shoulder. The old High Head jumped, reached up to grasp the hand, and looked at the Magician. "Magician, what are you doing? Go over and sit down. You're interrupting my concentration. Here I am, shutting off the world, trying to think, and you're bothering me."

"I understand, old friend."

"Stop whining like an orphaned fawn."

Tall Man appeared stricken. Star Shell could see that another light had gone out of his soul—just as it had from the famed High Head Elder's blind eyes.

Not since the days of Wolf of the Dead's father had so many canoes been assembled. More than ten tens of warriors had crossed the Khota border and landed their canoes on this island in the middle of the Ilini River.

The river came rolling and twisting down from the north. The beach, so recently underwater, remained littered with bits of wood and other flotsam. The cottonwoods behind him had fuzzed out in new green, and the leaves on the willows were already full. High overhead, waves of birds blackened the sky on their northward migration. This was a good day for a meeting—sunny, though he could smell rain on the wind.

Fortunately, Wolf of the Dead's head had remained clear, his thoughts as sharp as fractured obsidian. Now, in the midmorning sun, he faced Silent Owl, leader of the Hazel Clan. A narrow strip of sand, muddied by the recent flood, separated them.

Silent Owl spoke first. "I thought you'd come." The Ilini accent always inclined Wolf of the Dead to rage. Once he'd caught an Ilini who spoke the language so poorly that he'd had the wretch's tongue cut out and discreetly fed to a Trader who had been traveling north. The amusement came from the thought that the Trader would have shit the boy's tongue out in the very village where he'd lived.

And that remained exactly what Wolf of the Dead thought of the Ilini pronunciation of an otherwise beautiful language.

"You thought I'd come?" Wolf of the Dead, of course, ignored the lisp his lack of teeth gave to his own words.

Silent Owl crossed his arms. The Ilini warriors lined out behind him fingered their war clubs, clearly uneasy at the number of feared Khota who'd crossed the boundary. "We've heard the most curious stories. Four Traders stopped here last night.

Among their other brags, they claimed to have killed . . . let's see, yes, two tens and one of your warriors.''

"We will eat their hearts!" Round Scar hissed.

Wolf of the Dead raised a hand to still his warriors. The rage in Charcoal Thumb's face would have cowed a tornado itself.

"I believe they might have exaggerated the number," Grizzly Tooth interjected, glancing worriedly at Wolf of the Dead.

"Indeed they did," Wolf of the Dead replied easily. "These Traders killed two young boys who stumbled upon their camp. Now the murderers have turned the number to two tens and one? Four men?"

Laughter followed as Wolf of the Dead gave the cue behind his back. Grizzly Tooth looked relieved. What did he think, that just because of a blow to the head, Wolf of the Dead had lost all sense?

"Three men, and a woman," Silent Owl replied, an intensity in his eyes. "We, of course, doubted the number ourselves."

Wolf of the Dead crossed his arms. "Were such individuals to have arrived in Khota territory, we would have been suspicious. It would have been our policy to hold them on some pretext or another, and perhaps to send a canoe to inquire of our northern cousins as to the true nature of the claims."

Silent Owl nodded, a faint smile hovering about his lips. "Under other circumstances, so might we. However, this was no ordinary Trader. You've heard of the Water Fox? I believe your father killed his uncle when the man sidestepped your robbers one time too many."

So they were after the Water Fox. Well, good. That was an old score to settle—one that Wolf of the Dead had put off for too long. More than one rumor had passed up the river that the Water Fox repeatedly slipped through Khota lands like a ghost. That he'd traveled so far through their territory before Eats Dogs had stumbled upon him proved the point. How had the Trader known of that little island, anyway?

"But beyond that," Silent Owl continued, "he was in the company of a Contrary, a man called Green Spider."

"Perhaps a trick." Wolf of the Dead waved it away, aware of what such rumors would do to the morale of his men.

"I would have thought so, too," Silent Owl said quietly. "However, I had a watch put on all of them. The Contrary slipped away in the night. I was alerted immediately, and with my own eyes, I saw him playing in the moonlight."

"Playing? You saw him *playing*?" Wolf of the Dead laughed, his warriors following his lead. "Then maybe he's just a lunatic. Playing with what? Himself? No woman would have him?" More coarse laughter.

Silent Owl and the Ilini warriors remained steadfast, expressionless. "No, Khota leader, he was out in the fields playing with a big, black wolf. A wild wolf that no one had seen until the Traders arrived. Several of my young men tried tracking the animal this morning. As you know, the rains and floods have left the ground soft, muddy. A child could track in these conditions, but this wolf has vanished. It's as if it never entered the fields—and never left them."

"Some can track, and others . . ." Wolf of the Dead raised his hands to avert attention from the wolf story. "What of this woman?"

"Pearl, a woman from the—"

"I'll spit the bitch on a green pole and roast her!" Grizzly Tooth roared, stepping forward, his fists clenched.

Wolf of the Dead placed a restraining hand on his friend's swelling biceps. "Later, my friend."

Silent Owl appeared unimpressed by the outbreak. "You had better be very good, War Leader. Just before the sun rose this morning, I watched the warrior traveling with her practicing with his war club. He moves like magic, almost as if in a whirling dance. His club is heavy beyond what a man should be able to wield gracefully, yet he twirls it like a straw." Silent Owl paused, then added, "Having seen him, I could almost believe that two tens and one men would fall to his skill."

"What does he look like?" Grizzly Tooth demanded. "I have never met the man who could face me."

"This one is big, muscular. Arms thick, like most men's legs might be. His skin is scarred all over, from many fights. You will know him when you see him, because his face is broken, one cheek crushed. The jaw sits at an angle, and when he's mad, or upset, the muscles in his face twitch."

"The canoe," Wolf of the Dead said, getting back to the palpable things. "It has the fox head carved on the front?"

"That is the boat," Silent Owl agreed.

"The Water Fox carries Trade goods?"

"Many packs, all looking full."

"Then he won't be moving fast."

"I would think not."

"Silent Owl, we would ask permission to cross your territory. This Water Fox has committed crimes against us. We will cause no harm to your lands or people. What we need, we will pay for. If any Khota warrior harms an innocent person of the Ilini people, he will be disciplined by me before he is turned over to the clan he has offended for their fair retribution. On these words, I will let my blood, so that you will know the truth of what I say."

Wolf of the Dead reached into his belt pouch and withdrew a large flake—itself a wealth of sacred chert. Refusing to flinch, he sliced his skin over the wrist before dropping his arm so the blood would trickle down and drip off his fingers and onto the sand.

Pensive, Silent Owl stood watching the blood drip in red star-bursts on the mud-tan sand. What thoughts passed behind those calculating eyes? Wolf of the Dead glanced at Grizzly Tooth, the big warrior now as tense as a bent hickory stem. Something was missing, some clue that Wolf of the Dead didn't quite grasp. What? Silent Owl seemed too sure of himself.

"Very well, Khota leader, you may pass the Ilini lands on the terms that I, and all of my warriors, have heard. We will accept your blood, and your bond."

Wolf of the Dead smiled grimly at Grizzly Tooth. "You know my orders. Tell all of my warriors so that they will understand the agreement reached by Wolf of the Dead and Silent Owl."

And now we race northward to find these four killers.

To Silent Owl, he said, "We will stop on our way back downriver. I will show you these three men and this one woman. You will see a bit of their death, but not all of it, for they shall die slowly."

Silent Owl sat in his canoe, the vessel rocking with the waves as he watched the Khota warriors assembling on the parley island. Wolf of the Dead had well over fifteen tens of warriors, and more coming.

Silent Owl watched . . . and worried. The largest Khota war party since the conquest of the lower Ilini was forming before his eyes. Either it was a ruse to decoy the Ilini, or the Water Fox and his party had indeed dealt Khota manhood and pride a severe blow.

The Contrary's words echoed in Silent Owl's memory. His most fervent desire had always been to break the Khota stranglehold on the lower river. Was this the opportunity he'd only been able to fantasize about?

"I don't like this," Three Legs whispered.

"I don't either." Silent Owl rubbed his chin. "But let's think, cousin. The Water Fox didn't want Black Skull to tell us about the dead warriors. I don't think that was a trick. The Water Fox was clearly dismayed. The Contrary could have warned the Trader that Wolf of the Dead would follow them while they were still out on the river. He waited; and then— if he really is the Contrary I believe him to be—he played with the wolf where we could see him. A wolf? Curious, don't you think?"

"But to have so many Khota warriors on *our* territory!" Three Legs threw his hands up. "What if they find the Trader in the next couple of days? Just how good is Wolf of the Dead's oath?"

My question exactly. Silent Owl made his decision. Yes, it was a gamble, but the Contrary's words continued to plague him. Silent Owl began to see how it might work. "I want three canoes dispatched. Pick our strongest young men. One canoe shall take the east side of the river and warn our people. The other shall take the west side and give similar warning. Along with the alarm, they shall ask for warriors to head south. Surreptitiously and carefully. We will assemble back from the river at the place where the rosebushes grow.''

"And the third canoe?"

"The fastest of the three, I want to race upriver and find the Water Fox. If he's smart, he's already making good time. I want to see to it that he knows just what is after him and how fast it's coming.''

"You're going to help him get away?" Three Legs wondered.

"Absolutely. Pass the word that any help that can be given to him, must be given. The Hazel Clan will reimburse for any food, equipment . . . or anything else.''

"I don't understand.''

"Dear brother, I believe the story that Black Skull, Pearl, and the Water Fox told about killing those warriors. All of them. Nothing else would explain why Wolf of the Dead and Grizzly Tooth are so desperate to catch them. Wolf of the Dead is off balance. He's not thinking clearly, and neither is his war leader. They have promised, in blood, to pass peacefully, and we know that the Water Fox is headed for the Fresh Water Sea.

"Wolf of the Dead cannot allow the Water Fox to escape. He *must* capture the Trader's party or the Khota will have lost their luster of invincibility. Now, if Wolf of the Dead is willing to strip twenty tens of warriors, or more, out of his territory—"

"Maggots and flies!" Three Legs nodded in understanding. "You're the right choice for clan leader, all right. This is our chance!''

"Indeed it is. I'm hoping the Water Fox can lead Wolf of the Dead clear across the Fresh Water Sea.''

"Blessed First Man!" Three Legs cried, clapping his hands. "And may none of the Khota ever make it back! I think I know just who to send with each canoe. If the Water Fox is slow, he'll know what's behind him by afternoon. If he's fast, by tomorrow midday.''

Twenty-nine

For three sets of barracuda jaws that the Ilini would make into necklaces, and for palmetto-frond mats that they would use to cover their floors, Otter had received several baskets of dried fish, three jars of hickory oil, and two deerhide parfleches full of desiccated berries and hazelnuts. For a broken conch shell that the Ilini would cut up for beads, Otter received a finely woven hunting shirt to replace Pearl's Khota garment, and a new paddle, which he presented to her.

The paddle—fittingly decorated with jumping fish—had been crafted from white ash. The knob at the top of the handle had been carved into the likeness of a raven's head—just right for this expedition.

As the sun broke over the eastern horizon, *Wave Dancer* nosed her way down the creek and into the swollen brown waters of the Ilini River.

To Otter's surprise, Green Spider looked perfectly rested, as if he'd enjoyed a blissful night's sleep. To glance at his happy face, you'd never guess that the Contrary had spent the night out in a field playing tag with a wild wolf. Now he whistled and clapped his hands with delight as he stared at the reflection of the sun on the water. From his glowing expression, it might have been a totally new experience to him.

"He's fascinated by the simplest of things," Pearl murmured to herself, stroking easily with her new paddle.

"Simple?" Green Spider wondered as he leaned over the side to stare inquisitively at the sparkles of sunlight on water. Catcher, too, perched on the edge of the gunwale, tipping the boat as he tried to fathom Green Spider's latest interest. The dog's tail waved back and forth lazily.

"I call it idiocy," Black Skull told them from the bow.

"I don't know." Green Spider scratched his head, perplexed. "Puzzling, I'd say."

"And why is that, Green Spider?" Otter asked.

"Well, the sun bounces off the water. You've all seen that. Why doesn't your face get wet?"

"Wet?" Black Skull demanded as he surveyed the river for other canoes. "What does that have to do with being simple?"

"The sun shines through the water." Green Spider made a circle with his hand, one into which he could fit the sun's reflected orb. "If I pat my hand on the water, my hand gets wet. The reflection ought to get wet, too!"

"Of all the lunatic ideas!" Black Skull muttered, shaking himself like a dog shedding water.

Catcher continued to peer at the water with rapt attention as Green Spider stretched out and precariously tried to splash the sun. "Look! I can break the sun into lots and lots of little pieces!"

"You're getting me wet!" Pearl yelled as droplets of water went awry from Green Spider's splashing.

"Me, too!" Black Skull bellowed, twisting around to glare at Green Spider. "Stop it! Right now, fool, or I'll crawl back there and pinch your head off at the neck!"

Green Spider grinned at the wide rings of ripples he'd made and sat up straight, his face thoughtful. "There! I saved the world."

Pearl resumed her rhythmic use of the paddle, and the jumbled rings were left behind in *Wave Dancer*'s V-shaped wake. "How's that, Green Spider?"

"If I'd have kept up that splashing, the sun might have gone out. Then wouldn't the world be in a real fix? It would have taken days to find all those pieces of sun floating around and put them back together."

Otter shook his head. The problem was that with Green Spider, you were never sure just when he might be telling the truth.

And that, my friend, is a frightening thought indeed.

"Green Spider?" Pearl asked, trying for all the world to be casual. "Are we headed for any danger today?"

"Lots of it. We'll all drown today . . . and I almost put the sun out. That would have been pretty dangerous. We'd just have to bump around in the dark."

"The reason you didn't put the sun out was because I threatened to kill you first." Black Skull looked back. His lopsided grin didn't communicate humor, no matter what the warrior's intent. "It's a nice thing to know that I can have that kind of influence on you, fool. A little threat on my part, and the world ends up saved. Think of that next time you want to splash water on people."

Green Spider's curious gaze seemed to sharpen. "How true, Killer of Men! Of all the people I know, you have the greatest of all influences!" He paused. "But tell me, do you think the water heard you?"

"The water?" Bewildered, Black Skull glanced around the canoe as it slipped across the glassy river.

"Surely the water," Green Spider returned. "For I just stopped the splashing. It was the water that stopped jumping all over you. It didn't have to stop splashing just because I did."

"Of all the ridiculous . . ." Black Skull swiveled back to his rowing, but from the set of his shoulders, Green Spider had touched a hidden sore spot.

"Canoe." Pearl noted, but the oncoming vessel turned out to be two boys returning from an early morning check of snare sets.

Most of the canoes they passed veered in their direction to shout a greeting, and the others at least waved. As Black Skull had noted, it was indeed a busy river.

The crow appeared around midmorning, squawking and flapping as it circled the boat. The birds had been ominously absent ever since Black Skull killed the one down south. This bird, however, seemed intent on *Wave Dancer*.

"Black Skull," Otter warned, "leave this one alone."

"I've learned my lesson, Trader. Don't worry about me." The warrior glanced up with nervous eyes. His expression had gone ashen—but then, so had Green Spider's.

The fool stood up, spreading his hands wide as the crow clucked and *thwock*ed while it flapped in tight circles around the canoe. Green Spider shouted, "No!"

The crow chattered, the musical cries clearly angry.

"Well, what do you expect? I couldn't just ignore him!"

The crow tucked and dove, skimming just over Green Spider's head, a long screech adding to the effect as the Contrary ducked.

Green Spider regained his stance in the wobbling boat and shouted, "I didn't tell him anything! I mean . . . nothing important! He just wanted to talk, that's all!"

The crow erupted in chatter and fluttered in place just out of reach.

Green Spider shouted, "What do you mean, you don't believe me?"

With a final burst of clacks and caws, the crow flew off to the east, its wings rasping the air.

All eyes were on Green Spider, who sighed heavily.

"What was that all about?" Pearl asked uncomfortably.

Green Spider's befuddled gaze drifted over the horizon. "Did you know that a good sense of humor isn't appreciated by just anyone?"

Otter tightened his hold on his paddle. "Green Spider, last night the wolf—"

"Dancing 'round and 'round," the Contrary chortled. "Up and down, down and up, the crow is chasing 'round the wolf pup." And he laughed hysterically. Laughing and laughing until tears streaked his triangular face.

"Green Spider?" Pearl asked uneasily. "Are you all right?"

"I couldn't be better," the Contrary said, sniffing and wiping his eyes. "All is peace. Such tranquillity." He sat down backwards then and draped a blanket over his head.

For long moments, the canoe drifted while they looked uneasily at each other. Otter finally ground his teeth, raised his paddle, and started them northward.

The storm blew in from the west at midday, preceded by fluffy patches of cloud that fled before the tempest. As sheets of cold rain lashed down, *Wave Dancer* traveled on, her paddlers cloaked in blankets and capes. But Catcher, curled in a black, white, and tan ball, lay wet and shivering until Green Spider managed to shelter him under a portion of blanket.

"Are we going to find a clan house to stay in?" Black Skull stared up at the tormented sky.

A fine, misty rain fell, casting patterns on the choppy water and either beating on Otter or relenting long enough to allow him a quick gauge of their progress. Was this the crow's doing?

"No!" Otter had made his decision earlier that day. "Pearl heard some talk among the Ilini last night. Half of them wanted to turn us over to the Khota; and being a good Trader, I can understand the attraction. For another thing, the Khota *will* follow us. Wolf of the Dead can't afford to let us go. Too much Khota honor is tied up in this. First, Pearl whacks him over the head and burns his house. Second, we wipe out one of his war parties." Otter grinned. "What would you do, warrior, if someone did that to you?"

"Run him down and kill him—" Black Skull slitted his eyes "—in a manner that would chill the guts in anyone thinking about attempting the same."

Otter continued. "Stopping at a clan house always takes time—greetings, prayers, feasts, rituals, everyone wanting the news. We'll spend half the night talking and not sleeping. No, I say we camp along the way. Concentrate on making time upriver."

So they did, camping on a low knoll formed from a narrow neck between oxbows that had been pinched off when the river changed course. Previous travelers had appreciated the knoll's proximity to the river as well as its elevation over flood stage. Trees provided protection from the wind and allowed them to erect shelters from the storm. Charcoal smears, burned bone, fired limestone, and even an old house site, remained on the rounded crown.

Otter carried the last load of supplies up from *Wave Dancer*, slipping in the slimy brown mud left by the receding floodwaters.

"Can a person eat that?" Black Skull stared at the fish that Otter had bartered several stingray spines and a couple of shark's teeth for. They'd Traded with a fisherman who'd come alongside in his canoe, the huge gray fish in the bottom. The thing was as long as a man's leg, not counting the long, flat bill that stuck out of its nose for another arm's length.

"It looks like a shark," Pearl declared but shook her head when she fingered the smooth sides of the fish. "Too tender. Where I come from, we use sharkskin for sanding wood."

"It's a paddlefish," Otter told them. "And this one is small. They live in the backwaters and oxbows. I've heard that they stir up the mud with their bills, use them like digging sticks.

You can't catch them with a hook and line, but must spear them, or net them.''

Black Skull cocked his head skeptically; Green Spider made cooing noises as he poked at the creature's eyes, tiny for the size of the beast.

"Now, when you cut it up," Otter cautioned, "you'll find two kinds of meat, red, like deer, and white, like fish—"

"I'll eat the red meat," Black Skull declared. "Red meat is always stronger than white."

Otter dropped the pack down beside their little fire. Tiny droplets of rain, more a mist actually, continued to filter down through the branches overhead. "That's fine, but I'll warn you now, the red meat tastes like mud, whereas the white is sweet, tender, and delicious."

Pearl used a sharp flake to slice the fish open. "No bones! Not a one!''

When the fish had cooked, Black Skull made a show out of eating the red meat—but Otter noticed that most of it somehow slipped from the warrior's carved wooden platter into Catcher's mouth. After a decent interval in which to save face, the warrior went back to the half-eaten pile of white meat and proceeded to stuff himself.

Black Skull and Green Spider unrolled their blankets under the lean-to they'd constructed, but Otter hunched at the fire with Pearl. She was using a crooked branch to poke at the coals, her damp hair hanging down on either side of her delicate face. The flickers of light accented the contours of her skin and the fullness of her lips.

How did you end up here? Some man should be loving you, admiring you for all that you are. He stifled a sudden desire to reach out and touch her. During the day, his gaze kept straying to her slim waist, the full, rounded curves of her buttocks, and the way her glossy hair hung down her back. He'd watched her as she paddled, hoping for a glimpse of her profile, attracted by the smooth motions of her paddling.

I should be thinking of Red Moccasins. He frowned at the coals Pearl poked with her stick. After the Khota, Pearl wouldn't be interested in any man.

He said, "I'm surprised you're still up. After last night, I thought you'd head for your robes first."

She smiled, firelight highlighting her perfect cheeks. "Too much to think about, I guess. But you're right. I am tired. Look at these blisters. How did I ever get so soft? Can you believe that I used to paddle day in and night out?"

The blisters looked red and angry. He wished he could take her hand, soothe her hurts. She'd smeared something shiny on them. "What did you use to treat the blisters?" he asked.

"Grease from that curious fish we ate."

"They have another curious fish up here, the white sturgeon. It gets even bigger than the paddlefish."

She propped her elbows on her knees and looked at him. "These people, they don't have corn. Just goosefoot, marsh elder, and things like that?"

"Traders have brought corn to the Ilini before. I don't know if it will grow this far north."

She pursed her lips, thinking. "I've been sitting on that sack for months now. First in the Khota canoe, and now in yours. I thought I was being silly when I wouldn't leave it for Wolf of the Dead. Now I think it might have been a smart thing to do."

"How's that?"

"Well, it's the best corn the Anhinga know how to grow, sorted from the healthiest of plants. It's seed corn, Otter."

"All right, so it's seed corn."

"Are you always this slow, or do you have a mind like stone? I don't have any stake in this journey."

"You don't need to—"

"I *want* to Trade my seed corn. These people up here are mostly farmers. Maybe corn will grow this far north. Sure, it will never replace goosefoot, marsh elder, little barley, or sunflowers as a major food crop—but it would give them a little change of diet. It's a luxury, Otter. People pay for that."

He smiled then, ducking away from the smoke that seemed to want to go wherever he did. "Very well, Pearl, let's Trade your corn. I would never have thought of seed corn as something to Trade, but maybe you're right."

They sat in silence for a time, Otter aware that she was studying him furtively. A very bright girl, this one, and he had to admit that she was a better-than-average hand with a paddle. She seemed born to a boat and water.

"How come no woman has sent her clan to ask for you, Otter?"

He smiled. "We're not like the Anhinga. Among my people, I would ask my clan to approach the woman's clan about a marriage."

"Among the Anhinga, women ask for men." She gazed wearily into the fire. "Maybe that's why I didn't believe it when the Khota asked for me. It was like some kind of curious joke. It couldn't be true."

"People have different customs when it comes to marriage, Pearl. As a Trader, you realize just how many ways there are for men and women to get together."

"So, you didn't want to marry?" She gave him a sidelong glance. "You're all right, aren't you? I mean, you're not disabled or anything?"

He raised an eyebrow. "I'm a healthy male—in all ways." And he avoided her eyes, afraid he'd betray himself.

As she waited for him to go on, the last of the flames blinked out on the smoldering coals. Otter said, "She married my twin brother."

"He's a Trader, too?"

"No . . . no, as a matter of fact, he's everything that I am not. He's brave, strong, dedicated to clan, lineage, and family. He's smart, clever, and reasonable. One day he will be a great leader—both of the White Shell Clan and hers."

"You speak of him with love."

"Outside of her, he's the most important person in my life. We share souls, and so much else . . ."

"Is that why you became a Trader? Because she married him?"

"Just the opposite. She married him because I was a Trader. I've belonged to the river from the time I was an infant." He laughed. "And that's the answer to your question, Pearl. No woman with sense would want me."

She nodded soberly, and he noted that she had a habit, when in thought, of sucking her lips in and staring intently at some remote point. "I was the same way. As you belonged to the river, I belonged to the southern waters. The best days of my life were spent out in the swamp, or out on the great sea. But, beware, Otter. They get you in the end."

"Who?"

"Your clan. It's the way we live, don't you see? Everyone has to serve a purpose for his clan. Everyone has a role, a place, a duty. And when you don't fit, they make one for you. We're not free, Otter. We're enslaved to our clans and lineages . . . just as if we were taken in battle. But we're born into it, and we never know the difference. They'll marry you off someday. Just wait and see. You'll land your canoe, and they'll have a bride waiting on the beach for you."

"Don't be so gloomy. It's all right. You're free now. You've escaped."

She gave him a puzzled look. "To what?" She gestured at the land around them. "Let's say that I find a nice Ilini man who wants to marry me, and I want to marry him. He, too, is enslaved to his clan. Are they going to let that man marry a woman without family? To them, without the clan alliance and kinship to back me up, I have no name or history. I'm little more than an animal—although among the Khota, you're an animal even with a clan."

Otter let her wrestle with the anger for a moment. Then he said, "I think I've made my peace with my clan. Until now, I didn't understand what Grandmother was giving me . . . at least not really. It's your way out, Pearl."

"What? What's my way out?" She watched him warily.

"Trade. That is, if you want it. It doesn't come free, of course. At times, it's a lonely life. You spend months being cold and hungry, with your muscles aching. In summer, it's hot and muggy; the air is filled with mosquitoes, and you fight a constant battle to keep your goods from spoiling. But then there are those wondrous moments, like sunrise on the water, when the ducks and geese are calling and the sky lights up in every color. At those times, you can feel the very heartbeat of the Creator, the Mysterious One. And, too, you see new things, meet new people. It's worth every moment of discomfort."

"I've traveled with Traders before. I know the life. For a while, I just wasn't sure." She hesitated. "I had a bad experience with a dolphin. Maybe it's over, paid for."

"Think about it. Trade could give you everything you want, Pearl. And yes, let's see what we can do with your corn. Who knows? It's often the simplest of things that makes Trade work."

Unexpectedly, she smiled at him, and his soul leaped. She patted his leg, the touch sending a thrill through him. "Then I have a stake in this expedition. A real one."

"You have a stake." He wanted to hold her, to reassure her, but he forced himself to stare at the fire instead.

"Good," she said. "I'll take that, because I've lost everything else."

Star Shell winced as she straightened her protesting back. She stood with her feet braced wide apart. Every muscle in her shoulders had knotted. Cramps burned hotly in her hands, and as she shifted the adze from one hand to the other, she worked her fingers, aware of the peeling skin on her palms.

"Look, Mama. There's another!" Silver Water pointed, then bounded off with happy enthusiasm toward yet another sapling.

Star Shell glanced up at the heavy, dark sky. Miserable work, miserable day.

"This is truly a mess," Tall Man observed as he slowly surveyed the enclosure.

"I have done the best I could," Stargazer said with resignation. He walked where Tall Man led him, one hand on the Magician's shoulder. In the somber daylight, the old man was rail-thin, the color gone from his flesh. From the looks of him, he'd break like a dry stick if he so much as attempted the task of chopping out saplings.

Overhead, the sky remained dark, overcast, and threatened rain. Gusts of wind snapped around them, only to be followed by periods of unpleasant stillness. Star Shell followed after Silver Water, hefting the adze in her hand. This sapling, too, she hacked off, cutting deeply into the rich, wet soil to sever the roots. The little tree dripped sap, ready to burst into spring. The buds waited, their leaves tightly packed in the dark hulls, for a life they'd never enjoy.

"It seems a waste," Star Shell observed. "All these little trees, all those leaves. They'll never feel the sun."

"Leaves? A waste?" Tall Man wondered. "By fall, they'd be piled on the ground, dead."

"That's what I mean!" Stargazer cried. "What is the purpose of all this? Why must everything live and die? Nothing lasts forever! Where is the Mysterious One's purpose in having us constantly relearn things?"

"Maybe he's forgetful." Star Shell's adze smacked dully as she severed another tree at the roots.

"What?" Stargazer demanded.

Star Shell plodded forward to chop at yet another seedling. "Let me ask you this, Stargazer. If you were creating a world, how many times would you make mistakes because you were caught up in visions of the final product and forgot the basics? How many mistakes do you make when you build a house for the first time? Or even in clearing a field? If you'd never made a ceramic pot, would you produce a fine StarSky burial bowl on your first try?"

"Obviously not!"

Star Shell grunted as she destroyed a young oak. "You surely don't expect the Mysterious One to be perfect, do you? If so, it's a bit presumptuous, don't you think?"

" 'Don't I think?' " Stargazer pulled himself up straight. "Let me tell you something, *girl*. No one, no one, knows more about the sky than I do. Since my initiation, I have spent every clear night out there on that central mound. I have all that my Elders could teach me right here, inside this head. For instance—and I'm only telling you this because no one cares anymore—did you know that some stars go backwards at times, then proceed on course again? But only a few, and I'll not tell you which ones. I didn't discover that, girl. I was told it by a man who was told it by a man who was told, and so on. Now I have told you, but you won't make use of that knowledge. You can't. And when I die, it's gone. Will you pass it on? Perhaps, but without the other knowledge of when and where to look, it will be meaningless."

Star Shell hacked another seedling out of the earth as Tall Man led the Elder along in her wake. "Maybe it's meaningless, anyway. If some of the stars change directions, is that important for me? Will it put food in my plate? Keep my daughter warm?"

"And what if I tell you that it won't? Isn't there more to life than just scurrying to survive?"

Star Shell pointed her adze at the old man. "My concern is staying alive. And by doing that, I'll keep my daughter alive, and healthy, and safe from the Mask. I've lost everything I loved, except for Silver Water. I'm hunted, tired, cold, and sore from bending double to chop out your trees. Most of my troubles are the direct result of your 'old knowledge.' The sooner I'm done with it, the happier I'll be. Let it die."

Stargazer fingered his drooping jowls. "Such bitterness. How hard you sound, for a woman so young. Let it die? Is that what they teach now? Whatever happened to hope? To aspirations for the future? This future, here, now?"

"Ask Many Colored Crow." Star Shell slashed at another of the baby trees. An image of Greets the Sun tried to form in her mind, but she thrust it away with a vehemence equal to that she used to dispatch the seedlings.

"No hope, no future." Stargazer shook his head. "You don't know what's written in the sky. Well, mark my words, girl. Open your ears and hear this, because one day the fate of people will depend on what they find among the stars. Some, like you, will turn away from the heavens, and when you do, you will condemn us all to stagnation and death."

"You've read this in the stars? They teach that?" Star Shell propped her hands on her knees.

"And more . . . but not in a way you could understand. Not with such anger and futility seething in your soul." He sagged then, curiously defeated. "What about you, Magician? You've been oddly quiet, given your usual proclivity for obnoxious comments."

"I think all things must die and be reborn," Tall Man said quietly. "I think that's the way the world was made. Men, trees, animals, rocks, and rivers. All must die."

"And knowledge?" Stargazer asked.

"Knowledge, too, I suppose." Tall Man followed Star Shell to the next of the little trees, Stargazer's hand still resting on his shoulder. "It's the death of that knowledge that bothers you, old friend. You believe in the old way, that knowledge is sacred, a thing to be cherished. You treasure the old traditions, find security in them, peace."

"And you don't?"

"I wish I could, but it was the old ways that made us vulnerable to the Flat Pipe peoples in the first place. While we sat up at night to watch the stars, they were planting our fields. You are mourning for knowledge the way most men mourn for a dying wife. It gives you a desperation I'm not accustomed to hearing in your voice."

"Do you know what it's like to spend your life watching the death and decay of everything you hold sacred? Magician, I've watched my world fading away. The students stopped coming, stopped learning, or they scoffed and left to be Traders or pipe carvers." Stargazer gestured with a sweep of his free arm. "What do you see out there beyond the perimeter wall? Tell me, right now. What's out there?"

"Trees," Tall Man said reasonably, though he was too short to see over the wall.

"Trees!" Stargazer agreed. "And when I was a boy, the farmsteads stretched for as far as the eye could see. We didn't talk of death then, but of life, of learning. The Dead we revered, but the goods we left in their burial mounds were given out of respect and admiration. What do I hear today? That the young are racing to accumulate wealth so that they can be buried in opulence. And why? So that they'll be revered—people of status among their ancestors."

Stargazer thumped his chest. "I *remember* those ancestors, Magician. I remember them, and what they told me about their ancestors, and those who had gone even before that! They will despise these strutting fools in their shining ornaments, the same way a hunter secretly despises a strutting, gobbling turkey as it parades in its flashy feathers and arrogance—unaware of the bola that will soon flash around its neck. That's how they'll treat these foolish newcomers!"

"You can't expect the stars to stand still."

"No, but even the simplest fool should understand that when you go to the Afterworld, you'd better understand your ancestors and what they believed—because if you don't, you'll be outnumbered, ridiculed, and eventually exiled for your stupidity!"

"So what would you do?" Tall Man wondered. "You'd have to change the world."

"I would ... if I could." Stargazer stamped a foot in the

marshy grass. "But I've been robbed, Magician. My students were stolen from me. My people were stolen from me. The things my people believed were stolen from me. My future was stolen from me. And now, finally, my sight—my ability to learn more from the stars—has been stolen from me."

"You still have what you know," Star Shell called over her shoulder. "Leave here. Go to StarSky and teach it."

"Leave here?" He pointed to the poles that rose from the perimeter embankment. "Do you know what those are? Each of the posts has a carving. If I'm facing correctly, the one immediately to your right, girl, has a falcon's head on it."

"It does."

"That's the point on the horizon where Falcon rises during the moon after the fall equinox. And why is that important, girl?"

"I don't know."

"Ignorance, it's everywhere. The reason Falcon is important is that the sap stops running in the trees when he appears. The fast hunter is warning the world that winter is coming."

"We call that day the Badger's Dance," she answered. "It's the day when Badger's eye appears over the horizon in alignment with the southwest line of the Octagon."

"There, see," Tall Man soothed. "It's the same constellation, just a different name."

Stargazer glared hotly in Star Shell's direction. "That's just the point! Why does everything need a different name? The old ones are fine. Even you, *you* Magician, running around with an angry Flat Pipe girl who'd shit in her father's bowl before she'd learn something of value! You're just as corrupt and rotten as the rest of them." Stargazer spun on an unwieldy heel and strode off unerringly for the little house on the northwest side.

"That's why he won't leave," Tall Man said unhappily. "He knows this world inside the Circle, as alone as he might be."

"He calls *me* angry?" Star Shell flung the adze away, arching her back to ease the pain. "If he'd lived through what I have in the last couple of—"

"Easy, young Star Shell." Tall Man raised his hand to stop her. "He's lived it, just as you have. For you, it's been a quick death . . . mostly compressed into the last year or so. For him, it's been slow and lingering. He's watched his world die by the year instead of by the hour."

She bit her lip then and looked away.

"He shares your anger . . . and your desperation." Tall Man walked over to pat her on the hand. "Unlike you, he hasn't the means or the physical ability to do anything about it."

Star Shell reached down and took the Magician's hand. "I never thought of it that way."

"Mama?" Silver Water came rushing back. "I found more trees growing over by the moat."

"Good work, Tadpole. I suppose I should—"

"No, leave them." Tall Man squeezed her hand. "After this morning, I think this place is fine as it is. He sees the horizon and the rising stars clearly enough."

Star Shell nodded, looking around the abandoned Circle. Once Power had been centered here. People had studied, learned, and observed. They'd set the observation posts and instructed their young initiates in the arcane knowledge of the stars, moon, and sun. Now the trees would take it all back. The knowledge had moved on to places such as StarSky.

And what about StarSky? Will it ever be forgotten and overgrown like 'The Heavens'?

Impossible! The farmland was too rich, the confluence of the rivers too important. She'd heard the Traders speak as they walked in awe. In all the world, no place had such mighty earthworks! And the sacred chert would always be vital to all people. No, StarSky was eternal.

Thirty

Some stars go backward, like me.

I've been studying one star for a whole moon now, a brilliant, blazing star that forms the tip of Running Badger's long nose. It's reversed its course, making it seem as though Badger has cocked his head to survey the glittering belly of the heavens. Each night his head twists more. Where once he gazed longingly toward the western darkness, tonight Badger has one curious eye fixed on the east.

Waiting . . .

It has made me think.

Perhaps I, too, should look toward the Light. Maybe I could do it. I don't know. I suppose I could go backward in the other direction. It would feel strange, walking toward the sunrise with my back to Father Sun. Maybe if I closed my eyes, it would be all right. That way, I'd still be able to see the Darkness, but the Light would warm my back. It would feel very good, I think, being warmed by the Light. I've been feeling so cold lately. Cold down to the marrow of my bones.

But just thinking about this makes me hurt. Would going backward toward the Light mean that I had turned my back on the Darkness?

"You had heard about us," Tall Man said as the night rains pounded on the bark roof. For as old as Stargazer's society house appeared, the roof was still serviceable—a fact they could all be thankful for.

Star Shell had been playing nose tag with Silver Water. Now she turned her attention to Stargazer.

The nightly fire—as usual, they were burning wood that Star Shell and Silver Water had collected—cast flickering light on the star-dotted blue fabrics that draped the walls of Stargazer's tidy house. The object of the orderliness, it had turned out, was that as long as everything was in its place, the old man could find it.

"Heard about you?" Stargazer sat in his robes before the fire and waved his arms. "I've heard many stories about you. My idiot son came up here at the darkening of the last moon. Everyone is looking for you—and this obsessed war leader, Robin, has stirred up interest in the Mask of Many Colored Crow. I have heard from Two Hands and some of the other traditional

Elders. They wondered what we should do. Two Hands knows the Power of the Mask and what that silly Flat Pipe man let loose when he robbed that burial up on the mountain. The Mask isn't a thing for the Flat Pipes. It never was.''

"The Mask isn't a thing for any human," Tall Man replied. "That was precisely why our ancestors hid it, and exactly why I'm carrying it around now: to take it away from people, any people, all people. It just brings trouble."

"This Mica Bird wasn't strong enough—"

At Star Shell's gasp, the High Head Elder turned in her direction. "Oh, hush, girl. That business of the name bringing the ghost is foolishness."

"Not among her people," Tall Man interjected, "and I will appreciate it if you respect her beliefs about the subject and not mention his name again."

"Why not? What does she, or anyone, for that matter, care about what I or my ancestors believe? That's the point! You can't have one without the other, or you have a sort of tyranny! Are her beliefs more important than mine? If I want to blurt out a dead man's name, why can't I? I don't ask that she abide by my beliefs, do I?"

"It scares me." Star Shell glanced sidelong at the pack with its terrible Mask. "He was a suicide, Stargazer. A horrible, angry man. Please, don't call him here."

"Ghosts aren't that easy to call," Stargazer insisted. "Ask the Magician, he used to spend enough time and energy calling them up. Was it as easy as saying their names?"

"No," Tall Man said flatly. "But calling a ghost and getting it to do things for you are two different things."

The sudden fear swelling within Star Shell threatened to rob her of breath. "You? You used to call . . ."

"A long time ago, child. Yes, yes, but that was a different time, a different people."

"Different how? High Heads are still the same people, aren't they?"

"Some activities fall from favor over time." The Magician made a face, glaring his irritation at the smug Stargazer. "Power simply is, Star Shell. I've told you that. Once, among a certain society within the High Heads, it was common to call ghosts.

Sometimes they would come. Generally, they didn't appreciate being disturbed any more than you enjoy being yanked away from your duties. Ghosts have lives, too, you know."

"Call a ghost!" Silver Water cried, sitting up straight, her expression enchanted, eager.

"No, baby. This is a joke, that's all." Star Shell encouraged her daughter to lie down again and resumed stroking the child's hair. "Just a . . . a joke, Cricket. Now you go to sleep . . . and think about jokes. Maybe ones we could tell Grandma."

Stargazer grunted in disgust.

Tall Man, if anything, seemed even smaller than usual as he fingered one of the geometric designs incised on a pot. It looked like a highly stylized duck.

"The Mask . . ." Stargazer thoughtfully tapped age-spotted fingers on his sagging chin. "It's not evil. Not in itself."

"No," Tall Man said. He took a deep breath, paused, and placed a hand on his right side, just below his ribs, as though a pain nagged him there. "The trouble comes from the kind of men who want to wear it. This Robin, he wants the Mask in order to gain status and authority—exactly the kind of abuse you were railing against this morning."

"What have you heard about us?" Star Shell interrupted what was sure to turn into a harangue. "Stargazer, tell us what your son said. Who is looking for us? What kinds of things are people saying?"

Stargazer cocked his head. "Well, they're saying that the Magician is using the Mask to engage in sorcery, that he's out calling up . . . er, the ancestors . . . and committing evils here and there. That you, girl, are his new apprentice. That you're learning the ways of the Mask, how to kill men with a look. Some of the more ridiculous stories have you eating babies, that sort of thing. If people weren't so ignorant these days, and obsessed with death—"

"They say that? About me?" *How could they? I'm not like that! It's not fair!*

"Oh, not everyone." Stargazer seemed to think on it. "The weak-minded will always believe whatever sounds the most audacious and unlikely. It's their nature. The world isn't wondrous enough for them. They seem driven to concoct atrocious fantasies. But your husband *did* kill himself. You *have* stolen

the Mask away, and finally, you *are* traveling with the Magician
... well, what do you expect?''

What do I expect? A void continued to grow within. "We
should go, then. Leave here as soon as possible." Star Shell
glanced down at her daughter. "We're wasting time when we
should be heading north."

"You're not going far with the rivers flooded," Tall Man
stated. The pain in his side seemed worse. He bent forward now,
and rocked slightly as though trying to ease it. "Half of the
trails will be under water, and the rivers are out of the question.
You can only travel by the back trails. If you travel by water,
people will note your passing, and, I must say, we're somewhat
conspicuous. You don't find that many dwarfs traveling with a
beautiful young woman and a child."

"We're not going to make it, are we?"

"Yes, young Star Shell, we are." Tall Man straightened and
gave her a reassuring smile, but he kept his hand tenderly at his
side. "Had you really understood the odds against you last winter, you'd never have believed that you'd make it this far."

She wanted to believe him, but somehow ... Perhaps it was
Stargazer's eloquent sense of defeat and desperation that depressed her.

Silver Water had fallen asleep, her head tipped toward the
fire. Star Shell ran her fingers through her daughter's silky hair.
Thunder cracked and shook the world. Rain continued to batter
at the bark overhead. Star Shell could sense time running out
for all of them.

She glanced at Tall Man; the dwarf's face was like cast copper in the firelight. What was his real purpose? "What kind of
sorcerer?"

Tall Man shrugged. "Another time, Star Shell. I don't want
to talk about it now, not here."

"No," Stargazer said sourly. "You'll draw one of your old
ghosts. And the Mysterious One knows, you've created enough
of them." He peered blindly at Star Shell.

"Yes, she knows," Tall Man answered the unasked question,
waving it away as though unimportant.

"All of it?" Stargazer asked.

"Some."

"Tell me all of it," she demanded.

"Tomorrow, when there's no chance of being overheard." Tall Man pointed at Silver Water.

A sudden smile had formed on Stargazer's face. " . . . Would be a way to . . ."

"What?" Tall Man asked. "Speak up! What are you talking about?"

"Saving the old ways," Stargazer answered. "Yes, a way . . . if one had enough Power . . . enough personal strength."

"The world has changed," Tall Man insisted. He let his hand drop from the spot beneath his ribs, as if the pain had gone. Something he'd eaten for supper? "Our time is over. Let it die, my friend. Let it go in peace."

"Perhaps . . ." Stargazer mused, his eyes fixed on something high overhead. "See? The Duck is rising. There, just under the horizon."

"The Duck?" Star Shell whispered, her uneasy gaze on the Elder.

"The constellation of Spring. The sign of the renewal, rebirth, the Planting Moon, what have you."

"Stargazer, go to sleep!" Tall Man growled.

"No, old friend. I'm just waking up. So is the world." He jerked up an arm, pointing. "See! The Truth is there! I *will* see the stars again! So will everyone . . . they will learn the proper names."

"Yes," Tall Man agreed, apparently resigned that any other response would just bring on another argument. "You'll see the stars again."

Star Shell narrowed her eyes. *And tomorrow, Magician, you and I will have a long and serious talk about who you are and what you've been!*

With that, Star Shell rearranged Silver Water's bedding, placing herself between her daughter and the Mask that stood on the opposite side of the house.

She didn't see Stargazer late that night as he sat before the smoldering coals, his sightless eyes focused on the pack that held Many Colored Crow's Mask.

The Ilini was a good river to navigate, broad and slow, with a sluggish current that did little to impede progress. *Wave Dancer* made good time as Otter steered them upriver, avoiding the main channel. The floodwaters had dropped, but the cloudy skies periodically broke open to soak them, while lightning flashed and thunder boomed. In the chilly aftermath, hints of sunlight would peek through the tumbling clouds, and the faint fuzz of new leaves turned ever greener.

They'd stopped for a midday meal, pulling up on a thinly wooded island—really just a sandbar that had lasted long enough for adventurous cottonwoods to take root among the sparse grasses. The feast consisted of cold paddlefish, goosefoot bread, dried berries, and mint tea poured from a ceramic jar.

"We're making good time," Black Skull noted as he wiped his carved wooden bowl clean and popped the last piece of bread into his mouth. The way he chewed, with his off-center mouth and crooked jaw, had always amazed Otter.

"Better than I would have expected."

"Slow, too slow," Green Spider agreed as he squatted with both knobby knees jutting outward so that he resembled a giant skinny frog.

"The only thing slow around here is your thinking," Black Skull fired back. "Did I ever tell you, fool, that you irritate me way down in the depths of my soul? There are times when I want to wrap my arms around you and hug you so tight that every bone in your body snaps and pops."

"A hug? We could be lovers. Have you ever thought of that?" Green Spider gave the warrior a happy grin. "I never knew you loved me that much. You know, you shouldn't keep such things to yourself. Secrecy rots the soul, and devotion such as yours thrills my heart."

Black Skull reddened, his mouth opening and closing as if he were a flopping fish. Then he cursed, threw down his bowl, and stamped away up the island.

Pearl smothered her laughter until Black Skull was safely out of range.

Otter chuckled and wiped his own bowl clean. He inspected the rich grain of the walnut, a piece carved by Four Kills and polished by Red Moccasins. Why did he keep it? Every time he looked down into it, his heart ached.

"How do you know how far to push him?" Pearl asked Green Spider. "Is it because you can see the future?"

"No," Green Spider responded. "It's because I can't see anything."

"I don't know, Green Spider." Otter rapped his bowl with his knuckles. "I think you just like to tempt fate."

Green Spider focused on a fly that was buzzing about. He frowned, narrowed his vision, and sprang at the little beast, flopping full-length across the damp sand to make a grab for it. He missed.

When the Contrary looked up, his vision had cleared slightly. "Black Skull will get mad only if you're not honest with him. Pearl, you must always tell him the truth. Because if you ever lie to him, he'll kill you."

"But you just lied to him. Didn't you? Are you *berdache* as well as Contrary?"

Green Spider shook his head. "No. No. No. No! *Berdache* are between the worlds. Bridges between men and women, light and dark. Me, I'm going forward through a world that's going backward."

Otter stepped down to where *Wave Dancer* lay canted on the beach and placed his bowl inside. He laid a hand on the carved fox head and looked back at Green Spider. "What do you do with women, Green Spider? Are they too backward for you?"

"Do?" Green Spider turned over onto his back. "If I coupled with a woman, I'd ruin her. She'd never want another man. How could she go back to just any *ordinary* fellow after I'd taught her the secrets of pleasure? You see, it all has to do with the way a man uses his penis. Mine is trained; it knows just where to swell up and just where to prod."

"I'll bet," Pearl scoffed. "Being a Contrary, you probably stay limp until after you're done."

Green Spider grinned happily. "Is that a challenge? I love challenges. I guess, since Black Skull turned me down, I'll crawl into your robes tonight."

The joke was suddenly gone. Pearl's smile had turned icy, and Otter could see the slightly crazy glint in her eyes. "You're welcome to crawl into my robes any time, Green Spider." He was halfway to his feet when she added, "But when you finally crawl out, you'll be short one penis, two testicles, and any desire you might have had for a woman—forever.''

Green Spider promptly grabbed his crotch, let out a hideous wail, and flopped on the ground again. He writhed around, curled into a fetal position, and bleated in horror.

"You wouldn't!" Otter raised an eyebrow.

"Try me," she said coldly.

Otter saw her panic—and knew its roots: *Wolf of the Dead. . .*

Green Spider wailed a little louder. "Destroyed! She's made me a woman! I'll have to squat to pee! And I loved her! With all my heart, I craved her. Foul betrayal!''

"What happened to him?" Black Skull asked. His return had been covered by Green Spider's noisy antics.

"Pearl just castrated him," Otter said as he emptied out the leaves from the mint tea, avoiding Pearl's glazed gaze.

Black Skull turned to Pearl, bowing low. "My compliments! I wish we'd rescued you clear back when we first passed those cursed Khota canoes. I'd have fought all forty of them to give you a chance at the fool. But . . . where's the blood?''

"I didn't need a knife." Pearl was picking up the last of their camp, her head down. "Words were enough."

"Too bad." Black Skull turned. "You should have waited and let me help you. I have an incredibly sharp piece of obsidian here someplace."

Green Spider sat up, his hands still on his crotch, and stared downriver. "I wonder what took them so long? A little sooner and I'd have been saved from mutilation.''

Otter wheeled about. A slim war canoe was paddling relentlessly toward them. A tingling sensation invaded his belly.

"Just one," Black Skull said.

Pearl came to stand beside Otter's shoulder, her hands shading her eyes. "It's full of young men. I'd say six. About half are paddling. She's moving fast. Water's boiling at the bow.''

"You can see that?" Otter asked. "At that distance?''

"Better get the weapons," Black Skull muttered, and with those words, Green Spider leaped up and ran for cover in the trees. Black Skull ignored him. "It makes me nervous to see a canoe pushed that hard. It's almost like someone wanted to catch us—and urgently.''

"It does indeed," Otter agreed. "And if it were me, I'd rather meet them out on open water. That way, it's canoe against canoe. They can't use numbers against us. And if it does come to a fight, *Wave Dancer* is large enough to provide a stable shooting platform for the atlatls."

"Good thinking," Black Skull agreed as he turned back for his bowl.

"*Wave Dancer* isn't as nimble as a war canoe," Pearl reminded as they started down to the water.

Black Skull bellowed, "What the . . . *may maggots eat his filthy*—"

Otter turned as Black Skull violently kicked a cascade of damp sand into the air, and with it, his bowl. "What's wrong?"

"That stinking little *worm*!"

Catcher began barking with excitement, bounding this way and that, unsure of the reason for the commotion, but not wanting to be left out.

"Where'd he go?" Black Skull's fists had knotted, his biceps swelling and bulging while dark rage burned in his face.

"Do you mind?" Otter demanded. "There's a war canoe bearing down on us. Catcher, rot you, get in the boat! *Now!* Where's Green Spider?"

Black Skull shook his fist. "That stupid *idiot*! Do you see him? Where is he? I'm going to reach down his skinny throat and rip his heart out!"

"*Black Skull,* get down here! Green Spider? *Green Spider,* where are you?"

The warrior came cursing, pausing only long enough to dash his wooden bowl into the sand. Then he threw his weight into shoving *Wave Dancer* off the beach. "I don't know where the fool went, but vanishing was uncommonly smart on his part. If he's even smarter, he's already cut his own throat!"

"We'll have to come back for him, I guess," Otter called as they scrambled into the canoe. Then he muttered, "That is, if we survive this."

Black Skull was breathing loudly through his mouth, struggling to regain some of his vaunted self-discipline. His thick shoulders rippled as he used his oar to bring *Wave Dancer* about. "All right, Trader, now what? Do you want to take them—or to see what they want before we kill them?"

Otter winced. The warrior was more than ready for a fight. "When in strange country, Black Skull, always talk first and fight last." Otter used his oar to send *Wave Dancer* at a diagonal out from the island. He'd picked the side that seemed to have the more sluggish current. The band of trees on the shore gave him the distance of a dart's cast for maneuvering room.

"One thing's sure," Pearl told them. "It would be difficult to outrace that boat."

Otter silently agreed as the slim craft flew across the water like a cast dart. He stood, cupping his hands to his mouth. "Greetings! Who comes in such a hurry?"

A figure rose in the approaching canoe's bow. Across the smooth water, the reflection added to the man's height, doubling his human form. "Greetings! Water Fox? We come from Silent Owl. We're to warn you! Heave to! We bring news!"

Otter glanced at his companions. "A trick?"

"Maybe." Black Skull's fists were knotted, his muscles bulging. "I hope so."

Green Spider? Why now? Otter rolled his eyes. Delicate negotiations might be required, and Black Skull wanted to kill something.

Pearl squinted at the approaching canoe. "We do have a slight advantage."

"What's that?" Otter glanced around, seeing no place to run if things turned nasty.

"They don't know that I speak their tongue." Pearl lifted a delicate eyebrow. "If they're going to try to trick us, I might get a warning."

Otter nodded, shouting back, "We're heaving to!"

The Ilini pulled abreast, the trim hull's gunwales barely three fingers above the water. Of the six men within, three had been paddling; their muscular bodies glistened with sweat despite the blustery day.

"Greetings, Water Fox." The young man smiled. "I am Long Throw, of the Hazel Clan. My clan leader, Silent Owl, judged you correctly. He said that if you were a smart man, we'd catch you at midday today. You've made good time."

"What is your news?" Black Skull's eyes were smoldering.

"The Khota . . . Wolf of the Dead. He has brought many warriors. At the time we left in pursuit of you, at least two tens of tens had arrived at the parley island. He made a blood vow to run you down. Silent Owl had to give him passage through Ilini territory.''

''*Had* to?'' Black Skull cried.

''I understand,'' Otter said, seeing the young man's expression at delivering what amounted to a death warrant. ''Silent Owl owes us nothing. Sending you to warn us puzzles me. It's not that we don't greatly appreciate your effort—and as Traders, we'll reward each of you handsomely, and Silent Owl as well—but why is he sticking his neck out for us?''

The young man shrugged. ''That is the prerogative of a great leader such as Silent Owl. He has his own purpose. We have been sent to warn you, and to help you in any way that we can.''

''Help how?'' Black Skull asked as he webbed his scarred fingers over the knob on the end of his paddle.

''In any way that we can.'' Long Throw gestured to his companions. ''If you need help in rowing, finding food . . . anything. The Hazel Clan will repay any debts you incur with the other Ilini Clans upriver—just so you make good time.''

''Ah!'' Otter saw the pieces fall into place. ''I begin to grasp Silent Owl's wisdom in this.''

''I don't,'' Black Skull growled, glaring at the Ilini in their canoe.

''How far has Wolf of the Dead promised to chase us?'' Otter asked the Ilini.

''Until he catches you!''

Otter let his gaze drift southward. Uncle's ghost still stalked the lands down there. Perhaps even as he thought about it, Uncle might be walking around Levee Island, nodding in approval. It would be a Trade well made—assuming that Silent Owl was smart enough to seize the opportunity. ''We'll make the best time we can, Long Throw. Do you have relatives along the river? Someone who can take word back to Silent Owl?''

''I do,'' another of the men said.

''Then we'll do our best to make sure that Wolf of the Dead follows us all the way up the Ilini River and out into the Fresh Water Sea.''

''What are you doing?'' Black Skull's hot glare switched back and forth from Otter to the Ilini.

"Baiting a trap," Otter replied. "And we're the bait."

"I don't quite understand." Pearl was stabbing at the water with her oar. When she looked up, the desperation in her pained him.

"I told you, I lose all of my sense where the stinking Khota are concerned. Let's just say that I'm paying back old debts. And doing a little gambling on the side."

The muscles in Black Skull's face were twitching like termites in a punky log. "When you make decisions that I don't understand, I get nervous. Trader, just what, exactly, are you gambling on?"

"Me, you . . . and maybe the Contrary. By the way, what did he do to you back there?"

Black Skull scowled menacingly. "While we were looking at the Ilini canoe, he squatted down and crapped in my bowl! Left a big, wet, stinking brown turd right in the middle of it."

Pearl began to chuckle, then broke into unrepressed laughter.

"It's *not* funny!" Black Skull's fingers flexed as if he wanted to reach out and choke her.

"What is this?" Long Throw asked.

Otter waved it away. "Nothing. Just a bit of truth-telling. Come on, we need to return to the island for the Contrary. After that, we'll show you boys just how fast you can drive a big canoe upriver."

Otter's paddle dug into the water to bring them around. Black Skull continued to glare his disgust at Pearl, who just laughed harder, her paddle dragging limply in the river.

"By the way," Otter called across to the Ilini. "Is there any chance we can Trade for a good wooden bowl?"

Star Shell awoke to the predawn chirping of the birds. She blinked hard and rubbed at the film that had formed in her eyes. For some reason, she'd slept hard, vivid Dreams twining around her soul. She'd seen wild, tattooed men dressed in skins and carrying wicked-looking darts. Bits of a winding maze had floated out of a watery past, seeking to ensnare her—and a huge, awkward-looking bear had cornered and killed a giant wolf in a terrible battle of blood, fur, and foaming jaws. Yet, when it had been over, a man's pitiful corpse had lain in the grassy clearing.

Wasn't that what it always turned out to be? A pitiful corpse? *Maybe we do put too much emphasis on death.*

Star Shell reached out, then sat up instantly. Silver Water's bedding was empty. Star Shell came fully awake and threw off her blanket.

"Silver Water?" She stirred the fire for coals and blew on them before adding wood. The red eyes gleamed and burst into a few preliminary flickers of light. Enough light that Star Shell could see the Mask pack safely propped against the wall beyond Tall Man's humped blankets.

"Silver Water?" Star Shell pulled her tattered blanket around her shoulders before stepping out into the cold and wet. The rain had ceased, and the dawning sky looked clear; the last of the stars were still visible in the west. The birds continued to call, but otherwise, silence hung heavily over the forest. Dew lay thick and silvery on the new grass; her breath puffed whitely. She stared around at the large enclosure of the Heavens, the observation posts leaning this way and that in the gloom. Power pulsed as if in time to a giant heartbeat.

Where would her daughter be? *"Silver Water?"*

"Mama?"

"Where are you, baby?"

"Here. We're looking at the stars."

Not Stargazer! If he'd dragged her daughter out into the chill just to point out stars, she'd . . . she'd *break* his ancient High Head neck like the piece of old wood it was.

Led by the voice, Star Shell hurried toward the center of the Circle where the low mound stood. She could see them. Stargazer's withered arm pointed at the western sky.

How dare he take a little girl out into the dampness of a cold morning? What possessed the man? Star Shell bit off a curse as her moccasins whipped through the wet grass.

Not until she passed the outward-tilting posts did she notice the difference. Stargazer's head looked larger. Ungainly. Inhuman.

Silver Water sat firmly snugged in the crook of the old man's arm. She was following his hand as it swept across the sky.

"Look!" Stargazer cried out happily. "The last of the falling stars!"

Star Shell peered in that direction and saw the dot of light draw a line against the dawn.

She stopped short, a hand to her breast. How could the old man . . .

Stargazer turned his head, and the long black beak appeared, the irregular ruff of feathers fluttering in the morning breeze.

She started to tremble.

"And there—" his voice carried in the soft dawn "—if you draw a line between those two stars, they will point you straight north. You'll never be lost again, little Silver Water. The stars and I will always show you the way."

Silver Water grips Stargazer's old arm and turns halfway around to look at her mother, who is running away from the mound, waving her arms and shouting for Tall Man. This scares Silver Water. She sinks back into the hollow of Stargazer's bony chest and forces a swallow down her tight throat. Her mother hates the Mask—she knows this. But she wishes that her mother weren't so afraid. Silver Water would like to be able to talk to someone about her grown-up voice.

The Mask is whispering to Stargazer, making him smile, reminding him of things he's forgotten about the night sky. Silver Water wonders where she will learn these things. Legends speak of Dreamers who have been carried up into the sky to talk with the Star People. She frowns at this thought. Do their voices sparkle? Water makes a sparkly sound when it runs over rocks. Are the Star People's voices like that? Maybe they boom, like Sister Lightning's voice.

This last possibility makes Silver Water uneasy. She snuggles against Stargazer, and his arm tightens around her shoulder. The sky above them is polished blue slate sprinkled with ice crystals.

"Yes, yes," Stargazer whispers. "Of course, I remember that."

Silver Water twists to peer up at him. "Remember what?"

Stargazer uses the Mask's beak to point due east. "In about

one hand of time, you will see the sun and the new moon rise at the same time. They will set at the same time, too."

"They will?"

"Oh, yes, and it's very important to know such things, little Silver Water. Every day the moon rises a little less than one hand of time earlier than the day before. This means that the moon's year has three hundred and fifty-four days, whereas the sun's year has three hundred and sixty-five."

"You mean it takes the moon less time to get back to the same place on the horizon?"

"That's right." He nods, and the Mask's black ruff flutters like Raven shaking out his feathers after a dust bath.

"The moon is a fast runner."

Stargazer chuckles. He leans down so that the Mask's beak rests in the middle of her chest and she can look through the eye sockets into Stargazer's eyes. They are the faded color of driftwood. "I will tell you a secret, Silver Water," he whispers. "This is something that only members of the Star Society know. But you will be a member someday, and so I will tell you—"

"I will?" she shouts excitedly.

"Of course. Hasn't the Mask told you? Well, you will." He lifts the Mask's beak and places the tip against Silver Water's nose. It smells cold and musty, as if it has been sleeping in a cobwebbed hole in the ground for tens of tens of tens of winters.

Stargazer whispers, "I want you to listen very carefully. Will you?"

Silver Water tries to nod her head without breaking the contact between her nose and the Mask's black beak. "Yes."

"Good." He peers at her unblinking. In the sky behind the Mask, wisps of cloud are changing color, growing purple hearts. "All of our earthworks are laid out based upon a standard unit of measurement. Do you know what that means?"

Silver Water thinks about it, then shakes her head. "No."

"It means that we measure everything to assure that it's perfect. Each member of the Star Society carries a coil of twine with him. These coils are exactly the same length, and if you stretch out that coil eleven times, from end to end, you have one unit of celestial measurement. Everything we do is based upon the number eleven. Why do you think that is?"

Silver Water whispers, "Why?"

The beak presses closer, so close that her nose is flattened out. Air whistles in and out of her nostrils. Stargazer speaks softly. "Because there is a difference of eleven days between the moon's year and the sun's year. That is a very sacred number, little Silver Water. You will find that every earthwork laid out by the Star Society and constructed by the Engineer Society possesses a base of eleven. You may have twenty-two or forty-four units of measure, or even five and a half, but they still relate to the number eleven."

Silver Water's voice has a nasal quality. "But . . . but how long is the twine, Stargazer? I mean—"

"Ah, that is the greatest secret of all." He lowers his voice even more, so that it hisses at Silver Water like an angry bobcat. "It takes seven hundred and nineteen regular units of measurement to make one celestial unit. Now, if you look at your own hand, you will find the source for a regular unit—"

"Silver Water!" her mother screams hoarsely.

Silver Water jerks to stare over Stargazer's shoulder. Tall Man and her mother stand at the base of the small mound, breathing hard, their eyes wide and frightened.

"Silver Water? Hurry! Come to me!" Her mother kneels down and opens her arms. *"Do it now! Hurry!"*

Silver Water's teeth clench. She tenderly pats Stargazer's old chest, loving him for telling her about the stars. She has never disobeyed her mother, but . . . All of these secrets are baby eagles, trying to learn to fly inside her. She feels their wings beating at her ribs.

"Do you want to hear the rest?" Stargazer asks. "Or to go to your mother?"

Silver Water looks up at the rapidly fading stars. She starts to cry. But no tears come. Just her throat is crying. The baby eagles flutter wildly, and Silver Water aches with their longing for the sky.

"I . . . I want to hear more," she answers, choking out the words. Then she turns around so she can't see her mother's face. "Please, tell me more?"

Thirty-one

What is the present? And where is it inside me? I can't find it.

I watch the banks of the river passing, and glimpses of the future flash at the edge of my vision...

What fools human beings are.

We live our lives unaware, like bodies without brains or hearts. The present appears at the edge of our understanding, but comes into focus only after it has become the past. So we never really see the present when it's happening. That part of our lives is purely illusory.

For me, the future has melded with the present.

Both are in the process of "becoming."

But until they are the past, I can't trust what I see. Though I feel those fragments of scenes to be real, they are still... flimsy, unfocused.

One of the infinite sorrows of Truth is that you can't see it until you are already too far away to touch it.

Does that mean I should stop trying to touch it? Maybe Truth isn't something you're supposed to be able to hold in your hands. No matter how much you want to study it or cherish it. Maybe Truth is like a cup that's slick with hot bear grease. If you ever do manage to get your hands on it, you wind up breaking it into tiny fragments that don't even resemble the original cup.

Perhaps that's the lot of humans—the harder we try to hold the Truth, the more likely we are to crush it.

...Is that what the Wolf is trying to tell me?

"Are we stopping? I thought you would paddle all night again, Trader." Sarcasm laced Black Skull's voice as Otter used the last bit of daylight to guide *Wave Dancer* toward the beach.

"This seems as good a place as any," Otter responded. Indeed, better than most. Part of winning a long-distance race was in the pacing.

The last carnelian rays of sunlight bathed the trees that grew so thickly here, tricking the eye to see the new spring leaves as delicate pink flowers. A grassy meadow could be seen through a small break in the forest. Two deer grazed at the far edge, their ears pricking when they spotted the canoe. All manner of migratory birds chirped in a riot of song and decorated the branches with dots of red, blue, and brilliant gold.

As they jumped out and dragged *Wave Dancer* ashore, Otter gave Black Skull a sidelong look. The warrior had been his old obnoxious self all day. Every comment he made cut like a knife, and that fiery gleam had returned to his eyes. But then, Black Skull had a right to be a little irritable after what Green Spider had done. When they'd returned to the island, they'd found the Contrary laying spread-eagled on the beach, sound asleep in the sunshine. Since then, Black Skull had been throwing the grinning Contrary increasingly murderous looks.

The Ilini pitched their camp just to the south. The hollow, smacking sound of a stone ax rang through the evening, and their laughter carried to Otter. He pointed to the meadow where the deer had been. "Let's set up camp there," he said. "We'll be out of the wind."

Black Skull grumbled but began hauling bundles from *Wave Dancer* and carrying them to the campsite. While everyone else bent their backs to the chores, Green Spider whirled around the meadow with his arms extended, laughing like a giddy child. Spinning and laughing, spinning and laughing, until Otter wondered why he didn't fall flat on his face and throw up.

Black Skull began to build a rain shelter to protect his bedding. He wove saplings and poles into a framework to which he would lash one of the tanned hides. Anger betrayed itself in his quick movements and the twitching of his facial muscles.

"Trouble?" Pearl quietly asked Otter when she paused next to him.

"I don't know," Otter confided as he built a fire in a shallow pit he'd excavated with a digging stick. "He gets this way—and usually it takes bloodletting to get him out of it."

Her eyes filled with a dark wariness as she watched the warrior. With a slim hand, she pushed back a strand of coal-black hair. "I'm not sure what to make of him."

Otter shook ash from his fire pot, blew on it to find a glowing coal, and eased it into the tinder. Fanning the ember induced flames to thread through the dry grass and tickle the twigs he'd steepled over the basin. "He's a curious man. He's always looking over his shoulder, as though pursued by more than just the Khota . . . perhaps by who he is and who he's been." Otter paused. "He's just as lonely as the rest of us, I suppose."

The warrior unrolled the thick hide over the poles, lashing it with cord.

Pearl said, "When I drove that dart through Eats Dogs' back, I hoped it would allow at least some of you to escape. I never had the slightest notion that Black Skull would make it a battle to the death."

Otter watched the warrior working, no move wasted. Everything about him bespoke control and grace—except his temper. "Power chose him for a reason. Without his skill, we'd have died back there. At least Black Skull, Catcher, and I would have. *Wave Dancer* would have been taken, along with all the goods. I don't know what would have happened to Green Spider." Otter glanced around. "Incidentally, where is he?"

Pearl added a couple of small branches to the fire. "He and Catcher disappeared into the woods. I'm not sure whether Catcher is your dog now or his."

"It worries me that Green Spider has taken to disappearing. He didn't do that on the way upriver."

"Are you thinking about that night when we saw him playing with the wolf?"

"I suppose. Yes."

She turned sober brown eyes on him. "He never answered that question about the crow that day. I don't know him, but I thought he looked scared, Otter."

"I've been worrying about that. That bird was angry."

"What if Many Colored Crow has abandoned us?"

Otter rubbed his jaw, aware of her level gaze. What, indeed?

Every time a crow got mad, something bad happened. "I don't know. I—"

"Greetings, Trader!" Long Throw called as he appeared out of the shadowy trees. "I have come to ask if you need anything?"

The young Ilini glanced around, expressing satisfaction at the tidy camp. Stringy muscles covered his thin body, and he had a habit of cocking his head slightly to favor his right ear. He claimed to have hurt his left while diving for freshwater mussels. Generally, a diver clutched a big rock, using its weight to sink himself. The faster a person got to the bottom, the more time he could spend finding the shellfish and stuffing them into a bag. Broken ears were a common hazard, as were missing fingers from the "discovery" of a snapping turtle while poking around in the muddy dark.

"We're doing fine," Otter replied.

Black Skull had walked up to the fire, his broken face guarded. "Perhaps some Khota for me to kill? I have needed to kill something all day."

Long Throw gave Black Skull a wary appraisal. "No, warrior. Khota are not among the supplies we willingly carry."

"Too bad." Black Skull's mouth twisted sourly.

Long Throw scuffed his moccasin in the flattened grass. "Warrior, if I might ask, did you really kill that many Khota back at Levee Island? I mean, so many, and they are so fierce . . ."

Black Skull plucked up his heavy war club from where it had been propped against a tree. As he ran callused fingers over the wood, the copper spikes gleamed in the firelight. "I crafted this with all of the skill the Trader used in carving his canoe. The balance is suited to me, to the way my hands conform to the wood. My Spirit, as well as my blood, has joined with the wood, stone, and metal. Each of the decorations cut into the stock brings the Power of my four Spirit Helpers into the weapon— and both flesh and blood from each of those Spirit Helper animals have been rubbed into the club. My weapon has soul and Power of its own. No hand touches this weapon except mine!"

And with that, Black Skull twirled the mighty club over his head. The deadly whistle grew louder as he began his ritual. The whirling club began to blur as the warrior leaped, danced, and pirouetted around the fire. On feet as quick as a ferret's, he slipped and darted, circling the astonished Long Throw. The young Ilini gaped and then jumped backward as Black Skull suddenly froze, the stillness so sudden that he seemed to appear out of nothingness. Long Throw's mouth worked silently as his eyes sought to focus on the gleaming spikes that had stopped within a finger's width of his nose. The pointed stone hovered just over the center of his skull.

"So you see," Black Skull said easily, withdrawing the club and hanging it loosely over his shoulder, "the club and I are one. The essence of the warrior is harmony. I share that harmony with my atlatl, and with the darts I have labored so long to perfect. Your answer, my friend, is yes. We did kill those Khota rabbits."

Long Throw's throat worked in a way suggesting he was having trouble finding either words or saliva.

Black Skull grinned, reaching out to slap the youth on the shoulder in a friendly way. "We do not need anything, Long Throw. Go back to your friends and tell them we're doing just fine."

Long Throw nodded and backed away. As he retreated into the shadows of the trees, his knees didn't look any too steady— a situation Otter could well remember after more than one confrontation with Black Skull.

The warrior settled himself before the fire, the third point of a triangle. With his war club across his lap, he extended his scarred hands to the flames, his expression thoughtful as Otter settled a pot of stew in the ashes to heat.

"I don't know much about Power, or how men work for or against the Spirit World, but that fight with the Khota changed things." Black Skull glanced sideways at Otter. "I can sense the difference. It is very much like the way the world altered for me on the day lightning blasted the temple and burned it to the ground."

"Is that why you just scared the very soul out of that boy?" Otter used a stick to stir the fire with. Pearl had shifted closer to him.

Black Skull sighed. "Yes. I think it's all part of what we're doing. We haven't had much time to talk, you and I. But I want you to know. I've had a great deal of time to think, to try to understand."

Otter straightened a little. This might be an interesting switch. "I'm still so lost, I'll take any help I can get. What have you discovered?"

Black Skull had extended his hands again; frown lines deepened in his gnarled brow. "It's a matter of discipline, Trader. That eluded me in the beginning. I wasn't . . . No, think of it like this. My duty changed from responsibility to the clan to responsibility for this journey. I may still fail to understand why we're doing what we're doing, or what part the fool plays in it—but I *will* do my duty. In this case, I can't help but think we've broken the Khota, or at least started their destruction."

I'd give my soul for that. Are you listening, Uncle? "What does that have to do with our journey to save the Mask?"

"I don't know, Otter. Maybe the Spirit World doesn't like the Khota. Nobody else seems to. Maybe we were just a handy way to start the process."

"They've been in this from the very start," Otter thought aloud, wanting very much to believe the warrior's words. "I watched them pass with Pearl . . . way down at White Shell territory. You saw them pass when you were bringing Green Spider and the Clan Elders to White Shell."

"And we camped at just about every one of their campsites on the way upriver," Black Skull added.

Pearl sat listening, jabbing her stick into the fire until it caught flame, then smothering it in the damp soil. "All of us . . . chosen," Pearl barely whispered. "Why? What do the wolf and the crow have to do with it?"

For long moments they stared into the fire, each wondering about the Contrary, and about the Spirit forces that were shifting around them.

Black Skull glanced toward the forest. "I don't know, Pearl. A moon ago, I killed a crow . . . and I've regretted it ever since. I hope the fool knows what he's doing."

Otter cocked an eyebrow as he wondered at the changes in Black Skull's manner. The warrior seemed uncomfortable as he glanced back and forth at Pearl and Otter, as though trying to read their reaction to his words.

"I hope so, too," Otter said seriously. "For the moment,

we're going to have to let the Contrary worry about Power. We've got to worry about Wolf of the Dead. He's coming for us . . . and if he catches us, it won't be pleasant."

Black Skull cocked his head. "Was Power using Pearl as bait? Was that why she was supposed to marry Wolf of the Dead?"

Hot passion flashed in her dark eyes. "Given the choice of marriage to a Khota man and a leech, I'll take the leech any day. After living with the Khota, a leech looks pretty good."

"Another coincidence?" Black Skull wondered, rubbing his hands together. "The Khota came to this land because of a woman, a bride. Now another bride, Pearl, has been sent north— and she has escaped in the same way her Ilini counterpart did four generations ago. I find it a curious parallel."

"So do I." Otter stared up at the dark trees surrounding them. Occasional voices carried from Long Throw's camp. "That Ilini woman was killed, wasn't she? Is that the story I remember?"

Pearl angrily jabbed her stick into the flames. "Yes. But I'm no wilting Ilini—nor are the Anhinga. If the Khota want to take revenge on my people, they'd better be very, very good in the swamps. Those who would war with the Anhinga end up feeding alligators."

"But we are headed the other way," Black Skull noted. "Northward, to the Fresh Water Sea."

"Would Green Spider tell us? Give us some hint about the future?" Pearl asked.

"Oh, he'd tell us something," Black Skull assured her. "But you'll find yourself more knotted up trying to figure it out than if you simply use your own suspicions and study the signs."

"Signs?" she wondered.

"The pattern," Otter supplied. "What are the patterns, and how do they tell us that Power is working?"

The stew had begun to boil. They retrieved their bowls— Black Skull sneering at the replacement the Ilini had found for him—and dipped out the evening meal. Otter stared thoughtfully at the steam rising from his bowl. Patterns. And where was Green Spider? What was he doing out there in the darkness?

Pearl finished the last of her stew, stood, stretched, and walked over to stow her bowl. Otter couldn't ignore the way her hips swayed, the way the fabric conformed to that thin waist as she bent over.

"I think," Black Skull murmured quietly, "that Red Moccasins has started to fade from the Trader's memory."

Otter shot him a warning look. "I don't have time for women."

"Then perhaps I should consider inviting Pearl into my blankets."

It irritated Otter that he had to force a neutral response. "That would be between you and her. I can only tell you that she doesn't appear to be interested in any man."

Black Skull's expression softened. "I think the Khota hurt her. I have seen such women before. Sometimes they can fight the demons let loose by the violation. Other times the demons destroy them. Pearl could go either way." A pause. "Be very careful with her."

Otter hardly heard. Pearl was unfolding her bedding. "Careful? About what? I told you, she's not interested. Neither am I."

Black Skull had a brotherly expression Otter had never seen before. "If you'd like, I could start reminding you that you're not interested every so often," he said.

Out over the slate-colored water, a flock of crows winged southward, cawing and thocking to themselves.

Otter gave the warrior a suspicious look. "What's the matter with you? You're beginning to act human. It worries me."

Black Skull lifted a grizzled eyebrow. "Not nearly as much as it would worry me if I thought you were right."

Pearl lay in her blankets listening to the voices of the men hunched by the fire. What had begun as worry had twisted itself around like a wrung-out fabric, to become strained fear. Why did so many parallels exist between her and the Ilini woman who played such an important part in Khota legend? That woman, no doubt fleeing a man every bit as despicable as Wolf of the Dead, had died wretchedly, tortured for days while the Khota and their Ilini prisoners watched.

She pulled the thick blanket snug against her chin. *Is that the fate Power has in store for me?*

She shivered at the memory of hard hands groping her breasts, the pain of his penis driving itself into her. The shivers increased at the thought of all those wide, awed, Khota eyes witnessing her humiliation.

Pearl hugged herself, biting at her lip to keep from whimpering. A single tear escaped her tightly closed eyes to trickle hotly down her cheek.

There would be no forgetting, no healing, not of the wound that festered in her soul.

"Where have you been?" Otter's voice asked.

"Everywhere! At least, to all the places I've been." Green Spider cried. "And now I'm here!"

"What's that you're—"

"Shhh!" the Contrary shushed. "Delight stalks the land in human form."

Pearl clamped her eyes shut, blocking the idiotic ramblings from her thoughts. Tonight she *had* to sleep. If the dreams came haunting, reminding her of Wolf of the Dead and his—

She cried out when she felt the blanket being drawn back, and clawed in panic for the fabric.

"Shhh!" Green Spider whispered as he tried to settle in beside her. "We don't want to make too much noise. Otter and Black Skull will be jealous. All their juices will dry up and we'll never get upriver!"

"Green Spider! What in the name of—" And then something poked her in the side.

"I'm fulfilling a promise! I've come to share your robes! To lead you to the ecstasy only a Contrary can give a woman. You will never want an ordinary man in your bed again."

Pearl shrieked, rolling away and jumping to her feet.

Green Spider leaped up, his breechcloth hanging like a short tent over a huge sassafras root that protruded from his crotch. To Pearl's horror, two large gourds were dangling and shaking at the base of the long root.

"I don't *believe* this!" She backed away while Green Spider hooted and jumped, the dry gourds rattling with seeds. The sassafras root bobbed suggestively.

"What the . . ." Black Skull emerged from his lean-to, gaping at Green Spider, who bounded and pirouetted toward Pearl. Otter had a silly smile on his face—one that Pearl vowed she'd smack away at the first opportunity.

"A promise made!" Green Spider cried. "Come, Pearl. Let's couple and share bliss! This is only the beginning. Wait until it gets *really* big!" He spread his arms to show the anticipated length, and arched his back, which caused the sassafras root to jab like a lance.

Pearl circled, keeping the fire between them. Otter appeared frozen, as if disbelieving what he saw.

"Curse you, Trader, *do something*!"

"Green Spider," Otter suggested calmly, "I don't think this is a good idea."

"The worst! The worst!" the Contrary cried, moving closer to the fire.

In the gaudy firelight, the sassafras root cast weird patterns over Green Spider's bare belly, and the hollows of his eyes had taken on a skull-like appearance. The first edgings of true fear sank talons into Pearl's soul.

Black Skull crept up from one side as Otter closed protectively on Pearl from the other, but she couldn't hear this world any longer. The whisperings of a thousand Khota voices roared in her ears.

Black Skull dove, pinning Green Spider, who whooped and laughed, the sassafras root and gourd testicles gleaming in the dancing firelight.

As the Contrary struggled with Black Skull, the root wagged into the fire and the tip crackled into flame. Being sassafras, it began popping and showering glittering sparks in all directions.

Green Spider's eyes suddenly crossed and his mouth formed a circle of astonishment. His gaze fixed on the phallus as the fire climbed the length of the root and caught his breechcloth on fire.

"The river!" Otter's arms waved in panicked gestures. "Throw him in the river!"

Before Black Skull could react, Green Spider twisted loose, screeching and howling, running in frantic circles. Black Skull chased after him, and Catcher immediately joined in, barking and yipping delight in their wake. Green Spider made one quick circle of the camp, the sassafras root popping and spitting sparks as the Contrary's wild gyrations fanned the flames. Black Skull dove to tackle the screaming Green Spider. He missed, landing face-first in the muddy sand.

Green Spider vented a high-pitched howl and raced down the slope in a shower of sparks and smoke to charge headfirst into the river.

Pearl flopped on the ground with a thud and gaped at the wreckage of the camp. Her blankets lay strewn around. The packs had been kicked over and half the contents spilled out. Black Skull groaned and rolled over, coughing as he sat up. The air smelled of smoke and burned cloth. She could hear frantic splashing from the river.

"Pearl? Are you all right?" Otter asked, bending down with concern in his eyes.

She scowled up at him. "Why didn't you stop him?"

"When he walked into camp, it was so ridiculous. I didn't think—"

"Well, he's gone too far this time," Black Skull growled, his hands clutching sand. "First my bowl, and then this! We're going to have it out with him, Trader. Enough is *enough*!"

"That depends," Otter stated tersely. "I wonder how badly he's burned."

As Otter helped Pearl to her feet, she realized that the splashing had stopped. Together, the three of them walked down to peer at the dark, silent water.

"Green Spider?" Pearl found her voice. "Are you all right?"

The water looked unnaturally still.

Torches appeared on the bank above them as the Ilini arrived, peering this way and that, their atlatl's nocked with long, deadly darts.

"What's happened here?" Long Throw demanded.

"The Contrary," Otter replied. "He caught himself on fire. Bring those torches down here."

"What? His clothing? His hair?" Long Throw asked.

"His root," Black Skull growled.

With the aid of the torchlight, they could see pretty well, but the black water seemed to have swallowed Green Spider. Not even ripples suggested where he might have drowned.

A sudden wrenching feeling of loss grew in Pearl's soul. "It was only a joke," she whispered. "That's all. Not worth Green Spider's life."

"He'll be fine," Otter reassured. "He's got to have—"

"What are you doing down there?" Green Spider called from behind them.

Everyone spun around, seeing his skinny, stark-naked body outlined by the campfire.

"You miserable cur!" Black Skull thundered. "When I get my hands on you—"

"You can't kill me!" Green Spider leaped high, twisting in the air while Catcher barked and jumped beside him. "I'm going to be a father! A father!"

Black Skull started forward purposefully, but Pearl placed a hand on his brawny arm. "It's all right," she said. "He didn't mean any harm. Not really."

"A father?" Otter asked as he climbed the slope. "How?"

"I just impregnated the river!" Green Spider shouted, leaping and dancing. "The river won't ever want any ordinary man again, either!"

"I'm going to fetch my obsidian flake, and he's going to be lucky if I stop at his testicles!" Black Skull promised.

Only after the Ilini had left, muttering among themselves, and she and Otter had seen that Green Spider, indeed, had no blisters or burns, did Pearl return to her bedding. Someone had gathered up her blankets from where they'd been strewn around and laid them out perfectly again.

Cautiously, she slid inside. When her thigh touched something cold, she threw the blankets back and let out a sharp cry.

"What is it?" Otter called. "Are you all right?"

Pearl glowered at the charred sassafras root and two burned gourds, all carefully hidden and neatly tied up in a bundle of grass. "I'm fine," she called back. "Go to sleep."

Before she lay down again, she pulled out Green Spider's "gift" and placed it in front of her on the sand. The more she stared at the bundle, the more amusing it became, until laughter bubbled up in her throat. She couldn't stop laughing for a full finger of time.

Shaking her head, Pearl patted the charred root. She slept in perfect peace that night.

"We need to talk," Tall Man said. "Come walk with me."

"I can't go!" Star Shell insisted. "He has my daughter. Look at them, sitting together on that mound. I called to her and she wouldn't come! She wouldn't leave Stargazer's lap. Blessed Spirits, what can I—"

"Follow me. Hurry! *Now!*"

Having no alternative, Star Shell complied, walking in a panicked daze as Tall Man led the way through the eastern gap in the circular wall and down toward the marshy river bottom. Moisture had blackened the bark on the trees, turning them into solemn, brooding giants. The morning sun hid behind low-hanging billows of cloud that threatened more rain.

"How could this happen?"

"The Mask is doing everything in its Power to find a keeper." Tall Man walked downhill slowly, his hands clasped behind him, his head down. The damp leaves compressed under his diminutive feet.

"It's *my* daughter! That's who the Mask is after! You didn't see them!"

"No. But I certainly heard your screams." Tall Man stepped over the rotted remains of a downed maple. "That tantrum has earned you Stargazer's malice."

"I will *not* lose my daughter to that *thing*!"

"Oh, yes you will, if you challenge Stargazer just one more time. It will be whispering to him as he wears it, telling him how he can use the Mask to eliminate his enemies. And now you're marked as one."

Star Shell placed her fingertips to her temples, pressing as she closed her eyes. *Think. There's a way out of this. Just grab your daughter and run!*

"We must take the Mask back," Tall Man said sadly. "And I'm afraid that doing so will kill my old friend."

"Tall Man," she said, coming to her decision, "I'm leaving. I'm going back up the hill, taking my daughter, and leaving."

He looked up at her, familiar wisdom in his wrinkled face. "Do you really think it will be that easy, young Star Shell?

You'll win today. I'm reasonably sure of that. Stargazer will let Silver Water go. But what about tomorrow?''

"I don't *care* about tomorrow! I'll have my daughter safe . . . and far away from here!''

"For how long?'' The Magician steepled his short fingers. "Listen to me. Listen to me with great care and attention, Star Shell. Your daughter has been touched by the Mask. Just as your husband followed it back to the place his grandfather had taken it, so will Silver Water. Oh, she won't do this immediately. Over the years, her resentment of you will fester. You can't hold her forever, Star Shell. She'll come back . . . maybe as a young woman. And what will she find?''

Star Shell's legs had gone wobbly. "Stargazer, and the Mask . . . waiting.''

"I doubt it will be Stargazer. He's old, close to death, as I am. No, it will be a young man, one the Mask can use the way it did your husband. By the time Silver Water is old enough to escape you, she'll be ready for him.''

"What? That's crazy!''

"Is it?'' He gave her a flat appraisal. "The Mask has touched her soul, Star Shell. Whether you or I like it or not, she has an affinity for Power, and that affinity grows with each exposure to the Mask. Now, if we are going to save her, we *must* get that Mask back, and hurry—*run*—northward to the Roaring Water. It's our only chance.''

"I'm taking her away. She won't come back here.''

"It will be an *obsession* with her, the way it was for her father!''

Star Shell hesitated. "Why Stargazer? Why did it pick him?''

"He's perfect.'' Tall Man resumed his pace down toward the flats. "The Mask has offered him what he most desires. When he wears the Mask, he can see the stars again. And with its Power, he can lure young people back to study, and reestablish the ancient ways. For those two things, Stargazer would indeed Trade his soul. And for the moment, so would Silver Water. You were too frightened, too angry, but I saw.''

"Saw what?''

"The stars reflected in your daughter's eyes.''

"I'm taking her and leaving.''

"I hope not.''

"Do you expect to stop me?"

The Magician shook his head. "No. You will stop yourself."

"You have a great deal of misplaced faith in me."

"No, young Star Shell. I have a well-placed faith in you. You will not leave, because you are no fool. Right now you are speaking with the voice of a mother who is frightened for her daughter. Deep in your soul, you know that you can't run. Power never left that as an option for you. You must win against the Mask, or watch your own destruction."

The last of her defenses crumbled. "I never asked for any of this."

"No. I think, however, that we may all be thankful that Power chose someone with your strength and endurance."

An image of her husband's body flashed in her memory. The brooding darkness of the clan house filled her soul as it had that night. She could feel that biting chill—a coldness of the spirit. The rope that choked his puffy neck creaked just beyond her hearing.

And the Mask has touched my daughter.

She glared at Tall Man. "Stargazer called you a witch, a sorcerer."

He shrugged, glancing off through the saplings.

"You've killed a lot of people, haven't you? You're not just the kind benefactor you would have me believe."

He sighed. "I know a little of the plants, of Power and its uses, that's all."

She studied him, aware of his discomfort, though he hid it admirably. He lifted his hand in a futile gesture. "The High Heads are an old people, Star Shell. Our sacred societies were already filled with ancient mysteries when the Flat Pipe peoples were still battling squirrels for hickory nuts. We knew, some of us still know, secrets that would—"

"Just how Powerful are you, Magician? Why is it that until I met you, I had heard your name spoken only in hushed tones? Why have we always followed back trails on this journey? Is it just to avoid Robin and his warriors? Couldn't we have struck off to the northeast? Into the Walnut Clan territories? Or would they have gathered their people and hounded you?"

"I have acted prudently. You know this to be true."

She bent down, staring into his veiled brown eyes. "Well,

it's beyond prudence now, isn't it? Stargazer is wearing the Mask. He's Powerful, too, and the Mask is counting on that, isn't it?''

Tall Man licked his thin lips. "This will have to be done very carefully—which is why I had to bring you away, out of the Circle, down here, where we could talk.''

"He's never going to let the Mask out of his grasp. Just how do you expect to get your hands on it? To muffle it with the wolfhide?''

"He can't sleep while he's wearing the Mask. It will whisper to his soul, meddle with his rest. He'll have to lay it to one side.''

"But the Mask will warn him the instant we attempt to take it! It will know what we're plotting!''

Tall Man fingered his receded chin. "Does the war leader engage a battle in the fog?''

"Don't be silly. He can't see the disposition of his warriors on the battleground.''

Tall Man smiled. "But not all battles are won by attacking headlong. Some attacks are best carried out in the fog.''

What are you after, Magician? "We're talking about Power and a Mask, not a head-to-head fight.''

"Exactly.''

Star Shell crossed her arms, glaring at the little man. "How do you expect to sneak up on the Mask? How can we do this without placing Silver Water in greater jeopardy?''

Tall Man reached up to finger his copper ear spools. "Star Shell, it is an old saying that two people can keep a secret—as long as one of them is dead. I have a great many secrets that I would not wish to be shared. Trust me.''

"No. We've gone far enough on my trust. My *daughter* is at stake. You've made the decisions—and I'm not sure that they haven't led us to worse straits than if we'd simply run to StarSky, enlisted the help of my father, and pushed on to the Roaring Water.''

"Well, that would not have—''

"*Talk* to me! Tell me who you are!. Rot you, Magician. If you want trust, you're going to tell me why I should trust you to fool the Mask. Where would you find the skill to *trick* a thing with the Mask's Power?''

"Star Shell, there are times you simply have to believe what I tell you."

"My daughter's soul is at stake!"

He slowly relented under her hot glare. "Very well. I'll tell you a bit of my—"

"All of it. You'll tell me now! You've murdered, and for what? For lust! You've lied, tricked, killed. What else? Stargazer called you a sorcerer."

"Among other things." He clasped his hands below his chin, gazing on her with eyes that seemed to expand into black pits. "You would know it all before you will trust me to get the Mask back? Before you'll agree to help me?"

Come on, Star Shell. You've got to face him down. Her guts twisted under that hypnotic stare. "If I'm to go on risking Silver Water, I must know who you are."

"You are aware that we are called the Serpent Clans by most of the people in the world. Do you know why?"

Star Shell opened her mouth to answer, and stopped short, frowning.

"Ah, indeed, that is a hard one to answer. The big river to the south of us, the Serpent River, is now the center of the High Head lifeline. Like a snake, it runs through the High Head world, and many of my people's clans are now found to the south of it. But why Serpent, why that name?"

"Witches are called serpents," she whispered. "Like snakes, they blend in with the surroundings, soundless predators who hunt the night."

"You're a smart woman." His expanded eyes tried to suck her down into their depths. "Several days' journey to the southeast of the Many Paints' territory, you'll come across a hilltop fortification. That's now Flat Pipe territory."

"I know of it."

"But to the southeast of that lies the Viper Clan territory."

"Flat Pipe are not welcome there—almost no one is. Not even the High Heads, at least not that I know."

Tall Man's gaze had pinned her the way a bone awl skewers a roasting rabbit. "The Serpent Society has its center there. I went there as a very young man. What I tell you now must remain between us, for if you should betray it, the Serpents will kill you. Like the poisonous snakes that we are, we will come in the night, hidden among the people, and you will never see the deliverer of your death."

She tried to blink, locked in his stare. Her mouth had gone dry, and even the effort to swallow cost her.

"On a ridge top overlooking the Viper River there lies a giant Serpent. The legend says that First Man fought the beast, that it bit him on the ankle, and First Man hovered near death for four days. With each dawn came a new vision of the world's future. On the fifth day, First Man recovered his strength and did battle with the Serpent. But by this time, the Serpent's venom had mixed with First Man's blood, and neither could kill the other.

"Finally, Serpent stopped the fight and made this bargain with First Man: 'I will no longer fight you, First Man. You cannot destroy me, and I cannot destroy you. As a result, I will make an agreement with you. The Serpents shall become small and be hunters of the shadows and low places. When left alone, the Serpents will in turn leave men alone. When molested, they shall strike. I, the Great Serpent, will lie on this ridge, and some people will be drawn to me. Those I will swallow into my belly and devour their souls. When they pass, they shall be mine forever.'

"First Man agreed to the Great Serpent's offer. From that day, snakes have crawled on their bellies and hunted the low places. When disturbed, they have generally sought to avoid trouble, but when cornered, they strike—as is their right. Humans, too, have kept the bargain. As I did as a young man."

"You are a member of the Serpent Society?"

"I am one of the Elders." Tall Man nodded. "My Power is that of the Great Serpent. You see, I was prepared in the egg he clutches in his mouth. When I was initiated, he devoured me, and I made my passage along his length. I made the passage of the stars, the moon, and the solstices, each marked by a curve of his body. In the end, I was passed, and made my way back to the world through the spiraling maze."

"I don't understand what you're saying."

"I should hope not. You asked me to convince you that I could trick the Mask. Very well. The Power of the Great Serpent runs in my veins. Understand, Star Shell, that the Mask is Powerful, true, but it is not incredibly clever. I shall conjure a fog through which it cannot see. A diversion. We shall attack it from a blind side.''

A sorcerer, a witch! A being balanced between Darkness and Light. The Serpent brought instant death, or breathed life into the dying. Giver and Taker. *Which do you serve, Magician?*

"You're a frightening person."

"I regret that you had to find out." He turned away and walked into the forest. "Come. Out here among these trees we will find the wreckage of old houses. These were once prosperous fields where men and women worked. They hoped here, loved and conceived. Their children were born on this soil, and many are buried in it. The forest retakes the land so quickly. You'd never know that people lived here once—but perhaps they left what we will need."

Thirty-two

Moonlight played over the water, dancing off the ripples that ran before the evening breeze. Musky smells of mud, water, and the greenery of spring hung on the air, accented by the smoke from Otter's fire.

The cloud-strewn sunset lit the western horizon, broken only by the undulating tree line that followed the course of the river. In the distance, Singing rose from an Ilini village that Long Throw said lay up one of the tributaries.

Long Throw and his party had gone there to be feasted by their relatives tonight, while Otter's group had decided to forgo the festivities and collapse on a high knoll overlooking the river. Composed of discarded shells left by previous occupants of the site, even this little stand of high ground was losing way to the river, which had undercut some of the bank. Now shells gleamed whitely as they protruded from the charcoal-stained earth. Bits of stone had been intermingled with the rich soil, and a low stand of isolated sumac leafed out at the crest near their fire.

Pearl had reclined against a pack with a blanket across her lap, and now she stared at the fire with drowsy eyes. Otter watched her, as he did so often these days. Wind teased her hair into a fluttering raven halo around her beautiful face. She seemed oblivious to the strands that occasionally tangled with her long eyelashes. When she moved, her skin glistened like burnished copper in the pastel light.

Across the fire, Black Skull braced his elbow on a fat roll of palmetto-frond matting—an item Otter would have long since Traded had this trip been normal.

Long Throw's camp lay on a larger shell midden slightly back from the river and separated from them by a lazy creek overgrown with bulrush and cattail. A village had once stood in the flats behind them, fed by the bounty of the river, now reclaimed by marsh.

Green Spider had wandered off to do whatever he did after dusk faded. Sometimes his absence stretched into half the night.

"Where do you suppose he is?" Black Skull asked. "For the past five nights, he's wandered away like this. Do you suppose that maybe one of these days, he'll just disappear and we can go home?"

"He'll be back." Pearl yawned, pulling her blanket more snuggly over her long legs.

Otter had memorized those legs: muscular, firm, and silky skinned. He winced and forced himself to stare at the fire. Thoughts of her legs led to thoughts about other things, and that led to madness.

Think about Red Moccasins, he told himself. *Pearl isn't interested in you.* But she'd become a problem, sitting just ahead of him in the canoe, the movements of her body and that melodic laugh conjuring desires better left dormant.

A wolf howled in the distance, the call mingling with the Singing from the distant Ilini village.

"He's out chasing around with that wolf," Otter said to redirect his thoughts. "I'm sure I've seen it. Every now and then I'll get a glimpse, just a flash of black in the brush."

Pearl cocked her head. "Do you think it's following us?"

"And that crow's been staying close," Black Skull added. "Last night, just before dusk, I was back in the trees, and I heard him cawing and squealing. I also heard Green Spider's voice—which is undoubtedly what irritated the crow so much. At first I thought the fool was arguing with himself. Now I'm not so sure."

Pearl closed her eyes, sighing as she leaned her head back. "Wolves? Crows? I feel like I'm being sucked around and around in a whirlpool."

And Power is at the center of it, trying to suck us down.

Otter massaged his arm, aware of the lethargy that rode his muscles. They'd been maintaining a killing pace. Life consisted of paddling, eating, and sleeping. On those instances when the urge arose to slacken the pace, he needed only to look over his shoulder—back down the flat expanse of water—to know that Wolf of the Dead and his warriors followed relentlessly.

"Maybe it's Wolf of the Dead. Grizzly Tooth said he turned himself into a wolf." Firelight caressed Pearl's face. "Maybe it was more than that mask."

"If you see this wolf—" Black Skull stifled a yawn "—tell me. I'll wing a dart through it and we can go look it over."

"I don't want to remind you of the day you killed that crow," Otter said glumly. "Bad luck came from that. Maybe that's what Green Spider's arguing with the crow about. Saving your hide for offending Power."

Black Skull turned his head away, studying the night. "In the last couple of moons, I've learned a great deal, Otter. I would go back . . . change that day if I could. If it just wasn't for Green Spider. He makes me crazy . . . twists the world around so no one can see anything straight. And he does it on purpose."

"Of course. He's a Contrary." Pearl stared up at the white disk of moon. "Didn't you ever learn about Contraries?"

"My art and passion is war. Granduncle never taught me anything else. If you know about Contraries, tell me this: Why does he have to be such a trial?"

Otter swatted a mosquito. "Power makes Contraries to remind us of human folly. All that clowning is deadly serious. When you think about it, we're vain creatures. Absorbed with wants and desires that are no doubt trivial in the eyes of the Spirit World. Wealth? Status? Honor? What do those things mean in the end, anyway?"

Black Skull's crooked jaw worked back and forth. "They mean *everything*, Trader."

"I think Contraries keep us from taking ourselves too seriously." Pearl frowned at the fire. "I mean, if humans disappeared from the earth, would it make any difference? Would the robins stop hunting in the grass? Would the catfish stop eating minnows? Would the trees stop growing?"

Black Skull chuckled humorlessly. "We wouldn't have to paddle like slaves all day, because those accursed Khota wouldn't be around to chase us. And, of course, we wouldn't be around to be chased."

Otter rubbed his face. "I'm starting to think that might not be a bad state of affairs. But, Black Skull, you'd never make it back to the City of the Dead to receive a hero's welcome, either."

"Trader, I doubt that I will ever see the City of the Dead again. My ghost will be lost up here, somewhere. My ancestors will enjoy the Feast of the Dead without me."

"What a cheery thought." Pearl bent her head back to stare at the moon where it peered through a hole in the patchy clouds.

Otter watched the way her thick black hair fell over her shoulders and brushed the sand behind her. She should be back among the Anhinga, laughing with her relatives, telling stories about alligators, and hunting.

I would send you back to them if I could.

He closed his eyes, encouraging memories he'd tried so hard to drive from his soul. The river behind her, Red Moccasins walked toward him, her naked body silhouetted by moonlight. Yes, that made more sense. Better to desire a distant woman he couldn't have than one who sat so close. He'd memorized Pearl's scent, the way she made even the simplest gesture.

"Perhaps Power chose us because no one will miss us," Pearl said softly.

"The Anhinga may not miss you, woman, but my people will certainly miss me," Black Skull insisted. "The next time the Copena come down the river, they'll desperately wish I were there."

"The Copena have fought with the clans for generations before you were born," Otter said. "And since some things never change, they'll be fighting with them long after your ghost is propped on its own burial mound."

Black Skull shook his head, climbing to his feet. "Between

you and the Contrary, I'm almost inspired enough to open my veins. I'd better make a quick scout around the camp and ponder these truths you've imparted.''

Black Skull picked up his war club and ghosted into the night on silent feet.

"Doesn't he ever get tired?" Pearl wondered.

"If he does, he'll kill himself before he'll let anyone know."

They sat silently, listening to the night and the distant Singing.

Pearl stirred. "What is that? The Singing, I mean. It sounds like a celebration."

"Planting Moon." Otter pointed up to where the clouds had slipped across the glowing orb. "Tomorrow they'll all be in the fields, working like mad to get the maygrass and little barley in."

She turned those soft dark eyes—guardians of so many mysteries—upon him. "I meant it when I said that none of us would be missed. As for me, I can understand. I didn't accept my place. Wouldn't marry and do my duty for the clan. What about you, Otter? You're a puzzle. You're a man. You don't have to be responsible, don't have to take your place in council. Did you do something wrong? Commit a crime?"

"Among the White Shell, men do have to be responsible. We have to clear fields, teach our nieces and nephews, and a great many other things. And no, I didn't commit any crime. But I thought we weren't going to talk about that. Remember? I don't ask about the Khota, and you don't ask about me."

She pursed her lips, the frown lines deepening before she shot a glance in the direction Black Skull had taken. "All right. Let's talk." She sat forward and let out a deep breath. "There are too many secrets between us to allow us to be real friends. And I . . . I want to be your friend."

Otter's gut tightened. "You can be my friend without—"

"The Khota . . . the night we arrived, they took me up the hill to Wolf of the Dead's house. It's up on the bluff, overlooking the Khota clan grounds."

"Yes, I've been there. I know the place."

"I was promised to him. A deal. Marriage to establish a Trade relationship." Her fist knotted on the blanket. "I came to hate the Khota on the way up the river. They're practiced at taking slaves—and that's how they treated me, like a slave. When I couldn't escape, I fought back, used my knowledge of plants. It wasn't the right time of year to find good poisons, but I made them about as miserable as they made me.''

"They never found out?"

"Grizzly Tooth suspected, but he could never catch me at it." She paused, wetting her full lips nervously. "Then they . . . I . . .''

"Pearl, you don't have to say more, I—"

"Please. Green Spider knows. He's given me back to myself. Him and his sassafras-root penis." Her slim brown hands made an orderly gesture above the blanket. "That night . . . they took me to Wolf of the Dead. Deep inside, I'd resigned myself to being Wolf of the Dead's wife. I thought it would be handled like a marriage anywhere else. Feasting, stories—'' she listened to the faint Ilini songs "—Singing and Dancing.

"Instead, before I had the slightest hint of what was coming, they stripped me." She closed her eyes. "Threw me down on all fours . . . and he . . .''

Otter laced his fingers and created one tight fist before him. "I've heard the stories. I understand. But that's past now."

Her breathing had gone shallow, quick. "No. Not past. Those memories live inside me every moment. A person can't forget something like that. He took me like a dog, like a camp bitch. Right there in front of everyone."

Otter nodded. He had heard worse stories than hers about things Wolf of the Dead did to his wives after the first night. Horrifying things. Torture. Mutilation. Hadn't Pearl ever wondered why a man of Wolf of the Dead's status did not currently have a wife? Pearl didn't know how lucky she was to be sitting here. "Too bad you didn't kill him."

"Yes." She smiled bravely. "Evidently Power needed him for something. And now this black wolf is following us. Sometimes my muscles cramp and I want to break down in tears, but I drive myself that much harder, knowing he's back there, those canoes closing the distance."

"We won't let them have you."

She glanced up at him. "You have a great deal of confidence in yourself, Otter." A pause. "And so . . . now that you know my secret, tell me why you always seem so sad. If you didn't commit a crime, why did you come on this trip?''

Otter's mouth pressed into a hard white line. He fought with himself for a moment, deciding what to say, what not to. ''Her name is Red Moccasins. She married my brother.''

''You mentioned that once. So you killed him? Is that why you're here? Condemned with us?''

''No. No, I could never do that,'' he said in surprise. ''I love my brother a great deal. And I love her. She's a smart, capable woman. She'll be a great leader of the people, and she needs a man who is also a great leader to help her. Four Kills was that man. I was not. The river claimed me when I was a baby. I am as different in my way as you and Black Skull are in yours. Grandmother understood when she gave me my freedom. Better to have me gone, serving the clan through Trade, than obsessed with an unfulfilled love for my sister-in-law and lurking around the clan grounds.''

''Is that the longing I see in your eyes? For her?''

He lifted a shoulder. ''I didn't know it was there.''

She gave him a guarded glance, ''I think this Red Moccasins made a terrible mistake. You're a good man, Otter.''

''So is my brother.'' *And he Dreamed my death at the Roaring Water.* ''We're twins. We share souls. And sharing those souls, I can tell you that he is a much better man than I.''

She shifted to stretch out across the sand on her stomach, staring up at him. Did those eyes have to be so enchanting? ''Three outcasts and a Contrary. Power must be desperate to choose the likes of us.''

He laughed. ''Indeed.'' And reached over to pat her extended hand. ''Thank you for telling me your story. You're a very brave woman.''

''Really? For someone brave, I'm constantly strangling on fear.''

''That's what bravery is. Doing what you have to, no matter how afraid you are.'' He glanced at the brush. ''Black Skull has learned that lesson better than all the rest of us put together.''

''It's hard to think of him ever being afraid.'' She rolled onto her side and pillowed her head on the pack while she watched Otter. The blanket had conformed to the curves of her body, emphasizing the twin curves of her breasts, her narrow waist and full hips, the tawny length of her muscular legs. What was it that he saw in those doe-like eyes?

"I knew about you before we met," he said, steering for a safer course, one that he could manage. "The wild girl of the swamps. I even saw you a couple of times in the Anhinga grounds. I thought then that you were striking, alive."

He forced himself to watch the fire. Better to go night-blind than to start dwelling on a sensuous body like that. He reconstructed Red Moccasins' body the way it had looked that night on the river, in moonlight half as bright as this. There she had stood in naked splendor, back straight, breasts high and full as they cast soft shadows across her muscular belly. The thick mane of her hair spilled down over those smooth shoulders.

"I was alive then," Pearl said regretfully, breaking the spell he'd cast for himself. "Looking back, though, I think I ran to the swamps because something was missing in my life. I always went to the wild places to find it."

As I went to the river.

"You'll find it again," he promised, faking a yawn, unwilling to deal with the crazy thoughts that had begun to play with his soul. "We'd better try to sleep. Morning will come early. The river will be just as long, and the paddles just as unforgiving."

"Sleep well, Trader," she whispered, snuggling down farther into her blankets.

He feigned sleep, watching her.

Wolf of the Dead, that's two I owe you for. One for Uncle, one for Pearl. I hope to the Mysterious One and the Spirits that I can repay each in full.

Somewhere in the fantasy of choking the life out of Wolf of the Dead, he fell asleep. He vaguely heard Black Skull return and give Catcher an order to be quiet, then the rustling of bedding, and finally, the triumphant howl of a wolf in the distance.

Catcher's low growl came as Otter's first warning. The smell—even through the mists of sleep—came as the second. Black Skull's muffled curse was the third.

Otter sat up, blinking in the faint light of false dawn. Pale blue glints danced on the river and in the windblown leaves of the trees. At first glance, the camp seemed normal, but Catcher, sitting at the foot of Otter's blankets, had his ears up, the growl harsh and full of threat.

Black Skull sat bolt upright in his blanket, muttering to himself as he glared at Green Spider's bedding. The blankets were hunched as if the Contrary had rolled himself into a ball. The skunk smell burned in the air.

"Ancestors keep us..." Otter said, sitting up cautiously. "Where's the skunk? Do you see it?"

"The raving *lunatic*!" Black Skull cried.

Pearl had awakened and now scrambled from her bedding, too, pinching her nose. "Skunk in camp. Why didn't Catcher warn us?"

Otter shook the final filaments of sleep from his clotted thoughts. "Wait a minute. Green Spider brought a skunk into camp?"

Black Skull gritted. "*I* did! Any human being with the sense of the ancestors would have screamed, run, something. But look at him! And now... well, look! He's in there *sleeping* with it!"

Otter opened his mouth, but skunk air entered and almost gagged him. "You brought a skunk into camp? *You?*"

"And you put it in Green Spider's bed?" Pearl laughed out loud.

"He deserved it... after all the grief he's brought. You remember when he crapped in my bowl?" Black Skull flung his arms about, as if trying to indicate what he couldn't say, or to get rid of something stuck to his hands—the effect was the same. "*I had to get even!*"

"Are you sure he's in there?" Otter took a cautious step closer to Green Spider's bed, at the same time signaling Catcher to stay where he was. "Green Spider?"

"Good morning, Otter." The Contrary's voice sounded cheerful, if muffled by the blankets. "Black Skull brought me a friend."

The warrior exploded: "Rot you, fool! Get up! Get out of there!"

"Quiet!" Green Spider cautioned from his nest. "You'll frighten Black-and-White."

"Black-and-White?" Otter glanced uneasily at the warrior.

He knew that look; Black Skull wanted to kill something, and desperately.

"Look at this little nose," Green Spider asserted from the mass of blankets. "It's beautiful."

"I don't want to think about noses," Pearl told him. "Mine's already clogged." Turning, she asked Otter, "How can he breathe in there?"

Otter gestured for calm, more to quiet himself than to still anyone else. No one, it appeared, was going to do anything foolish. No indeed, that part had already been taken care of.

Black Skull exhaled as if his lungs had been punctured; his crooked jaw set with frustration. "That *fool*! He crapped in my bowl. My *good* bowl! The one I brought from home. It was a gift!"

"All right, yes, we remember."

"Well . . ." Black Skull groped for the words, his eyes gone glassy, either from the skunk stink or his anger. "I tried, Otter, I really did. I didn't kill him, did I? Not even when every one of my instincts told me to twist his head off, I didn't. I said to myself, 'Just get even.' And last night while he was out doing whatever it is that he does out in the dark, I caught this skunk. Grabbed it by the tail real quick, you see. Kept it from spraying me. Well, I came back to camp, and shushed Catcher to keep him from giving it away. Then I put the skunk in the fool's bedding and wadded it up!"

Otter winced. "You *did* that? In the name of Many Colored Crow and the ancestors, *why*?"

Black Skull's face had gone red, the muscles twitching like a bag full of mice. "*He* plays tricks on everyone else! How come *he* can get away with it and *I* can't?"

Otter wrinkled his nose, aware that the smell continued to grow worse. *Now what do I do?* "Green Spider, you can't keep the skunk."

"Black Skull gave it to me."

Otter flayed his brain. "Yes, well, not every gift . . ." No, that wasn't the way. "Um, Catcher will be very hurt. He thinks he has the duty to guard the camp. Now how will he know if it's Black-and-White or another skunk that's come to raid?"

"Dogs can tell the difference, just like they can with people. They can smell it."

Otter wet his lips, then thought better of it because he could taste that pungent stink. "So can everyone else, Green Spider—"

"Trade," Pearl said suddenly, a light in her frantic eyes. "Trade something for the skunk! Anything! How about Black Skull's new bowl?"

"What do you mean, 'How about Black Skull's new bowl!' " the warrior exploded.

"No, that'll never work." Otter glanced up at the morning sky. What could he Trade? The magnificent reddening haze of dawn gave him his answer. "Green Spider, I would like to Trade with you. You have a—a wonderful skunk. I have this gorgeous sunrise!"

"Sunrise?"

"Yes, Green Spider. It's a beautiful sunrise. But I've always wanted a skunk!" *Just like I'd want another Contrary in my life.* "I would Trade with you. Black-and-White for this sunrise."

"I don't know," Green Spider responded. "How would Black-and-White feel? It's a terrible thing to be Traded first thing in the morning."

"Well, at least he won't miss this beautiful sunrise. It's more gorgeous than you can imagine! Come on, Green Spider, Trade with me. This beautiful sunrise for Black-and-White."

"And two badger bowls!" Green Spider countered.

Otter glared at Black Skull. "You drive a hard bargain." Especially since he was out of badger bowls. "I'll have to get the badger bowls later, Green Spider, but, yes, if you can wait to receive them, I'll Trade you the sunrise and two badger bowls."

"All right." Green Spider threw back the blankets, and the very air seemed to wilt.

"Ugh!" Black Skull groaned and backed away.

Pearl ran.

The Contrary sat up with a very upset skunk cradled in his arms. Black-and-White's nose wiggled and his beady little eyes took in the camp, the people—and finally, Catcher. The tail went up and Otter could see the off-color spray being blown all over Green Spider's clothing. The reek came hot on the heels of the mist.

"Oh, no . . ."

Catcher took off like a shot, his tail between his legs, toward *Wave Dancer*. Pearl followed in hot pursuit, one hand pinching her nose.

"Here!" Green Spider extended the skunk, holding it out to Otter by the scruff of the neck. Black-and-White clawed desperately at the air, hissing and growling at the same time.

"Just set Black-and-White down." Otter pointed, trying to keep his eyes from watering.

Green Spider instantly clutched the skunk against his chest, and the panicked animal sprayed yet again.

"No! I mean, yes! Hold onto the skunk! Strangle him, Green Spider! Don't let him go!"

Green Spider stopped, suddenly unsure. He glanced solicitously back and forth between Otter and Black Skull. "He might decide to leave."

"No, no, I'm sure he'll stay." Otter couldn't help but cough. Every nerve in his nose had caught fire.

Green Spider shrugged and set Black-and-White on the ground. The skunk waddled off in a beeline for the sumac grove, and the Contrary sighed.

Black Skull propped his hands on his hips. "No one, *no one*! would ever have imagined that you would—" His eyes went wide as Green Spider leaped and threw his arms around Black Skull's neck. "*Ahhh!*"

The Contrary hugged him tightly, the fresh skunk smell rubbing into Black Skull's clothing. At the same time, Green Spider was crying, "You're the *best* friend I ever had! I didn't want to Trade the skunk you gave me, but look at this magnificent sunrise! And I promise, I'll give you one of my badger bowls when I get them!"

Black Skull grabbed Green Spider by his shirt and breechcloth, took a short run, and pitched him headlong over the edge of the shell midden into the river.

. . . It didn't help.

Stargazer awakened after a day of fitful Dreams. Images of the past—of the old days—had returned to haunt him. Out beyond the perimeter of The Heavens, people had farmed the lush fields on the floodplain of the Red Buck River. In the sunlight, those fields had waved emerald in the summer breezes.

He'd stood on the lip of the earthen embankment and looked out at the Sky Clan holdings while he listened to the Songs of praise and work. The wind, warm and scented with the smell of prosperity, had stroked his face and clothing. The land swelled with the harmony of the people.

When he turned back to The Heavens, he saw the manicured grace of tailored grass contrasting with red, brown, white-and-yellow clay surfaces—the colored soils carried in by the basketload and placed in the proper order to reflect the balance of the ordered world.

The marker posts stood straight in the curve of the perimeter wall, freshly painted, and the effigy heads that marked the locations of the constellations were crisp and uncracked in the newly carved wood.

And there in the center, on the observation mound, initiates sat by rank, listening to the Second Star give a lecture about the sky, and the lights that moved through it according to the Mysterious One's plan. Their faces had been rapt, awaiting yet another layer of the ancient knowledge to be revealed, like the skin peeled from an onion.

What a wondrous Dream. It would live again. He groaned, aware of a heaviness in his chest. Then he opened his sightless eyes to the insides of his house, once the main temple of the High Head Star Society. This forlorn place would be deserted no longer. The Mask had promised that the old ways, the old Power, would return. The disciples would be back, sitting at his feet as he lectured through the Mask.

Of all the horrible truths of old age and death, another death—that of his people's ways and the knowledge of the ancients—had tormented him the most. Even his grandson had tired of hearing him talk about the vanishing ways.

Didn't they understand? Those "ways" were the very blood in their veins! Monuments like The Heavens had been built upon years of study. The rituals had been given to them by the Mysterious One and the great Spirit heroes. Many Colored Crow had walked upon this spot.

Such precious and sacred knowledge must not be allowed to die.

I shall live to see the Dream fulfilled. Yes, perhaps that's what the Dream was trying to tell him. He hadn't been seeing the old days, but the new. That Dream, so vivid and bright, would be the future of the Heavens. Those were not ghosts, but people he would know soon.

A thin smile formed on his lips as he fingered the Mask lying on his chest. The wood felt so smooth, the feathers on the ruff crisp and forgiving.

And he had his first student. Silver Water had listened intently as he pointed out the stars, her face shining in wonder. She would inherit his position; the Mask had already told him so. After her initiation, she would become the First Star. And after that, upon his death, she would be the Stargazer, the keeper of the ancient wisdoms.

Enough. Evening was falling. The time had come to rise, to find young Silver Water and take her out for yet another night of instruction in the movements of the heavenly bodies.

And best of all, he would *see* again. When he wore the Mask, the heavens returned to him in radiant clarity, as sharp as an obsidian blade. That gift, if no other, brought joy to his soul.

That Star Shell woman would scream again, but Silver Water was no longer her daughter. Not as long as he wore the Mask. This Star Shell—Flat Pipe that she was—didn't deserve a daughter so filled with wonder.

You've lost her to me. Stargazer cuddled the Mask as he sat up. He found the cord, a bit thinner than he remembered, and slipped the Mask over his face—only to remain in darkness.

"Mask?" He reached up, feeling carefully at first, then with frantic fingers. The lines were wrong, and then the long beak came off in his fingers. Panic stunned him for one horrifying moment as his exploring fingers discovered the telltale truth. The feathers came off in his hands, so loosely had they been glued to the fake.

"Magician?" He lurched to his feet, grabbing the wall for support. He scrambled to the place where the Mask pack had been. Vacant. Empty space. The irony of it twisted inside him like a rabbit on a stick. As he had taken the Mask through stealth, so had the Magician returned the favor.

Stargazer rushed for the door, slamming a shoulder painfully and staggering out into the dusk. *"Magician!"* Only the twitters of birds answered. He sank down on pain-filled knees, his joints crackling, and tears spilled down his cheeks.

"Bring it back! Please, Magician. Bring me the Mask. I will do anything you want!"

He sniffed, rubbing his sleeve across his dripping nose. "Don't you see? It's not just me who will die. But our people! *Your* people! Does that mean nothing to you?"

Silence answered. The evening breeze carried the cooing of a dove to him.

"Magician?" The old man bowed his head until he felt the ground, cool against his burning skull. Nothing would be saved. Not his sight, not his heritage, not even this place. The Heavens would vanish with him.

Perhaps the trees might remember as they spread their branches across the area where long-dead men had once charted the stars and read the heavens.

The aching loneliness hammered in his heart.

Thirty-three

My companions call me a fool, but who is the real fool? I ride in the canoe, seeing the present at the sides of my vision, looking back down the river at where I've been. That which appears beside you is the present. In life, we know only where we've been, looking over the back of the canoe . . . guessing at what will appear at the side of our vision as we round the next bend.

Is that not how all humans live?

So who is the real fool? Which of us are really traveling backward?

Or are both directions really the same?

"Where are we going, Mama?" Silver Water asked as they walked along the river path. The branches rustled overhead, their new leaves bursting with the fresh green of spring. In the growing dusk, a raccoon thrashed away from them and disappeared into the shelter of the forest.

The cool air carried the scents of rich damp earth, pungent new vegetation, and water. Finches, redstarts, and warblers flitted from the riverside brush up to the treetops in splashes of color as they sang before the night. An owl hooted back in the forest, the flute-like sound a promise to rodents, hares, and other small creatures of the darkness.

"North, baby. We'll travel up the Red Buck, then follow a path Tall Man knows to the hills again. After that, it's going to be a long walk." Star Shell looked back. The Magician's short legs were pumping vigorously to keep up. The Mask rode in the hunched pack. Was it her imagination, or had his expression gone gray? Was the set of his mouth pinched, as if against pain?

Is it your conscience, Tall Man? Are you already suffering, repenting Stargazer's broken heart?

As if reading her mind, Silver Water said, "Mama, Stargazer was going to teach me about the sky. He knows so much! We have to get back to The Heavens by full dark. That's when the Planting star will cross the horizon."

"Yes, baby, I know it will. But we're going to see it from a different place."

Silver Water pulled at her mother's hand. "We've got to go back *now*!"

"No! We can't, baby. We have a very important thing to do in the north. Then, and only then, can we learn about the stars. Both of us, I promise."

Silver Water craned her neck to look back over her shoulder. "What about Stargazer? He was going to teach me. Just me. I'd be his First Star. And later, I'd become the Stargazer and save the people. Then I could wear the Mask."

Star Shell's blood froze. "You must listen very carefully, Silver Water. Remember your father? The Mask tricked him, and later it killed him. It will do that to *anyone* who puts it on. I love you, baby. If you love me, you will promise on your soul to never, *never* wear the Mask! Do you hear me?''

''The Mask isn't bad, Mama. It's—''

''Daughter!'' Amidst gathering panic, Star Shell struggled to keep her voice calm. ''Do you remember what your father did? Did you see him dig up his grandfather's bones?''

Silver Water's mouth puckered, and she dropped her eyes.

''Answer me.''

''Yes, Mama.''

''And do you remember what your father did? How he died?''

''Yes.'' The little girl's voice could barely be heard.

''If the Mask ever speaks to you, promise to tell me, all right?''

''I won't wear the Mask, Mama, but can we go back to Stargazer's so I can learn about the sky, and the ways of the ancient ones?''

Star Shell bent down, taking her daughter by the shoulders, searching her earnest face. ''Listen, little Cricket. We can't always do what we want when we want to do it. Do you understand? I'm not trying to be mean. We just don't have any choice. I don't, you don't, and Tall Man doesn't. We must go north.''

''To throw the Mask into the Roaring Water. Isn't that right?''

Star Shell released her, turning back onto the trail. ''Yes, daughter. I want you to understand. We'll do whatever you want after we finish our journey. I'll take you back to The Heavens, and you can study with Stargazer. But until then, you must act like an adult. Can you do that? Be grown up for me until we finish what we have to do?''

''When will that be, Mama?''

''Soon. Another moon, maybe two.''

''By summer solstice?''

''I think so, yes.''

''And then we can go back and learn about the sky?''

''Yes, baby.''

Silver Water sucked her lips for a moment, the action puffing out her cheeks. ''And you could go back to Greets the Sun?''

''If you want, we'll talk about it.''

"That usually means no."

Star Shell forced a laugh she didn't feel. "This time it means we'll talk about it. Mama got hurt at Greets the Sun's—the way you are being hurt by leaving Stargazer. We both have to live through these little hurts, and then, by solstice, we'll never be hurt again."

"Promise?"

"I promise. Do you promise to never wear the Mask?"

"I won't wear the Mask. I promise. But I don't want to throw the Mask into the Roaring Water. It doesn't want to die."

Star Shell glanced back at Tall Man, who was plodding along impassively. "It has to, baby. Tall Man has seen it in a Vision. It's the only way."

The Planter's Moon had crossed half of the sky before Star Shell finally called a halt in a small clearing. Despite the threat of rain, they rolled out their blankets, and Silver Water fell asleep immediately.

Star Shell lay on her back, staring up at the network of branches that locked the sky away from her. How far could she trust Silver Water's promise? What did a little girl know about the kind of deceit and trickery the Mask was capable of? The rustling night sounds mocked her.

"What now, Magician?" she asked tonelessly, aware that he, too, was awake.

"Northward, like you said. The Red Buck heads a day's walk from here. Over the divide, we can go in one of two directions."

"That's StarSky territory." *It's time. You've got to do this.* The plan had been forming inside her since they'd left The Heavens. She forced her voice to remain firm. "Funny, all these months of running and hiding, and I'm right back where we started. Very well, we'll cross StarSky holdings. I'll see my father long enough to let him know that I'm alive, and we'll cut straight across to the upper Moonshell. We can steal a canoe at Buckeye clan grounds, paddle north to the headwaters, cross to the Spirit Frog River, steal another canoe, and float down to the Wind Sea."

"I don't think that seeing—"

"That's how we'll do it, Magician. Like I told Silver Water earlier, we don't always get to do what we'd like. Had we run north three moons ago, we'd be there, and already rid of the Mask."

"Star Shell, don't you remember the look in Robin's eyes?"

She stared up at the dark branches overhead. The moon had vanished behind the clouds. A nightjar cooed. "Yes. But I also remember the look in the old woman's, and in Greets the Sun's, and in Silver Water's tonight. Would you make any bets on how Stargazer is looking right now? No, sorcerer, you wouldn't. You know what we brought that old man. Disaster, just like everyone else we've touched so far."

Tall Man pulled his blanket up to his chin. "And yet you want to see your father?"

She winced, hoping he didn't see. Fear clawed hungrily at her soul. "He's already suffering, wondering what happened to me and his granddaughter. I don't want him near the Mask—and we won't stay longer than to tell him that I'm alive."

Tall Man sighed. "You're a hard woman, Star Shell."

She gazed absently at the filigree of branches, remembering the horrifying rituals he'd performed to create the false mask they'd given to Stargazer. Tall Man had frightened her deeply. "What about you, Magician? Did your soul turn to stone when you were in the belly of the snake? You said the snake devoured you. Did its stomach juices eat your soul like acid and turn you into the heartless monster you became?"

"I've never believed myself a monster, Star Shell. Though, indeed, I have made mistakes."

"Your spell worked on Stargazer. That and your gumweed-and-wild-lettuce concoction to make him sleep harder. I must admit, however, that when you were acting like a wolf, wearing the hide and calling on First Man, you made my hair stand straight out from my head."

"We have the Mask, don't we?"

"Yes. We have the Mask, and Stargazer—not that he deserves much—has lost his Dream."

"Sleep, Star Shell. You're tired."

"Tell me, do you get enjoyment out of tricking people? That false mask probably fell apart in his hands."

"It served its purpose."

"But did it feel good to cheat him like that?"

"No, Star Shell," he said through a tense exhalation. "It did not feel good. I share his sorrow over the death of the old ways. Unlike him, I will not risk wearing the Mask to save them. We've entered a new age. Traders, wealth, and grandeur are what the future is about. If the wisdom of the High Heads had truly stood them in good stead, we'd still be making our observations from The Heavens—and not from StarSky."

"So The Heavens should die?"

Tall Man waited, then finally replied, "Everything dies, young Star Shell. Plants, men, rivers, mountains, and eventually the very earth herself. Why should peoples and beliefs be different?"

"A truth from the belly of the snake?"

"If you wish to think so."

"If I wish to think so? Tell me, sorcerer, what did you get from the Serpent Society? Wealth? Prestige? Authority?"

"All of those things, and more. And when I was young, I used them ruthlessly. I am older now . . . and a great deal wiser."

"But just as ruthless."

He rolled over to face her, and moonlight broke through the clouds again and flowed into his wrinkles, making him look a thousand years old, and very tired. "Yes. Perhaps not even age can erase that from a man's soul. But please remember that I am ruthless only when I see no other way. Do not betray my confidence in you, Star Shell."

"Or you'll destroy me like you have so many others?"

"To give you an idea of how far I would go to ensure that the Mask is destroyed, I want you to think about this: If it became necessary . . . *I* would don the Mask."

His eyes gleamed in the darkness, like a circling wolf's in the light of a campfire.

Quietly—despite her quaking heart—she rearranged her blankets and turned her back to him. The nightjar cooed again.

The Ilini had narrowed until it barely merited the designation of "river."

Long Throw's lighter boat, with its six paddlers, pulled ahead of *Wave Dancer*. On the way past, Long Throw told them, "I'm going to find a cousin. He lives at Dead Owl mounds, but the passage across Mud Lake is just below his holdings. I'll meet you there with guides, and help in case the passage can't be navigated."

"Good! May Many Colored Crow bless you and speed you onward!" Otter replied, waving.

"Stay away from skunks!" was the parting comment.

"What did he mean?" Pearl asked, pausing for a moment to inspect her callused hands before she returned to paddling. "Why can't we navigate? It doesn't get much narrower than this, does it?"

They'd been paddling straight east for three days now. The bluffs, so long their companions, had sunken into mildly rolling countryside. Here, through breaks in the trees, open land could be seen, undulating and rounded by hillocks. The patches of prairie had drawn a sigh of wonder from Black Skull, who'd lived his entire life within the security of the forest.

"We just made the northeastern bend," Otter replied. "A couple of clan holdings lie along here, but the big Ilini clans, the ones Long Throw is referring to, are north of the passage we'll take to the Fresh Water Sea. The passage itself is through a marsh called Mud Lake—and it can be just that. After the spring rains, the marsh can have water in it as deep as a man's waist. If the rains haven't come, or later in the year, it will be a sea of mud."

"And if it's mud?" Black Skull asked, clearly uneasy at the way the matted green brush hung down the sides of the banks. A lurking assailant could literally jump into the canoe.

"There's a trail that skirts Mud Lake. We might have to hire men to portage—carry *Wave Dancer* and the packs—for a day's walk until we find water deep enough to float in again. Once there, we'll be across the divide and have a straight shot into the Fresh Water Sea."

"I don't mean to be disheartening," Black Skull called back, "but *Wave Dancer* isn't an easy canoe to carry."

"That's another reason Long Throw is going ahead. If we

have to carry her, I'll bet every one of his relatives is there to help.''

"And your Trade goods?'' Pearl asked. ''You could lose them all in paying for the help.''

Otter shrugged. ''What if I do? My guess is that Wolf of the Dead is less than a day behind us. In the end, if the Ilini get all of my packs—and we get away, well, First Man bless them.''

"Less than a day?'' Black Skull half rose to look behind them. ''Do you think they're that close? We've pushed awfully hard, Trader. They'd have to check all the tributaries, make sure we didn't double back.''

"Wolf of the Dead had enough warriors to do just that,'' Otter reminded him. ''A war canoe can make better speed than *Wave Dancer* can. I'll be honest. I expected them to catch us a couple of days ago. That they haven't is nothing but the good-will of the River Spirits and Many Colored Crow.''

Pearl swiveled to search his eyes. ''You're sure? A couple of days ago?''

"I know rivers, and I know boats. I think I'm better at reading water than any Khota, and that bought us a little time. But when Green Spider started to help with the paddling two days ago, I knew Wolf of the Dead was close.'' *And I didn't want to frighten you so that you couldn't think, or sleep.*

Pearl held his gaze, a flash of anger deep in her brown eyes. ''I'll keep that in mind for the future.'' She turned back to paddling, and he noticed that she did so with more vigor, the water swirling in the wake of her powerful stroke.

Otter chewed on his lip, looking past the brushy wall of green that hemmed the narrow channel. Red-winged blackbirds flitted back and forth, stopping to cling with awkwardly spread feet to waving cattails. The sky seemed a deeper blue here, as if it pressed more closely to the ground. To the north, a black, towering mass of thunderstorm rolled across the prairie.

"Why don't the trees grow out there?'' Black Skull asked, nodding his head toward an open, grassy patch.

"Fire mostly. In the fall, it can get pretty dry. When that happens, the fires burn off the trees out in the flats. The black oak can resist, but you'll notice the sugar maple, elm, and ash all stand where water protects them from the west wind.''

"Not enough rain? Fire? What kind of country is this? And

look at those hills. You'd swear they were earthworks.'' The low, mounded ridges and humped earth were indeed different from anything the warrior would have ever seen.

"We'll see a great many marvels by the time we make the Roaring Water," Otter declared.

"I've already seen enough," Pearl muttered. "From the islands out in the ocean to this. I'll take a little quiet swamp, some water moccasins, and a bit of hanging moss."

Wave Dancer's wake lined out on either side to vanish into the thick brush that overhung the dark water.

"What do you say, Green Spider?" Pearl asked. "Are we going to have to carry *Wave Dancer* across Mud Lake? Or will we float?"

Green Spider's gaze was wandering, disconnected as usual. "Horrible time," he said. "Dry, cracked ground, dust blowing around. And the Khota . . . cheerful and happy, paddles dragging in the water . . . will wish us onward."

The tension was back in Pearl's shoulders as she plied her paddle. Otter watched the muscles moving under the smooth brown skin of her arms. Where had that need to touch her come from? And worse, why did it continue to plague him?

I'm not in love with her, am I?

"All right," Black Skull called from where he sat behind the fox-head bow. "We'll be able to float across Mud Lake. But the Khota are closing in behind us. Slime and leeches, I'm starting to understand him!"

"It does sound that way." Otter squinted ahead, seeing a major fork in the channel. Two Ilini markers indicated the channel he wanted. "Gets tricky up here. Lots of channels and backwaters. Black Skull, keep your eyes open. Our route is marked by owl symbols on the posts. The land is all jumbled up here."

Patches of brush, plum, blackberry, and ground cherry were all leafed out and competing with the colorful splashes of wildflowers on the hilly slopes.

Otter's imagination caught him walking those slopes with Pearl, watching her white teeth flash with laughter while the sunlight cast bluish tints in that long raven hair. What would she feel like in his arms?

"May the accursed Khota get lost and go around and

around," Pearl whispered, the vehemence breaking Otter's reverie.

"Straight!" Green Spider chimed, half ducking out of the canoe as he grabbed for shining minnows in the water. Catcher watched intently, trying to determine just what this new game was about. "Khota are like dart shafts, always driving straight ahead, never going around and around."

At that moment, the black crow came circling out of the lazy sky, sunlight glinting on black wings. The bird flapped, hovering overhead and squawking.

"What?" Green Spider called, watching the bird. "Of course we will." He turned around, searching for his paddle. "Time to slow down and go backward. Help me, Catcher!"

Pearl cast a nervous glance at the bird, which glided off downriver. Otter could see the strain in the set of her pert mouth. She renewed her paddling with grim efficiency.

Otter leaned forward, summoning the strength from some deep reserve, and pulled *Wave Dancer* ahead.

They passed a clan ground on the south bank. People called to each other and ran down to shout greetings and an encouragement to stop and Trade. Otter politely declined but tossed several sharks' teeth to the boys who ran along the bank. After all, a little generosity never hurt any Trader.

The sun had slanted across the sky by the time they met Long Throw, waiting with three canoes. The Ilini had a grin on his face. "Good passage, Water Fox! Come, we can have you to the Fresh Water Sea by dark. These are my cousins. They've come to help."

"And get a good reimbursement in return," Pearl muttered, but Otter could see that her arms were shaking, the movements of her paddle clumsy.

How much could she stand before she collapsed? "Take a rest now . . . catch your breath. We may need some additional effort soon." He'd caught himself glancing back downriver, the hair starting to prickle on the back of his neck. To Long Throw, he shouted, "The Khota are getting close. The sooner we're across, the better!"

"How do you know?" Long Throw demanded.

"The Contrary is paddling. The harder he paddles, the closer the Khota!"

"Right! This way!" Long Throw's cousin turned them off into a watery slough, more like a backwater than a channel. The way was well traveled; rushes and cattails had been beaten down into an easily defined path. The air had taken on the musky pungency of marsh: water, plant, and decay all mixed together. Red-winged blackbirds watched them pass, clinging sideways on slender cattail stalks. Through gaps in the bulrush and cattail, they could see herons, cormorants, and ducks. Occasional sea-gulls skimmed overhead.

"Don't want to veer off into the side routes," Otter decided, noting the channels that led off in various directions like a series of oversized muskrat runs. Here and there, floats marked the locations of fish traps, each bearing the distinctive mark of its owner.

Black Skull called over his shoulder, "What do these people do? Just fish?"

"The land is rich here. They harvest the usual nuts: hazel, walnut, hickory, butternut, and the rest. Those funny rounded hills we passed through grow onions and dogtooth violet by the basket. Wild rice grows up here, too; they harvest it in the marshes along with cattail. Sumac, blackberry, hawthorn, grape, plums, ground cherry, and other berries are important foods. Fishing is good, of course, and so is the hunting—even down to occasional buffalo and elk. And, as you've seen, they grow goosefoot, little barley, knotweed, sunflowers, squash, and all the other normal plants."

"You'd think the trees would grow here." Black Skull shook his head.

"I can take you to places where you can travel for days on end and never see a tree beyond the river."

"Up here? Where we're going?" Black Skull gestured toward the canoe they followed through the narrow marsh trail.

"No, much farther west. Up beyond the buffalo lands. And if you go even farther, you'll find mountains that reach so high they pierce the sky. Those are the obsidian lands. Most people don't believe the stories, but they're true."

This time when Otter looked back, he could see only the marsh. This part of the journey would slow the Khota, force them to navigate carefully, searching for the main current. Unless they, too, found themselves a guide.

Otter sighed. And they would, of course. The Dead Owl Clan wouldn't want two hundred prowling Khota warriors hanging around. Much better to show them the passage and send them on to harass some unlucky clan out on the shore of the Fresh Water Sea.

The sun had sunk to within a handsbreadth of the western horizon by the time the marsh began to narrow, high ground visible to north and south. The transition proved gradual, but Otter detected a current moving with them—not much, just twigs and bits of debris drifting past cattail stalks.

"We've crossed Mud Lake," Otter noted, and was rewarded by Pearl's answering grin. She looked wan, hollow-eyed from the grueling pace they'd maintained.

All that, and not a word of complaint. This was a woman to be proud of. *And face it . . . Red Moccasins, no matter how realistic and capable, couldn't have survived this trip the way Pearl had.* The thought was the most horrible betrayal he'd ever committed.

In the north, the storm had continued to build. Slanting sunlight gleamed off an endless pile of white, fluffy clouds that extended as far as the eye could see. Pray that it kept its course and passed to the north.

The channel widened slowly, and Otter maintained the stamina to continue paddling. The wind blew at his back, helping them along, but then, it would do the same for the Khota. And who knew how close they might be? Green Spider still paddled, half the time humming to himself, half the time leaning forward to tickle Catcher's foot while the paddle dragged in the water.

If he starts to sweat and paddle like mad, we're all dead.

No well-defined riverbanks existed here—just marsh spreading out to either side and slowly blending into isolated stands of trees. Occasional humped dunes, covered with waving grass, thrust up to give the only feature of the land beyond marsh and sky.

"Look!" Pearl pointed to the wheeling white birds. "Gulls! Lots of them! I almost feel like I'm home."

"We're close." Otter worked his aching hands, resting them. How did Black Skull continue without a single falter? The man had no feeling in his body. No other answer could explain his inexhaustible strength.

And then they were through, winding around a bend and out into a sandy delta with nothing but blue water ahead of them. Evening sunlight sparkled on the water, fading out into the flatness of the sharp horizon. Unlike the ocean, the Fresh Water Sea looked remarkably calm, without surf crashing on the white-sand beach.

Black Skull rose slowly, feet braced, massive legs flexed, his paddle dripping as he stared at the endless expanse of water. He seemed spellbound as Long Throw's canoe drifted alongside.

The young Ilini gestured and grinned. "You're through the passage, Water Fox. We've still got a finger's worth of daylight to spare. Come, we'll share a last camp with you. My cousin knows a place just up from here. Besides, he says that a big storm is coming tonight. Bad winds and hard rains."

Otter stretched, hating the ache in his shoulders. "Green Spider? Are the Khota right behind us? Will we die if we spend the night here?"

The Contrary looked back, his eyes nearly focused for once. "Oh, you'll be safe, Trader. Snug as a worm on a leaf with a bluebird to keep guard. Sleep well tonight, for you will live long and happily." He frowned slightly. "We'll Dance along the dunes, Trader. Forever. Dancing and whirling, whirling and Dancing."

Otter shrugged wearily at the Ilini. "We're going on, Long Throw. Wolf of the Dead is too close. Black Skull, throw that pack . . . *Black Skull!* Wake up, man! Throw that big pack over to Long Throw." The warrior looked back, his eyes slightly glazed, then moved with a curious lethargy. "There, that's the one."

Otter reached across the water, clasping Long Throw's hand. "My friend, you've enough conch shell wrapped in southern hanging moss there to see you and your cousins through a dozen weddings and half that many buryings, but there is one other thing we would like to give you for your help."

He motioned to Pearl, and she propped her paddle beside her knee and reached for the sack of corn. Sadness glinted in her eyes when she handed it to him. Even when it rested in Otter's arms, she fingered the sack as though reluctant to let it go.

"You're sure?" Otter said softly.

"Yes. It will be less weight we have to carry, and these are good people."

As Otter held out the sack for Long Throw to take, Pearl said, "Among my people, this is a very precious seed. This was selected from the finest of our corn plants. It was supposed to be a gift to the Khota. I would ask only that you share it with all of your clans. Plant it, nurture it, and remember Pearl of the Anhinga when you harvest."

Long Throw's brows drew together. "Corn," he said slowly as though trying the name out on his tongue. "We shall do so, I promise you that. So, we have made our Trade."

"We have," Otter agreed, looking at the empty gaps left in his goods.

Long Throw shook his head, staring at the booty. The large fabric sacks swelled over the sides of his narrow war canoe. "Then we bid you farewell and good luck!"

Otter gave the Ilini one last wave. "Take care, Long Throw, and be sure to let Wolf of the Dead know that we laugh in his face and spit on his ancestors' graves. Tell him he's not even half a dog, and if we didn't have important business on the east end of the Fresh Water Sea, we'd hang around and kill another three tens of his warriors."

"Do you want me to tell him where you're going?"

"Absolutely." Otter jerked his head toward the expanse of water. "The last thing you'd want is for him to linger here, along your coast. He might forget his promise to Silent Owl."

Pearl straightened, speaking in Khota, a language the Ilini could understand. Slow grins spread on their faces, and several laughed in that male manner of half-bark—the one that indicated a well-handled insult.

"What did you say?" Otter asked as the Ilini turned their canoes back toward the passage.

"I asked them to carry a message from me to Wolf of the Dead."

"What message?"

Pearl took out her paddle again and dipped it into the water, ready to go. "That he should turn back now, because if he catches us, this time I won't just knock him in the head and burn down his house. This time I'll cut off his testicles and roast them like hickory nuts before I feed them to Catcher."

"You do know how to entice a man, I'll say that for you," Otter replied and looked back. Both current and wind were carrying them out into the open water. "Which way, Contrary?"

Green Spider pointed back toward the Ilini canoes.

"Figures." Otter lifted his paddle, his arms numb like pieces of stone. "The shoreline, as I remember, curves to the southeast here and then turns north just past the dune fields. That's our direction."

Otter bent to the paddle, driving them out from shore. For the first time, Black Skull wasn't paddling but simply sitting there, his paddle clutched in his hands as he stared at the darkening water.

Otter barely heard the faint shout from behind them. Shading his eyes against the sunset, he could see the bend beyond the mouth of the river. One of the Ilini canoes—Long Throw's cousin—had paddled back into sight. The man was waving furiously for them to hurry.

Needing no more warning, Otter muttered angrily to himself, setting his paddle and straining to propel *Wave Dancer* out to sea.

"Otter, what are you doing?" Pearl asked, her eyes still on the Ilini canoe that waved them on. "It's going to be dark soon. Where are you going?"

"Out there." He pointed straight out across the Fresh Water Sea. "Where else can we go? They can spread out, search. Anywhere along the shore, they'll find us."

He tried not to see the lightning that flashed whitely along the black underbelly of cloud bank to the north. Big storm, huh? That was the nice thing about traveling on an errand for Power—you had your choice of tempests to face: natural, or Khota-driven.

"You're as crazy as the Contrary," she told him, adding her effort. The wind at their back had already pushed up the chop. Black Skull still sat rigidly in the bow, staring fixedly between the fox ears.

Behind them, in the dusky light, Otter could just make out the Khota canoes as they broke from the river mouth. How far? Six, seven dart casts? Across the waves, the judgment of distance grew tricky, more so when the light was failing. The wind bore the sound of victorious shouts.

"Paddle! *Hard!* They've spotted us. They're coming!"

"I'm glad you let me rest," Pearl told him fervently. And she threw her all into the effort.

Green Spider—facing forward now—had also begun to paddle madly. Despite his zeal, more water got splashed back on Pearl than was translated into headway for the canoe; but she seemed oblivious, driven, if anything, to greater effort by the frenzy of the Contrary's effort.

Only Black Skull sat unmoving in the bow.

"Warrior?" Otter cried. "Black Skull!"

Behind them, the slim Khota canoes began closing the distance, deadly darts lined up for casting. Otter bit on his lip, using pain as a means of fighting his leaden fatigue. What was wrong with the warrior? Otter could see the muscles knotted up and bulging like rocks beneath his shirt. A panicked man might react that way. "Black Skull!"

"Forget him!" Pearl shouted, but her eyes softened when she glanced at the big warrior's back, as though she'd seen such a response before. "Just paddle! What's worse? The Khota behind you or the black sea ahead?"

River Traders didn't paddle across open seas. They had shorelines on either side, and a current to tell them in which direction they headed.

But Otter paddled ferociously, scared to death that he'd get lost out here, die of starvation, or be eaten by some deep-water predator—any one of which was better than the fate offered by the Khota.

Grizzly Tooth turned in the narrow canoe and looked into Wolf of the Dead's eyes. "In a short time, we won't be able to see them anymore."

Wolf of the Dead rose to a half-crouch, staring at the black dot ahead. How far? Five, six dart casts away? He glanced around, aware of the anger burning in his brain. So close! For the first time, he could see them! There in the fading distance, Pearl paddled—accompanied by the Water Fox, the Trickster, and the murderer!

His head throbbed; a warrior's pragmatic sense told him to back off, to return to the beach and camp for the night. Around him, three tens of canoes raced along with the wind. In the growing dusk, Wolf of the Dead could see the mixture of emotions on the faces of his warriors. Some shot worried glances at the endless expanse of indigo water before them; others had focused their attention on the far-off dot of the enemy, anxious only to close and kill.

Ancestors, tell me, what do I do now? The fiendish woman and the murderers of his people were so close!

"I have three tens of canoes," he mused.

"Against one," Grizzly Tooth said with a grim smile. "Even if we send only half of our canoes out into the dark, one of our boats should be able to find them, capture them."

A spear of pain shredded his thoughts for a moment—a reminder of the Anhinga woman's blow. Wolf of the Dead didn't need to ask the ancestors. Once before, a woman had tried to kill her husband—as this Pearl had tried to kill him.

"Go!" Wolf of the Dead stood, his shout reaching across the water. "All of you! Follow them! I want them alive! I want to take them back and kill them slowly. All the peoples of the world will know the Khota—and how we deal with betrayal!"

Whoops rose on the evening breeze.

"When you find them," Wolf of the Dead continued, "turn back into the wind. That will bring you back to shore. Look for the smudge. Thick black smoke will mark the location where we have made camp."

Wolf of the Dead seated himself again and chewed thoughtfully on his thumb. Someone would catch the Traders. That big canoe couldn't outrace the light, fast hulls of the Khota. Tonight he would see Pearl's face again.

"Like the wolf pack that we are, we'll run you down, Anhinga bitch. And when we do, every man shall plant himself in you. I won't begin to kill you until every Khota warrior has had his fill, and then I'll cut you apart piece by piece, and you and your Trader friends can watch me eat the pieces."

As for the men with her, she could watch as they suffered their own little deaths. In the end, however, their skulls would be polished and placed on the trophy wall of the clan house. The Water Fox's could rest beside his Uncle's.

Long Throw stood atop one of the taller dunes. The wind whipped at his back, fluttering his clothes and bouncing the red-slate gorget that hung from a thong around his neck. The tall grass, so newly grown among the brown strands of last year's, sawed at his bare legs.

Long Throw cupped his hands to shade his eyes, not from the dying light of day, but from the whipping wind. He barely noticed his thin cousin who climbed up beside him.

"Are they all gone?"

"They are," Long Throw said. Then he glanced northward at the piled clouds and the inky blackness beneath. Even as he looked, the murky depths of the storm were shattered by flashes of lightning. "Are you sure about this storm?"

"I'm the Weather Teller, remember? Just wait. By midnight, you'll wonder if it's the end of the world. This is supposed to be the calm month out on the water, but that doesn't mean it can't whip up a real blow. And that, cousin, is one of the worst that I've seen in a long time."

Long Throw nodded, losing sight of *Wave Dancer,* now so far from shore. Even the bobbing Khota canoes were disappearing in the growing darkness. "Tomorrow I'll leave before dawn. My clan leader needs to know that the Khota have made it to the Fresh Water Sea."

"And the Water Fox?"

"If this storm comes with the fury you predict . . . well, I wouldn't want to be out there on that much water." Long Throw made a face. They'd been good people, honest, courageous, and polite. That they'd put forth so much effort just to drown in a storm . . . But no, they'd taken the fiercest and finest of the arrogant Khota warriors with them.

"In a couple of days, cousin, I too shall send a message to your clan leader." The Weather Teller paused. "I will be able to tell him that none of the Khota have returned to our shore."

"Don't be too sure," Long Throw warned.

A huge gust of wind nearly blasted them from the high dune. "Oh, I'm more than sure," Long Throw's cousin said with a gap-toothed grin. "Only a man experienced with deep water will outlive this night. I hope that Trader friend of yours has not spent all of his life plying the inland rivers."

Long Throw placed a hand on his cousin's shoulder. *Water Fox, I will make offerings to your ghost. Perhaps then your Spirit will rest a little easier down there in the cold, black water.*

Thirty-four

As the canoe dances and bobs, I stare up at the wind-torn sky. Spatters of water driven from the sharp-tipped waves pelt me like grains of angry sand and soak my thin clothing until I am shivering miserably.

I might die tonight. We all might.

Wolf, I wish you were here in this boat with us. How I'd like to see your expression when we capsize and sink into the cold darkness of the waves. In the end, you, and your brother, may both be tricked by Power.

I smile thinly, feeling the icy water trickling down my face, knowing this is only the beginning of the terror, knowing how much hinges upon this night. . . .

Black Skull clung frantically to the sides of the canoe, his fingers crushing the wet wood. His arms ached from the effort, but with each rise of the fox-headed bow, his hold tightened before the inevitable plunge into the black abyss. Behind him, he heard Pearl shouting commands to Otter, teaching him the ways of the storm, telling him what to do to counter each new peril. But most of the words were lost in the heaving terror that suffocated Black Skull's soul.

He closed his eyes tight against the driving rain, but the careening and jostling only worsened.

Nothing had prepared him for the sounds, the combined fury of wind and water raging, screaming, at him. All . . . deafening!

This isn't happening! It couldn't be. They had to hit shore soon. The Fresh Water Sea couldn't go on forever, could it? That image of endless water stretching flat across a purple horizon, with no land in sight, coiled and slithered like a poisonous serpent in his belly.

Another gust of wind howled out of the blackness, bringing cold rain and spray to batter Black Skull's back. He tensed, his jaws clenched and aching because of his misaligned teeth. Not even that pain could mitigate the wretched fear pumping with each beat of his heart.

Wave Dancer bucked, pitched, and rolled, tormented by the heaving water and driving gale. A dying animal twisted and writhed in this same way.

Dying! We're all dying! And the water would suck them down into the terrible blackness. His corpse would descend, arms limp, legs outstretched, head hung low as if searching for a muddy termination.

He cried out as the canoe caught a wave and shot upward. In that split instant, Black Skull wondered if his hands had been torn from their hold—and then *Wave Dancer* dropped out from under him, the fox head crashing, driving so deep into the trough of water that Black Skull saw white spray, ghostly in the darkness, peeling out to either side.

His mother's voice crept in from the edges of his panic. *"Stupid, filthy child!"*

"No . . . I'm not. Go away! Please!"

"You're nothing more than a worm . . . stupid little boy. Stupid."

He sobbed, so sick that his stomach roiled and tickled. Weakness had eaten his heart out. So sick, he bent to the side and threw up into the pitching blackness. Shamed. So horribly shamed and frightened.

"Filthy child!" his mother's voice hissed out of the blackness. *"Disgusting weakling! You're no good, boy. A fool and a coward! Look at you, so frightened you shiver like a puppy before the stew pot!"*

He wanted to scream, "Mother? Granduncle made me kill you!" But the words stuck in his vomit-clogged throat.

"*Black Skull? Is that what you call yourself now? Arrogant as well as foolish! You've made yourself a name, little boy, to keep the world from knowing who you really are!*"

"I'm Black Skull! Black Skull!"

"*You're Little Mouse, remember? That was your boyhood name, but I called you something else . . . or has your stupid mind forgotten?*"

"Slug! You called me Slug!" He broke down then, sobbing his humiliation. The nausea, the fear of the mountainous waves, the aching urge to vomit, again called up those memories. He'd felt like this when she played with him. Disgusted, so disgusted.

"*You little slug!*" Her lip had risen in a sneer as she inspected him standing there before the fire. "*Let me see you. Come here! I've seen more naked males than you!*"

He'd begun to tremble, and the fear had tormented him, wanting to make him throw up. He'd closed his eyes, only to whimper when she slapped him.

"*Look at me! Yes, look!*"

And he'd stared into those crazed eyes of hers, seeing the delight as she fed upon his fear and self-disgust. Her hands were always cold when she touched him.

"*Look, see? See what I'm doing? Does that feel good? Hmm?*"

And he'd have to look down and watch her hand as she gripped his little penis and ran those callused fingers under his fear-shrunken scrotum.

"*And you think you'll be a man!*" She threw her head back and laughed. "*Water runs in your veins. If you had real blood, you'd be as hard as a hickory stick by now.*" The lip rose again, disdainful. "*Get away from me. Go cover yourself up and hide that dangling slug from my sight.*"

He'd run, tears leaking down his face as he dove into the blankets. By the time he'd covered his shame, she'd have left, gone out into the night searching for other little boys.

Little Mouse would lie there, buried under the blankets of his bed. Most nights, he'd wish he were dead, and sometimes he'd wish that his mother were dead, or that at least she'd stay away. Often the night passed without her return, though usually she'd come back giggling, with male laughter for accompaniment. Then he'd listen to them as they coupled like weasels, and his mother would sound like a wounded bear, or the man would curse as she bit and clawed at him.

"*And you're still worthless, you little worm,*" his mother's voice keened in the storm. "*You split my skull that night . . . crept up from behind . . . as I'm doing to you! Tonight, Slug, you'll drown . . . drown down in the cold blackness!*"

Little Mouse bent his head, hardly aware that it banged against the wooden carving before him. The muscles in his hands were weakening, and soon he'd be unable to hold on. His broken sobbing had already lost itself to the storm and terror.

Wave Dancer pitched again, pounding downward and dashing spray upward, so the wind blew back on Little Mouse's doubled-over body. He gagged, trying to throw up, but only dry heaves cramped in his stomach.

Lightning flashed, giving him an image of endless horror, of water ripped and torn, water piled into wave-scalloped peaks, the crests shredded and rent by wind. Moving, crashing, even in that brief instant of lightning flash. Surging and roiling, all that hellish water was churning toward his panicked death.

She was coming—coming to kill him. Out there, dancing among those rising and falling ridges of dark water. Slashing rain was pounding on her split skull, pattering on the jagged bone and tapping on her exposed brain.

His ghost would end up here, forever trapped in the black, endless water. Little Mouse could only sob his defeat.

A thin, high voice cut through the storm. The fool! Yelling! "*Black Skull? Black Skull! Did you know that ghosts live in the present moment all the time? I wonder how they do that?*"

In all of his life, Otter had never been this terrified. He struggled to keep his balance, to keep his grip on the water-slick paddle. The slanting rain lashed down on them, while gusts of wind hammered out of the blackness. The violence! *Wave Dancer* lifted as if riding the back of a monster, and then fell, plummeting to the depths, only to lurch upward again. Every time the canoe dropped out from under him and that tickling hollow swelled in his gut, he wanted to get sick, or to cry in terror.

Rain rattled on the hull as it pummeled the black sea with its powerful fists. Spray, blown from the twisted and frothing peaks, pelted him like sleet. He could barely keep his eyes open.

In a lightning flash, he glimpsed Pearl kneeling in front of him, a ceramic pot in her hands. The sudden flash of light had caught her in the act of bailing—pitching water like a silver smear in the whiteness. Her knees had been braced, her drenched face expressing determination. In the afterimage, Otter couldn't see anything, let alone anyone else—or the canoe bottom. He had no idea of how much water had accumulated.

"Keep your back to the wind!" Pearl shouted as disjointed thunder rolled over the churning water. Wet, black hair had glued itself to her face. "This is getting worse! Have you ever ridden out a storm like this before?"

"No! Not one like this." Otter's soul seemed to ebb with the water sloshing around his feet. *I made a mistake coming out here.* A mistake . . . mistake . . . The thought repeated over and over. Each time he lifted the paddle for another stroke, the wind tore at it, trying to grab it away and fling it into the madness of pitching waves.

In yet another flash, he could see the packs moving, sliding back and forth as *Wave Dancer* rocked from side to side and front to back, all at once. Otter watched the bow rise. Green Spider's face was tipped up toward the lightning, an expression of gleeful abandon on his thin, triangular face.

"We're all right!" Pearl shouted. "We're not shipping much water!" But her voice sounded shrill against the howl and roar of the storm. "Keep *Wave Dancer* running before the wind. If the stern starts to swamp, tell me. We'll have to come about, turn the bow into the wind and try to hold her that way."

He flinched as the wind blasted stinging spray across his face. All trace of his bone-weary fatigue had vanished with the storm's assault, replaced by vein-bright terror. And where were the Khota? He'd been able to hear their calls faintly on the wind. How would those narrow war canoes do in this?

Better to die in this storm than at your hands, Wolf of the Dead. This would be quick, a sudden twist of the canoe as it capsized, then the cold insult of the water . . . choking, gagging, splashing, and finally, panic would subside to cold blackness . . .

Lightning arced in jagged tendrils, a weird, spindle-legged monster that crisscrossed the silver sheets of rain and danced over the tortured sea. The image froze forever in Otter's memory: endless, battered black waves, topped with foaming white, caged in the arms of a huge, glowing spider.

This was crazy! How could water do this? Become this possessed?

"And if we come about and still ship water?" Otter struggled to keep his sanity. *Think, Otter. You can't panic, or we'll all die.*

"Then we throw things out for more freeboard," Pearl told him.

"Those are my *Trade goods* you're talking about throwing overboard!"

"It's our *lives* I'm talking about saving," she yelled back.

Jagged lightning pulsed blue-white just overhead, giving Otter a glimpse of *Wave Dancer* as she dove headlong into the depths of a trough as deep as the canoe was long. *This is it!* His belly knotted in anticipation of being flung into the cold.

To his surprise, the canoe surged upward, somehow bearing them safely out of the disaster. He worked his paddle as wind tore at his back.

Wave Dancer soared upward yet again, then immediately plummeted down, running the swells, surging and diving so steeply he felt certain they would all be cast into that black oblivion beyond the hull. Lightning gave him a view from the heights: endless, twisted crests and valleys, all raging hungrily.

He wiped a hand over his dripping face.

"We're not going to make it!" he shouted at Pearl, but the deafening *crack-boom*! of thunder hammered his words into infinity.

"Keep her stern on to the wind!" Pearl cried as a wave tossed them sideways. "If you don't, we'll be swamped!"

Otter paddled frantically, struggling to hold his course. Was anyone else paddling? Green Spider? Black Skull? He couldn't tell. "Pray for land!"

"No!"

"What?"

"I said no! We're safer in deep water than in shallow. The

surf will be running so high that it'll smash us onto the beach, splinter *Wave Dancer,* and most likely kill all of us!''

He could imagine that final drop, the impact under the breaking wave. Otter flushed it from his thoughts.

''Hold the course,'' Pearl called, shifting. ''I've got to bail!''

''What's Black Skull doing?'' Rot the darkness, anyway . . . if only he could see. But then, with the rain and spray blowing into his face, he'd be half-blinded, no matter what. ''Is he paddling? I can't see him!''

''How should I know? He might be overboard for all I can tell, but Green Spider is paddling like mad.''

Thank the Mysterious One, but Many Colored Crow himself would have been desperate to save his soul at a time like this.

Wave Dancer lived out the essence of her name, leaping, twisting, bucking. Otter could do nothing more than fight to keep her from rolling over.

''Are you scared?'' Pearl called as she threw a pot of water over the side.

''Yes!'' He saw her smile, just a glint of white teeth.

''So am I!'' she answered.

''Sure you wouldn't rather go back and chance the Khota?''

A flash of lightning caught her still scooping water with her pot, wet, bedraggled, yet defiant. ''You've never seen anyone so happy to be right here as I am, Trader. I'll take this storm over those bits of walking filth any day! And we're certainly doing better than the stinking Khota. In those skinny war canoes, they're shark food by now.''

Yes, Otter, keep that thought. If Wave Dancer *is hard-pressed by this, they're back there dying.* What would it be like, trying to cling to the rounded bottom of a war canoe capsized in this chilling black horror? He could imagine them splashing, beating at the water as they rose and fell in the giant waves, water pouring into mouths that gasped for air.

Stop it! The images conjured were too real.

''How are we doing?'' Otter dug in with his paddle, feeling *Wave Dancer* turning as one of the swells rose and the wind threw them suddenly to the right. A man might be riding on the back of a fighting monster.

Wave Dancer dropped out from underneath him. Otter felt weightless. His stomach leaped, and then the canoe rose with a tremendous splash and lifted him again. How big were these waves? Taller than three men, that was sure. And the fourth moon was supposed to be the most peaceful time to cross the Fresh Water Sea?

"I'm glad you're here!" Otter shouted over the hissing roar.

Pearl grinned, still bailing. How did she keep her balance? "So am I. It may end up being a short trip, but it's been worth it. I'm me again!"

"You've always been you!"

She fell silent, and Otter concentrated on the paddle, on the storm, aware that despite his fear of dying, he could feel the ache in his muscles now. *How far can you push yourself? How long can you keep this up?*

Pearl's voice surprised him. "No, I lost myself for a while . . . after the Khota. But now I've got myself back."

"Just in time to drown!"

"You just keep your back to the wind and we'll live!"

The storm tore down on him, its shriek that of an animal fighting for its life. Otter squinted into the darkness, aware that water ran from his body in sheets. Once again he was wet to the bone, only his exertion keeping him from desperate shivering.

Pearl braced herself close and he caught her delicate scent, woman mixed with rain and night. "I can bail us out faster than the water comes in. We're doing fine!"

"I wasn't aware of that."

She laughed, the sound of it startling against his utter terror. "I see the pink beauty in every sunrise, Water Fox, because I've learned that traveling with you, I'd better."

"Is that right?"

"Of course! I enjoy each one because I have the uncomfortable feeling that they're numbered."

"Smart woman!" In that moment, he began to love her. Despite himself, Otter smiled at her teasing tone and drew from her courage, from the sense of shared danger and spirit. Prickles of euphoria hovered around his soul . . .

. . . and vanished when *Wave Dancer* leaped high into the air. Otter would have sworn the canoe jumped clear of the water before she dropped and plunged nose-down again.

"Where's Catcher?" Otter cried in sudden panic. In this inky blackness, and as rough as the ride had been, the dog might be overboard and gone before he even knew it. "Pearl, look for him! Is he still with us?"

"I don't know!" Pearl moved away from him, and Otter took a moment to run his sopping sleeve over his face. He squinted out at the blackness, amazed to see the faint white smears of rain on the jostled black water. His fingers cramped with the struggle to hold on to the slippery paddle.

Pearl made her way back to him, each movement braced. "The Contrary says he's long gone! Washed away and drowned. I assume that means he's asleep under one of the tarps."

"Catcher's all right? You're sure?"

"Yes, don't worry. The Contrary's being Contrary!"

Pearl bailed, and Otter strained to keep the boat moving with the wind. The giant waves rose and smashed down, as if trying to crush them in fury.

How fragile and insignificant we are. If only I could see something . . . anything. He followed Pearl's instructions because she had been right so far. He did not understand how she knew the secret to staying afloat in these colossal waves, nor did he care. She was keeping them alive.

The image of the drowning Khota kept bobbing up in his thoughts. "If we go over," Otter called, "hang on to the keel! That will be the only thing to grab on to."

"Your keel is all that's saved us so far!" Pearl shouted back over the roaring of wind and water. "Where'd you learn that trick?"

"From the Salt Water Traders."

Lightning exposed her again, her muscular body bent as she scooped her jar across the hull. A second flash caught her tossing the water, flickers of lightning giving him ghostly stop-and-go images of her movement.

Pearl told him, "They may have saved all of our lives!"

For an instant, the tearing wind lessened and he thought he heard crying . . . , no, heartrending sobbing. Who? Where? Green Spider?

Then the storm drove down with renewed strength, water breaking over the stern, pooling behind him and rushing forward. The fury had worsened.

"We've got to turn!" Pearl bellowed into the gale. "Otherwise, we'll be awash!"

"Tell me how!"

"It's terribly dangerous, and we'll have to time it to the waves. If we're abreast of the wind at a crest, or if we catch a wave partially quartered, we're sunk!"

Otter licked his lips, aware that his throat had gone dust-dry in the midst of a universe of water. "All right, on your call! Tell me when!"

Pearl threw her pot aside and picked up her paddle, leaning forward to talk to the Contrary.

"Paddle hard! Right side!" A pause. "Now!"

Otter felt *Wave Dancer* drop off the crest of a towering black wave and threw all of his energy into driving the big canoe around, fearing the way the wind lashed at him so suddenly. *Wave Dancer* did an about-face so quickly that he wasn't prepared for the wall of water that crashed down upon him as though they'd driven into the wave's very heart . . .

He heard Pearl shouting, felt her striking him, telling him to paddle.

We're going to die now.

The young man appeared to be healthy and influential. He wore a finely woven red shirt under a heavy brown traveling cloak. An atlatl hung from its strap on his belt, and his knee-high moccasins showed the signs of hard travel.

Robin watched through the doorway as the young man approached the Blue Duck clan house, guided by Woodpecker. The ceremonial escort was ritually correct. After all, the High Heads placed a great deal of emphasis on ritual and procedure, and this man came from the Sky Clan, one of the most traditional of the High Head groups.

Robin dropped the door flap and retreated to his place on the other side of the fire. This must be about the Mask—nothing else would explain this man's presence.

The empty-eyed trophy skulls stared with curious detachment from their places on the pole-and-thatch walls. He could feel the presence of the ancestral ghosts who watched from the shadows, or sat in spectral silence on the conical jars and storage bowls. Overhead, sacks of herbs rustled slightly at the passage of unseen forces. Tension reflected from the old war clubs lashed to the roof supports. He could smell the reek of burned blood; the screams of death and dying lay just below the threshold of his hearing. Warnings . . . but about what?

Robin placed a fist in his other palm and tensed his powerful chest muscles so that the human-jaw breastplate rattled.

You're being foolish. The ancestors value courage, and no one has more courage than Robin of the Blue Duck. So it will be said down through the generations as the young warriors offer blood at my burial mound. "Robin of the Blue Duck." My name will be chanted forever.

Woodpecker cast the door-hanging aside, crying, "High Feather, a man of the Sky Clan of the High Heads, has arrived to see Robin, war leader of the Blue Duck Clan."

"May the noble High Feather enter and be welcome." Robin watched the High Head enter, bow politely, and walk to stand across the fire from him. Despite the thin young man's elegant politeness, Robin could read his reluctance. The reason could wait until after the formalities.

"Please." Robin gestured to the colorful fabric folded on the cattail-mat floor. "Be seated. Woodpecker, have food and drink brought for our guest." Then Robin began the recitation of his clan, the first of a series of recitations that he would be forced to perform.

The rituals galled Robin. Granted, the Flat Pipe peoples were relative newcomers to these fertile lowlands, but placating High Head sensitivities always smacked of the implicit inferiority in the Flat Pipe society.

As Robin patiently chanted the blessings, he studied the young man who had crossed the hills to see him.

The youth's head had been bound as an infant to augment the swell of the forehead and flatten the back of the skull. His straight, triangular-shaped nose balanced the wide mouth and high cheekbones. Clear brown eyes, eloquently intelligent, perceptively met Robin's gaze.

The droning of clan lineages was finally completed and the stone pipe lit with a mixture of tobacco and willow shavings.

"Blue Duck Clan bids you welcome," Robin said after the pipe had been smoked and food and drink brought to the guest. "I am Robin, war leader and clan spokesman for the Blue Duck lineages. Eat and drink in peace, and may all the blessings be bestowed on you and your ancestors."

"I am High Feather, of the Lean Tail lineage of the Sky Clan. As you know, I have come to you from the Red Buck valley. I came at the bidding of my grandfather. He was the Stargazer, the last of the High Elders of The Heavens. That place, The Heavens, is one of the oldest of observatories."

"I have heard of it," Robin replied as he refilled the pipe, lit it, and passed it back to High Feather.

High Feather took the pipe, puffing and blowing smoke toward the oblong smoke hole in the roof. "My grandfather is very recently dead. He died of witchcraft."

"I am sorry to hear that." Robin forced himself to relax. *Take your time. He'll get around to the point. These old clans have lots of silly rules of protocol.*

"I found him on his deathbed, complaining of a pain in his chest. He told me that the sorcerer who killed him was gripping his heart, squeezing the life out of him."

"Such sorcerers should be severely dealt with."

"Indeed, it is so. I myself must return to my clan and attend to the ceremonies for my grandfather. He currently lies in the charnel house. He will lie there for four moons while the flesh cleaves from the bone and can be stripped away. Then, as is the custom, we will paint his bones with red ocher and build a tomb—a special tomb, since he is the last of the Stargazers. I will be needed to see that all the ceremonies are carried out properly."

"You're a worthy grandson for so fine an Elder," Robin agreed sagaciously. *Get to the point, rot you.*

The High Head drank from his bowl of stew and fished out the pieces of venison and squash that floated in the bottom. He chewed, a most proper expression of appreciation on his face. When he'd emptied the bowl, he placed it neatly before him. The belch was socially perfect, from deep in the gut and with just the right resonance and duration. Then he inclined his head and said, "I am in your debt for such an excellent meal. You do me too much honor with your fine hospitality."

"You honor me with your praise of such a humble offering."
Now, tell me!

"My grandfather was a most venerable member of our clan and moiety. Not many of the Elders, with their wealth of knowledge, were left to us. His counsel, therefore, was highly valued in all matters that might be of import to my people."

"A wise man indeed," Robin agreed with an expansive wave of the hand.

"Thus it was that we informed him of the activities of another of our Elders, a man of Power and reputation unsurpassed. Grandfather, therefore, knew the circumstances when, to his surprise, this Elder arrived at The Heavens."

"Tall Man!" Robin snapped in violation of all High Head etiquette. At the look on High Feather's face, he added, "Forgive me my outburst. Mention of the Magician stirs the passion of my soul."

"And so he stirs mine. And before that, my grandfather's." High Feather gave Robin a look of disapproval. "I would not have come here except at the behest of my grandfather. As he lay dying, he insisted that I inform you of the Magician's sorcery. I am to tell you that he travels with a young woman, her daughter, and the stolen Mask of Many Colored Crow."

Robin resettled himself, an elbow on one propped knee. "And does the noble High Feather know the whereabouts of the sorcerer and this young woman? Might they be in the territory of the Sky Clan?"

"At this time, no. I do not think so." The High Head made a gesture of regret with his thin hands. "Some of our hunters, however, noticed tracks heading northward, toward the headwaters of the Red Buck. Not knowing of the Magician's perfidy, they naturally suspected that a woman and two children had passed that way, although in one set of tracks, the feet were large for the length of the stride. Only later did they come to realize that a dwarf would have made that same track."

Northward! Toward StarSky. Robin considered. He'd come close to losing his prestige and the respect of his warriors the last time he'd gone north looking for Star Shell and the Mask. And all the time she'd been so close—virtually next door.

His eyes narrowed as he considered further. He could call up the best of his warriors; he'd need no more than twenty men loyal to him and his lineage. Light and fast, they would head northward.

Robin extended his hand again, a smile on his face. "Would the noble High Feather have any other information that might increase Blue Duck clan's indebtedness to the Sky people?"

"You pay me too much honor with your talk of indebtedness. I come bearing but a trifle of news for you. However, since the noble war leader would ask, I should probably tell you that they were heading north, their final goal the Roaring Water, or so my grandfather believed at the time of his death. Apparently, the little girl, Silver Water, told him the particulars one night while he showed her the stars. Such information is offered only as speculation, given the age and experience of the source. I would not have you think it reliable, and hence be misled."

"Your concern is understood and appreciated. I thank you for your candid honesty." Robin smiled grimly, adding bluntly, "And if I catch them, I shall bring you the Magician's head. Oh, I might keep the skull, but you can have the jawbone—cut into two pieces and braided on a string for a chest ornament."

High Feather's nostrils flared in distaste and his eyes widened. "If you will excuse me, I must be returning to my duties."

"Very well," Robin grunted, getting to his feet. "If that's how you feel, I'll keep the jawbone, too."

Thirty-five

Star Shell walked beneath a canopy of emerald, where the oaks, shagbark, beech, and maple intertwined overhead in the lush bright-green of new foliage. Wild grapevines—as thick as a man's thigh—hung from the forest giants. Silver Water's laughter came with the freshness of a babbling brook's as she ran from vine to vine, trying to swing.

Birdsong rose endlessly, bringing a modicum of joy to Star Shell's weary soul. Starflower spread its umbrella of leaves just above the forest floor, catching the last of the spring light before the canopy closed.

Outcrops of gray limestone thrust through the leaf mat, and even here, on the edge of the flat-topped ridge, the waste of quarrying activities could be found. This was the eastern limit of the sacred chert deposit from which StarSky achieved so much wealth and influence.

Star Shell led the way through a low gap and onto the level surface of the ridge top. Through the boles of trees, she could see the undulations and pits, some of them as deep as three men's height, that had been hacked out of the earth. Around them, giving the land a lumpy look, piles of broken limestone and cracked chert mounded the surface.

"It's been a long time," Tall Man sighed as he stepped up beside her. "Once, as a very young man, I came here and dug my own sacred chert from the ground. With it, I scarified my breast at my first summer solstice as an adult."

"Before or after you were devoured by the snake?"

"Before. When I was younger and more innocent."

Star Shell climbed up on one of the spoils piles and looked into the hole, seeing where leaves had blown into the pit. Down in the bottom, the miners had followed a winding vein until it had become too bothersome to chip out the limestone and lesser-grade chert.

Tall Man squatted and picked up a piece of waste. "You know, there are people who would gladly trade a fine pot for chert of this quality. But here, they throw it away."

"They make blanks here." Star Shell pointed to a pile of flakes where a flint knapper had sat. "They chip off the nodule and turn it into a flat piece about the size of your hand. It's a lot easier to transport in that shape than as big round rocks. The blank can be turned into anything—a point, knife, scraper, or drill tip."

And they made blades, of course: long, thin slivers of stone that were driven off of rounded cores. Those were Traded all across the world for use in sacred rituals, bloodletting, and offerings to the Dead. The only stone that could compete with the sacred chert was obsidian, from far off in the west.

She turned, looking at the dwarf. He'd killed a Trader who

specialized in obsidian. But then, ritual stone, no matter what its origin, touched the lives of all the people.

"Come on. Let's go. We've got a long way yet, and even if we hurry, we won't reach my father's until after sunset."

Star Shell hadn't been to the sacred chert quarries in many years. She'd been Silver Water's age . . . and now her own daughter ran around the quarry holes, looking down, throwing rocks into them, and climbing happily to the top of the spoils piles.

I remember them with her eyes, giant holes in the earth. Now, so many years later, they don't seem as deep, as forbidding. But there were so many of them! As she continued walking from pit to pit, following the Trading trail that ran the length of the long ridge, she could verily believe that a gargantuan battle had been fought here in the distant past. Worse, she could imagine another, this one fought by men. What carnage could be wrought with so many hiding places and defensive concealments?

Is that all you think about? War, and death, and conflict? She should be proud that her lineage administered these quarries upon which the entire world depended for ritual stone.

"Look!" Silver Water came charging up, a chert nodule in one hand. "You can see every color! Look, Mama. Red and blue and purple and yellow and green are all swirled together."

Star Shell inspected the find. The piece had been split in two, the bulb of percussion humped out over the colorful surface. Who knew why the Trader had left this behind?

"Beautiful, baby."

"Is it really monster blood?" Silver Water demanded.

"Of course it is, Cricket. That's why it's sacred. First Man killed a monster up here in the first days of the world. The drops of blood streamed out and turned to stone, making this ridge top."

"Does monster blood have all these colors in it?"

"Usually it's as red as any other blood," Tall Man said. He sat cautiously on a rock and hunched forward, as though suddenly tired, but Star Shell saw the ashen look, the hand that rose to his right side. Gently probing. "But in this case, I think the colors were just the way they showed up in the rock. This monster had special Power, you see."

Silver Water nodded solemnly before trotting off with her precious find.

"And you, Magician?" Star Shell asked. "What color is your blood?"

"Red," he told her. "Did you immediately think of me when I mentioned monsters?"

"They do come in all shapes and forms, don't they?"

He got to his feet again and exhaled a halting breath. "Yes, I suppose they do."

"I don't understand. You killed people, and you did it because you were paid for it, correct? I could have come to you and offered you shell, or freshwater pearls, or copper plate, and you would have killed someone's soul. Just like that. What if that person didn't deserve to die?"

"There's more to it than murder. Star Shell, human beings must be who and what they are. People like me, sorcerers, keep everything in balance. You were the prized daughter of a respected and influential clan. If you and the ones you loved were harmed by another, the prestige and authority of your lineage demanded and received an accounting. Justice was served, was it not?"

She said nothing, and he raised his hands in a gesture of acceptance. "Among the people who have no such clans, another way must be found to obtain justice. Let us say that a man such as Robin, also influential and respected, commits an atrocity. In this case, we will say that he violates a little girl of the Frogwort Clan."

"The who? I've never heard of a Frogwort Clan."

"That's my point. Let's say they exist, a small clan eking out an existence someplace up in the hills. If one of their Elders goes to Blue Duck, what sort of hearing would he receive? Do you expect that the clan would pressure Robin's lineage to redress the wrong?"

"They'd do nothing. But there would still be whispers; the seed of suspicion would be sown."

"Not if Robin lied with tact and brilliance. He could survive without a blemish. His only suffering would be the minor irritation of having to concoct a palpable lie, or to plot the further destruction of the little girl's reputation."

"Yes, I know things like that happen."

"And that's where a sorcerer comes in."

"But just anyone can come and pay you to kill someone. Is that right?"

"Mostly it is. Let's return to the Frogwort Clan. Their Elder has been rudely rebuffed at Blue Duck, and he comes to me. I listen as he tells me about the offense against this little girl. I listen to him and then ask to see the child. I have her tell me about what happened. I ask the Elder what he wants done. He tells me that the little girl was raped, that her life is now ruined because the chances of marrying her are gone. The little girl panics and screams whenever a man comes near her; her soul has been seriously wounded. She may never recover. The Elder wants Robin to pay. He demands the war leader's death. I tell him that if I must kill Robin, it will cost Frogwort four big pieces of copper."

"Which is almost more than they can pay."

"Absolutely. Their willingness to pay so much tells me a great deal about the seriousness of the charge. Consider: If they would pay me only four jars of goosefoot seeds, then it is probably not an important charge that they are making against Robin. If they will pay four copper plates, that tells me that if this thing is not brought to a resolution, Frogwort may be driven to send warriors in retaliation."

"So they're willing to give you the wealth."

"Then I go to Robin and tell him that Frogwort is very upset. What is his side of the story? He tells me, but I see the lie in his soul, the place where it is twisted and evil. I tell everyone—him, his lineage, and the Blue Duck Clan—that Frogwort must be compensated, and the little girl provided for by means of land, alliance, marriage, or tribute.

"Blue Duck Clan talks it over and decides that they have no obligation to pay. War Leader Robin's lineage claims that they are not responsible either, and any decision is Robin's. He, of course, refuses."

"And then?"

"Then I kill him. Frogwort pays me four big pieces of copper plate, and people are back in balance."

"More or less."

"More or less." Tall Man rose and began climbing down a

loose slope where the Traders had dug out the trail following a vein of chert.

"That's a nice story, Magician. If you had always done things the right way, the just way, you wouldn't have felt so guilty about having murdered that Trader in an attempt to get the woman you loved. Stargazer wouldn't have made you fidget like a fish on a spear when he mentioned the angry ghosts, would he?"

Tall Man walked in silence for a time, his head down as he watched the trail disappear under his short feet. "No. I didn't always do things the right way."

"And why would that be, Magician?" She lifted an inquiring eyebrow.

"Power, Star Shell, is neither good nor evil in its nature. It simply is. People can use it for whatever they will. We are imperfect beasts, flawed at our best. I was . . . well, young. And, yes, I would have to say vain as well. After all, I was a dwarf, coveted, prized, innately Powerful. I brought people good luck, and I could do no wrong. When you grow up like that, you don't see things the way they really are. Everyone pampers you; if I asked for something, I received it from glad hands."

"And you asked for everything."

"I got it, too. But, you see, a person always wants more. I went south to the Serpent Clan and petitioned for Initiation. Suddenly I wasn't someone special. At first I enjoyed the anonymity, the ability to test myself against others. You must understand, I've always been blessed with the ability and intelligence to obtain what I wished, and through hard study, I rose to the top. Again, being a dwarf helped—not so much with my teachers, but among my peers. They still held that inborn belief in a dwarf's natural superiority. And I used it."

Star Shell reached down and flicked a wood tick from her leg. "So you who commit judgments on others are no better than your victims?"

"Human beings are no more than they are." He sighed as he watched a promethea moth disturbed by their passage. It fluttered to one of the maples before flattening itself conspicuously on the bark. "Power has a way of evening things, young Star

Shell. I make no excuses. I did a great many things wrong . . . and knew it at the time. Poisoning that Trader was but one of my evil deeds. There are others, many more distasteful than that; but you should know that I am repaying my debts to Power, and to the ghosts."

"Are you? I could almost believe that you and the Mask are more alike than different."

"We are very much alike, young Star Shell. I would point out, however, that a man learns much more quickly than a Mask."

"Mama! Look!" Silver Water came racing through the dark boles of trees, a box turtle tightly clamped in her hands. "I found him! He was in a place he'd hollowed in the leaves. Can I keep him?"

"Baby, I don't know how. Anything that we'd put him in, he'd get out of."

Silver Water frowned, staring down at the pretty shell, the yellow splotches on horn-brown. "We could eat him. Then we could make the shell into a rattle. I could run around and rattle it at everything that might have a ghost in it."

"And ghosts don't like rattles?"

"No, Mama. It bothers them, because the sound of a rattle makes them want to Dance. Ghosts don't always want to Dance, just at the ceremonials. How would you feel if people started shaking rattles at you when you didn't want to Dance?"

"I never thought of it that way. How do you know that ghosts feel like Dancing when they hear a rattle?"

Silver Water pursed her lips, the action making her cheeks look plump. "Someone told me."

"Who?"

"Someone. I said I wouldn't tell who."

Stargazer? "It's all right, baby. We'll go back, and you can learn the stars—just as soon as we take care of what we need to do up north."

"It's no use, Mama. Stargazer is dead." Silver Water continued to stare down at her turtle, the shell opening the slightest bit as they came to a complete stop.

"Why do you think that?" Star Shell asked softly, aware that Tall Man watched her daughter with thoughtful eyes.

"I just know, that's all."

Star Shell glanced uneasily at the Magician. He shrugged his own bafflement.

"Baby, you can't know that Stargazer is—"

"I *know*, Mama!" she said miserably. "I just know!" At that, Silver Water ran into the forest with her turtle clutched to her chest.

Star Shell stood stunned. "What's this? She's never acted like this in her entire life!"

"Fear, perhaps?" Tall Man spread his arms as he climbed up to her. "Or anger? With her father's death and our constant running, it's just amazing that she's been as good as she's been."

"Well, I'm going to chase her down, bend her over my knee, and—"

"Star Shell, let it go," Tall Man said gently. "If it becomes a habit, you'll have plenty of time for discipline."

Star Shell watched her feet as bits of trail disappeared under her moccasins. The question repeated within: *How could she know that Stargazer is dead?*

And if he was, were she and Tall Man responsible?

The dwarf followed along in his rolling gait. The humped pack containing the Mask gave him a grotesque appearance.

A shiver tickled through Star Shell's guts. Another trial loomed on the horizon, and this one would be for much higher stakes.

Silver Water sits beside a small pond. Moss furs the rocks at the water's edge, creating a soft green blanket for her. She gazes down into the turtle's shell. It has pulled its head inside, but she can still see its yellow eyes. It blinks each time a hot tear rolls down Silver Water's cheeks and plops on its face.

"He's dead," she whispers as she tips the turtle sideways to wipe her eyes on her sleeve. "He . . . he came to see me . . . at the end."

The turtle opens its mouth and hisses at her.

Silver Water props it on her drawn-up knees and strokes its shell tenderly, feeling the raised patterns slide beneath her fingertips. She concentrates on the coolness. The shell. The water. The air.

Her heart is on fire. It won't stop burning.

That same hurts-to-look-at brilliance hides in the secret place in her soul, with flames that eat her belly and hot tears drowning her face.

"Poor turtle," she croaks, and uses a finger to dry the tears on its shell. "Are you drowning in there?"

She turns it upside down and shakes it, just to make sure it's not. A few tears fall out. The turtle's legs flail wildly at thin air for a moment before it pulls them inside its shell for good.

Silver Water stares at the teardrops on the moss. Seven of them. All have stars inside, glistening.

Her eyes widen.

"Stargazer told me! He told me that once I really understood the sky, the stars would come to live with me."

Hesitantly, she looks around, and sees them winking in the pond . . . and on the tree leaves . . . and flashing with the specks of dust that pirouette through the air. All are Dancing.

Laughter bubbles up in her throat and surprises her.

She misses Stargazer.

He died of loneliness.

Silver Water sets the turtle down on the soft moss and uses her hands to prod all of her inside parts. Liver, kidneys, stomach, backbone. Before he died, Stargazer didn't have any. The loneliness had chewed and chewed, until it hollowed him out.

She is lonely, too. More lonely than she has ever been in her whole life. Her father used to terrify her. Now her mother does. If only her mother would talk to her about the Mask. . . .

Silver Water lies down on the moss beside the turtle and curls into a tight ball, trying to make a shell from her arms and legs, hoping it will protect her from jaws she can't see.

Thirty-six

I sit hunched over my prize, staring down into his broken face. Waiting. Desperate for it to be over.

The storm has subsided; now I will see what the tempest has wrought. And pray that it is enough to save us when the time comes.

Few can manage to balance on the edge of the abyss without falling in. Even fewer have the courage to pull themselves out if they slip. . .

Little Mouse huddled in a ball, Dreaming. This Dream, of all Dreams, was special: This time, Little Mouse Dreamed his death.

He'd Dreamed the manner of this dying before, the sinking, the horror of his mother's curses, but he'd awakened before that actual onset of death. Now he experienced the afterward, and his soul suffered in lonely captivity.

He floated in darkness, drowned, his corpse drifting weightlessly on the currents. His head, arms, and legs hung downward; sightless eyes stared at the rippled mud. His limp toes and fingertips dragged, stirring up puffy swirls of silt.

Where life had been, only a hollow, aching loneliness remained. *This is how it feels to be a ghost.*

He noted the sensations: cold, his skin white and water-swollen, weightless silence. The rocking and drifting actually soothed him as he hovered in the darkness.

Will I be alone now? Is that my ultimate curse? Down here, at the bottom of the Fresh Water Sea, he'd never share the camaraderie of other ghosts. His soul would be forgotten. No feasts would be given, no respect shown by the unborn generations.

He would know only loneliness, darkness, and cold.

Forever.

How did a Spirit deal with that? Where did he find discipline in this empty solitude? Discipline for what? Discipline implied a goal. A goal? What goal? How did one measure success in a black nothingness devoid of almost all sensation?

You will endure . . . because there is nothing else. The thought didn't comfort him. He might rage, scream into the murky silence, thrash and whip the darkness into a frenzy. And no one, nothing, would notice or care. Weep? Break down and sob? Bury himself in the misery of his hopeless condition? But only he could relish the wretchedness of his Spirit. Beyond that, when the emotions had exhausted themselves—as emotions always must—he would have returned to this same inevitable reality. No wiser, just a bit more weary and foolish.

In all of his imaginings, he'd never anticipated such a desolation of the soul.

He'd hoped to die in the heat of battle as he struggled against worthy foes—his remains to be carried back to the City of the Dead. There his corpse would be washed, gently oiled, and allowed to decompose in the charnel house. Finally, his carefully prepared bones would be placed in a special tomb by worshiping hands. When the ceremonials had been attended to and the Spirit World made aware of his arrival, he'd pass through that veil and into the realm of the ancestors, there to be greeted with the respect and admiration due a man of his status and reputation.

Not this . . .

Aloneness. Floating. Forever.

How did this happen?

"*You needed to die,*" a sympathetic voice told him.

"Where are you?" A faint spark kindled in the peace.

"*Right here, Little Mouse. Your head is in my lap.*"

"I'm dead, Granduncle."

He *wasn't* alone! As that single reality surged through him, the thrill rivaled that of sexual release—and that, of course, conjured images of his mother.

"She did this to me, Granduncle. Avenged herself on me for splitting her skull. But I had to, didn't I? You told me that it was my duty. She was sick and twisted in her soul. She was hurting people. She . . . she hurt me.'' Only on the journey up-river with Otter had he come to understand how much. He'd made a friend, almost in spite of himself. If only he could take back that day when he killed the crow—and shamed the only men he'd come to care about.

"Yes, I know. But that has passed behind you now. Your soul has healed." A gentle hand patted his head, loving and reassuring, imparting a warmth to the cold darkness. *"You're safe now, Little Mouse. You've found yourself. Found all the threads that came apart because of your mother. They're beginning to weave together again. You're growing whole."*

"I've found myself." The curious truth burned anew within him. He became aware of the warm lap upon which his head was pillowed. He could feel his body rocking and bobbing, and somewhere a gull cried out.

A second sound, that of wood bumping hollowly on wood, caused him to start, and Black Skull opened his eyes, blinking at the familiar gunwale of the Trader's canoe. For a long second he simply stared at the battered wood while his thoughts churned in confusion.

Wave Dancer! And that meant . . . that he wasn't dead after all. The reassuring hand still lay on his head, a realization that sent blind panic racing along his bones.

Black Skull fumbled to get his arm beneath him, then pushed up, aware that morning light streamed across the water. Sunrise bathed both the fox-head bow and the underside of the low-hanging clouds in gaudy, reddish light. Water stretched in all directions, endless, smoothly undulating until it met the flat horizon.

Only then did Black Skull turn to stare into Green Spider's unfocused eyes. The Contrary's hand, fingers splayed, still lingered over the damp blanket in his lap. Black Skull could see the impression left by his head.

Green Spider gave him a quizzical look, that narrow mouth puckered. "Good evening, Killer of Men."

Black Skull, shivering in the cool morning, licked his lips. Every bone and joint ached from the cramped position in which he'd slept. His tongue stumbled, unsure of what to say. He could see Otter and Pearl huddled together under a blanket in the stern.

Catcher had propped himself on a soggy pack just behind the Contrary, and now he raised his head, his ears pricked.

"Last night . . ." Black Skull's voice cracked.

"Peaceful and tranquil," the Contrary told him blandly.

"I thought . . ."

"I never think."

"I know that, fool!" Black Skull bent over, supporting his head with one hand. Through the web of his fingers, he stared at the water sloshing so harmlessly in the bottom of the boat. "Last night . . . what was real? What was Dream?"

"Warrior, the only realities are Dreams. When you're awake, everything you see or do is made up. A trick . . . illusion. Last night it finally grew light enough for you to see."

"I thought I was dead . . . my soul floating."

"We're all dead. Dead. Dead. Dead. More so when we're obsessed with living than at any other time."

Black Skull winced, wishing that just this once, the fool would speak like a normal man. "It seemed so real, so eternal."

"Little Mouse, I will tell you this truth: The made-up things are those that last the longest. The harder you seek, the poorer your ability to comprehend. Last night when you let go, you finally found yourself. Do you understand?"

Black Skull rubbed his offset jaw as he squinted out at the endless expanse of water. The low swells reflected the blazing sky in the stillness of the morning. He'd never seen water so glassy, as if it alone in all of the universe were pure and unsullied.

"Then you know what a coward I was?" Shame began to leak out from the place where he'd tried to hide it.

Green Spider's gaze began to wander. He picked mindlessly at a splinter on the side of his paddle. "You should fight all battles with such courage."

"Don't mock me, Contrary. Not now, not this morning."

Green Spider's gaze cleared, and he stared with eerie intensity through Black Skull's defenses, into his very soul. "We all face our storms, Killer of Men. Last night you faced yours—and you've awakened to a new dawn, having survived. You will come to understand. It seems like cowardice to you because you don't know the difference between what is brave and what is spineless. Last night I saw you being true for the first time."

"True? I was so frightened that I . . ." He closed his eyes. What would Granduncle have said?

The Contrary's hand rested for a moment on Black Skull's shoulder, the touch birdlike and fleeting; it imparted, all the same, a sense of understanding. "No man should regret such courage. Facing oneself is the hardest thing of all."

Black Skull swallowed with difficulty, aware of the naked loneliness in his soul. Every one of his defenses had been battered or shattered. In this new confusion, how was he going to put himself back together again?

He tried to look away, but when he finally met the Contrary's eyes, he saw respect there.

"Thank you, Green Spider."

Green Spider made a face and stuck out his tongue. Tongue still protruding, he added in a very slurred speech, "I did nuht'-ing."

And Black Skull couldn't help but chuckle. "Very well, fool. But I think you did." He paused. "Which is a truly terrifying thought."

Green Spider sucked his tongue back in and pretended to swallow it. "Scares *you*? Think of what it does to me!"

Black Skull sat with his arms braced on his knees, his hands dangling loosely as he watched the water around his feet swaying in time to the movement of the canoe. For the moment, he was content just to breathe, to enjoy the feel of air entering and leaving his lungs, and to listen to the shrill calls of the gulls.

He lifted his head to stare around at the eternal water. The sun would be obscured by clouds soon, and any sense of direction would vanish.

"Which way, Contrary? With no landmarks, how do you tell directions out here?"

"Seas are like souls." Using both hands, Green Spider pointed this way and that. "At dawn, as at birth, the way is clear. In midlife, all goes adrift in the glare of the noon sun. Only in the evening of life do we look back and wonder at where we've been, what we missed, and why."

"So, it's morning. There's the sunrise. Where's shore?"

"That way!" Green Spider pointed west, which at the moment lay off the right rear of the drifting canoe.

"East it is, fool." Black Skull found his paddle, waterlogged and heavy, shoved between the packs and the hull. He settled himself and began paddling toward the sunrise.

How many are left? Wolf of the Dead scanned the expanse of white beach visible from this high dune. To his astonishment, the blue water was placid, as if the Fresh Water Sea slept in dreamless oblivion. He and his warriors had barely escaped drowning out there in the mountainous violence. Had those been *these* waters?

Shading his eyes, he studied the pale sands that stretched northward in a slight curve around the still water. Those tiny dots far to the north might be some of his warriors. That, or Ilini. A shiver of doubt stole along his spine. It was one thing to cross Ilini lands at the head of two tens of tens of warriors . . . and quite another to be a small Khota party in hostile country.

He narrowed his eyes, the crow's-feet deepening in the side of his face. Like the wolf from which his legendary ancestors had sprung, he scented the quiet air, drawing the damp freshness of the morning into his soul. A grim smile played around his mouth, the skin puckered like beaten copper.

Grizzly Tooth climbed up from below, a worried look on his face. The bear-tooth necklace clattered with each step. The warrior's hard fist had tightened around the atlatl at his belt. "Do you see anyone?"

"I can just make out a small party of people up there." Wolf of the Dead pointed. "From this distance, I can't tell who they are. Maybe Ilini. This accursed land is too full of them."

"Perhaps. Their actions don't look dazed enough to be Khota." Grizzly Tooth took his time, shading his eyes as he searched. "Nothing, only water and sand dunes and more of that thin grass."

"How many do you think might have survived?"

Grizzly Tooth sighed and seated himself on the sand. He looked out over the water. "I don't know. We'd have drowned out there ourselves if Round Scar hadn't had the sense to head us right back into the wind and race for the safety of the shore. As it was, we just made it.''

"And Pearl and the Water Fox?" Wolf of the Dead turned his attention eastward, toward the horizon, searching vainly for any dots that might be boats.

"Who knows?" Grizzly Tooth scooped up a handful of sand and let it trickle through his fingers. "That Trader's canoe is big; it floats high in the water. Would the wind have capsized it? Or would they have been able to ride out the storm?"

"How should I know? What do I know about the Fresh Water Sea? Or of canoes in water like that? Maybe they drowned. We came within a thread of swamping.''

Are you alive, woman? And you, Water Fox? Are you out there? Laughing at me? Wolf of the Dead closed his eyes, searching with his soul. What was that hint of feeling? Could he detect them? Sense them out there? In the end, he bowed to a warrior's pragmatism. "I think . . . I think they are alive out there. That big canoe, with its keel, might have saved them. We must assume they live.''

Grizzly Tooth grunted as sand streamed between his fingers.

"Our only salvation is to hunt them down, kill them, and bring their heads home as a signal to all peoples that no one insults the Khota." Wolf of the Dead ran his tongue over the gap in his front teeth. "Now, show me how this Fresh Water Sea lies upon the land.''

"I have been told it looks like this." Grizzly Tooth drew a long loop in the sand. "We crossed the passage here, on the southwest side. This shore, south of us, curves gradually eastward along a series of giant sand dunes. Then the coast runs northward." Grizzly Tooth drew another loop like a big thumb. "This is the land beyond the eastern shore. You'll notice that it's a big peninsula. More of the Fresh Water Sea lies on the other side. I've never been here before, let alone to the other side of the peninsula. I only know what I've learned from the Traders. They say it's a long way around.''

"What kind of lunatic would paddle right out into the middle of the Fresh Water Sea with a storm coming on?" Wolf of the Dead glared angrily at the silver sheen glinting off the water.

"A desperate one." Grizzly Tooth rubbed his map away and

looked up. "And speaking of desperation, what do we do? If our warriors have survived, they'll be scattered all along this coast."

Ah, old friend, you do not wish to mention the fact that I may have killed the finest of our young men. And for that small favor, at least, Wolf of the Dead felt a welling gratitude. "You used the word desperation. What choices are left to us? Retreat back to our territory? I think not."

"You are right, my leader. No matter what, we must proceed." Grizzly Tooth shook his head. "The Ilini would see our weakness. On top of the stories of Water Fox's massacre, we can't allow them to spread this news."

Wolf of the Dead nodded. Another of his blinding headaches was building. By afternoon, the hammering pain would sap him into uselessness. "If the Ilini see the remnants of our party slipping home like cowed dogs, we will be condemning our people to destruction. On the other hand, if we gather those whom we find alive and continue the chase, the Ilini will not know the disaster that has fallen upon us."

Grizzly Tooth rubbed his face wearily. "I think you're right."

"You don't look pleased."

"I'm not. I would have liked a moon at home. After all those days in the canoe watching Pearl's inviting body, I'm ready for some time under the robes with my woman. But enough of that. Yes, we should do as you say. And if we can find enough men alive, we should send one canoe back to reassure people that all is well." Grizzly Tooth frowned, his fingers pressed to his lips. "Have them . . . yes, tell a story about how we tied all the boats together, rode out the storm. Some of the canoes broke loose and you and I took it upon ourselves to scout for those missing boats. The others, meanwhile, are paddling straight across the Fresh Water Sea."

"And we will meet them after ensuring that Pearl and the Water Fox didn't double back."

Grizzly Tooth thought about it. "It will work. Even with the survivors we find. If we do this correctly, we can still win."

"Exactly." Wolf of the Dead grinned to cover the futility that drained his soul. "What other choice do we have? The Ilini *must* think that our warriors survived—and that we'll be coming back."

Grizzly Tooth watched the water with dull eyes. "It's my fault. I brought Pearl upriver."

"No, my friend." Wolf of the Dead placed a hand on his blood kin's shoulder. "You did as I asked. We'll survive this. The Ilini told us that this Water Fox is headed for a place called the Roaring Water, on the eastern side of the Fresh Water Sea. We'll follow him there and kill him and the woman. On the way back, we'll do a little raiding, accumulate all the wealth and slaves we can handle, and return. That way, the Ilini will see triumph—and we can tell them that our warriors are holding new lands that we have taken on the other side of the Fresh Water Sea."

Grizzly Tooth was playing with the sand again, scooping it up and letting it run through his fingers like escaping dreams. "Do you really think it will work?"

"We must hope so. I can't see any alternative."

Grizzly Tooth threw his last handful of sand down and stood, smacking the clinging grains from his legs. "Then come, let us build a signal fire. Any survivors will be looking for that. To keep the damage to a minimum, we will tell those who arrive that others have already gone on. As long as we keep them from panicking, we can maintain our leadership."

Wolf of the Dead nodded and took one last look at the shining water. How could that smooth body of water have betrayed him and his people so thoroughly?

"Do the ghosts of my drowned warriors look up as I am looking down? Do they weep?" *As I shall one day weep ... unless I can avenge their deaths.*

Otter had awakened several times during the day to stare around with a half-opened eye and then drop back into exhausted slumber, reassured that everything was all right. He'd resettled several times, cramped on the wedged packs but fully aware of Pearl's warm body conformed to his body. All else had faded into the oblivion of a man too long pushed to the edge of his endurance.

When the wind had finally dropped and the water had turned

from terrifying to simply unsettling, he and Pearl had taken shelter under a blanket while the unabated rain continued to fall. Relentless lightning flickered through the clouds before thunder rolled across the sundered heavens. Arms around each other in camaraderie, laughing about the danger and the fear they'd shared, they'd nodded off to the staccato of drops on the blanket and the whisper of rain on the waters.

Otter's bladder finally forced him to full wakefulness. He yawned and ran his tongue around his mouth. The taste reminded him of moldy, mouse-soiled blankets left too long on the dirt floor of an abandoned hut.

What a vile thought! But, Otter, isn't it great to be alive to think it? He chuckled at himself, gazing at the marred gunwale of his canoe. The cypress wood had been bumped and bruised over the years by countless impacts of the paddle. Nevertheless, his sturdy canoe had survived its greatest trial. He reached out to run gentle fingers along the wood. Did he sense the canoe's satisfaction?

Pearl stirred in his arms, and he paused to stare up at an evening sky. Scattered clouds were scudding to the east. In the bow, Black Skull paddled mechanically, heading eastward, and the Contrary lay curled on the packs. Catcher slept in the hollow of Green Spider's stomach.

Otter spun a strand of Pearl's hair between his fingers. How soft it felt after the rain. Her smell was pleasant, that of a healthy woman. For the moment, he could imagine savoring that scent for the rest of his life. He could enjoy all of this, the rocking of the boat, the feel of the woman against him. The satisfaction of having shared danger and, together, having triumphed.

He recalled how she'd laughed in defiance, daring the storm. How she'd whooped when *Wave Dancer* dropped into the depths, to splash and rise again. She'd saved them all. Her knowledge of deep water and swells, her skill and resources, had kept him from making mistakes that would have swamped them in the darkness.

Pearl, you don't know what a wonderful gift you gave me last night.

An old, familiar sensation, that of contentment, lingered in his breast. He hadn't felt this way since his early days—days on the river with Uncle. Since Uncle's death, that sense of accomplishment had been but a shadow. Now it burned bright again. They'd beaten the storm! He wanted to laugh, to shout with joy, but instead, he kept it all hidden—a secret exultation saddened only by the speculation that when she awoke, that special camaraderie they'd shared in the midst of the storm would have evaporated like the puddled water on the packs.

Yes, well, you can't blame her. Not after what the Khota did to her. And he was suddenly conscious of the firm fullness of her breast where it pressed against his left arm. He closed his eyes, seeking to absorb the feeling of her, the warm security of her body against his. This he would keep carefully locked away to retrieve on cold and lonely nights when he and Catcher camped beside the river.

Then, as the fire crackled, he'd remember the storm, the fury of the wind, and the long hours of darkness. *Wave Dancer* would buck and jump in the crashing waves. Rain would lash him again, and the hopelessness of their situation would loom frighteningly real. He'd hear her shouting, hear the laughter that had broken from her wet lips in the most desperate of moments. He'd worship her then—and recall this well-earned rest with her hip against his, the pressure of her thigh so warm. On those damp, dark nights, the warm softness of her breast would haunt him.

Such memories could last forever if they were properly stored. The way he lived and the solitude of his Trading allowed him to cherish more of the past than people who lived in constant companionship, and he had more time to explore it.

He stared absently across the water, seeing a wavering mirror of the sunset on the glassy surface. Water turned to sky. Even a Contrary would be confused.

He battled with his bladder, enduring the misery of the body for the bliss of the soul. If only . . . if only . . .

She finally stirred and stretched just at dusk, groaning as she sat up and looked around. Otter took the opportunity to rub his arm where it had fallen asleep. Her warmth would dissipate now, to become but another memory.

"Where are we?" she asked, making a face and rubbing her shoulders. "Every joint and muscle in my body aches."

"But we're alive," Otter reminded. "Thanks to you."

"Thanks to all of us."

"Are you awake? Good," Black Skull called from the bow. His paddle continued to dip regularly into the water. "I don't know where I'm going, only that I'm headed east. Is there land anywhere?"

Otter suffered through the tingling of reestablished circulation before he politely crawled forward over coarsely woven packs, rolls of palmetto matting, and what had been carefully packed jars, to allow Pearl privacy—such as there was on a canoe in the middle of the Fresh Water Sea. Some of the ceramic jars had broken, the seeds scattered among angular sherds of pottery. Others had cracked, no doubt from the hull slamming down into the swells. Nothing appeared to have been lost, and considering what they'd survived, the damage was minor.

Otter found Green Spider sound asleep on a roll of palmetto matting. He picked his way carefully over the Contrary, then attended to his own needs before he hunched down behind the warrior, staring up at the deepening indigo sky.

Black Skull dropped his voice. "I wasn't much help to you last night."

"It's all right. I remember how you feel about water. I'd have stayed close to shore if I could have. The Khota just didn't give me any choice."

Black Skull never missed a stroke with his paddle. "I fought a battle of my own last night." A new vulnerability was in his eyes when he looked back. "Since that day at Hilltop, I . . . well, I've been seeing myself differently. Last night, something just . . . I'm sorry, Otter. I should have been there."

Otter clapped the big man on the shoulder. "You're doing just fine. We all survived. We just did it in different ways."

Black Skull took a deep breath. "It's hard for me, but I have to tell you that I was terrified. Me, of all people."

Otter stared out over the rolling water. "We all were. I've never seen a storm like that. We've all ventured into unknown territory, Black Skull."

"Will you forgive me for grabbing you by the throat that day?"

"You're long since forgiven, warrior."

After a long pause, Black Skull asked, "Why didn't the joke with the skunk work?"

"It would have . . . with anyone but a Contrary."

They both laughed at that.

Black Skull gestured ahead. "Is there land out there?"

"There's land all around us . . . or so I've heard. Traders who follow the shoreline make their way clear around the Fresh Water Sea. Now, if you can trace the shore all the way around, it follows that we'll hit land somewhere, doesn't it?"

Black Skull grunted under his breath. "All right, I guess that makes sense. So, tell me, Trader, where are we? Do we go north or south? East or west? At dawn, Green Spider said to go east. Perhaps we should wake the fool and ask, just to—"

"No. No, let him sleep." Otter rubbed his neck. "I don't know, Black Skull. The roaring water is east—that's all I can tell you."

"And when it gets to full dark, which way is east?"

Otter looked up, seeing the first stars. The trouble with stars was that they changed throughout the year. A constellation that shone in one part of the sky in fall glimmered in another part in spring.

"East?" Pearl asked from the stern, where she'd been washing her hair. She craned her neck sideways as she twisted the long strands to wring the water over the side, then pointed. "That way! We're headed a bit north of true east."

Otter asked, "You know how to read the stars?"

In the fading light, he could see her teeth gleaming as she smiled. "I've been to the islands way out in the Saltwater Sea, remember? If you don't know the stars, you'll die out there. And you can't take too long about making your crossing, either. Unlike the Fresh Water Sea, you can't drink the water."

Otter took his bearings, watching the heavens. They'd change with the night, but he'd start learning. "Black Skull, you've been awake all day?"

"Someone had to stay awake and keep watch. Even the fool nodded off within a hand's time after dawn."

"Sleep now. Pearl and I . . . we'll keep the course through the night. In the morning, you'll have the sun—and Green Spider, for what he can tell you—to steer by. If we keep headed east, we'll find land somewhere."

At the warrior's nod, Otter retraced his way to the stern. Unknown territory? In more ways than one. He was curious about the changes wrought in Black Skull's manner, and he felt awkward over the feelings that Pearl inspired in his soul. He could almost wish for another storm and its simple challenge of survival.

"How come you never learned the stars?" Pearl asked as she

fluffed her hair to dry it. "I'd think a Trader would do that first thing."

He shrugged, refusing to meet her eyes, embarrassed by his desire to hold her again. "Rivers have only two directions: upstream and down. When we traveled, Uncle taught me the currents, the plants, the animals, how to read the water for dangers. You know, what the River Spirit was trying to tell me. And then, as I mastered that, there was so much more. Which tributaries led to whose territories, the various histories and customs of the different peoples. For instance, did you know that I have twenty-six wives?"

She stiffened, her eyes suddenly cool. "You told me . . ."

He chuckled. "You must understand about Traders and Trading. Four of my wives are dead. Most of the others are happily married to other men, having their children, and doing their duties to their clan. You see, among some of the peoples one Trades with, one must be part of the family—related to the people—or you're not a full human being."

"What do you mean, a full human being? You've got the right number of legs, arms, and . . . well, the other things."

Otter settled himself in the stern, gauging where east ought to be from the evening star she'd pointed out. His hands, shoulders, and back protested at the feel of the paddle as he began the age-old rhythm of paddling. The awkwardness was growing between them. As he'd feared it would.

"Ah, but parts do not make a man. Relatives do. Just like you and Wolf of the Dead. Make a marriage and you've joined two clans, no matter how dissimilar. That, or you adopt. I have . . . let's see, sixteen, no, seventeen, additional brothers, and more than a handful of fathers scattered around the country. After all, a man wouldn't cheat, trick, or betray his own family, would he?"

"I can tell you he would if he were Anhinga." She stared bitterly out at the evening. "It's so quiet here. Not a sound."

He smiled, paddling, wishing he knew what to say that would make her feelings as smooth as the water.

"These wives," she finally said. "You live with them when you visit their clans?"

"No. Well, except for She Panther."

"She Panther?"

In her profile, he could see the arched eyebrow. "One of my, uh, wives. She Panther is at least six tens of years old. She's a woman of the Morning Star people, who live high up the Muddy River. I think she's married to half of the Traders I know, and when we go up there to Trade for buffalo, antelope, prairie turnip, or Knife River flint, we stay in her lodge. She's like . . . well, we all call her Grandmother. But I gather that she created quite a sensation as a young woman.''

"A sensation, you say?" The eyebrow hadn't dropped entirely. "I guess I'd never thought about it. But some Traders do have different wives, real ones, don't they?"

"I know Traders who have six or seven families along the river, spending time with each as they follow their routes. It wouldn't be a bad way to live, I suppose."

"Then why didn't you?"

"I had my reasons."

Pearl nodded in sober understanding. "Red Moccasins was a fool."

"No. She was very, very wise." But Otter had to admit that for all her wisdom, she'd have lain shaking in the bottom of the canoe last night. Knowing that—and having witnessed Pearl throw her laughter to the fury of the storm—had changed something inside him.

He paddled silently, trying to figure out what to say, anything to keep her looking at him. "Would you teach me the stars? I mean, point them out. Which ones do I need to know?"

She leaned back toward him, her silky black hair cascading down her back, and he could smell her delicate odor again. It soothed him deep down.

"That is Blue Crab, the Scavenger," Pearl told Otter, pointing to the south.

"We . . . my people, the White Shell, call that the Snail."

"People have different names for things." She stared up at the sky, remembering the warmth of his body and how he'd held her. *You're a fool, Pearl,* she told herself. *You know better than this. One man pulls you out of trouble with another man and you're ready to latch on to him like a barnacle to a mangrove root?*

"That's Black Drum, there, to the west of Blue Crab. He's turning in the water . . . with his mouth open. See, you can follow the stars and imagine his outline." To sleep in his arms had been so pleasant after the terror of the storm. How secure she'd felt, as if she belonged there. How could a relative stranger kindle such warmth and security within her?

He's not a stranger. I've been traveling with him for over a moon now.

She frowned in the darkness. No man had ever made her feel as secure as Otter did; it was as if they'd been together forever, despite the fact that each day was a new beginning, fresh and exciting.

So, what are you going to do with him, Pearl?

"We make two constellations out of those groups of stars." Otter continued to paddle. "One-legged Man, and part of Flying Squirrel."

It simply wasn't fair! In the height of the storm, they'd worked so well together, shared that sense of desperation, and . . .

And what, Pearl? Did you imagine that was some magic moment? Think, girl. He loves this Red Moccasins. The man is probably mired in guilt because he woke up with his arms around you.

She pointed to the east. "We call that one the Wedding Bowl. You know that women ask for men in Anhinga society. The story is that once a young woman fell desperately in love with a handsome young man. Her family went to his and asked for the marriage. When he agreed, she was the happiest girl on earth."

"What happened?"

"Among the Anhinga, a special bowl is made and decorated to show the symbols of each lineage. At the end of the marriage ceremony, both man and woman drink from the bowl." *What's wrong with you! Your voice is almost trembling!* "The new couple returns to their house—generally one borrowed from one of the girl's relatives for the wedding. After they've coupled and he's planted his seed in her, they break the bowl and set the fragments outside to indicate that they are man and wife and that the union is complete."

"I've seen that," he murmured. "So how did the bowl get into the sky?"

Pearl took a deep breath, images of Khota hands grasping at her thoughts, tearing them like fabric. "After they went to the house where they were to spend that first night, he ducked inside first and turned. That's when he told her that he could not couple with her. He said he was in love with another woman, who would be in his heart forever. That woman, however, had married another man in order that her clan might gain great wealth and new fishing grounds. He, in turn, had married for the same reason, and even if he could never love her, never join with her, they could break the bowl and no one would ever know."

"The man was a maggot," Otter growled at the night.

Pearl studied him for a moment, watching the steady swing of his arms as he paddled. He seemed thoughtful, his attention on the water. Was he thinking of Red Moccasins even now?

Or of the fact that Wolf of the Dead planted his seed in you? Is that it? Does he think you're soiled, polluted by Khota semen? She felt that way, why shouldn't he?

He'd seemed so uneasy after waking with her in his arms. Was it something she'd done? Said?

Buck up, Pearl. Stop being a fool. Only an idiot expects a man to take care of her. Like Grandmother always said, it's not in their nature, so start taking care of yourself. She took a deep breath, steadying herself. It had to be fatigue driving her crazy. Yes, that was it.

"The young woman's heart was broken. She couldn't break the bowl. She had to do something. She walked to the doorway . . . and threw the bowl up into the sky. High. So high that it caught up there, and we can see it still." *Which is a lesson for you, Pearl. No matter how kind this man seems, no matter how you enjoy that twinkle in his eye, you must not expect anything more from him.*

"It's a sad story," Otter told her.

"Yes, it is." She turned and rearranged the packs so she herself could paddle. *But then, Trader, life is full of sad stories.*

Thirty-seven

Star Shell knew where to look for her father as they crossed the eastern side of StarSky City. They paralleled the bluff overlooking the muddy water of the Flying Squirrel River. Ahead of them, a group of people stood in a knot, huddled under rain-soaked blankets and capes.

In defiance of the rolling thunder and the misty rain, a number of engineers worked with their strings and pegs. Star Shell couldn't ferret out the meaning of all the measurements, lines, and angles, but she understood the construction process. What able body, born and raised at StarSky, didn't?

She, Silver Water, and the Magician had walked down from the ridge trail at first light. The night had been spent with a young couple—members of the Fast Squirrel Clan—whose holdings stretched up a small tributary creek south of Duck River. From them, Star Shell had learned that StarSky would be building a new earthwork, construction to begin at the close of the summer solstice ceremonials. And, of course, that's where her father would be.

Star Shell had draped her blanket over her head for protection against the misty rain. Her worn and stained moccasins were already soaked from the wet grass. Silver Water, too, used her blanket as a watershed. Her little fists—shiny with moisture—clutched the blanket firmly. Tall Man walked bareheaded, beads of water adding silver to his tight hair bun.

"You Flat Pipe people amaze me," the Magician said as they walked through the wet grass. "How much more can you build here? What will you do? Cover the entire world with mounded earth?"

She smiled grimly. "Stargazer would be appalled."

"He said that people forget too much," Silver Water reminded them solemnly. "After a few tens of years, nobody knows why things work the way they do."

The new earthwork would be a semicircle on the terrace above the confluence of the Flying Squirrel and Duck rivers. A series of paths had been worn between the terrace and the sloping banks of the river. Traders generally landed at this place. But only the Star Society knew whether that had anything to do with choosing the location. Similarly, only they could determine the shape of the earthwork to be built there.

Once the determination was made, the Elders of the Star Society went to the clan leaders, and the project was discussed in an open council. Then, if the people agreed to construction—for whatever reason the Star Society offered—the engineers would be called in to translate the vision of the Star Society into reality.

Star Shell now observed a step in that process. The outline of the proposed earthwork had been established with pegs and string. The engineers were good at that sort of thing. They carefully guarded their knotted measuring ropes, pegs, and cords, along with the secrets by which they figured angles and distances.

After the pattern had been laid out on the ground, a course of stones was placed to mark the outline. Then the strings were taken up. In the following months, the Star Society astronomers made celestial observations from the site, ensuring that the orientation was precisely correct. Perfect alignment often necessitated several rearrangements of the stone courses and recalculations by the engineers. On occasion, squabbles over the details had become severe enough to split societies, and, on extraordinarily rare occasions, whole clans.

When both the engineers and the Star Society were satisfied, the clan leaders—such as Hollow Drill—were called in. They represented the necessary labor.

As any leader knew, coordinating people had its own endless list of potential troubles. Was the planting on schedule? How many bodies could be spared from clan duties for the construction? Which individuals would excavate the soil, and which would carry it? Did the clan have enough burden baskets on hand for the number of people involved? Enough digging sticks? Who cooked the food for the toiling workers? Who repaired broken baskets? Which clans had the greatest responsibility for finishing the project? Because the necessary red soil came from deposits belonging to one clan, did that clan need to contribute as much labor as the others? If one clan did a majority of the construction, would it also be required to do the maintenance work?

Not to mention the myriad smaller problems. Could a given person be dismissed from that day's labor because of a sore back? What happened if an important relative within the clan died and half the people had to leave for the mourning cycle? Could so-and-so be excused from work for a week to attend an in-law's wedding? And, naturally, someone was always fighting with someone else and had to be put on a different part of the project.

Hollow Drill and the other clan leaders would be included in all of the planning for the earthwork. Each clan would carefully tally its resources and then decide how the proposed construction could actually be completed.

Star Shell's heart ached as she approached. She recognized him standing with the group of Elders at one end of the stone alignment. Despite the distance, she saw that he looked different, fragile. Here and there, strings had been placed and stretched taut. A heated debate between two of the engineers and one of the astronomers had ended with flapping arms and rising voices.

The clan leaders stood as amused observers. Hollow Drill looked in Star Shell's direction, seemed to dismiss her, and then reacted with a visible start. He said something to the Broken Pot clan leader and strode purposefully away.

Star Shell stifled a gasp of disbelief.

"That isn't quite the warm welcome I anticipated," Tall Man said. "By the ancestors, he couldn't possibly know . . ."

"Know what?"

The Magician winced, pressing tenderly at his side. "Nothing, girl. The musings of a tired old man."

Star Shell slowed, trying to understand why her father would walk away—and then she caught Hollow Drill's subtle signal. He pointed to the right, toward the Squirrel clan burial mound.

"Something's happened," Star Shell said quietly. "He doesn't want to be seen with us. This way." She cut across the wet grass toward the mound. *Funny, I've lived here all of my life, and I can't remember which Elder was buried here, or why he was important. Maybe old Stargazer wasn't so wrong after all.*

A burial mound wasn't built for just anyone. Great Shell, who had founded the lineage, rested under the mound at the western passageway into the Octagon. Thus, from the observatory on the summer solstice, an observer would see the sun rise across Great Shell's mound and, in effect, see through his eyes.

"Don't forget, everyone is looking for you," Tall Man reminded her. "A man on a high ridge does not seek shelter under an oak tree in the middle of a thunderstorm."

"Because an oak tree draws lightning," Star Shell finished. "I only have to tell him that I'm alive, that he shouldn't be worried about me."

"A messenger could have done the same thing." Tall Man looked around nervously. "I can't help but think this is a mistake."

"Then at least it's *my* mistake."

"Far be it from me to hinder your ability to make mistakes. The ancestors know, I've made plenty of my own." He paused, warily eyeing the burial mounds.

Why? What did he have to fear from any ghosts at StarSky City?

Hollow Drill had dropped over the terrace, out of sight of the Elders and the engineers. He circled under the lip of the terrace and came up behind the grassy burial mound. Here they would be shielded from the others. For a moment, Star Shell could only stare at the haunted expression, the drawn lips. Even the familiar tattoos had faded. When had he aged so? The lines had deepened; his flesh was oddly gaunt. Was it her imagination, or had his warm eyes sunk in the skull? The man she remembered as hearty, hale, and so strong, stood before her now little more than a walking rack of bones.

"Father?"

"Star Shell. My beautiful baby." A faint ghost of that old smile bent his lips. "I . . . I've been so worried."

She rushed into his arms, hugging him. Silver Water hung back.

"Baby?" Star Shell broke loose. "Come here, Silver Water. This is your grandfather. Come meet him."

Silver Water's blanket had slipped off her head. She stared at Hollow Drill with distrustful eyes, a finger in her mouth. She approached with halting steps.

"Hello, Silver Water," Hollow Drill greeted, dropping to one knee. "You're every bit as beautiful as your mother."

Silver Water nodded, clearly unconvinced.

"What's happened to you?" Star Shell's nervous fingers picked at his clothing. "You look as though you haven't eaten. Why did you point me in this direction? Isn't my brother feeding you? You haven't been sick, have you?"

"Only in my heart," he said gently, standing and taking her hands in his. Looking into his eyes, she could see torment just beneath the surface. His skin looked ashen and cold.

"What is it, Father?"

"Robin, the Blue Duck war leader, came here. Looking for you, of course. We came very close to a war with the clans in the Moonshell valley." He clasped her to him, patting her anxiously. "The ancestors help me, I've been so worried about you. Frightened. And at night, your mother's ghost is near. She's trying to tell me something. She seems angry, wailing, but I . . . I can't quite understand."

"I'm all right, Father." She held him, aware of bones where muscle had once been. "You need to go back. Finish with the earthwork planning. I'll wait at the house. We'll—"

"No. You can't." He pushed away, blinking at tears and sniffling. "It's too dangerous for you here. I've got to hide you somewhere. Let's see. Maybe among your mother's clan, down on the—"

"Father!"

He raised his hands, the gesture more for himself than for her. "Daughter, people are afraid. Afraid of you and the Mask and of what it might mean for them. You *must* leave here. Go to safety. Your mother's clan will take you in. They're—"

"They're a moon's walk to the south! I have to go north, Father."

He frowned, confused. "North? We don't have any relatives up that way."

"I know. It's my responsibility to take the Mask to the Roaring Water. You heard Tall Man's words the night of Mother's cremation. Don't you remember?''

He nodded, looking miserable.

''I just wanted to let you know that I was alive, to spend one night with—''

''No, child. It's too dangerous.''

''This is my home!''

He lowered his eyes.

She knotted her fists, frustrated with the whole miserable mess. ''I should have known. No matter which way I turn, there's nothing left, no place to go.''

''I'm so sorry. I . . . I'll come with you. Join you. Help you to—''

''No, Father.'' She steeled herself. ''But you can do something for me. Take Silver Water. Keep her safe.''

''Mama?'' Silver Water asked, bending her head up to stare with fear-wide eyes.

''Tadpole, it's the best thing I can think of. That's why we came here. Your grandfather can—''

''Do nothing,'' Hollow Drill interrupted dully. ''She's a member of your husband's lineage. Her clan is Sun Mounds, daughter—not StarSky. They'll discover that she's here with me. I would do anything I could, but you know that her people will ask for her. They'll consider her abandoned, an orphan.''

''They won't have to know who she is! She's just a little girl! Send her to cousin Slow Foot. He lives out on that farmstead all by himself. Who'd know?''

Hollow Drill frowned. ''You're not thinking clearly, daughter. Are you that desperate? Think, girl! You're at the center of the biggest storm to blow across this land in generations. In the last moon, the Many Paints have gone to war against the Rattlesnakes. Evidently they're going to settle that old territorial feud in blood. The story is that trophy heads are being taken. Like circling hawks, everyone is watching the StarSky Clan. Silver Water will be seen. Perhaps not immediately, but certainly within a moon. Someone will notice an extra little girl— even at Slow Foot's. They will tell someone else, and the speculation will begin. You know where it will end.''

Star Shell shook her head, refusing to believe. ''I must find a place to keep her safe.''

"Now do you understand?" Tall Man asked as he stepped forward. "I did not take the back trails by accident. Your father is quite right. There is no safe place. As long as the Mask is abroad, men will not rest."

Star Shell searched her father's face, looking for any sign of salvation—and saw only wretched sadness in those haunted brown eyes.

"I'm sorry, daughter. She's safer with you." He tried to smile, but even that effort failed him. He reached out with a trembling hand and laid it on her shoulder.

"You were my last hope," Star Shell murmured. "And now it's as if I don't even know . . ." *You.* But she couldn't say that. Not to this empty husk of a man whom she still loved so much.

Tall Man had stepped up beside her. He peered at Hollow Drill. "I'm sorry, old friend. I hope that one day you will forgive me for all the terrible things I've done." He paused. "Sometimes we learn too late in life."

At that, Tall Man reached out, touched her father's unresponsive fingers, then walked slowly past them to stare out over the narrow ribbon of sinuous brown river.

"Not even for one night?" Star Shell asked.

"It would be too dangerous, girl. Does anyone know you're here? Did anyone recognize you?"

"We stayed with—"

"Then go. Go now! Quickly." His gaze wavered. "Are you sure you don't want me to come with you?"

"Mama?" Silver Water asked. "Are we going now?"

Star Shell nodded. "Good-bye, Father. May the ancestors bless and keep you."

"And you, daughter."

For a moment, she tried to see him as he'd been when she was a girl, but failed. The present, this vacant husk, couldn't be denied.

Her feet had gone stone-heavy; nevertheless, she started toward the Magician and the trail northward. Everything in her life had rotted out like an old log. She forced herself to turn and look back one last time. He stood motionless, shoulders bent, as the misty rain spun down around him—a testament to futility.

She understood then that she would never see him again.

Thirty-eight

Wave Dancer rose and fell on the endless cycle of swells. Otter had never seen water as blue as out in the middle of the Fresh Water Sea. He'd grown so used to it that at first he didn't recognize the change in the horizon. A slight band of green had separated from the blue water by a thin white cord.

They'd cleaned up most of the storm damage, thrown the broken pottery overboard, scooped up the wet seeds and cast them into the water as if in some sort of offering to the depths. Packs had been shuffled so that the last of the seeds could be wiped up. Rags soaked up the last of the water and were wrung out over the side. Then packs were turned to air lest they mildew, matting dried, and at last, a tidy *Wave Dancer* followed the undulations of wave and wind—the only spot of color in a blue world.

How does it feel? Otter rubbed his jaw and squinted at the greenish haze on the horizon. *You've found land.*

Where were they? He had no idea. What sort of place was this? Did the inhabitants recognize Traders? Did they even know Trader pidgin? And why couldn't he shake the sudden feeling that danger lurked behind those white dunes ahead?

"Look." Otter reached forward to point past Pearl's shoulder. Unease had haunted them throughout the night. She'd begun to obsess him. She filled his dreams, and during the waking hours, he watched her. His imagination conjured erotic thoughts of her breasts against his chest, her arms around him. Her dark, secretive eyes warmed as her full lips parted in anticipation. If he closed his eyes, he could feel her long, silky hair falling around him as she leaned over him and smiled.

Stop it! The last thing you can do is let her know that you have those kinds of thoughts about her. She'll feel like she's back with the Khota again.

Throughout the night, silence had proven a more comfortable solution.

"Do you want to make land?" she asked. "If not, I'd stand off, follow the coastline. We need to head north, don't we?"

"I think so. At least we do if this is really the eastern coastline, not just some island."

She gestured at the graying dawn. "You can't get any more east than that."

"Then north it is."

Black Skull woke at the sound of their voices, sat up, and studied the shore with obvious relief. He shot a crooked grin back toward Otter. "Well done, Trader."

Otter used his paddle to steer *Wave Dancer*'s course northward. "If you need to thank someone, thank Pearl. We'd be nothing more than waterlogged corpses and drowned souls but for her."

"We all use what we have—" she glanced sadly at Otter "—and we do what we have to, don't we?"

Black Skull turned sober eyes back to the shore. "We do what we have to." He nodded to himself, then kicked at Green Spider's blankets. "Get out of there, fool."

"Careful," Pearl cautioned. "You didn't give him another skunk, did you?"

To Otter's surprise, Black Skull laughed.

Green Spider and Catcher emerged from the huddle of blankets, and each yawned, stretched, and shook in perfect synchronization. Then Green Spider climbed to his feet and lifted his hands to the sunlight. He beamed happily at the morning, and the sun illuminated the planes of his triangular face as he bent over and broke wind in Pearl's face.

In reply, she used the paddle to splash water at him. "What did you do *that* for?"

Green Spider turned Dream-haunted eyes on her and smiled. "I wanted you to be able to see the root of your troubles more clearly, Pearl. You must stop thinking you're the only impure one in the canoe."

"What?" She looked from Black Skull to Otter and back

again to see if they understood. Each shrugged. "You broke wind in my face! And I'll tell you this. Do it again and I'll hammer a hardwood plug into you so you blow up like a fishing bladder."

"Good idea, Anhinga." Black Skull thumbed a nick in the blade of his paddle. "But he'd probably just belch twice as much to even things out—and who knows what it would be like if he threw up?"

Otter sighed as he placed one of the packs of hanging moss underneath his blanket for a cushion. The Contrary had been watching him with narrowed eyes. Why? Had his words for Pearl been aimed at Otter, too? What could impurity have to do—

Otter turned abruptly to watch Pearl settle herself, feet toward him, on the rolls of palmetto matting. The day would be warm; nevertheless, she pulled her blanket up to her chin, shading her face with a curled cattail mat.

For a moment, their eyes met, and he sensed the regret she hid so well.

He took a breath, longing to crawl forward and tell her how much she'd come to mean to him, how he'd felt his heart opening to her.

Don't be an idiot! his responsible side cautioned. *The last thing she wants is a lover, not after what the Khota did to her. She must still feel . . . tainted.* He forced himself to close his eyes, breaking that contact. *Just be her friend. That's all she wants, Otter. Just friendship.*

He slept through most of the day as Black Skull and Green Spider paddled them north, paralleling the endless sandy beaches. In his dreams, Red Moccasins taunted him, forever warm and inviting, always retreating just out of his reach. The more desperately he loved her, the more fervently she rejected him. And somewhere in the background, Pearl laughed at him before she broke into tears.

Locked in the misery of his dream-self, he met a sad-eyed Four Kills coming toward him along a burned forest trail. *"The waterfall is waiting, brother. Red Moccasins is no longer yours. Hurry, Otter, northward. Down there in the foaming, clear water, you'll end your misery once and for all."*

Pearl awakened to the evening. She stirred and banished the tormented nightmares of firelight flickering golden-yellow on a man-wolf monster that loomed over her. She'd been cowering, naked and staring in horror at the beast's serpentine penis as he bent over her. Helpless, she'd been unable to do anything except tremble in anticipation of the painful violation.

Otter had stood in the shadows, watching with impotent eyes. Each time she'd called out to him, he'd turned his back on her and her tormentor.

If only she hadn't come to care so much for him. She'd never known a man as strong and gentle. From the moment he'd pulled her out of the river, he'd shown her nothing but kindness, respect, and equality. In the center of the storm, they'd worked as the perfect team. She'd searched all of her life for that feeling of unity.

And now that you found it, he won't let himself touch you because of what the Khota did to you. She turned over to stare at the hewn side of the canoe and the thick weave of the heavy brown pack she lay on. Faint images of Otter's strong hands floated up. She could imagine them, warm and soft, on her skin. She could see that glint of desire in his gentle eyes. Enough of sleep's fog remained that she could run her hands under his shirt, trace the swelling muscles of his chest and belly with her fingertips. As she held him close, the beat of his heart matched hers. She knew how his body felt against hers, and knowing that, the ache for him went deeper and deeper.

Any chance that such fantasies might become reality had died that night when Wolf of the Dead took her. His taint would last for the rest of her life.

What life, Pearl? Where can you go? What can you do? You are a woman without a home—without a clan, or a family. You've become nothing.

She removed the sunshade, threw off her blanket, and rose, looking back at Otter. He lay on one side, curled up as if he'd been kicked in the stomach. His head was pillowed uncomfortably on the curved stern.

If only he'd said something, indicated that there was any hope that I might be anything but a remote friend... Pearl took a deep breath and sighed. The Trader would probably spend the rest of his life torturing himself over this Red Moccasins who had married his twin brother.

Face it. Trying to compete with Red Moccasins would drive you as mad as the foaming-mouth disease.

She stared out at the shoreline, illuminated by the dying sun. Dark waves slowly rolled away from the canoe, getting smaller and smaller in the distance before bursting into a surf that melted whitely into the sandy beach. Beyond, rising ranks of sand marched inland, capped by thin stands of grass. The tree line—where it could be seen between the dunes—made a hazy green mat in the distance.

The fact is, you don't have a future. She pulled her hair back with a slim hand. On the river, fleeing the Khota, she'd only had time for the struggle to survive. But here, with nothing but the captivity of sky and water, the reality of her situation had to be faced. She couldn't return to the Anhinga. What people would want a clanless woman? She now must live without roots, without place or people.

The future had turned lonely and cold. What did a woman alone in the world do to survive? Pray that some family would feed and shelter her in return for labor in their fields, for hauling their firewood, grinding their flour? That placed her one step higher than a camp dog.

Build a canoe, go into Trade the way Otter suggested? She thought of the Ilini. Patrilineal peoples had different ideas about women—and even among her own Anhinga, Trade was conducted by men. Would they deign to barter with her? Or would they just take what they wanted from a clanless woman?

She pulled uneasily at her hair. Otter had fictive kin all up and down the river. How would she manage that? The social reality was that males could marry any number of wives, get them pregnant, or refuse to couple with them, then leave to go Trading, all with no hard feelings. But since she had no property, any man who married her would want to consummate the relationship ... and that could be disastrous. Granted, she knew the plants to use for douches and how to take precautions during the month, but somewhere along the line, she would conceive a child.

So many complications, and no answers. *Who are you, Pearl? Where are you going? What are you going to do?*

The slanting afternoon sun gleamed golden on the expanse of water that stretched to the western horizon.

"Canoe!" Black Skull called, pointing ahead of them.

Pearl shaded her eyes to see as Otter jerked awake, staring wildly. He seemed to shiver, perhaps recovering from a nightmare.

The approaching vessel turned from a bobbing silhouette into a small dugout that carried two men with a pile of netting mounded between them. Sunlight flashed on the paddles.

When they were close enough, Otter cupped his hands and shouted, "Greetings!" in Trade pidgin.

"Greetings!" the reply came in pidgin; then, to Pearl's surprise, they changed to Ilini. "Who are you? Where are you from? Do you speak our tongue?"

In pidgin, Otter called out introductions, but the men in the canoe waved their hands that they didn't understand, shouting back in Ilini, "We know very little Trader talk. We speak only Ilini! Who are you?"

Pearl cupped her hands, shouting in her Khota tongue, "May the blessings of Many Colored Crow be bestowed on you and all of your clan. We are Traders from the far south. We are just passing through. I am Pearl of the Anhinga. I am accompanied by Otter, the Water Fox, of the White Shell people, and Black Skull, a warrior of the City of the Dead, and Green Spider, of the Blood Clan."

As they closed, the two men appeared unduly wary. Pearl could tell that they grasped atlatls, each nocked and carefully held just below the gunwale of their canoe.

The call came back: "Greetings, Traders! I am Trout. This is Thin Belt. We're of the Northern Hummingbird clan. Our clan grounds are about a day south of here, and then two days' east, upriver and inland. You are welcome to come there. Our Elders would feast you and make you comfortable."

Pearl translated as the Ilini paddled closer.

"Find out where we are," Otter said. "And tell them they won't need their weapons. We're Traders."

Pearl cupped her hands and shouted Otter's words, somewhat relieved that he hadn't been unaware.

Trout and his companion raised both hands above the gunwales. The Ilini responded, "Ilini territory lies to the south of here. To the north, however, you get into the country we call the Wild Lands. Forgive us for being wary, but the people there are warlike. They grow little of their food, but mostly hunt, fish, or harvest the rest out of the lake and forest. They are a lot like animals."

"Will they attack us?" Otter asked, glancing thoughtfully northward.

"Only once," Black Skull promised.

Pearl translated the Ilini answer. "It depends. Trout says that you just can't tell with those people. It would be better if we turned south again and Traded with their clan."

"How far?"

"Three days," Pearl answered. "A day south along the coast and two days upriver, past the dune fields and pine forests. Then you reach the oak-hickory forest, where this clan has its fields."

Otter cast a suspicious glance at Green Spider. He appeared completely oblivious to the Ilini. His head hung over the side of the canoe, one hand cupped to his ear as if listening for something. "What is your advice, Contrary?"

"South! South! And never look back." Green Spider didn't even flinch as a wave slapped the side of his head. "Did you know that if you listen real hard, you can hear fish talking?"

"And I'll bet they say things that are a lot more important than you do," Black Skull growled irritably. Then to Otter: "I think we'd better keep going. But I'd like to know more about these wild men."

"Agreed." Otter motioned toward the beach. "Pearl, ask them if they'd land and share a meal with us . . . maybe Trade a couple of shark's teeth and some shell for information."

She turned to the Ilini, who maintained a careful distance. "Will you camp with us tonight? Perhaps Trade?"

"It would be our delight!" Trout turned the canoe shoreward, and he and Thin Belt bent to their paddles.

Pearl realized that Otter was trying to gauge the surf. "Have you ever landed a canoe in breakers?"

"No. You just race in, don't you?"

"There's a trick. When I give the signal, everyone paddle hard. We should be able to ride *Wave Dancer* right up on the sand."

She timed the waves and called, "Paddle!"

Otter whooped as the canoe caught the wave and rushed forward. Catcher barked and jumped from side to side as they were borne up onto the beach. As the wave receded, *Wave Dancer* canted to one side on her keel.

The Ilini were already ashore, unpacking and bearing goods up to the white sand beyond the scalloped line of the surf. Killdeers, phalaropes, and gulls retreated, leaving the stick-littered beach to the humans.

"How high does the water rise . . . you know, the tide?" Pearl asked the Ilini.

Trout spread his arms wide in bafflement. "Unless there's a storm, the water will be the same. It doesn't get any higher or lower."

What? No tide? That didn't make sense to a person used to saltwater. Pearl inspected the Ilini. Trout was young, a little older than she, muscular, tall, and with a subtle humor in his warm brown eyes. Clay earspools hung from his earlobes, indicating a man of modest means. A strong jaw, firm cheeks, and straight nose made him extraordinarily attractive.

Thin Belt, on the other hand, had been built short, round, and stout. Those fleshy lips were meant for smiling, and laugh lines had indeed formed on his chubby face. He wore a battered shirt, the fabric frayed around holes that had worn through on the elbows.

Trout's attention fastened on her, and when he smiled, straight white teeth flashed. "This shall indeed be a pleasure. We don't always meet Traders of your beauty and charm." He glanced over at Black Skull, who had picked up his weapons and was trotting toward the dunes on his usual evening scout. "Your husband is a warrior?"

Clever man, this Trout. "No, my *friend* is a warrior. My other friend, Otter, is a Trader, and the skinny man, Green Spider, is a Contrary—a most holy man."

"A real Contrary?" Thin Belt stared, his mouth open.

At that moment, Green Spider didn't look particularly holy. He had dropped on all fours to follow Catcher around their camp. Each time the dog urinated on a piece of driftwood, Green Spider lifted his leg and tried the same. From the trickles streaking his thigh, dogs were more efficient.

"He sees things, does things differently than we do," Pearl said. "I don't understand, but Power fills him." Only an idiot would try to explain Green Spider.

Trout's grin had widened. He bent down to scoop out a fire pit, nodding a greeting when Otter walked up with a pack. Pearl noticed that Trout looked Otter up and down, giving him a full inspection. Sizing up the competition?

She paused thoughtfully. "You are married, Trout?"

Thin Belt smiled and poked his friend in the ribs. "What do you tell her, eh, friend? That you're married to your canoe and nets?" He glanced at Pearl. "That's the joke told about my friend here. We're all still waiting for him to come back to his senses."

Trout rubbed the gleaming white sand from his muscular brown hands. "My wife was killed two winters ago. We had a difficulty with the Badger people—the wild men who live north of us."

Thin Belt glanced at Pearl and then at Trout, a sly smile on his lips. In a low voice, he said, "Caution, cousin. Always beware of a woman who travels with three men."

Pearl felt her face going hot. "Let a Trader give you a word of free advice, Thin Belt: A smart man never accepts a situation at face value. But if you are the sort who does, then you're just the one I'd like to Trade with. Everything you've got, for everything I've got. Interested?"

Trout laughed, jabbing his cousin in the side with a hard fist. "Beware, cousin. I think this Pearl is more than a match for you."

Scattering in different directions, they collected the driftwood that littered the beach and piled it up beside the hearth. Pearl supplied dry grass as tinder. Trout added an ember from one of his little ceramic jars, and a crackling fire blazed to life.

Otter came up with the last of the packs, rummaging for the ritual paraphernalia of pipe and tobacco.

"What have they said?" he asked.

"Small talk mostly. The people north of here are called the Badger people. They fought a war with the Northern Hummingbird Clan two years ago. Trout's wife was killed. Thin Belt says he stays married to his boat now."

She could sense a trace of reservation in Otter, one not normally present in situations like this.

After the ritual smoking, prayers, and formal introductions, Otter got right down to business. "Ask them to show us where we are."

In the sand, Trout made a long line running north-south, then bent it around in a big loop to the east and back north again. He pointed to the western side of the loop. "The Ilini lands from which you came are on the west side of this part of the Fresh Water Sea. My clan, along with other Ilini clans, came here—" he pointed to the eastern side of the loop "—several generations ago and took these territories from the wild people who lived here. We still Trade with our relatives, of course, and marry back and forth to keep those ties."

"What if we wanted to go east, to follow the Fresh Water Sea as far as it will go?"

Trout propped his fist on his muscular brown thigh. "That's a long way, my friend. We are here, about halfway up the coast. Most of the trees around here are beech and sugar maple. Hickories are widely scattered. Then, as you go farther north, birch trees, hemlock, and stands of pine take over. It's not good land for farming or for harvesting nuts."

Trout drew the coastline farther north, then bent it to the east. "This is a narrow passage. Be careful. The Badger people sit on the narrows at this time of year, hunting the big sturgeon. Sometimes they're friendly, sometimes they want to kill. It depends on the signs they get from their Spirits, I guess. Who knows how those people think? They're not really human."

"So we'd best avoid them," Black Skull noted.

"My thoughts, too," Otter agreed.

Trout drew the line east, then back south again and pointed to a spot across the peninsula he'd drawn. "Over here you'll find some people to Trade with, but they're way inland. Along the shore here, the Spotted Loon people live. They are fishermen, and warriors, too, but normally they don't bother Traders. In exchange for Trade, they'll show you the way to head south into yet another freshwater sea."

"Another?" Otter asked when Pearl had translated. "I thought there was just one."

Trout mused on that for a moment. "If you live long enough to reach the Spotted Loon people, they'll be able to tell you more. I can only tell you what Traders have told me. They say that to go east to the lands of the Serpent Clans, you must go down a river to another freshwater sea."

"If we live long enough?" Pearl asked, lifting an eyebrow.

"The Badger people are north of here." Trout pointed up the beach. "We still haven't found a way to deal with them. In all-out war, we beat them every time. But they keep coming back, sneaking out of the forest to attack us, stealing a child, or a woman, ambushing a hunter. They're as trustworthy as weasels. Be very careful."

"We will do that." Otter studied the map in the sand and sighed. "I'd thought we'd be closer to the Roaring Water by now."

When she'd translated, Trout studied Otter skeptically. "The Roaring Water? I've heard of it. It's over here someplace." He pointed far to the east, then rubbed his jaw. "You've a long way to go. And it will be very dangerous. I've heard the Traders talk. Terrible storms. Fierce warriors raid back and forth. Monsters live in the waters there—big ones that rise out of the depths and eat men whole."

Otter continued to study the drawing in the sand. Despite his stern control, Pearl could read worry in the set of his mouth and the shadows in his pensive eyes.

Otter said, "Tell Trout that we all thank him for sharing this with us. Pearl, offer him some of our nicer shells, maybe that matting, I don't care." He stood and walked silently out into the dusk.

"He didn't seem pleased," Trout noted.

"He has just realized how far we have yet to go," Pearl said. "He thought he was closer to the Roaring Water than he is."

"You're of his clan?" Trout asked. "A relative?"

"No, my clan is far to the south. Where the Father Water empties into the Salt Sea."

"Then you have no tie?"

Pearl smiled wistfully. "If you are asking if I am tied to Otter, no. We met in the Khota lands. It seemed expedient at the time to travel together.''

''Ah! The Khota.'' Thin Belt shook his head. ''We've heard of them. Not nice people, according to the stories. I thought you had an odd accent.''

She raised her eyes, aware of Trout's appraisal. His attention and interest eased a nagging doubt deep in her soul. If a woman had to be noticed, it helped when the man was handsome, clear-eyed, and endowed with a charming smile that promised other things.

''How does a woman from so far away end up here—and speaking in a Khota accent?'' Trout began to stir the coals. Thin Belt had returned to the canoe and now approached, bearing two monstrous trout. Green Spider was backing his way toward the fire, making growling sounds.

''It's a long story.''

''I'd like to hear it.''

Pearl met his stare, reading challenge as well as desire and concern. *Very well, let's see what you make of this, Trout.* She began to talk as Thin Belt used a chert flake to fillet the fish and then propped them on sticks to roast and smoke over the fire.

Green Spider flopped down in the sand, rubbing his belly and claiming, ''I'm so fat and heavy I'm sinking into the sand. That fish looks horrible.''

Night settled as the fire crackled and the fish cooked. Trout listened as Pearl told of her trip upriver. Otter and Black Skull seated themselves when Thin Belt removed the steaming fish from the coals. They talked quietly while eating their fill of the flaky white trout meat. When the others had finally sought their robes, she sat staring at the fire. Only Trout remained in the fire's glow, his gaze fixed on her.

''About out of firewood,'' he noted, getting to his feet.

The moon had risen and light was slanting across the dunes. From logs to sticks, driftwood littered the sand. Gathering didn't take long.

''Come,'' Trout took her hand. ''Finish your story.''

As she talked, Pearl studied him. Half a head taller than she, he walked with a confident stride, and his hand was warm around hers. He looked up at the moon, pensive, the slight frown on his face somehow inviting as she studied his profile, the way the moonglow played on his muscular chest.

She told him about escaping the Khota, about Otter pulling her from the river, the pursuit, and the storm on the lake. But she didn't tell him everything, and was curious at her reticence.

"You could stay here," he said as they walked along the shore. The waves rolled and washed, but not with the phosphorescence she knew on the gulf.

"Stay?" she asked. "You've heard the story. I have no clan to speak for me. I'd be a homeless woman with no relatives. What would I do? Live like a . . . slave?"

His grip tightened. "You don't understand. Just north of us—up there—are a bunch of savage people who will kill you as soon as look at you. This territory is the northernmost outpost of the Ilini. We don't pay as much attention to forms and ceremonies as our cousins down in the secure Ilini valley do. We're a young and vigorous clan. We've only begun to clear and plant. We're building here, making a new way. A woman of your skill and courage could find a place with us."

"And my friends?"

"They'd be welcome, too. This foolishness of trying to reach the Roaring Water—it's a place of legend. Pearl, you'd be safe here. No Khota are going to be chasing after you. And what if they did? We would protect you."

She studied him from the corner of her eye. "Why do you make this offer to a woman you only met today?"

He stopped, taking her other hand. "Because I think you might fill the empty place in my heart. When I saw you walking up the beach, your body illuminated by the setting sun, you looked like one of the Sea Spirits, too beautiful to be real, your stride sure, your hair blowing free around you. You are a woman for a man to be proud of, to share his life and his dreams with."

She closed her eyes when he pulled her close. For long moments, they stood, holding each other. He reached down, running his fingers along the curve of her face, and she could hear his breathing deepen.

"I want you," he whispered urgently.

"What if I told you I was raped by the Khota?"

He backed away slightly, frowning. "Does that make a difference? I *wouldn't* hurt you, Pearl."

"But to know—"

"Hush. The butchers who killed my wife raped her repeatedly before they finally cut her head from her body. I wouldn't have cared what they'd done to her if I could only have had her back. Don't you see, I want to love like that again. To cherish and hold someone. To smile down into a woman's face and see her smiling back at me."

Pearl nodded, aware of the magical moonlight on the water, flickering silver as the endless waves crashed against the white sands. "And what if you find that I'm not the right woman? What if—"

He placed fingers to her lips, stilling her. "I know you're the right woman, Pearl. I can feel you in my soul. Stay with me."

Otter snapped awake. The rhythmic sounds of surf and the faint pop of the fire mingled with the breeze blowing in from the water. He sat up in his blankets, tormented by dreams of blood and terror. Rubbing his face, he looked around, thankful for a night on shore instead of in *Wave Dancer*'s cramped stern.

The fire had burned down to coals, and he rose to add a couple of sticks to ensure strong embers in the morning. Catcher lifted his head to look, then flopped back on his side with a sigh.

Otter added wood and sat for a moment, watching the moonlight as the flames built. Where had this sense of foreboding come from?

Pearl's bedding was still rolled in a bundle. He glanced over, seeing Thin Belt where he slept soundly. Black Skull's rasping snores couldn't be mistaken. So where was Trout? And where was Pearl?

Otter leaped up and walked carefully from the camp, looking up and down the moon-washed beach. He stepped down to the Ilini canoe and peered inside, finding only netting. *Wave Dancer*, too, was unoccupied.

Did he dare call out? No. To awaken the camp might bring him humiliation. Instead, he started circling, trying to work out the tracks the way Black Skull would—and found two sets headed northward along the water.

Fists knotting, he trotted on their trail. What did she think she was doing? Trout might not understand that she'd been hurt by the Khota. *And by the ancestors, if he's hurt her, I'm going to beat him to within a finger's width of his life!*

The anger continued to build, warming the pit of his gut.

He barely noticed the white mound of sand, intent only on the footprints on the beach. Somewhere out there, he'd find a black blot of two human bodies, and when he did—

The mound of sand exploded, spooking Otter half out of his wits. As he stumbled backward, he could hear muffled giggling, followed by, "Who fools the fool?"

"Green Spider?" Otter squinted through the sandy haze. "What are you doing out here?"

The Contrary sat up from the wrecked sandpile. "I was listening to the waves underground. The problem is that people never really listen. They let their thoughts clog everything up so that they couldn't hear if they tried. Have you listened recently, Otter?"

"I think so." He stared absently out at the water.

Green Spider's supple fingers were tracing patterns in the sand. "Where do waves come from? What motivates them? Think about it. Would you start way out in the depths to just race forward and splash on a beach?"

Otter swallowed his heart back down to its rightful place. "Green Spider, *what* are you doing out here?"

The Contrary looked up. "Wondering, Otter. You've worked yourself into a wave. Why?"

"A wave? What wave? What are you talking about?"

"You left the far shore . . . just a little tiny ripple. But in the deep water, the wave built, a swell that lifted everything before it. And now, here, I've watched you come rolling down the beach, ready to wash everything away, and in the end, all you'll do is make a splash. The gleaming round pearl will flee to the big fish, who will swim away, the victor of an unfought fight. And you, my friend, despite all of your foaming fury, will turn and slide back toward the water in defeat just as another wave washes over you."

Otter growled, "Black Skull is right. Just once, I wish you'd act like a real human being. Can't you talk straight?"

"Black Skull says that only when he isn't listening—as you aren't now." Green Spider's uncertain gaze went to the sand packed between his legs. "Why are some beaches sandy and others not? I mean, where does sand come from?"

Otter raised his hands. "All right, one more time. What are you trying to tell me?"

"That which you pursue the hardest, flees the fastest."

"She might be in trouble."

"She might not be."

"Meaning she is, right?"

"Meaning she isn't, wrong."

Otter propped his hands on his hips and scowled down. "Do you want to come with me to find her?"

Green Spider leaped up, sending sand every which way. He placed a calm hand on Otter's shoulder. "Go ahead, run down the beach and find her. You'll sleep peacefully for the rest of your life, glad that you made her decision for her."

The Contrary's tone had gone gentle, as though speaking to a silly child, and Otter's anger faded into a kind of throttled anxiety.

"What decision?"

Green Spider's eyes had a curious gleam in the moonlight. "Once I told you how to find yourself. Do you remember?"

"By losing myself," Otter recalled. "Which doesn't make any sense at all."

"It makes all of the sense in the world."

Otter sighed in confusion. "Tell me what to do. Shall I walk down the beach to check on her, or not?"

Green Spider's curious eyes were darting this way and that, like a butterfly in flight. "Oh, yes, go! Hurry! Charge away, ripping up the sand like a snorting buffalo in the passion of rut! Bellow and rage, paw and trample! Lock horns with the rival foe and batter each other to bloody meat!"

Otter swallowed uneasily, turned, and walked back toward the fire. Each step drained a bit more of his soul into emptiness and defeat.

In the moonlight, the Contrary raised one leg like a resting heron, cocked his head, and stoically observed Otter's retreat.

Star Shell and Tall Man had camped in the heart of the forest, the night as dark as Star Shell's soul.

Nothing might have existed in the world except rain, the boles of trees, branches, vines, and dead saplings. Overhead, the misty precipitation fell from torn black clouds to collect on slick leaves. Droplets formed, tossed on the breeze from leaf to leaf as they worked through the interwoven branches and finally fell free to splat in heavy round drops on the blanket that shielded Star Shell's small camp. They'd stretched the blanket between four trees and propped a stick under the middle to keep the sag from collecting water. A smoky fire—fed with wet wood— smoldered under one corner, protected from the rain but close enough to the edge that the smoke didn't collect. The blanket steamed in the faint flickers of firelight.

Star Shell rested against one of the tree trunks, her knees drawn up and her chin propped. Nothing was left of her life except her daughter. Everything else—dreams, hopes, and aspirations—had vanished like mist in sunlight, as though they'd never been. Defeat lay heavy on her soul.

The Magician sat across from her, staring at the smoky flames. Between them lay Silver Water's bedding. The little girl's shape was nothing more than a hump under the damp blankets.

Star Shell rubbed her face, hardly aware of the dirt she smeared in the process. Tendrils of unkempt hair hung at the edges of her vision. When she looked down, it was to see tattered clothing soiled with soot, mud, and grass stains. Black half-moons lay under her fingernails, and dirt was ground into the webbing on her hands. She could smell herself. The only cleansing she'd had time for was the rain's.

She turned gritty eyes toward the Magician. "Why are you here? The Mask might have been manufactured by the High Heads, but that doesn't explain your involvement. Power could just as easily have picked someone else. What did you do that you deserve this?"

She'd given up trying to figure out why she'd been chosen.

But the Magician, a sorcerer, should have been able to avoid the desperate heartbreak of this cold, miserable flight.

He looked at his small hand, as if studying the lines. "We each pay for our mistakes in the end."

Star Shell tilted her head, wondering why she still cared. "Mistakes? What mistakes? Someone you killed? You remain cleverly quiet about your past. It seems that the only time you talk about yourself is when you don't have any other choice."

The dwarf shrugged. "Do I hear you bursting to reveal your deepest secrets to me? Come, Star Shell, what's the worst thing you ever did? Tell me your darkest regret. Of all the mistakes or misdeeds that you've committed, which would you change?"

I was beautiful once. "I wouldn't have married my husband."

Tall Man added a piece of wood to the fire. "That's not what I'm talking about. Tell about the worst thing you ever did. An indiscretion? A theft? What malicious deed did you commit that you will regret forever?"

"Malicious deed?" Star Shell shook her head. "Outside of marrying my husband, I really don't have any regrets. Oh, I'd go back and change some things. I wish I'd never told my father that I'd never forgive him for making me grind my aunt's goosefoot seeds. I'll regret that forever. I threw away at least two big jars of it. When no one was looking, I dumped it in the creek to wash it away. Aunt was half-blind. She never noticed the difference."

"*That* was malicious?"

"What would have happened if we'd had a really bad winter? She was up there alone on the farmstead, old, half-blind, and a silly girl dumped two big jars of goosefoot. Why? Because I was spoiled and lazy." *I was too proud. The beautiful daughter, too good to grind flour for an old woman. And look at me now.*

"But you must have done something purposely evil, Star Shell."

She frowned, thinking back. "Worse than dumping the goosefoot?"

"Much."

"Well . . . there was a girl I didn't like in the Pale Flower lineage. Stone Rose was her name. She was always causing me trouble. She thought I was pampered, arrogant . . . and too pretty." *Which I was.* "We hated each other. I got more attention from the boys, and she didn't like that one bit.''

Star Shell picked at the dirt under her thumbnail. ''I found out that Stone Rose was involved with a married man of the Fast Squirrel Clan. One time when he sneaked off to be with her, I sent a message to this man's wife. Had a friend of mine tell her that her husband wanted to meet her down by the river in the willow patch.''

''And that's where Stone Rose lay with the woman's husband?''

Star Shell nodded, seeing into the past. ''I would change that if I could. No matter that I didn't like her. It wasn't right to harm her like that.''

Tall Man sighed and winced, involuntarily placing a hand to his right side. The stitch of pain seemed to have grown worse over the last few days. ''Is that the *worst* thing you've ever done?''

''Other than marrying my husband? Yes. He brought me nothing but pain.''

''You didn't know he was going to become a monster. You didn't do anything wrong. I mean, it wasn't a malicious act, something that you knew was wrong when you did it.''

''If I knew it was wrong, why would I do it?'' She gestured the futility. ''I felt so wretched after dumping Aunt's goosefoot seeds that I swore I'd never do anything like that again.''

Tall Man sighed and shook his head. ''I find it hard to believe that you were such a perfect child.''

I wasn't, Magician. I was proud, vain, arrogant in my beauty and privilege. She tipped her head back, listening to the big drops spattering randomly on the blanket. ''My parents brought me up to be responsible, I guess. They always were. My father took his duty to heart. Mother was the same way. Everyone loved her, and not just because she was married to the clan leader.''

''Yes,'' Tall Man said wearily. ''Everyone loved her.''

''She was a beautiful woman. Right up to the end.''

''Like a fantasy woman come to life.''

''I'll miss her. I just wish Silver Water could have known her.'' Familiar grief tightened in the back of her throat. She glanced at the pack that contained the Mask, silently hating it.

"So will I." Tall Man bowed his head, lost in his own musings.

"So," she said with a sigh, "we are back to my original question. Why you? I would think, Magician, that Power would have understood your character and left you alone. Or didn't your sorcerer's ways work?"

"They always worked very well, Star Shell. Too well."

"But you're still here, running just like me. It hasn't been any more pleasant for you than it has for me. Can't you cast a spell, or conjure a fog, and slip away?"

He gave her a sober appraisal. "My abilities are given by Power, girl. First Man showed me what was in store for me. And I understood and accepted his offer. What is given must be taken. Balance is the heart of everything."

Star Shell shifted, trying to find a more comfortable spot. Her feet hurt, swollen and chafed from her rain-soaked moccasins. She picked at the stubborn laces, caked with mud, and peeled them off. Her feet looked pale and shriveled. Had the leather of her moccasins not been superbly tanned and smoked, they'd have dried hard by now, and shrunk so small that not even Silver Water could have worn them.

"You must have done something terrible to deserve this," she insisted. "What do you think it was? I told you the most terrible things I ever did. How about you? You poisoned a man because you wanted his wife . . . and then you sired a child off of her, but couldn't make yourself live with her. You killed people for hire—maybe for good reasons, maybe for bad. Did you steal babies' souls? What single thing do you take as your most malicious?"

Tall Man stared vacantly at the fire, his turtle-like face expressionless.

"Fair is fair," she said. "We made a bargain. What single thing would you change? Come on, Magician, why are you here?"

The wind rustled the leaves high overhead, and within seconds, a pelting of drops spattered their blanket. Cold, wet. Would it ever be warm again?

He frowned slightly, then said in a weary voice, "It's the spiral. Circles within circles. The Light must always balance the Dark. Of all the things I've done, I'd change quite a few."

"Like letting the Power go to your heart?"

"Just like that." His smile seemed remote. "For such a little man, Power expanded within me. And I used it for myself, for my aims. What is given is taken away. What I misused now misuses me."

"What does that mean?"

When he sat silent, she reached over and cuffed him. "Tell me! You've hinted, weaseled, and misdirected. I gave you my secrets, rot you, now give me yours! It has something to do with the Mask, doesn't it? I *must* know!"

She stretched over Silver Water's sleeping form and shook him. "Tell me, Magician."

Tall Man licked his lips, nodding. She released her hold and backed away carefully, aware that she'd come perilously close to waking her daughter.

Tall Man's mouth pursed as though he'd eaten something bitter, something he wanted to spit out but couldn't. "A little more than two tens of years ago, I was asked to perform a Healing by a High Head Clan. The patient was dying, and there wasn't anything that could be done. Power runs its course. Lives are lived, be they long or short, and the soul departs. That's all there is."

Tall Man closed his eyes as if in pain. "She had arrived just before I did. I remember that my heart skipped when I first saw her, and I could do nothing but stare. Her sister had sent for her, and she lived quite far away, in the north. She had kinship ties with the High Heads . . . strong ones. Not only had her sister married a High Head, but they were descendants of prestigious High Head clans."

"Like me."

He seemed to stumble, adding quickly, "Yes, like you. I was enchanted, completely obsessed with her. I admit that I'd known a great many women of passion and beauty. You met one in the Blue Duck holdings—but this one, she was different. Not just a beauty. She had a poise, a bearing like no other woman I'd ever known.

"When she looked at me, my soul melted like beeswax on hot rock. She moved with a stately grace, and her gestures were those of a dancer. Her body sang to mine with every curve and motion. Those incredible dark eyes carried me into worlds of soft fantasy. Her face might have been the Earth Mother's, full of promise.

"I barely managed to conduct my duties, and, of course, the man died. She stayed for the funeral; her sister needed her. I made sure that I, too, stayed.

"Everything she did sprang from some presence of the soul that I had never encountered before. She was kind, gentle, caring, concerned with everyone and everything. Here, before my eyes, was a *perfect* woman! Do you understand? She was the complete fulfillment of every man's fantasy. Charming, beautiful, sensuous, intelligent, and compassionate. Body and soul, she might have been sent to me by the Mysterious One himself."

"And did you tell her of your love?"

Tall Man hung his head. "Yes. On the night of the cremation. She listened, hands in her lap, and then she told me this: 'Dear Tall Man, your words are most flattering and complimentary. I treasure your eloquence and earnestness. However, I am happily married to a wonderful man. Were I not his, and he mine, your warmth might lead me to reciprocate. Instead, I shall honor and cherish your kind words, and I hope you will do the same with mine.' "

"She did that very well," Star Shell said warily.

"As she did everything." The dwarf fingered the hem of his shirt, his stubby fingers rolling the material back and forth. "I couldn't leave it at that. Not I, not the Magician! Through my skills, I determined the route she would take north, and left several days before she did. I was waiting at the clan house where she would spend her last night before arriving home.

"Imagine her surprise when, upon her arrival, she found me. Nor did she disappoint me. That keen soul of hers didn't let her down and she understood immediately what I was about. With that perfect control, she told me that there could be nothing between us. And in that moment, I understood just how sincerely she meant it."

"But you couldn't leave it be, could you?"

Tall Man shook his head. "I made up my mind instantly. You see, a sorcerer can have anything he wishes, Star Shell. Power grants you that. I wanted her, and that night, I had her."

"And she didn't claw your eyes out?"

"You still don't understand, do you? A witch, a sorcerer, has ways of bending people to his will. To her, I'm sure it seemed like a dream—and I don't doubt that she thought I was her husband. You see, as I was coupling with her, she raised her head to look at me with such love and adoration that I couldn't stand the thought of those eyes looking at me with hatred. And she would have hated me with all the passion with which she loved the rest of the world."

"So you left her with the illusion?"

He nodded sadly. "I saw her off and on for the rest of her life. On those occasions when I could manipulate the circumstances, I used my Power to take her. And always, I left her with the illusion that she had dreamed of her husband. To her, I was just a very good friend—one with whom she shared the secret of my confessed love, and nothing else."

"You *are* vile!"

If he heard the disgust in her voice, he simply accepted it. "I went to see her when I heard that she was dying. I arrived too late. I'm not sure what I would have done. Perhaps I could have saved her, kept her alive for a while longer. In the end, however, the results would have been the same. Her soul would have been freed of her body, and veils of illusion would have fallen away. She's dead now, and her ghost knows."

Star Shell turned the moccasins she'd laid to dry by the fire. "Let me guess. You're starting to worry. You're not a young man anymore, Magician. Her ghost is waiting for you, isn't it?"

"You are a smart woman. A fact that grieves me a great deal. Yes, she's waiting. Too many of the ghosts are waiting for me. Most I can face and bear. But how can I face her?"

"And that's why Power sent you on this journey? First Man is willing to bargain? If you help to eliminate Many Colored Crow's Mask, First Man will help you avoid facing this woman whom you . . . you . . . Sacred ancestors! I can't even speak it! You *violated* her."

Tall Man's eyes had lost their luster. "I don't think you understand. I'll have to face her, young Star Shell. First Man won't save me from anything. I may, however, be able to redeem a bit of myself before I die. For most, the opportunity comes too late. I'm struggling to earn at least a sliver of atonement—so that I don't see hatred in her eyes when we meet.''

Star Shell shook her head. ''You had better be glad that she's not me. I wouldn't forgive you for what you'd done, no matter what good deeds you attempted in penance.''

Tall Man's expression seemed to sharpen, some of the depthless quality returning to his gaze. ''Oh, I don't know. A Trader would point out that we all have something with which to purchase a little good will.''

''You'd have to give her something back as precious as you took.'' Star Shell reached down, placing a loving hand on Silver Water's sleeping form.

''Yes,'' he mused as he watched her hand. ''I intend to do that. And perhaps in the end, she will forgive me.''

Thirty-nine

I have found that a sickness lies in wait for Dreamers.

A soul sickness.

It eats and eats at even the most devoted.

When you can see through the moss-colored pool of the world to the rocks lying on the bottom, you begin to wonder why the pool exists at all. What purpose is served by making it hard for humans to see the rocks? Why doesn't Power just make all pools clear, or drain them away so the rocks are easily visible?

I understand that this is why Contraries and Tricksters are made. I do understand.

The bottom of the pool is invisible. So someone must pick up the rocks and throw them at people, because only a good bash to the brain will make a human stop rushing long enough to consider standing on his head for a better look around—and this includes Dreamers.

But it hurts just the same. Bashing and being bashed.

Yes, it hurts . . . The pain of those near me increases every

*day, and I feel their suffering like a disease inside me, sapping
my strength, filling me with questions, sometimes with inexplicable bouts of rage, or grief . . .*

And all I can do is to keep throwing rocks.

Pearl had the fire crackling and one of the big round ceramic
pots boiling when—accompanied by the waking cries of the
gulls—Green Spider danced out of the false dawn. He looked
like a skinny urchin, whirling and skipping through the bluish-
gray mist that clung to the shores of the sea. As he squatted
down next to her, he stuck his thin, hawkish nose over the pot
and sniffed.

"That's really wretched-smelling. Why don't we dump it all
out so no one feels like throwing up?"

"Glad you like it," she replied, using a piece of water-worn
wood to stir the contents. Then she settled back, wrestling with
the dilemma inside her. Her glance drifted to Trout, where he
lay sound asleep in his blankets.

"I hate going down trails," Green Spider mumbled as he
flopped beside her. "So many forks and branches . . . and all of
them go someplace. Isn't that interesting? It doesn't matter
which trail you take, you always end up somewhere."

Pearl nodded. "Yes, and when you get there, you'll usually
find another bunch of trails to choose from."

"I never choose. I just sit down and cry."

Pearl gazed out over the pale blue water, nodding absently.
"Green Spider? You know, don't you? I mean . . . that Trout
wants me to stay here, with him. I—I said I'd decide by morning. I guess it's morning faster than I want it to be."

"As the moments pass, it gets lighter and lighter, and ever
harder to see." Green Spider wiggled around and found a
wooden bowl. He dipped up the hot stew and blew noisily across
the steaming surface. "Did you ever notice that steam always
goes up? Why doesn't it ever go sideways?"

"Trout would make a very good husband. He's a reliable
man, a good provider, and he'd let me fish and hunt with him.
It would be like it was at home. No clan obligations."

"Are you steam?"

She stared at the patterns she'd drawn in the sand. "Am I what?"

"Steam. That, or you can be stew. But it's one or the other. Steam always has to get out of the bowl; so it twists and turns and dances, until it escapes. In the end, it vanishes, but you remember the glorious patterns. Stew sits in the bowl, absolutely contented. But someone always seems to eat it, so I guess it vanishes, too. The difference is that people remember what steam looked like—and with stew, people may or may not remember the taste."

Pearl brushed a long strand of wind-teased hair behind her right ear. "Just once, would you say what you mean?"

Green Spider frowned at his bowl. "People tell me that more and more. You'd think that after this long, they'd learn to hear things right."

Pearl leaned her head back, letting her tangled wealth of jet-black hair tumble down her back. "I'd have a home again. Think of that. A roof to sit under when it rained and snowed. Four solid walls."

"Just like stew," Green Spider asserted. "Of course, it's easier to keep track of children that way. You can imprison them inside those solid walls."

Children? Once she settled down and put on a little weight, she'd probably catch. Once again she glanced at Trout, the clean lines of his face visible now. Yes, he'd be a good father, warm and caring. Unlike Anhinga men, he would help raise them. A father, not an uncle.

And for her: a partner, not a husband. Partner. She liked the sound of that.

So why had she held back? Last night, with his arms around her, she'd wanted to savor that feeling of companionship and warmth. He'd led her to a high dune crest, and there, holding each other in the stark light of the moon, they'd talked about so many things.

She poked angrily at the fire with her stick, remembering the warm tingle as he caressed her and nuzzled his face into the hollow of her neck. His hot breath had sent shivers through her, and she'd trembled when his gentle hand cupped her breast. She'd felt the insistent pressure against her hip of his erection as it strained at his breechcloth. In the end, however, she'd stopped herself on the brink—not out of fear, but from a last instant of confusion, not knowing what she really wanted.

And Trout, his blood literally aboil and his flesh aching for her, had acquiesced at a word. To douse the flames, both had charged into the cold waters and swum themselves into acceptance. He'd been perfect as they played tag in the water. She'd delighted at her ability to swim circles around him, and he'd taken it all in good humor.

Later, they'd walked back to camp hand in hand, she to consider her answer, he to sleep.

"What am I going to do, Green Spider?"

Green Spider shrugged and continued eating. The Contrary was on his third bowl of stew by the time Black Skull sat up, yawning and rubbing his broken face. The warrior rolled up his blankets, grabbed his club, and vanished over the grassy dune for his morning duties.

Thin Belt coughed and groaned himself awake, blinking owlishly at the dawn as he clambered to his feet and tottered off for his own morning chores.

Otter came bolt-upright, startled by something in his sleep, before sending an uneasy glance her way. This morning he didn't smile, and she simply met his gaze with her own, trying to understand the rush of emotions churning in her chest. To her surprise, he stood and walked off without a greeting. Something heavy and cold, like stone, settled on her stomach.

"Good morning," Trout whispered in her ear as he sat down beside her. He clapped his hands, delighted as he sniffed at the stew. "You did this?"

"I didn't sleep," she told him dryly, and then smiled. "I had a lot of thinking to do."

"And?"

She took a deep breath. "And I . . ."

"Don't know." Trout glanced up as Black Skull walked over the dune, his war club on his shoulder and a fine film of sweat gleaming like oil on his scarred skin. "That is one mean-looking man."

"You ought to see him fight," Pearl said.

The others joined them and they ate, talking in desultory

tones. To Pearl, it seemed as if everyone were watching her and Trout, Thin Belt in particular.

She grabbed up one of Otter's packs and walked down to *Wave Dancer*. When she turned, Black Skull stood right behind her.

"You and this Ilini, is there something between you?"

She fingered the fox head on the canoe. The red wood felt oddly warm under her fingers, familiar. "He's asked me to stay with him. I don't know, Black Skull. He and I, we talked all night. I like him." She slapped the wood. "It's a *good* offer. I'm a woman without a clan, without a family. He'd make a good husband—and he likes to do the things I like to do."

Black Skull fingered his broken jaw and glanced awkwardly at the dunes where Otter had disappeared. "What about the Trader?"

"What about him?" She realized she'd balled her fists.

Black Skull paused uncertainly, then smiled. "I think he would be very disappointed if you left. Myself, I will ask you to go on with us."

"Why?" She crossed her arms, curious at this new part of Black Skull that she'd never seen before.

"For two reasons. First, I ask you for myself, Pearl. You are a warrior woman, and we may need you. Besides, you have become my friend. And second, I ask for Otter, who has also become my friend."

"Why ask for Otter? He doesn't care . . . does he?" Her heart thumped against her ribs. "I mean, I . . . Look, he's still in love with Red Moccasins. You know that better than I do."

"A man may care for more than one woman at the same time."

"And if I decide to go?"

He reached out with one muscular arm and dragged her to him in a strong embrace. "Then I will send you off with wishes for your happiness and safety."

She looked up at him. "You're a good friend, Black Skull."

"And so are you. You can fight on my side any time." At that, he loosed his hold, turned on his heel, and went back for another of the packs.

As Trout carried his blankets to his own canoe, he glanced

repeatedly at Pearl. After he'd finished stowing, he slowly walked over. "Are you all right?"

Pearl struggled with a tightness in her chest, glancing up at the dunes to where Otter had disappeared. He loved his Red Moccasins. Any other woman would always be a shadow. But . . . if only he'd smiled at her this morning . . .

"I guess I'm going to stay with you." And it took all of her control to keep from tears.

Trout gave her an understanding look. "I'll make sure that you never regret it."

In that instant, she felt cut adrift, her soul bobbing in uncertain currents. Summoning all of her courage, she tried to smile bravely.

They'd loaded the canoes, and the fire had burned down to glowing coals when Otter walked down from the dunes. She steeled herself.

"Otter?" Why were the words so difficult. "Trout has asked me to . . . to stay with him, here, and I . . . I said I would." She made herself look up into his eyes, seeing the familiar lines of his face. She fought the sudden desire to reach up and lay her fingers along his cheek. A tightness pulled at the corners of his wide mouth.

"It's all right. I told you we'd find a place for you." Otter reached for one of her hands and lifted it to his lips.

In that instant, she began to tremble, and she pulled her hand back before he could kiss it. "Take care, Water Fox. Don't let the sneaky Khota—or these Badger people—catch up with you."

"I'll try not to."

He let his hands fall and quickly stepped past her, his head down. She turned, realizing that everyone was waiting at the canoes. She walked up to Trout and smiled. He'd moved her blankets to his boat. Black Skull, Green Spider, and Otter wrestled *Wave Dancer* around, facing the big canoe toward the water and sliding her into the waves. Only Black Skull continued to watch Pearl with regret in his eyes.

"Oh!" Otter broke away and ran back through the waves. He pulled up, smiling at Trout. "Take care of her. She's the best woman there is." He reached into his shirt, pulling out a folded mat of grass as he turned to Pearl. "Here," he said, briefly meeting her eyes. "I think this is yours. I don't know what your prayers were . . . but I hope they'll come true."

He patted her hand gently and backed away. "Good-bye."

As he trotted for his canoe, Pearl stared at the prayer mat, remembering those carefully tied knots; each represented a moment of despair or terror.

"Pearl?" Trout asked anxiously.

Her fingers traced the folds in the plaited grass. He had to have found this on the river, carried it all that way in his shirt, next to his heart. Why? Did he know the ways of her people? That they believed warmth stirred the soul in the mat, fed it, kept the prayers alive? Maybe that was why she had managed to escape the Khota. Because he had cared enough about an unknown woman and her terror to . . .

"Trout?" She could barely speak. "I . . . I can't go with you."

"Why not, Pearl?"

"I'm steam, not stew." She sniffed, fighting for the words. "Because I love Otter."

When she turned, her eyes shimmering with tears, *Wave Dancer* was already slicing through the waves, driving out into the water under the furious paddles of its crew. Only Catcher looked back, his ears up, tail wagging.

A hand clapped over Star Shell's mouth, bringing her wide awake. She stared out at the moonlit meadow, the grass and wildflowers ghostly white before the dark wall of trees.

"Shhh!" Tall Man whispered in her ear. His elderly little face hung over her, the wrinkles drawn into an expression of fright. The polished moon-gleam sheathed the leaves of the sumac grove behind him. "Don't make a sound! Wake Silver Water and take the packs. Crawl back into that sumac, and as your ancestors are witnesses, *be quiet!*"

"Why? What—"

"Hush! I've done almost all that I can for you, Star Shell. One thing remains. Then you will have to rely on your own wits. Trust no one! You know by now that the Mask can pervert the strongest of souls.''

He backed away, his small feet sinking into the thick grass. He made calming motions with his hands, perhaps more for himself than for her. Then he turned, taking little twists of sticks and grass from his wolf-headed medicine pack and driving them into the ground as he hurried down the trail toward the dark trees.

At the far edge of the clearing, he paused and shoved another of his crossed sticks into the rich earth. In the blink of an eye, he vanished into the weave of forest and night.

Star Shell threw off her blankets, rolled them and slipped the Mask pack over her shoulder, trying all the while to hear beyond the thunderous pounding of her heart.

She woke Silver Water the same way that Tall Man had awakened her. ''Come with me, baby. We have to be very, very quiet!''

''Why, Mama?''

''Shhh!'' Star Shell pushed her belongings and the Mask pack before her and crawled into the smooth sumac, looking back to make sure that Silver Water followed. In the heart of the thicket, she looked up at the moonlight, barely visible through the rows of lanceolate leaves. Night sounds, crickets, faint rustlings in the grass, and the distant hoot of an owl merged with the whisper of the leaves high overhead in the forest.

''Mama?'' Silver Water whispered. ''I'm frightened.''

Me, too. ''It will be all right, Tadpole.'' But what were they doing? What had Tall Man discovered that would—

''This way!'' Robin's voice called from the trail.

And Star Shell clamped her jaw so hard that her head trembled. She tightened her grip on Silver Water's coat, barely allowing herself to breathe. She rested her face on the leaf mat, the smells of earth and mold filling her fear-bright senses.

''There he goes!'' Woodpecker cried. ''Capture him! He's headed for StarSky!''

''Does he have the Mask?'' Robin cried, and footsteps pounded up the trail.

Star Shell huddled on the ground with Silver Water pressed against her. The little girl's shallow breaths warmed her throat. On the cold night wind, scents and sounds seemed to magnify tenfold. The chirping of birds and crickets competed with the pungent odor of a nearby skunk.

"Mama?" Silver Water asked.

"Quiet, baby," she whispered. "We have to be as silent as ice on a pond."

Silver Water peered through the tangle of branches, her little hands nervously crushing and releasing the spongy leaves.

The faint, plaintive sound of a whippoorwill floated eerily through the night air.

Star Shell shifted to prop herself on her elbows, trying not to think about the grisly Mask on the ground to her right. Did it know that Robin and his warriors were combing the forest? Was it trying to signal them? Or had the Mask called them, invaded their Dreams and told them where to search for her and Tall Man?

We were so close! The upper Moonshell lay less than a day's march from here. Tall Man had told her of a man who lived near the Buckeye clan grounds, a man who took in Traders and knew the route. He would give them directions to the Roaring Water. But they would never make it now, not with Robin's warriors sniffing out their tracks.

What are you doing, Magician? She longed to make a run for it, but she was too afraid for the moment to try—and the overwhelming fear made hiding here, according to Tall Man's instructions, so much easier.

The moonlight had moved enough to cast new patterns on the thick stems around her. A glossy wealth of silver triangles and rectangles lit the brush. The penetrating scent of the sumac filled her until she could sense the sap rising in the stalks, feel the leaves breathing and building in the spring night. She sought to meld herself with the plant, to share the soil, winding down into the rich earth in harmony with the roots.

The rustling of leaves and the soft murmur of voices forced her to clamp a hand over Silver Water's mouth.

" . . . Got to be here somewhere."

"The little runt could have lied."

More thrashing about.

"We ought to wait for morning. We'd have better tracking light."

"We saw him just up the trail. They would have to be here.

This clearing is about the only place to camp on this side of the ridge.''

"Here's the fire pit!" one cried. "This is the place, all right."

They stood so close that Star Shell could smell their sweat; it twined sourly with the wet fragrances of damp earth and tree bark. She tried to swallow, but her throat had constricted so tightly that she couldn't.

"In there?"

"No. That's poison sumac. Star Shell's anything but a fool."

"Even a fool will do something silly if she's desperate."

Star Shell glanced up at the leaves. *He's crazy! This is smooth sumac. The edges of the leaves have little teeth! Even a child would know the difference.*

"Well, I'm not crawling in there," one of the warriors muttered. "I say we— What's that?"

Star Shell tensed. A faint cry carried through the forest, high, shrill. She knew that voice, though she'd never heard it filled with such pain. Silver Water's eyes widened to huge brown moons. She knew, too.

"Robin is making the Magician howl," another of the warriors reported with a laugh. "I think that if I were that little Trickster, I'd be wishing I'd never been born."

"He's braver than I am, doing that to a dwarf. Mark my words, Robin will die a terrible death for treating the Magician this way."

"He had a Dream. Power is tied up in this. Robin knows what he's doing."

Another growled, "Come on, keep looking around. Do you see anything?"

"You're sure the Magician said they were camped here?"

"You heard. Probably a trick."

"Well, if you ask me, they're long gone—dashed into the forest, running for their lives. Would you stay? Just wait to be captured?"

"Why would the Magician betray his friends, anyway?"

"Torture has a way of loosening the strongest men's tongues."

Star Shell's fist knotted in the musty leaves. How could Tall Man have been caught? A sorcerer of his Power should have been able to escape! Couldn't he have cast a spell to distract his pursuers? Or changed himself into—

"This is impossible!" one of the warriors bellowed. "Come on. Let's go tell Robin. The Mask isn't here. The woman has it . . . wherever she is."

Star Shell lay rigid as they retreated through the rain-drenched underbrush.

"Mama?" Silver Water murmured against her hand.

Her lips to her daughter's ear, she whispered, "You stay right here! Don't you dare move—no matter what. I have to see if I can do anything. You stay! Do you understand?"

Silver Water jerked an unhappy nod.

Star Shell crept silently out of the sumac. Would the warriors have left a guard, someone to watch the little clearing? Could this be a ruse to create a sense of security so that she'd break cover—and step right into their arms?

Another anguished cry echoed.

What are they doing to you, Magician?

She used the trees as cover as she followed on the heels of the warriors. A shadow in a world of shadows, she traveled on silent feet. Now she could be thankful for the caked mud and the dirt that smudged her clothing and skin. With it, she blended into the forest.

The warriors hurried along the deer trail she and Tall Man had followed down the sloping ridge that evening. Who would have guessed that Robin would have been this close?

How had he found them so late at night? The fire! With the wind, the smell of smoke must have drifted up to the top of the ridge. A lookout, a hunter, or even a man out relieving himself, might have smelled it. Only Tall Man's vigilance, or his Power, had kept them all from being captured.

Star Shell crossed the uneven outcrops of weathered sandstone and retraced the trail until she came to a place where lightning had blasted an oak. Before her stretched an old burn where the wind had carried the flames. No more than fifty strides ahead, Robin had set up camp. A fire burned, sending eerie reflections to wander among the trees like an army of shadows. At least a dozen warriors stood around, laughing, watching . . .

Star Shell started to shake so hard that she had to brace a hand against the lightning-scarred tree and lock her knees. She shoved the knotted fist of her other hand into her mouth to mute the anguished sobs that rose from her horror-choked throat.

They'd hung Tall Man from a stout oak tree next to the fire, and then they'd slit open his belly. Robin was slowly feeding the dangling intestine to a pot of boiling water.

The little man cried out again. His entire weight hung by his wrists—his arms bound behind his back. To hang so was terribly painful, and if hung so for long, the arms never worked right again, for the muscles tore and the ligaments separated.

She could see the firelight bathing Tall Man's sweating face. He wouldn't last long. The hanging position, coupled with the strain on the diaphragm from evisceration, impaired the lungs, causing shortness of breath.

"Where *are* they?" Robin bellowed, bending close. "Tell me, Magician! Tell me, and I'll let you die in peace."

"South!" he croaked. "South . . . toward Star Shell's mother's clan."

"South?" Robin fingered his chin, the human-jaw breastplate gleaming in the firelight. "Then why are you up north, little man?"

"Decoy," the Magician rasped. Then he turned his head and looked straight at the trees where Star Shell hid. "Look . . . for the Trader . . . snakes on his cheeks."

"What? What Trader?" Robin demanded.

Tall Man's eyes bugged out, and his tongue protruded. Again he managed to lift his head and stare at Star Shell, gasping: "*Trader . . . snakes on his cheeks!* Tell him I would have—"

"He's delirious," Woodpecker decided. "Too much pain from the steam backing up into the tubes."

Tall Man's voice dropped. "Forgive . . . me . . ."

Star Shell stumbled backward on clumsy feet, her retreat covered by a final shriek that split the night. She staggered into the trees and rushed blindly over the crest of the ridge, heedless of the rocks she tripped over.

They'll find our tracks at first light. We have to leave. Now! She dashed downward, reeling off of trees, ripping through the vines. Dead saplings slapped at her as she tore her way toward the thicket.

"Mama?" Silver Water whispered from the sumac. "Mama, I'm scared!"

Star Shell dropped to her knees, gasping for breath and sanity. Tears welled to blind her, and she sobbed, pulling at her hair.

"Mama?"

Star Shell glanced at the hiding place, stunned. There a thicket of poison sumac was bathed by the moon's white light. She shook her head, remembering the little sticks and twists of grass that Tall Man had left as he backed away. Had he used all of his Power to shield them while he forced Robin's warriors to chase him down?

She scrambled forward, throwing the Mask pack and her blanket over her shoulder, then gripping her daughter's hand and dragging her out.

"Come on, baby. We've got to run again." *Trader . . . snakes on his cheeks. . .* Tall Man had said those words to her, and to her alone. How had he known she could hear?

Never mind! Run!

"I know, Mama. I don't want to get caught like Tall Man."

Star Shell licked her lips, staring around wildly. "Then you know what Robin will do to us if he finds us."

"I don't want him to kill me." Silver Water started down the trail, adding, "But he'd rape us first, Mama."

"You're too young to know about such things, baby."

"I'm too young to know about a lot of things—but that can't be helped, can it, Mama?"

"No, sweetheart, I guess not." And as she hurried down the trail, she began to settle down, steadied by her daughter's cool appraisal of their situation.

Star Shell tried to erase the image of Tall Man, his stomach sliced open, the gray entrails running like snakes to the steaming pot. She'd heard of people being killed that way—about how the cooking guts created pressurized steam that swelled the tubes and tried to vent both ways, until the tissue finally burned through. Except that a master torturer kept that from happening.

Robin was a master. Had the Magician not sacrificed himself, all three of them would be lying up there now, dying. After, of course, Robin and his warriors had taken their fill of her . . . and of Silver Water.

"Run, baby! Run as fast as you can!"

She clutched Silver Water's hand and pulled her along as they wound down through the trees, following the game trails that wove in and out of the moonlight.

Star Shell cocked her head, hearing faint laughter. Her spine tingled when she realized that the sound came from within the folds of the wolfhide that bound the Mask.

Four canoes. Ten-and-seven warriors, including himself and Grizzly Tooth. Wolf of the Dead pressed his fingertips tenderly to the side of his head where the Anhinga woman had struck him. This was all that remained of his war party. They had searched up and down the coastline, leaving trail markers—signals to any other survivors who might reach shore.

Lodged amidst the driftwood, they'd located fragments of the canoes, cracked, splintered, and scattered like the rest of the flotsam. But only two bodies had been discovered as they paddled around the coastline in pursuit of the Water Fox.

Two tens of tens left our homeland. Of them, only ten and seven remain. The knowledge burned in Wolf of the Dead's head as he looked back at the three canoes following his, paddles flashing in the sunlight.

What a terrible land this was. Nothing but water and sand. In places, the dunes piled high and towering, like cropped-off mountains. On their desolate crests, grasses battled with wind, sometimes winning, sometimes losing to long, concave blowouts that scattered a haze of particles over into a treacherous slip face.

Were it not for their nets and bolas, the Khota would have starved. In the evenings, the warriors dove for freshwater mussels to augment the thin stews of fish, duck, goose, heron, and any other creature prey to their weapons.

"Ahead!" Grizzly Tooth cried with rising elation. "Two canoes . . . but they're standing out, thick of hull." His voice was dropping. "Not war canoes."

And hence not Khota. Wolf of the Dead raised himself and saw that the boats appeared to be working together, dragging a fishing net.

"Let us go and see," he suggested. "Look around. Tell me

if you see anything else. Any sign of other canoes. Perhaps smoke back in the dunes. Your eyes are better than mine.''

As they approached, Grizzly Tooth scanned the water, as did Wolf of the Dead. Just two canoes? Where did they come from?

They were close enough now to make out the details of the nearest canoe. One man, two women. From the silhouette on the water, the second canoe contained one woman and two men. Stretching between the dugouts bobbed a line of net floats.

''Greetings!'' Wolf of the Dead called, using Trade pidgin.

''Greetings!'' the answer came back in the Ilini tongue. ''Who are you? Where are you from?''

''Tell them we're from the Hazel Clan,'' Wolf of the Dead said. ''Try to sound more like an Ilini and less like a Khota.''

''Hazel Clan. Far to the south!''

The Ilini began to haul in their net, bundling it neatly into the boats as they pulled themselves closer to each other. The spokesman shouted, ''Have you come to visit? Or perhaps to Trade?''

Grizzly Tooth muttered, ''Do you suppose they have a holding somewhere near here?''

''Ask them. If they do, and if they believe that we are really distant cousins, perhaps we can turn this to our benefit. Tell them we're searching for the Water Fox. That . . . that he took something that wasn't his.''

Grizzly Tooth cupped his hands to his mouth. ''We're following a Trader who stole from us. Are your clan holdings near here?''

''Two days,'' the man shouted back. ''What Trader stole from you?''

''The Water Fox. He took a sacred object from our clan house.''

By this time, the fishermen had hauled their catch to the surface. Wolf of the Dead could see silver tails flopping in the net. His stomach growled in complaint. He glanced around, noting the hungry stares of his warriors.

''The Water Fox?'' one of the women called. ''We've heard of him. A man from our clan met him. He's far to the north by now. You'll have to travel hard to catch him.''

''There's another way,'' the second woman said, her voice barely audible as Wolf of the Dead's canoe closed the distance.

"They could travel up past the clan territories, portage across the hills, and follow the Dry Grape River to the Upper Lake. If they paddled hard, traveled light, they could make that crossing before this Water Fox can go all the way around."

Grizzly Tooth had begun to grin.

By this time, they were close enough to be seen clearly. The man was beginning to frown. "You are not Ilini! Who are you?"

"What would you say if I told you we were Khota?" Wolf of the Dead answered.

The man turned pale. He licked his lips, instinctively trying to backpaddle, his effort impeded by the women, now stopping in confusion. They didn't seem to realize what was wrong.

"You can't escape," Wolf of the Dead told him. "Our canoes are faster."

"You killed my cousin!" the man shouted. "I'll *never* help you!"

The women, comprehending at last, simply stared wide-eyed, as if monsters from children's stories had appeared before them. One of the women, Wolf of the Dead realized, was not only young, but very attractive.

"Grizzly Tooth, my friend. Here we find two canoes full of fish, three women, and only three male Ilini dogs to guard them."

"What do you suggest, my leader?"

Wolf of the Dead rubbed his jaw, aware of the Ilini man's growing panic. He'd started to paddle frantically. It would be a shame to waste all that fear. "I think, my friend, that we will camp on the beach tonight. We will eat all the fish we can hold, and our beds will be warmed by these women. You and I, of course, will share the young one there. Our other warriors may satisfy themselves on the other two."

"And the men?" Grizzly Tooth asked.

"They must know a great deal about the territory, the rivers, this portage the woman mentioned. After all, we can't all be using the women at the same time, can we? While we're waiting our turns, we'll see what the men can tell us about this route to catch up with the Water Fox."

"I'll tell you nothing!" the Ilini declared, but desperation had crept into his voice.

"We'll see, camp dog. Khota are good at making people talk."

The second canoe was fleeing now, aware that something had gone terribly wrong. Two fast Khota war canoes were already heading them off.

Wolf of the Dead stared at the young woman, watching her breasts rise and fall as she began panting with fear. Her dark eyes reflected a growing terror. A trapped fawn had eyes like those.

That night, Wolf of the Dead stuffed himself with fresh-roasted fish. As the driftwood fire crackled, the Ilini men alternately screamed, cried, begged, and whimpered.

Wolf of the Dead considered what he'd learned. They'd have to change their appearance, look more like Ilini and less like Khota. The war shirts had given them away, as had the style of their hair buns. However, there was a way to cross the thick neck of land by following the rivers and then making a portage. He could catch the Water Fox on the way to this Roaring Water—and avoid this terrible lake that had drowned most of his warriors.

Grizzly Tooth gasped in delight, his body stiffening. Then he groaned and rolled off the limp Ilini woman to stare up at the stars.

Wolf of the Dead reached down, scooping up more of the flaky white fish meat and stuffing it into his mouth. He stood, walking around Grizzly Tooth's inert body to stare at the naked young woman.

"Pearl would have fought longer and harder," he told her as he settled onto her breeze-cooled body. Her eyes had taken on a dull listlessness. The feel of her was enough to excite, but she showed no response to his entry.

He coupled with her absently, his mind on what they'd learned from the dying men. It could be done. Follow the Hummingbird River inland, portage for two days, then follow the Dry Grape River out on the eastern side of the land. There they would find another body of water, Upper Lake, that would take them to the Roaring Water.

One of the men screamed as a burning branch was thrust up his anus.

I'm coming for you, Pearl. How ironic. The Ilini are going to help me catch you. And then, Anhinga bitch, I'll pay you back in kind for each of my dead warriors.

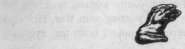

"What do you think?" Otter asked, watching the sun as it was swallowed by the shining, fiery waters in the west. A glinting flood of golden light spilled out and captured *Wave Dancer* in its path. The carved cypress wood turned a deep yellow. To the east, smoke—turned amber in the sunset—rose from behind the dunes. That much smoke at this time of year meant people. Trout had also made it clear as to what sort of people these Badger folk were. Dangerous.

"I say we avoid trouble." Pearl studied the hazy smoke.

"I recommend that we keep paddling," Black Skull said. He stood in the bow to stare at the wooded shore. "It's one thing to meet canoes on the water in daylight. It's a whole different matter to find yourself ambushed on land in the middle of the night."

"Oh, no!" Green Spider stuck his skinny arms out in protest. "No one would dare ambush us! We're Powerful heroes headed into the Unknown."

Black Skull gave the Contrary a disgusted look. "Don't call me a hero, fool. I know from experience. Heroes are the easiest men of all to kill. They run around fearlessly, acting like squawking grouse because they've convinced themselves Power is protecting them. One smack in the side of the head, that's all it takes to prove otherwise."

"I think we'll continue on." Otter took a close look at the handle of his oar. Long ago, the wood had turned a rich, dark brown, dyed by his sweat and body oils. How justly fitting, for in many ways, it *was* part of his body. He'd crafted the pointed paddle from the finest of hickory, and with it, he'd traversed most of the world. Now they would travel night and day, seeking to circumnavigate the great projection of land that Trout had drawn in the sand.

They all pitched in, paddling hard as the last of the sun dipped into the western waters. The section of shore screening the fire was left far behind them.

What are you going to do now? Otter was right back where he'd started. He'd have cut off his arm to keep Pearl in the canoe . . . and now he didn't know what to say to her.

She'd thrown in with them, Trading everything that Trout offered—safety, caring—for more days of sleeping on the packs. For having to hang her bottom overboard every time nature called. As well as for eating cold food from jars and suffering aching muscles from paddling. What did a man say? Thank you?

"Same order?" Black Skull asked. "The fool and I by day, you and Pearl by night?"

"I have a lot of stars to learn," Otter answered. "And in the daytime, you can't get too seriously lost. Just stay out far enough from shore that we can't be seen easily."

"Black Skull and I are never lost! We both live inside our bones," Green Spider insisted as he jabbed his paddle down into the water and watched it bob up again.

"Fool," Black Skull muttered. "The only thing that lives in your bones is idiocy."

Otter dropped his voice for Pearl's ears alone, his eyes on the dark and ominous shore. "You can still live to regret this."

"We can all live to regret a great number of things." She turned, those lustrous eyes wide. "Will I always have to walk in Red Moccasins' shadow?"

"Is that why you thought about staying with Trout?"

"I couldn't stand the thought of loving a man who loved another woman—one out of his reach. Such loves become almost magical. The living can never live up to the legend. I guess I . . . well, the story about the wedding bowl struck too closely to home. That, and Trout was handsome, fun-loving, and kind. Had I met him instead of you, I would have been very happy with him. We understood each other."

"Pearl . . . about Red Moccasins." Otter searched for the right words. "Sorry, I guess it's a little difficult. I—I'll always love her, Pearl. I can't help that, any more than I can help but love Four Kills.''

She arched one of those delicate eyebrows. "You never slept with your brother."

"Of course I did! We shared cradleboards and blankets until we were—"

She slapped her paddle in the water and sprayed him. "That's not what I meant, and you know it."

"What's wrong back there?" Black Skull called as the canoe rocked.

Green Spider answered, "I liked it better when they were afraid of each other."

"We're still afraid of each other. Now shut up, turn around, and paddle," Otter ordered.

Green Spider dropped his paddle to clatter in the bottom of the canoe, clambered back on the packs, and sat with his hands cupped to his ears to hear better.

"Contraries!" Otter yelled, while Pearl grinned despite herself. "Very well, Green Spider, listen closely because Pearl and I want you to hear every word and be engrossed by our entire conversation. We really *want* you to hear our most private thoughts."

Green Spider vented a sigh of resignation before returning to his spot and retrieving his paddle. To Otter's amazement, the Contrary held on to the blade, this time stroking with the handle in the water. Otter opened his mouth, then thought better of it. He couldn't be sure of what kind of lesson the Contrary might be trying to teach this time.

"You were saying?" Pearl asked.

"Hmm? Oh . . . Red Moccasins." Otter continued to shoot nervous glances at the Contrary. *Be honest, Otter.* "It's gone forever. For instance, let's say . . . let's say that Four Kills divorced Red Moccasins. She wouldn't take me, Pearl. And I wouldn't take her. I know better, and so does she. Before she married, we could be wild and irresponsible, fool ourselves about who we were. But she'll never leave Tall Cane holdings— except perhaps to travel to the City of the Dead for a ceremony. And I'll never stay home and be a responsible husband."

Pearl turned halfway around to meet his eyes. The sun had bronzed her skin to a deep golden brown, highlighting the sepia tones of her eyes. "I can't live in her shadow, Otter."

He told her seriously, "You cast your own shadows. In the storm, I realized how much I'd come to love you."

"Why didn't you *say* something?"

Black Skull turned his head at her outburst but quickly returned his concentration to his paddling. Green Spider was churning froth with his upside-down paddle, apparently fascinated by the sound the handle made in the water.

Otter shrugged unhappily. "Why? Because I was afraid. Afraid that you'd be frightened. After the storm, you seemed hesitant."

"I was—but that's because you looked as guilty as a thief!"

"That's because I thought the last thing you'd want was to fight off another man! I didn't want to make you uncomfortable when all you wanted was a friend."

She bowed her head and stared down at her reflection in the water over the side. It wavered in the ripples from Green Spider's upside-down paddling. "When it comes to women, do you always have to act like you're walking around water moccasins?"

"It doesn't take much to become unwelcome." Both he and Pearl had stopped paddling.

"By the sacred ancestors, from now on, will you just talk to me? I'm over that, Otter. Over what the Khota did to me. Green Spider, well, the night he set his sassafras root on fire and charred those gourd balls of his, he gave me an escape hole through the pain. I don't understand how, really, but he did."

"He's special, isn't he?" Otter looked up at the sky, seeing the first of the evening stars. He filled his lungs, savoring the cool smell of the water.

"Yes." She smiled at him, reaching back to take his hand. "And Black Skull, too. Each of you, in your own way, has become more like family to me than my real relatives." She paused. "But, Otter, tell me, how will it be when we go back to White Shell clan grounds? Will I have to suffer in Red Moccasins' presence?"

He rubbed the back of her hand with his callused thumb. "Suffer? In her presence? I don't think so. Assuming we live through this and do go back, it wouldn't be for long. I've made my deal with Grandmother. She won't try to hold me."

"And if she did?"

"I'd just leave. I've done that often enough in the past. Grandmother understands me better than I thought she did. Strange, isn't it? The older I get, the smarter she turns out to be."

"That doesn't solve the problem, Otter. What part do I have in your life?"

He leaned forward, drawing her back into his arms, feeling her resistance as he settled her into the position that he'd held her in after the storm. Yes, like this, the way he'd memorized.

"This is as honest as I can get," he told her, using a finger to push strands of black hair away from her soft cheek. "Red Moccasins was my lover once. Her responsibilities led her to make the choices she made—and they were the right ones. But now . . . I want you to let me love you, Pearl. Will you? On the night of the storm, we were partners, working together, doing what we both love, and I can't imagine any other woman who'd want to share my crazy life the way you do."

"Partners," she whispered, her body finally conforming to his. She glanced sideways at him, a soft glow in her eyes. "And if we should become lovers? What's in the future, Water Fox? Partners for how long?"

"Forever, if I have any say about it. Maybe you'd even marry me one of these days."

"You'd better think about that." She tilted her head questioningly. "What is a wife to you? Explain the term to me. These Ilini, they trace their lineages through the men. A woman's children belong to the man. Property belongs to the man. Therefore, Trout could say to me that he'd marry me.

"But among the White Shell, your mother has the right to say whom you may or may not marry. My clan has already given me to the Khota, and they wouldn't be happy to know that I dishonored them. I suspect that my brother would kill me if I ever returned. Given that fact, do you think your mother would allow you to marry me?"

"I'll ask my clan to adopt you."

"And why would they? All that trouble—not to mention expense—just for you? A runaway grandson who dodges clan responsibilities?"

"Put that way, Trout sounds like a much better catch than I am."

She held his hand to her lips. "Perhaps, Water Fox, but I chose you. And these things we're talking about will be only the first of many problems we'll have to deal with."

"What problems?"

"Well, let's say we manage to marry and Fat Frog—" she gigged him in the ribs with a pointed elbow "—has her child, and then maybe another one. Do you expect to raise a family right here in *Wave Dancer*?"

He scratched his ear. "You know, I never gave it much thought."

"Well, we're going to have to." She lifted an eyebrow. "Or have you spent your entire life planning only for the moment and letting tomorrow take care of itself?"

"I've always let tomorrow take care of itself."

"Someone has to be pragmatic—unless you want to rely on Green Spider for the rest of your life."

Otter winced.

Pearl gave him a crooked grin. "See? You need me, Water Fox. Of course, I lived that way myself until the Khota got me onto the river. And I guess I had another bout of it when you gave me back my prayer mat."

"Did you? I felt sick when we pushed *Wave Dancer* out and you weren't here." He glanced at the deep lavender that was fading into darkness in the west. "I didn't know what to do."

Pearl pressed her open palm to her cheek. "Fortunately, I did."

The loud splash brought Otter and Pearl upright. They'd been so busy staring into each other's eyes that they hadn't seen what happened.

"What the . . ." Black Skull wondered.

The canoe quivered as splashing sounded and Green Spider shouted, "Help! Help! I'm dying of thirst!"

Catcher leaped back and forth on the packs, barking and yipping, his tail whipping the air as he stared over the side. The Contrary had fallen overboard.

Otter, Pearl, and Black Skull scrambled across packs in the rocking canoe, each reaching out for the floundering Contrary. Black Skull grabbed a hand, pulled Green Spider close, and bodily lifted him into the boat. The Contrary promptly shook himself and scrambled after Catcher. He hugged the dog to his breast, running his fingers through the thick black, white, and tan fur.

"What happened?" Pearl and Otter demanded in unison.

Black Skull, perched on the gunwale of the tipping canoe, shook his head. "The fool was emptying his bladder. I heard him asking, 'I wonder where all the bubbles come from.' You know how he is. I guess he got so fascinated watching his water make bubbles that he just sort of pitched headfirst overboard."

"You're joking?" Otter asked dryly.

The dripping Contrary was using Catcher's shaggy tail to dry his face with. Black Skull jerked a thumb at him. "Who'd joke about a thing like that?"

High overhead, a falling star streaked the sky.

Forty

"Do you know the difference between a fat Caribou woman and a grizzly bear?" Pale Snake carefully placed a pack in his canoe, resting on skid logs set into the mud of the landing. Other canoes lay upside down nearby, their hewn bottoms like peeled logs. The place had that earthy smell of water, wet earth, and greenery. The Upper Moonshell was a narrow meander here, barely worth the name of "river." A wiry youth could pitch a stone across those lazy, muddy waters.

Behind him, up the slope, the earthen enclosure of the Buckeye Clan bustled with activity. People were passing through the opening in the earthen wall, calling their blessings to the ghosts of the ancestors. Just the tips of the peaked thatch roofs could be seen, and the breeze carried most of the sound away to the east.

Stone Wrist thought for a moment, lines deepening in his fat face, then said, "No."

Pale Snake grinned. "If you offer a copper ring to the bear, he'll just eat you and it's over with. But offer the ring to the fat Caribou woman, and you're married to her forever!"

Stone Wrist laughed, then tilted his pudgy head. "What's a Caribou woman? And why is she fat?"

Pale Snake rubbed his neck as he looked across the river at the irregular fields and the lush forest beyond. The brown dirt had been planted, and puckered mounds of soil marked the location of seeds. The problem was, some jokes couldn't be translated. These Serpent clan people didn't understand who the Caribou people were, or what they were like. The Caribou people came out of the forest in midwinter, when their yearly migration brought them south. By the deep cold, they would have made their kill off of the wintering caribou herds. They would appear then, traveling behind sleds pulled by dog packs, to Trade for manufactured goods—copper, and lightweight, portable foodstuffs such as goosefoot-seed cakes.

Stone Wrist tapped his arm. "Do you know how many Traders it takes to fill a clan leader's bed?"

"If you're talking about me—just one; but I'd better not come back that way, because when I've worn her out, she's never going to look twice at another man. And I'll remember that the next time I come to Buckeye clan grounds. I'll expect you to be married by then. Your sister is going to be disappointed as it is. She worries about you."

At that moment, a crow came spiraling down from the blue sky to caw excitedly. Pale Snake had barely looked up before the bird flapped off to the north with a rasping of wings. He frowned, wondering.

"Married? Me? Do you think I could ever find a woman willing to bear this much weight?" Stone Wrist slapped his rotund belly with both hands. "But then, I suppose you'd be visiting all the time, eating my food, trying to bed my wife." Stone Wrist tugged at his belly, a most astonishing mountain of flesh. "You and your stories about women! Why do I think it's all bluff? Eh?"

Pale Snake caught sight of a woman walking down the muddy slope. She'd be beautiful if the grime were washed off—and appealing if she weren't towing a little girl, which meant that she'd be married to someone who'd object to his interest.

The Trader punched his friend in the gut. "You wouldn't want me visiting too often, old friend. With as much belly as you've got sagging there, your manhood couldn't find its way to a woman in the first place . . . and you'd crush her dead in the second."

"That, or suffocate her. Ah, well, I can always dream." Stone Wrist watched as Pale Snake placed the last of his packs in the canoe. "I'll miss you. It's such a treat when you come. And only once every two years. Why did you insist on living out at the edge of the world? You're as far as you could get from here and still be someplace!"

"I like it that way. It's a long journey back and forth. Two passages to make—and one never knows what, or who, might drift down from the north."

"So be it. May Many Colored Crow go with you and keep you safe."

"And may your ancestors keep you, Stone Wrist." They clasped hands and hugged each other. Pale Snake bent down, starting to shove his loaded canoe out into the brown floodwaters.

"Wait!"

He stopped, turning with Stone Wrist to see the woman and her child running toward them. Something about the child's gaze was most unsettling. A cold chill ran down his back. He knew that look.

"You are a Trader?" the woman asked. Her hard eyes had narrowed at the sight of the snakes tattooed on his cheeks. He could see the muscles in her jaws tense. The humped pack on her back, her frayed clothing and loose black hair bore spatters of mud. To look like that, she might have lost a wrestling match with a raccoon. The little girl looked no better.

"I might be a Trader, but then, it would depend on what you might want to barter. I've got a canoe as full of goods as I can get it. Unless you're interested in sacred chert, slate pipes, copper awls, and goosefoot seed, I don't have much to offer a local."

She would be gorgeous if she were washed and those clothes taken out and burned. And what's in that pack?

She straightened under his gaze. "I need to travel to the Roaring Water. Do you know the place? A friend of mine . . ." She glanced uneasily at Stone Wrist. Then she took Pale Snake's arm and led him several steps to the side. "Would you know the High Head Magician, Tall Man, by any chance?"

Pale Snake tensed, and his soul chilled. Of all the things she could have said, nothing would have captured his interest so completely. Who was this hard-eyed woman? Her speech was that of a prestigious Flat Pipe lineage, one with a long tradition of authority. From the fine shape of her face and the delicate nose, she must be of the northern Serpent Clans. This woman, despite her appearance, wasn't used to rags—and he'd heard of only one such association with Tall Man. "You're Star Shell."

She didn't react: proof of either complete confidence or unmitigated idiocy. "And you are?"

"Pale Snake." *And if I had the sense the Mysterious One gave a mosquito, I'd turn on my heel and walk away!*

"You haven't answered my question. Can you take us—"

"And in that pack," he mused, "is the Mask of Many Colored Crow."

A faint smile played at the corners of her full mouth. "I wouldn't get any ideas, Pale Snake. You look like a healthy man, and one satisfied with life. With the exception of my daughter and myself, the only people who have seen this Mask in the last four moons are all dead."

"What do you want from me?" he asked coldly. *And what does Tall Man have to do with this?* Pale Snake kept glancing at the hills, half expecting the dwarf to come charging down the slope. *And then what would you do? Break his neck on the spot? Or just twist his arms off?*

"Transportation. For myself, my daughter, and the Mask. We need to go to the Roaring Water."

Pale Snake examined the little girl. His soul prickled at the Power he saw in those big brown eyes. "Who sent you to me?"

"Tall Man . . . just before Robin killed him last night."

Pale Snake peered into her eyes, seeking to read her soul. "Are you sure that Tall Man is dead? Not just some ruse?" *Dead? Really? Seriously?*

"War Leader Robin boiled his intestines last night," she told him levelly. "I doubt that even the Magician could make a sleight of that."

"No, I doubt that he could . . . although I'd have to wonder how Tall Man would have allowed himself to get caught.''

"You're not an ordinary Trader, Pale Snake.''

"What makes you think that?''

"I can mention Tall Man's name and you don't glance about in sudden fear that we might summon his angry ghost here.'' She studied him, her eyes narrowed. "No, you're not ordinary in any sense.''

He could feel Stone Wrist's growing interest. He hadn't much more time. *You're a fool, Pale Snake. You ought to just say no, get in your boat and travel as fast as a frightened mallard for home.*

Instead, he placed a hand on Star Shell's shoulder, turned toward the canoe and said, "I'll tell you what, Yellow Snail, I'll take you and Little Salamander here as far as the Acorn holdings. From there, you can catch the trail to the Butternut clan grounds. Fair enough?''

"You've made a deal.'' Star Shell gestured at the canoe. "Come on, Little Salamander. We can't keep the man waiting all day.''

Silver Water clambered into the boat, stepping over the packs and folding her blankets to sit on. Star Shell waded out into the water, found a second oar where it had been stowed, and took a seat in the bow.

Pale Snake pulled at his ear and made a face for Stone Wrist's benefit. "I don't know. She's only got a burden basket in that pack of hers, but she claims that a relative at Acorn will throw in a good copper plate.''

"Uh-huh.'' Stone Wrist shook his head uneasily. "Take my advice, dunk her in the water four or five times if you're planning on letting her crawl into your blankets at night. Otherwise, you'll be picking fleas and ticks out of your scrotum for a month.''

"I don't think I'll be doing that. The River Spirit might sink me in return for the defilement.''

"I'd make her walk,'' Stone Wrist declared as Pale Snake pushed his canoe off.

"See you in two summers!'' the Trader called back.

"And say hello to my sister!''

"I will!'' Pale Snake began paddling, turning into the current and away from the shore.

Star Shell said angrily, "I heard what he said. If you think I'm getting anywhere close to your blankets—"

"I have no intention of any such activity." *Especially if you've been mixed up with Tall Man.* "But at the same time, I don't suppose that you'd like Stone Wrist speculating on the nature of my interest in transporting you. One of the secrets to Trading is understanding where your opponents' weaknesses lie. Fortunately, Stone Wrist is so delightfully full of weaknesses that I've yet to find a strength."

"You're a slick talker, Pale Snake." She was slashing the water with her paddle, more than a little of it wetting the Trader's clothing and packs.

"Easy," Pale Snake said. "You want to set the paddle in the water and pull it straight back. It's one smooth motion."

"That's what I'm doing."

"Crow feathers! You're using it like it was a digging stick, or a war club . . . I'm not sure which."

"Just get us to the Roaring Water. You do know the way, don't you?" But she changed her grip on the paddle, doing better.

"I believe so," Pale Snake answered. For a moment, he sucked at his front teeth, then asked, "I realize that you've been hounded, hunted, and chased by just about everyone for the last half a year or so, but that doesn't mean I have to like that tone of voice."

"And what, pray tell, are you going to do about it?"

"I might just take old Stone Wrist's advice and chuck you in the river. You and the Mask can float your way right back down to Robin and his little group of weasels."

She half-turned, shooting an icy glare his direction. "Unlike most, you don't seem to take a great deal of interest in the Mask. I find that interesting . . . and not just a little suspicious."

He chuckled, setting a strength-saving pace with his paddle. "I guess you would. But then, I suppose that you'd find quite a bit about me interesting."

"You have a rather high opinion of yourself."

"It's taken years to fully develop. I have to admit, I'm rather pleased with the results."

Star Shell turned to gape. "Why on earth would the Magician

ask me to seek you out? Of all the Traders headed north, you'd think he'd have found someone . . . reputable.''

"Oh, I'm about as reputable as they come—outside of my origins, that is. Origins are always a problem, and not necessarily one that you can do a whole lot about. Friends, you can choose. Now take me, for instance. You see, I never saw eye-to-eye with my father. We were sort of on different levels. The result was that we fought all the time.''

"If that's the case, I'm sure I'd like your father.''

"Can't say. He was a despicable tyrant filled with his own importance, a scoundrel, a scheming thief, and a general pain in the nether portions.''

"I see that you've inherited all of his charming characteristics.''

Pale Snake chuckled. "I think I'm going to like you, Star Shell. You've got spunk right down where you need it." He paused, aware of Silver Water's unnerving stare as she studied him from her position behind her mother. "What do you think, Silver Water? Does your mother have spunk?''

"She doesn't need spunk. She has the Mask.''

Pale Snake tried to smile, but the attempt dried on his lips. "You've seen the Mask, haven't you, Silver Water?''

The little girl wet her lips. Was it his imagination, or were those eyes trying to suck him in? In an almost hopeful voice, Silver Water asked, "You're a sorcerer, too, aren't you?''

At her daughter's words, Star Shell spun around so quickly that the canoe bobbed and rocked. She peered at Pale Snake with her mouth slightly ajar. "A sorcerer? Is that why you have those snakes tattooed on your cheeks? Did the Serpent devour you, too, Trader?''

He shrugged. Star Shell's paddle was dragging in the water, steering them inexorably into the tree-lined banks.

"Oh, he tried, Star Shell. He really did. The problem was, I just gave him a bellyache. Uh, would you mind either paddling or keeping the blade out of the water so we don't crash into those trees?''

She helped him straighten out the canoe, her paddle waffling as she pulled it through the water.

Pale Snake avoided Silver Water's eerie gaze. "If you don't mind my asking, what are you going to do with the Mask once you reach the Roaring Water? Poison the Mist Spirits?''

"I'm throwing it over the edge."

"Poisoning the Mist Spirits!'' Pale Snake noted the growing intensity in Silver Water's eyes. Didn't Star Shell see that? Didn't she understand what it meant?

He exhaled wearily. Under his breath, he said, "I should have pulled out of Buckeye in the middle of the night."

"What did you say?"

"Oh, nothing. Nothing at all, Star Shell. Just looking forward to the trip."

Otter watched the coastline pass endlessly along *Wave Dancer*'s right side. Twice they were hailed by parties in canoes shouting: "Trade! Trade!'' in pidgin. Most of these people were dressed in tailored skins with long fringes. They wore their hair loose, or braided with feathers, or held in place with shell hair clips. The men had a smoky-eyed inscrutability that left Otter uneasy. Long strands of black hair that looked very much like bits of scalp cut from human heads had been sewn to the shoulders of their tan shirts.

In both instances, they'd held up fish, for which Otter offered stingray spines, a hank of shell beads, or a bundle of hanging moss—the latter of which these Badger people had never seen before.

At the insistence that *Wave Dancer* stop to Trade at their camps, however, Otter politely refused. Once the canoes had veered off, they'd bent to their paddles, placing as much distance as they could between them.

The moon had begun to wane against the graying dawn as Otter and Pearl finished their nightly turn at the oars. A stout wind bore down out of the west, and the coastline had gradually turned to the east. Here the beaches gave way to steep cliffs topped by a thick wealth of mixed conifer and maple-oak forest.

To the north, they could see more land narrowing down toward them, as if to funnel them into a slender vein of water.

"This has to be the entrance to the northern passage,'' Pearl told him. "The place where the Badger people hunt for the big sturgeon."

"I remember. Trout said it was dangerous through here." He shook his head. "I wish we could have crossed this stretch at night."

In the rough water, *Wave Dancer* leaped and fell with the long, flat swells. She seemed to ride differently now, as if the Fresh Water Sea had seeped into her soul. Of course, Otter had to admit, they rode higher on the water, with so many of the packs flattened and gaps where rows of jars used to sit. He still had several rolls of palmetto matting, two sacks of conch shells, one parfleche of sharks' teeth, two jars of stingray spines, three sacks of yaupon, a jar of barracuda jaws, four big bags of hanging moss, six bundles of White Shell fabrics, some Tall Cane pottery, and two packs of tobacco leaves. That was it—and nothing to show for the return trip, since they'd eaten everything they'd Traded for.

"Look up there." Otter pointed to a series of sparkling fires that twinkled under the dark canopy of trees. "Looks like quite a village."

"We're coming to the straits, all right," Pearl said thoughtfully as she studied the shoreline. "Trout told me that we'd recognize it. The land hooks, remember? Perhaps like that bay we circled last night. This might be the last headland."

Otter watched the fires gleaming on the cliffs off to the right. "Did he say what it would be like on the other side of the straits?"

"We'll be able to see land on both sides. We stick to the near shore and follow a wide channel between the mainland and an island."

When they rounded the high headlands, Otter could see nothing but water to the east.

Green Spider sat up in his blankets, stretching his thin arms as he threw back his head and yawned. He blinked, rubbed his eyes and relieved himself over the side, obviously still fascinated by the bubbles.

"Men! At least the wind's not blowing in my face," Pearl muttered over her shoulder.

Otter turned his attention to the north shore as it became visible in the morning twilight. Faint patterns of mist were fleeing with the increasing breeze that blew down their backs to expose more wave-cut cliffs topped by high-peaked spruce, fir, and pine. The trees rose like dark somber spears among the brilliant green of the newly leafed maples and oaks. On both shores, monoliths of rock reared up, perhaps Earth Mother's guardians of this realm of water. Otter could see that fierce storms had lashed the battered banks and cast the corpses of huge trees high onto the rock.

"I'd hate to pass this in a storm."

"Me too," Pearl agreed.

"They are always a little bit late," Green Spider declared.

"Who?" Otter asked, glancing around.

"Those wild people."

"What wild people?" Black Skull asked, sitting up in his blanket and blinking away his slumber.

"Well, I certainly wouldn't look over there to see them." Green Spider pointed to a recessed cove.

Otter shaded his eyes. Men were rushing down a narrow trail on the pockmarked cliff. They looked like ants as they leaped and scrambled over the rocky drop. On the beach, canoes had been pulled up above the wave line. Most of the scuttling men carried what appeared at this distance to be sticks.

"Black Skull! I don't like the looks of this. These guys might be worse than the Khota." Otter threw his back into paddling; a picky little voice insisted on reminding him that they always ended up paddling for their lives just when they ought to be settling down for a well-earned rest.

"Green Spider," Pearl suggested, "you might not want to paddle 'backwards' with as little effort as you can muster."

The Contrary settled himself, digging in with his paddle. *Wave Dancer* fairly flew through the water, rising and falling as she raced the windborne waves.

Otter spared no breath for talk but kept an eye on the canoes that launched from the little harbor. One by one, they pushed off in pursuit, until nine dark slivers shot toward them.

"Stop and Trade?" Pearl wondered.

"Maybe they're friendly . . . and again, maybe not. Would you like to gamble? And why would that many warriors carry darts? No, I say we run like mad."

"At times, you demonstrate surprising logic, Trader," Black Skull noted.

Otter gauged *Wave Dancer*'s rate of progress. They were flying along the shore, headed right into the bloody orb of the sun that barely broke the straightedge of the horizon. The pursuers paddled smaller boats, with more warriors—but they were cutting across the angle. He was running the Khota race all over again.

"We're not going to make it," Otter declared.

"Then we must string them out," Black Skull called. "One against one, we've got a chance."

Otter threw a glance over his shoulder, guessing the distance of the pursuers. By the time the sun hung a finger's breadth above the horizon, they'd be within range. He managed a fresh burst of energy.

They passed another cove, and to Otter's dismay, three more canoes came racing out to join the chase. The cries of the wild men carried on the wind: joyous ululations.

"This isn't going to be good," Otter growled. "Pearl, I wish you'd stayed with Trout."

"Well, I didn't. Keep paddling."

Green Spider turned and said very seriously, "If she hadn't stayed with Trout, she'd be here to save us right now."

Nonsense? At a time like this? *"Paddle!"* Otter ordered, and to his dismay, the Contrary shrugged and laid his paddle down on the pack. "All right! *Don't* paddle." After Green Spider had returned to work, Otter muttered, "There are times when he makes me want to cry."

"Save us how?" Pearl asked, shaking her head slightly as she puzzled on it. The wind was whipping her hair around, but she didn't take time to fix it. "Green Spider? How can I save us?"

"You know," the Contrary told her without losing his rhythm. "These river men would never think of it."

"Does he mean I'm really going to save us . . . or kill us all?" Pearl wondered.

"Just paddle!" Otter urged.

He'd plotted the intercept course about right. The sun hung big and red. If Otter could have spared a finger, it would have fit between the horizon and the sun's bottom.

The first dart arched out of the sky to strike the water behind them with an odd *thoosh*ing sound. He didn't need to look over his shoulder to see it bobbing in the waves. It would float point-down, the nock up in the air where a hand could retrieve it.

"We're being shot at!" Otter called. He would have liked to redouble his efforts, but his reserves of stamina were depleted. He panted now, his skin sticky with sweat—as was Pearl's. Only Black Skull's tremendous strength carried them forward.

Another dart *thoosh*ed into the water no more than a man's length to the right of *Wave Dancer*'s hull. Before the shaft bobbed up, Otter idly noted the white stream of bubbles that marked the location.

Black Skull stood in the bow, looking back. "That lead canoe is well within my limit."

The warrior nocked a long dart in his atlatl. Bracing himself against the axis of the canoe, he waited, dart poised into the wind. *Wave Dancer* continued to rise and fall as she coasted over the rolling swells. Black Skull's release shivered the big canoe.

The deadly missile soared up, caught the wind, and fell short of its mark. Howls of glee erupted from the hunters.

"This wind!" Black Skull growled, reaching for another of his darts. "When they cast, it carries their missiles to us. Me, I have to try to throw past them, gauge the amount of drop." And he did, grunting with the effort.

Otter glanced back, chewing on his lip as he watched that slender dart winging through the rouged morning sky to whistle downward.

Black Skull whooped as it thunked home into the dugout's wood. The answering cries betrayed outrage this time, but the pursuers dropped back.

"Good cast!" Otter called, and Black Skull returned to his paddle, having brought them a short reprieve.

The lead canoe might be holding back, but the others were catching up, and Otter closed his ears to the jabber of orders called back and forth behind them.

Black Skull gritted his teeth. "They're not going to give us the opportunity to kill them one at a time. They've figured out that they can outrun us."

Otter's gut squirmed when he looked back and saw the warriors paddling their canoes wide, spreading out to encircle them. "Time appears to be on their side."

"If it just wasn't for this wind!" Black Skull roared. "And, Trader, they have more darts than we do for this kind of drawn-out fight. They can retrieve what they shoot at us. Our darts are gone forever with each cast."

At his words, the wind picked up again, scalloping the surface of the waves, whipping up bits of scud.

"The wind . . ." Pearl whispered.

Another dart made a *thoosh*ing sound as it smacked the water and bobbed up, the fletched shaft angled leeward.

One by one, darts dropped down around them, one splintering a groove out of *Wave Dancer*'s gunwale. Each time, Black Skull would turn, only to see the attacker's canoe drifting back out of range.

Thunk! and Green Spider gasped, looking down at where a still-shivering dart had pinned his shirt to the hull.

"Rot this wind!" Black Skull raged. "Why will it not help us?"

Pearl laughed then, and dove for the packs, lifting the heavy sacks away from the matting.

"What are you looking for?" Otter asked. Arms aching and leaden, he tried to wet his dry lips and blinked sweat from his eyes. A burning—as if his chest were going to rip apart—followed each gulped breath. *This time, we're not going to make it.*

Another dart hissed down to *thoosh* into the water just ahead of the fox-head prow. This one Black Skull snagged out with the barest break in his paddling.

And what are you going to do? You know what they'll do to Pearl. He would die slowly, tortured and screaming. But before they got their hands on the woman he loved, he'd use his paddle one last time. She'd never know, never feel a thing.

Pearl, meanwhile, had displaced Catcher to rise with a big roll of palmetto matting. A grin widened her face. "Pray for more wind."

"That's the last thing we need!" Sweat streaked the side of Black Skull's face as he cast a worried glance over his shoulder.

"Help me," Pearl told Otter. "Hold this other side. Don't just stare at me like I'm daft, *do it!*"

"You mean you want me to stop paddling?"

"Yes! Now!"

Otter scrambled forward to take one side of the tightly woven matting. Palmetto fronds made strong, yet light mats, and this one was a fair-sized piece, as tall as a man and twice as wide. He'd threatened to throw it out—and would have Traded it long before now had the journey not been so rushed. Pearl spread the mat, and when the wind caught it, it jerked Otter forward so fast that he nearly went overboard.

"That's it!" Pearl cried. "Use it to catch the wind!"

And Otter saw how it could work.

"This is what the saltwater Traders do!" he cried as he braced a foot on the polished gunwale. "I've seen them. They—"

"Of course!" The wind whipped her hair around her face as the mat bulged and swelled. *Wave Dancer* surged ahead, and Otter scrambled as he struggled to keep his balance and stretch the heavy mat with trembling arms.

"Black Skull, keep us on course! Steer us!"

The warrior looked back, shook his head, then paddled all the harder.

Otter squinted into the wind at the pursuing canoes. Would this give *Wave Dancer* the edge they needed? For the moment, they seemed to be breaking even, and holding the mat might be deadening to the arms, but now muscles different than the ones used for rowing were trembling. White spray was leaping from under the fox-head bow to spatter on the dark, crystal-blue water.

Ancestors, help us! Pearl might have found a way to save our lives again! She gave him a ravishing smile, sparks of joy dancing in her eyes. He whooped, living for the moment, enjoying that surge of vitality they'd shared in the storm. "Did I ever tell you that I love you?"

"No!" Green Spider chirped. "But I'm glad you do, Otter."

"Not you!" Otter snapped, then added, "Green Spider, hold your paddle up here in the middle of the mat . . . help us support it." At the Contrary's blank look, Otter pleaded, "Just this once, Green Spider, don't force me to think in reverse! Just *help* us."

A wan smile curled the Contrary's lips as he climbed back and used his paddle as Otter directed. Otter could feel the additional push it gave them, and in response, he leaned out, hanging over the water to stretch the matting wider.

The Badger people held about even, but now all hands were paddling—and the wind seemed to be stiffening again.

"If the wind holds . . ." Otter tried to stretch the mat even wider, leaning out perilously. To his surprise, *Wave Dancer* had come alive and was skipping over the waves. Black Skull switched sides in the bow, paddling like mad to bring the canoe back on line with the wind. Without the keel, it would have been a maddening job.

Otter sensed the abrupt drop in pressure as the wind lessened. Nevertheless, they'd opened a lead on the pursuit. The Badger people were now well out of dart range, and sunlight flashed on frantic paddles.

"How are we doing?" Black Skull asked, his view blocked by the mat.

"We gain some, we lose some. Right now, we're losing." But as Otter spoke, the wind freshened.

"There's our island," Pearl noted, nodding toward it. "The channel we want is to the right, but it's at an angle to the wind."

Otter contemplated the strength of the wind and the position of the pursuers. Just as they'd poured all of their heart into *Wave Dancer*'s initial sprint, the Badger folk had now used up a burst of energy in trying to bring their quarry to bay.

"And on the other side of the island?" Otter asked. "If we go north, what do we find?"

"Open water . . . I think."

Otter worked his tongue around his dry mouth, wishing he could reach down and cup up a drink. "All right. If we head for open water, we can use the stars. Paddling straight south should take us right back to the coastline, shouldn't it?"

"Who's afraid of open water?" Pearl asked.

"I am," Black Skull retorted. "Mostly."

"Stay with the wind," Otter decided. "Black Skull, take us straight east."

Again the wind strengthened, and again *Wave Dancer* pulled ahead, only to have the fickle wind die away to the point that Otter, Pearl, and Green Spider dropped the mat and began paddling.

Shouts of renewed hope carried faintly to them as the hunters rekindled their chase.

The big, humped island slowly passed off to their right. The rolling slopes appeared to be thickly wooded behind a wave-cut shoreline. The white beach was littered with driftwood. Several small fishing camps could be seen on the shore, but the people there only shaded their eyes to watch them pass.

Relentlessly, the hunters closed the gap, but fewer of the boats remained, the others having either exhausted themselves or lost interest and turned back.

"Are we going to make it?" Pearl continued to stroke with her paddle despite trembling arms.

"I don't know," Otter told her. The wind blowing on his back was no more than a pleasant breeze.

The sun had moved high into the sky as they cleared the last sandy spit and headed out into open water. Ahead of them, nothing but magical blue sparkled against the glaring horizon. Puffy white clouds had formed to march across the sky.

A dart *thoosh*ed into the water behind them.

Paddle, Otter told himself grimly. *All you can do is to paddle.*

His bones ached, and his muscles cramped and knotted with fiery exhaustion. Maybe it would be better just to let the wicked Badger hunters kill him.

You can't let them have Pearl. He glanced behind him. The sinking sensation of defeat was tempered by the fact that only two canoes had followed them past the tip of the island. All of the others had turned back.

How many ups and downs could a man have in a day?

"One thing's sure, they'll have earned it," Pearl stated matter-of-factly.

"Yes, I guess we know that they weren't the friendly sort. No one would work this hard just to Trade for a couple of sharks' teeth and some shells."

Another dart *thoosh*ed down to bob up in front of them.

"That's enough," Black Skull growled, throwing down his paddle and picking up his atlatl. "The wind's gone. I'm going to show these tree-crawling maggots what atlatls can do."

Otter glanced back over his shoulder, horrified at the closeness of the nearest canoe. As he watched, Black Skull cast, his dart dropping on the lead warrior. The man screamed and pitched backward before the canoe veered off. The second boat slowed, paddles dripping as it coasted.

"Let's go back. I can kill them all if we do." Black Skull

fitted a second dart into his atlatl. He braced on *Wave Dancer*'s pitching deck and cast; the dart embedded on the distant canoe's hull with an audible thunk.

"Let them go," Otter said wearily as the two canoes shied off, the paddlers heading back toward the island.

"I guess they'll think a lot about chasing us again," Green Spider asserted as he poked his finger through the dart hole in his shirt.

Pearl collapsed onto the packs, moaning. "Blessed Spirits, how soon, Green Spider? When will they be back?"

"Before we're ready for them, that's for sure."

Pearl rubbed her face briskly with both hands. "I wish I were drowned."

Under other circumstances, Otter would have considered heaving her overboard for the fun of it. Instead, he just slumped. The wind was picking up, but he couldn't care less. "We'd better try to get some sleep, Pearl. Looks like we're going to need the rest."

"Which way?" Black Skull rubbed his off-center jaw and gazed uneasily at the endless water.

"South. Look for land." Otter reached over the side to cup up all the water he could drink. Then he reshuffled the packs and stretched out, holding his blanket open for Pearl to crawl in beside him.

"We made it," she whispered, snuggling close.

"You saved us again." He kissed her temple.

"Hmm?" she murmured, eyes closed.

"Your wind trap. It saved us from capture. The wind trap was just enough to make the difference." When Pearl didn't respond, he raised his head to look at her. Her chest rose and fell in the slow rhythm of sleep.

He tucked an arm around her. "Good idea."

For the briefest of moments, he was aware of *Wave Dancer* rolling on the waves. The big canoe seemed more than pleased with herself.

Woodpecker trotted out of the trees as he followed the winding deer trail. Sweat gleamed and accented the rich brown tones of his skin. His muscles rolled smoothly, betraying the power in his shoulders and arms. Robin could read nothing in his wooden face as he approached. Since the killing of the dwarf, things had been changed. Woodpecker might have pulled an invisible blanket between them.

"Nothing," Woodpecker reported between gasps. "If she's between us and StarSky, she's either turned herself into a rock or melted into a tree. We've crisscrossed the hills, checked the farmsteads, and inspected the trails. If she's there, she's not leaving tracks. Can the Mask enable her to walk on air?"

Robin grimaced as he walked out into the clearing and savagely kicked the humped dirt in front of a woodchuck hole. "So where, then? The Magician wouldn't have deserted her—and he wouldn't have left the Mask behind."

Woodpecker walked close, and Robin could smell the musk of the man's hot body. "Cousin, I must ask you, is this necessary?"

Robin arched a hard eyebrow. "Necessary?"

Woodpecker wiped the sweat from his face and stared up at the treetops. "This Mask, we've sought it for almost half a year now. We're less than two moons from the summer solstice. Your warriors are beginning to chafe at the long absences from home."

"And you, my cousin?"

"A death has been avenged; that ghost can rest easier now. I would suggest that we take the Magician's skull back to the clan house, let the crows and magpies strip it clean, and hang it on the wall. Then we can go back to our familial duties."

"I sense something else."

Woodpecker gave him an inscrutable look. "Some are wondering if they haven't lost their luck."

"Because I killed the dwarf?" Robin glared suspiciously at the warriors who lounged in the shade of the trees. Quit? Had the time come to go home with Tall Man's skull and allow the ghosts to relax?

No! I was Powerful enough to capture the mighty Magician! To kill him! I will be Powerful enough to recover the Mask! In his soul's eye, he could see the high burial mound they would make for him—the whole of it capped with bright red clay to shine in the sun. That mound would be his. It wasn't just for the present, but for eternity that he struggled—and Star Shell carried the key to that eternity.

I will be buried with the Mask—that all will know the Power and prestige of Robin, war leader of the Moonshell valley!

He reached out to run callused fingers over the smooth bark of a beech. Then he turned, stating, "We will make one last hunt. I want everyone to spread out and search toward the Buckeye clan grounds. If we discover no sign of Star Shell, her daughter, or the Mask by the time we reach the Upper Moonshell, it will be a sign from Power that we should give up. However, if we do cross her trail, Power will have declared that we should keep searching for her."

Grunts of assent broke from the warriors, and Robin could see the affirmation in their eyes. No matter how homesick, they would fulfill the will of Power in this business.

The end would come soon.

Forty-one

Star Shell sat across the fire from Pale Snake, studying him cautiously. Why did he seem so at ease? He knew all about her, and more important, about the Mask. How could any human be comfortable in these circumstances?

For their camp he had picked a little wooded oak-and-maple grove on a terrace above the confluence of a reed-and-bulrush-filled creek and the sluggish Upper Moonshell. The canoe had been neatly pulled into the willows behind the screen of the rushes, and wild plum growing along the edge of the terrace hid their camp from view. The wispy blue smoke from the fire was effectively disseminated by the leaves overhead. Soft grass covered the ground. All in all, he couldn't have chosen a better camp.

"He's making goosefoot cakes, Mama," Silver Water said, her eyes glowing with anticipation. She rested on her stomach, button chin propped in grimy hands.

"Some of the best ever," Pale Snake told her. "I learned this trick long ago. I mix flour with a little grease and some of the special starter I keep in this jar. I let it set for a bit and it fluffs up. Then I mash it flat again and put it in a pot to bake."

"You seem to be most proficient at what you do," Star Shell told him, keeping a hand on Silver Water for reassurance. She still hadn't managed to decide whether she liked him or not. Disdain for him gave way to grudging acceptance that slid back into annoyance.

True, Pale Snake was a handsome man, of medium height, muscular, and carefully dressed. An atlatl hung from his belt, along with several pouches, the contents of which Star Shell could only guess. The sinuous snakes tattooed on his lean cheeks were the most notable of his features. They seemed to coil for a strike every time he smiled—and Pale Snake, she'd discovered, smiled a great deal.

"This won't be ready to eat for a while yet." He puckered his lips. "But the night is warm, and we have a screen of willows to block us from the main channel. Why don't you two go down to the creek? It might be the last chance you get to wash up."

"And leave the Mask here, I suppose?" Star Shell cocked an eyebrow. *Let's hear it, Trader Pale Snake.*

"If you'd like. Better yet, why don't you take it with you . . . and while you're down there, heave it into the middle of the current?"

"I don't trust you," Star Shell said as she stood up, taking Silver Water's hand. The Mask stayed in its pack on her back.

"That's because you don't understand me." He used a stick to rearrange the coals.

"Oh, how wrong you are. I do understand some things about you. You're a man, at the very least. Should I worry about you peeking through the bushes while I'm washing?"

Pale Snake gave her a mild smile. "Of course you should. You see, I know some things about you, too. You're the worrying type. Now, accepting the fact that you're a worrier, you wouldn't feel right down there naked without tormenting yourself as to whether or not I was wiggling through the grass on my belly to feast my eyes on your feminine allure. Such as it is. My advice, therefore, is that you go right ahead and worry . . . you'll feel better about it."

"You are not funny. You are despicable!"

"No, no, now, that's my father. We never did get along. In fact, I figure that's why he sent you. It's the sort of thing he'd do. Some sort of punishment or torment inflicted on me . . . just out of spite."

Father? Star Shell hesitated. Her weary thoughts tried to find order, but they couldn't string themselves together. *What did he mean by that?* While she thought about it, she retreated through the plums with her daughter.

"He's a strange man," Silver Water said. "He's scared of me."

"No one should be scared of you, baby." *But we are, aren't we? Pale Snake saw the changes in you that I want only to ignore.*

She studied the spot he'd told her about. A clear creek flowed out of a mat of brush and was screened by tall rushes before it emptied into the river. The evening carried a chill, but the water did look wonderful. She need only look down at her sleeves, at the stains and caked grime, to know what a mess she was. *So much for the privileged maiden of StarSky.* But then, that maiden had vanished a long time ago.

"Come on, baby. Let's make ourselves clean." She swung the Mask pack down where it would be close and peeled out of her clothing. As she waded into the water, she caught herself glancing up the slope, waiting for his leering grin.

She flinched at the cold but settled herself into the stream, gasping as the frigid water lapped around her stomach. Silver Water watched from the bank.

"Come on, baby."

"It looks cold."

"It looks *clean*. I haven't felt this way since . . ." But she couldn't say Greets the Sun's name. Not anymore. That dream, too, had been laid in its tomb. *If I lose any more of myself, there won't be anything left.*

Silver Water pulled off her dress and waded in, her face contorting in displeasure. Star Shell grabbed one of her arms and dragged her into the deeper water, the action accompanied by shrill squeaks.

"Let's get really clean."

"It's *cold*!"

As Star Shell scrubbed her daughter down, she kept glancing up the slope. Pale Snake perplexed her. He seemed to know everything about her—and the Mask—and he could joke! A sorcerer? Afraid of Silver Water?

Star Shell bit her lip. *How much have you denied, Star Shell? You've seen the changes. She doesn't act like a little girl anymore.*

But how could she, after everything she'd been through?

"Ouch!" Silver Water tried to twist away. "Not so hard, Mama."

"Sorry, Tadpole. Here, let me do your hair. When did it get so tangled? You've got sticks in here . . . and what's this? A tick?"

Silver Water made suffering sounds as Star Shell plucked the partially engorged tick from her scalp and let it float away in the water. After the time spent crawling through the woods, it was a wonder that they weren't covered with the bloodsuckers.

"Star Shell?" Pale Snake called from above. "I've some clean clothing. Heads up! I'm sailing it over the edge in a bundle."

Before she could say no, a rounded mass launched over the terrace in an arc, thumped onto the grassy slope and rolled to the very edge of the water. The fabric looked new. She looked back up to where she expected to see his beaming face.

"Nothing for Silver Water, I'm afraid. Poor planning on my part. I do hope you'll forgive me."

"Thank you," she called back, and in a lower voice, "But I'm sure we can do without your rags." Their own would be fine.

She shook her head as she let Silver Water escape to shore. Then she waded over to retrieve her daughter's clothes. She scrubbed them out as best she could, aware of Silver Water's shivers as the girl jumped up and down, arms crossed.

"I'm freezing, Mama!"

"Go on up to the fire. That Trader may not be worth much,

but his fire is. Go get warm. But, baby, don't let him touch you, all right?''

"Yes, Mama." Silver Water sped up the slope, driven by shivers.

Star Shell scrubbed herself as clean as she could and washed out her hair. The mats and tangles would take a while to pull free. She discovered a painful bruise on one shoulder and wondered when that had happened. Perhaps in that mad rush through the trees after Tall Man's . . . Wearily she wondered how she'd managed to block that horror from her soul.

You're tired, Star Shell. Not thinking clearly. She splashed water on her face, staring at the wavering reflection in the water. *I need all of my wits now.* But her thoughts seemed as muddy as the water she looked into.

She turned and laid Silver Water's clothing out on the grass. The child was nearly in rags. She clicked a sound of dismay with her tongue as she started to work on her own garments. The pitiful remnants had been a beautiful dress once, moons ago.

It's all right, Star Shell. One day, maybe in a moon or so, you'll be able to act like a woman again . . . make a comb, mend your clothing.

She wrung the last of the water from her hair, gooseflesh pricking her skin. She did feel clean, and somehow better about herself. Pale Snake had been correct about that. She started to don her wet dress; then, out of curiosity, she opened the bundle he'd thrown down.

A thick new blanket enclosed a brand-new woman's dress and a pair of heavy moccasins. The dress was stunning—the bodice adorned with bone, shell, and copper beads laid out in chevrons. Long fringes hung from the sleeves and down the yoke in the back. Instead of the fabric she'd expected, she fingered finely tanned buckskin that had been scraped to a perfect thinness and softened until it melted against the skin. She lifted it, inhaling the rich aroma of hickory smoke.

It's so beautiful. She sank envious teeth into her lower lip, then looked back at the worn rags she'd been traveling in. Why would he give her a dress like this? How deep would she place herself in his debt if she accepted it?

He wouldn't have thrown it down here if he didn't expect

something from you. Nevertheless, her fingers kept running over the soft leather. It would be so warm. And she hadn't been warm in a long time.

The humming of a mosquito broke the logjam of her indecision. She pulled the wonderful dress over her head, sighing at the way it conformed to her cold skin. She smoothed it over the swell of her hips and looked down. Leather molded to the body, of course, but the dress was just the slightest bit too small; it fit like a second skin. She flushed at the way it accented her full breasts, flat stomach, and narrow waist.

The knee-high moccasins had been dyed a lustrous crimson and were made of a thick leather she'd never seen before. When she slipped them on, it was with a gasp of delight, for they might have been cut for her feet alone. Thongs secured them firmly to the calf.

Finally, she rolled up their old wet clothing, slung on the Mask pack and made her way to the top of the slope.

"Stand still, little girl," Pale Snake demanded.

At the sound of his voice, Star Shell charged forward; whatever was happening, it couldn't be good. As she cleared the plum bushes along the edge of the terrace, she could see the fire. Silver Water stood before Pale Snake, a defiant look on her face. He was doing something to her hair. Only as Star Shell closed for the kill did she see the comb.

Pale Snake looked up with annoyed eyes. "Doesn't the child own a comb?"

"No. And stop that! I'll comb her hair . . . and when she's *dressed*!"

Pale Snake lifted an eyebrow. "Does it make a difference? I've been combing hair for . . . well, for a long time. It combs as easily dressed as undressed."

"That's not what I mean."

He made a smacking sound with his lips, as if being forced to eat something gruesome. "Hold still, Silver Water. Just because your mother's sure that I'm a filthy leech, it doesn't mean that I am. And as soon as we get this last tangle, you'll be as pretty as polished conch shell."

Star Shell stopped short. "Do not interfere between me and my daughter."

He glanced up at her, noticing her attire for the first time, his eyes widening. "Now I know the old demon sent you to torture me. By the ancestors, Star Shell, you're a beauty."

"Not yours," she told him coldly. "And as soon as my clothing is dry, you may have your dress back."

He finally freed the comb so that it traveled smoothly though Silver Water's hair. "There you go, little one. Now, you just stand there and let the fire dry your hair. As soon as I get your mother straightened out, we'll comb it one last time."

He walked over to Star Shell, forcing himself to look her in the eyes. He lifted the comb and raised an eyebrow. "Turn around."

"You're presumptuous!"

"Very well, do it the hard way." He laid the comb on her bundled clothing and returned to the fire. With a stick, he stirred the coals banked around the pot. Even from where she stood, Star Shell could smell the aroma. Her stomach, so long empty, growled in distress.

Pale Snake pointed to a framework of saplings he'd built beside the fire. "You could put the wet things there to dry out. I don't think you'll be too uncomfortable in that dress, but Silver Water will want hers dry before it gets too dark."

Star Shell forced herself to move, draping the clothes over the drying rack, then placing the Mask pack close to her as she combed out the snarls in her hair. Maybe he'd been right, it might have been easier if he'd done it. But he could rot like a log first.

"Were you one of his women?" Pale Snake asked softly.

"One of his . . ."

"Tall Man's?"

"No. I wasn't. He always treated me with a great deal of respect. Almost . . . sadness." She glanced at him. "Doesn't it worry you to say his name like that? His ghost is somewhere, and believe me, given some of the things he admitted to, it's not a very happy ghost."

Pale Snake studied her from the corner of his eye. "I'm sure of that. Tell me, did he ever give you anything? Twists of grass made into human shape? Little leather bags with arms and legs? Bundles of feathers tied together?"

"No. Should he have?"

Pale Snake frowned before reaching up to feel Silver Water's hair. "About dry, little one. If Mama will toss us the comb, we'll make it shine."

"I'll do her hair. Come here, baby." As Star Shell ran the comb through Silver Water's hair, she shot a suspicious look at Pale Snake. "Is that how he did it? He said that he'd used his Power to fool one woman, to take her . . . and make her dream he was her husband."

Pale Snake poked at the embers with more vigor than he needed. "Then he told you a great deal about himself. That, Star Shell, was a most unusual confidence. I wonder why he did it."

She shrugged. "He had his reasons. And I suppose you have yours. This is quite a dress. Who is it for? Your wife?"

He chuckled in that irreverent manner of his. "I killed my wife seven years ago."

"Killed?" The comb stopped motionless, halfway down Silver Water's hair.

"She was sleeping with my father—of her own free will, I might add." He studied the glowing embers. "I might have let it go, even so. She said some things . . . well, enough to make me bash her brains out."

"With your father?" Star Shell could only gape. "What kind of family did you come from?"

"The worst . . . but then, you'd know all about that."

She swallowed hard, remembering her husband, and the rope creaking in the darkness. "It was the Mask that made Mica Bird do the things he did. He wasn't that way . . . before."

"He wore the Mask?" Pale Snake licked his lips uneasily. "Listen, Star Shell, why don't we just throw it in the river and be gone? I'll take you wherever you want to go. The Mask, it's nothing but pain, heartache, and trouble. It's already working on Silver Water."

Tendrils of dread ran down her arms. "What? What do you mean?"

"Can't you see it? That look in her eyes? Haven't you seen the changes?"

An ache began in Star Shell's throat. "What . . . what changes?"

"Power is talking to her." He turned, his voice gentle. "Isn't it, Silver Water? Teaching you Songs?"

Silver Water glanced imploringly at her mother, as if she wanted to answer but was afraid to; she squatted down and stared at the fire. Looking for faces? Like the old woman had told her about?

Pale Snake walked around, knelt, and placed a reassuring hand on the girl's bare shoulder, smiling at her—but he spoke to Star Shell. "It will be all right. We have time."

Star Shell's mouth had turned dry. "What . . . what do you see that I don't?"

"She's been touched by Power, that's what. With a child's innocence, it simply follows her whim and will. Power isn't evil by itself. Human beings use Power, and sometimes it uses human beings."

"My husband . . . hung himself. Did terrible things. Killed. The Mask made him do those things. Are you suggesting—"

"No." Pale Snake shook his head. "It only used what was already lurking in his soul. That's why I'm surprised that Tall Man wore the Mask."

"He didn't."

"But you said he did. When we were talking about families."

"I meant my husband." She shook her head. "Wait a minute. I'm confused. Tall Man feared the Mask. He came to me at the winter solstice. I was in StarSky . . . for my mother's funeral. Tall Man was there. He'd heard of the Mask being used for evil. My father took me to see him just after Mother's cremation. The Magician understood what was happening, and he told me that First Man had given him a Vision. He knew how to recover the Mask, how to use the wolfhide to dampen its Power. But he said that only throwing the Mask into the Roaring Water would neutralize it forever."

Pale Snake playfully tugged at Silver Water's hair as he watched the fire. "That doesn't sound like him. Since when would the Magician care if a Mask was terrorizing half the world? Let alone his little corner of it."

Star Shell bit off her response, glancing away.

"You know something else." Pale Snake lifted an eyebrow suspiciously at her. The serpents on his cheeks wiggled uncomfortably as his jaw muscles tensed.

"It was a confidence." She bristled. "I'm sorry, but I don't trust you . . . or anyone. I've watched my life, the lives of my father, mother, and husband, destroyed . . . and if what you say about Silver Water and the Mask is true, my daughter's life may be in greater danger than I know. I've seen people die, one after another. Robin is hunting me, trying to kill me as he did the Magician. I *can't* trust anyone . . . not anymore. Especially not you.''

He nodded, his expression thoughtful again. ''But, Star Shell, you trusted Tall Man. Now isn't that a curious twist of fate? I'd sooner stick my hand into a basket full of rattlesnakes than allow him within a week's travel of me.''

''Why? What did he ever do to you?''

Pale Snake's eyes narrowed, and the slow, pulsing anger was measured by the tightening of his muscular fists. ''Everything he could. In the beginning, I wanted to be like him in every way. I blamed myself for outgrowing him. That was the first disappointment. No matter how I tried to follow in his footsteps, I was different. The more I despised him, the more he hated me.''

''Tall Man? Hated you?''

''Everything he was, I was the opposite.''

She bowed her head. ''He was kind to me.''

''That's what bothers me.'' Pale Snake reached over to the drying rack, feeling Silver Water's clothing. ''A little while longer.''

''If he hated you so much, why would he send me to you?'' She absently pulled the comb through her long black hair.

''None of this makes sense—except that he knew I'd be enough of a fool to save you no matter what. I always was a sucker for a hard-luck story. It makes me a mediocre Trader at best.''

''You didn't sound like a nice man when I heard you joking with Stone Wrist.''

''I'm not a nice man. Whatever filled you with such non-sense? I killed my wife, remember?'' He glanced unhappily into the fire. ''Tall Man was always too deep, too devious, for his own good. That's what Power granted him.'' He wove his fingers together. ''And he wouldn't have missed one last oppor-tunity to hurt me. Is that it? Did he send you to hurt me?''

Star Shell slowly shook her head. "I'm not here to hurt any-one. All I want to do is to get the Mask of Many Colored Crow to the Roaring Water, pitch it over the edge, and then . . . then . . ."

What? She stumbled on emptiness. What happened after she'd finished this?

"You're a trap," Pale Snake decided. "Though I'll grant that maybe you don't know you are. That slimy weasel had to take one last slap at my peace." He paused, thoughtful attention on the dress and the way it accented her slender curves. She was on the verge of a hot retort when he asked, "You're sure that he didn't give you any kind of charm?"

"Yes, I'm sure! Stop looking at me like that!"

He seemed not to hear. "I can't figure it out. You're perfect. Beautiful, young, intelligent, and courageous, extraordinarily healthy—just the sort he'd have to bed."

"*Bed me!* Don't be a . . ." The words died as she realized that he was watching her with eyes every bit as wary as her own. "Would you . . . would you explain that?"

"Women were his passion. He lived for seduction. Perhaps it was because he was a dwarf, perhaps because nothing was ever denied him. We should all be born so lucky." Pale Snake's expression had turned to stone. "That's why he had to have her. And not with any charm, but on his own."

"Your wife?" Star Shell guessed from Pale Snake's slumped posture. "But I thought you said that your father . . . By the sacred ancestors . . . no." And it all came clear—the confusion, the words aimed past each other.

The stony expression didn't change. "You didn't know?"

She shook her head numbly. "I'm so tired, I can barely think at all. I just wonder what other obvious things I've missed lately. He said he had a son. I never . . . He didn't give me a name."

"It's time to eat," Pale Snake said woodenly. "Silver Water, your clothes are dry. You'd better get dressed before the night chill nips at your bones."

As darkness takes hold, prickles run up and down Silver Water's backbone. But it is more than the cold.

The owls and bats have gone silent. No frogs croak. Not even the wind dares to breathe tonight. Everyone here is afraid.

Silver Water kneels before the fire and studies Pale Snake from the corner of her eye. He is a sorcerer. She wishes she could talk to him—about the Mask, about the creatures moving in the forest. He sits only five hands away, but her mother is watching. Besides, he has his head down, and his jaw is clenched so tight that his cheek muscles are jumping. He doesn't look like he wants to talk to anyone.

Silver Water bites her lower lip. A log breaks in the fire and bursts into flame, hissing and spitting.

Her stomach knots.

Beyond their camp, there are shadows. They slither through the trees like ghosts, their dark tongues flicking out. Tails flash as they slip between smoke-colored trunks. She doesn't know what they are, but they . . . they look like snakes. Silver Water's breathing is shallow. There are so many of them. Bright golden scales shine when the light hits them just right.

"I'll be back," her mother says suddenly, and Silver Water jumps, her eyes following as her mother walks away toward the forest.

Should Silver Water warn her about the snakes?

No. She will shout at me. Ask me how I know. Ask if the Mask told me.

Desperate, she watches long after her mother has disappeared into the maw of blackness.

Silver Water glances back at Pale Snake. He is studying the Mask pack, which sits on the other side of the fire. The Mask has been strangely quiet, as though it has run out of words to say. Or maybe it is just tired.

Pale Snake fingers his chin thoughtfully, and Silver Water leans toward him, whispering, "The Mask is sleeping."

Pale Snake turns. His brows draw together. "I know," he whispers back, as though understanding that she doesn't want her mother to overhear their conversation.

Bravely, Silver Water shifts to face him. She wrings her hands, opens her mouth, but the words fly away.

Pale Snake waits for her to speak, then smiles. "What do you want to say to me?"

Hoarsely, she asks, "Do you see them?" She uses her eyes to point out the serpents in the forest.

Pale Snake lifts his chin and surveys the forest carefully. Tilting his head, he answers, "No. Though I *feel* something out there. What do you see?" He looks down at Silver Water very seriously.

Words flood out of her mouth. "I—I see snakes. Lots of them. They have shiny scales and long tongues and . . ."

Her voice fades as a frown carves lines around his eyes. Firelight retreats from those lines, leaving them deep and dark. Scary.

"Snakes," she repeats, barely audible. "Out in the trees."

The lines go away as his face slackens. He looks at the forest again. "Where? Show me. Point them out for me."

Silver Water jumps up and runs to sit beside him. "There!" She points at a big one. "See it? Behind the bushes. It's crawling toward us."

"Is it?"

"Yes, and it . . . it's huge. It could swallow us whole." Her hands are shaking.

Pale Snake peers down at her meditatively. Gently, he smooths a hand over her clean dry hair. "Has the Serpent spoken to you?"

She shakes her head.

"Well, I'm sure it will."

"Why? Why would it?"

A faint smile warms his face. "I think that's why it's here. For you, little one. I've already met that Serpent, so it can't be after me. And your mother, well . . ." He sighs. "She's not the sort the Serpent would want to swallow."

Silver Water's heart thunders. "But I . . . I don't want to be eaten by that snake!"

"Maybe not yet," he answers, "but someday you will." The lines are born again around his eyes. He lowers his voice, and it comes out like the deep rumble from a mountain lion's throat. "Someday soon, I imagine."

"No. No, I—I don't—"

Silver Water whirls when her mother steps out of the trees

and starts back for camp. Pleadingly, she looks up at Pale Snake, trying to tell him that she wants to talk more, but . . .

Her mother sits down on the opposite side of the fire, and Silver Water quickly scoots back to her former place and stares wide-eyed out at the forest. Her back teeth groan against each other. They are elk antlers, spiky, locked in a death struggle. She can't pull them apart.

"What's the matter?" her mother demands, looking first at Silver Water, then at Pale Snake.

"Not a thing," Pale Snake says and laces his fingers over one knee. "Did you see anything move out there in the darkness, Star Shell?"

"No. Why?" Suspicion fills her mother's voice.

Pale Snake laughs softly. "We didn't think you'd see anything," he says. "No, not in ten tens of years, Star Shell. Not you. You're just not the type."

"I don't know why you always have to insult me when I least expect it."

"Don't be silly. That's the only time to insult someone. I mean, if you wait until they're expecting it—"

"I'm going to bed!" her mother announces. "Come along, Silver Water. I'm very tired."

"Yes, Mama." Silver Water jumps up and runs to grab her mother's cold hand.

As they pass Pale Snake, he winks at her, and Silver Water can breathe again. Her lungs fill with cool air.

Pale Snake mouths the words, *Don't worry.*

She cranes her neck to watch him as her mother drags her away. He stands and starts kicking dirt over the fire. With each kick, dust puffs, and the snakes slither away into the forest and vanish.

Silver Water's mouth drops open. She looks around, searching for them. But they are gone. All gone. He has killed them.

Glancing at her mother to make sure she isn't watching, Silver Water lifts a hand to Pale Snake. He smiles again, and a tiny smile tugs at the corners of her own mouth.

For just a moment, the world changes.

The tree leaves aren't black, they are coated with starlight. Everything gleams, the rocks, the blades of grass. The clouds.

And she knows that if she can just break her heart and let the stars in, she will be all right. All the shadows will go away.

The snakes will not eat her.

. . . At least not until she wants them to.

Naked and dripping, Black Skull waded out of the cold water and onto the pale sand of the beach. Shivering, he turned and looked out across the glossy Fresh Water Sea to where the rising sun lay just below the horizon. They'd rounded the peninsula. Soon the sun would rise out of the water and spread over the land as they headed south. Shreds of high clouds drifted across the sky, forming patterns like glowing-red fish meat.

He raised his hands, and from his heart a Song of welcome and thanks rose to his lips. He'd stolen the Song, of course; it belonged to the Blood Clan, but after years of hearing it as he practiced with his war club, he supposed they wouldn't mind if he Sang it. Though, if they heard his cracked and coarse voice rising off-key and toneless, they might kill him for desecrating such a thing of beauty. The Singing made him feel better, at peace with himself.

As he returned to his clothing and war club, he noticed Otter walking loose-limbed up the beach, thumbs tucked in his belt. *Wave Dancer* lay just behind him where they'd pulled her up on the sand. The painted designs had faded and weathered, but the fox-head prow still watched alertly.

"Good morning, Trader."

"Good morning, Killer of Men." Otter pointed toward the silver-crested water. "I see you haven't lost your reckless spirit. For a moment there, I thought you'd gone down for the last time."

"I like to dive deep," Black Skull said, rubbing the water from his hide. "That's one cold, dark bottom down there. Look at that! My balls are pulled up so tight, my heart will barely beat."

"Find any ghosts down there this time?"

"No." Black Skull paused reflectively as he studied the smooth surface of the sea. "Not even a sneaky Khota. But then,

I myself once feared losing my soul down there. Feared it more terribly than I've ever feared anything." He gave Otter a side-long look. "The night of the storm. I got hold of my soul and tucked it into a safe place inside me. I no longer fear it slipping away as I once did. I know I wasn't of much use to you that night."

Otter reached down, picking up a flat piece of weathered shale and skipping it out across the glassy water. "To be honest, I was so terrified during that storm, I think I fouled myself. I'd never dreamed of such raging wind and water."

Black Skull picked up his shirt and batted the sand from the fabric. "I thank you for the lie, Otter. You've become a friend to me. But we both know the truth of that night: I broke."

The Trader skipped another rock. "Don't you think that's the wrong word? To me, 'broke' means unfixable, or at best, something that can be patched up, maybe glued, with a thong run around it—like a pot. But never as strong as it was in the beginning. You seem even stronger now."

"The fool used that analogy at White Shell clan grounds that day. Do you recall? He said you could see a life in a pot." Black Skull curled his toes in the coarse sand. "I didn't understand."

"None of us did. But we're here."

"Saved again by Pearl. She steered us south by the stars all night, didn't she?"

Otter studied the next rock he picked up, as if judging its quality before skipping it. "She did. Again. That wind trap was quite an idea, too. Too bad it works only when going with the wind."

"It will never replace paddles." Black Skull tied on his breechcloth and picked up his war club, testing the balance before he rested it on his shoulder. "Tell me, Trader, did you ever think we'd make it this far? Look at that. Water as far as you can see, just like on the other side of the peninsula. How much water is in the world, anyway?"

"I don't know, my friend."

"Nor do I, but a sense of wonder has been born in my soul. Otter, sometimes I look back . . . think about how I lived at the City of the Dead, and shake my head. That life . . . I know it was real, but it seems like a Dream now."

"Because it's hard to be away from home?"

"No. Not a Dream of something I want, but one that you wake up remembering. I wouldn't Trade any of this, not one moment—well, maybe two moments."

"Which two?"

He paused, nerving himself. "Killing that crow on the river just before we reached the Hilltop Clan . . . and grabbing you by the throat that day."

Otter placed his hand on Black Skull's shoulder, the grip firm. "It was a lesson . . . for both of us."

"What do you miss the most, Otter?" They started walking back toward the canoe.

"Oh, I don't know. Nights with Uncle, I suppose. I think he rests easier now. Maybe I miss a little of the innocence that was once mine. Green Spider has taught me a great deal. I'll never stand back like I used to."

"And Red Moccasins? Is she still tormenting you?"

"Sometimes . . . in my sleep." Otter clasped his hands behind him. "Since I've been with Pearl, those dreams come less and less frequently. Pearl and I seem to match, like two pieces that fit together. At other times, I look forward, toward the future, and wonder what will become of us. I would make her my wife, Black Skull, but we're each clanless in our own way. A man has few rights among the White Shell when it comes to marriage. The Anhinga will disown her when they hear what happened with Wolf of the Dead."

"You worry too much, Trader. Believe me. I know you for the conniving and slippery eel that you are. You'll find a way."

Otter grinned. "How about you? When this is over—assuming we live that long—what are you going to do? You'll be a great man, respected, almost worshiped, at the City of the Dead."

Black Skull shrugged, scooping sand with his foot to fling it in a wide arc. Individual grains stippled the water. "Maybe I'll take up catching skunks for a living."

"Yes, well, you do have a talent for it."

Black Skull squinted into the sun's red glare as the first arc crept over the flat horizon and set the water on fire. "Trader, I think I've begun to understand what it is about this life that possesses you. Once you break free, travel beyond your clan, you can never return again. What will I tell them?'' He gestured to the east. ''About watching the sun rise out of the Fresh Water Sea? Will they believe that? About the storm whipping the water into waves as tall as a clan house? About these wild lands, where men haven't heard the word of Many Colored Crow? They'd just stare at me with blank eyes.''

''But you can grow tired of it after many voyages.'' Otter skipped yet another pebble, the stone spatting off the surface in a trail of rings. ''Uncle did, and he wanted to go home, to marry and have a family. If Pearl and I can find our way together, we'll want to raise a family someday.'' He cocked his head seriously. ''You know, 'Fat Frog' can't do that on the water.''

Black Skull chuckled. ''All these worries—and we're not even to the Roaring Water yet. Forget them, Trader. If Many Colored Crow is generous, you'll have time to consider these things. But for now, there are more important things to think about.''

''You mean the Badger people?'' Otter glanced at the dunes, glowing red-orange in the morning light.

''They are the least of our worries. Back there, somewhere behind us, the Khota are still following—or do you foolishly believe that they all drowned? Meanwhile, ahead of us, unknown challenges wait. This fine beach Pearl found us last night is but a reprieve, a small gift from Power so that we might build up our strength again.''

''You're right. We may all be dead before this is through.'' Otter glanced at the bedrolls up the beach. ''If I could keep her safe . . .''

''You can't. You don't have the right to. She's part of this journey.''

''But what if something happens to her?''

''What if something happens to you? What of it? You think her heart won't break? You need to talk to the Contrary about that habit of blaming yourself for everything. If she dies, Otter, you'll mourn her, I'll mourn her, and I think the fool will mourn her. The same if you die. You'll put a hole in all of our souls. But then, that's the way life is, isn't it?''

''It is, but I don't have to like it, do I?''

Black Skull eyed his friend. ''So why are you down here walking around instead of up there in Pearl's blankets?''

"We haven't found the right time for that yet. This is the first time we've made shore since leaving Trout's camp. She was dead tired. I couldn't sleep. And to be honest, we're not safe yet."

"You could just come out and say that you're both still scared of each other."

"Well, yes, I could . . . but I'm not going to."

Black Skull smiled. "You'd better go up and get some sleep. I'll keep guard in the meantime. When the sun reaches its highest, we'll start south again."

On the north side of their camp, Green Spider was running down the beach behind a group of seagulls, flapping his skinny arms like wings, unable to get off the ground. Finally, he fell over, and across the distance, Black Skull could hear his cackling laughter.

Otter glanced at the sun, now hanging redly over the horizon. "I'd like to come back someday, travel these shores when it isn't a race."

"A race," Black Skull said slowly, following his gaze. "A warrior develops a sense for things like this. Wolf of the Dead is still coming—and ever more desperate to catch us."

Forty-two

To doubt a Spirit Helper requires at once valor and despair.

   They are immortal, after all.

   Yet I have found they are also imperfect—or perhaps perfectly blind, each in his own way.

   Neither First Man nor Many Colored Crow sees the whole. That is why they are locked in constant struggle and the world rocks back and forth in a heroic lullaby of tragedy and ecstasy, Light and Dark.

   Their war is everlasting.

   Perhaps that is the only unalterable Truth.

But I keep thinking, praying, that a bridge must exist. A bridge that stretches above the war and allows mortal Dreamers to traverse the battlefield without being captured by either side.

A Contrary is the embodiment of those eternal opposites. But opposites crossed. I stand at the middle point between the two, which allows me to see both sides. And I do see both. But I don't see a bridge. Just the relentless conflict.

The Clan Elders used to speak of the Mysterious One's quiet soul.

And I wonder if this is not the bridge I am seeking. But how do I find it? Where is it?

Is it inside me? Or outside? . . . Or both at once?

Inklings stir the back of my soul, as though I already know the answer to that question . . . I just haven't seen it yet.

Stone Wrist sat on a stump before his house, enjoying the sunshine. Spring had been particularly dull and rainy, but warmth bathed the land today. His modest house lay several dart casts beyond the earthen enclosure of the Buckeye clan grounds. He could see the conical roof of the clan house and the faint smear of bluish smoke rising from the incense burning in the charnel house. This close, the walk back and forth wasn't punishing—and he was close enough to know most of the goings-on.

This morning he had found himself enchanted by the distant cries of children involved in a game of stick. Women were working the fields to the east, bobbing as they plied chert hoes to chop out pesky weeds from around the newly sprouted goosefoot. The hearty laughter of men could be heard from the canoe landing, and from somewhere behind him, the dull *tunk-a-thunk* of a pestle carried on the hazy air.

High above, two buzzards twirled about each other, the sole threats to the few puffs of cloud. A man could do worse than to live with this kind of simple happiness.

Stone Wrist had become a broker of sorts—a Trader's host, offering a friendly household and plentiful food in return for pleasant companionship. The Traders who stayed with him generally left a special something behind as a token of appreciation.

Those pieces of shell, obsidian, mica, or copper allowed him to Trade with friends and relatives for enough goosefoot, sunflower seeds, squash, or whatever else he might need to nourish his legendary belly.

Of late, he'd noticed pains in his groin, but they seemed to lessen when he lay down, and such discomforts were minor when compared to the ease of his life.

Today would be very nice. His sole duty consisted of enjoying the warm sunshine and contemplating Pale Snake, his most recent guest. Now there was a truly peculiar man. So delightfully amiable, yet curiously secretive. Sometimes he claimed to belong to an old High Head Clan, other times to the Many Paints, and sometimes to the Serpent Clan of the north—whatever that was. Nights spent with Pale Snake generally overflowed with merriment, as well as with jokes just off-color enough to be genuinely amusing without offending good taste.

I could stand a bit more of his company. Stone Wrist nodded to himself and leaned his head back to catch the full benefit of the sun. What did Pale Snake do up there in the north? Too bad he came by only every two years.

"Stone Wrist?"

He glanced up, then had to use the flat of a hand to shade his vision from the sun. "Greetings! You're new. Looking for a place to stay?"

"Not particularly." The man stepped out of the sunlight, and Stone Wrist could see that this was no ordinary Trader, no indeed—not with split human jawbones hanging down his chest like a breastplate.

"How then might I be of service, warrior?"

"I'm looking for a woman."

"Looking for a woman? Aren't we all?" Stone Wrist noted the travel stains on the warrior's high moccasins. Similar blotches could be seen on the shirt, and on the rolled blanket he carried. Other stains, a bit more rusty looking, had to be blood. Human or animal?

"Her name is Star Shell. Perhaps you've heard of her?"

"Oh, yes. Everyone has, I daresay. And about the Mask . . . and that man, a warrior from down at Blue Duck, who has vowed to find her."

"I am that man. I am called Robin."

Stone Wrist straightened, a hand to his chin. "The same? You don't say? What brings you to me, noble War Leader?"

Robin hunched down beside him, and Stone Wrist was reminded of a supple cat ready to spring. Ropy muscle corded under supple bronze skin. That narrowed gaze cataloged the approaches to Buckeye clan grounds. This was a hard man, and those unforgiving eyes now turned to Stone Wrist. "I told you, I'm looking for a woman. I've heard that a woman and a little girl left here a couple of days ago . . . and that you were there. I think that woman was Star Shell."

Stone Wrist cocked his head. Robin spoke softly, precisely, and sounded all the more dangerous for it. Something in the human soul can sense a killer's Power—the ability to deal practiced death. That awareness now chilled Stone Wrist's fat-encased heart. "I know of no Star Shell, great warrior."

"But you do know of a Trader who took a woman and a girl from here? Perhaps in a canoe?"

"Ah! You mean Pale Snake! Yes, a woman and girl. But her name was Yellow Snail, and . . . let me see." He furrowed his meaty face, scratching at his stubborn memory. "Little Snail? No, the woman was Yellow Snail. Little Snake? Little—"

"It doesn't matter. Describe the woman."

"Filthy. She looked like she'd be handsome enough, though. I told Pale Snake to dip her in the creek to clean her off. She and the child as well."

"She had a pack? Not too heavy? Over her shoulder?"

"Yes. With a burden basket inside. She told Pale Snake he could have it . . . and a copper plate, yes, that was it. A copper plate when he reached the Acorn holdings."

"Upriver."

"That's right. But it wasn't Star Shell. It was Yellow Snail. And . . . I remember! The girl was Little Salamander!"

Robin remained squatted with his arms braced on his thick thighs. "You're sure it was Acorn clan territory that she said she was headed to?"

"Positive."

"Northward."

"That's right."

"She didn't mention the Roaring Water?"

"No, I'd have . . . Wait. Yes, there at the very first. I think she did. But Pale Snake told her he would take her to Acorn territory.''

''She didn't mention taking the Mask someplace?''

''No.''

''Did she appear desperate that this Pale Snake take her? Look nervous?''

''A bit . . . at first. Then when she drew him to the side, she talked with him in a real low voice. She seemed, well, confident, if you understand. Like a woman who knows very well what she's about. I assumed, naturally enough, that she promised to warm his bed in exchange for carrying her and the girl north.''

''Yes, I suppose you would.'' Robin stood effortlessly. ''How long ago did they leave?''

''At mid-morning . . . yesterday.''

''Thank you, Stone Wrist. A blessing to you and your ancestors.'' And Robin loped off, not rushing like his namesake, but with the grace of a cougar stalking a wounded deer.

Star Shell paused as she followed Pale Snake and the porters he'd engaged to help them portage over the divide. She looked back down the trail toward the Red Feather clan grounds on the flat terrace next to the winding, tree-lined head of the Upper Moonshell. There a large, circular earthen enclosure had been attached to a huge square—the joining of High Head and Flat Pipe symbols. Two squat mounds rose within the clan grounds. Beside them stood four oblong charnel houses. Bark-roofed society houses clustered around the peripheries. Smoke twined up to the cloudy morning skies in sinuous blue columns.

Irregular fields had been chopped from the forest, and faint lines of green stippled the rich earth where goosefoot, sunflowers, and squash sprouted. Men and women were already at work in them, bending down, plucking weeds and unwelcome sprigs of grass or newly sprouted trees.

The trail Star Shell now followed would cross the low saddle in the humped hills to the head of the Spirit Frog River. They had traveled as far as they could on the Upper Moonshell. Her once familiar river had now become little more than a twisting creek—narrow to the point that in some places, the brush and branches had to be chopped away to keep the channel clear enough for canoes to pass.

At Red Feather, they'd Traded the canoe to a friend of Pale Snake's. One of the lineages who lived at Red Feather Traded in nothing but canoes, supplying the Trade. In exchange for shell beads, the young men of another lineage had agreed to carry the packs across the divide to the Wind clan territories, where Pale Snake would engage yet another canoe.

"They shuttle these canoes back and forth?" Star Shell asked as she turned and followed the Trader. Ahead of her, the young men marched at a brisk pace. The trail they followed was a deep rut beaten into the brown earth. A lot of feet had tramped this path.

"Trade is difficult between the lakes," Pale Snake told her as he led the way. "From the Serpent Clans to Upper Lake, there's no passage for a canoe. The same between Upper Lake and Lake of the Winds—unless, of course, you want to try to paddle over the Roaring Water. In the event that you do, I would imagine the thrill would be the cap of a lifetime—but too short-lived for most people's tastes. The big problem, of course, is what you'd encounter at the bottom, down in all of that crashing spray. The legends say that only the most Powerful Dreamers have ever gone over the falls and lived."

She ignored him, trying to get back to the point. Were she to return this way, she might need this information. "Then a good Trade in canoes does exist?"

"It does. It's the same big family, actually—the Bear lineage. They have holdings at Red Feather, Wind, and Bear clan grounds. They make canoes just for the Trade. Like so many, they've specialized as more Trade develops. When we reach the Wind Clan, we'll dicker with a fellow I know—a member of the Bear lineage—for another canoe. He'll get a carved pipe, and when we reach Bear clan holdings, we'll leave the canoe with my friend's cousin. For another pipe, we'll hire men to help carry our goods around the Roaring Water. And there, finally, we'll find my canoe where I cached it on Wind Lake. Then it's just a long paddle home."

"Wrong. That's where *you* will find *your* canoe for the long paddle home." She glanced back to ensure that Silver Water followed behind her. Her daughter had plucked a blade of grass and was flicking it back and forth. "How did you end up clear on the north side of Wind Lake?"

"It's as far as I could get from my father and still be among people I understood. I didn't even really want to make the journey back to the Serpent Clans—but I share the duty with a friend of mine. He's married to Stone Wrist's sister, so it works out well. I do all of my Trading at Buckeye—and have a place to stay. Stone Wrist is a reasonable sort, even if he's fat and lazy and lecherous."

"What do you do way up there in the north?"

"We farm, harvest wild rice, hunt, fish, trap, and Trade with the Caribou people, who come down from even farther north."

"The Caribou people?" She glanced up at his broad shoulders and noted the easy grace of his walk. She tried not to think of his slim waist or the rounded curves of his muscular back.

"Migrating hunters who follow the herds. Nomads, mostly. They live in skin huts that they pack on their backs, or on their dogs. They make beautiful carvings of ivory and bone, and sometimes they skewer their noses."

"And you can marry their women for a copper ring?"

"Your ears are too sharp for your own good. Actually, I made that up. If Stone Wrist knew the truth about them, he'd be insufferable with his questions about their sexual practices. You don't need a copper ring. Depending upon the clan and lineage, a man will offer you his wife as a matter of hospitality."

"How charming." Was this another joke . . . or an attempt to goad her?

"Not at all. They are a very practical people. Neither husband nor wife is interested in being charming. They want the seed. Like I said, it depends upon the clan and lineage."

"The seed? To make a child?"

"That is the desired outcome."

Star Shell winced. "It sounds very . . . well, different."

"Oh, I don't think so. Conceiving a child generally means that a man couples with a woman, no matter what people they're part of. At least I've never heard of conceiving a child without the seed being planted inside the—"

"Do you always deliberately misunderstand what someone means?"

He chuckled, stepping high over a root as they entered the shadows of the trees. "Not always, but I've worked very hard to become as irreverent as I can."

"Why? You don't need to be so flippant. It . . . it doesn't become you."

"I become anything I want—from owls to snails."

She could see the sparkle in his eye when he glanced back. "Can't you ever be serious?"

"I can. You've even seen me being serious. But I don't like being that way."

"Anything to be different from your father?"

"Absolutely." He ducked under a thick, wild grapevine. "You see, once upon a time I was the most serious man alive. It cost me my wife, my family, and my soul. The night I killed her, I fled my home like a slinking wolf and ran away into the darkness, pursued by every demon a man can conjure: guilt, rage, sorrow, vengeance, and terror. I had no idea of where I was going, or of how I was going to get there. On the shores of Upper Lake, I stole a canoe—almost went over this Roaring Water that you're so interested in.

"One day I heard about a clan holding, a tiny place, freshly built on a little lake lush in wild rice. I went there, and they took me in, asking few questions beyond whether I could fight and work. After almost a year, I laughed again, and on that day, I resolved that I would laugh forever."

Star Shell stepped over a rotting log covered with moss and toadstools. She couldn't help but admire the crimson moccasins he'd given her. "And you found yourself another woman?"

He walked in silence, his head down despite the green grandeur of the leafy canopy overhead. She thought he'd ignored her question until he said, "I loved once, Star Shell. I opened my soul as wide as I could, and she ripped me apart as a cougar does a fawn. Never again."

She resettled the Mask pack on her back. "You father's dead now. You could go back."

"I don't think you understand. There's no going back. There never was."

She thought of her father, of his eyes that last day as they stood there in the rain. Of Stargazer, seeking to restore the past.

Of herself in Greets the Sun's little valley. Of Clamshell watching the embers to see the past.

"What was your mother's clan, Pale Snake?"

"Many Paints. Why?"

How many children did Tall Man leave behind? One from Clamshell, at least. Did he leave one with every clan—just for good measure?

He said, "You're not thinking of eligibility, are you? If so, get it out of your head. I'm not interested in you. You keep too many questionable friends and acquaintances."

"Don't flatter yourself. I imagine I'd find a Caribou man more attractive than you."

"Some aren't too bad. But I'll warn you now, they don't bathe with the regularity expected by our people. Then again, given the way you looked when you appeared at Buckeye, that may not be of much concern to you."

Star Shell groped for a response and finding none, scooped up one of last year's walnuts. With a well-aimed pitch, she hit him with it—square in the back of the head.

Hello, Trader!" The call carried across the water.

Otter squinted against the light, and Black Skull rose to look, standing braced in *Wave Dancer*'s rocking bow.

"What now?" Pearl asked, sitting up in her blankets. She shielded her eyes against the glare of sunlight on the sparkling water.

"A canoe." Otter pointed shoreward. They were well out from land, far enough to maintain sight but not readily visible.

"Friendly or hostile?" she wondered.

"Hostile!" Green Spider blurted. "Going to kill us and pull Catcher's tongue out of his head so he won't lick me anymore."

Catcher wagged his tail as though he'd heard, then leaped on Green Spider with his long pink tongue extended, trying to reach the Contrary's nose. Green Spider threw up one arm and screeched in mock terror. The canoe rocked as they wrestled.

Otter scanned the waters, then the beach, seeking smoke or

signs of a settlement, straining to see against the slanting afternoon sun. "I don't see any others."

Pearl stretched and began hunting around for her atlatl. "That last canoe-load of Traders saved us having to paddle around that inlet. Maybe we've stumbled on more Traders."

"Let's hope so. Or at least, friendly people." From what the Traders had told them, four days of hard paddling would bring them to the southern shore of the Fresh Water Sea. There a narrow inlet would carry them into a river that flowed southward into a small lake—"small" being relative to these people, Otter had discovered. When the river emptied into the lake, they should paddle straight west, pick up the shoreline there and follow it south until yet another outlet carried them into yet another channel. Through that, they would be in what was called the Upper Sea.

Otter stood to inspect the approaching canoe. Three paddlers, each looking young, propelled the crudely hollowed-out log in their direction. A mound of netting filled the front of the unwieldy boat.

Otter cupped his mouth, shouting, "Greetings! Where are we?"

"Not far!" The tallest of them rose to his knees. At least they spoke Trade pidgin.

Otter frowned. "Not far from where?"

"From Wenshare . . . Shinbone's village!"

They were closer now, and Otter could make out three friendly faces. The speaker was a young man of about twenty summers. A younger boy and a young woman sat behind him. All three were naked, grinning, and more than happy to have found them.

"What can you tell me about Shinbone's village?" Otter gave them his winning smile. He saw the youths get their first good look at Black Skull. The smiles faded.

"Oh, don't mind him!" Otter made a throwaway gesture. "He looks that way because we test tool stone on him. We hit him in the head with greenstone and basalt mauls. If the stone breaks, we don't Trade it!"

"Oh, yes he does Trade it! And at the first opportunity— usually to the blind or enfeebled," Black Skull corrected. "You watch him carefully. If you want to know the good stone from the bad, ask me. As he says, I am clearly the expert.''

The smiles had grown wide again. ''You would come to Shin-bone's village and Trade?''

Otter perched himself on the gunwale. ''That depends. Where is it? We're heading for a river that empties from the Fresh Water Sea. We've been told that it's down south near here, along this shoreline.''

The elder youth smacked his paddle against the side of his canoe. ''We have our village just a short way down the channel . . . on the east side. You have reached the Spotted Loon lands. Follow us. We'll show you.'' Then he grinned. ''For Trade, right?''

''Right. But . . . up north, we were chased.''

''Yes, we know. Wild land people. They're not like us. We are Shinbone's people. You are safe here. We like Traders. Make a Trader mad and he won't come back, right?''

''Right!''

''Follow!'' And they dug in with their paddles, turning the awkward dugout.

''I think we're all right,'' Pearl said as she located her paddle. ''Trout mentioned the Spotted Loon people. He said we'd be safe when we reached their lands.''

''Shinbone?'' Otter rubbed his cheek. ''And he's down our river?''

''Maybe,'' Black Skull mused, ''we're back among normal people. Shall we see what the night brings, Trader?''

''Wretched night!'' Green Spider declared. ''Gutted and splayed, our flesh rotting in the sun. Look at us . . . bones all broken. All that pain—and me, starving to death, stuck to the floor.''

''Stuck to the floor?'' Black Skull wondered. ''By what? You're not planning on making somebody so crazy he'll drive a dart through you when you're asleep, are you?''

Green Spider nodded vigorously, his eyes wide and serious.

Pearl glanced back, winking at Otter. ''Well, if it gets rough, Black Skull can just kill a few people and bail us out again.'' She arched her back. ''I'm ready for another night on shore . . . where the ground is flat and nothing moves.''

''Thought you liked deep water,'' Otter goaded.

''I'd like hot stew, too. And maybe a thick roll of backstrap freshly cut from a deer and roasted down deep in the coals until the meat can be picked apart with the fingers.''

"All right. Enough," Otter groaned. "Let's paddle."

The youths in the lead canoe paddled with happy abandon, fighting their stubby craft through the water, periodically calling back encouragement.

When Otter shaded his eyes, he could see a shoreline rising out of the water ahead of them. What began as a broad, tree-lined inlet narrowed to a sluggish river, pulling them onward.

"Now this," Black Skull declared, "is more like it."

In places, the forest ran right to the water's edge, then gave way to stretches of sand and occasional marsh. Lines of crooked sticks protruding from the clear water marked the location of weirs and fish traps. Here and there, floats indicated nets or trotlines.

"Starting to look inhabited," Otter stated.

"How beautiful and peaceful," Pearl whispered happily as they coasted through the trees mirrored in the tranquil water. After endless waves, the lush river came as a relief. Catcher stood on the packs, his tail waving back and forth as he sniffed the fragrant air. Birdsong created a symphony in the verdant maple, oak, hickory, and beech that rose in high splendor.

The sun had disappeared behind the trees, leaving them in shadow, when their youthful escort cut left, following a lazy stream. Here a marker consisting of several planks tied together had been placed on the bank. The painted yellow surface bore a blue squint-eyed face with a protruding tongue.

Otter used his paddle to guide *Wave Dancer* into the narrow stream. People shouted from back in the forest, and the youths answered. Otter could smell wood smoke and the characteristic odor of a village. The locals appeared from among the shadowed boles, running down to stare and wave.

Men wore hide breechcloths with wide flaps that hung down to their knees in front and back. Each was decorated with a design: a bird, bear, or other emblem. The women were bare-chested but wore skirts that ended just below the knee. One or two carried infants under one arm, while children and dogs materialized as if magically from the forest depths.

They landed their canoes at a place where the bank had collapsed.

Canoe-building, Otter discovered as they beached, was not a high art here. Generally, the Spotted Loon people hacked down a tree, peeled the bark away and hollowed out the trunk by means of fire, adze, and gouge—but without the finesse he was accustomed to. Some crude chopping was done to create a bow of sorts, but little else.

"Trade, right?" Otter called, and after helping to pull *Wave Dancer* up on the beach, he gave each of his grinning guides a couple of sharks' teeth. Instead of the usual response, he received blank stares as they turned them over and over, perplexed.

"Sharks' teeth," Otter repeated.

"Don't know." The elder youth ran his thumb along the sharp, serrated edge of the triangular tooth.

"From big fish in the Salt Water Sea."

"For jewelry," Pearl stated as she stepped up beside Otter. "Drill holes and make a necklace. Like a gorget. No one else will have one—and not from so far away." She took the young woman's hands, guiding them up so that she could model a hanging ornament between her round young breasts.

Then the smiles grew. People began crowding around them, chattering and gesturing. Catcher, back on full-time guard duty, snarled and barked as he walked back and forth on the packs that bulged within *Wave Dancer*'s canted hull.

People gave way for an old man, gray of hair and white in one eye, as he strode forward imperiously. His bony fist clutched a long wooden staff that swung with each pace, the end tapping the ground. His breechcloth bore the image of a ferocious bear, long-toothed, with widespread claws. Wrinkled skin hung from the Elder's visible ribs, and his belly was rounded, the navel sticking out like a walnut on a river rock.

He stopped, studying the landing with his one good eye. "Greetings, Traders. I am Shinbone. Welcome to Wenshare village."

"Wenshare?" Otter asked, stepping forward and bowing politely. "We do not know that word, respected leader."

The chief cataloged Otter and his companions, then took in *Wave Dancer* and the snarling Catcher. He spoke one word—an order—and people retreated, calling and cuffing their dogs back. The Elder then stated, "In Trade tongue, it means 'the place where the big nuts fall.' Have you come from far away?''

"I am known as the Water Fox, a man of the White Shell Clan. This big man is Black Skull, of the Winter Clan of the City of the Dead. This woman is Pearl, of the Anhinga people. Finally, this is Green Spider, a Contrary. Yes, we have come from far away. Some of us have come from the shores of the Salt Water Sea, many moons' travel to the distant south.''

Shinbone frowned at that. "I know of no Salt Water Sea to the south. I have heard of the one to the east . . . beyond the mouth of Wind Lake.''

Otter pointed to the southwest, his arm making an arc as he talked. "We came up the Father Water . . . the great river. Then we made passage up the Ilini River to the Fresh Water Sea on the other side of the land to the west. We paddled all the way around and had to outrun some of the wild people. The Badger people, we think.''

Shinbone nodded thoughtfully. "Ah . . . you have come from far. I have heard stories of the passage to the Father Water in the western land of the Ilini. Traders have told me.''

Shinbone turned his attention to *Wave Dancer*, stepping down to touch the carved fox's nose. Catcher growled a dire warning, lips curling on his long muzzle. "But I have never seen a canoe such as this." He looked at Black Skull, who stood with his club neutrally balanced on his shoulder. "Or a man such as this. A warrior, yes?''

"A Trader," Black Skull replied easily, "who was once a warrior.''

Shinbone smiled, making a motion with his hand. "Come, Traders. I declare you my guests. Upon my word, your packs and goods shall be safe. Join me and my band of the Spotted Loon people. Trade with us, and tell us of your adventures.''

Amidst the chattering of excited people, Otter took Pearl's hand and led the way forward—but for Green Spider, of course, who followed backwards. Shinbone's people pointed, exclaiming to themselves, obviously curious, some even worried.

"Don't be afraid of him," Black Skull said. "He's just demented.''

Those who understood Trade pigeon nodded, more out of politeness than belief, since a glance told them that they reserved the right to be suspicious of anything a man that ugly might tell them.

A winding path carried them a dart's throw from the river to a village on a rounded hillock. There longhouses, twenty to thirty paces in length, stood, looking uniformly new—last fall's construction at most. Tall and arched, they had been sided with strips of bark lashed to a substantial framework of logs and poles.

Shinbone led them to an open plaza in the middle of the houses, where a fire pit smoldered in the twilight. At a clap of his hands, youngsters scurried away to return with firewood that was then unceremoniously dumped into the big hearth. Shinbone motioned everyone to sit, and a gray-haired woman bearing a pipe bag emerged from the mouth of one of the houses. She wore a white-leather skirt and walked with a limp, but despite the ravages of time and weather, the sparks of intelligence and beauty remained. She offered the pipe bag to Shinbone and nodded at Otter's party.

Shinbone produced a beautiful stone pipe carved in the shape of a loon, the bowl in the bird's back and the mouthpiece in the tip of the tail feathers.

Otter offered tobacco, which Shinbone gracefully accepted. The Elder packed his pipe, used an ember to light it with, and puffed, blowing the smoke to the four sacred directions, to the sky, and to the earth.

"Let it be known that Shinbone and his village open their hearts and their homes to these Traders from far away. Let us act in peace, in harmony, and in honor. Great Father Sun, bless us with health and wisdom. Mother Earth, may the deer continue to offer his flesh and soul that we may grow strong. May the fish continue to fill our nets that we may live long. May the nuts fall thick in the fall that we may stay fat through the winter. May the ducks and geese give themselves that our souls may fly. For all these things, we thank the Spirit World and First Man. We ask now that these new friends share our hearts and our fire, and that we all honor the Spirits of the land."

The old woman took the pipe from his hands, inhaling and then stating: "I am Tall Fisher, wife to the great Shinbone. I call out to my people to make food and warm tea that my guests may eat and refresh themselves. To you, honored guests, I bid welcome to my home and fire.''

Otter took the pipe and drew before exhaling the sweet tobacco smoke to the sacred directions. ''We echo the hopes and prayers of our brave and wise host, Shinbone. And thank the venerable Tall Fisher for her welcome. We are strangers to this land, and unfamiliar with its Spirits and ways, but in our land, we always ask the blessing of Many Colored Crow and First Man. So do we now. We ask them to bless Shinbone's village with health and prosperity, that their hunts be successful, their nets always full, and that the nut harvest fill all of their baskets.''

He handed the pipe to Pearl, who lifted it to her lips and inhaled.

''What about asking the blessings of the ghosts?'' Black Skull asked softly in their own tongue.

''Don't mention ghosts until you know what the people believe,'' Otter muttered back. ''Some peoples are scared to death of ghosts.''

''How anyone could be frightened of their ancestors mystifies me.'' Black Skull took the pipe and smoked before handing it to Green Spider.

''We have heard of Many Colored Crow, and we—'' Shinbone stopped suddenly when Green Spider blew into the pipe instead of inhaling. Glowing embers and dottle flew everywhere, drifting down over Green Spider's thin, smiling face. ''He *is* a Contrary!''

''You have no idea.'' Black Skull batted at a glowing ember that had landed on his shirt and burned a hole in the fabric.

Shinbone cleared his throat, nervous eyes on Green Spider. ''As I was saying, we have heard of Many Colored Crow, and respect his message and the peoples who live as he taught them. We are bounded upon the west by such people, and upon the south and east as well. We Spotted Loon people, however, have our own ways. The Sky Mother gave us this rich land full of fish, turtles, shellfish, birds, nuts, berries, and game. I think each people must listen to the Spirits of the land and the teachings of the heart.''

''We agree with your words of wisdom, great Shinbone,'' Otter said warmly. ''As strangers to your customs, please inform us if we should happen to offend your ways.''

Shinbone's eyes twinkled as he looked at the Contrary. "We will make special exception for you, Water Fox."

Evening had settled; the birds of day grew silent as the crickets and creatures of the night began to stir. The fire popped and shot sparks to twirl into the cool air. Otter relaxed and took Pearl's hand. The aroma of food in preparation caused his stomach to gurgle in anticipation.

"And what of your journey?" Shinbone asked. "Please tell us."

Otter stood then, so that all of the people could see him in the firelight. Drawing on his talents, he related the story of Green Spider's Vision of the Mask, the long moons on the river, the race with the Khota, and the storm on the lake. He told of meeting Trout, and of the passage above the peninsula where the wild people chased them, of Pearl's wind trap, and of the long voyage south.

"And now we are here, willing to Trade with Shinbone and his people, and curious about the way that lies before us."

Old Tall Fisher nodded, glancing at her husband and then speaking. "We have heard of this Mask. Several Traders have passed during the last moon. They talk of trouble among the Serpent Clans. It is said that one Star Shell, a woman of the StarSky Clan, and a High Head dwarf, a magician known as Tall Man, have taken the Mask and vanished. The Blue Duck Clan covets the Mask and will do anything for it—even start wars."

"At the mouth of the Serpent River, we heard that war was coming," Otter said. "Has this happened?"

Tall Fisher rubbed her bony hands back and forth. "We cannot tell you, Water Fox. We live a long way from the Serpent Clans. News takes a moon or so to reach us. We have not heard of serious fighting, but tensions are still high."

"A woman named Star Shell," Black Skull murmured to himself.

"What of this dwarf?" Otter leaned forward, his chin on his hand. "The High Head respect dwarfs a great deal."

"Tall Man, the High Head Elder." Shinbone's white eye gleamed in the firelight. "He is considered to be very Powerful. Among the Serpent Clans, he is known as the Magician."

Tall Fisher was watching Green Spider play peek-a-boo with

several of the little children who had wiggled their way through the ranks of adults ringing the fire. Now she said thoughtfully, "Star Shell and the Magician have taken the Mask . . . and the Water Fox comes from the south with Green Spider, a Contrary, to take the Mask back? And you say you are to go to the Roaring Water?"

Otter nodded, suddenly uneasy. Pearl squeezed his hand hard in warning, but he wasn't certain of what. "That was Green Spider's Vision from Many Colored Crow."

"Not me!" Green Spider closed his eyes tight and proceeded to feel of everything within his grasp—a rock, a giggling child's moccasin, a woman's calf. He spent a little too much time there; the woman jerked away. "I never see anything! I just run into trees and fall over roots and bump into things all the time. Look at how bright it is in here!"

Black Skull asked, "And what of the way we must go? South, into the Upper Sea?"

"That's right," Shinbone told them. "Follow the river and you'll find yourself in a large lake. On the southwest side is another river like the one you took to get here. That will carry you south, right into Upper Lake. From there, your way lies to the east. A great many rivers run into Upper Lake, but only one river drains out of it, on the far eastern shore. There, on that river, you will find the Roaring Water. Don't get caught in the rapids, however . . . you might go over the Roaring Water, and it's said to be a long way down."

"This Mask." Tall Fisher pressed her palms together and placed her fingertips under her chin. "Are you sure it's such a good idea to rescue it? It is said that Star Shell's husband, Mica Bird, committed suicide over this Mask. We were told that Sun Mounds burned the clan house with his ghost trapped inside, and that they are going to cover it with earth at the solstice. We have heard of nothing but heartbreak, war, and trouble when the Mask is mentioned."

Green Spider stood then, stepping close to the fire to look down into the flames. His voice came out hushed and somber. *"This is the way, man of the people. I show you the way to salvation."*

"What?" Black Skull asked as he shot a glance at Green Spider.

The Contrary turned, his vacant gaze chasing around Black Skull's face like a mouse in the daylight. "Wolf, of course. He chewed on Flies Like A Seagull's body. He was darted and eaten for that. I wouldn't chew on the old woman's body myself. Someone might shoot me—and it would be a terrible thing to have the blood drunk out of your heart and then have it eaten."

"What's he saying?" Shinbone asked.

Anxious conversations broke out among the gathered people.

Black Skull made a nervous gesture. "His babbling always means something to someone, but it's rarely clear what or who. Don't worry. After he's been around for a while, you'll realize that he's an idiot. After he's been around for a while longer, you'll realize that you're more of an idiot than he is. It's a puzzling experience."

"Do his words have something to do with the Mask?" Tall Fisher asked as she watched the Contrary pensively.

"I don't know." Black Skull rubbed his broken jaw. "Trader? What do you think?"

Otter raised his hands. "I'm not sure."

At that moment, Green Spider clapped his hands and began whirling around. With outstretched arms, he Sang:

> "You. Born of Father Sun.
> Laid in the light next to night.
> Choose, my people.
> Dance the Father you don't know.
> South, ever south we go . . .
> Arise, people of the Spotted Loon!
> Dance! Dance with the Contrary!"

Green Spider continued to Sing as he whirled around the edge of the fire. His face was beatific, a radiance shining out into the evening, touching and warming everyone in sight.

"Come on!" he cried. "Get up! All of you! Get up! Dance with me! Sing! Power moves the earth! Wolf and Crow twist and circle!"

Green Spider reached down and pulled up the young woman who'd been in the canoe. As he taught her the steps, her friends rose to join in.

Pearl leaned over to whisper to Otter, "Green Spider said that forward. He must be seriously worried about Tall Fisher's talk of the Mask.''

''It does seem that way.'' Otter watched warily. Green Spider Danced and Sang as never before. Distracting them all? For what purpose? Wouldn't everyone benefit from hearing more about the Mask?

Pearl gripped Otter's hand and tugged on it. ''Come on. There's probably something sacred about this Dance anyway. Let's do it.''

She laughed at the look on his face as he stood, and they began to imitate Green Spider's shuffle, hop, shuffle, hop, step.

Tall Fisher ceremoniously stood, helping her husband rise, and when he, too, took the step, following the circle to the left around the fire, the rest of the people joined in. They learned the Song, and voices rose and fell with the chant. Dust kicked up from bare feet, and the fire seemed to burn with a greater intensity as shadows wavered blackly on the house walls surrounding them.

Black Skull sat quietly, his heavy war club in hand as he watched the people passing around him. Only when a brave young girl tugged him to his feet did he, too, join the Dance.

Otter Sang, holding Pearl's hand, enjoying the moment. Nevertheless, he continued to watch the Contrary's face.

What does he know? One thing was certain. Pearl was right. Green Spider hadn't wanted Tall Fisher to talk about the trouble the Mask was causing. That was particularly perplexing. *Does Green Spider fear that such information would make us abandon our quest to save the Mask?* And who was this Star Shell? A woman of the StarSky Clans?

His thoughts vanished when Pearl put her arm around his waist and forced him to match steps with her. Apparently, he'd lost the rhythm.

Green Spider is hiding something. And a High Head dwarf, a very Powerful and feared man, is involved. Why? To counter the Power of the Contrary?

Power had chosen its champions, was that it?

Blessed Mysterious One, why hadn't Green Spider told them? Had the skinny little Contrary known all along that going after the Mask would thrust them into the midst of a StarSky clan war?

Otter gazed across the circle at Black Skull, Dancing in the company of two smiling young women. The warrior looked happy, truly happy, for the first time.

Then Otter's gaze met Green Spider's.

And fear filled Otter's breast. Those usually joyous brown eyes, untouched by anything in this world, brimmed with tears. They traced lines through the dust on Green Spider's cheeks. . . .

Forty-three

Black Skull allowed himself to flow with the Song, his feet rising and falling to the Contrary's lead. Not since he was a child had he Danced like this. And even now, he held tight to his war club, ever a partner in a different kind of Dance.

The spreading warmth in his chest caught him by surprise, and he grew light. He could imagine himself floating on the rhythmic chant of the people, all Singing in their own language, the words as close as they could come to the Contrary's Trade pidgin. The words themselves didn't matter. Green Spider had touched their souls—and that shared awareness had become a spirit with a Power all its own. The harmony and step flowed over and through them, becoming one with the night, one with Black Skull.

How long did they Dance? Circling around and around the fire, faces caught the yellow light, white teeth flashed in ecstatic smiles, gleaming black hair swung with the gyrations of bodies and the clapping of hands.

Black Skull didn't care. Set free for the first time in more years than he could remember, he Danced and Danced until his legs ached and trembled. Only then did he realize that most of the older people had stopped and that he alone remained in the circle with the young. The problem with the youngsters, he reminded himself, was that they could always replenish their resources.

Black Skull continued to Dance anyway, holding on to the wondrous sense of freedom and life that flowed in his veins, until at last he drifted to the edge of the circle and sank down beside Green Spider and Shinbone. He gasped happily, wiping at the sweat that ran down his scarred body. Green Spider, too, he noticed, had been sweating profusely. Beads of moisture clung to his eyelashes.

A bowl of food was thrust into Black Skull's hands, and he plucked up bits of fish and meat with gusto. A gourd of water came his way, and he drank with complete satisfaction.

"You do make a man welcome," he told Shinbone.

The one-eyed chief nodded, a thin smile on his lips. "I think, rather, that you carry enjoyment with your Contrary." Shinbone looked back at the shining bodies of the Dancers. "Look at them, smiling, laughing. The solstice is little more than a moon away. No one is getting married at any time soon. This unexpected celebration is a welcome pleasure for them."

Black Skull ate the last piece of fish from his bowl, which magically seemed to be refilled. Green Spider still Sang, clapping his hands as he watched the Dancers with sparkling eyes.

"This Star Shell," Black Skull asked, turning to Tall Fisher. "She's known as an evil woman?"

The old woman sighed and plucked at one of the wattles on her neck. "I'm not sure what to tell you, Trader. We'd barely heard of her until all this trouble with the Mask began. According to the stories, Star Shell is a beautiful young woman of the StarSky Clans. She married a man of the Sun Mounds, this Mica Bird . . . and it was he who used the Mask to terrorize the clans. In the end, he hung himself. Sun Mounds burned the clan house where he died and then placed posts up as wards to keep the angry ghost hidden deep within. Star Shell fled with the Mask . . . and in the company of the Magician. She's being pursued by Robin, a war leader of the Blue Duck Clan."

"And what do you know of him?" Black Skull finished yet another serving of meat and fish, aware that a lovely young woman was ladling more into his bowl. When he smiled, she gasped—and only then did he remember what he looked like when he smiled. Instead, he winked, and she shot him an embarrassed grin before handing him the water gourd again.

Shinbone spoke. "Robin is an ambitious and respected man. I have met him before. He lives only for the increase of his own authority and influence. I think he hopes to become one of the most Powerful men among the Serpent Clans." Bitterness twisted the chief's lips. "I do not think he cares how he gets to this end, either. He has quite a collection of skulls, all polished and painted, on the walls of his society house."

"And Tall Man?" Black Skull asked. "This Magician?"

Green Spider stopped Singing in mid-sentence and turned to Black Skull. "He's dead. Robin slit him open like a fish and roasted his guts. Pop and sizzle, sizzle and pop." He shook his head morosely. "You should hear his ghost plead for forgiveness."

"Dead?" Shinbone asked.

"Or alive?" Black Skull asked. "Are you talking forward or backward, fool?"

Green Spider grinned and reached up, trying to wiggle a finger into Black Skull's flaring nostril. The warrior pinned him in place with an armlock. Green Spider, unfazed, told him, "As I speak, a warrior carries the Magician's skull south to rest on the wall of Blue Duck clan's Warrior Society house. Pity the Magician's ghost. No place to go. Hounded, chased, even as pretty Star Shell is chased by Robin."

Black Skull let him loose, frowning.

"Contrary, how do you know this?" Shinbone asked as he took his wife's hand. They seemed to share the sudden tension.

Green Spider bowed his head and let out a weary breath. "Fear not, great Shinbone. You and your people are safe. Tomorrow we will be gone and you will have fine goods and memories of our stay. Tonight is important only for us. Here in your village, we will each find our way."

"And what way will I find, fool?" Black Skull asked.

"A way," Green Spider whispered. "That's all I know."

The Contrary drew a circle in the dirt, and beside it, a spiral with little points jutting off from the last whorl. He stood, throwing back his head. From his lips burst a perfect howl, that of a lonely old wolf abandoned by its pack.

Surprised, the Dancers stopped to stare.

In the awkward silence, an answering wolf's howl echoed

through the trees. Green Spider grinned and clapped his hands, shouting, "Dance! *Dance!* Lift your souls and hearts to the beat of your hands and feet!"

The Dance started again, right where it had paused, and people laughed as Green Spider Danced backward through the crowd, making four circles—only to disappear between the houses.

"He is a frightening man," Shinbone observed. "You have had a most interesting time with him, I would say."

"Indeed," Black Skull said, staring at the drawing the fool had made. The circle was the people's sign for a star—the spiral with the outer spikes, the design of a conch. Black Skull could read it with crystal clarity.

Star Shell. The woman fleeing with the Mask. But why would that matter to Black Skull?

Pearl danced in the radiance of the smiles that Otter cast in her direction. After days within *Wave Dancer* 's confines, the ability to move, to feel her soul Dancing, sent a burst of sheer bliss to charge her muscles. She clasped Otter's hand, unaware of anything except him and the graceful steps that they shared—a blending of souls and Songs and weaving bodies.

When she finally tugged him out of the circle, it was to drop, panting and exhausted, among some of the Spotted Loon people. These were Elders, smiling, offering bowls of food. Pearl dipped up sweet pounded nuts and, yes, even a roasted chunk of meat was handed to her.

"You got your prize!" Otter cried, the smile still living on his lips.

She savored the juicy meat, and admired him. The strong lines of his face had softened in the firelight. His straight nose and strong brow had flushed with the exertion of the Dance. His head still bobbed in time with the people who shuffled and hopped past them.

"Quite a night," Otter said happily, his hands tracing down her arms as he pulled her close. "The Contrary did this, turned it into a celebration."

Pearl swallowed the last of the meat and licked her fingers. "Better that than allowing Tall Fisher to talk about the Mask."

"He did that rather well, didn't he? Maybe I should have let Black Skull pull his arms and legs off back there on the river. He might have told us more about this insane venture."

Pearl settled back against Otter, feeling the warmth of him penetrating her shirt. Otter's expression had gone grim.

She jabbed an elbow into his ribs. "Stop thinking like that. Whatever it is that Green Spider didn't want us to hear tonight, he'll tell us when the time is right. He doesn't have a conniving bone in his body. You know that."

"Yes. That I know."

Pearl closed her eyes, enjoying the feel of Otter's arms around her. Nearby, a girl giggled and a young man laughed. Youth was meant for young lovers.

She freed herself from Otter's arms and pulled him up, saying, "Come on. Walk with me."

She held his hand as she led him past the houses and down into the shadowed darkness of the trees.

"Where are we going?" he asked.

"How should I know? I've never been here before. Are you coming, or do I go alone?"

"I'm coming." And his arm went around her shoulder. They matched step as they followed the dark scar of a path that wound along the forest floor.

"Otter, when this is over, I think I want to go south again."

He walked quietly and then said, "All right. We might even be able to beat the weather. Downriver is always faster than up." A pause. "Where would we go?"

She shrugged under his arm. "Somewhere with a swamp, some alligators, a little hanging moss, and warm winter evenings."

"Alligator Clan? Or is that too close to the Anhinga?"

She sighed. "It's always going to be difficult, isn't it?"

"It usually looks more difficult from afar than close up."

They broke out of the trees and onto another of the rounded knolls. The whole country seemed to be made of rolling hills. Fire had cleared this one—perhaps a fire from a lightning strike, since the rise appeared taller than the others. From the height, they could survey most of the surrounding country in the slanted light of the crescent moon.

"I hope you're right." She led him to the top of the knoll and stopped to stare southward, following the stars to the place where her home should have been. "I had a wonderful life down there."

"Can I ask . . ." he started uncertainly, " . . . why would they Trade you off like goods?"

"No one wanted me." She pulled him down, snuggling under his arm and hugging him close. "Among the Anhinga, a woman has responsibilities. I turned my back on them."

"You're a beautiful woman. I should have gone after you the first time I saw you."

She reached up to stroke his face. "Your heart was in a different place then. Are you sure you've made peace with that?"

"She's my brother's wife."

"And what am I?"

An owl hooted in the trees, and a faint breeze stirred the leaves.

"The woman I love," he said softly.

She ran her hands along his arm, her fingers tracing the swelling muscles. She could feel him tremble, and that stirred the warmth within her. "I'm afraid we'll be riding out one storm after another, Otter."

"I think I'd like that." Slowly, gently, his hand smoothed her breast. "I don't want to . . . I mean . . ."

"I'm not afraid, Otter."

"That's right, you and Trout . . ."

"No, we didn't. I couldn't, Otter." She smiled up at his shadowed face. "That night I wanted arms around me. The problem was, I wanted *your* arms around me."

"You don't know how close I came to . . . I was storming down the beach, and Green Spider saved me. I'd have made a real fool of myself."

"Why?" She ran her hands up under his shirt and onto the corded muscles of his chest.

"I didn't know how much I loved you until then. I was afraid that Trout—"

"Green Spider was right to have stopped you. I needed that time with Trout."

Her pulse had begun to race, and she worked him out of his shirt. She undid the knot in his belt and pulled back the flap of his breechcloth. "For the longest time, Otter, I wondered if you cared about me."

"Now you know."

She pulled off her shirt and skirt and laid them out behind her, aware of his musky scent as he bent down to take her breast in his mouth.

When he moved up, she held him for a moment, her hands on either side of his head. "I love you, Otter."

"Pearl, I love you with all of my soul. I want you with me forever."

She reached down to guide him to her, and gasped as he slid into her warmth. Then she locked herself around him. "One storm after another, Otter. Remember that I warned you."

Pale Snake pulled at his ear and shook his head in disgust. In the two days since leaving the Wind clan grounds, he'd done everything he could to scourge, beat, and batter Star Shell from his thoughts.

Now, as they paddled down the winding course of Spirit Frog River, he made himself look at the banks, identify the trees, count the number of woodpecker's raps—anything but look forward to where she sat in perfect oblivion.

Giving her that dress had been the worst mistake of his life—well, second worst, after marrying his wife. He should have left Star Shell safely encased in her filthy rags. The soft leather of this new dress had melted onto every curve of her body. As she paddled, that slim waist moved sinuously over those rounded hips and the fullness of her muscular bottom. The bodice had conformed to her full, rounded breasts, which had begun to haunt his imagination. In the sunlight, her hair gleamed bluish, catching each golden ray and intensifying his desire to reach out and run his fingers through that thick wealth.

Instead, he bit his lip and paddled furiously, driving them on down the river.

Silver Water perched on the pack in front of him, not quite

big enough to block his view of her mother—the infuriating object of desires he'd thought long dead.

Bad as it was, life in a canoe with Star Shell was a great deal easier than life in camp with Star Shell. There, he not only had to watch her walk around in that most unsubtle dress, but he had to look into her eyes. They enchanted him . . . large, black, and liquid enough to make his heart swim. He could imagine those rich red lips pressed against his. Her facial features were delicate and perfect. That soft skin—radiant with health and energy—begged to be caressed. On those rare instances when she smiled, his soul ached.

You did this to me, Father! That's why you sent her. You knew—you wretched little demon—that I'd find her irresistible. And even if she did show an interest—which she never would— he couldn't allow himself to touch her for fear that she'd been one of his father's things.

Just then that sensual and melodic voice of hers broke the silence. "You've been quiet, Pale Snake. It's not like you."

"I've been thinking."

"No wonder you've been silent. Thinking must be so novel that you've been awed by the entire process. Tell me, are you considering making it a habit?"

Pale Snake bit his lip harder. *Yes, that's it. Try to hate her. Maybe your testicles will unwind a little.*

At his silence, she turned around, contrition in those luminous eyes. "I'm sorry. That was unkind of me. Please forgive me."

All of his hard work crumbled to dust. He was back to the insufferable misery of desire.

Well, perhaps talking about another man would help. "Tell me about your husband, Star Shell. What was he like before the Mask got to him?"

He could see the tension in her shoulders. "I guess . . . well, I really don't know. I remember him as a serious boy when he first came to StarSky City. My father introduced us, and he spent most of the day just staring at me. At the time, I thought it was idiotic worship in his eyes. Maybe it was then. Later, I learned it was obsession."

Don't I know! "Didn't you like him?"

"Not that first time. The night before he left, he talked me into going out for a walk with him. When we were far enough away, he tried to make me couple with him. I said no, and he pouted. That was when he promised he'd marry me.''

''So you did?''

''The next time I saw him, it was several months after his grandfather had died. He was different, self-confident, a young leader. Father was impressed, and I guess I was, too. It looked like the perfect alliance for my lineage and clan, a marriage to my advantage.''

''And, of course, you stepped into a nest of vipers.''

''Interesting phrase for a Serpent sorcerer to use, don't you think?''

The expected loathing wasn't rising within him. Try again. ''He must have loved you, though. There had to be instances of tenderness between you. You produced a daughter, after all.''

''Tenderness?'' she asked wistfully, and shook her head. It made the tumbled black locks shine bluish as they caught the sun. ''I'm not sure what I felt. Him? Maybe, but I doubt it. There's a difference between making love and the rut. One is intimate, the other is for procreation. Looking back, I'd say that my husband and I started with procreation, and that things went sour from there.''

Pale Snake winced. ''I'm sorry, Star Shell. If I could go back and . . .'' *What are you saying? Shut up!*

''Change things?'' she finished for him. ''You're kind to think of that, Pale Snake. I'm afraid it's too late. What a naive fool I was. StarSky's pampered little darling. I had everything . . . station, family, beauty, and admirers. Once, my friend, I reveled in that admiration. Now I realize it for the curse it was.''

''Curse?''

''What else would you call it? If I hadn't been so desirable, *he* wouldn't have desired me.'' She'd grown accustomed to the paddle now, driving it deeply into the water and pulling it strongly. He caught himself enjoying the way she moved, and he forced his attention to the brown fabric of the pack in front of him.

''But you must have had a lover . . . someone.''

Her laughter carried notes of bitterness. ''All right, Pale Snake, I'll tell you. His name was Greets the Sun, a—''

''Not my demented brother!''

She turned, staring at him, the paddle dragging in the water.

"Your . . . brother?" She blinked. "Wait. You said your clan was the Many Paints."

"That was my mother's clan," he admitted sullenly. "I was raised among the Paints. Greets the Sun was my *half* brother. He lived with a High Head Clan over on the Red Buck."

"Tall Man's . . . son?" Star Shell paled.

"Did you see his mother? If you had, you'd know why Tall Man had to seduce her. She was too much woman for him to pass up. Why do you think they put Greets the Sun way up there in the hills? His very presence was a reminder to everyone in that clan that Tall Man had impregnated a very important man's wife."

"On the way out, Tall Man avoided a farmstead, said the man had a vicious dog."

"I'll bet. More likely it was a studded war club named 'Bad Dog' . . . or maybe 'Killer of Dwarfs.' "

Star Shell half-turned in the canoe, and Pale Snake's heart melted at the fragile look on her too-perfect face. "No matter who Greets the Sun might have been sired by, he was kind. He gave my soul peace. I . . . I would have stayed with him, enjoyed the solitude of his little valley. I would do anything to see him smile again, to share that humble innocence."

"Perhaps I underestimated him. I met him but two or three times. The Magician was looking for yet another son to follow in his footsteps, especially after I disappointed him so completely."

Star Shell glanced up. "In the end, I think he was a trap, Pale Snake. A lure, like a feather on a hook dangled before a bass's mouth. I snapped it up."

"What happened?"

"While I was loving Greets the Sun, the Mask was talking to Silver Water. I had decided to stay with him. But when I saw my daughter talking to the Mask, I knew I had to leave."

Pale Snake ground his teeth, continuing to paddle. "If I'd only known, I'd have come south . . . rescued you from the little demon. I don't know what it was about Tall Man. I've known other dwarfs . . . delightful, normal human beings. They weren't all twisted like he was."

"Pale Snake, please." She'd rested her paddle crossways on the gunwale. "He wasn't all twisted and weird. He knew what to do when my husband hung himself. He saved me a number of times. He wasn't all bad.''

"Name something he did that was unselfishly good.''

She gave him a look of irritation—a look that thoroughly charmed him. "He offered my father a very beautiful stone tablet for my mother's tomb. In doing so, he recalled service that she'd rendered to a High Head Clan once during an illness. At the time, that offering was most important to my father.''

"Let me guess. It was then that he asked permission to accompany you back to Sun Mounds, right?''

Her spirited eyes flashed. "Do you attribute *everything* to a mercenary motive?''

"When he's concerned, yes.''

"He saved my life that first time at the Blue Duck Clan when Robin would have killed me.''

"Of course. You were his escort into Sun Mounds.''

She shook her head in disgust and turned away. "What about yourself, sorcerer? You've heard about me, so what about you? Did you ever love, Pale Snake? Or do you just brag about it with Stone Wrist?''

She'd discovered a subject that could drive his thoughts completely away from the allure of her body. He paddled for a time, aware of the challenging stare she shot over her shoulder.

"Yes, I loved. It was after my father and I had parted company at the Serpent—at the earthwork where the society keeps its grounds and secret artifacts.''

"Viper clan grounds,'' she said.

"Yes, you know of the place then. The final fight we had was rather spectacular. I'd come to know him for what he was, conniving, sneaky, lustful. I went home, having vowed to have nothing to do with him anymore. I moved in with my mother's people, saying little, conducting a Healing now and then. I was young, and Power ran strongly in my blood. The news of my skill and ability began to spread, and people came from all over to see me.''

You don't want to do this. It's just picking a scab off an unhealed wound. But he kept talking, absently aware that he wasn't going to stop.

"The first time I saw her, my heart leaped. She was small, with long black hair that hung like a mantle down past her knees. And when she turned and looked at me, her eyes shone with an impish sparkle. She didn't have your classic beauty, but a more petite charm, as if she were a doll, to be cherished and held.

"I was entranced, totally and helplessly. And she, of course, saw me as a promising young man who could provide her with everything her clan couldn't. She came from down south of the Serpent River, having traveled north with her father to visit relatives—and, of course, to seek a husband. My mother's lineage was important among the Many Paints, and her father saw it as the perfect solution to both his daughter problem—he had seven of them, she the oldest—and a way to align his clan with the Paints."

"Did she love you?" Silver Water asked from where she lay on a pack, watching him, her chin propped on her hands.

"At first maybe. I don't know. I was young, and deadly serious about what I was doing. Mostly, what I was doing was rising in popularity among the Many Paints. I supervised the lineage labor during the building of the outer square of the enclosure."

"To be placed in charge of labor indicates a great deal of respect," Star Shell said. "My father was doing that the last time I saw him."

"Yes, a great deal of respect." Pale Snake remembered the fresh dirt they had piled up, basket-load upon basket-load, along the creek terrace. He'd climbed the ridge to the north with the clan leaders, looking down on the finished work, where the great central mound and the society houses had been laid out in perfect order.

A time to be proud of.

"And then Tall Man came?"

Star Shell's question shook him from his thoughts. "How could he ignore me? My fame and reputation were expanding. The new, young leader among the Many Paints! And I was doing it on my own. Almost in spite of him."

"Why didn't you throw him out when he showed up?"

"When he arrived, I was gone . . . to my wife's clan to perform a Healing. She was pregnant with our first child, and it was my thought that she shouldn't risk traveling. Silly of me now that I think about it, for that was my second mistake."

"And your first?"

"Not telling her about my father and what a slime he was. You see, I thought that such things were between a man and his son and not the business of other people. My mother knew, but since she herself had once fallen prey to him, she didn't like bringing it up and reminding herself. Perhaps I got that trait from her.

"Be that as it may, Tall Man arrived at our farmstead in a driving rain, and my innocent wife took him in. To be sure, he was his charming and delightful self—all the time feeding her teas and herbals, which to this day I credit with causing her miscarriage. He, of course, was there, kind, thoughtful, exploiting the fact that I was far away in her time of need."

"And your mother?" Star Shell asked. She'd picked up her paddle, causing curls to spin backward in the water as she helped to propel them downstream.

"After some days, one of my cousins mentioned that Tall Man was at my farmstead—but since she, too, gave him more credit than he was due, she considered him simply solicitous of my wife's condition."

Pale Snake made himself relax, aware of how hard he had gripped the paddle, his fingers white and bloodless as if he were trying to strangle the wood.

"Sorcerers don't always recognize sorcery. One illness followed another among my wife's people. By the time I returned home, nearly three moons had passed. My wife had miscarried during the first, and for two moons, he had soothed her, wooed her, and perhaps given her one of his charms.

"One of his Spirit Helpers warned him of my coming, and he was gone before my arrival. I should have recognized the dreamy look in her eyes, the distance I felt when we lay under the robes. Naturally, I attributed it to her losing the child and the uncertainty that comes of such things. She said he'd been there for only a short time."

"Are you sure he did this?" Star Shell asked. "Are we really talking about the same man that I traveled with for so long?"

"I presume so. Short, about so high, fleshy nose, copper ear spools, carried a little bag with a wolf's head in which he kept poisons, aphrodisiacs, and charms?"

"That part sounds like him."

"If you weren't one of his women, the rest would, too."

"I *wasn't* one of his women."

He looked at her. "I left again within two moons for, of all places, StarSky. I accompanied my mother's father and the Elders there to discuss an access for mining sacred chert, and also to settle a boundary dispute. Tall Man arrived on my doorstep the day I left. Within a span of days, he was in my wife's bed, and this time, without the benefit of charms."

"Why?" Star Shell demanded. "Why would she bed your father? Didn't you tell her what sort of man he was?"

Pale Snake's paddle dangled over the water, and he rubbed a hand over his curiously hot face. "I'd told her not to let him in. That I didn't want him in my house. We fought. She didn't believe me. Maybe that's why he had so little trouble parting her legs. He'd left by the time I'd returned, and I thought we could live the way we had before the baby. I didn't know that she was laughing at me the whole time."

"Maybe she wasn't laughing. Maybe you just think that. A way of salving your guilt for murdering her."

"Oh, I wish it were that easy, Star Shell." He stared up at the sky, watching clouds rolling in from the west. "She was probably easy for him. After all, he was the Magician, revered, Powerful, and influential. He was everything her people had taught her was admirable. You yourself know how charming he could be. Me, I was young, serious, and he knew me. From my toes to the depths of my soul, he knew me. He could tell her things—things about what I would say—and then twist them, you see?

"I left again, this time to accompany the Elders to a marriage at Six Flutes. Within a day of my leaving, he was back in my wife's bed. That time when I returned, I could feel the difference. She didn't care to have me share her bed. Said she was feeling unwell, and in fact, she was. Every morning she was ill. Are you beginning to understand? It was winter. I'd been gone almost three moons with the delegation to Six Flutes."

Star Shell turned, her face pained. "Oh, no."

Pale Snake ran his fingers down the wood of the paddle, over a knot that had resisted smoothing. "He claimed that he'd never had a woman he didn't plant a child in. That was part of what drove him. It took me a moon, stupid bumpkin that I am, before the realization came to me.''

"I'm sorry, Pale Snake." Star Shell shook her head. "Why didn't you just cast her out? Send her back to her clan?"

"Because of what she said to me. Because she laughed at me, at my manhood. She had to goad me, tell me that she would bear her child and that my father would raise it. That it would be everything that a failure like me wasn't. He filled her, she said . . . while lying with me was like coupling with water."

He worked his hand on the wood. "And something in my soul went black and evil, and when I came back to myself, she lay dead on the floor."

The canoe was drifting, turning slowly in the mild current. Silver Water blinked. When he looked at her, it was like staring into a bottomless pool.

He shook himself, casting out the demons. "So there, Star Shell, you have it. The horrible, wretched secret of the man you're traveling with. Now you know why I ran, and why I went as far as I did. The only thing you don't know is why I let you come with me . . . and to be completely honest, that baffles me, too."

She watched him with a crystalline fragility, as if on the verge of tears, and lifted a gentle hand toward him, then dropped it and turned away, placing her paddle in the water to turn the canoe back to the channel.

You're here to hurt me, Star Shell. I'd like to believe that you don't know, that you're not part of it.

But he just couldn't.

Black Skull awakened with the suddenness of long familiarity. Sunrise would come soon. He blinked, aware of the warm presence beside him.

If it's that crazy fool, I'm going to grab his nose and twist it off his face.

Squinting in the near darkness, Black Skull could make out tumbled black hair. The dim light failed to hide the girl's full breast or the dark nipple that peeked above the edge of the blanket. Then it all came back.

He remembered the Dancing and the sense of freedom he'd felt—enough so that after his discussions with Shinbone and Tall Fisher, he'd stood and Danced again, sharing smiles with the young girl who'd kept his plate full and brought him water.

In the late hours of the night, the Dancers had begun to drift away in ones and twos. The girl had smiled shyly, leading him here to this quiet end of the longhouse. She'd deftly laid out the blankets, undressed herself, and drawn him down into her soft arms.

Now he reached out, hugging her to him. She murmured happily and curled against him. The firm warmth of her bottom against his hip stirred a longing he'd rarely felt within his often-wounded soul. The incongruity of his blunt, callused fingers against her satin skin surprised him.

"I must get up," he told her quietly. "It's morning, girl."

She smiled at him, yawned and stretched, running fingers down his chest and making satisfied sounds.

Only one part of Black Skull's body rose, and the girl didn't seem to mind at all. Instead, she slipped her arms around him and pulled him down on top of her; then pleasant sounds came from her throat as they found each other.

After they had spent themselves, Black Skull stared down into her soft brown eyes. "Why did you want me, girl? I'm a horribly ugly man, with an even uglier past."

She traced slender fingers along his broken face. He started to rise, but she grabbed onto him, holding him tightly as she murmured softly in her own tongue.

"I must get up. Sunrise is coming." Again he tried to withdraw, and once more she held him, slim legs locked around his hips. She spoke softly, insistence in her voice. Black Skull was on the verge of prying himself free when her undulating hips evoked another response from his body. To this, the girl happily giggled and brought him to yet another delightful release.

This time, she threw back the covers and from a small bag retrieved a fired-clay ball that she carefully inserted into her vagina.

Black Skull studied her uncertainly, but she gave him that ravishing smile before finding her dress and slipping it on.

"All right, girl. If that is your custom." He dressed and picked up his club, then walked down by the river. She followed him. He was used to being watched, and she gaped as he began his morning ritual with the club, happy to hear her clap her hands as he Danced. Not for the first time did he wish she could speak his language.

"Very good, Black Skull," Shinbone called from the path. The Elder leaned against a maple trunk, his white eye gleaming in the morning light. The girl chattered excitedly, that huge smile on her face.

Shinbone nodded, hugging her, then faced the now perspiring Black Skull as he twirled his club for the last time. "My daughter tells me that you've planted a child in her."

Black Skull almost dropped his club. Sudden unease crept up his spine on chilly feet. "She came to me after the Dance, great chief. I assumed, since she initiated it, that it was among the customs of your people. I hope I have not committed an error."

Shinbone hugged his daughter again. "Black Skull, you are a great Trader, and a guest among my people. My daughter chose you for your courage and your strength. She also tells me that you were kind and gentle, and she worried about that before making her decision. She tells me now that she chose well."

"I do not understand."

"For a father," Shinbone replied.

Black Skull frowned thoughtfully. "You must know that I have to go with my friends to the Roaring Water. I hadn't planned on becoming a father." *By the ancestors, I'm not married, am I? Otter, where are you?*

Shinbone's wrinkled face betrayed a subtle amusement. "Let me ask this. You have planted a child. What would you say if I told you that you must now marry my daughter?"

Black Skull took a deep breath and fingered the smoothly worn wood on his club, glancing at the smiling girl. She was comely, with long black hair that gleamed in the morning light. Any man could fancy the sensation of those warm breasts pressed against his chest. And the thought of that firm bottom against his hip returned to plague him.

"This could be difficult," Black Skull stated. "Can she come with me? Return to my country after I fulfill my obligation to my friends?'' Lightning and thunder! The girl couldn't even talk in a human tongue!

Shinbone nodded to himself, chattering to the girl. She stepped over to Black Skull and hugged him. Slightly bewildered, he could do little but pat her on the back.

Shinbone began laughing. ''You are a man of honor, Black Skull. I congratulate Tall Fisher on choosing so well for her youngest daughter. But I must tell you, you look as if a sentence of death has been passed on you.''

''The news that I'm to marry has . . . let's say, come upon me by surprise.'' He shrugged. ''And I would have to admit that had I known, beautiful as she is, I would have turned her down last night.''

''You are a worthy man, Black Skull.'' Shinbone spoke to his daughter, who tightened her hug, looked up into Black Skull's face and spoke earnestly.

''What's she saying?''

''That you've given her the most wonderful of gifts. She hopes that your seed will grow within her and that now she will be eligible for marriage.'' Shinbone made a gesture with his hand, as if to include all the earth. ''Among our people, a girl is not a woman until she is heavy with child. A man does not marry unless he knows that a woman can bear him a family. My daughter has been waiting, and twice before she has tried without result, but those were young boys, friends of hers. This time she wanted a man.''

Black Skull rubbed his jaw with one hand while he patted the girl with the other. ''Shinbone, a man's seed doesn't always take with one night.''

The chief made an airy gesture. ''I don't know of such things. Tall Fisher does. She tells me a woman counts the days between her bleedings. My daughter has a good chance . . . and I think she wants to marry Big Net, of my cousin's clan. They've been eyeing each other for years.''

Black Skull nodded, lifting the girl's chin. ''I wish this Big Net luck, health, and wisdom. And perhaps we have both given each other a gift.''

She smiled as Shinbone translated.

Green Spider appeared on the trail, spinning around and around, his arms flailing the air like the wings of a gawky eaglet just learning to fly. A silly grin split his thin face.

"Greetings, fool! You've been off cavorting with wolves again?"

"Never!" Green Spider cried. "I slept! Slept with the single-minded intent of a log in the forest." He wobbled to a halt, eyes wide as he pointed at the girl in Black Skull's embracing arm. "Trouble there, Killer of Men! Beware."

Black Skull ignored him. "Have you seen Otter and Pearl?"

Shinbone said, "In the village. They were being most generous with their Trade goods." The chief squinted. "Like my daughter, they seemed to glow this morning. Have they been lovers for long?"

Black Skull looked over to where *Wave Dancer* waited. Catcher was perched on the packs, paws pattering on the hull at Green Spider's appearance. "Yes, Great Chief, they have. It's just taken them a while to discover it."

Green Spider hopped around like a rabbit, his nose twitching. He stopped, staring at the girl as if having trouble seeing her, and then squinted and backed away from Black Skull as if the vision were too much. "You, Killer of Men, have made the most curious of discoveries this morning. Beware, Black Skull, you're losing touch with what you were. The earth shakes, the land trembles. Whence came the wrath of the Black Skull?"

"I didn't feel any wrath, fool. I felt . . . honored. And perhaps that is not such a bad thing." The warrior ran gentle fingers through the girl's hair, musing on the fool's words.

Otter and Pearl emerged from the forest, a once bulging but now empty pack over one of the Trader's shoulders and Pearl safely tucked under the other arm.

A following crowd of well-wishers helped launch *Wave Dancer*, and Black Skull took his place behind the fox-headed bow, while Catcher barked. Several canoes followed them as far as the lake they'd been told about.

A crow came spiraling out of the cloud-mottled sky and chattered noisily as it circled around them.

Otter groaned uneasily, and Black Skull saw him glance suspiciously at the Contrary.

At that, Green Spider stood, spread his arms wide and shouted up, "He's not wrong . . . and neither are you!"

More squawks.

"I *don't* know!"

Was it Black Skull's imagination, or was Green Spider's voice pleading?

"Green Spider," Otter called evenly, "is there something you want to tell us?"

"Everything! All the things that there are to be told in the whole world!" the fool said as the crow winged its way eastward.

Black Skull cast occasional glances over his shoulder. Either his lack of sleep the night before was clouding his judgment or the Contrary looked slightly sick. Maybe he'd eaten too much of the fish.

Throughout the day, Black Skull paddled, driving the boat westward toward the shore, then south in search of the outlet to Upper Lake.

"You're quiet," Pearl finally called.

Black Skull was remembering those happy eyes staring into his. "I could have changed my life. I could have married that girl."

Pearl gave him a reassuring smile. "Could have changed your life, warrior? What? Again?"

"I suppose I never thought of it that way. But, yes!" *And I never even knew her name.*

Forty-four

I suspect I am one of the few Dreamers in history to be so beleaguered by Spirit Helpers. They won't leave me alone. I can't sleep, I can't eat, I can't even go into the forest to relieve myself without being accosted by howling wolves or fluttering black wings.

They tug me back and forth, back and forth, so Powerfully that sometimes I fear they will tear me in two.

Maybe I should let them do that . . . let each rip off and devour half of me.

In the empty space left between the halves, maybe I can find the present moment.

I have come to believe in that moment.

Indeed, I have convinced myself that it is the bridge across the battlefield.

Wolf of the Dead let out a whoop as the slim bow of his war canoe cut a V-shaped wake into the open water of Upper Lake. Behind him, the rest of his canoes raced out of the river's mouth and into wind-patterned water. The thickly wooded banks of the Dry Grape River lay behind them now, marked only with the standards of the clan holdings upriver. For Wolf of the Dead, the present was here, now, on this vast body of water. Somewhere out in that vast blue, he'd find Water Fox, Pearl, and their party.

More shouts of triumph followed as the warriors stared at the long-sought sea. They shipped paddles—the entire war party—just looking, savoring this sight they'd labored so long for. The canoes barely rocked on the rippled waters.

"Where do you think they are?" Grizzly Tooth wondered. "I see a lot of water out there. Where do we begin?"

Wolf of the Dead ran his tongue through the gap in his teeth, trying to sense the direction . . . and found only a blank. "This Roaring Water, it lies on the far end of this lake." He studied the shoreline, noting that it seemed to run north-south. They had indeed come out on the western shore. But which way was the closest to the Roaring Water?

"Look!" Grizzly Tooth pointed at the sky, his human-and-bear-tooth necklace rattling. There a bald eagle soared to the northwest. "A sign?"

Perhaps, but then if not, it would serve for the moment. "That way!" Wolf of the Dead pointed to the northwest.

Seventeen paddles bit into the water, the lean shapes of the war canoes arrowing out into the lake.

The country changed as they followed the Spirit Frog River westward, then north. Where the river meandered through low hills in the beginning, it now cut lazy esses through gently undulating forest. Here and there, they passed fish weirs, clan totems, and occasional fields. They met two or three canoes, calling out greetings, or waving at people on the shore, but the land was wilder here, more forbidding than south of the divide.

Little was said as they landed and built a camp on a high bank under the trees. Pale Snake had tugged the canoe up on the mud, unloaded the packs, and with his usual efficiency, started a fire before setting about cooking a meal. Star Shell and Silver Water had foraged for firewood and then retired to bathe.

A grove of red oaks sheltered them. Just upriver, they'd passed the Acorn clan grounds. The decision had been made, however, that there would be no stopping and socializing. Their goal was to travel as far as they could each day—and the fewer who knew of them, the better.

Dinner was a quiet affair, and Star Shell found herself oddly disturbed that Pale Snake's usual ebullience had vanished. It surprised her to discover that his irreverent attitude had buoyed her spirits.

"Mama?" Silver Water asked as Star Shell rolled out her blankets. "Will Pale Snake be all right?"

"Yes, baby. He's just being sad, that's all."

"He's not a bad man, Mama. I can feel it."

"I know. You sleep now."

When Silver Water had rolled over and hugged her blanket around her, Star Shell went back to the fire and seated herself across from Pale Snake. Lost in thought, she picked up a broken branch and poked it at the coals, slowly burning it away. As the end would catch fire, she'd twist it in the dirt to put it out, then place it back in the fire again.

At last she looked up, aware that he was looking in every direction except at her. "I don't blame you. Stop struggling with yourself."

He laughed at that, but it sounded dry, forced.

"It's just that, well, your stories of Tall Man bother me," she said, doing a bit of struggling on her own. "I could almost believe he was two different people. The demon you knew, and the repentant sufferer I knew. He called us heroes once."

"Heroes?" He stared thoughtfully at the fire, and she noted the weariness in his face. Tendons and veins stood out on the backs of his clasped hands. "You, maybe. He was up to something."

"He did mention that woman's ghost. The woman he'd wronged. He told me that in life, she'd never known of his trickery, but that when she died, her ghost would know everything, of all the times he'd deceived her and coupled with her. He said that with his charms, she'd always dreamed that her husband was inside her."

Pale Snake made a hissing sound. "He saw his death coming. That's all."

Star Shell looked up.

"He was a sorcerer, Star Shell, like me—only a great deal better, because I let my skills slide after ... after ..."

"He knew he was going to die? And that's why he had to make amends ... by doing a good deed. Yes, he told me once that he'd made a bargain with First Man. That if he helped me to remove the Mask, maybe First Man would speak for him. That this woman's ghost wouldn't exact the revenge it was due."

Pale Snake smiled grimly. "Well, that settles a bit of the crawling feeling in my gut. At least I know the old bloodsucker had a reason for not doing something horrible to you."

She reached out, placing a hand on his. He seemed to freeze, his eyes on her slim fingers. "Pale Snake, maybe he wanted forgiveness from you. Maybe that's why he sent me to you. He said something about forgiveness just before I turned and fled into the forest."

Pale Snake trembled and pulled his hand back, still refusing to meet her eyes. "I don't ... I can't believe it, Star Shell. I'm not dying, and even if I were, I wouldn't seek revenge. Just the opposite. I'd be afraid that he'd see my death as just another opportunity to hound me."

She moved beside him, trying to put her arm around him, but he sidled away. "Pale Snake?"

He glanced up, eyes shining. "Don't, Star Shell. You're trying to be comforting, and that just makes it worse."

"What?"

"You."

She shook her head, baffled, but kept her distance. "I was *not* one of his women."

Pale Snake smiled at that, spreading his hands wide. "I've actually started to believe that. No, it's something else. Some trap he's laid. And it's got to be you, Star Shell."

"I don't know of any trap. I've told you the truth, Pale Snake." But even having to admit it dismayed her. "I'm not going to hurt you."

A frightened smile curled his lips. "I think you believe what you're saying, and I almost can myself. No, it's not that simple, Star Shell. It would be subtle, like the way I've started to feel."

She suddenly found herself anxious to glance away. The blackened tip of her stick had become very interesting. She nerved herself. "And how is that?"

He paused before he said, "From the time that my wife died, I've had no interest in women. Until you."

"Pale Snake, please."

"Oh, don't worry, Star Shell. Even if you threw yourself at my feet, I'd back away."

Why did that crush her? She'd come to like him, true, but she'd never thought of him as a lover. "You'd back away?"

"I want you too much. It's . . . unnatural."

"The Mask," she whispered hoarsely. "It has to be some trick of the Mask's. So far, everyone I've been close to has died, or been terribly hurt. Only Silver Water and I are all right, and Silver Water . . . That's why I had to leave Greets the Sun."

"Do you understand?" he asked warily. "I wish I'd never given you that dress. It stirs parts of me that have been dead for a long time."

She studied her hands on the crooked branch. "If you'd like, I'll change into something else, a basswood-fiber sack maybe."

He pulled at his ear and shook his head. "It's not so bad now that we can talk about it. You just won't mind if you see me staring and flushed, will you?"

"No. It might even be good for me. I don't feel very attractive these days. I only feel . . . tired." She shook her head. "So tired

I can barely force myself to move, or even to think.''

"You are the most alluring woman I've seen in years, Star Shell. That's what's been driving me half insane. I'm sure that Tall Man knew that I'd want you—and somehow, he's baited the trap so that I'll be destroyed by the very wanting."

She tapped the branch on the dirt. "You're sure he'd do something like that?"

"Positive. If he'd ruin my wife, turn her against me like he did—and I told you the undecorated truth—he'd find a way to strike one last blow."

"He never mentioned you."

"I just can't figure it out. He has to know that I'd be suspicious."

"Maybe that's just what he was counting on. That you'd be wary enough to see me through the dangers." Star Shell jammed her stick into the fire and rubbed her eyes. "Pale Snake, let's get the Mask to the Roaring Water. We'll pitch the thing over the edge, take a deep breath, and then sort all this out. Who knows? Maybe by that time, you'll realize just what a trial I can be and you'll have lost any interest."

He studied her, a wry smile on his lips. "Tell me, do you think it will be that easy?"

She shook her head and glared at the humped pack. "The Mask isn't going to allow us to just walk up and fling it into oblivion, is it?"

"I doubt it." He frowned and closed his eyes. "I haven't used Power in a long time, and I'm a bit rusty, but when I search for the Mask's soul, I can feel it, waiting. It's as if it's biding its time."

"What would it try?"

He remained silent for a moment, then blinked lazily before his expression sharpened. "What would it try? Anything that would help it to survive."

Star Shell looked at Silver Water, now only a small mound under her blankets. "No matter what, Pale Snake, I won't let it have my daughter. Do you understand?"

"I do indeed. She's a good girl, Star Shell."

"I . . . I want you to promise me something."

"What might that be?"

"That if the Mask makes a move and I have to die to stop

it, you will make sure my daughter is safe. Will you do that?"

He rubbed his hands together, his pensive thoughts on Silver Water's sleeping figure. "If I can, Star Shell. And if Silver Water is the trap?"

"How could she be?"

"I don't know. I just don't know. And it scares me half to death." He rubbed his arms briskly, as if suddenly cold.

Otter's flute music carried on the evening breeze as Pearl walked down to the curling, knee-high breakers on the white sand. The new moon barely streaked the top of the waves that rolled along the long spit of sand and dashed together in patterns out in the open water.

Traveling down the north shore of the Upper Lake, they had come to this place. But for the patterns of the low waves and the oppressiveness of the dank odor, she could almost believe she looked out upon the southern Salt Sea. This, however, was not the beach of her youth, but a point of sand that extended out like a giant fang into the heart of the water.

Otter's music rose and fell in a haunting melody. It drifted soft and soothing on the cool night. Her feet dimpled the sand as she walked out to the tip of the point.

"Like the bow of a canoe, isn't it?" Black Skull crouched there, his club over his shoulder. He gestured at the living waters. "You can almost see the land sailing out into the waves."

"I'd think you would have had enough of sailing." She settled down beside him, tucking her knees to her chest and clasping them with her arms. "You've looked pensive for the last couple of days. Still thinking about the Wenshare girl?"

Black Skull nodded. "It's at times like this that I try to remember who I was. Was it a dream, Pearl? Did I really kill my mother? Was I the most feared of warriors? Did the Copena tremble at the mention of my name?" He laid his war club aside and drew a diamond in the sand. "It's as if the City of the Dead—and the man that I was—never existed."

A log floated by in the water, little more than a bobbing line that the waves slid over. Two gulls perched atop it, sound asleep. "People change, I suppose."

He scooped up a handful of sand, looking at the white crystals. "Sometimes I wonder if I didn't die in that storm. Maybe this is my ghost." He raised his head toward the sliver of moon. "All of this, it's the afterlife. Black Skull really died out on the water that night. When I woke up the next morning with my head in the fool's lap, it was as a Spirit."

"Then we all died together," she mused. "But for me, death came at the hands of Wolf of the Dead in the Khota clan grounds."

"Death, life, change. I wonder if a person really knows when he goes from living to being a ghost. I mean, some must. If you look down and see a war dart sticking through your heart, that would be a pretty good indicator that you were dying, or dead."

Pearl shuddered. "True. The same if you woke up in a tomb covered with dirt."

"Or had your head cut off. Now that would be an interesting way to live as a ghost, wouldn't it?"

She smiled at their bizarre conversation, letting her soul travel out over the water. "So, you're down here trying to decide if you're dead or alive. And all because a girl chose you to father her child?"

He chuckled. "It's not the choice, you see, but the reason for the choice. Women have always wanted me because of my fame. They wanted to couple with the Black Skull, the great warrior. They wanted the reputation, not the man. Shinbone's daughter wanted me because of who I am . . . as a man, I mean. Until we walked into their camp, she'd never heard of the Black Skull."

The muscles in his face had begun to twitch. He continued more slowly. "I frightened her in the beginning. She didn't want to be close to me. But somewhere during the Dance, she managed to see past the scars. The wonder of it is that she *liked* what she saw!"

"That bothers you? I like you, too. A lot. So does Otter, and even the skinny lunatic."

He sighed. "I've never been a likable sort. I never wanted to be. Look, *I* didn't really like me—and I lived with me all the time. That's why I wonder if I died out there, drowned and floated away. I dreamed that. Maybe it wasn't a dream.''

"Maybe all that drowned and floated away was the part of you that you didn't like.'' The waves danced new patterns in the darkness, the lapping and splashing mixing with Otter's flute music. "Do you like yourself now?''

The muscles in his crushed face relaxed. "I think I do. When I looked into that girl's eyes, I saw a reflection of myself different than I'd ever seen before. When I touched her, it was with different hands than I had ever touched a woman with before. I've found myself regretting that I didn't stay so I could keep on seeing that reflection in her eyes.''

"You could go back.''

He tossed a handful of sand into the water. "By the time we could get back, she'll have determined whether the child is planted or not. She had a husband in mind. I don't know if I could stand that. Not yet.''

She reached out, placing a hand on his muscular arm. "You had a taste of honey, and now you want the entire hive, regardless that the bees of ordinariness would sting you mad in the end.''

"Possibly.''

"Probably. Tell me, can you even go back to the City of the Dead and live as you used to? From what I've heard, you lived like the effigy on a stone pipe, with only one expression—hard, unchanging. To see the image was to see the reality. This was the Black Skull. No matter how many times you looked, the image was always the same.''

"You are right, Pearl. I'm not certain I can go back to that life, either.''

"What *are* you going to do when this is over?''

He shrugged. "First we have to see whether Power will let us live through it, and then we'll have to travel all the way back to the Father Water, I guess. What do you think? Do I make a good Trader?''

"I'm not sure. I hear that you have a real problem getting value for a badger bowl.''

He rubbed his distorted face and vented a short laugh. "I've got to work on that. And on catching skunks, too.''

Like wolves of the night they moved, each foot placed carefully, hands parting the branches to allow their silent passage through the darkness.

A thrill fit to burst built in Robin's breast as his warriors crept soundlessly out of the pitch-black brush screening the canoe landing.

I trained these men. I taught them these stealthy skills!

The Wind clan grounds lay like a sleeping monster, dark, humped, irregular against the landscape. Robin and Woodpecker had planned this approach downwind, away from the keen noses and ears of the camp dogs. Two small houses had blocked their path, but they had passed them without raising any alarm.

Robin needed enough canoes for his twenty warriors. The Wind Clan provided canoes, placed as they were on the Trade route north to the lakes; however, it was common knowledge that the clan didn't just lend their canoes. They'd want something in Trade, and all Robin had to offer at the moment was the skill and daring of his warriors.

Woodpecker's form molded into the brush, and Robin raised his hand in signal. Every man instantly froze. The taint of wood smoke carried down from the clan grounds, along with the green smell of vegetation and the pleasant musk of damp ground. Crickets trilled in the night, and water lapped along the banks of the Spirit Frog River.

Woodpecker eased forward, slipping through the brush like a shadow. Robin followed. He could see the canoe landing now, and tightened his grip on the war club in his hand.

Woodpecker glanced at the first of the canoes drawn up on the beach, then went on to the next. There he made a slashing gesture, and Robin stepped out, motioning to his men. In a line, they rushed forward, counted off the number the boat would carry, and without a word, lifted the canoe and bore it to the water.

Meanwhile, Woodpecker had proceeded to the next canoe, rejected it, and moved onto the next. Here again he made the slashing gesture; the next batch of warriors carried the second craft to the water, slipping it into the current before climbing in, finding paddles, and sending the boat downstream.

"What's going on here?" a voice asked in Trade pidgin.

Robin's heart leaped, but he smiled quickly and stepped forward. "Greetings! Who's there?"

"I am called Copper Tooth, a Trader of the Gray Owl Clan of the Ilini People."

Robin could see the Trader now. He was sitting in the largest of the canoes lining the bank. Evidently, like most good Traders, he slept with his packs. Robin walked forward, his club balanced on his shoulder.

"Copper Tooth, we're off to check our fish and crawdad traps. We want to be on our sets by morning."

The Trader's head, little more than a black ball in the night, turned, staring out at the water. He glanced back just in time to cry: "Wait! Don't—"

Copper Tooth's skull cracked loudly under the impact of Robin's whistling war club. The sound seemed to sunder the night— at least to Robin's sensitive ears. A nervous fluttering of arms and legs sounded as the corpse spasmed. Then silence filled the night again.

Robin spun on his feet, head cocked for any sound: the cry of alarm, the running patter of feet, a barking dog alerted by the sodden splitting of the skull.

Only the faint rustling of a vole in the grass gave his heart the slightest tremor, and that passed as the rodent skittered down its runway.

None of Robin's warriors had moved. Now Woodpecker stirred to gather paddles, handing them one by one to the men.

Robin inspected the Trader's canoe, a well-made craft filled with packs. He smiled, and gave the slashing gesture. Immediately, the rest of his warriors descended, grunting and struggling as they slid the heavy Trade canoe down to the water.

"What about the Trader's body?" a warrior whispered.

"When we're downriver, we'll get rid of it," Robin hissed. "Now, let's go!" He clambered into the big Trade canoe, heedless of the warm corpse he squatted on. Backing water, they moved out into the current, heading the canoe into the narrow channel.

Woodpecker glanced back when they'd passed out of hearing

of the Wind clan grounds. "Why did you take the Trader's boat?"

"I wanted these packs we're sitting on." Robin used the paddle to adjust their course away from a shadowy bank. "Who knows where this chase will take us? I'm sure we'll need the supplies or goods to Trade for information, food, or maybe even for canoes, eh?"

Woodpecker chuckled. "You're a crafty one. Indeed, I can believe that you will be the greatest leader of all. In ages yet unborn, they shall sing your praises."

Robin smiled. That would indeed be the case. As soon as he controlled the Mask, the entire world would know it.

When morning broke, they had traveled a considerable distance from the Wind clan grounds. The corpse Robin sat on had grown cold, and he could smell the blood, urine, and feces that had leaked from the body.

Copper Tooth's body slid into the water with barely a splash. When Robin looked back, it floated facedown, the broken fragments of skull already washed clean around the crimson-clotted gore of the wound.

He would have liked to have kept the head for his wall, but it would have been burdensome, and besides, he had gained no honor in the taking. Star Shell's skull, and the little girl's, however, would rest beside the Magician's, no matter what manner of death Robin dealt them.

As they paddled past the last silhouetted spit of land and into Upper Lake, Star Shell marveled at the immensity of the water. There, to the north, shining in the sun, stretched a burnished eternity of wave and motion that faded into a still horizon.

"I never knew there was so much water in the world."

The image of the Dream bowl, and the world within, refreshed her memory. Yes, she'd seen, but a person didn't understand the magnitude of sky and water, the vastness of distance, and the stunning insignificance of a human being in this wet world. In the forest, humans marched large, but on the open water, they vanished into obscurity.

"This much and more," Pale Snake said behind her.

"Mama? We won't drown, will we?" Silver Water asked.

"No, Tadpole. Pale Snake and I will make sure that you're safe. Won't we, Pale Snake?"

He laughed at the sudden concern in Star Shell's voice, fully aware that Silver Water had just felt that first panic that people can't help but experience on open water.

"I think we'll be quite safe. We're going to follow the south shore all the way to the river that takes us to the Roaring Water. As you can see on the shore, all the driftwood piles up on the beach. Wind and current both move eastward here—and even if the canoe tips over, just hold on to it. It will wash ashore before long."

"I feel *so* much better." Star Shell gave her full attention to being scared as they entered the swells rolling past the last protective point of land. The little canoe rose and fell, the sensation disconcerting. Bars of light danced downward into the depths, leading the eye into a hazy, cold infinity, greenish here, unobscured by silt. But where was the bottom?

"Relax," Pale Snake called. "Move with the canoe as it follows the waves, not against it. What is this? First I have to teach you to paddle, and now I have to teach you how to ride a canoe?"

"I've never been off the river!"

"Believe me, I can tell."

At the sarcasm, she forced herself to relax. *Star Shell, people paddle across this water all the time. It can't be that hard.* Nevertheless, her soul bleated that each movement of the canoe presaged immediate disaster.

"Mama? Is there a bottom to this water?" Silver Water asked.

"I think so." But as she looked at the shore and then into the murky depths, she couldn't be sure. The land looked more than a dart's cast away. Even on the Lower Moonshell, a man could cast a dart across the river, except in times of flood. And the Serpent River, which she'd seen only once, had shores that a person could reach in a short time. That however wasn't the question that suddenly plagued her. Did land float on water, or did water lie on land? In a river, a person knew. He could dive down and touch the bottom. The shellfishers and pearl hunters did it all the time. What about here?

"Pale Snake?" Star Shell asked hoarsely. "Is there a bottom?"

"Along the shore, there is. You can feel it with net sinkers, or plummets on a fishing line. Once you paddle farther out, the bottom drops away. Maybe it's there, maybe not. No one's ever tied a rock onto a cord long enough to find out. Myself, I suspect that there's a bottom down there somewhere."

"Why?" She wished she could grab onto the sides of the canoe and close her eyes until they'd beached again.

"Because the Upper Lake is surrounded by land. If you can see bottom all the way around the edges, it's most likely that it goes clear across . . . unless, of course, there's a big hole in the middle." He paused. "But if there was, wouldn't all the water drain out?"

"Not if that's where the water's bubbling up from," she responded, and felt a little queasy.

"Like a gigantic spring, you mean? Hmm. Interesting thought."

"What happens if a person drowns out there?"

"The same thing that happens if a person drowns in the Upper Moonshell, the Red Buck, or even the Paint. He dies. Say, you're not about to panic are you? You drown just as dead in shallow water as you do in deep."

"I may be about to panic."

He had the audacity to laugh at that. "Silver Water, your mother is about to panic. I'm not sure, but perhaps we should get her to turn around so we could see better. It's never as much fun to watch someone panic from the rear. From the front, you can watch their face turn colors and their eyeballs roll around in the sockets."

Silver Water cried: "Turn around, Mama! Turn around!"

"You are impossible!" Star Shell was shamed into picking up her paddle. She struggled to keep the canoe from wobbling, and paddled despite the terror in her heart.

"That's it," Pale Snake praised her.

"How far are we from the Roaring Water?"

"I'd say we'll be there by the solstice."

"That long? You said it was at the east end of the lake."

"It is."

"How *big* is this lake?"

"Like you said, all the water in the world."

She struggled to keep her concentration while gulls whirled around, inspecting them for fish or other treats. "But this is the Upper Lake. Wind Lake is this big, too?"

"It is. I live on the north side of it. I told you it was a long trip."

"Tell me about it." *Anything to keep my mind off of where I am—and how soon I'm going to drown!* "The place where you live, I mean. Is it like StarSky, or Many Paints?"

"Something, yes. But we have more lakes . . . lakes everywhere. Lots of ducks and loons, and more game. The people there are different. It takes some learning to understand the dialect they speak, but it's very close to ours. The rituals and beliefs are quite dissimilar, though. We worship a Sky Mother instead of a Mysterious One, and we don't follow all of the ceremonies with the slavish intensity that the Serpent Clans do. Among my people, the lineage is more important and more influential than the clan is."

"Do you have societies?"

"Yes, sort of. But the societies aren't as strong or as established as the ones you're used to. Think of them more as social clubs."

"It sounds like chaos. How do you get anything done?"

"With a lot more fun than your people do. I even built a serpent—a mound like the one you've heard about. Everyone pitched in and built it." He paused. "I suppose I did it in defiance of my father. He'd scream if he knew that uninitiated hands had dared to erect such a mound."

"He can't scream, Pale Snake," Star Shell said. "Robin pulled his guts out."

"You've been around me too long. My fabled sense of humor is rubbing off."

Star Shell peered at him through narrowed eyes. "Don't be insulting. . . . So lineages run things, not clans. And you don't have real societies, just social clubs. What else is different? Who tends to the fields? Decides the planting?"

"Star Shell, we don't have that many people. It's not like the Moonshell or the StarSky country. We see the land differently;

it doesn't belong to a lineage or a family. If you want to plant goosefoot, you just go clear a field and do it. If anything, we put more emphasis on survival than on rules. That extends to our Trade, too. Most of the silver comes through our centers, as do the fine northern furs, bears' teeth, and caribou hides.''

''And sacred chert?''

''Among us, it doesn't have quite the reputation that you are used to. We don't use it for bloodletting or sacred carvings. Most of our chert comes from the clans on both sides of the Roaring Water. Bear Clan for one. In fact, while I'm there, I'll Trade for some.''

He stopped paddling long enough to push hair out of his eyes. ''I guess I'd have to say that we don't take status quite as seriously as people do farther south. Maybe because we don't plant as much of our food. We trap and net fish, dive for shellfish, and collect rice from the lake and berries and nuts from the forest. Through fall and winter, we spend more time hunting, especially when the deer yard up in their large winter herds. It leads to . . . I guess you'd say to fewer interests in politics. I like to think we're a little more flexible.''

She had picked up the rhythm of the open water now, and as they'd made it this far without capsizing, she began to hope for survival. ''If you're so happy up there, why do you return to the Serpent Clans? Why not stay forever with your undisciplined northerners?''

''I'm one of the few who don't have a family, and no one misses me while I'm gone. It's not like the south, where Traders follow the rivers and bring you things. We have to travel back and forth, do our own Trading with the Serpent Clans, as well as with the Stone Hunters to the south. Silver is especially important. We Trade for the nuggets and pound them into shapes for Trade southward.''

''Mama?'' Silver Water asked. ''Can I go hunting when we get to Pale Snake's clan holdings?''

Star Shell almost said yes, then paused. *What are you going to do when you leave Roaring Water?* To Silver Water, she gave the response that every mother uses to frustrate her children to the point of tears: ''We'll see.''

''You can hunt all you wish,'' Pale Snake told Silver Water in a kindly voice. ''I even have a little friend about your age.

His name is Mink Stalker, and he's going to grow up to be one of the bravest and most skilled hunters we have. You'll like him.''

Star Shell fought the sudden urge to slam the paddle down and turn on him. What made him think that she wanted to go to his northern land with its Caribou people and lakes? For all she knew, the place swarmed with mosquitoes and flies, and ticks hung on every blade of grass.

Is that really why you're so angry? She made herself paddle, her eyes ahead to where the white sandy shoreline rose to the wave-cut bank. Above that, green forest spread in a leafy mat that followed the gentle undulations of the dissected landscape.

No, the truth was that she was starting to actually like Pale Snake. That impudent attitude refreshed her, somehow lessened the burden of her responsibility.

She stifled the urge to shake her head. He'd see, and with his sorcerer's Power, probably understand her thoughts. It was crazy! The man was her last lover's half-brother! Tall Man's son! A renegade who'd murdered his wife for sleeping with his father—and conceiving an incestuous child!

Against all the warning fires burning uncomfortably in her soul, she couldn't help but admire the way that he moved. During those hidden moments, she loved to catch sight of his private smiles and the way they affected the snakes tattooed on his cheeks. The twinkle of gentle humor in his eyes haunted her. She'd bitten off more than one sigh as she'd watched his muscular body, irritated at her awareness of his lean hips and wide shoulders.

He'd made her laugh, and somehow he'd managed to return a part of herself that she hadn't known was missing.

But do you want to leave everything behind? Travel with him to the north, Trade for silver and caribou meat?

She stole a glance southward, trying to see her father, Hollow Drill, in her soul's eye. A lifetime of habit and intimacy lay there.

She paddled harder, releasing the frustrations of indecision. *You can't fall in love with Pale Snake, Star Shell. He's right, there's a trap somewhere. But it's the Mask that's plotting evil. I'll never believe that Tall Man sent me to Pale Snake as a final act of unkindness toward his son.*

The Mask—the hideous demon that rode in its pack on her back—had suddenly begun to grow warm. Warmer and warmer. As though it were awakening from a long sleep. That responsibility would have to be dealt with first. And then, only then, could she decide about Pale Snake and what to do with what remained of her life.

You're trapped, Star Shell. Trapped . . . but you just don't know how.

Forty-five

Wave Dancer made good time, helped by a stiff wind from the west. Pearl's wind trap pushed them along, water frothing under the fox-head bow as Otter used his paddle to steer them. They'd found from the beginning that by staying far out in the lake, they avoided the coastal fishing peoples, all of whom wished to Trade but had little more than fish to offer. In deeper waters, *Wave Dancer* could fly along unhindered as she rode the swells.

Otter savored this day of sunshine, wind, and sparkling water. *If only I could make this last forever!*

Clouds raced before them, as if the entire world were heading east. Catcher perched on his packs with the usual ease, nose twitching with the wind until he curled up and sighed before dropping off to sleep.

"Being a dog wouldn't be so bad." Pearl winced at the stiffness in her arms as she struggled to hold on to her side of the wind trap. "Just guard the packs, play, and sleep."

Across from her, Black Skull nodded, his big body leaning out over the water as he stretched his side of the palmetto matting. "There has to be a better way to do this. Maybe use sticks instead of people to hold the mat."

"You'd still have to prop the sticks somehow," Otter told them, happy to let the wind blow strands of hair across his face.

"Drill holes," Black Skull countered. "Then you could drive

the sticks into the wood. Attach them to the boat.''

"Not my canoe, you don't!"

The warrior growled something under his breath.

The wind flattened Pearl's milkweed-fabric shirt against her skin, and Otter could see every line and curve of her breasts and flat stomach as if she were naked. He'd begun to learn all those curves, exploring each exciting new part of her.

Black hair whipped over her shoulder as she struggled with the wind trap, eyes flashing, the hint of a smile pulling at her lips as she fought the wind. She looked wild, untamed, thoroughly enraptured with the challenge of propelling the canoe. From the flush in her smooth cheeks to the firm muscles in her shapely arms, her blood pumped with the living thrill of the day.

Of all the women in the world, I have been blessed to find this one . . . if only for so short a time.

The wind shifted, and Otter twisted his paddle slightly to keep them stern-on to the blow. To his amazement, despite the chop and swells, they seemed to speed across the water, the bow slapping out spray that the wind whipped away.

"This is the way to travel!"

"Only because *your* fingers aren't cramped into agony," Pearl declared as she braced her legs against the bucking hull.

Black Skull turned his head, asking, "Tell me, fool, will your wolf be able to keep up? That was him that you slipped away from camp to see last night, wasn't it?"

From the other side of the wind trap, the Contrary cried, "The Spirits are slower than even the fastest of men, warrior. Of all people, Little Mouse, you should know the ways of Power."

"Little Mouse?" Otter asked. "Did he call you Little Mouse?"

Black Skull's wounded face paled. Defensively, he muttered, "The fool's just raving again, Trader. Forget it, Green Spider. Just forget that I ever mentioned your miserable wolf."

Green Spider lifted his hawkish nose above the middle of the wind trap and sniffed in Black Skull's direction. "The ways of Power, yes. You stink of Power these days, Little Mouse. It was that brilliant daylight during the storm. You learned to live inside your bones that night. Remember! Remember! You'll always remember!"

Pearl smiled, white teeth flashing, as she glanced back at Otter and winked.

Little Mouse? Otter studied the warrior with a new curiosity. Who would have thought . . . but then, everyone had a childhood name that they outgrew. Somehow he'd imagined a sullen, angry little Black Skull, a child-sized war club over his shoulder, flailing anyone or anything in his path.

They camped that night on a sandy hook that protruded out into the lake and curled around to the east like a beckoning finger. After camp had been established, Otter looked at Pearl and nodded toward the lee of the hook. "Want to swim?"

"After today, I'm about as energetic as a twisted rag. Sure."

While Black Skull made his nightly rounds and Green Spider squatted before the fire, Otter and Pearl peeled off their clothing and ran out into the shallows. Catcher bounded along, barking and splashing until he had to paddle, nose up, ears pricked. Pearl dove cleanly into the clear water, stroking under the surface like a graceful brown fish.

Otter gave chase, attempting to overcome the woman's natural grace with his superior strength. She darted ahead of him, breaking for a breath, and, belly muscles flexing, jackknifed away, trailing silver bubbles and streaming hair.

Otter broke the surface, gasped a quick breath—and floundered as she pinched his rear from behind. Ducking underwater, he found her grinning; then, like a minnow, she twisted and escaped his thrashing advance.

Finally winded, he tread water, flipping his wet hair from his face. A final pinch on the butt proved difficult to ignore, but he did so. She surfaced in front of him, parting her hair with slim brown hands. "You're easy to pinch."

"I ought to drown you."

"Try it," she challenged, and slipped below the surface. This time she didn't pinch his bottom, but irreverently yanked on the member that dangled in the front. Otter growled and resumed the fruitless pursuit. By the ancestors, she was half fish!

In desperation, he gave up and stroked lazily to shore while she literally swam circles around him. In the shallows, they both stood, grinning. The sunset accented her skin with red, glistening in the droplets of water that streamed from her shoulders to curve around the high swell of her breasts and down the smooth concavity of her sides.

"You look happy," he told her.

She reached for his hand. "I am, Water Fox. But one thing's sure, you're no otter. A real otter should be able to outswim an Anhinga any old day."

Catcher had given up on them and now pranced along the shore, dragging a sandy stick in his mouth. Water trickled from his tricolored fur.

As they waded toward shore, Black Skull appeared over the crest of the dune. He approached with that assertive step Otter had come to associate with trouble.

"What's wrong?" He dropped Pearl's hand as he retrieved his wadded shirt from the sand. Pearl was twisting her thick hair to wring out the water. Despite his concern, Otter couldn't help but watch the muscles play in her sleek brown forearms.

"Something I think you should see," Black Skull said dourly. "I don't know if it's immediate trouble or not. Green Spider didn't show any of the usual signs of coming disaster; instead, the fool gulped down some berries from one of the pots and disappeared inland. We'll probably get a visit from a mad crow tomorrow."

"What is it you want us to see?" Pearl asked as she shook her damp hair back and shrugged into her shirt.

"Come." Once they were dressed, Black Skull led them up over the low, grass-covered dunes. Where small ponds had been trapped by the sand, shoots of cottonwood now rose above the tall grass. Here and there, logs—cast up during storms and partially buried—now rotted, each a home for mushrooms and insects. To Otter's surprise, maple and elm had started to send up occasional saplings.

Black Skull led them down to the beach on the windward side and turned northward. Finally, he stopped, gesturing with the flat of his hand. "All right, Trader, tell me what you see."

Otter approached warily, still holding Pearl's hand. The skid marks in the sand, along with the stippling tracks to either side, were self-explanatory. What might have been imagined as a giant centipede's mark was where a canoe had been dragged up and then back off the beach. Four such marks were visible.

Catcher had forgotten his stick and was now hunting around, nose wiggling, as he checked the scents.

"So someone landed here," Otter replied. "Given the number of fishing canoes on this coast, I don't see—"

"Look at the fire pits up here," Black Skull said. "And you two be careful where you put your feet. Try not to step on the tracks they left."

Otter and Pearl stared at the charcoal-filled fire pits. Otter bent down and felt the warmth that still radiated. Last night's camp, then. He glanced at Pearl as she squatted beside him. "Does this mean anything to you?"

"It looks like a fire pit. This is where they scooped the sand out, and over here—" she stood, leading him to the flattened marks in the sand "—is where they laid out their blankets." She frowned.

Black Skull had dropped to one knee. "You might look at this, Trader. It's a very interesting footprint."

Otter left Pearl and her pensive study of the flattened areas to bend down next to Black Skull. The imprint of the moccasin had been made in wet sand and had dried in perfect condition.

"I see a moccasin print. It's a man's, from the size of it, and he seems to have curled his toes from the way the front of the print is pressed down. Um, let's see. The seam runs up the instep of the moccasin, which generally means it's a high moccasin, right? Low types usually just have the seam in the back."

"You're better than I expected. But what you don't realize is that we've seen this track before." Black Skull's eyes had narrowed.

"Khota," Pearl said suddenly, backing away. She wiped her palms on her skirt, and a hard swallow went down her throat. "That's . . . that's what it is. At every camp we made, they laid out their beds this way. Head toward the inland, feet toward the fire. If it had been stormy, they'd have camped on the opposite side of the island and built partial shelters from the wind. Last night was peaceful. No wind."

Otter reached down, his fingers barely tracing the track. "We've seen this track? You're sure?"

"I'm sure."

Pearl crouched down beside him and studied it. "Grizzly Tooth," she stated.

Otter felt a chill go down his back. "How? I mean, it's impossible! We'd have seen them. They couldn't have passed us without our knowing!"

"They must have traveled another course." Black Skull rubbed his off-center jaw. "We circled that loop that Trout drew. What if the Khota knew of a way across the bottom? The land is riddled with rivers, and just like the Ilini River, some must have passages, or a short portage at worst."

"But why wouldn't we have heard?" Otter shook his head, refusing to believe.

Black Skull pointed to the scrape marks in the sand. "Those are light war canoes, Otter. I see ten and seven beds up there. How far can four warriors carry a light war canoe in one day? Look at how narrow the marks in the sand are. These canoes could be paddled up very small creeks. Places we could never take *Wave Dancer*."

Pearl walked away from them, up into the grass, searching carefully for something. She bent down, then stood, her face strained. "I think I know this one, too. He's got a tapeworm in his guts. The last time I thought about that was when I was watching him hang his bottom over the side of the canoe on the way upriver."

"How could you know a man has a tapeworm?" Otter asked.

One of her delicate eyebrows arched. "I fed it to the slimy weasel, that's why. He was lucky. You should have seen what some of the others ate."

"I'm never going to make you mad at me," Black Skull promised and strode down onto the beach, his lips twitching with disgust. "What do we do now, Otter? They're ahead of us."

Otter looked out at the sunset, feeling the cool wind that rustled the trees and watching the surf that curled down the beach. "They're in shallow draft canoes. They've got to stand in close to shore, avoid rough water. *Wave Dancer* can take a fair sea, and the wind's with us."

Black Skull tucked his thumbs in his belt, skepticism in his eyes. "Thinking about outracing them again?"

"We've got the advantage. We know they're here, and we know how many of them there are."

"Maybe," Pearl objected. "He might have split his party,

sent half north along this shore and the other half along the southern.''

Otter glared at the marks in the sand. "Yes, he could have. But one thing's sure. He knows we're headed to the Roaring Water. If he gets there first, he can set up camp, scout the country, and lay any kind of ambush he wants. If we get there first, we can lay a trap for him."

Black Skull nodded. "Now you are talking like a warrior." He glanced out at the water. "I wish you'd forgotten to mention where we were headed, though."

"Yes, well, me, too. But at the time, it seemed the thing to do. Anything to draw Wolf of the Dead and his warriors out into the Fresh Water Sea. I'd like to know how any of them survived that storm."

"Just because a man is Khota, it doesn't mean he can't be as desperate as an ordinary man." Pearl turned hard eyes on the deserted camp. "And maybe the Water Spirits that live in the Fresh Water Sea didn't want their kind of ghost fouling the depths. Who knows, Wolf of the Dead's corpse might poison a fish."

Otter nodded. "All right. Let's go find Green Spider, eat as much as we can hold, sleep until the middle of the night, and then Pearl and I will take the first watch."

"It takes three people to use the wind trap," Black Skull noted.

"As long as we can use it, we can Trade off. Green Spider is a little troublesome, but maybe he can steer. That's not too much of a challenge."

They started down the beach, Catcher coursing back and forth, nose to the ground, tail up.

"Well," Otter sighed, taking Pearl's hand, "it was great while it lasted." Images of her athletic body lingered in his memory; he'd been planning on running his fingers along those same smooth lines the water had run down. Leave it to the Khota to shatter such pleasant dreams.

"It's a long time until the middle of the night," Pearl whispered.

"I thought that after seeing Khota—"

"All the more reason to have you close tonight." She tightened her grip on his hand, shooting a dark-eyed glance his way.

"Maybe we can fill our souls with other dreams for now. The Khota will intrude enough as it is."

He managed a smile, but then he'd always had the ability to smile, no matter how horrible he felt.

The wind mixed with the pounding of the surf and the hispering grass. Pearl had nodded off after their last desperate coupling, but Otter couldn't sleep. A melancholy sense of loss had begun to coil around his insides.

"I had a Dream last night. Water falling in endless cascades that turned from crystal-clear to a white as bright as snow. Thunder . . . everywhere . . ." Four Kills' voice crept from the depths of his soul. Sleepless, Otter stared up at the night sky, naming the stars Pearl had shown him.

Pearl mumbled something under her breath and turned over. Her breathing deepened.

". . . The body came whirling about in the sucking whirlpools. A ray of sunlight pierced the sky then, shimmering through the dancing spray, silvering the droplets and striking gold from them as it lit your face."

Yes, he remembered. Four Kills had been so desperately sure that the dream was a Vision. Otter reached over, rolling a strand of Pearl's thick hair between his fingers, thinking of how perfect the day had been, of how happy he'd felt.

"You were dead, brother, and your soul was still Dancing in the water."

Was that how it had to end? Was that the price to be paid for saving the Mask?

Otter slipped out from under the blanket, motioning Catcher— curled at the foot of the bedding—to remain on guard. He used a piece of driftwood to weight the corner of the blanket against the prying fingers of wind, and dressed before crossing the grassy dune to the campsite.

To his surprise, a low fire flickered and wavered in time to the wind that raced in off the water. Green Spider sat hunched there, his triangular, hatchet face and knobby knees illuminated by the flames.

"Can't sleep," Otter confided.

"I sure can." Green Spider reached over and dropped another piece of wood onto the blaze. "Fire is curious, isn't it? Have you ever wondered what makes it turn so dark?''

''I'd never thought about it.''

''Look at this, Otter. So much darkness, it spreads around so that the eye can see in the brightest of nights. And yet, the next day, what do you have left? Pale wood. Is it because fire takes all of the light out of the wood that you have charcoal?''

''That makes sense. I never thought about light being locked in a piece of wood. Maybe that's why charcoal is black—but you can burn a piece of charcoal again and it will glow red until it's all down to white ash. Brown to black to white.'' Otter smiled. ''At least in my way of thinking.''

Green Spider's vacant eyes remained fixed on the fire. In a mournful voice, he said, ''I can't answer all of your questions, Otter. Some. But not all.''

''Why not, Green Spider?''

''Because I don't know all of the answers yet.''

Otter took a deep breath. ''It's not going to be as easy as the Vision portrayed, is it? Not with Khota and High Head magic involved.''

''Only the hardest things are easy. But, no, Otter, this isn't going to be like the Vision.''

''You were out with the wolf this evening, weren't you? Is it the same wolf we saw that night outside of the Ilini clan grounds?''

''His name is Watcher.'' Green Spider's lips pinched. ''He's a very old wolf... at least his soul is. He's taken me places, and I've seen amazing things, Otter. I've met Foxfire, and old White Calf, Sunchaser, and Bad Belly. And Heron—the First Woman—who lives in a cave with a tree growing up through the middle. I've kissed the roots of that great tree of life, the red cedar, and felt its branches where they touch Father Sun.''

''What's happening, Green Spider? What are we heading into?''

Green Spider's focus seemed to sharpen. ''Oh... Otter, I only see parts. You see, the poorest of all gambles is made on the human soul. Not even Many Colored Crow, who understands so much about people, understands completely.''

''Does this have to do with saving the Mask?''

Green Spider smiled. ''Sometimes the only way to save something is to allow it to perish.'' His eyes widened, his gaze wandering, seemingly distracted by each flicker of the fire. "You see, there is this bridge . . . where opposites are reconciled. Earth and Air. Water and Fire. All rising, twining. That's the Power of the Roaring Water."

Green Spider's mouth opened slightly, as though he wanted to say more but didn't know quite where to begin. Confusion, or perhaps hopelessness, glimmered in his eyes. The look made Otter's stomach muscles clench. He'd seen it before . . . on the night of the Dance at the Spotted Loon village. The night that tears had traced lines down the Contrary's face.

Otter leaned forward. "Green Spider, I know this may be hard for you, but . . . has Many Colored Crow abandoned you? Is that why you no longer—"

Green Spider laughed out loud. Then his mirth dropped to periodic chuckles as he shook his head. "Oh, yes. He's left me all alone in the wilderness, with only myself to talk to! The animal! To do such a thing to his chosen Dreamer! What a beast."

"But I—I don't understand. I mean, I thought—"

"Otter." The Contrary squeezed his eyes closed for a long moment, as though concentrating very hard. When he spoke, the words came out soft and strained. "I . . . I don't know the end of this journey anymore."

"But you did when we began."

"I know that there is mist," he said with great precision, as if speaking like a normal man required great effort now. "And I know that the bridge is there in the heart. But I can't see it. Do you understand? The mist is so thick, I . . ."

Otter gave him more time, but he added nothing further. Otter said, "Green Spider, tell me. What about the Khota? I don't care about myself, but can you promise me something? Can you ensure that Pearl will be safe? And Black Skull?"

"You would give yourself up? To ensure their safety?" The Contrary turned glassy eyes on him, and Otter's soul quaked.

"I remember Four Kills' Dream. At the time, I scoffed, but that's the price, isn't it? My death? Very well, I'll pay it. For Pearl and Black Skull . . . and to ensure *your* safety as well."

"Why? Tell me, Otter. Why, when your soul has begun to Sing again, and your flute music charms the stars . . . why would you give that up for the rest of us?"

Otter rubbed his hands together, lost in the fire himself, hearing Four Kills relate the story of his Dream. "I'm to drown, aren't I? Four Kills saw that. You know about his Dream. The only way you could know is if you saw it when Many Colored Crow granted you your Vision. My corpse, spinning around, Dancing in the water."

"You don't have to. You can still save yourself."

Otter's heart ached. "I suppose. But I think I finally understand what you meant that day at White Shell when you told me that to find myself, I had to lose myself. I have found love, Green Spider. The love of a man for a woman. Pearl gave me that. And I have discovered the love of friendship . . . through Black Skull." He lifted his tightly clasped hands and pointed at Green Spider with that single fist. "And you have taught me a love for the Sacred, Contrary. But I think I see now that to protect these things, I may have to lose them—by giving myself up to save them."

Green Spider smiled sadly. "Power chose well."

"Black Skull will attempt to thwart me." Otter swallowed hard, seeing it in his mind. Black Skull would do everything in his power to save Otter. "It's in his nature to think he ought to sacrifice himself to save others. But I *do not* want him to die, Green Spider. He'll try to justify it through some eloquent speech about duty and being a warrior. But, Green Spider, you'll see that it's me instead, won't you?"

"And if he seriously wishes to lose himself to save you?"

Otter rested his mouth on his clasped hands. "You and Pearl will need a warrior to lead you through the Khota. Black Skull is the only one who can do that. You need him to protect the Mask. So you see, I have practical reasons."

"And Pearl?"

Pain constricted Otter's heart like strips of wet leather tightening as they dried. Speaking became difficult. "I regret that we had so little time . . ." He forced a breath into his lungs. "When this is all over, Green Spider, when you have the Mask and have escaped the Khota, if Pearl and Black Skull should look at each other with love in their eyes, you'll tell them that it's all right, won't you? That they should not forfeit happiness over thoughts of what I might be thinking or feeling in the City of the Dead."

Green Spider twined his fingers in the fabric over his heart. "Your words are here, Otter. I will tell them."

"And yours are in my soul, my friend." He paused. "Green Spider, there may not be time to say this when we get to the Roaring Water. I want to thank you . . . for everything. For all the gifts of laughter and delight, and for the lessons you've taught. I hope I learned them well."

Green Spider met Otter's eyes with a crystalline intensity. "Knowing you has brightened my soul, Otter."

Otter smiled and stood. The cool wind coming in off the water whipped his long hair back over his shoulders. He absorbed the bite of the wind, inhaling the watery fragrance of the lake.

The deal had been struck.

And all he felt was relief that the Contrary, Pearl, and Black Skull would be safe.

I'm sorry, Four Kills. But were you here, in my place, you'd do the same.

He dropped a hand on Green Spider's narrow shoulder and squeezed, then turned, heading back to the woman he loved.

Black Skull lifted his head as the Trader disappeared over the dune. As he'd listened to his friend's agonized words, his head had begun throbbing.

Catlike, Black Skull crept from his blankets, scooped sand over them to keep them from blowing away, then quietly headed for the fire, where Green Spider sat so placidly. The Contrary stared out at the vast indigo sea, lit only by silver waves that crawled relentlessly toward the shore.

Black Skull sidled up to the fire and squatted down next to Green Spider, oddly uneasy as the fool added another chunk of wood to the fire.

"Look," he said straightforwardly, "I know what the Trader's up to. If it hadn't been for the wind, I'd have missed it, but as it was, enough words were blown to me that I could get the gist of what he had to say."

"Isn't it a funny thing about wind? How it changes sound, I mean. Don't you ever wonder about that, Little Mouse?"

"Well, no, I guess not."

"Air is something. You can feel it, breathe it. When the wind blows, a stillness fills the land."

"Because the wind covers the sound?"

"Only the loudest of noises become complete silence."

Black Skull's brows drew together, and he heaved a sigh. Flames licked up around the piece of firewood. "Otter thinks that he should be the one to drown. That's silly, and you know it."

"Why? Tell me, Killer of Men."

"I'm the one to do this thing. Listen." Black Skull could feel the muscles in his face jerking, though no violent emotion lay behind the spasm, just a vague sense of desperation. "I wasn't chosen to travel all this way just to kill a few Khota on that Levee Island. If so, I'd have drowned in the storm that night. Power has kept me alive because it's me. *Me,* Green Spider. I have not fulfilled my purpose yet. And I would do that. It is my right to see it done."

"Are you saying you want to die?"

Black Skull smiled, aware that it chased the twitching muscles into hideous contortions. "You asked me once if I would be the most beautiful man or the most ugly when we reached the Roaring Water. Well, Contrary, I can tell you. I'm both."

The Contrary's gaze centered on the flames. "Can you be two things at once, warrior?"

"Of course, fool. Steam and ice are just different ways of being water. That girl at Wenshare chose me because she saw me in a way I never had. When I looked into her eyes, I was beautiful."

"Death will rob you of that feeling. Why do you seek it?"

Black Skull folded his hands. "I always expected to die in battle. Dying's not hard. But to go on living, knowing that my death might have saved my friends . . . I would never see myself as beautiful again. Do not condemn me to that, Contrary. I ask you as my friend. Let me be the one."

"You are asking that I ignore Otter's plea."

"Yes." Black Skull felt oddly at peace inside himself, as though his soul knew the rightness of this decision. "You didn't see him on the beach with Pearl today. They came rising out of the water like Spirits, each so taken with the other's love. I would buy them eternity if I could.''

"Otter thought that perhaps you would take care of Pearl." Green Spider craned his neck to peer more closely at the fire, as if he saw a Vision forming there. "Fire is Powerful. Little Dancer barely understood."

"Who? Don't try to distract me, fool! I love Pearl, of course. She is a warrior, and my friend. But don't you see, I *owe* her this. She saved my life, and by doing so, gave me the chance to be reborn. If my death can save Otter for her, then that is the most precious gift I can give her in return.'' He slumped back on the sand and glared at Green Spider from the corners of his eyes. After several moments of silence, he added, "And don't give me any of your backward crap, either. I know this to be true."

"You love them both that much?"

"And you, too, you silly fool." He chuckled then. "I think the world needs a Green Spider more than it needs a Black Skull. I've taken a lot of lives, Green Spider. I'll take a few more Khota with me, too. But I would give mine to keep yours in this world a little longer. You keep going backward, and maybe a few more idiots like me can go forward. That's a reasonable strategy, don't you think?"

Green Spider gazed at him through wide, clear eyes. "But how will we get home without you and your strength?"

Black Skull shook his head. "I can't get anyone home. I don't know the rivers, the customs. I was just lucky that I didn't start a war by coupling with Shinbone's daughter. If the two of you hadn't had the sense you did, I might have gotten us all killed at Meadowlark, or Hilltop, or who knows where. The point is: Otter is the *only* one who can make sure that everyone—and the Mask—gets away safely." He jammed a callused thumb into his chest. "I *can't*."

"I see."

Black Skull sighed, finally summoning his courage. "Green Spider, I ask you this as a friend. I don't know the whys and ways of these things, but work it out with Power. I'll take care of the Khota, whip them all, right down to the last breath in my body. Tell Power I want the chance to save my friends. My life, for all of yours. Otter can live with his Pearl, and you will be able to go on teaching people . . . teaching them . . . well, teaching people how to live inside their bones.''

"Do you seek glory, warrior?"

"I no longer know what that means. But, no. If necessary, I'll slip away, face the Khota alone. My name and my ghost may be forgotten. My body can rot among the leaves or in the darkness under the falls. I wish only the safety of my friends.''

Green Spider smiled and reached out to pat Black Skull's broad shoulder. "You're a good man, Little Mouse. I will speak for you. Many Colored Crow was a warrior once—he will understand.''

Black Skull gripped Green Spider's hand and pulled him forward, embracing him so hard that he drove the air from the Contrary's lungs in a gush. "May the ancestors bless you, my friend. Take care of Otter and Pearl. Help them. That is the last thing I will ask of you.'' He tightened his embrace one last time, unaware of the look of suffocation on Green Spider's frantic face.

Black Skull rose and headed back toward his bedding.

Pearl listened to Otter's deep breathing, and with deliberate care, slipped out from under his arm. She rose and used the same piece of driftwood that he'd used to hold down the heavy blanket.

She walked a short distance and answered nature's call. Only then did she wonder what had kept Otter, and why he'd left so furtively. The reflection of the fire on a dune face piqued her interest, and she was almost over the crest when she saw Black Skull, his hands moving with such an intensity that he seemed to be pleading with Green Spider. The Contrary, in contrast, appeared completely absorbed by some Vision in his head.

Pearl hesitated, then circled the camp, dropping to her belly and slithering forward on the sand until she could hear Black Skull's words. The blood froze in her veins as she listened.

Otter had drifted away to buy her safety with his life? And now Black Skull, fool that he was, was trying to do the same?

She waited, truly touched, as the warrior ended his impassioned plea and then hugged the Contrary. Green Spider's eyes fairly popped from their sockets under the embrace.

Pearl allowed Black Skull's broad back to vanish into the night, gave him a moment lest he return with some last words, and then rose, brushing the sand from her skirt as she walked up to the fire and squatted beside Green Spider. She turned her back to the wind so she could watch for either Otter or the warrior.

"They're crazy, Green Spider," she said calmly. "Are you sure that someone has to give himself up for the Mask? Tell me 'backward'—was that part of the Vision?"

Green Spider's unfocused eyes drifted this way and that, as if seeking an answer, and he ended up by placing another piece of wood on the flames. Sparks shot out and swayed upward in the gusting wind. "I flew with Many Colored Crow, and I saw someone in the swirling mist below the falls. A great many Spirits live there. This Spirit looked familiar, but the face was different . . . dark, misshapen."

"Black Skull? You mean Black Skull?"

"Not a human face, but one more misshapen than Black Skull's . . . surrounded by a black halo. A beautiful face, with large, dark, glowing eyes. Swimming, stroking through the mist like a fish in water. The shape whirled around me, almost teasing, and I tried to reach out and touch it, but it was too fast. Afterward, I rose, spiraling like silver in the sunlight, twisting around, watching rainbows of color arching through the air, growing, circling me as I rose on high."

"A black halo? A beautiful face with large, dark eyes?" She propped her chin on her fist, frowning into the fire. "Then there isn't any reason why it couldn't be me."

"There isn't any reason why it should be you, either," he countered, reaching down thoughtfully to rub his dirty moccasins. "Otter and Black Skull have both asked to be this Spirit."

She closed her eyes, her soul aching. "They would, wouldn't they? Well, they're both fools." She reached out, laying a slim hand on his arm. "Green Spider, if Power must have a soul in exchange for this Mask of yours, I'd rather that it had mine."

He blinked, squinting as he turned to try to bring her into focus.

"I'm the obvious one," she stated positively, aware of the

rightness in her soul. "I've nothing left. No family, no clan, no place to go. Not only that, I can't let Otter or Black Skull go in my place. I'd *never* forgive myself. Not for Otter's death, not for Black Skull's, and certainly not for yours."

She leaned forward. "If someone has to go, I'm the perfect one. The Khota wouldn't be here but for me. It's *my* fault, don't you see? None of this would have happened if I hadn't drawn the Khota out on the hunt by bashing Wolf of the Dead over the head and burning his house down. It's *me* they want. My part in this is finished. I've taught Otter all I can about deep-water travel. He can read the stars as well as I can now. He knows how to weather a storm, how to read the swells."

"And your love? It doesn't mean anything to you?" Green Spider made a face, as if he saw something just over the top of her head that he didn't like.

She whirled to look, saw nothing, and let out the breath she'd been unwittingly holding. "Green Spider, if Otter dies for me, my soul will die with him. How can I love Otter and you if I know that Black Skull died trying to protect me? In the end, that knowledge will eat at my soul like acid on shell. If either of them dies in my place, I am condemned."

"And if you die? Are they?"

She glanced sadly into the fire. "Black Skull will mourn, but his soul is a warrior's, accustomed to such loss. He'll find it acceptable in the end to spend the rest of his life honoring me. In that way, he will survive. As for Otter, he's been crushed by love before. He will hurt, Green Spider, but he'll have you to help him. They'll both have you to help them—and you'll do that for them, won't you? You'll help them?"

"I never have any choice," he whispered. "Front is back and the insides always come out."

"Good," Pearl said without quite understanding what he'd meant. "Now, there's another thing we have to consider. This Mask of Many Colored Crow . . ." She squeezed his forearm tightly. "Green Spider, look at me." He did, though it seemed to her that nobody was at home in those eyes. She continued, "Tell me now, is the Mask wicked? And if so, why are we all talking about throwing away our lives to save it?"

"It is not evil, Pearl."

A sigh of relief escaped her lips. "It's worried me ever since the night at the Spotted Loon camp. I just couldn't understand why you would . . .''

He tilted his head in a gesture so vulnerable that she longed to comfort him. "I'm doing the best I can, Pearl."

"Oh, Green Spider, I know you are. I have always believed that." She crumpled the hem of her skirt with nervous fingers. "The Mask is the most important thing there is. But second is you. You're Power's chosen Dreamer. You know how to deal with the Mask, how to care for it, where to take it. Next comes Otter, and then Black Skull, each as vital as the other. Black Skull's right. He doesn't know the people or the rivers, or how to handle a boat. But without Black Skull, Otter's completely vulnerable. He needs Black Skull's muscle to speed *Wave Dancer* through deep water. Otter can get by on rivers, but that won't save the Mask if someone pursues *Wave Dancer* after this business at the Roaring Water is over. And you know as well as I do that Black Skull can protect the Mask—as well as everyone else—until you can get it home again."

She took a deep breath, fists clenching. "The Khota are here because of me. They *want* me. Well, all right, they can *have* me."

Green Spider closed his eyes as though suffering. "And so the decision can be made without considering the passions of the heart: love, hate, despair. Is that what you would have me believe?"

She lowered her eyes, aware of a warmth rising along her cheeks. "No, my friend, I would not lie to you. I'm scared to death of what the Khota will do to me. It won't be a pleasant way to die, but I'm strong enough and stubborn enough to buy you the time to rescue the Mask and make your escape, especially if you keep those two heroic fools from realizing what I'm doing until it's too late. It would be just like them to rush off to rescue me . . . and have all three of us die while the Mask goes over the falls into oblivion, and while you're . . . I don't know, probably Dancing and Singing, or something silly like that."

Green Spider smiled. "Yes. Something silly like that."

She added, "Green Spider, we can't afford such a disaster, so you'll have to help me. Cover for me. Tell them something, anything, to keep them from knowing until you're all safely away with the Mask.''

Green Spider's mouth trembled. He opened his eyes to stare at her. ''But what of your soul, Pearl? The Khota will leave it homeless, angry, roaming forever.''

''I'm already homeless,'' she replied, though she'd been hoping, hoping desperately, that perhaps she had gained one with Otter. ''I'll be very happy in the lonely places, talking to the deer, whispering to the juncos, and Singing with the crickets. As a ghost, I'll go see all the things I didn't get to see while I was alive. Maybe drift back into Khota country and look up Otter's Uncle.

''Besides,'' she said with a wan smile, ''I won't be angry, Green Spider. I have freely chosen this death. There are seventeen Khota. They'll all want to rape me as many times as they can. If I play my part right, I can buy a couple of days for you that way. Then Wolf of the Dead will spend another two days on different means of torture, and all I have to do is to outlast him, and . . . and, yes, finally I'll confess to him that Otter and Black Skull are coming back in a couple of weeks, passing right back down the river with the Mask.''

She nodded, seeing it all in her head. The plan was simple, and she *could* outlast the Khota. ''If I am strong enough, he'll sit right there on the river, waiting for the Mask of Many Colored Crow until you are all far away.''

''Only a coward could be so brave,'' he whispered.

Pearl massaged her forehead. Her hand was cold. ''That's backward. Only the brave can be so cowardly. You should feel my heart—I'm already terrified. But this time, Green Spider, I'll be ready for the filthy maggots. Last time, I wasn't.''

''Last time it wasn't a prolonged murder,'' the Contrary reminded her in a remarkably straightforward manner.

''Last time I wasn't saving the lives of my friends . . . or the life of the man I love. I'll do my part, Green Spider. The only thing I need to hear from you is that you'll do yours.''

His eyes had lost focus again, and he grinned idiotically. ''Never! No, never! And never again! All is lost! Otter, Black Skull, and the silly Contrary, dead, dead, dead! Only Pearl lives in the glory of the lights—the sparkling, wondrous lights of so many colors.''

Pearl took his hand and placed it to her lips. ''Thank you, Green Spider. If you hadn't burned your root off that day on the Ilini, I'd have never found the courage. You've given me a great deal. I'll be worthy, I promise. I'll make you proud of me.''

With that, she rose and stepped around the fire. She cast one last smile Green Spider's way, then walked thoughtfully back to where Otter lay sound asleep.

Once she'd slid back into their blankets, she slipped an arm over his stomach and placed her head on his chest, listening to his breathing, to the steady rhythm of his heartbeat.

''Um?'' he said, half-waking.

''I'm just loving you,'' she whispered. ''Go back to sleep.''

He tenderly nuzzled his chin against the top of her head and drifted off again. Tears trickled silently down her cheeks while she watched the stars gleaming and twinkling high overhead.

I sit and watch as the fire burns down, the embers shifting and glimmering in the wind. In one of my Dreams, White Ash told me of seeing Wolf Dreamer's face appear in the wavering coals.

And so I wait . . . and watch . . . considering the words of my companions. Each so desperate.

I cannot help the sobs that swell my chest. The dignified resignation of Otter, the simple faith of Black Skull, and the horrifying pragmatism of Pearl—all have left me feeling empty, as if their love for each other has transported me, and me alone, to the barren windswept plains of Power.

And all I see around me is a wasteland.

Nothing lives here. Except Death.

A gust of wind assaults the coals, and sparks spiral up and twist away, flying out over the moon-dark lake, where they vanish in the mist.

I stare harder at the wavering coals. As hard as I can.

. . . But I see no face.

The battlefield seems to have gone suddenly quiet.

So.

The decision is left to me.

Which of my friends do I condemn to Death, that the Mask of Many Colored Crow might live?

I bow my head, close my eyes, and laugh with wild abandon.

Forty-six

Pale Snake shifted uncomfortably as the wind changed and disturbed his fire. Brilliant yellow sparks twirled with the rising smoke to swarm around him in a warm haze. He turned his face away until the sparks subsided. "The answer lies with Tall Man."

Behind them, the beach became rocky and rose in a gentle slope to an unscalable wall of crumbled soil mixed with rock that had been undercut by millennia of terrible storms. Before full dark, Star Shell had been able to see huge cedar roots grasping frantically at the air, beseeching the lost soil to return, for any further erosion meant death amidst the detritus at the bottom of the sheer drop.

This night was particularly black. Wind came moaning out of the darkness, bearing the sweet scent of water, and white-crested waves pounded the pale beach.

Star Shell lowered her eyes, refusing to look at Pale Snake. She stroked the locks of Silver Water's dark hair. The little girl had rolled up in her blankets and stretched out before the fire, leaving the wind to tousle her hair atop Star Shell's extended legs.

"I think you're wrong," Star Shell said. "I think it's the Mask. As it has been all along."

Unabated, the waves pulsed upon the bleached sand, each foaming advance racing up as if to tag the rear of their beached canoe—then falling back in a white rush and undercutting its successor.

Frustrated, tired beyond exhaustion, Star Shell blurted, "Tall Man? Does it always come back to him? Can't you stop hating your father long enough to think? You're a sorcerer. What about the Mask?"

"It's fearsome enough." He gave her a somber appraisal. Firelight accented his strong cheekbones and black eyes, and the wind tugged at his pulled-back hair. "But, Star Shell, you've got to remember, a Mask is just that, a home for Power—neither good nor evil. It reflects or projects, and a person looking through it sees as Many Colored Crow does, that's all."

"It speaks to my daughter."

Pale Snake looked at Silver Water, who peered at him with luminous eyes. He asked, "Does it tell you to do bad things?"

Silver Water's lips tensed, and she shook her head, refusing to meet Star Shell's eyes.

"Does it ask you to hurt anyone?"

Silver Water shook her head again.

"Tell me," Pale Snake said gently, "what does the Mask ask you to do, Silver Water?"

"Nothing, but it . . . it shows me things. I mean, sometimes when I Dream, it shows me people and places that I don't know. I hear voices talking in strange words, but I understand what they're saying."

Star Shell nerved herself, forcing her voice to remain calm. "Does it ever ask you to kill?"

Silver Water shook her head. She lay with her hands shoved down beneath her blankets and her back arched. She looked like a very unhappy little girl.

"Does the Mask ask you to do good things?" Pale Snake asked. "To help people? To keep them from being hurt? Maybe to warn them of trouble?"

Silver Water blinked and shook her head again.

Pale Snake smiled reassuringly. "Silver Water, do you ever want to hurt anyone? Or to help them, either one?"

She looked up at Star Shell, her eyes pleading.

"It's all right, baby. Just tell the truth. I love you."

Silver Water shook her head. "Pale Snake, I don't know what I want anymore. Except . . . maybe . . . to go home."

Pale Snake smiled and reached out to ruffle her hair. "I can understand that." He glanced up. "Star Shell, I want to see the Mask."

Her soul recoiled, and she raised a hand as if to fend off some terrible monster. "No! It *kills*!" She swallowed hard. "Don't you understand? Everyone who has laid eyes on it is *dead*!"

"You're not. And neither is Silver Water." He watched her, totally calm, his voice completely reasonable.

"But the old woman, my husband, Stargazer, Tall Man . . . maybe even Greets the Sun, for all I know."

"From what you yourself have told me, the Mask didn't kill my father. Robin and his warriors did." Pale Snake sighed. "I can feel the Mask, Star Shell. It's calling to me. And there's no wickedness in the summons—though it's capable of that. I don't feel goodness, either. Though it's also capable of that. It's waiting, and it knows something that I think we need to know."

"I don't care what you say. Tall Man is *dead*. And he was a far more Powerful sorcerer than you are." She winced, regretting her words.

Pale Snake, however, simply said, "Everything that you say is true. But listen to me. Tall Man never wore the Mask, did he? Did you ever see him actually don it? Look through the eyes?"

She shook her head. "No. He said . . . said he was afraid of it. Of its Power. Of what it would do."

"I see." Pale Snake then added, "Star Shell, he's dead. But you must understand, being killed *by* the Mask is different than being killed *because* of the Mask. Now, which way did he die? Did the Mask kill him outright?"

She shook her head.

"Do you trust me?" he asked, giving her that level stare. "After having traveled with me, after everything I've told you, do you trust me? I think you do."

She wet her lips, aware of Silver Water's eerie gaze. "Yes. Yes, I trust you."

He seemed to deflate a little, exhaling wearily. "Thank you, Star Shell. I didn't realize how important it was to hear that from you."

"But I don't want you to even look at the Mask." She closed her eyes, imagining horrible scenes. "I don't want to lose you."

"Well, in that case, maybe you'd better just tie a cord around my neck—or bind my feet perhaps."

She smiled, rubbing her eyes before she could look at him again. "The Mask is trouble, Pale Snake."

"I quite agree, but I have a suspicion about it that I'd like to investigate. To do so, I don't have to wear the Mask or look through the eyeholes. I simply need to ask it some questions. I cannot do that until I have your permission."

Star Shell glanced down at Silver Water, who quickly looked away, clearly afraid . . . not of the Mask, but of her mother. In that instant, Star Shell began to grasp the extent of the rift that had grown between them. And all because of her own hatred of the Mask.

"Baby? You . . . I mean, do you think this is a good idea?"

Silver Water stared unhappily at the fire.

"Silver Water?" Pale Snake asked gently. "You know the Mask better than either your mama or I do. Do you think it would hurt me?"

Silver Water slowly shook her head, and a pain grew in Star Shell's chest.

"All right," Star Shell said hoarsely, refusing to take her pleading eyes from her daughter. "Look at it. Get it over with."

"Not so fast," Pale Snake warned. "The Mask is a thing of Power, not a simple fetish. I'll need to prepare myself."

"Prepare yourself?" Could she repair this wound between her daughter and herself? Was it just a temporary misunderstanding, or had the Mask claimed yet another victim?

"Prepare myself, yes. Your ears worked correctly the first time."

She glanced up, suddenly confused, hurt, and scared, her soul torn so many ways that it didn't know which way to run.

"Easy." Pale Snake leaned forward to place his hands on her shoulders. On his face, betrayed in the firelight, she could see his terrible yearning for her, the unfulfilled love that he longed to bestow on her.

"Why?" she asked. "Why are you doing this?"

"The Mask might tell me where the trap is, or if there even is a trap. I'll know the truth of Tall Man's words after I talk to the Mask. Did he ever touch it? I mean without using the wolf-hide as a protection?"

She thought back. "Yes, when he . . . the first time. In the clan house. Just after my husband—"

"All right. That's good. That means the Mask had direct contact with his soul." He tightened his grip on her shoulders.

She could feel her soul touching his, beginning to surrender. How she wanted to rely on someone who could comfort her, reassure her that everything would be well.

"I'd better go," he said, his voice gone husky. "I need to Sing and Dance to prepare my soul. It won't take long."

She nodded, reaching for Silver Water's hand. As he let her go and walked away, she whispered, "Baby, I'm sorry. So sorry."

Silver Water looked up, and with her free hand, wiped away one of her mother's tears. "It will be all right, Mama. The Mask won't hurt him."

From up the beach, his voice rose, strong and resonant as he Sang in a language she didn't know. Some of the words sounded familiar, and she thought that Tall Man might have used them on the night he fixed the charms to blind Stargazer. . . . Stargazer. She shook her head. Why wouldn't the old High Head Elder have known to prepare before donning the Mask?

Old, a voice told her. *Too much forgotten.*

She closed her eyes, aware that Silver Water had kept hold of her hand. Odd, how comforting her daughter's touch was. As if she, too, were preparing.

Pale Snake approached out of the darkness, Singing, and Star Shell started at the sight of him. He'd rubbed black onto his cheeks to cover the snakes and had drawn a crow effigy on his forehead with charcoal. Twists of grass circled his arms, and sprigs of red cedar appeared to have been rubbed over his body and tucked into his breechcloth.

A tranquillity filled his handsome face as he knelt before her, his arms held high to wave a cedar frond in the air.

Star Shell trembled as she unslung the pack from her back and delivered it into his hands. At that moment, she seemed to float; her soul turned airy.

Pale Snake raised the pack to the fire and then, his voice dropping into a melodic chant, began untying the laces.

With one hand, Star Shell grasped Silver Water's hand again, and her other hand rose to her throat as if to alleviate the tightness there.

Pale Snake lifted the wolfhide, glorious and shining, from the outer pack and slowly unfolded it from the gleaming jet features of the Mask.

"Blessed Mysterious One," he whispered. "It's beautiful."

Star Shell gasped, for the Mask seemed to glow, and she could feel the Power, resonant, surging with the wind.

"Look!" Silver Water cried. "It's pretty, Mama. It sees in many colors, like dark fire!"

Pale Snake bowed his head, the chant ending. Then, slowly, he began speaking in what Star Shell recognized as High Head—the old language, that of the Elders now all but gone.

The pounding of the surf grew louder, as if it carried a thousand voices. A breeze whipped at the fire, whirling the sparks around. From somewhere out in the night, a curious bellowing sounded, the roar of some huge, trumpeting animal. Then the Singing seemed to spring from the very air.

"Look, Mama!" Silver Water cried. "A big white animal with two tails! One in front, one behind! And curly long teeth!"

Star Shell blinked, looking at the whirling sparks, and there, staring back at her from the flames, stood a proud warrior, scarred, but strong. His misshapen face should have frightened her, but a strength radiated from those black eyes. He tried to smile, but the muscles in his broken face betrayed him. He sighed, saddened, but his soul seemed to shine, like polished copper in the sun.

"It's all right," she told him, trying to reach out. "I see your soul."

And then he was gone, vanished into the glow of the fire.

"Wait!" she cried, rising to her feet. "Come back!"

But the fire only snapped and popped, and the surf rolled and pounded, and whispered down the shore.

Pale Snake sat with his head down. He returned the Mask to its pack. Silver Water stared wide-eyed into the fire.

"I think I have the answers I needed," Pale Snake said, looking up with numb eyes. "Star Shell, we must go. We must leave here now. I'm twice a fool, and maybe three times so. I should have guessed that they would follow."

"Robin?" she said dully.

"Yes, we must leave. Now." He seemed broken. "I'll get you as far as the island. I need to drop my packs, and then you'll be on your own."

"My own?" She frowned. "Pale Snake?"

"You were meant to destroy me, Star Shell."

"Destroy you? How?"

He rose to his feet, stepping close to run trembling fingers along her cheek. She almost cried out at the pain in his eyes. "I'll tell you as we travel. I don't know all the facts. You'll have to help me piece it together. Come, let's pack. We can make the river by tomorrow night. This wind will help us along. It will be hard paddling, but if we don't work like dogs, Robin and his cutthroats will have us first."

His expression went grim. "I saw a Vision of your skull, neatly cleaned and polished, hanging from Robin's wall, right beside my father's."

"What . . . what else did you see? . . . Pale Snake?"

"You were meant to love, Star Shell. The greedy demon understood that."

And with that, he began loading the packs into the canoe.

The image faded into swirling flames, sparks and smoke whipping around as searing heat forced Black Skull to duck behind the hard hickory of his war club for protection.

He cried out and jerked awake. *Wave Dancer* rode the swells, powered by the wind trap and the fierce gusts that drove out of the west to push them across the black waters.

"Are you all right?" Pearl called from where she held one side of the wind trap, her form barely visible in the blackness.

"Dream," he called back and shook his head. He could see Green Spider struggling with a corner of the wind trap. Those knowing eyes were fastened on the warrior.

Black Skull fought to regain the image, and, yes, there she was, reaching out to him through the firelight.

When he blinked, though, it was to see only night. Wind roared off the whitecaps, and the bow splashed whitely into the black water as the canoe dipped and rose.

Black Skull crawled back onto the packs, staring up into Green Spider's owlish face. "What was that?"

"The Mask," the Contrary told him in a curiously pained voice. "Its Power was unleashed tonight, drawing on the wind and water, twinkling with the stars. Didn't you hear it calling?"

"I was Dreaming," Black Skull admitted. "Funny thing. I've never Dreamed of being a bird before, but there I was, soaring, flying high over the lake, and I saw these canoes paddling along. Naturally, I dropped down to see if they were Khota, but no, a different group of warriors, angry men, blood on their minds and clothing.

"But what were they pursuing? I let the wind carry me, ever eastward along the southern shore. And there I saw a camp with a man, a woman, and a little girl. The man was Dreaming, locked with Power, Dancing around and around as they Sang and chanted, and the woman looked up at me with fright in her eyes as I landed.

"I knew all of a sudden that the warriors were chasing her. Just having flown over them, I knew how closely they pursued. Just as I was going to warn them, I really saw her . . ." He paused, slowly shaking his head. "The most beautiful woman in the world. Right there, holding the child's hand and looking up at me."

"Star Shell," Green Spider told him. "The little girl is Silver Water. Her daughter."

"And the man?"

"A medicine man of some sort. I've never seen him before tonight."

"Her husband?" Black Skull's heart fell.

"No. Though he would like to be. I can sense that he loves her, and she . . . she doesn't know how to feel about him."

"I must save her, Green Spider." And so he would. For this other man, no doubt. "Your Vision at Wenshare village was wrong, Contrary." Black Skull lowered his voice so that Pearl couldn't hear. "I will die for her, too. I will fight these Khota, and these other warriors who pursue Star Shell and Silver Water. I will die for all of you."

Green Spider smiled sadly in the darkness. "Yes, my friend. You, the ugliest man in the world, will die for the most beautiful woman. The Contrary has spoken."

Black Skull nodded firmly, sinking down on the soft pack, lost in his thoughts.

"Tell me, Killer of Men," the Contrary whispered, "if you could have her, would you change your mind? Would you live, knowing that you could love her for the rest of your life?"

Would he? His heart had skipped at the sight of her—looking so alone and frightened. She'd stared up at him with those wondrous eyes, and he'd felt his soul melt.

He glanced over his shoulder at Pearl, struggling with the wind trap. He couldn't see Otter at the stern, but he could imagine the happy set of his face as his canoe ran faster before the waves than it ever had.

Black Skull raised himself again. "No, Green Spider. First I will save my friends. Only then will I attempt to save her. That is enough for the Black Skull. But if this other man doesn't treat her correctly, my ghost will come and pay his soul a visit."

Green Spider nodded. "Power knows your heart, Killer of Men. It has heard your words."

"Good! Then my friends, and perhaps the beautiful Star Shell, will be safe." He smiled at that, aware that his facial muscles worked better in Dreams than real life. But Star Shell hadn't cared, she'd seen his soul.

Black Skull pulled at his blankets, stopping only long enough to pat Catcher and scratch his ears. "When I'm gone, Catcher, you guard them well. I'm putting a lot of faith in you."

The dog licked his crushed cheek, and Black Skull resettled himself, closing his eyes. The swaying, the sound of water splashing, and the occasional droplets of spray that spattered him brought a sense of well-being. And to think, he'd once lain here, in this exact spot, cowering and quivering with terror.

He reached out, giving *Wave Dancer* a reassuring rub, and then closed his eyes and tugged the blanket up against his chin. Yes, he could still see her on the fabric of his soul. He studied the lines of her delicate face, seeking to learn them so that he could picture her even long after he was dead, killed by the Khota, or by the sniffing foxes that drove Star Shell toward him.

Death held even fewer fears for him now. And it wouldn't be long. A couple of days at the most.

Star Shell's legs ached from the cramped position in the canoe. Wind ripped at her, thankfully coming from behind, but it carried just enough spray that she stayed perpetually wet and chilled. Despite having become slightly familiar with canoe travel on the big lake, she was still afraid of these huge swells. Riding them in the darkness, in the gusting wind, and hearing the whisper of the whitecaps, didn't reassure her any.

She tried to paddle hard enough to keep the cold at bay, but not so hard as to exhaust herself. She couldn't allow that, not with Robin so close.

From the sound of the breakers rolling along the shore to their right, and by the surging white foam of the waves, Star Shell could mark their location. The night had dragged on—and Pale Snake refused to speak. When she looked back, she could see his dark form paddling mercilessly. But then the wind would whip her hair and cause her eyes to tear.

"Pale Snake? What did you see?" The first lifting of the night sky in the east indicated that a new day was fast approaching.

And—as he had done all through the night—Pale Snake said nothing. He might have become soulless, driven only by the flashing of his paddle and the swaying of his body with each stroke.

Star Shell gazed at her daughter where she slept huddled in water-silvered blankets.

Why won't he speak? Fear fluttered like sparrows' wings in her belly. Had the Mask done something to Pale Snake? Eaten his soul? Turned him against her? Was he even now planning on how to deliver her up to Robin?

Pale Snake felt dry and forlorn, as barren as dust.

He barely heard her pleading entreaties to talk, to explain what had happened. He locked his jaws, driving himself to paddle that much harder. The Mask had answered his questions.

Yes, Tall Man had sought to trap him—and the scheme had worked, partially at least. The ultimate betrayal had not yet occurred.

"But why?" he'd asked. "Why did my father send her to me?"

"*Justice*," the Mask had told him, and before Pale Snake's eyes, there flashed a series of scenes from the past. Those images had burned into his brain, and now he could begin to sort them out.

"Is Star Shell a trap? Will she destroy me?"

"*Yes.*"

"How?"

The Mask had given him the key to finding out. "*Ask Star Shell about the woman that Tall Man wronged.*" And then had come the warning: "*Flee! Fast! Robin and his Blue Duck warriors are almost upon you!*"

Now, as dawn began to ease the eastern darkness from its hold, Pale Snake concentrated on the images the Mask had shown him. Images of his wife, of his father, and of himself.

To keep his soul from screaming, he forced himself to paddle, rechanneling his fury into the wood and water. He drove himself, heedless of the sweat that ran down to soak his clothing. He was a man pursued, fruitlessly fleeing the demons conjured in his mind.

To Pearl's surprise, her soul hovered in a blissful serenity as she used her crow-headed paddle to steer *Wave Dancer* toward the brilliant orange dawn. She'd lost the shore last night and had veered ever northward, but the swells had seemed to bear them toward their final destination. Still no shoreline appeared, but as long as they were headed toward the northeast, they'd find either the north shore or the east, and then correct.

Otter lay asleep in the blankets in the bow. Black Skull chastised Green Spider for letting the air slip through the wind trap, and the Contrary muttered something nonsensical in reply. Pearl smiled at the exchange.

She surrendered to the wonder of the morning: of *Wave*

Dancer, the canoe's spirit alive with the rush of wind and water, as if it had found its element; of the warrior and the Contrary, each battling to stretch the wind trap; and most of all, of Otter, her lover, as he slept.

They would all continue because of her. For the first time in her life, she finally understood what it meant to be a woman. Not to serve her clan, or to comfort her children, or to please her husband. Her role was to preserve the ancient ways and to protect her loved ones, no matter what the cost. She might bear the young and raise the family, but beyond that, she had to be willing to swing a war club with all her heart, or home and family had no chance.

That floating sense of tranquillity expanded, buoying her, instilling a new courage. Every instant she bought for Otter and her friends increased their odds for survival, and in the end, gave her purpose. No matter what pain the Khota inflicted upon her, she would endure.

I can do this, and do it well. In this instance, the advantage would lie with her. She knew what the Khota thought of women. They would never imagine that her endurance was planned and that by goading them to inflict more suffering, she was winning.

If only there was a way to do all this without the pain. She knew she would scream when they burned her, and whimper when they cut, or twisted, or hit, but that was an admission of the flesh, not of the soul.

You must make the flesh last, Pearl. That is all that matters. You have to keep yourself alive for as long as you can.

Her soul would be the weapon she would use to defeat the Khota ... the one weapon they refused to recognize that she possessed.

Otter awakened from a fitful sleep. He lay curled in an uncomfortable ball, and the warm softness tucked into the curve of his stomach turned out to be Catcher, not Pearl. He stroked the dog gently while he whispered in Catcher's ear, telling him how much he owed him, how much he loved him, and how Pearl would take care of him and feed him when Otter was gone.

Catcher wagged his tail at the soft, tender sounds.

"You have been my finest friend," Otter said, his lips against the silky black-and-tan ear. "I'll look for you on the other side."

Catcher wiggled, twisting to expose his white-furred belly for scratching at the same time he snuffed and ran his warm tongue across Otter's cheek.

Otter propped himself on one elbow and became instantly aware of the fatigue that saddled him like packs too heavy to carry. *You'll be able to rest soon,* he told himself, *and the water will bear your Spirit around and around, Dancing as in Four Kills' Dream. That's not such a bad death.*

Black Skull and Green Spider each leaned out as they held the wind trap. Pearl would be steering, using her paddle to keep them parallel to the shore. To everyone's surprise, the wind trap had worked, even when the wind changed and blew off of one of the stern quarters. *Wave Dancer* continued to hold her course, given a little effort with the steering paddle and provided a person didn't mind the canoe tipping a bit.

Otter closed his eyes for a moment, savoring the last strands of sleep as they parted from his thoughts. This might be his final awakening. He had no idea of when they would reach the Roaring Water. Maybe today.

He heard Pearl's laughter, indistinct through the rhythms of wind and water, and he ran his fingers through Catcher's thick fur. *It will be all right, Pearl. The river claimed me in the beginning, perhaps just for this purpose. You and my friends will live, and smile, and share the warmth of the sun.*

A man could do worse with his life. Red Moccasins would have healthy children by Four Kills, and that, after all, was still Otter's blood. The Mask of Many Colored Crow would be safely entrusted to Green Spider's care and Black Skull's guardianship. And his own life with Pearl, though short, had been wonderful.

"And you, my old friend," Otter said softly, placing his cheek against Catcher's soft head, "you have an easy life ahead of you. Pearl will probably feed you so much that you'll get fat and lazy and spend all your time sleeping in the sun. Do as she and Black Skull tell you. Guard their packs for them."

Catcher yawned and licked Otter's nose as he tried to stretch his legs in the confined space.

What would it be like to drown down there in the cold, clear water? Soon he would know firsthand. If not anxious, at least he was ready.

Perhaps Power hurried them to their goal, or perhaps *Wave Dancer* had communicated with the Spirits of the water, for even as they sighted the shoreline ahead of them, Black Skull could tell that this must be their destination. A flock of crows wheeled in the sky above a narrow inlet. All along the eastern horizon, the tree line extended in a solid, unbroken mass of green.

The wind had finally abated, and in its wake, high clouds mottled the sky, dispersing the light into the most extraordinary display that Black Skull had ever seen.

"Look," he said softly, pointing.

Green Spider followed his finger. "It's all gray to me."

"Magnificent, isn't it?"

"Ugly, warrior, as ugly as you've become."

"Very well, fool. I've made my bargain. Just tell me one thing. Are the Khota here? Did they beat us to this point?"

Green Spider's gaze wavered. "So far ahead of us, warrior. They wait with such intensity that the trap is unsprung."

Black Skull ground his teeth, unsure. "Point the way to them, Contrary."

Green Skull pointed at the mouth of the inlet, and Black Skull grinned. "Then with the wind trap, we've passed them! Excellent. Very well, fool, let's go find your Mask, and the beautiful Star Shell. And then, when all are safe, I shall find the Khota! Will they come from water or land, Contrary?"

"Water, water, always water. With their moccasins still dusty and their canoes ready for pursuit."

Black Skull hesitated, then reached back for Green Spider's hand and patted it hard. "Thank you, my friend. As soon as you have the Mask and Star Shell is safe, order Otter to cast off and paddle like mad back upriver. When the Khota step out of the trees with their accursed wet boots, then the Black Skull shall be among them.''

The Contrary's gaze drifted here and there like a butterfly in flight. ''Among them! Indeed, a whirlwind of death. Dance, Killer of Men, and your wind shall blast away the treacherous souls.''

Black Skull took a deep breath and nodded, grabbing up his heavy paddle, the wood richly stained with his sweat. With an unaccustomed vigor, he dipped his paddle and sent *Wave Dancer* flying for the inlet.

As they entered the channel, he was surprised to see a number of houses on the high banks, many with mounded shell middens running down into the water.

''Greetings!'' Otter called to the first canoe they passed. ''Is this the way to the Roaring Water?''

''Yes, Trader. But beware!'' a man called, waving. ''The river splits up ahead. Follow either branch, for it is only the River Spirit seeking to avoid the drop ahead. Past the island, when the channels come together, you must stay close to shore. If you get into the rapids, you are lost!''

''We understand. We must avoid the rapids!''

''Yes.'' The fisherman hesitated. ''You can't get past with a canoe that big. Not even the Bear Clan will help you portage such a boat. Why don't you stay and Trade with us, here? We'll take you down in a small boat to see the Roaring Water.''

''Thank you. We're not going over the falls. Here!'' Otter tossed the man a great pink conch shell. ''We'll be back. That's for giving us information!''

The man caught the shell, a happy smile curving his lips. He lifted it, nodding appreciation. ''Remember! Avoid the rapids at all costs!''

''We will. Thank you!''

Black Skull studied Otter's face, seeing the resignation, the indomitable courage, of one who believed in his destiny.

I should tell him. But of course he couldn't. Otter would do something foolish like diving headfirst over the side just to deny Black Skull his rightful death.

Pearl, too, seemed to be steeled for something. Had the Trader told her of his planned demise? Was it a knowledge shared between them?

No, it couldn't be. She still looks at Otter with a warm love reflected in her eyes. No woman, no matter how brave, could look at a man like that when she knew he was going to die. Whatever Pearl thinks, she doesn't believe that Otter is going to perish. It must be that being so close to the end has turned her pensive.

Black Skull squared his shoulders then, plying his paddle. His atlatl felt warm beside his thigh. The darts were laid out with the usual care, and his war club waited close at hand. Every now and then he'd steal a touch to instill Spirit into the wood, stone, and metal. For soon now, they would be ready for their final challenge.

A War Song, one his granduncle had taught him, rose in his throat, and as they approached the island the fisherman had spoken of, Black Skull began to Sing softly to himself.

This was the way a man was meant to die.

Forty-seven

Star Shell marveled as they coasted into the mouth of the Roaring Water River. The entrance was broad, wider than even the Serpent River in the south. She could sense the current pulling her toward the end of her trial, and despite the horror that she knew loomed just ahead, she put what little remaining strength she had into paddling. Rapidly, they passed fishing weirs, net floats, shell middens, and canoe landings.

She could see farmsteads and fields through breaks in the trees, and people hailed them from canoes as they hurried by.

She glanced up, aware of the slanting afternoon sun. She had never witnessed a sunset like this, the rays of light streaking through the high clouds, shimmering in colors of pink and purple, rose and violet. The very light seemed to have burst into a halo of the heavens.

The water, too, was clear, deep and dark, possessed of a

Power she'd never felt before. Despite her exhaustion, she straightened, paddling onward. The end lay up ahead somewhere, frightening and reassuring at the same time.

She glanced back at Pale Snake. The snakes tattooed on his cheeks stood out, dark against his unnaturally pale skin. Only his eyes blazed, a reflection of the fire that burned in his soul.

Silver Water sat quietly behind her, watching with sober, dark eyes as the banks passed and the water swirled and eddied in the sinuous coils of the river.

Star Shell looked up at the clouds again. What caused them to glitter in such gem-like fashion? Had the majesty of Power, the infinite swelling and contracting of earth, water, and season, all gathered here to see the Mask of Many Colored Crow reach its final, watery end?

"There." Pale Snake spoke as the river split into two forks. "Land on the point. Right there on the sand."

Star Shell pointed the canoe toward the low beach, wondering which fork one took to reach the Roaring Water. She felt, as well as heard, the hollow grinding as the canoe beached and the wakes rippled into obscurity along the sandy littoral.

Pale Snake sighed, then winced as he rose to his feet. He stepped out, tossing his paddle onto the shore, where it clattered on driftwood.

Star Shell didn't move but watched his jaw muscles as they clenched and quaked, giving life to the serpents on his cheeks.

"Pale Snake, what are we doing? We can't camp here, can we? How far is it to the Roaring Water?"

He lifted the first of his packs from the canoe. Then he extended his hand to her, helping her to her feet and out onto the shore. She locked her knees, aware that until the pins and needles of renewed circulation had finished making her miserable, she'd be just as likely to pitch forward onto her face as to make a step.

With characteristic gentleness, he lifted Silver Water from the canoe.

"Don't go far, Silver Water," he told the little girl. "Your mother will be leaving very soon."

Silver Water nodded and walked down the beach, picking up shells and bits of driftwood. She bent down to peer into the clear water that lapped the shore.

"This place," Pale Snake said, "is special. Here the river splits—it is said that it does so because it does not want to leap over the edge of the Roaring Water and plummet so far down onto the violent rocks below. Only when it can no longer deny the inevitable does it come back together and rush toward the terrible precipice." His jaw trembled and then steadied as his voice lowered. "Here I, too, must encounter the inevitable."

"What did you see last night?"

He grimaced and propped his hands on his hips. "Did you know that Tall Man was dying? That he'd seen his own death?"

"You mean that he knew Robin was going to catch him?"

"No, not that at all. A terrible sickness had penetrated his body and was eating his liver. A disease that not even he, with all of his Power, could cure."

"No, I didn't. But . . . he kept having a pain on the trail." She pressed a hand to her right side beneath her ribs. "About here."

Pale Snake grasped her by the shoulders, staring into her eyes, trying to see into her soul. "The Mask said I should ask you about the woman, the one Tall Man talked about."

She swallowed hard, unable to tear her gaze from his. "Tall Man said that he'd met a woman, the most wondrous of women. She came to a Healing. He . . . he fell in love with her, went to a place he knew she'd be and offered his love. She told him no, that she could love only her husband."

"And then what did he do?"

"He said that he used Power to take her. That he made charms so that when he coupled with her, she Dreamed that it was her husband who had entered her. He said he did that whenever he could, and that she never knew."

"He usually told them eventually. Why didn't he tell her?"

Her heart had begun to race, her blood fearful in her veins. "He said that he had truly loved her and could not have endured seeing hatred for him in her eyes. And then . . . then she died."

The words came tumbling out of her, rushing like the river toward a torrential plunge into chaos. "Her ghost, it knew what he'd done. He said that he was trying to atone, to lessen the ghost's anger by helping me to remove the Mask of Many Colored Crow. He said that he'd be doing a great good for the woman . . . that by helping me, perhaps he'd earn her forgiveness for the evil he'd done.''

Pale Snake's hands tightened on her shoulders, and Star Shell bit back a cry at the pain. "Did he tell you her name? The woman's *name,* Star Shell!''

"No . . . just that she'd recently died.''

Pale Snake's throat worked, as if convulsively. "Where . . . where did you meet Tall Man? When?''

A fist seemed to close about her throat and choke off her air. "No! *No!* It can't . . .''

The corners of Pale Snake's mouth turned down. "Did he mention any Healing at that time? Any that your mother might have . . .''

Star Shell closed her eyes, nodding. She remembered . . . back to the time just before the carved stone tablet was offered. Now she wanted to fall, to crumple down onto the wet sand and die. *Mother? He . . . did that to you?*

"Star Shell.'' Pale Snake's voice brought her back from the gray abyss. "I see the trap now. It's not Silver Water.'' He turned loose her shoulders, looking curiously broken. "I thought he'd had you after all. You, the most beautiful woman alive, would have been ripe for him.''

He balled a fist, watching the tendons leap in his wrist as the muscles swelled. "I thought he'd charmed you, taken you. And in spite of that, I would still have loved you. Made you my wife. I would have known that Silver Water was his daughter, and I would still have loved her, helped her to become the great Dreamer that she will someday be.''

"What?" Star Shell cried. "Silver Water? His . . . You've lost any sense you might have had!''

He shook his head, and grief welled in his eyes. "No, he never took you, Star Shell. He wouldn't. But the desire he must have felt for you gave him the idea to trap me. Or perhaps it was the crime that you were committing with my idiot brother, Greets the Sun.''

"What crime?'' Star Shell backed away as quickly as she'd pursued.

"Tall Man wanted you to leave Greets the Sun, didn't he?'' Pale Snake glared at her. "He did *anything* to get you to leave, didn't he? Even coaxed Silver Water to talk to the Mask that night. He knew that would break you away from Greets the Sun!''

''What are you *talking* about!''

His lips curled. ''*Incest, Star Shell.*''

Words strangled themselves in her confusion.

Pale Snake's smile soured. ''He loved your mother. To have charmed her that way, he must have been obsessed by her. He would have planted a child within her, Star Shell. He conceived you. And when your mother died, he went to you, to save you from Mica Bird's mad rages.''

''You . . . you're as mad as Tall Man!'' Incest? She felt dazed and directionless. *Incest?* Of all the horrible crimes . . .

''No, Star Shell. I'm just another of his victims, like your mother, like you. I'm sure that in his desperation, he really thought that your mother, the fine woman that I'm sure she was, might truly forgive him if he saved you.'' Pale Snake closed his eyes, and tears began to leak down his cheeks. ''He didn't send you to me until he knew that his death was close at hand.''

She shook her head dully. None of this could be true. None of it!

''He knew then. There, on the verge of death, he knew that she'd be shrieking her hatred and anger for what he'd done. So he sent you to me. I was there, in the right place, and he took the gamble that I would feel sorry for you and help you, because I would believe you to be one of his many victims. I don't know if he planned that you—my sister—and I would commit incest, or whether in the last moments, he knew only that I would save you. It doesn't matter. He certainly knew that I would love you.''

Star Shell had backed yet another step away. ''I don't believe any of this.''

Pale Snake pointed at the Mask pack. ''Do you think the Mask did it? Fool, the only reason Mica Bird went crazy was that he wasn't strong enough. He wasn't prepared. You have to learn how to exist with Power before you can use it. A stripling boy can't just pick up the Mask and see through a great Spirit's eyes. He'll go mad!''

''Why didn't Tall Man look through it? He knew the ways of Power.''

''Because he was using the Mask. Blaming everything on it,

covering the tracks of his *own* evil! Power isn't evil, any more than it's good. Human beings, people, are either—'' He jerked away, staring upriver. ''No! Not yet! I'm not through!''

Star Shell turned, and her breath caught in her throat. Up the channel, four canoes rounded the bend.

''Silver Water!'' Pale Snake shouted, waving his hands.

Star Shell watched as her daughter came trotting back, a grin on her face.

''Into the canoe, sister,'' Pale Snake ordered grimly. ''I'll do what I can. Quickly, paddle like you've never paddled before. That, or Robin will be roasting your pretty intestines before sunset. I'll earn you as much time as possible, but *save the Mask*! And yourself, if you can.''

''Save it? *Save it!* I came here to destroy it!''

''Don't! Now go. Hurry!''

As Silver Water clambered in, Pale Snake shoved the canoe into the current, pointing to the west. ''Take that channel. It's shorter. They haven't seen you yet. Stay close to the bank until you're out of sight.''

Star Shell paddled frantically, barely taking time to look back. Her last image was of Pale Snake, his feet braced in the water, shoulders squared as he awaited the coming of the Blue Duck warriors.

In desperation, she paddled closer to the overgrown bank, struggling against the tears of disbelief that shimmered in her eyes. *Incest? Not me . . . not me!*

''Mama?''

''Hush, baby. We have to run now. We have to save ourselves.''

Unless, of course, it was already too late.

The canoes shot across the calm surface of the Roaring Water River, their V-shaped bow wakes mingling as they passed in stealthy silence. Robin rode in the bow of the Ilini canoe, scanning the tree-covered banks as he paddled.

Uneasy glances were cast back and forth by his warriors. It was one thing to talk about the Roaring Water, another to be driving down upon it. The race, however, had grown desperate. Star Shell might already be at the falls, and even as he thought about it, she might be casting the Mask out, over the edge, to fall into the depths below.

And if that's the case, I shall make her die a thousand deaths.

"Paddle!" he ordered. "Harder!"

The men strained, as they had already been doing throughout the long day. *How could the woman have made it this far?* Unless she knew how close he was. Perhaps they'd glimpsed his pursuit and traveled all night. Or had they enlisted others to paddle?

He paused long enough to touch the sets of human mandibles that he wore for a breastplate. Star Shell's would be there soon. Mask or no Mask.

A warrior called, "Leader? Which way?"

Robin lifted his head to study the split in the channel. He barely noticed the man standing on the beach—a fisherman, no doubt, someone from the settlements. Then he gave the man a second look. He'd know the way.

Before Robin could draw a breath, the man on the beach cupped his hands around his mouth, the strong voice carrying across the water: "Robin, War Leader of Blue Duck Clan! Heave to!"

Robin rose, balancing, shouting back. "Who are you? How do you know me?"

"I am Pale Snake! A sorcerer of the Serpent Society! A warrior who fights for Many Colored Crow! I bear you a message from the Dark Twin. Turn back, you men of Blue Duck Clan. Those who pass this point will never return. Your death will be followed by an eternity of wailing, your ghosts trapped beneath the Roaring Waters. You will hear only the pounding roar beating you down and down into the darkness . . . forever!"

Robin chuckled over the sudden uncertain buzzing of his warriors. "A sorcerer, you say?" They'd coasted in toward the shore, the men backwatering to hold them in place. "The *last* sorcerer we dealt with screamed for hours while we cooked his guts in boiling water."

"Tall Man's ghost told me!" Pale Snake called grimly. "But did you know that he was dying? Already possessed of an evil that was eating his insides? Do you think you caught him by accident, Robin? He *went* to you, knowing full well what you intended to do.''

Robin continued to chuckle, but uncertainty nibbled at his soul. ''No man, sorcerer or not, allows himself to be captured when he knows his intestines will be boiled.''

''Oh, yes he does.'' Pale Snake thumped his breast. ''Were I possessed by a black evil that was inside me, killing me, eating *my* soul, I'd walk right into your hands.''

''I see . . . in fact, it appears that you have.''

Pale Snake threw his head back and laughed. ''Oh, anything but! I don't need to have an evil driven out of me. *Driven,* I say. Do you understand, Robin? By boiling the Magician's guts, you drove the evil from within him. Of all the curious ironies, you helped him!'' Pale Snake continued to laugh. ''Which of your warriors do you suppose the evil entered when it fled Tall Man's body? Eh? You, Robin? Is that why you are so obsessed with the Mask?''

His warriors gasped.

''Move up!'' Robin ordered. ''Take him.''

''Wait!'' Pale Snake held up his hands. ''Hear me. I am but the messenger of Many Colored Crow. If you pass, you shall die and your souls will be tortured in blackness! Turn back!''

''I think I'm going to cook your guts.'' Robin lifted his paddle and edged the craft forward.

''Not *mine,''* the sorcerer replied with a wry grin. ''Before you're even close, I'll dive into the water, turn myself into a fish and be gone. Oh, by the way, those wishing to die will need to go that way!'' He pointed toward the western channel. ''It's the shortest route to death. Star Shell took it.''

Robin drove the canoe forward. Even as he did so, the sorcerer dashed into the water, diving cleanly. He barely created a splash as he cleaved the surface and disappeared.

''Spread out!'' Robin ordered. ''The water is clear here. You'll see him.''

His canoes drifted, the men looking over the sides into the pale green depths.

Robin glanced around. ''Don't just look down, you idiots! He's got to come up for air sometime!''

They continued to drift ever closer to the shore. The warriors looked about warily, exchanging a few anxious words.

"There!" two warriors cried simultaneously. And others in their boat scrambled to look to where the two pointed. Then they glanced back at Robin.

"Do you see him?"

"We see a big fish, War Leader." Woodpecker looked at him with tormented eyes. "If that is the sorcerer, his words were true. And . . . and you saw the swelling in the Magician's liver! It was pustulous and bleeding. How could this sorcerer know about that evil?"

Mutters broke out among the warriors. Robin heard two men heatedly discussing his drive to find the Mask, speculating that Tall Man's evil had *indeed* entered him and taken over his soul. Others were muttering that they'd been foolish to kill a dwarf. Everyone knew that dwarfs were good luck.

Robin cursed, driving his canoe toward the eastern fork of the river.

"That way was shorter." One of the warriors—his eyes half-panicked—pointed to the west.

"He *wanted* us to go that way."

Woodpecker's voice carried across the water. "War Leader, let us return to our homes. We should not pass this point! I am willing to hunt for Star Shell but not to cross Many Colored Crow."

Robin turned. The three other canoes were still backing water. "You are ordered to come!"

Woodpecker stood up and dared to smile as he cupped a hand to his mouth. "I refuse, cousin! This is no longer a thing for our clan. The Mask is gone from our territory. Our holdings, our clan, are safe. For me, that is enough. A death has repaid a death."

Robin reached down, untying his atlatl from his belt. He picked up a war dart and nocked it to the shaft. "You will follow me!"

"I will not! Nor will my warriors!" Woodpecker crossed his arms over his chest.

Robin fought the sudden trembling as he straightened his arm, ready to cast. Only the sudden rocking of the canoe stayed him, and he turned just as a warrior slipped over the side. Another of his warriors half-rose and dove cleanly into the water. One by one they went, each stroking for the other canoes, heedless of his deadly dart, until he alone remained in the stolen Ilini craft.

"Will you kill us all?" Woodpecker shouted, gesturing to the warriors swimming away from Robin's canoe. "We are your relatives!"

Anger drove heat into Robin's heart. "I will find the Mask, cousin! And when I have it, I shall seek out each of you and make you stare into it! You will see your cowardice—and your souls will flee your bodies!"

With that, he dropped his weapons, grabbed his paddle and drove his canoe eastward, seeking the fastest portion of the channel.

"I'm coming," he gritted, roused to a strength he'd never experienced before. "I'm coming for you, Star Shell. You . . . and the Mask. I'll have you both or I'll never have anything again!" The canoe leaped forward, spurred by his rage.

And as to Woodpecker and his warriors, a curse take them! He never looked back.

Forty-eight

If I gain the Mask for the whole world and lose one of my friends, will the world be richer, or poorer?

I grieve over this question.

I cannot imagine anyone who would want to live in a world that had been suddenly stripped of Otter's kindness, Black Skull's strength, or Pearl's courage.

What would be the point?

And yet the Mask's Power is very great. Many Colored Crow assures me that in the right hands, the Mask can do more than just bring glory and greatness to multitudes of people. He says it can perform miracles, cure disease and poverty, alleviate the suffering of thousands.

Can it?

Even First Man agrees, says "yes."

. . . Will it be able to cure my suffering when this is all over? First Man tells me "no."

And so I have become my own vulture. Every moment, I consume more and more of myself, picking, tearing, swallowing . . .

Will there be enough of me left to make the necessary decisions by the time we reach the Roaring Water?

Otter sensed the quickening of the river even as he heard the first muted roar on the cool, spring-scented wind. *Wave Dancer* might have been a thing alive as he used his paddle to bear them toward the southern shore.

"The rapids!" Black Skull rose and braced himself behind the carved fox head.

"We're putting over," Otter called, edging toward the bank. "The farther upstream you are, the less current you'll have to fight on the way back. Listen to me, learn this! Absorb it into your souls. A canoe can make only so much speed. If the water runs faster, you must be pulled downstream, no matter *how* hard you paddle. *Do you understand?*"

"Yes, yes." Black Skull stared at the rising bank. "But we'd better find a place fast, Trader. This river is down-cutting."

"There!" A creek emptied down a rushing set of rapids, but it allowed them a landing. Together, they heaved *Wave Dancer* up on the bank, leaving her canted in toward shore. Otter ran his hand over the carving of the fox head. "You must see them safely back upriver, good canoe. Uncle and I, we put the best of our souls into your wood. Cherish Pearl, Black Skull, Green Spider, and my faithful friend Catcher as I have cherished them."

"What did you say?" Pearl asked as she walked up behind him, Wolf of the Dead's atlatl in one hand, darts in the other.

"I told *Wave Dancer* to stay put and not to go exploring," he lied as he walked back for his own weapons. Not knowing what might lie ahead, he added his pack and a coil of heavy rope—the rope that Four Kills had made himself and given him on that day so long past at White Shell. He took his flute, in the hope that he could fill the afterlife with music. Finally, he beckoned to Catcher. "You, too, old friend. Come. No one will bother the packs here."

Loyal Catcher had the right to share this last adventure, as he had shared so many others through the years. To have left him behind would have been a betrayal. Catcher must see Otter die, or he would be forever waiting for him to return.

Black Skull and Green Spider had already climbed up along the broken black rock and into the green brush that choked the bank.

Otter held Pearl's hand. They forced their way through the sumac and raspberries, each flinching at the scratches left by the thorns.

A beaten path paralleled the shore, and Otter looked at Green Spider, who now walked around in circles, hunched over, his nose quivering. Catcher immediately recognized the behavior and began sniffing on his own.

Black Skull's face reflected dismay. "It's my fault. I made the mistake of asking him if he could sniff out the way to the Mask."

"I think we'd better sniff downstream," Otter replied. "Whatever is going to happen is going to happen at the falls. Isn't that the Vision, Green Spider? A woman in the water, a little girl, and the Mask, all of them at the edge of the falls?"

Green Spider looked up at Otter with love glowing in his eyes. He simply nodded.

That gaze felt like a physical blow. It made Otter's heart ache. He matched Green Spider's nod and gestured downriver. "We should hurry, then."

Together they walked through the shadowy forest, aware of the slanting light that filtered through the colored clouds above. They walked in silence, their steps absorbed by the spongy ground. The smells of the forest, the sound of the rushing river, the brilliant colors of butterflies and flowers, the shafts of green-tinged sunshine—all were amplified in the senses.

When they looked at each other, warm smiles played about their lips. *Here are the finest of friends.* That message passed between them in a shared glance, the familiar gesture, the glint of an eye.

The roaring increased. At a break in the trees, Otter looked out at clear water rushing in a smooth hump over a rock. "Look." He pointed. "See how fast the current is? You couldn't paddle a canoe out of that."

"What would you do?" Black Skull asked. "Just go over the edge?"

"No, head straight downstream and point for the closest bank. I want you to remember this for the journey back. You've got to keep steerage. The canoe must move faster than the water or you'll just spin. And in waters like these, if you spin, you spill." He illustrated with his hands. "If you can, drive your boat ashore. If not, bail out when you're next to the bank. You'll lose the canoe, true, but if you're close enough, you can climb ashore. That way, you lose everything but your life."

The roaring continued to build as they walked along. Otter chewed at his cheeks, aware that he hadn't expected it to look like this—such a *huge* roaring river, cascading rapids, and country so wild! Now, as he looked out over the crashing white water, he couldn't help but wonder how Power could hope to save anything from this roiling chaos.

Star Shell and Silver Water cleared the southern tip of the island, only to find the river veering westward. The sun had slanted into eventide, throwing gaudy bars of orange and purple light across the sky in a majestic starburst display.

Every muscle in Star Shell's body ached. She had never worked so hard.

Desperation, she told herself. That, and the lurking awareness that as soon as she relented, Pale Snake's words were going to crush her soul the way a stone mallet flattened a hickory nut.

My father . . . Tall Man. Incest? No, not me. Never! She battled the oar, trying to speed onward, rushing to the final reckoning.

Save the Mask! Pale Snake's final order burned within her. Whom did she trust? Had Tall Man really lied through those six long, cold moons of winter? Had he been hiding his own misdeeds as they slogged through the rainy mud of spring? Or did Pale Snake's hatred of his father speak now?

"Are you evil?" she asked the Mask, throwing the query over her shoulder. "I must know!"

"No, Mama." Silver Water's frightened voice ate at Star Shell's soul. "It's not evil."

"I want the Mask to answer me!"

"It won't, Mama. It . . . it says talking to you would do no good."

"Tadpole? That last night in Greets the Sun's house. Do you remember? The night we left?"

"I remember."

"Did Tall Man ask you to talk to the Mask?"

Silver Water paused. "Yes."

"You're sure?"

"Mama, he opened the pack, even pulled back a flap of the wolfhide. He said it would be all right, just that once."

A fist closed on Star Shell's battered soul. "I believe you, baby." But did that mean that Tall Man was malicious? Or just trying to save her from committing incest? And if she'd conceived a child? The horror of the thought sent shivers through her. She licked her dry lips, wishing she could slow down and drink, but she was afraid to lose even that much lead on Robin's closing canoes.

No matter how, Tall Man had been right to drive her and Greets the Sun apart. *Sacred ancestors, she'd slept with her brother!*

"Silver Water?"

"Yes, Mama."

"No matter what, I want you to know that I'm sorry. I wish . . . I wish you could have been spared all this trouble. I wish I hadn't been so hard with you. I only wanted to protect you."

"I know, Mama. I love you."

"I love you, too, Tadpole. Now, I want you to keep a lookout. Tell me if you see any canoes behind us."

"I will."

Star Shell glanced at the wooded shores, wishing she could land, hang her head and cry. Above, a flight of crows circled, cawing to each other as if amused by her plight.

"Mama," Silver Water called unhappily, "a canoe is back there."

Star Shell shot a quick look over her shoulder, slightly relieved to see but one canoe bearing down on them. In that hull sat a lone man, his muscular arms stroking as if he were enraged. The relief vanished. She could recognize him despite the distance: Robin!

She shot a pleading look at the color-streaked clouds and the whirling crows. "Help me! Please!"

The rest of her effort went to the paddle, and she flew past the big canoe on the southern bank. The barest of thoughts flashed in her mind . . . *beautiful craft . . . oddly canted on its side*.

Her effort was paying off. No matter that she panted on the verge of exhaustion, the trees moved past with ever greater speed.

She cast a look over her shoulder. The canoe was closer, close enough that she could hear Robin shouting at her, saying things she couldn't make out but could imagine. Hate-filled words.

Fear spurred yet another burst of energy, and she sailed past the first of the rocks, vaguely aware that water slid over them, rushing and bubbling. Only then did she look up and see the white water. The soul of the river had turned vicious. Her canoe bucked and jolted through the rapids, shooting ahead as if alive. Terror ran bright in Star Shell's blood.

"Mama!" Silver Water cried.

"Hold on to the boat, baby!"

Star Shell sighted people on the shore. They'd rushed out of the trees, waving their arms, and—she supposed—shouting.

The big man, somehow familiar, used his whole body to beckon her. Star Shell paddled toward him. Her canoe rose and fell, bucking, dashing, jolting her off the hard hull as it battled the waves and banged on the rocks.

The shore . . . must make the shore!

Water splashed, soaking her. She fought her way closer. Not far now. The bank rushed past. Not far . . .

When they hit the boulder, the effect was like a mighty fist that ripped her paddle away with a numbing shock that paralyzed her arm.

An instant later, the canoe crashed down into a frothy hole of white water and Star Shell screamed as the current spun the boat end for end, whipping it around, bashing it against rock after rock.

Silver Water's mouth opened in a frightened scream—a scream that couldn't penetrate the roar of the water. Star Shell froze in terror, watching as the canoe slammed into a huge boulder that thrust up out of the water.

The jolt sent her flying, up and out, into the pounding rush and violating cold.

"Silver Water!" she shrieked as she broke the surface. "Silver Water! Where are you?"

Star Shell was sucked under, into bubbling, blue-green cold. She fought, surfaced, floundered, went under again, trying to locate her daughter. When she opened her mouth to breathe, only water entered, and she coughed.

There!

Not more than two body-lengths away, Silver Water flailed the water. Alongside her, the Mask pack floated free.

Star Shell struggled against the overwhelming current, reaching for Silver Water. For the briefest of instants, elation ran like fire through her veins. She grabbed for her daughter's dress . . . but the child was whisked away by the boiling current.

In desperation, Star Shell clawed at one of the angular black rocks, her fingers groping along the slick surface. She found a crack and pulled herself up—just far enough to shoot a quick glance after her daughter.

Then she lost her grip, jerked away by the rage of the river, and she felt her body being sucked into the midst of the terrible maelstrom again.

Forty-nine

Pale Snake let the water wash over him as he stared out from behind the curling root that looped down from the bank and into the water.

The three canoes bearing the Blue Duck warriors were paddling resolutely upriver. Pale Snake exhaled wearily. With careful strokes, he swam back along the curve of the island and waded up onto the beach.

A fish, he thought, amazement at human culpability vying with his torment. He'd done better than he'd hoped for in his effort to buy Star Shell time. Who would have guessed that Robin's warriors would have been so close to bolting?

He climbed up to where he'd left his packs in the brush and sat down, staring glumly at the bend where the Blue Duck warriors had disappeared.

"I loved you, Star Shell. Not as a sister, but as a man loves a woman." He twisted water out of his hair and wiped at his wet face. Well, so be it. At least Tall Man had failed in his final endeavor to hurt him.

"I did not commit incest for you, old man. You won't have that to hold over me when I pursue your ghost in the Spirit World."

He blinked, startled at the four canoes that had reappeared around the bend. Flattening out on his stomach, he carefully wormed back into the brush, screening himself with saplings.

As they closed, he could tell that these were not Blue Duck warriors; their clothing and hairstyles were different. But they were warriors nonetheless, dressed outlandishly in long yellow shirts and high moccasins. Further, upon reaching the fork in the river, they pulled up speaking in an unfamiliar tongue.

One warrior finally pointed to the west, and with paddles dipping in unison, the slim war craft slid out of Pale Snake's sight.

He rolled over, rubbing his eyes. Should he pursue?

How? he wondered. *On foot?* The battle would be long over by the time he reached the fighting.

But he had to try.

Pale Snake stood, tried to brush the dirt, sticks, and leaves from his wet shirt, and dropped his hands in disgust.

Good luck, Star Shell. Blessed Spirits, I pray you live.

But the Mask . . . If that Power object went over the falls, he'd know. He'd feel its terror in his soul.

I told you the truth, Star Shell. He pushed through the brush, found a faint trail back into the trees and broke into a run. . . . *The truth. No matter how much it hurts us.*

The hollow rapping of the pileated woodpecker echoed through the forest.

Is this it?'' Grizzly Tooth scanned the silent forest on either side. Ahead, he could see what appeared to be another channel. "Maybe this land off to the right is an island?''

"Perhaps so.'' Wolf of the Dead glanced around uneasily. "For the time being, I'm more than happy to be off that accursed sea. Water is meant to have banks around it!''

"Tell that to the warriors who drowned,'' Grizzly Tooth answered. "At least this time we had the sense to follow the shoreline.''

"We're close,'' Wolf of the Dead said soothingly. And why shouldn't he expect his people to be short-tempered? They'd been gone for almost three moons, and for what? Nine out of ten of his warriors had drowned or were missing. They'd tramped, fought mosquitoes and ticks, sweated in the sun, shivered in the rain, and felt their souls quake as they crossed yet another immense body of water in narrow war craft that could scarcely withstand whitecaps on a river, let alone storms on great seas.

"Will they be here?'' Grizzly Tooth asked. "What if they've come and gone?''

That same fear had echoed hollowly in Wolf of the Dead. "I have faith.''

But the problem with faith was that it could crumble like sun-dried sand when any pressure was placed on it. "If they're not here, we'll rest for a couple of days, fish and recuperate. If they haven't arrived in ten days, we will paddle back upriver and raid those settlements we passed. Acquire supplies, and perhaps a few women to amuse us as we travel.''

"And what do you have in mind?'' Grizzly Tooth continued his inspection of the banks as the rivers joined and the channel bore them straight into the west. The direction of home.

Wolf of the Dead rested his paddle across his lap. "Consider' this. Several portages lie south of this lake. Follow the rivers, portage across the headwaters, and you end up flush in the middle of the Serpent Clans. They have a great deal of wealth—just waiting to be plundered.''

''And I'll remind you that the last time we tried that, they sent your father and his warriors home—whipped!''

''But they knew we were coming,'' Wolf of the Dead objected. ''Every Trader on the river had heard of my father's plans. Word ran like fire through dry grass, pushed by the west wind. No, my friend. This time we drop out of the north with no warning. We'll be among them before they know it. We loot their clan houses, take their clan leaders and society chiefs as hostages, and we're gone, flying downstream to the Serpent River. There we raid the holdings, and we return home with such wealth as has never been seen. The reputation of the Khota will be restored, my friend. No one, no one will ever have committed a raid of such devastation. Traders will be talking about it for . . . for generations!''

Grizzly Tooth lifted his chin, rubbing his throat thoughtfully. ''As long as we don't get too greedy, weight down the canoes with booty, it might work.''

''It *will* work!''

''Is it my imagination, or is the channel running faster here?'' Grizzly Tooth peered nervously over the side of the canoe.

Wolf of the Dead craned his neck, letting his practiced eye study the roiling river water. ''Faster. Look, you can see it in the current, as if the river itself is growing excited.''

Grizzly Tooth paddled warily, studying the surface, seeking the better channel. ''I think we should—'' He gaped.

''What? What do you see?'' Wolf of the Dead rose, warily searching for a snag.

''Put in!'' Grizzly Tooth cried. ''There, that canoe. Do you see it?''

''Yes, but I—''

''It has a keel . . . a *keel*!''

Wolf of the Dead stared at the beached canoe, lying canted away from the river. The long keel ran the entire length of the hull.

''Land there! Warriors, prepare yourselves! Be ready!'' And

Wolf of the Dead strangled his desire to whoop. He would have Pearl now. Her and the Water Fox! And when he'd finished, he'd still swoop down on the Serpent Clans and deal them a blow they'd never forget!

Black Skull raced down the bank, bursting through brush, leaping deadfall. From the corner of his eye, he'd seen the canoe dash over a rock, spin around in the wash and flip end over end, spilling the woman and her little girl into the raging white water.

He tore around a beech tree, gauged the distance and leaped to the rocky strip of beach, then pounded into the water. He could hear only the roar as he swam out into the current. Flipping water from his face, he got enough purchase on a rock to lift himself high, catching a glimpse of the little girl as she floundered and grabbed a buoyant pack—and after that brief instant, bobbed out of sight.

Black Skull struggled in that direction, barely feeling the rocks he scraped by. He caught another glimpse of her as he was carried over a rock and then down into the swirling backwash. The water sucked at him, dragging him under, but it spat him back up.

There she was, clinging desperately to the pack and the trapped air it contained. He stroked after her.

Like your canoe, Trader. You've got to keep steerage. And he managed to sink fingers into the girl's wet shirt where it rode high from the air bubble inside.

"Hold onto my neck!" he shouted in pidgin as he pulled her close. "That's it. Crawl onto my back!"

"Where's my mama?" the girl cried. "Where is she? Did you see her?"

"No. Now hold tight!"

He began battling toward the shore. As he was washed over yet another of the rapids, he caught sight of a raft of driftwood piled in the rocks. He made for it, only to be pinned against the thick logs by the surging current. He shoved the girl and her pack up on top of the mess.

He himself started up, casting a glance out across the water.

The canoe, upside down, whirled past and vanished into the leaping spray and crashing water. Then he saw the woman, up the river, hanging precariously onto a rock. She looked back at him. Black Skull held up her daughter. Some of the fear left the woman's face.

His perch on the logs was anything but secure. The entire raft was held in place by a single log that had wedged between two rocks. Looking down, Black Skull saw their sanctuary shuddering and giving under the force of the rushing current.

The shore lay farther away than it had any right to be, ten body-lengths, and when Black Skull glanced behind him, the canoe hadn't bobbed back up. In fact, nothing was bobbing anywhere behind him. All appeared to vanish into a curving nothingness. He could see the swirling mists rising beyond, from a long, long way down. He crouched at the lip of an incredible waterfall.

He shook his head, refusing to believe what he'd just seen, and looked back upriver in time to see the woman's hold loosening. She slipped into the rush, twisting and splashing in the water as she shot down toward him.

"Stay here!" Black Skull shouted at the petrified girl. She'd twined one hand in the pack, the other clutching the driftwood raft.

Black Skull groped frantically and found a splintered pole in the mass. Tugging it out caused part of the pile to break away and whirl off over the cascading falls. The girl let out a sudden shriek.

"Thrice-cursed wood," he muttered, struggling for balance on the heaving debris. The woman might have been a plaything, the way the current tossed her this way and that.

In the midst of that insanity, Black Skull caught a momentary glimpse of a ludicrous sight. A second canoe, this one painted in Ilini designs, plunged down the river, rising and falling in the rapids. It took only moments before it went over the edge of the falls. Sunlight flashed on some kind of bone breastplate. The single occupant paddled on air, his mouth open, the scream lost as he continued to paddle outward, downward, beyond the curvature of the falls.

Black Skull turned back. The woman rushed toward him. Wet black hair covered her face, but her dark eyes were insane with fear. "Help me!" she screamed. "Please! Help me!"

"Mama! Mama!" the little girl cried.

Black Skull jabbed his stick into the rushing water, like a spear, throwing his weight against it, praying the wood wouldn't shatter when it hit bottom, or that the force wouldn't wrench the raft from underfoot and kill them all.

He roared as he struggled to hold the pole so she'd have something to grab onto.

"Try to grab the pole!" he shouted.

In that last desperate instant, she twisted, got hold of the slippery wood, and he was able to drag her into the lee of the rock, where the backwash swirled. From there, he could pull her close enough, and finally reach down to drag her up, shaking and terrified, onto the driftwood raft.

Immediately the woman grabbed her daughter, crushing the child to her breast, so engrossed that she didn't see another section of their perch break loose and pitch over the falls behind them.

She wept as she hugged the girl, cooing in a language Black Skull didn't understand.

He wiped the spray from his face, trying to assess what was left of their crumbling nest. With their combined weight, they were literally crushing their perch beneath them.

Black Skull leaned down, shouting in Trade pidgin, *"Don't move!"* and pointed to the sagging wood.

Star Shell understood immediately and nodded, frightened into motionlessness. The little girl, too, stared down with panicked eyes.

Black Skull muttered under his breath, searching around, looking for something, anything, that would give them a chance. And that's when Otter broke out of the trees. Catcher was dashing along, barking, doing his best to stop Otter, and that touched Black Skull.

"Come on, Otter. Stay on shore. Think of something for me to do out here!"

Another piece of wood broke free, and Black Skull forlornly watched it drop down into the backwash, twirl around a couple of times and finally tumble over the edge.

"Trader? If you don't think of something, you're going to have to take on the Khota by yourself. You and Pearl and the fool." He got another glance at the falls, four body-lengths be-hind him, and shook his head. One thing was sure, it would be quick, no lingering bleeding, suffocating, or hurting. Just that sick sensation of the long fall, then smack! And a person would be gone.

He bent down, bellowing into Star Shell's ear again. "If what's left of the raft starts to go, I'll jump off! I'm the heav-iest." He pointed to where Otter was running along the shore, now followed by Pearl. "My friends will find a way to save you!"

She looked up, and he couldn't tell if those were tears in her black eyes or just the water from the spray of the falls. "Why? Why would you save us?"

"It's part of my friend Green Spider's Vision. Now I'm going to climb down—get partway into the water. Take some of the weight off before I break it up more."

Black Skull turned to see Otter unwinding a rope, tying the end around a small rock.

"The crazy fool, he can't hold my weight!"

Otter slung the rope around his head, the way he might a bola, and it sailed out over the river. The impact on the water knocked the rock out of the knot. The rope came twisting and slithering in the dashing wash. It passed just near enough that Black Skull could clamber down and catch the end.

"All right, Otter. So I've got the rope. Now what?" He pulled it tight, fighting the drag as the current caught the taut rope, tugging and straining at his hold. Black Skull glanced up to see Otter tying off on a slim maple—not the best, but the only anchor available.

Another bit of their raft broke free, jarring them, and bringing forth sharp screams from the girl. Black Skull growled, and, battling with the rope, beckoned Star Shell to him. She crawled forward carefully, clutching the child under one arm.

Black Skull bent down, shouting into her ear. "I'm going to tie the rope around your shoulders."

"What about you?"

"Next time! I don't think it will take the three of us!"

He leaned back, taking up slack, and with Otter's help, man-aged to pull the rope tight. Star Shell helped him as he took a figure-eight loop around both of her legs, adding, "It will hurt, cut off the circulation to your legs, but as long as you hang onto the rope, my friends will get you to shore."

She nodded uncertainly.

"You *must* hold on! No matter what. Even if you go underwater."

"Yes!" she cried.

Black Skull gave her a nod, then signaled Otter, who held up a hand in acknowledgment and started working on the rope, stretching it tight again before tying off.

Black Skull took a deep breath. "Ready?"

Star Shell nodded, clearly scared out of her wits. She twisted the rope around and around her arms while Silver Water crawled onto her back.

"Take a deep breath!" Black Skull ordered. "Both of you. And kick if you can. Stroke if you can. Fight! You must fight with all your heart!"

"All right. We're ready!" Star Shell nodded, but she was clearly afraid to let go of their precarious driftwood raft. Black Skull whispered a prayer to the ancestors and eased her into the water.

Star Shell whipped away from him, twisting around, immediately pulled under.

"Hang on, girl! Don't let go of your mother!" Black Skull's heart leaped as Star Shell and Silver Water bobbed up to the surface, then sank again. Would the little girl have the strength to hold on? Or would she panic and be swept over the edge?

Otter and Pearl dragged the rope in as it swung shoreward. No one could work the rope hand to hand in that powerful current, but Star Shell seemed to be trying. The maple tree bent under the strain. Pearl went knee-deep into the river, catching the rope, hauling their prize to shore. A wet, bedraggled Star Shell—her half-drowned daughter no doubt strangling her—was washed against the sand at the very edge of the falls. From his vantage, it appeared to Black Skull that Star Shell's feet hung over the edge.

He inhaled then, realizing that he hadn't been breathing.

Pearl worked to untie the rope.

The wood shifted under Black Skull's feet, and he windmilled for balance as half of the raft broke away and went rushing toward the edge.

Surveying his situation, Black Skull climbed down, immersing himself to the waist, letting the water push against him while his driftwood haven continued to disintegrate.

Here at water level, the river wasn't quite so frightening, but then, a person couldn't look over the edge of the falls. He waited, feeling, rather than seeing, another section of the raft break away. The rope washed up against him.

Grabbing it with one hand, he started to climb up onto the perch—when the key log cracked and gave way. In that instant, as he fell, Black Skull wrapped the rope around his wrist, drawing a deep breath as the current savagely jerked him under. Beneath the water, the river roar's dropped to a low rumble, like a pack of panthers closing for the kill.

He grabbed for more rope and wrapped it around his arms as he swung toward the shore.

Suddenly, the terrible, deafening roar returned as he broke the surface . . . and was swept over the falls.

Pearl screamed when she saw Black Skull go over the edge. A moment later, the rope ripped out of the water, snapping taut with enough force to blast a silver spray from the stretching fibers.

"Otter!" she screamed, running for the lip of the falls. "Otter, he's still holding on! He has to be close. There was only enough rope . . ."

She fell on her knees at the water's edge, and there, just out of her reach, she could see the rope that dangled Black Skull over the abyss. He hung in that crashing water, his body twisting and turning, straining under that awesome cascade.

Pearl lunged into the shallows, running, hating the pull of the current as the water deepened.

"Pearl! Wait!" Otter thrashed into the water behind her. "Grab the rope!"

They both dove for it and grabbed on, straining muscle, back, and bone to pull it to the side, out of the brute force of the current.

"Hold! Rot you, hold!" Otter was screaming, his muscles

bulging as they backed step by step into the shallows.

Pearl glanced up the length of the straining rope. If the knot gave, or if the slim maple pulled free, or if the rope parted, they'd all be swept into the boiling mist beyond the precipice.

Side by side, she and Otter felt their way to the rocky lip, where Otter leaned out over the edge of the falls, struggling, heaving. Pearl looked back to shore where the woman and child stood dripping wet, watching in terror. She yelled, "Grab hold of the rope! Help us pull!"

They probably couldn't hear her. Pearl waved toward the maple where the rope was tethered, and the woman seemed to wake from her dreadful sleep. She ran for the rope and grabbed it, throwing herself backward in an effort to help pull them to shore.

"We're winning!" Otter shouted. *"We're winning!"*

Splashing and yelling, trampling each other, they fought their way back.

Still in the wash of the river, Otter flopped down, staring over the edge of the falls. "Pull! He's not up yet! Come on, hurry! I don't know if he can breathe down there."

Pearl glanced over the edge, seeing Black Skull hanging there, so limp, his arms wretchedly cut by the twining rope.

"Hurry!" she screamed.

The three of them braced there on the rock, each grunting and straining as they hoisted Black Skull up, bit by laborious bit. Otter whooped when he got a grip on Black Skull's rope-cut hands and dragged him up by brute strength, flopping him onto the shore.

"Is he alive?" Pearl shouted as she threw down the rope and bent over him.

"Get the rope off!" Otter was doing his best to unwind the thick rope, but his fingers were ineffectual, for the rope had cut deeply into the skin of the warrior's arms. Black Skull's broken face twisted in agony, and water was leaking out of his nose and mouth.

Pearl reached down to the trailing end and pulled it back, unwinding it gently from the crisscrosses that had tied Black Skull to his lifeline.

Otter pointed to a frayed section of rope, grinning worriedly.

"Must have been where it got hung up on the rocks! We came that close to losing you, Black Skull."

As if in reply, the warrior coughed, water spraying. Another racking cough brought Catcher to lick his battered face. Black Skull's eyes opened, and he managed the grimace that normally passed for a grin, or was it an expression of intense pain this time?

Pearl pulled the last of the rope free and bent down, aware of the woman taking Black Skull's other arm to assess the damage. Skin had been torn away, the tissues deeply bruised, and now, as circulation seeped into the injured areas, blood began to mingle redly with the water.

"Can you stand?" Otter asked.

Black Skull turned over, vomiting onto the ground. He coughed again, shaking with the effort. "I'd rather die, Trader, but yes, I think I can."

"Help me," Otter said, and Pearl draped one of Black Skull's mangled arms over her shoulder and helped him to his feet. The woman had taken her daughter's hand, as well as the pack, and she followed them up the slope. A faint trail wound through the trees. The ground here was damp and moss-covered.

They laid Black Skull onto the leaves, letting him cough more water from his lungs. Here, back from the edge, they could at least hear each other speak without shouting.

"Black Skull?" Pearl asked, taking one of his hands and wincing at the raw patches of bleeding flesh. "Are you all right?"

He coughed, then clamped his eyes shut. "My arms! I think they've been pulled from the sockets. And the pain! Ah! I haven't hurt this bad since . . . No, I've *never* hurt this bad."

The woman leaned down to study him. She laid a hand gently on Black Skull's crushed cheek and said in Trade pidgin, "You were in my Dream."

Black Skull coughed violently, struggling for air. Then he looked up at her. "And you . . . in mine. Greetings, Star Shell. I am Black Skull. Your daughter . . . how is your daughter?"

"Well. Silver Water, come meet Black Skull."

As the girl stepped forward warily, Otter asked, "Is the Mask here?" He looked around, searching the grass and trees. "I am

Otter, from the White Shell Clan, and this is Pearl, an Anhinga woman.''

Star Shell nodded to them, then pointed to the pack the little girl carried. ''The Mask—how do you know about it?''

Otter shrugged. ''Many Colored Crow sent us to rescue it. You're from the Serpent Clans, aren't you?''

She nodded, much too sadly it seemed to Pearl. ''StarSky. And after that, Sun Mounds.''

''What has happened to Mica Bird?'' Otter asked. ''For many years I've heard stories about your husband and the Mask.''

''He's dead. He hung himself. I wish you wouldn't use his name again.''

''Otter,'' Pearl said, ''we'll have time for this later.'' She lifted a hand to shield her eyes from the orange glare of sunset. ''Where's Green Spider?''

''I don't know. I haven't seen him since we saw Star Shell's canoe out in the water.''

Black Skull moaned against the pain. ''That was a good rope you had, Trader.''

''It was specially made at White Shell. Four Kills braids only the best. It was a gift from him, and I am forever grateful.'' Otter turned then and gazed pensively at the pack. ''That really holds the Mask of Many Colored Crow?''

Star Shell turned to face him. ''It does. And if you have half the sense of a rock, you'll leave it in that sack. It's not a thing for men. Not anymore. Ta—my father . . . had a Vision that it should be thrown over the falls. Killed. So it could never hurt anyone again.''

Otter studied her thoughtfully and nodded. ''I'll take your word for it.'' Then he grinned forlornly. ''I guess Black Skull is our hero. He saved you and your daughter. It was all in Green Spider's Vision.''

Pearl studied Black Skull's flayed arms. ''We have Khota behind us somewhere.'' *And I must know when to leave. Green Spider, where are you?*

''Khota,'' Otter said sourly as he bent down. ''Black Skull, we have to make our way back to *Wave Dancer.* Can you do that?''

Black Skull looked up, and dismay tensed his face, as though suddenly he feared he was incapable of fighting anyone. ''If it kills me. But, Otter . . . Otter, find my club. I *need* my club.''

Pearl hated herself for the pain she caused as she gently placed Black Skull's arm over her shoulder. She could hear him gasp, his offset teeth grinding as they started back for the canoe.

They hadn't made three paces before Catcher began growling, his black hair rising on his back. Warriors sprinted from between the tree trunks, as silent as shadows, circling them. Pearl stumbled, staring in shock, and slowly slipped out from under Black Skull's heavy arm. She heard Otter murmur, ''Blessed Spirits, what do we do now?''

Black Skull's eyes narrowed, and he spread his legs to brace himself. ''*We fight,*'' he whispered.

''Greetings, Pearl,'' Grizzly Tooth said as he strode forward, his war club balanced in his hand. ''I think you remember my clan leader?''

Wolf of the Dead stepped out from behind the thick trunk of a maple. ''How nice to see you again, *wife!*'' he slurred. ''And what's this? The Water Fox?'' His mocking grin exposed the gap in his teeth. ''How happy we are to see all of you!''

Still more warriors emerged from the trees behind them, spreading out like a pack of hungry wolves.

Fifty

''Who are these people?'' Star Shell asked in pidgin. She eyed the newcomers warily. Better the Blue Duck warriors than these . . . barbarians!

''Khota,'' Otter told her. Then: ''Catcher, go guard the packs.'' The dog looked up in confusion, ears pricked. ''You heard me! I said to go guard the packs!''

Catcher whimpered, but he loped away, back toward *Wave Dancer,* and Otter let out a shuddering sigh. ''They'll kill him first, and I—I couldn't stand that. I want him to make it out of this . . . even if we don't.''

Who were these new enemies? Star Shell had never heard of the Khota. They must live very far away. Then what were they doing here? Had the entire world turned upside down?

Silver Water clutched the Mask pack to her chest. Star Shell lowered a hand to her daughter's shoulder and bent down. "Baby, listen to me," she whispered. "When you get the chance, run. Run as hard as you can. Go into the trees and find a place to hide. I'll come looking for you when this is over." *If I can.* "Do you understand?"

Silver Water wet her lips and nodded anxiously, her dark, knowing eyes shifting from one warrior to the next. Her panicked fingers tightened on the pack.

Star Shell straightened, only to have a hard hand shove her forward. A man's voice spoke in pidgin: "Don't move. I'm right behind you, woman."

She glanced back at the yellow-shirted warrior. She couldn't even guess where he and his friends might come from; the accent was too strange.

The one called Wolf of the Dead said something to Pearl.

"I won't dirty my tongue with your words again, leech. If you want to talk to me, speak in pidgin." Pearl boldly stepped forward, bracing her feet while she untied the atlatl that hung from her belt. She extended it like a club, gripping it with both hands, waving it about tauntingly. "Let them go, Wolf of the Dead. It's me you want. So here I am. See if you can take me, you filthy Khota slime!"

The Khota grinned and laughed, nodding eagerly.

Pearl smiled back, yelling, "I offer myself—for my friends. Do you hear that?" She sneered at them. "If you can take me, you can have me! But I make you this wager. Eh, Khota *girls*? You can have me! But you will *never* beat me into submission." More laughter from the men, some with their heads thrown back.

Pearl laughed, too, a low, threatening sound. "Want to try? Hmm? I see that gleam in your weaklings' eyes, Wolf of the Dead. They want me! Let my friends go! Then we will see if your water-souled warriors are up to it. How about you, Round Scar? Do you have any strength left after that tapeworm I fed you?"

The man in question—who stood no more than three paces

from Pearl—blinked; then, as realization dawned, he growled, "You did that? You bitch in heat! You—"

Pearl lunged and deftly smacked her atlatl across the side of his head before she danced away to the cheers of the other warriors. Round Scar fell flat on his face and groaned, a hand clasped to the side of his head.

Pearl jeered and leaped sideways, pointing at another man with her weapon, waving it in front of him. "And what of you, Rotten Mouth? How about a little more dogbane in your food? You'll spend so much time hanging your butt over a log and shitting that you won't have time to break me!"

Star Shell gave Silver Water a shove, whispered, "Go!" and felt her daughter slip away.

"Pearl!" Otter cried. "What are you doing?"

"Shut up, Otter!" she growled. Then: "Do you hear my challenge, you filthy Khota pigs? Let my friends go, and we'll see who can outlast who!"

Three of the Khota warriors had begun piling wood near the edge of the trees—enough to make a huge bonfire.

"Pearl, no!" Otter shouted. "Please! Don't—"

Pearl laughed at the Khota warriors. "I'd have killed Wolf of the Dead the first time if his silly war club hadn't been made of rotten wood. But it's the same with all things Khota, isn't it? They're filled with decay, putrid to the core."

Wolf of the Dead stepped right in front of Pearl, close enough to run a finger down the side of her jaw. "No, woman," he said in a silken voice. "I think we'll keep all of you. Take your heads back to the clan grounds. I've made my promise to Power. No one will ever dare to mock the Khota again."

"Everyone mocks the Khota," Black Skull rasped, squaring his massive shoulders, heedless of the blood dripping from his swollen and lacerated arms. "A few skulls on the wall will not change that." He braced himself, standing tall and strong, and Star Shell couldn't imagine how he managed it. "Killing Khota is like killing rabbits in a catch pen!"

"Not rabbits . . ." Otter's face had frozen into his charming Trader grin. He had cautiously moved away from Black Skull, working to the left, so that he and Pearl and Black Skull created a perfect triangle. "More like netting fish. Rabbits at least have the sense to run, but build a little fire and the Khota come swarming like whitefish to a torch. Just so you can dart them!''

Star Shell glanced around. Silver Water was gone. And with her, the Mask. She shot a glance at Pearl. The woman looked like an enraged she-bear, ready to take on anything to save her litter of cubs.

And I've become one of her cubs. If she can offer herself to save me—a woman she doesn't even know—then . . .

Star Shell closed her eyes, saying a small prayer, inhaling a deep breath. If felt good to be alive. She couldn't deny that, despite everything. An ironic smile touched her lips. She clasped her hands before her, making a tight fist, then spun around, slamming an elbow into the gut of the man behind her.

He gasped and staggered backward in shock. Everyone turned in her direction, including Pearl, who had an alarmed expression on her face.

"Let the men go!" Star Shell shouted, walking to stand near Black Skull. "Pearl and I both challenge you, Wolf of the Dead! What do you say, male worm? Can you stand to be laughed at by *two* women? Or is it enough to be scorned by just one?"

"What are you doing, Star Shell?" Black Skull asked, his voice tremulous, as though he could barely find the breath to speak. "This isn't your fight!"

"I have my reasons. Besides, you were willing to Trade yourself for me. Grant me the dignity—"

"Enough of this!" Wolf of the Dead shouted. He squinted, studying Star Shell in the translucent gleam of sunset. "You are most beautiful. Who are you?"

"I am Star Shell, of the StarSky Clan," she declared. Her knees had begun to shake so badly that she feared she might not be able to go through with this. "I am the daughter of the terrible High Head Magician, Tall Man. Sister of Pale Snake, the Serpent Society sorcerer. You ask who I am, Khota? I am your *death*!"

Star Shell forced her feet to take two steps forward so that she stared up into Wolf of the Dead's ugly face. "My husband hung himself from the clan house ceiling, and his body was burned as a suicide! Shall I call him?"

Wolf of the Dead's jaw muscles slackened. Fear glittered at the corners of his eyes, and Star Shell smiled. He flinched when she reached up and ran her fingers along the side of his cheek.

Then she extended her arms wide and yelled at the sky: "Mica Bird! Come! I call to you, my husband. Arise and come! These Khota *worms* want to see you!"

"*Stop!*" Wolf of the Dead struck her in the face.

Star Shell staggered. With great deliberation, she spit in his face.

"You shrew!" This time he drove a fist into her cheek.

Star Shell landed hard on the ground, gasping for breath, fighting the sickness in her belly. The blow had left her head spinning. His warriors broke into a riot of laughter and hoots, slapping their thighs in approval.

Black Skull bent down to pick her up, defying the pain that had to be screaming in his mangled arms. "What are you doing?" he said softly. "I didn't save you just so the Khota could kill you for insolence."

She whispered, "Silver Water escaped. I'm buying time for my daughter." And she was, among other things.

Black Skull's brows lifted. "You're as bad as the rest of us. Now, if we only knew where the fool went."

"The fool?"

"A Contrary. His name is Green Spider. It was his Vision that brought us here."

The Khota had started the fire. Wood crackled and shot out wreaths of sparks as the flames leaped higher. Otter had advanced, only to have a club-wielding Khota gesture him back. The Trader pointed at Wolf of the Dead. "Before this is done, I'm going to kill you, filth. I promise."

"Kill me?" Wolf of the Dead laughed, exposing the gap of his missing teeth.

"I owe you," Otter insisted. "Twice!"

Wolf of the Dead slapped the Trader with all of his strength; the blow snapped Otter's head sideways.

"Who are these Khota?" Star Shell asked as she watched Wolf of the Dead turn away from the Trader and begin conversing with his subordinate, the one with the bear-tooth necklace.

"Scavengers, grave robbers, thieves. Sneaky and mean as weasels," Black Skull answered.

"I gathered that," she whispered back. "But where do they come from? Near here? Or are they—"

Wolf of the Dead turned on his heel, crying, "Tie the men! They can watch, for the time being. Then bring the women. And be patient, my warriors. We'll have our fun, one by one. All will share. First, the women shall entertain us, and then, when we've tired of that, we'll let them watch while the men scream a little."

"Courage!" Black Skull whispered as two Khota grabbed Star Shell by the arms, shoving her forward to stand before the fire beside the defiant Pearl.

Very well, Star Shell. She glanced at Pearl. *Can you be as tough as this woman?*

Near a huge maple tree, thirty paces away, warriors brutally shoved Black Skull and Otter to the ground, forcing them to lie on their bellies while they drew up their legs and brought their arms around, tying hands to feet.

The big man, the one with bear teeth in his necklace, smiled at Star Shell. "I will take you first, Serpent-woman beauty." She closed her eyes as he ran his hands over her face.

"You think you will," she said. "Just wait—"

"No, you wait!" he shouted, grabbing her by the shoulders and throwing her to the ground, where he lay atop her, smiling. He had pinned her arms at her sides, using one hand and a knee to hold her down. With his free hand, he roughly groped her breasts. "I've never had a woman as beautiful as you. Perhaps, when it's all over, I'll keep your skull. Hmm?"

Out in the forest, a strange, high-pitched voice began Singing, the notes eerie and accompanied by the trilling of a flute. The Song rose and fell in the gathering evening. Grizzly Tooth had twisted a hand in the leather of her dress, ready to rip out the seams . . . but then he paused, his head cocked.

Star Shell shot a glance at Pearl, who had been likewise thrown to the ground. Pearl nodded, and together, they collected themselves, each glancing around, ready to run.

"What's this?" Grizzly Tooth demanded, rolling off of Star Shell before rising warily to his feet. The guards had turned their attention to the forest and were looking back and forth nervously.

"What is that sound?" Wolf of the Dead demanded, lisping through the missing front teeth.

"Power," Otter called from where he lay bound. "Star Shell called it! We came here for it, and now you may get a canoe-load of it, Dead Wolf."

Pearl sat up and laughed at that. "What do you think, Khota leech? That we're alone here? Have you ever heard of Many Colored Crow? We came here to save his sacred Mask! And we've got it. Do you think our Spirit Helper would abandon us now?"

Star Shell bunched her legs under her. It had to be the Contrary that Black Skull had spoken of. Raising her voice, she called, "Many Colored Crow! Hear us! A daughter of the High Heads, your children, asks you to come. In my veins runs the blood of your Mask's makers. Come! Hear me, Many Colored Crow. Come! Dance for us, Many Colored Crow! Come and Dance!"

In the forest, the flute music stopped. Then, to Star Shell's horror, she could hear Silver Water Singing. She knew those words, knew that Song—and knew where her little daughter had learned it.

Out of the deepening shadows came a whirling, Dancing form, moving to Silver Water's child-clear Singing.

"Sun God! Spiral, you god of gaudy colors!
Carry the plant upon your back.
Parch the seeds upon the rack.
Rocks like sky are passing by."

The spinning figure stamped and leaped, its skinny arms outstretched as it capered. In the torrid wash of sunset, Star Shell could see the Mask, the long beak shining, the feathers ruffling around the edge.

And Power. So much Power!

Star Shell started to shake. The Mask might have been gathering all the darkness from the shadowed niches in the forest, collecting it from beneath brush and under rocks, and forming it into a Spirit Being of enormous proportions. Even the trees seemed to bend away as the Mask traveled amongst them.

Silver Water's crystal voice grew louder, shivering off the branches . . .

"Feathers colored, the dead are laid.
Logs across and dirt is made.
Lazy sloth, in baskets carried—
Sun man, and woman, high are married!"

The pirouetting figure of Many Colored Crow Danced backward, circling, diving down toward the ground, then swooping up as if to shoot skyward.

The Khota warriors stood entranced, their eyes locked on the fearful apparition.

Silver Water's voice filled the world now, so fresh and sweet, like snowflakes on the tongue.

*"Built a mountain out of dirt.
Raised on sweat and hurt.
Rose so high over the river.
Eating plants! Bah! No Spirit in that,
Not like blood-filled liver."*

Many Colored Crow Danced his way into the circle. Nervous warriors shoved each other aside to make a path for him. And following in his shadow, Silver Water marched with her head back, Singing as her face glowed radiantly. In her hands, she carried the long flute.

*"You. Born of Father Sun.
Laid in the light, next to night.
Choose, my people.
Dance the Father you don't know.
South, ever south we go . . .
Find an end to the blowing snow."*

Many Colored Crow whirled and ducked, the Mask ending a bare hand's width from Star Shell's face.

"Greetings, Woman of the People. I hail you and the blood that runs in your veins. Your soul has lingered, Dancing Fox, and I barely would have recognized you in this guise."

Star Shell slowly shook her head. "I don't know what you're saying."

"One day, when you rise from the logs of your tomb, you

will know again. For now, you need only wait. Your way will become clear, Woman of the People. Once again you will nurture and raise a great Dreamer.''

Many Colored Crow wheeled, spinning and spinning, around and around, until he stopped abruptly before Wolf of the Dead. The Khota war leader stared into that terrible Mask, then fell back a step, breathing hard.

Many Colored Crow leaned forward, peering at the war leader. ''You are an abomination, *Wolf of the Dead!* How dare you parade in the guise of First Man's Spirit Helper.'' His thin arm rose, pointing into the forest where darkness had begun to cling like tar. ''Go! The Watcher waits. Wolf Dreamer metes out his own justice, and in this case, I will not argue with my brother. Go!''

Wolf of the Dead's eyes began to glaze as he backed up a few more paces, until surrounded by a group of his warriors. He hesitated, his head tilted against hunched shoulders.

Many Colored Crow began whirling again, faster and faster, the fiery brilliance of sunset flickering through his feather ruff in green, blue, and gold. ''Grizzly Tooth, I see the last of the Khota, arrogant, proud, and abandoned. Listen, Khota warriors! All of you! Hear this Song!''

A keening wail rose from Silver Water's lips as she Sang. The sense of loss and unbearable despair overwhelmed Star Shell, though she knew none of the words.

''Do you hear, Khota?'' Many Colored Crow whispered hoarsely. ''Listen to what has become of your people. People you abandoned to follow this foolish leader!''

Among the warriors, the effect of the Song and Many Colored Crow's voice was palpable. Many gaped, stunned, while others moved away like whipped dogs.

''The Song celebrates your doom! Do you hear? Even now, this Song is being Sung among the Ilini up and down the rivers. Your wife weeps, Grizzly Tooth, desolate as she receives an Ilini man's seed. She will bear her new owner's child—the infant that should have been yours! The Khota are gone! Drowned with the courageous flower of your nation.

''You, who took such pride in your arrogance, now find the Spiral turned full circle. What were Ilini lands once are Ilini lands again. Families who were slaves now enslave *your* families.

"Hear the lamentations of your children? They will grow up Ilini in nature and belief. It was you who followed Wolf of the Dead when he took the cunning Water Fox's bait! The wailing of your families began with the storm that blew in out of the dark night. It worsened when your cousins' drowned corpses bobbed on the surface of the Fresh Water Sea! *The Ilini have killed your brothers and fathers and enslaved your women and children* . . . because you . . . *you* abandoned them."

Many Colored Crow flapped around, pointing and cawing. "Which of you remains to pollute my sight? Leave here! Disperse! Do you wish to join your dead clansmen? Many Colored Crow has spoken!"

Several of the warriors on the outermost edges of the circle fled in panic, quietly disappearing into the forest.

In that moment, courage seemed to return to Wolf of the Dead. He began shouting in rage. Star Shell couldn't understand a word of it.

One Arm licked his dry lips, glanced around at the dwindling numbers, and in Trade pidgin, yelled, "I told you! I told you we shouldn't cross Many Colored Crow! I'm leaving!" He threw down his war club, bravely turned his back and stalked off up the bank of the river. Another pair of men did likewise and followed him, no one speaking, each with his back straight and stiff, as if expecting the impact of darts.

As though he wanted Many Colored Crow to understand, Grizzly Tooth bellowed in pidgin: "You cowards! You fear an *idiot* wearing a mask. You should have drowned in place of your brave friends. You are gutless dogs!"

One by one, warriors made up their minds, slipping away, until but ten stood by their leader.

Wolf of the Dead turned to the men who remained clustered around him. He began talking excitedly, gesturing to emphasize his points. Pearl apparently understood the words. Star Shell felt, more than saw, the Anhinga woman move, carefully easing away toward the forest. The Khota had broken into an enraged conversation, shouting at each other, pointing at the Masked figure that cackled as it bobbed and dipped like an intoxicated bird.

Silver Water had changed Songs now, adopting a lilting lullaby that Star Shell used to sing to her when she'd been a baby. Her daughter looked so beautiful; her long hair had dried to a lustrous sheen that reflected the gold of the building sunset. When she chanced to turn Star Shell's way, her eyes shone with an inner light that Star Shell had never imagined possible.

A Dreamer? My little girl?

Many Colored Crow continued to leap and whirl, swaying and dipping his arms like a bird in flight, soaring and diving, apparently oblivious of the Khota.

"*Enough!*" Wolf of the Dead finally blurted in pidgin. He glared at his edgy warriors. "Of course the Mask has Power! Can't you feel it? And look at what it did to your cowardly friends! Chased them away like cuffed puppies! How can you doubt the Mask?"

His warriors stared back and forth uneasily. Wolf of the Dead added, "But *I* am more Powerful than this Mask. With your own eyes you have seen me turn into a wolf! You've seen me rip out the throats of my victims! This Mask is worthy of me! I shall have it!"

Star Shell felt sick. Pearl had slipped away now. Otter and Black Skull still lay beneath the spreading limbs of the maple. They hadn't moved a muscle, bound as they were.

The Khota turned as one to stare at Many Colored Crow.

Wolf of the Dead settled into a crouch, his powerful legs flexed, arms wide as he advanced on the masked figure. His remaining warriors gripped their war clubs and spread out, moving to surround the bizarre bird-man who had started to stumble and laugh joyously as he spun out of control, the black beak of his Mask tipped heavenward.

"Now, southern obscenity, you will die!" Wolf of the Dead screeched in pidgin. "And we will take this sacred Mask for our own. No matter what has happened to our clan, if we have this Mask, we will avenge our families. We will wipe the Ilini from the face of the earth!"

Pale Snake had just waded through a rushing brook that tumbled into the Roaring Water River when he saw the canoes. The four slim war craft had been pulled up like deadly daggers behind a large, fox-headed Trading canoe that lay tilted to one side on the rocky outwash.

Pale Snake scrambled down the rocks, leaving wet tracks on the black stone and bruising the green moss. Ferns bobbed in his wake. He glanced inside the Trade canoe. Packs, blankets, ceramic jars, and rolls of matting lay within.

Pale Snake turned then and climbed back to the trail, trying to sort out the myriad of tracks that impressed the damp, humus-laden earth.

He heard the frantic whine and glanced up. The dog was mostly black, but tan eyebrows and legs contrasted with a snowy-white bib. The dog, looking over its shoulder, whined again, clearly unhappy about whatever it had left behind.

"What's the matter, my friend?" Pale Snake asked. "Where's Star Shell?"

The dog started at the sound, dashing to one side, highly alarmed.

Pale Snake cocked his head. The animal must have been headed back toward the Trader's canoe, for it surely hadn't been traveling with the warriors.

"Come on," Pale Snake called. "I won't hurt you. I—"

He felt the swelling of Power. It struck him like a kick in the stomach. *The Mask! Someone's wearing it.* He started forward, slapping a hand on his leg. "Come on, boy. Let's go. Star Shell and Silver Water need us."

He broke into a run . . . and saw the dog halt, looking between him and the canoe, clearly torn by the decision. Pale Snake trotted forward soundlessly, ducked beneath low branches and skirted the brush in the trail. In moments, the dog had caught up with him and was running at his heels.

Only by a chance glance to the side did he see the war club. How had the warriors missed it? The weapon lay canted in a patch of rosebushes. He felt the Spirit in it when he closed his fingers over the handle and lifted. Gleaming copper spikes protruded under a polished cobble that had been ground into two deadly points. But so heavy! What sort of man could swing a club like this?

Leave it! You couldn't fight with it if you had to. But he took it, carrying it in two hands as he hurried forward. The roar of the river was louder now, pounding as white water rushed toward the inevitable falls. He frowned as he listened. Mingled with the rising and falling of water he could hear . . . music? Was that a flute?

The dog still followed, ears pricked, whining in distress. Power seemed to ebb and flow with the sound of the lilting melody that wove through the growing roar of the falls.

Pale Snake ducked down and slipped under the hanging branch of a lightning-rent maple. It wasn't far now, was it? He could smell the mist, and when he looked up, he expected to see it in the slanting light of the late afternoon sun. In less than one hand of time, the sun would be down.

The dog growled, circling warily to one side, its long nose quivering as it scented the damp air.

"Are we getting close?" Pale Snake asked, again testing the heavy war club. It looked particularly vicious—and so big! If nothing else, he could hide behind it.

He wound his way forward, slipped around plum and willow bushes, and then darted behind a tree. He could hear a child's voice now, crystalline as she Sang—Silver Water!

At that moment, a frightened warrior came thrashing down the trail, slowed to a stop at the sight of Pale Snake—and went crashing off to the west, clearly in panicked flight. Pale Snake watched the man leave, keeping track of the yellow war shirt as the warrior dashed through the trees.

The dog had laid its ears flat, growling, but allowed the man to go.

Pale Snake could hear others passing, clearly running. *The Mask! But . . . who's wearing it?*

He worked his way forward until he could see a clearing. Through the weave of bushes, he caught sight of a big man, his hands and feet tied, lying on the ground. Pale Snake used a clump of wild roses for cover as he zigzagged closer. No, two men—each tied, and beyond them, people stood . . . Star Shell! Another woman was crawling through the brush to his right, toward the bound warriors. Everyone else's attention was riveted on a skinny figure that stumbled and jerked and laughed as it rotated like a leaf on the wind. The Mask pulsed with Power, surging, reaching out desperately.

The yellow-shirted warriors had begun to advance, war clubs in their hands, circling the spinning Dreamer who wore the Mask.

The strange woman crouched to Pale Snake's right. She cast a glance at him, warily taking his measure. Then she sucked in a breath and began pulling at the bonds of the smaller man. The dog crept up behind her and silently licked her hands as she worked.

Pale Snake got down on his stomach and edged forward to untie the bonds of the big warrior, aware that the man's wounded arms still leaked blood.

One of the yellow-shirted warriors shrieked a war cry as his men tightened the ring about the gyrating Dreamer. Why didn't the Dancer use the Power of the Mask? With it, he could destroy all of them! Why was he hesitating?

Pale Snake used the copper spikes of the war club to sever the fiber cord that bound the big man's hands and feet. The fellow looked back, saw the club, and his eyes lit with a ferocity that Pale Snake had never seen before.

"Now, good stranger, hand me my club. I've had just about a bellyful of Khota . . ."

From the corner of her eye, Star Shell caught movement near Black Skull. Had he shifted slightly?

The Contrary staggered sideways, then went around in a backward circle, trying to keep his balance as he chuckled delightedly. When he stumbled, Wolf of the Dead let out a hideous howl and rushed forward.

"Silver Water! Get down!" Star Shell yelled, and she leaped for her daughter. She tackled the little girl and dragged her to the ground just as shouts of rage erupted, followed by pounding feet and screams.

"Be still!" Star Shell ordered, covering her daughter's body with her own.

She didn't believe what she saw. Black Skull fought like a

man possessed, twisting, dancing, swinging a gigantic war club so fast that the movement became a blur. *Where had he found the strength?*

Otter snatched a dropped Khota war club from the ground and swung it up to parry a blow as a Khota warrior sought to crush his head. The Trader pivoted and used a side-handed riposte to hammer the warrior's ribs with a snapping *whump*. The man gasped, and Otter took that opportunity to brain him.

For a moment, Star Shell's mind refused to accept the fact that the third man who scooped up a war club was Pale Snake; his terrible grimace made the tattooed serpents on his cheeks coil and strike as he beat a stumbling Khota warrior to his knees, then battered through the man's defense to cave in his opponent's forehead.

One of the Khota thudded into the ground in front of Star Shell's eyes, his body flopping loosely with the impact. His face was skewed, one eyeball popped out; it took a moment for Star Shell to recognize the leaking, reddish-gray mass protruding from the side of his shattered skull: brains . . .

Black Skull twisted away in a blur to crack a charging warrior across the kneecap. As the man staggered, Black Skull twirled, broke the arm holding the war club, then crushed the spine with a blow to the back of the neck. Before the man could fall, Black Skull ducked under a whirling war club, jabbed the attacker in the hollow of the throat, and as the man jerked back, planted a foot and batted his victim across the face. Faster than a blink, he skipped sideways to strike down yet another of the Khota.

Catcher leaped to grab a man's arm as he started to swing a war club at Otter. The dog shook itself in unleashed fury, its teeth shredding its screaming victim's flesh. The unexpected weight pulled the warrior to the ground, where he shrieked in panic, fighting to protect his throat and stomach by kicking at Catcher.

And the Contrary laughed, hooted, and skipped through the carnage, clapping his hands like a child at a game of hoop-and-stick.

A sodden crack, like a melon being dashed down upon a rock, made Star Shell spin around. Grizzly Tooth took a half-step, his mouth dangling open as he dropped his war club in the dirt between Star Shell's feet. He reeled to one side before pitching face-first onto the ground.

Pearl stood there—eyes flashing like an avenging Spirit's—a war club in her hands. Star Shell glanced at Grizzly Tooth. The back of his skull had been crushed by her blow, but his body had not yet realized its death. The flesh twitched and spasmed in the final throes.

The world quieted suddenly. Only the endless roar of the falls spoke for the coming night.

As though the silent soul of the Mysterious One had descended, birds stopped singing. There were no moans, and no one panted, or exhaled in relief. Pearl's eyes had gone wide and still.

Black Skull crumpled to the ground. Otter cast aside the war club he'd been using to pound Wolf of the Dead's face into bloody mush and knelt at his friend's side, speaking softly.

Pale Snake stood motionless, blood dripping from his war club, his eyes on the Contrary.

Green Spider had one foot up and his arms extended like wings. In a voice almost too low to hear, he said, "Do you see it?"

"Yes," Pale Snake answered reverently.

Star Shell followed his gaze. A breathtaking rainbow had shimmered to life, spanning the river from shore to shore, the bands of color so clear they seemed crafted of the purest jewels.

Silver Water, Pearl, and Pale Snake started forward. Otter followed. Star Shell knelt to help Black Skull to his feet. She slipped his arm over her shoulder and together they went to stand behind the Contrary, seeing the miracle before them.

Summer solstice. The crimson sun hung molten and glowing above the treetops, shooting light out in gigantic copper-colored spikes. One of those spikes had pierced the mist that boiled up from the falls as evening cooled the air. Thick and sparkling, the mist resembled a blizzard of tiny winter snowflakes. The rainbow had been born in the mating of fiery light and glistening water vapor.

"The bridge . . ." the Contrary murmured and stood silent for a moment before bursting into insane laughter. He fell to the ground and rolled around, holding his stomach and kicking his feet like a clubbed jackrabbit.

Black Skull rasped, "What's the matter with you, fool? It's a rainbow!"

Green Spider replied from behind the Mask, "Yes, but I'm seeing it *now*." Such deep gratitude filled his voice that it brought inexplicable tears to Star Shell's eyes. "Now! Now! Now!" He roared with mirth. *"I'm here now!"*

Otter frowned and spread his hands. "When else would you be here? Tomorrow? Yesterday?"

Black Skull waved a weak hand. "He's raving again. Get him up off the ground and let's get out of here before someone else comes to kill us. I don't want to have to—"

A chilling howl rent the air, demanding, authoritative. Everyone whirled, and Green Spider rolled to peer into the forest. There, at the edge of the trees, a wolf stood with its ears pricked. Black as jet. Huge. It howled again. Agonized this time, like a beast in pain.

Green Spider grabbed up the flute—lost in the melee—and got to his feet, peering at the creature through the Mask. His voice came out soft, frightened. "You and your Dark Brother have both gambled poorly. You know that now, don't you?"

A snarl wrinkled the velvet satin of the wolf's muzzle, and long white fangs were bared. Green Spider fell back a step. The beast took a threatening step forward, and Star Shell felt Black Skull tense, ready to kill the wolf with his bare hands to save his friend. "No, wait," she whispered. "It's a Spirit Animal."

He looked down at her, but his muscles didn't relax.

"Let's not fight," Green Spider pleaded, gently accenting his words with waves of the flute. "Fair is fair." He glanced to the side, where Catcher was advancing, hair standing on end. "No, Catcher. Stay out of it, my friend."

His ears back, tail down, Catcher veered off from the wolf.

A coal-black crow dropped to a low-hanging branch, and an angry caw erupted from its feathered throat.

"No," Green Spider answered through the Mask. "I have made my decision. Neither of you can change it."

The crow's throat swelled. The bird shrieked and flapped its wings, as though in reprimand.

"You're worse than your brother," Green Spider said. "Both bad losers! Never bet on a human, Raven Hunter. We're not reliable."

The wolf bounded forward, scattering people, and Green Spider turned and ran flat out, leaping deadfall, slipping on moss and mist-slick rocks. He cried, "The rainbow! *The rainbow!* Where once a red spider Danced on the bridge . . . a green spider will now Dance!"

The wolf snapped at his heels.

"No!" Otter shouted. He had suddenly grasped Green Spider's words. The rainbow touched the bank just above the precipice. If Green Spider tried to . . . "*No!* Green Spider, wait!"

The wolf yipped and growled at Otter's pursuit, while the crow squawked as it flew above him, trying to drive him back. Otter batted at the diving bird.

And ahead of them all, the Contrary whooped and screamed, his ecstatic laughter carrying over the roar of crashing water.

Pearl lunged down the path after them, and Pale Snake grabbed up Silver Water, carrying her as he followed. Black Skull limped along as quickly as he could, Star Shell staggering as she helped him keep his balance.

Perhaps it was a trick of the foaming water, or perhaps the Mask gave him the luminosity, but Green Spider remained bathed in an unearthly light as he raced down the path crying, "I'm here. I'm here now! Do you hear that, you squabbling brothers? *I win! I'm here now!*"

"Get back here, fool!" Black Skull bellowed desperately. "Stay away from the water! I don't have the strength to save you!"

Green Spider charged into the rushing river and dove straight into the rainbow. Thick mist boiled out, sparkling so vibrantly that it swallowed him whole.

"No! Green Spider! *No!*" The cry tore from Otter, who splashed frantically out into the shallows of the river where the water curled clear and bright. "Green Spider, where are you? *Where . . . are . . . you?*"

A desperate Pearl lunged out and grabbed Otter, locking her arms around his waist in time to halt him from running downriver and into eternity. They both stood there, battling the inexorable current that coiled whitely around their legs as it sought to topple them. Otter struggled against her for a moment, then relented, allowing her to draw him back to the relative safety of stiller waters before he buried his face in the wealth of her hair. They clung to each other.

Star Shell stood quietly, using her hip to help bear Black Skull's weight. She couldn't hear Otter's weeping, but she felt it.

The rainbow slowly faded, dissolving as the sun sank below the horizon. Her eyes drifted to the west, where golden clouds floated on a polished amber background.

Pale Snake lowered Silver Water to the ground, and she walked to the water's edge and stared out across the falls. Her stubby fingers wove into Catcher's fur as they stood side by side, their eyes on the rolling white fountain of mist that billowed up from the chasm.

"Has he gone over?" Black Skull demanded. "Did anyone see—"

Star Shell pointed. "Look!"

Just upriver, Wolf stood with Crow perched on his back. Apparently they'd made peace—for the moment. Both Spirit Animals peered at the falls, waiting . . .

And from somewhere deep in her soul, Tall Man's words rose: *Only the greatest Dreamers have ever survived.*

"He's beautiful," Pale Snake whispered, his eyes gone curiously vacant. Star Shell followed his gaze in time to see Green Spider shoot out over the falls, his arms spread, flapping slowly as he fell, as lazy as an eagle on a warm summer updraft. He twisted in the air to tip his Masked face eastward, staring at the few dewdrops of stars that gleamed on the pale blue blanket of dusk.

Star Shell softly said, "I wonder what the stars look like through the eyeholes of the Mask. They must be glorious."

Silver Water whispered, "Oh, they are." A radiant smile lit her young face. "They truly are. He's living in the Light of the world now. . . ."

Epilogue

The dark piece of banded slate felt warm in Pale Snake's hands as he used a brown chert flake to carve the Contrary's head. He always did Green Spider last, after the rest of the carving was finished. He made one a year, always the same. He'd begin carving in fall from a block of banded slate Traded up from the Serpent Clans, and by spring, he'd have ground and polished a stone fetish of *Wave Dancer* and her famous crew.

He sat on the grassy shell midden, warm in the sunlight, and looked out at the sparkling blue waters of Rice Lake. Spring had come early this year, and—unexpectedly—so had the young woman who sat beside him.

On this day the trees had budded out into the bright green of first leaves. The grass on which they sat stirred at the slight breeze drifting off the lake. Where the waves washed at the black soil, white curls of old shells and triangular sherds of broken pottery leached out of the crumbling bank, along with burned bone from deer, ducks, and fish.

The sound of children playing hoop-and-stick carried from the village on the other side of the knoll-top clan grounds. A woman's lilting voice—the words indistinguishable—mingled with the *tunk-a-tunk* sound of a wooden pestle and mortar as she pounded seeds into flour. The Traders who had carried Silver Water here were even now being feasted and wrung dry of all the information they carried.

Above, and just behind them, stretched the Serpent Mound that Pale Snake had constructed here in defiance of his father. He'd woven it out of older mounds and incorporated them into the Powerful symbol of immortality—a concept that had now turned icy in his suddenly desperate soul.

The ghosts of the Dead buried in that mound hovered around,

listening, watching, savoring the Power that radiated from the young Dreamer beside him.

Silver Water remained quiet, thoughtful, no doubt fully aware of the ache in Pale Snake's heart. She wore a fawnhide dress tanned to a snowy white. It clung to her with a terrible persistence that revealed every outline of her supple body. When had the young started wearing such revealing things?

But then, the memory of her mother in another dress had plagued Pale Snake's dreams for years. And remembering only added to the grief that deepened with each beat of his heart.

"Things change," he said unsteadily.

"Next year, they'll make it."

"Of course they will."

He used the hard edge of the flake to make a delicate notch in the rounded knob of the Contrary's backward-facing head. Eventually it would be one side of Green Spider's nose. For one of his *Wave Dancer* carvings, Pale Snake could Trade for enough goods to keep him through an entire year. A man didn't need much more than that, did he?

"It's just part of growing old," Silver Water said gently. She had her mother's perfect face and doe-soft eyes, with long, lustrous black hair that draped down to her hips. "Think of it. The four of them have made the journey every year, always arriving at the solstice. This time it was just too much for them. They started, but by the time they reached Hilltop, they knew they'd never make it. Black Skull's joints ache so badly . . . well, last year he could barely hold a paddle."

"And your mother?" Pale Snake deepened the nose groove, resolutely pressing the chert against the softer slate.

"Beautiful, as always. Her hair is still black, like Pearl's." Silver Water clasped her slim brown hands around her knees, tilting her face up to the bright sun. She added playfully, "I notice a great deal more white in your locks, Uncle. And when did you turn to braids instead of a proper bun?"

"Braids are easier." Pale Snake glanced at her, worshiping her beauty. "You don't look like a sorcerer, girl."

Hard to believe that she'd been swallowed by the Serpent in her fifteenth year—and now traveled the land, Healing, Dreaming, conducting rituals. The great war that had broken out between the Six Flutes and Serpent City had stopped—just because she had appeared at one of the critical battles. Silver Water, then only in her seventeenth year, had dictated the terms of a peace that still remained scrupulously in effect. By her twentieth year, she'd become a leader of the Star Society at StarSky City and had gone to study with the last of the High Heads. It was said that no one knew the patterns of the stars better than Silver Water.

"I'm more than a sorcerer," she said evenly, glancing at him with luminous eyes. "You know that."

But you couldn't keep my friends strong enough so they could make the trip this year. He glanced down, rubbing a callused thumb on the smooth side of the stone canoe. In the beginning, he'd carved Catcher's image—but after the pain in Otter's eyes the year the old dog didn't make it, he'd begun leaving him out, so as not to grieve Catcher's best friend. Catcher wouldn't have wanted that.

"Uncle, age is inevitable." Her hand settled on his shoulder, and he could feel her Power, like lightning in his soul. "Not even the greatest Dreamer can stop the sun from crossing the sky, or the rain from falling. Trust me, they have a great many years remaining. In that time, they will continue to spread their wisdom. They just can't make it *this* year."

"But they will return again. You're sure?"

"Yes," she told him. "It will take a couple of years, but they will come. Their children will bring them."

His chert scritched on the slate as he worked on shaping the other side of the Contrary's nose. What would the solstice be like without them?

Every year Otter crafted a new flute, and on the evening of the solstice, he climbed out on the rocks overlooking the falls and played it as he stared longingly down into the chasm. Silver Water always stood behind him, Singing with her crystalline voice, their music mingling with the water's roar.

Pearl reverently burned a sassafras root and two gourds before casting the ashes into the mist.

And Black Skull . . . Black Skull always hobbled out on his aching knees and knelt down with his offering, a carefully prepared skunkhide cradled in a magnificently carved wooden bowl, and set it adrift in the river to tumble over the falls.

Star Shell sent another bowl down behind Black Skull's, hers laden with a crow's feather and a bit of wolf's fur.

"That's why I came early," Silver Water told him. "So that you'd know. And so that we could travel to the falls together."

He always hated that part, paddling himself down to the place on the south shore where the Roaring Water River emptied out into the lake. Knowing the exhaustion he felt in just crossing Wind Lake, he couldn't imagine how the Water Fox managed to get his party up so many rivers and across the Fresh Water Sea every year.

The ordeal involved more than just the physical demands of the journey—for everyone knew the story of the Water Fox, Pearl, Star Shell, the Black Skull, and Catcher. In every clan house, the story was told of Green Spider, the great Contrary who wore the Mask of Many Colored Crow and tricked both of the Hero Twins.

Pale Snake received enough of the attention himself. People would be out, standing in awe just to witness his passage as he paddled around the shoreline, headed for the yearly observance. This year they would have the treat of seeing Silver Water, the great Dreamer, as well.

I never wanted to end up as a mythic hero.

He could feel Silver Water's knowing eyes probing at him. "After the solstice, would you like to travel south with me? Maybe spend the winter with them at the City of the Dead? They would be so happy to see you, to have the chance to talk for moons. Especially Mother."

He shook his head, running a callused thumb along the smooth stone of the carving. His carvings were Traded with the understanding that they could never be used as grave goods, no matter how exalted and respected the piece's owner might be. Rather, they were good-luck pieces for courageous journeys—and *only* for journeys. That was the Power he instilled in them.

"No, I like it here. People know me. This is my place." And here he wasn't treated like a legend.

She nodded, returning her attention to the water, where four courting loons bobbed.

"You . . . you've heard the stories, haven't you?"

With a Dreamer's intuition, she understood which stories without needing to be told. "Yes, Uncle."

He sighed, turning the stone in his hands so that he could

start making the groove on the other side of Green Spider's nose. "I've felt him. I've never said anything, figuring it was just sorcerer's Power."

"I know." She seemed reluctant to talk about it.

"The Bear Clan," he said. "They tell stories about flute music in the forest. And sometimes, when the sunlight is right, they see the image of a spider perched on the rainbow under the falls."

"They tell more stories than that," Silver Water said neutrally.

"Yes, for years I've heard them speak of a strange figure, thin and awkward . . ."

She reached out to clasp his hand. " . . . that Dances backward through the forest in the moonlight . . ."

He tightened the grip. " . . . accompanied by a huge black wolf and a midnight crow, who circle and circle." He studied her, examining every subtle emotion betrayed in her face. "Silver Water, you were close to the Mask. Closer than anyone alive. Could it be?"

Her smile ought to have terrified him, but it soothed him, warmed his soul. "Uncle, under the bond of the sorcerer's blood, I will tell you this: I've seen him . . . Danced with him . . . but only on misty summer nights when moonlight floods the forests."

Selected Bibliography

Barnes, Burton V., and Wagner, Warren H. *Michigan Trees*. The University of Michigan Press, Ann Arbor. 1981.

Brose, David S., and Greber, N'omi. *Hopewell Archaeology: The Chillicothe Conference*. Kent State University Press, Kent, Ohio. 1979.

Buikstra, Jane E. *Hopewell in the Lower Illinois Valley: A Regional Study of Human Biological Variability and Prehistoric Mortuary Behavior.* Northwestern University Archaeological Program, Scientific Papers No. 2. Evanston, Ill. 1976.

Caldwell, Joseph R., and Hall, Robert L., eds. *Hopewellian Studies*. Illinois State Museum, Springfield, Ill. 1977.

Chapman, Carl H. *The Archaeology of Missouri, II*. University of Missouri Press, Columbia. 1980.

Chapman, Carl, and Chapman, Eleanor F. *Indians and Archaeology of Missouri*. University of Missouri Press, Columbia. 1983.

Clay, Berle, and Niquette, Charles M. *Middle Woodland Ritual in the Gallipolis Locks and Dam Vicinity*. Cultural Resource Analysts, Inc., Lexington, Ky. 1993.

Cleland, Charles E. *Rites of Conquest*. University of Michigan Press, Ann Arbor. 1992.

Cole, Fay-Cooper, and Deuel, Thorne. *Rediscovering Illinois: Archaeological Explorations in and Around Fulton County* (1975 Reprint). The University of Chicago Press, Chicago. 1937.

Converse, Robert N. *Ohio Stone Tools*. The Archaeological Society of Ohio. 1973. *Ohio Slate Types*. The Archaeological Society of Ohio. 1978.

Dean, Blanche E., Mason, Amy, and Thomas, Joab L. *Wildflowers of Alabama and Adjoining States*. University of Alabama Press. 1973.

Dennison, Edgar. *Missouri Wildflowers*. Missouri Department of Conservation, Jefferson City, Mo. 1989.

Dorr, John A., and Eschman, Donald F. *Geology of Michigan*. University of Michigan Press, Ann Arbor. 1970.

Erdoes, Richard, and Ortiz, Alfonso. *American Indian Myths and Legends*. Pantheon Books, New York, N.Y. 1984.

Erichsen-Brown, Charlotte. *Medicinal and Other Uses of North American Plants: A Historical Survey with Special Reference to Eastern Indian Tribes*. Dover Publications, Inc. New York, N.Y. 1979.

Fagan, Brian M. *Ancient North America*. Thames and Hudson, New York, N.Y. 1991.

Farnsworth, Kenneth B., and Koski, Ann L. *Massey and Archie: A Study of Two Hopewellian Homesteads in the Western Illinois Uplands*. Kampsville Archaeological Center, Research Series, Vol. 3. Kampsville, Ill. 1985.

Faulkner, Charles T. *Prehistoric Diet and Parasitic Infection in Tennessee: Evidence From the Analysis of Desiccated Human Paleofeces*. American Antiquity 56:4 687–700. 1991.

Ford, Richard I. *Prehistoric Food Production in North America*. Anthropological Papers; Museum of Anthropology, No. 75. University of Michigan, Ann Arbor. 1985.

Greber, N'omi. *Recent Excavations at the Edwin Harness Mound, Liberty Works, Ross County, Ohio*. MCJA Special Paper No. 5, Kent State University Press. 1983.

Gill, Sam D. *Native American Religions*. Wadsworth Publishing Co., Belmont, Calif. 1982.

Hockensmith, Charles D., ed. *Studies in Kentucky Archaeology*. Kentucky Heritage Council. 1991.

Hudson, Charles. *The Southeastern Indians*. University of Tennessee Press, Knoxville. 1976.

Hunter, Carl G. *Trees, Shrubs, & Vines of Arkansas*. Ozark Society Foundation, Little Rock, Ark. 1989.

Hutchens, Alma R. *Indian Herbology of North America*. Shambhala Publications, Inc., Boston. 1991.

Johnston, Richard B. *The Archaeology of the Serpent Mounds*. Royal Ontario Museum; Occasional Papers No. 10. 1968.

Kenyon, W.A. "Mounds of Sacred Earth." Archaeology: Monograph 9, Royal Ontario Museum.

King, Francis B. *Plants, People, and Paleoecology*. Illinois State

Museum Scientific Papers, Vol. XX. Springfield, Ill. 1984.

Kline, Gerald W., Crites, Gary D., and Faulkner, Charles H. *The McFarland Project*. Miscellaneous Paper No. 8. Tennessee Anthropological Assoc. n.d.

Kwas, Mary L., and Mainfort, Robert C. "The Johnson Site: Precursor to the Pinson Mounds?" *Tennessee Archaeologist*, Vol. XI, No. 1. 1986.

Lepper, Bradley T. "An Historical Review of the Archaeological Research at the Newark Earthworks." *Journal of the Steward Anthropological Society*, Vol. 18, Nos. 1 and 2, pp. 118–140. 1989. "Mounds Tell Us Much About the Past." *The Advocate*, Oct. 1, 1990.

Lumb, Lisa Cutts, and McNutt, Charles H. *Chucklissa: Excavations in Units 2 and 6, 1959–67*. Memphis State University; Anthropological Research Center Occasional Papers No. 15. Memphis State University, Memphis, Tenn. 1988.

Mainfort, Robert C. *Pinson Mounds: A Middle Woodland Ceremonial Center*. Tennessee Department of Conservation, Div. of Archaeology Research Series No. 7. Nashville, Tenn. 1986. "Middle Woodland Ceremonialism at Pinson Mounds, Tennessee." *American Antiquity*, Vol. 53, No. 1, pp. 158–173. 1988. "Excavations at Pinson Mounds: Ozier Mound." *Midcontinental Journal of Archaeology*, Vol. 17, No. 1., pp. 112–136. 1992.

Markman, Charles W. *Chicago Before History*. Studies in Illinois Archaeology, No. 7; Illinois Historic Preservation Agency, Springfield, Ill. 1991.

McGowan, Kevin P., and Kreisa, Paul P. *Research Trends in Midwest Archaeology*. Journal of the Steward Anthropological Society, Vol. 18, Nos. 1 and 2, University of Illinois, Urbana. 1989.

McNutt, Charles H., ed. *The Archaic Period in the Mid-South*. Occasional Papers No. 16, Anthropological Research Center, Memphis State University, Memphis, Tenn. 1991.

McPherson, John, and McPherson, Geri. *"Naked Into the Wilderness": Wilderness Living & Survival Skills*. Prairie Wolf, Randolf, Kans. 1993.

Morse, Dan F., and Morse, Phyllis A. *Archaeology of the Central Mississippi Valley*. Academic Press, Inc., San Diego, Calif. 1983.

Muller, Jon. *Archaeology of the Lower Ohio River Valley*. Academic Press, New York, N.Y. 1986.

Murphy, James L. *An Archaeological History of the Hocking Valley*. Ohio University Press, Athens, Ohio. 1975.

Parker, Arthur. C. *Iroquois Uses of Maize and Other Food Plants* (1983 Reprint). Iorcrafts Ltd., Iroquois Publications, Oshweken, Ont. 1910.

Perino, Gregory H. "The Pete Klunk Mound Group, Calhoun County, Illinois: The Archaic and Hopewell Occupations" in *Hopewell & Woodland Site Archaeology in Illinios*. Illinois Archaeological Survey, Inc., No. 6. University of Illinois, Urbana. 1968.

Schleis, Paula, and Suba, Ed, Jr. "Finding the Road." *The Beacon Journal*, Akron, Ohio, pp. 4–7. July 5, 1992.

Schneider, Allan F., and Fraser, Gordon S., eds. *Late Quaternary History of the Lake Michigan Basin*. Special Paper No. 251, Geological Society of America, Inc. Boulder, Colo. 1990.

Schusky, Ernest L. *Manual For Kinship Analysis*, 2nd ed. University Press of America, New York, N.Y. 1983.

Schwartz, Warren E. *The Last Contrary*. The Center for Western Studies, Augustana College, Sioux Falls, S.D. 1989.

Seeman, Mark F. *Cultural Variability in Context: Woodland Settlements of the Mid-Ohio Valley*. MCJA Special Paper No. 7. The Kent State University Press, Kent, Ohio. 1992a. "Woodland Traditions in the Midcontinent." *Research in Economic Anthropology*, Supplement 6, JAI Press, Inc., pp. 3–46. 1992b.

Smith, Bruce D. *Rivers of Change*. Smithsonian Institution Press, Washington, D.C. 1992.

Smith, Gerald P. *Archaeological Surveys in the Obion—Forked Deer and Reelfoot—Indian Creek Drainages: 1966 Through Early 1975*. Memphis State University Anthropological Research Center Occasional Papers No. 9. Memphis State University, Memphis, Tenn. 1979.

Squier, E.G., and Davis, E.H. *Ancient Monuments of the Mississippi Valley, Comprising the Results of Extensive Original Surveys and Explorations* (1973 Reprint). AMS Press, New York, N.Y. 1848.

Stafford, Barbara D., and Sant, Mark, eds. *Smiling Dan: Struc-*

ture and Function at a Middle Woodland Settlement in the Lower Illinois Valley. Kampsville Archaeological Center: Kampsville, Ill. 1985.

Stafford, Russell C. *Early Woodland Occupations at the Ambrose-Flick in the Sny Bottom of West-Central Illinois*. Center for American Archaeology, Kampsville Archaeological Center, Kampsville, Ill. 1992.

Struever, Stuart, and Holton, Felicia Antonelli. *Koster: Americans in Search of Their Prehistoric Past*. Mentor; New American Library, New York, N.Y. 1985.

Stout, Wilbur, and Schoenlaub, R.A. *The Occurrence of Flint in Ohio*. State of Ohio; Department of Natural Resources; Div. of Geological Survey, Columbus. 1945.

Sutton, Ann, and Sutton, Myron. *Eastern Forests*. National Audubon Society. Alfred A. Knopf, Inc., New York, N.Y. 1985.

Tanner, Helen Hornbeck, ed. *Atlas of Great Lakes Indian History*. University of Oklahoma Press, Norman. 1987.

Tooker, Elisabeth, ed. *Native American Spirituality of the Eastern Woodlands*. Paulist Press, Mahwah, N.J. 1979.

Underhill, Ruth M. *Red Man's Religion*. University of Chicago Press, Chicago, Ill. 1965.

Walthall, John A. *Prehistoric Indians of the Southeast*. University of Alabama Press, Tuscaloosa. 1980.

Webb, William S., and Snow, Charles E. *The Adena People* (1988 Reprint). University of Tennessee Press, Knoxville. 1945.

Woodward, Susan L., and McDonald, Jerry N. *Indian Mounds of the Middle Ohio Valley: A Guide to Adena and Ohio Hopewell Sites*. The MacDonald and Woodward Publishing Co., Blacksburg, Va. 1986.

LOOK FOR

Kathleen O'Neal and W. Michael Gear's

PEOPLE OF THE LIGHTNING

Available in paperback

from Forge Books

In the land we call Florida, eight thousand years ago . . .

His thoughts had grown blurry, indistinct. For long hands of time, he could remember nothing, not his name, nor his clan, not even the direction which led home, then it would all come back in a terrifying rush and he would break out in a dead run.

A short length of dart shaft protruded from the left side of his back. It wouldn't stop bleeding. He pressed his hand over the wound, and tremors of pain possessed him. Every move he made caused the sharp chert point to slice deeper. He'd tried pulling out the shaft, but couldn't get a grip on it through the blood. He'd broken the shaft off . . . broken it . . . when?

Cottonmouth's warriors, he forced himself to think. *They attacked . . . the dart pierced my side. I fell . . .*

He forced a swallow down his dry throat. Horrifying images of running men filled his soul.

All around him, tufts of fog lay like cattail down in the thick vines that looped the trees. As the evening cooled, the mist condensed and a constant patter of drops rained down upon the brown leaf mat of the forest floor, creating a faint drumlike cadence. Soaked to the bone, Diver shivered. Not even the hooded mid-thigh-length tunic he wore could shield him from the bitter wind. It sent probing fingers right through the fabric, taunting his skin.

Birds watched him with their feathers fluffed out for warmth, but few dared to chirp. The whole world had gone silent and glistening.

Only the mist moved.

Silver veils meandered around the broad bases of towering oaks, and climbed the trunks of pines to coil in their pointed tops.

Diver limped forward with ghostly silence. The single dart he carried had grown slick. He clutched it more tightly. He had tucked his atlatl, his dart thrower, into his belt. The weapon consisted of a piece of wood four hands long which had a shell hook in the end. When the butt of his dart was secured on the hook, the atlatl allowed him to cast his dart five times as far as he could have with his bare hand. Out on the sandy beaches, atlatls made lethal weapons, but in this dense forest he would be lucky to get a shot at all, let alone strike an enemy.

He pushed aside a curtain of hanging moss and saw a small pond ahead, crystal clear, ringed by lichen-covered logs. Mist haloed the surface. Desperately thirsty, Diver got down on his stomach and crawled toward it. Scents of wet leaves and grass filled his nostrils. He could not risk being out in the open for long . . . but he had to have water. He would die if he could not drink.

Diver stealthily dipped up a hand of the sweet cool water. He dipped another, and another, gulping the water, letting it run down his chin and throat, until he felt ill, then he sank into the grass and propped his chin on one hand. His soul, his reflection, stared at him from the calm surface of the pond. Knotted black hair framed his round face. That morning he had used charcoal from an old fire pit to paint his skin, but in the mist the designs had melted to gray smears which circled his brown eyes and flowed down around the corners of his wide mouth. A blood-caked lump the size of his fist protruded above his right temple. He stared at it, unable to recall being struck.

Blessed Spirits . . . what happened two days ago?

He had set out with a scouting party of eight to check the boundaries of their clan's territory. Stories had been filtering in on the lips of travelers that Cottonmouth planned to attack Windy Cove village again, to steal food and women, and kill anyone who stood in his path. On the second day out, Diver's party had run headlong into twenty of Cottonmouth's warriors. Diver remembered the initial attack, being struck by the dart . . .

He shook his head. But . . . what else? What else had happened?

For just a moment, he granted himself the luxury of closing his eyes. Musselwhite's delicate oval face formed on the fabric of his soul. He smiled. She was forty summers old, and silver strands mingled with her long black hair, but she had lost none of her beauty. Her full lips could still turn up in that ironic smile he loved so much, and her large black eyes still danced with mischief—though she let no one see those things but him. To the rest of the village she remained a hard-eyed leader: Musselwhite, the great warrior of the Windy Cove clan, hero of the Pelican Isle massacre. A woman to be revered, and feared.

Memories flashed . . . strange, mostly disconnected. He struggled to catch them, to piece them together. The night before the attack, he had been engaged in a violent argument with his son Blue Echo. Or . . . or had it been just moments before?

"We are all going to die! Do you hear me, father?"

Blue Echo's voice crept from the depths of Diver's soul. A wavering image of his son's face formed, angry, the mouth hard, eyes glazed.

"This scouting party was her idea, and she—"

"And what would you have your mother do?" Diver asked. He threw another stick of wood onto the fire. Sparks danced upward into the night sky. Trees canopied their camp, leaning over them as if listening. His oldest sons, Diamondback and Mole, sat across the fire, staring into their gourd cups of tea.

Blue Echo lurched to his feet. Against the shreds of mist, he seemed very tall for his sixteen summers, and on the verge of tears. He choked out, "And—and more of my friends will die this time. Maybe even my brothers or my father. And why? Why, father? Mother fights Cottonmouth at every turn! Why can't we just set our autumn camp further south, out of Cottonmouth's reach? It is *her* he's after, not us!"

Diver massaged the back of his aching neck. Cottonmouth and Musselwhite had been lovers, as the boy perhaps knew, but Diver would not discuss it. Only Musselwhite had the right to tell her sons about her past.

"I cannot believe my ears," Diver said, and pinned Echo with his gaze. "My son asks why his clan cannot simply move their autumn camp. Just set it up elsewhere! Why not invite Cottonmouth into our camp and ask him to kick us about like mangy camp dogs? The humiliation would be the same."

Their clan moved three times each cycle. From winter solstice to spring equinox they lived far to the south, harvesting the plants and animals which thrived along the big lakes. Then they packed up and journeyed northward to the inland rivers where they fished, stole birds' eggs, and collected tubers and roots. After Sun Mother's Celebration Day, they moved to their final camp near the ocean. Everyone loved this last camp most, because they could fish the fresh water rivers, collect nuts and berries, and dive for scallops, clams and lobsters off the coast.

"Echo," Diver added with a tired sigh, "the Windy Cove clan has kept the same autumn camp for generations. Twenty-two of your grandmothers are buried there. We can't just give it up because Cottonmouth wishes it."

"But why does he hate mother so? Do you know, father? It is almost as if she'd done something terrible to—"

"Don't," Diver warned in a low hoarse voice. He gripped his gourd cup hard. "I will not have it. Only your mother can answer such questions. If you had the courage to ask her, she might tell you. But no! You are too timid, too cowardly."

For a sickening moment, images whirled . . . leaves blowing from the trees, spiraling across the ground . . . Blue Echo's chest covered with blood, his eyes staring sightlessly at the tree boughs . . . leaves falling down, down . . . a dart thrusting up from Mole's stomach . . . men running . . . screams . . . horrible screams.

Diver opened his eyes. Darkness had flowed into the spaces between the trees, rousing the night insects. Had any of his warriors escaped unhurt? Made it home? Was Musselwhite even now racing through the forests trying to find him?

Blessed Spirits, if he died, too, what would happen to her?

His soul twisted. She would take her sons' deaths hard, but his death? Losing him would wound her very soul.

Diver plastered a cool leaf on the club wound, and tears filled his eyes.

"Oh, my wife, my wife. I have loved you so deeply."

Heart pounding, Diver picked up his dart and dragged himself to his feet. Blood gushed from his dart wound. He bowed his head, gritting his teeth against the pain. For a time, he stood shaking. The alligator's eyes watched him. Quiet. Speculative, probably wondering how much longer Diver could stay on his feet.

He forced his legs forward. As he entered the forest, Diver ducked low to clear a pine bough . . . and froze.

Cautious voices punctured the silence, coming toward him.

No. Oh, no.

Diver limped backward, then got down on his stomach and slid across the ground. The growing darkness might shield him if he could get far enough away from the trail.